MW01248105

THE FAR HORIZONS

THE FAR HORIZONS

Michael Wagman

A Jonathan David Book

DELACORTE PRESS / NEW YORK

Published by
Delacorte Press
1 Dag Hammarskjold Plaza
New York, N.Y. 10017

Manufactured in the United States of America
First printing

Published by arrangement with
Jonathan David Publishers, Inc.,
Middle Village, New York 11379

Typography by Jack Ellis

Library of Congress Cataloging in Publication Data

Wagman, Michael.
The far horizons.

"A Jonathan David Book."
I. Title.
PZ4.W13155Far [PS3573.A364] 813'.54 80-11790
ISBN 0-440-02815-9

To my Uncle Grisha,
who taught me to cherish my past.
To my son, Grisha,
who is teaching me to cherish his future.

For Jan
without whom there would be no child Grisha.

To my brother, Steven, whose insights, criticisms,
and support were invaluable sources of inspiration
and fortitude.

And especially to my parents,
whose love was, is, my
inspiration.

PROLOGUE

On May 15, 1881, one week after the incident on Reschelevskaya Street, Jacob Reubenovich Moisei finally rid himself of the most damning curse of his life: he converted to Christianity. As the cool drops of baptismal water touched his forehead Jacob felt a freedom he had not known before. And as he watched the brooding priest, haloed by the golden dome of the Cathedral of the Transfiguration, remove that same curse from his wife, Jacob wondered why he had avoided this moment for so long.

The sun streamed through the stained-glass windows, sending flashing glints of amber, red, blue, and green along the gilded columns that rose from the floor of the church to its hemispherical roof three hundred feet above. Five hundred candles stretched in a single row at the foot of the altar, their slender flames illuminating massive frescoes which adorned every wall. A Byzantine mixture of angels, saints, fighting knights, and an enormous mural of Satan, horned, hoofed, and tailed, breathing flame and smoke, forced the eye to the center of the altar. There, encased in a gold frame studded with jewels, hung a picture of the Virgin Mary. Her face was painted black, the head encircled with a band of emeralds, and the body and hands gilded. Suspended from the center of the dome was a silver chandelier which on Holy Days was lighted with three thousand candles. Almost directly beneath it was the baptismal font.

Jacob watched the prelate carefully open an ornate silver vial and stood mesmerized as he dipped a tiny silver-handled camel's-hair brush into the sparkling vessel, soaking the soft bristles in the sacred oil used for baptizing children.

"So he may only see good," the holy man murmured as he traced the sign of the cross over each eye of the young boy who knelt before him. "So he will only admit good." He anointed the child's ears. "So he will speak as befits a Christian." The oil sanctified the boy's mouth.

As the baptismal brush crossed the youngster's hands and feet, Jacob tried to keep himself from shouting in exultation.

"So he may do no wrong and tread in the path of the just," the priest of the Orthodoxy intoned.

Jacob looked at his wife. She stared back at him, not acknowledging the smile on his lips and the satisfaction in his eyes. The priest raised the silver vial and brush toward the heavens, distracting Jacob from his wife's stern glance. The man of the Church of Russia gazed upward, piercing the cathedral's dome with his zealot's eyes, and in a voice that seemed to rumble from Calvary asked God to accept these people into His realm. He beseeched the Lord to pardon them.

"Forgive them for having sinned. Forgive them for having been born Jews."

While his voice still echoed throughout the church, the priest peered down at the three converts. He extended a perfectly manicured hand, one finger decorated by a large jeweled ring. Gently, Jacob Moisei clasped the man's hand, solemnly pressing his lips against the blessed stone. In turn his wife and son did the same. Together they closed their eyes and bowed their heads. Without further word or gesture the priest walked away.

"It's done!" Jacob whispered hoarsely.

"Can we go now, Father?" Aleksandr, his eleven-year-old son, asked.

Jacob hugged the boy to his chest and then stood up. He

offered his hand to help his wife to her feet; she ignored it, gaining her own balance. Taking hold of Aleksandr's hand, Jacob led the way up the aisle. Naomi followed, her expression grim, her eyes fixed on the floor. As they approached the exit, children uniformed in navy-blue suits of a military cut, their jackets cinched at the waist by wide leather belts, swung open the great wooden doors of the cathedral. The sudden rush of white light blinded the Moiseis as they emerged from the church's shadowy interior. Jacob stopped and blinked, trying to adjust his sight. It took several seconds for the pink and yellow painted limestone buildings of Sobornaya Square to become distinguishable. Slowly, the dark green trees and velvety lawns of the pleasure grounds at the center of the square came into focus. Jacob drew himself up to his full height. He was almost six feet tall with a ruddy-complected square face, a curled black mustache, and closely cropped hair of the same dark color. For a man of forty Jacob was unusually trim, his body still firm. He had avoided the portliness so many of his friends wore as badges of success. They envied how fit he had kept himself, and Jacob was aware of it. Now, as he stood on the steps outside the Cathedral of the Transfiguration, Jacob Moisei wished they could see him. Forcing aside his thoughts of himself, Jacob looked down at his son.

"Well, Aleksandr, what did you think?"

The boy's blue eyes returned his father's steady gaze. "I was a little frightened, Father. The priest looked so angry."

Jacob squeezed his son's shoulder. "He wasn't angry. I can assure you of that."

"But all he did was frown. And his eyes weren't kind like Papu's, or Rabbi Eleazar's."

"Aleksandr! Do not mention Eleazar's name. Especially not at church!"

"Yes, Father."

Jacob patted the youngster's blond head. "How would you like to go to the sea?"

"Can we, Father?"

"Why not?"

"Can we buy some lemonade at the Promenade and could we go to the Arkadia and watch the sailboats?"

"Yes. And if you tell me which boat you like, I will have one built for you, exactly the same."

"I have to tell Ivashko!" Aleksandr exclaimed. Whirling around, he dashed down the flight of stone steps toward a burgundy-lacquered carriage with two matched bay horses hitched between the shafts. A liveried coachman stood waiting on the walkway.

Jacob stared after his son, entranced by Aleksandr's animated gestures and the excitement on his face as he spoke to the family's elderly driver. "After today there is nothing in Russia that cannot be Aleksandr's," Jacob said to his wife.

"The crown cannot be his," Naomi softly countered.

"These days who can be sure?" Jacob took hold of Naomi's elbow and ushered her down the stairs.

"Poppa, can I ride on top with Ivashko?"

"Yes. But hold on!" Turning to Naomi, Jacob asked, "Do you mind walking for a while?"

"If that is what you want, I will walk with you."

Jacob studied his wife's unhappy face. It seemed to him that she had worn the same disheartened expression for more than a week now. He tried to recall exactly when she had changed. *Was it when I told her about what happened on Reschelevskaya Street? Or when she learned we were going to convert?* Jacob shook his head. The events of the past week were a blur—except for what had taken place on Reschelevskaya Street. Those details remained distinct. Even in the new security of his conversion just the thought of it filled Jacob with dread. His skin felt cold and damp. And as they had almost constantly since first he heard them, the facts of Reschelevskaya Street still haunted Jacob.

It had been a perfect day that Sunday for strolling along the Promenade by the sea, or lazily window shopping on fashionable Deribasovskaya Street. The sky was mauve, and the usually noisy city was nearly silent, a blanket of heat muffling every sound. On Reschelevskaya Street, a residential avenue with stately homes that lined both sides of the road and towering elm trees that formed a canopy over the walkways, children chased one another while their mothers chatted with bearded old men who were bragging about how good their lives were. A grandmother, still strong of step and with an erect bearing, carried a sack containing green apples, raisins, brown sugar, and dough for strudel. At first no one paid attention to the distant shouts and sounds of racing hooves as they broke the peace of the spring day. But when fifty horsemen, their arms and legs splattered with blood, waving swords with pieces of flesh clinging to the blades, rounded the corner and galloped down Reschelevskaya Street, they all took notice. Mothers screamed as they raced to find their children. The old men, wailing loudly, hobbled into their doorways. And the grandmother, trying to run, shrieked when she tripped and fell, the ingredients for the fruit-filled cakes scattering all around her. In the middle of the block a terrified young girl and her frightened father started across the street, dashing for the safety of their own home.

"Let's put a torch to them!" one of the horsemen yelled as he blocked their path.

"No! The girl is mine!" bellowed another. "I want to cut off one of her tits and give it to my wife!"

"Let her go. Do anything you want to me, but let my daughter go!" the girl's father pleaded, clutching the leg of one of the horsemen. With a flick of a sword, blood spurted from the man's cheek. "I beg you, do not hurt her!"

A gunshot sounded and everything stopped. The girl's father lay dead, a bullet in his head. The man who had fired the shot jumped off his horse and grabbed the girl. He grinned, exposing a toothless mouth. Then, tearing the girl's dress from her body, he held her by the shoulders and displayed her nakedness to all who were in sight. The girl tried to cover her breasts with her thin arms. Snickering, the man wrenched her arms to her sides.

"Look, she is ashamed!" he roared. "If my wife had ones like that, she would not be ashamed!"

Another man, wiry, with a pockmarked face and one eye that turned outward, dismounted. As if he had rehearsed his part many times, he withdrew a knife from his belt and slit the clothes from the dead man's body until not a single thread covered the pale white flesh. Then, clutching the Jew's genitals in one hand, with a single stroke he severed the penis and testicles from the lifeless form. One of the others took hold of the dead man's daughter, threw her to the ground, and straddled her; the girl became hysterical, twisting and turning to free herself. With hairy hands, raw fleshy fingers, and long nails caked with dirt and manure, the man who held the girl fast forced open her mouth. His companion, holding aloft the prize he had won so all could see, knelt over the child's head and forced the dismembered genitals into her mouth. As her father's blood fell onto her tongue, the girl gagged and then vomited. The man who sat astride her convulsing body took his knife and cut open the girl's belly, twisting the blade once it was deep inside her. Not waiting to see whether she was dead, the two men kicked the girl aside, mounted their horses, and with wild shouts led the others away. Moments later Reschelevskaya Street again belonged to the Jews who lived there.

Jacob Moisei looked up at his son, who was perched on the coachman's seat. Aleksandr's beaming smile filled Jacob with a rush of love that erased his thoughts of the brutal attack on Reschelevskaya Street. "Ivashko, I think Madame Moisei and I will walk for a while. But follow close behind in case my wife decides she would prefer to ride."

"Yes, sir." The gray-haired man doffed his cap and climbed up to the driver's bench, settling himself next to Aleksandr.

Jacob nodded to his son, then turned to his wife, taking her hand and placing it in the crook of his arm. He took a deep breath and, reminding himself how momentous the occasion was, led the way from Sobornaya Square to the great Nicholas Boulevard. With each step Jacob remembered how he never before had taken a Sunday stroll along

Odessa's most elegant thoroughfare; Jews avoided the boulevard on the Christian Sabbath. But now for Jacob Moisei everything was quite different. Joining the other Sunday-morning strollers, Jacob felt a flush of excitement as he fully realized that from this day on he and his family, and all future Moisei generations, were legally and unquestionably true Russians. His exhilaration made him tingle, and in a rare impulsive gesture he leaned down and kissed his wife.

"Look at these Christians," Jacob said with a trace of contempt, "too lazy to go to church before noon."

"Perhaps it is not as important to them as it is to some," Naomi replied, a harshness to her words.

"And perhaps, my dear wife, they are unaware of its true significance."

"And you?"

"I know precisely what it means," Jacob shot back. "For the first time in my life I am no longer a cripple. That is what Jews are—*cripples!*"

Naomi gasped, her husband's words landing like blows. The hurt that welled within her turned Naomi's thoughts inward. With an angry silence separating them, Jacob and Naomi continued along with the throngs of men dressed in colorful coats and breeches, and women in fine silk dresses, their heads covered with wide-brimmed hats. Several times Jacob glanced at his wife, reassuring himself that she was as tastefully dressed and as beautiful as any woman on Nicholas Boulevard. Only slightly shorter than he, Naomi had an aristocratic bearing that Jacob liked. She wore her fine blond hair swirled upward from her neck in delicate curls carefully arranged atop her head. Her skin was fair and clear, and, though she was slender, the pink dress she wore displayed her ample hips and bosom, revealing an unexpected sensuality. But it was Naomi's face which intrigued Jacob most, with its finely formed lips, tiny nose, and eyes so blue they sometimes seemed possessed.

"Will we go to church every week?" Naomi asked, as they passed stone mansions whose corniced columns were ornamented with gold leaf.

"Every week. Every holiday."

"I am certain that Papu will be happy to hear that," Naomi retorted.

"Your father is a hypocrite. Otherwise he would have moved from our house long ago."

Naomi parted her lips as if to respond but changed her mind.

"Father, can I go down to the water?" Aleksandr called from his seat atop the carriage as they arrived at the massive flight of granite steps which led from the boulevard to the harbor almost two hundred feet below.

Receiving permission, and as soon as Ivashko had helped him to the ground, the boy scampered down the stairs to the foamy surf of the Black Sea which tumbled onto Odessa's beaches. Without asking his wife if she wanted to go along, Jacob touched her elbow and steered her down toward the port so he could follow his son.

Darting back and forth between the people who crowded the outdoor cafés lining the wharf, Aleksandr asked his father for the glass of lemonade he had been promised. Jacob obliged, and afterward allowed Aleksandr to tug him along until they reached the Arkadia Yacht Club. There, while Naomi stood apart from them, Aleksandr and Jacob watched the small white sailboats skimming across the peaceful bay.

"Father, look at that boat!" Aleksandr pointed to a sleek white craft running before the wind beyond the breakwater. "That's the kind of boat I want, so I can go out to sea, too!"

But Jacob heard nothing, his attention riveted on the heart of the harbor. There a hundred oceangoing cargo ships lay at anchor; each had come from some foreign port bringing goods that ranged from raw cotton to machinery. Now they were laden with Russian grain, beets, sugar, potash, and scores of other export items. Recognizing at least a dozen of the vessels as belonging to his employer, Nikolai Viska, Jacob wondered if someday Aleksandr might not own as vast a trading empire as Viska's. Maybe instead of merely managing Nikolai's affairs, he would be a competitor! Tears came to Jacob's eyes. *If yesterday I had dared to dream such a thing, I would have considered myself insane. But today, today everything is possible!*

It was nearly mid-afternoon by the time Jacob, Naomi, and Aleksandr wearily reached the final step of the long flight of stairs leading back up to the Boulevard. The waiting carriage was a welcome sight, and while Ivashko held the door open they quickly climbed inside. A moment later, the vehicle rolled along Nicholas Boulevard, moving rapidly past Odessa's finest hotels and restaurants. They passed the Exchange, Odessa's financial center, an imposing limestone building where Jacob's employer occupied an entire floor. In the principal room of the Exchange balls were often held during the winter season, none of which Jacob had ever been invited to attend. *Next season things will be different,* Jacob thought to himself. He looked up at the villas of the wealthy aristocrats which dominated the terraced hills above the city. Jacob was entranced by their opulence.

"I think I will buy a nightingale for our garden, Naomi. Just like they have." Jacob wondered if he could afford to buy one of the enormous stone mansions.

"I will buy a gilded cage. The best to be found in Odessa. And we will hang it from the orange tree." Jacob paused a moment, then laughed. "Maybe what I should do is buy one of those villas that already has a bird and a cage. It would be easier. I have no idea how one selects a bird."

"Jacob, I have no need for a bird. Nor do I want a villa on the hill."

Ivashko maneuvered the coach from the boulevard toward the center of the city. The streets narrowed, and, though the houses here were made of the same stone and painted in similar pastel shades, they were far smaller and less grand than the villas on the hillside. Except for a few children, no one was to be seen. The carriage turned another corner and entered Reschelevskaya Street. The only sign of life was a dozing horse hitched to an empty phaeton; the houses looked still and unoccupied. Behind thick wooden doors and heavily curtained windows, Jewish merchants worked their final figures for Monday morning while their wives prepared suppers of pot roast and potatoes, with noodle pudding and sponge cake for dessert.

"Papu said it happened here," Naomi whispered.

With his eyes riveted to the street Jacob said in a hushed voice, "Yes, it was precisely here."

Naomi turned away from the scene and rested her head against the back of the carriage seat. Ivashko urged the horses to a gallop. Aleksandr clutched the sill of the door, his eyes searching for anything that marked the incident. A sob escaped his mother's lips, and the boy turned to his father, a look of anguish on his face.

"Why is mother weeping?"

Jacob's eyes caressed his son's face.

"Why, Father?"

As if it required great effort, Naomi sat up straight, removed a handkerchief that had been tucked into her sleeve, and wiped the tears from her eyes.

"I am weeping because we are Christians. Because we *have* to be Christians."

The coach rounded the corner at the far end of Reschelevskaya Street. Aleksandr glanced back. The horsedrawn phaeton was gone.

"It looks like no one lives there," he said.

"No one wants to anymore," Jacob replied tensely.

"Is it better where we live, Father?"

"Yes, it is better."

"Is it the best?"

"No."

"Where is it the best, Father?"

"In a villa on the hill."

BOOK ONE

May 15, 1881 to Autumn 1895

And in time our name will be forgotten
And no one will remember what we have done . . .
So let us enjoy the good things that exist
Let us have our fill of expensive wines and perfumes
For this is our due and our destiny.

THE WISDOM OF SOLOMON

CHAPTER 1

The first snowfall in Kiev in November 1894 began with thousands of fragile flakes. It ended two days later, having grown from a storm into a blizzard. On the Lipki Heights, the crowning hills of the city which overlooked the Dnepr River, aristocratic men secured themselves in their opulent villas, from the drifting snows and vicious arctic winds. Dressed in suits of velvet, they sipped liqueurs while chatting with ladies in décolleté gowns and necklaces heavy with jewels that flamed upon enticing breasts. Uniformed servants rotated spits on which whole pigs were roasting. Standing where the light was brightest, couples talked too loudly, attempting to prove their conversations innocent while in shadowy corners less prudent men slipped hopeful hands beneath the skirts and along the thighs of other men's wives. Rendezvous were arranged as subtle lips whispered times and places into anxious ears. Those more cautious waited breathlessly for trusted intermediaries to deliver hastily scribbled notes. Drunk and jealous husbands, watchful of their coquettish wives, rushed through final efforts to cuckold others. Late good-byes turned into frantic races as sleds, pulled by two- and three-horse teams, dashed lovers to secret meetings. Even as the sun rose, making Kiev a city of blinding white, a few stragglers still remained at the Lipki villas, lingering as new affairs were being enjoyed or old ones bitterly resolved.

Below the heights, on a series of wooded hills which snuggled against the right bank of the Dnepr, stretched the rest of the city. The Lacra, the most revered convent in Russia, seemed more pure than ever, encased in its new walls of unblemished snow. The entrance to the catacombs of St. Anthony, where bodies of saints and martyrs lay preserved in open coffins, had been obliterated by the storm. Monks dressed in black gowns and fur-lined coats scraped away the snow from the mouth of the grotto so the host of pilgrims who filled Kiev year round might enter and kiss the stiffened hands of the men buried within.

On Kreshtchatik Boulevard, the center of the city's traffic, only a few hardy people pushed through the drifts. On the side streets playful children tumbled in the deep powder like joyful bears. In Podol, the lowest part of Kiev, by the river's edge, youngsters watched their mothers bake fruit pies while their fathers added vodka to the samovar to drive the winter chill from their bones. Beyond Podol, beyond the sturdy houses of the middle classes and the smaller ones of the poor, were the docks, now left unattended by workmen who huddled in cafés before wood-burning stoves. And beyond that, rising like ugly sores on the white landscape, were rows of wooden huts that leaned with age and shoddy construction, their outer walls sealed from the cold with daubs of mud, tattered rags, and newspapers wedged into cracks and holes. Windowpanes rattled as the north wind raced through the Ukraine, spitting snow beneath crooked doorways.

In a room as cold as the outside a woman of forty, shivering though she was fully clothed and wrapped in a blanket, stood before a small oval mirror which hung on a wall between a picture of Moses receiving the Ten Commandments and a faded painting, measuring eight inches by six, of a young girl wearing a long dress trimmed with flowers. *You were so pretty once, Esther,* the woman said to herself. She reached out to touch the image, running her fingers along the dark braid wrapped around the top of the girl's head. *And now you look so old.* She stared at herself in the mirror. The deep wrinkles in her forehead no longer bothered her, and she had learned to live with the roughness of her skin and boniness of her face. She ran her tongue over her cracked lips. The long dark hair she used to wear like a braided crown was now gray, and more often than not left hanging loose, uncombed. Only her eyes affected her. They looked lifeless. She closed them, no longer wanting to see the reflection of herself or the room behind her that served as a kitchen for her, a parlor for her daughter, a study for her husband, a place to eat and talk—a place for them all to hope. In one corner of the fifteen-square-foot room a wooden tub for washing dishes and clothes, and for bathing as well, leaned against the wall. Next to the tub stood a splintery wooden table covered with a stained cloth that had once been white. A dented tin samovar, several glasses, and a scattered pile of books hid most of the discolored linen. Surrounding the table were four crudely fashioned chairs. A few steps away, in the very center of the room, sat a scorched iron stove, its single cooking burner occupied by the empty kettle in which Esther boiled *lapasha.* Along two sides of the room, bookcases sagged under the weight of heavy well-thumbed volumes in Yiddish, Hebrew, and Russian. Against the fourth wall a sofa slumped before two small windows. On either side of the squares of glass hung colorless curtains and, as if an afterthought, a skimpy remnant of the same material, still retaining some of its original yellow color, was stretched over the sofa. At one time the walls had been washed white; now they had a grayish-cream cast. In many spots the mud used to seal the cracks between the slattings had seeped inside during the spring thaws, leaving permanent brown smears.

The wind howled. Esther clutched the blanket tightly around her. Sighing, she opened her eyes and stepped away from the mirror. She glanced at a doorway covered by a piece of material. She listened. There was no sound except the wind. *I might as well go to the police station now,* she said to herself. *Maybe Soybel will not awaken before I return.* Esther was thankful that her daughter was still asleep, grateful that slumber would keep Soybel from knowing that only two small sticks of firewood remained. It would take a day, perhaps two, to find more. With a grimace Esther unwound the blanket from her body and walked to the front door. From a peg she took a woolen coat that had been patched a dozen times, replacing it with the blanket. "Why I bother with this, I do not know," she muttered. "Instead of keeping the cold out, it keeps it in." Esther slid her arms into the coat, squirmed into a pair of boots lined with newspaper, and stamped her feet. The image of her husband's face, pasty-skinned and bearded, the memory of his smile, caught her unawares. Esther stopped moving. Through the dirt-packed floor the winter ice numbed her feet. She twisted her toes in disgust, remembering how each spring the thaw made the earthen floor ooze with worms and beetles and eyeless silver slugs. Esther's thoughts returned to Yehuda, her husband: why had he still not returned home? Where had he wandered to when the snow had begun to fall two days earlier? What had happened to him? He had been wearing the same pants and shirt he had worn every day for the last month, a high hat, and a jacket which was too thin for autumn, let alone winter. Esther stood silently, recalling the day she had finally convinced Yehuda to buy a warm coat. It was hours before he had returned home. When he did, instead of sporting a new coat on his back, an expensive hat adorned his head. Frustrated, Esther implored her husband to explain why he had bought the hat rather than a coat to keep his frail body warm. Yehuda smiled with a child's ecstasy and said: "A coat would be only for me. This hat is for God, too!"

Esther's recollection irritated her, and she became annoyed that Yehuda's unexplained absence was causing her to worry. And knowing that she would have to ask the police for help in locating Yehuda frightened Esther; the police frightened every Jew in the ghetto. Esther became angry with Yehuda for having disappeared, and she became angry with herself for caring that he had disappeared. But even though she disliked her husband—in truth despised him—Esther still felt concern for Yehuda: a caring borne out of the familiarity created by more than twenty years of marriage; an anxiety produced by the fear of having her friends and neighbors discover that secretly she scoffed at the sacred vows of marriage, had disobeyed the biblical laws of marriage. But mostly she dreaded that if she did not attempt to find Yehuda, everyone would know that she hoped Yehuda's disappearance had been caused by his having perished in the storm. And so, Esther Dubrovsky readied herself to search for her husband.

CHAPTER 2

The two-mile walk from Esther Dubrovsky's house to the ghetto police station was torturous. The roads, little more than rutted paths, were dangerously covered with thin sheets of ice. Wild dogs roamed free, ready to devour anything edible. Men skulked in alleyways, prepared to pounce on anyone carrying a bundle or appearing likely to have even a single kopeck in his pocket. Trudging along the nameless streets, past rows of indistinguishable hovels, Esther dreaded reaching the precinct building which squatted like a hungry frog waiting for insects. Esther knew that no matter how politely she behaved, she would be greeted, at best, with disdain, and with violence at worst; the wooden bats of the dreaded *politsya* were ever ready. Approaching the police station, Esther abruptly changed direction. There was no need to suffer indignities when the police would ultimately send her to the furthest edge of the ghetto to inquire about her husband. Shivering, Esther plodded on to the shed.

For years, after each heavy snowfall, Kiev's police stations had been crowded with people frantically searching for members of their families who had not returned home. In 1890, the local authorities, having concluded that the overwhelming majority of those who died in the brutal winter blizzards were ghetto Jews, ordered the construction of a large wooden structure at the very outskirts of the city. From then on, for a week following each snowstorm, peasants in horse-drawn sleds roamed Kiev and collected the frozen bodies strewn about the streets, bringing the corpses to the shed, and leaving them there to be claimed.

As she neared the shed, Esther Dubrovsky's apprehension increased. A gruff-looking peasant, draped in a limp, ankle-length woolen coat, and with a cap pulled low over his eyes, strutted out of the entranceway of the long rectangular structure. He stationed himself before a small fire built in the snow. Warily, Esther approached him.

"Can you help me?" Esther's voice lacked its usual raspy assertiveness.

The man eyed her suspiciously, his surly expression menacing. "Were you sent by the police?"

"No." The circle of heat drew Esther closer to the fire. Ice that had been melted by the burning wood seeped into her boots.

"Then why did you come here?"

"The storm is over and my husband has not returned home, so—"

"Perhaps the storm is just his excuse not to come home." The guard peered down at Esther. "For some men storms are a cover for their spending time at places more interesting than home." The peasant underlined his innuendo with a sly laugh.

Esther closed her eyes and shook her head; she focused her senses on the flame. "The only other place than home my husband would be is at the synagogue, and he is not there."

The Russian snorted and spat. "Then he deserves to be here."

Fighting a desire to remain close to the heat, Esther took a step toward the shed. "May I go in?"

"I do not care if you do or don't. But if you do, I hope you find him. The shed is overcrowded. And I could use the room." The warder wiped his runny nose on the sleeve of his coat. "And do not be afraid in there—those Jews are harmless."

Esther hurried past the Russian into the building. The interior was gloomy, lit only by flickering kerosene lanterns. Shocked gasps of "Poppa!" and "Momma!" ripped through the stillness. Slowing her pace, Esther shuffled along the dirt floor past wooden tables on which there lay more than a score of petrified bodies. She moved aside to let pass two young boys carrying the rigid corpse of an old man whose face bore a thankful expression. Carelessly, the boy in the lead banged the head of the dead man into one of the tables.

"If he wasn't already dead, he is now," the youth casually remarked.

His friend snickered. "Just don't drop him. If you do, he will shatter like glass. And then we will have to return the kopecks his wife gave us."

"Perhaps we should drop him. Then we can demand more money—because instead of one dead husband, she will have hundreds!"

Esther ignored the boys' laughter.

Those who mourn the dead should instead envy them. That is why God made suicide a sin—to torture us, Esther thought. She passed the body of a woman no older than herself whose face was lined with anguish: tears seemed to be frozen to the woman's face. Her right hand was tightly clenched in a fist, the fingers of her left hand were limp. Esther wondered if the guard had snapped the bones of the woman's hand in order to steal her wedding ring. Esther walked on, thankful that only a few bodies remained for her inspection. Then, on the very last table, she saw Yehuda. She paused, staring into his still-open eyes, and she looked at him with a tenderness she had never felt when he had been alive. Yehuda's corpse reminded Esther how temporary was her own life, how wasted it had been. Vividly she recalled the day when she was twelve and her father proudly announced that she was now engaged to fourteen-year-old Yehuda Dubrovsky, a promising scholar, a sage perhaps.

Five years passed before Esther and Yehuda were married. And in all that time, they never saw one another—Yehuda trusting firmly in the divine and just hand of God, Esther prevented from knowing her intended by the strictness of custom.

Sadly, Esther remembered how her life had changed from the moment her father and Yehuda's had signed the marriage contract. Immediately God and ritual determined her behavior. No longer was Esther permitted to indulge in the amusements of childhood. Dashing madly in games of tag, hide-and-seek, dancing in circles to the accompaniment of spontaneous songs, just sitting and daydreaming, were all suddenly forbidden, considered improper. Now Esther was tutored in reading and writing, instructed in the etiquette of marriage. Her mother taught her to prepare both everyday meals, and the special traditional recipes for holy day feasts. Her father described the life of the pious Jew, explaining in detail the prayers, rituals, and customs which guided every moment of a devout Jew's life. The rabbi's wife taught Esther how to count the days following menstruation to determine when she was permitted to lie with her husband. She was taught how to purify herself, how to maintain marital cleanliness by purgation in the ritual bath. Her head was shaved, her hair shorn almost to the roots so she would not luxuriate in her own beauty, and she was given a severe-looking wig to cover her baldness.

A trousseau was ordered for Esther—ankle-length skirts, wrist-length blouses with high-buttoned collars—all the proper garb for traditional women. Young matrons visited her to discuss housekeeping matters, teaching Esther how to sew, knit, darn, and bargain at the market. Yet, despite this whirl of activity, Esther was plagued by the absence of information about Yehuda Dubrovsky. More than once she inquired about him, hoping her father would reveal some facts about this man to whom she would be wed, information regarding his temperament, his features, the way he carried himself, the way he smiled. Often Esther fantasized that her husband-to-be would be much like her father: robust, with dark glistening hair, a beard of silky curls, eyes that graced her with affection, and a warmth and gentle humor. But all she learned was that Yehuda Dubrovsky was a scholar of great promise. She was told only that to be married to a man so brilliant and pious was an honor achieved by few women. When she passed young men scurrying between their homes and the synagogue or school with one hand clutching their books while with the other they kept their hats clapped to their heads, Esther selected the youth with the most pleasing features and wondered if he were Yehuda Dubrovsky, praying he *was* Yehuda Dubrovsky. At times, engulfed by the ardor of her blossoming womanhood, and having learned how that passion was quelled, Esther imagined herself embraced by a man as well-favored as the storied heroes of her childhood. Succumbing to her reveries, Esther often secretly entertained thoughts of choosing her own husband.

Frightened by the boldness of her unorthodox romanticism, Esther applied herself even more diligently to preparing herself to be a proper wife. And on the morning of her wedding day there was no sign whatsoever of the spirited child, the romantic young woman Esther had once been. Not one thought of those past years of abandon disturbed Esther's mind, yet the enormity of her transformation eluded her. And as she dressed for the ceremony of marriage, Esther experienced, not a joyful anticipation, but a melancholy she did not understand.

Not until Esther stood beneath the marriage canopy did she come face to face with her intended. Only then did she finally gaze upon this stranger who was to be her husband. A momentary feeling of revulsion made Esther tremble. This was not the handsome young man she had dreamed of. Yehuda Dubrovsky was homely, with skin the color of a fish's belly. His nose was thin, hooked at the tip, and his too-full lips gave him a simian look. Black earlocks, twisted like horns, lay over ears too big for his head. A beard and mustache of the sparsest kind made his face look unwashed. The suit Yehuda wore, though newly made, flapped when he moved, covering limbs so frail that it seemed they would snap under the slightest pressure. Aware of her own slimness of waist, fullness of hips and bosom, Esther recoiled at the thought of the womanly instructions given to her by the rabbi's wife and the midwife. The secret yearning she had felt while imagining herself as a wife ready to lie with her husband now turned to fear. When, as part of the marriage ceremony, Yehuda trod upon Esther's feet, symbolizing that forever more she would serve him, obey him, a shudder coursed down Esther's back. And with only a dim awareness of the event, Esther Dubrovsky née Furman agreed to the vows of marriage.

Following the wedding festivities and the Dance of Purity, Esther's mother led her to the nuptial chamber, where she was commanded to give herself willingly to her husband; "Be fruitful and multiply" was the first dictum of the Torah. Reluctantly, Esther undressed in the darkened room and put on a luxurious silken nightgown especially made for this moment. Then she climbed into the bed and waited. The mattress that she and Yehuda would share until "death did them part" seemed to encase her, holding her fast like quicksand.

A hesitant unlatching of the door announced Yehuda's arrival. The muffled sound of the wooden barrier being opened caused Esther to lie rigid. Cautiously, Yehuda entered the room and closed the door. The marriage chamber was pitch-black. The air was stale, the heat stifling. Yehuda undressed, the rustling of his clothes foreboding. Knowing not what else to do, Esther pulled her nightgown up to her neck. Yehuda's voice began to drone. Esther wondered if he were praying. The murmuring ceased, and though there was nothing but silence, Esther could feel the approaching presence of Yehuda Dubrovsky. Her breasts heaved spasmodically. Sweat stained her thighs. She was terror-stricken at the thought of her body being penetrated. Without warning Yehuda's weight depressed the side of the mattress at Esther's feet. Something coarse was placed over her legs and quickly drawn over her body up to her chin. Esther cried out in fright. "It is me, your husband, do not be afraid," Yehuda reassured her. Gingerly, Yehuda spread the covering so it draped over the sides of the bed. Knowing full well what the cloth was for, Esther permitted Yehuda to complete the ritual. When he was certain none of Esther's skin below her neck was exposed, Yehuda lightly touched his wife's hip through the fabric and traced a line to the center of her belly. He paused and emitted a soft, eerie wail. Esther closed her eyes and waited in anguish for her husband's hand to proceed downward along this specially prepared blanket, a solid piece of linen with an opening propitiously placed to permit his member to pierce the cloth and then his wife; a piece of scratchy material meant to prevent Yehuda Dubrovsky from coming in contact with his wife's flesh and thereby falling prey to lust. Yehuda's hand moved downward. Feeling the mound below Esther's belly, he slid his fingers from side to side, seeking the slit in the cover. Esther parted her legs, hoping that would hasten his search. Unable to locate the perforation, Yehuda became agitated. His probing grew vehement. With one hand he grasped the sheet and with it Esther's hair beneath. The fingertips of his other hand searched the linen in an ever-descending line. Esther spread her legs further apart. Yehuda's fingers, sheathed by the cloth, sunk into the deep folds of skin protecting Esther's private parts. The linen cover became moist, wet. Esther drew up her knees, set her feet firmly on the mattress, and completely opened herself up to Yehuda. Frantically, Yehuda sought his goal and without warning his finger stabbed through the slit in the material and fully entered her. Esther screamed with pain, with fear, with shock. As if in a fever, Yehuda knelt between Esther's thighs, hastily removed his finger from within her body, and urgently placed the hole in the sheet over his erect organ. Flinging himself on his wife's body, Yehuda thrashed about. His bony knees dug into Esther's thighs. His long toenails scraped her shins. His thin fingers clawed at her shoulders. His pointy elbows bruised her chest. His rapid breathing assaulted her face. And then it was over.

For a minute Yehuda remained atop his wife, spasmodically devouring chunks of air. Finally, and without a word, he rose, dressed swiftly, and left the room. Alone in the dark, still covered by the linen cloth, Esther Dubrovsky began to cry. Her hand reached down to where Yehuda's penis had thrust against her. A puddle of sticky matter made the sheet cling to her belly. Esther removed the cover from her body and let it slip to the floor. The weight of a great loneliness descended upon her. A disappointment she could not explain, a deep sadness, took hold of Esther and she wept. She touched the crusting pool of liquid on her stomach, and she wondered if Yehuda knew that he had not entered her, if he had any idea that the marriage of Yehuda Dubrovsky and Esther Furman had not been consummated.

The passing of time dimmed the events of Esther's wedding night, until it became a memory well hidden from her. Indeed, the fulfilling of her wifely duties, and then the swelling of her belly with the growth of her first child, permitted Esther no time to wander in the recesses of her mind. And with the tragic arrival of her firstborn, Esther was too shamed by her husband's accusing eyes to care about anything but easing his grief. For Yehuda had finally impregnated his wife with his seed and as her belly swelled, so did his pride. A serene satisfaction softened his usual pinched expression. On the day of her labor Esther's painful cries were music to Yehuda. But the silence that followed, the lack of the lusty shout of life, the news that his wife had produced nothing but a stillborn boy, plummeted Yehuda into despair. From then on there was a grimness to the Dubrovsky household that intensified when Esther became pregnant for a second time. When she gave birth to another boy, a screaming, kicking infant, Yehuda gave praise to God. A year later the child died, succumbing to scarlet fever. Again Yehuda Dubrovsky plunged into gloom.

Esther's third pregnancy brought constant apprehension. The excruciating pain caused by her passing the infant's unusually large head was ominous to her. And when the midwife announced that the loudly crying girl was healthy,

Esther feared that the woman was taunting her. But the infant survived the ordeal of birth. Week by week it grew stronger, thriving on its mother's milk. One year became two, three, four, and Soybel Dubrovsky still lived. Esther was joyous. She doted on the child, kissing her a hundred times a day, hugging her a hundred more. To entertain Soybel, Esther concocted tales of luxurious villas and princely men. She devoted hours to combing her daughter's thick dark tresses, and days to fashioning her dainty dresses. Indeed, everyone who knew Soybel Dubrovsky was entranced by her. Except Yehuda. To him, his daughter was meaningless. After all, she was not a son. And as time proved Soybel quick, clever, and perceptive, Yehuda resented her. For if she had been a son, Yehuda would have had someone he loved with whom to share his passion for learning. But this child lacked interest in everything except play and the pleasant diversions of fantastic daydreams. As she grew older, budding into maidenhood, and frivolous talk and visions of living on the Lipki Heights occupied Soybel's thoughts, Yehuda almost completely ignored her. Yet, Yehuda Dubrovsky never mentioned to anyone, except God, how much he disliked his daughter.

For eight years the Dubrovskys lived well, the dowry Esther's moderately prosperous father had agreed to in the marriage contract enabling them to enjoy a comfortable life while Yehuda did nothing but study and pray. Then in 1880 Esther's parents died, and the meager inheritance that remained after the government confiscated its share was quickly spent. With no one to support the Dubrovskys, Yehuda was compelled to seek employment. In prior years Yehuda had often been asked to teach in the yeshiva, and each time he had refused, preferring his scholarly solitude. Now there were no pedagogical positions available at the ghetto seminary; there was not even a place for Yehuda as an instructor at a *heder*. Forced to steal time from his own studies to find a way to earn even a few kopecks, Yehuda grudgingly accepted several youths as private pupils. Coupled with his own resistance at being a tutor, and the economic situation of Kiev's ghetto Jews, Yehuda had barely a handful of students. Money became scarce, and the Dubrovskys struggled to survive. Fruit tarts, honeycakes, and raisin scones became remembered luxuries. Sabbath meals consisted of thin broth and bread. Clothing was patched and repatched. Unable to provide for his family, Yehuda withdrew into a world of the Bible, Talmud, and prayer.

Having no other choice, Esther assumed her husband's burden. She mended clothes and washed laundry for the few Jews fortunate enough to have jobs; even so, what she earned was little. She made *lapasha,* rising each day before dawn to boil the noodles in a large iron kettle, then, until nightfall, hauled the heavy pot from one end of Kiev to the other, selling cups of the steaming food for a kopeck each. But that, too, provided only a pittance, and then nothing; there was no longer enough money for Esther to purchase the ingredients needed to make *lapasha.* So she took to begging, tortured inside by the indignity, and gradually a change took place in Esther. Her face became stern, her words sharp. Instead of castigating Yehuda silently, she did so to his face, purposely humiliating him. Even Soybel gave Esther no joy. In truth, Soybel caused her mother to become seized with terror. For as their situation worsened with each passing day Esther pictured her daughter the victim of starvation. Then came the first day when Esther found herself poking through the garbage of those able to afford food in search of discards with which to feed her family. And before long Esther began to loathe her husband, despising Yehuda's pious ways, his holy books. Before long Esther Dubrovsky ceased cleansing herself in the ritual bath and began to let her hair grow beneath the wig she had worn for twenty-three years.

Now, as she stood in the shed of death before her husband's emaciated, lifeless body, Esther Dubrovsky came to a realization that stunned her. Its awesomeness made her tremble. "I never loved you, Yehuda. But I never hated you, either," Esther said softly. Yehuda's head was uncovered, his bony skull looked as vulnerable as an infant's. Esther wondered what had happened to Yehuda's hat. "And when I cursed you, Yehuda, it was not you I was cursing." Esther removed her handkerchief and tied the corners together, making a cap. Gently, she lifted Yehuda's head and placed the cap atop it. "And if I could afford to, Yehuda, I would buy you a new hat to bury you in. But I cannot even afford to bury you." Carefully, Esther lowered her husband's head back to the table. "I hope you find more peace in death than you had in life. And I also hope that at sometime in eternity you can forgive my blasphemy. For it was not you, my husband, I denounced all these years. Nor was it you I loathed. Because it was not you who caused my life to be the way it was. It was God. And now I know that it was God I was cursing. Because it is God I despised."

CHAPTER 3

According to tradition, Yehuda Dubrovsky's body was laid to rest on a wooden plank in his home, his feet facing the doorway, a lighted candle next to his head. Then, after Esther and her daughter had been led away, the *chevra kadisha,* a group of men who prepared the bodies of deceased Jews for burial, readied Yehuda for his interment. First Yehuda was disrobed and immediately covered with a sheet. A handkerchief was tied around his jaw to keep it securely in place. Taking care not to uncover the corpse, Yehuda was bathed in lukewarm water: first his head, then his neck, the right upper half of his body, the right lower half of his body, the right foot, and then the same ritual on the left side. The fingernails and toenails were cleaned, and the few strands of white hair on his head combed. After placing straw on the ground, the *chevra kadisha* raised Yehuda's body to its feet. Twenty-four quarts of water were poured over his head and allowed to flow down the length of his body. Again Yehuda was placed on the wooden plank, dried and covered with a clean sheet. Finally he was dressed in a headdress, trousers, a gown, and a belt, all made of cotton. His prayer shawl, after some of its fringes had been torn, was wrapped around his body. With his head entirely covered by the headdress, the shroud drawn way down over the nape of his neck, Yehuda Dubrovsky was ready to be buried.

The funeral service itself was simple; there was little to say about Yehuda except that he had been a devout scholar, revered by many. Of the dozens of people who attended the rite, none were different from what Yehuda had been. All were the poorest of the poor: bakers who had become impoverished because government policy forbade them to purchase the ingredients to make rolls and cakes, and thereby make a living; cobblers who were not allowed to buy leather with which to practice their trade. There were others, those blessed with the gift of fashioning exquisite cabinets with their hands, but who were unable to acquire wood. Teamsters without horses. Hat makers without material. Tinsmiths without tools. And fixers who, with nothing but their ingenuity, somehow managed to repair everything. But most were *luftmenshn,* men who tried to earn a living from the air.

As they made their way to the Dubrovsky home, the majority were silent, remembering their friendship with Yehuda, recalling how they had shared their food with him, a glass of tea, and the belief that devotion to God would someday bring them eternal peace. Others spoke aloud of Yehuda, their ceaseless chattering keeping away the thoughts of their own frail existences. In the Dubrovsky home the blackness of the room where Yehuda lay was disturbed solely by the light radiating from the candles surrounding Yehuda's body. Pressed against every wall were lamenters, their eyes drawn to the hooded corpse at the center of the room. Huddled together, a pace nearer Yehuda, was his family.

Esther stood motionless, her face blank, her eyes barely blinking. For a moment she envied Yehuda's escape from the world. Feeling her fourteen-year-old daughter clutching at her arm, Esther glanced at her and wondered if Soybel would be able to avoid the agonies of life. Intently, Esther studied her daughter. Soybel's black eyes were absorbing every detail of the scene, her alabaster skin and long dark hair giving Soybel the appearance of a Byzantine Madonna.

The rabbi took two steps closer to Yehuda's corpse and began to speak. "Man is like a dream; like the grass renewed each morning. For though it flourishes each morning, in the evening it withers. And so it is with man. Our threescore and ten years are soon gone. So teach us to treasure the days that we have, and teach us to have wise hearts. And though the dust will return to the earth as it was, the spirit will return to the God who gave it."

After the last amen faded into silence, the rabbi asked for the pallbearers. Four old men stepped forward. They lifted the bier; its lightness surprised them. Bowing their heads, they carried it outside, past the mourners who had gathered beyond the confines of the Dubrovsky house, to a waiting horsedrawn sled. Gently, they placed Yehuda in the back of the runnered vehicle. The driver rippled the reins along the horse's flanks, urging it to move slowly, allowing the processional to gather and follow behind. Everyone else walked the three miles to the cemetery that bitter cold day; only the dead could afford a horse and sled. Esther and Soybel plodded alongside the vehicle, their bodies wracked by the wind, their faces chapped raw. Soybel watched the snow spray from her feet while Esther studied the tragedy in her neighbors' expressions. Like a brackish stream worming its way through a barren countryside, so moved the long file of grievers. They trickled past the deserted shops of butchers, bakers, grocers, past shabby warehouses empty of stores but crowded with the homeless families of jobless men. They shuffled past the *shul* where Yehuda had prayed every day of his life, past the *mikvah* where long ago Esther had bathed away her monthly uncleanliness. They trudged into the marketplace and past the well at its center where often Yehuda had stopped to speak to the young boys drawing water to test their knowledge of the Talmud. They tramped past houses rotting at their foundations, past people so impoverished that to them squalor was paradise—relentlessly they plodded to the only place that offered freedom from Russia. Leading the way out of the ghetto and into the bleak landscape beyond, the horse-drawn sleigh transported yet another body to the overcrowded cemetery of the Jews. As the sled passed the graveyard gate, the driver stood up on his footrest and looked for the telltale mound of dirt that marked the place of another hole in the earth. A nod of his head indicated that he had found Yehuda's final resting place. With a simple command the driver pressed his horse forward. When the vehicle stopped, the pallbearers carried Yehuda to a grave freshly chopped out of the frozen crust of the world. Carefully, the deceased and the plank on which he rested were placed on ropes that straddled the dark pit. The rabbi waited until the procession came to a halt and the mourners encircled the grave. Then he prayed. Two men let the ropes slide through their hands. Yehuda Dubrovsky's body slid into the ground; it bounced as it hit bottom. Soybel grasped her mother's hand, her eyes fixed on the shrouded corpse. Yehuda's body came to rest, and Esther wondered if a host of angels would suddenly appear to escort his spirit to the side of God; the bitterness Esther felt caused her to silently damn the Lord. The rabbi spoke his final words, and the men of the congregation began to recite the *kaddish,* the prayer for the dead. Yehuda's friends and neighbors rocked back and forth in rhythm with the dirge.

"*V'yisgadal, v'yiskadosh, sh'may raboh* . . . Magnified and sanctified be His great name."

"Amen."

"In this world which He created according to His will may He establish His kingdom during your lifetime . . ."

"Amen."

One man after the next took the shovel that was thrust into the mound of dirt and tossed earth onto the corpse. Moving more quickly than they had on their way to the cemetery, the mourners returned to the ghetto. Several accompanied Esther and her daughter to the Dubrovsky house to begin *shiva.* For seven days the men prayed and talked while their wives cleaned and cooked. The small mirror that hung between the picture of Moses and Esther's portrait was covered with a rag. No one wore shoes. And everyone sat on the earthen floor, the act of lowering the body a physical accompaniment to the desolation and remorse brought on by death's visit.

On the morning of the seventh day after the burial of Yehuda Dubrovsky, the ritual of *shiva* ended. The men who had prayed, had chanted the *kaddish,* their covered heads bobbing back and forth, all to keep Yehuda's memory alive, regretfully bade their good-byes. Their wives, whose task it had been to console Esther, to relieve her of every burden, also departed. Alone for the first time since Yehuda had died, Esther and Soybel found it impossible to talk, to utter even a word, the stillness emphasizing the void in their lives. The only sounds in the room were breathing and the occasional scuffing of feet as either Esther or Soybel made her way to the window to stare outside, unseeing, blinded to the wretchedness of the ghetto by their own despair. The sun completed its arc, and along with the perishing day the embers in the stove also died. A candle was lighted, but the wind, flitting beneath the door, permitted it only a precarious life. Darkness came. The candle burned lower until the room was almost as black as the night. The cold became unbearable.

CHAPTER 4

The seemingly endless months of winter left Esther with barely enough strength to survive. The bitterness she had felt toward her husband during their last years of marriage was now replaced by resentment of the impoverishment of her daughter and herself. She grew tired of the consolations of her friends and neighbors; their pity for her and the stories of their own hardships infuriated Esther. Very directly, she made it clear that she was no longer concerned with anyone's misery but her own. And when anyone attempted to speak of Yehuda in glowing words, Esther retorted that whereas her husband might have found comfort in God, she, Esther Dubrovsky, first wanted comfort in her home. The rabbi, too, became a victim of Esther's tongue. It was obvious, she told him, that God had abandoned her: "If He had not, would He permit my daughter and me to live in such a disgraceful state? And is it not so that killing is a sin?" Even before the rabbi had finished nodding in affirmation, Esther angrily added: "Then God is the most sinful of us all, for by permitting us to live as we do, He has condemned us to death!"

News of Esther's blasphemy traveled quickly among those who knew her; the rabbi wasted no time in relating his shock and horror at hearing the widow of Yehuda Dubrovsky speaking like a heathen. Almost instantly, Esther felt a change in the attitude of her neighbors and friends, all of them avoiding her. At first Esther was unsure of her ability to withstand their punishment; the fear of isolation gave her pause. Yet, when along with the Russian New Year of 1895 there came more severe snowstorms and increasing deprivation, Esther became obsessed with a fierce determination to escape the ghetto.

The decision to better her condition was based on more than Esther's emotional outbursts or haphazard thinking. She had a specific goal and a plan by which to achieve it. Day by day, unremittingly, Esther pursued it. She sold Yehuda's books, hoarding the few rubles she received for them, often rubbing the paper money between her fingers as reassurance that her dream of purchasing freedom from impoverishment was rooted in reality. Seeing how meager was the handful of rubles she had collected drove Esther to search for more, spurring her on as furiously as if there were a sword pressed against her back—for Esther Dubrovsky knew full well how many more rubles she needed to buy salvation. Knowing it was impossible for her to find any kind of employment, Esther accepted the fact that she would have to beg for money. And she did so, fiercely, with the same determination as if she were involved in a fine profession. Daily, Esther roamed the streets of Kiev, hobbling from the ghetto to the center of the city, pleading with everyone she met to part with a kopeck or two. She approached the holy monks of the Lavra and the Catacombs of St. Anthony. She pestered shopkeepers and brazenly approached businessmen and bankers as they stepped from their coaches. She even pursued the rabbi of Kiev's richest synagogue, demanding that he, of all people, should fill her outstretched hands to overflowing. Upon returning home, Esther would carefully count the kopecks she had collected, then drop them, one by one, into the hole she had dug in the dirt floor beneath the washbasin to keep her treasure safe. Every clink of the coins as they landed one atop another reminded Esther how paltry her savings really were.

Constant exposure to Kiev's bitter winter did not leave Esther unscathed. Her voice changed as water collected in her lungs. Her words began to sound fuzzy as the first signs of pneumonia appeared. A deep, convulsive cough tore the skin of Esther's throat, and an infection inflamed her windpipe, making it impossible for her to swallow without pain. A fever that fluctuated to extremes constantly threatened to erupt into a disease that would prove terminal. Sometimes for days on end Esther's feet stayed numb, crawling with fire within while remaining cold to the touch. Yet, Esther never missed a day searching the city for anything with which to sustain herself and her daughter and to add to her already accumulating sum of money.

Soybel, too, was pressed into aiding her mother's plan. Indeed, Soybel's part was most important. Gently stroking her daughter's hair, Esther apologized for sending a girl of fourteen, a child really, out into the harsh Russian world. Esther explained to her daughter why Soybel needed to find work, and yet, as desperate as was the need for money, Soybel's primary task was not the earning of rubles but rather something far more significant; and if Soybel failed her purpose, all would be lost. Understanding the importance of her mother's words, Soybel applied herself zealously to all that was demanded of her. In mid-January she even found work at the Fabrika Relekvya, a Russian manufacturer of ikons. Soybel's job, along with dozens of other young girls and women, was to devote fourteen hours a day to painting comely features, beatific expressions, on the cast-iron saints which adorned the crosses that were so popular among the pilgrims who crowded Kiev year round. Of the scanty wages Soybel earned, some was used to buy kindling sticks that were often so wet they did little more than smolder. Some was used to purchase food. But most of Soybel's earnings were taken by her mother, saved to procure the things that would be needed to flee the ghetto.

Indeed, despite the precariousness of her physical condition and the threat that Soybel would fall prey to a similar fate, Esther Dubrovsky denied both herself and her daughter wholesome nourishment, reasoning that for the moment it was more important to gamble with their lives than to deplete their savings. And so for weeks the Dubrovskys existed on rotten potatoes and stale bread, and the only real heat they had came from the samovar. Each morning before dawn, Esther would fill the large container with snow and then light the precious bits of charcoal in the chamber beneath it. Quickly, the frozen crystals would melt and drip through leaves of tea that had been used many times before. After several days all that was left was clear, steaming water, which the Dubrovskys drank anyway, thankful to have anything warm. But in truth, Esther was plagued by guilt for depriving Soybel of decent food. And yet, though she saw not a single sign that the future would be better, Esther Dubrovsky's ferocious resolve did not diminish.

"Momma?"

Soybel's lilting voice drifting from the back room caused Esther to finally take a match from the small metal box she held, and with a smart strike ignite its phosphorous tip. The sudden warmth of the flame touched Esther's icy fingers and for an instant she hesitated.

"Momma, are you there?"

Cautiously, Esther held the wavering flame to the only piece of wood in the stove. Esther fanned the spot of heat with her breath, careful not to extinguish the crackling pinpoint before it had attached itself to the kindling. Within seconds the bottom of the wood was aflame. *How long will that last—five minutes?* Esther silently muttered.

"Momma!"

"I'm here, Soybel, I am here."

"Is there any tea?"

To us it's tea, kinde, *others would call it orange-colored water.*

"Momma, answer me!"

"There is tea, Soybel. I'll bring you some." As she drew a cupful of the tepid liquid from the samovar Esther wished for the morning when there would be warm bread and strawberry jam for Soybel. Especially strawberry jam, it was Soybel's favorite.

"There is no need to bring it, Momma, I am getting out of bed."

Before Esther could reply, Soybel pushed aside the material that divided the one room from the other. In her hands she held a dress, undergarments, and shoes. Soybel walked to the stove, rubbed herself against it, and stretched. Already her slim fourteen-year-old body was graced with deep curves, and her breasts held the promise of fullness. "Maybe the sun will be warm today," Soybel purred.

Her mother sneered. "And maybe instead of it still being winter, it will suddenly be spring."

"Someday, Momma, it will be spring for us every day."

Esther was drawn to her daughter's oval face and large black eyes that did not just see, but seemed to draw in every thing about her like a spiralling vortex. Ignoring her mother's gaze, Soybel draped the clothes she held over the stove, pulled her woolen nightdress over her head, and then a second one of softer material. Soybel squeezed her eyes shut and waited a moment before attempting to remove the chemise she still wore. Suddenly she pulled it off. Her naked body shivered. Feeling a tug of envy, Esther found it impossible to look away from her daughter's hard nipples and, lower down, at the new shadow of hair that curled across her womanhood. Esther was pleased with how her daughter was maturing. Counting to three, Soybel dressed.

"When you finish your tea, I have something to show you," Esther said.

"Show me now."

Esther smiled. "When I was a girl, I, too, was impatient."

"Show me what it is, Momma."

"Not as beautiful as you, but as impatient." A flicker of sadness touched Esther's face and she sighed. "How ignorant I was when I was your age. Would you believe the girl in that picture there is me, twenty-five years ago? I was fifteen then. And my poppa was so proud that his Esther would someday be married to a great scholar. Two years later I was wed. The day was so exquisite that Kiev looked like the Garden of Eden. The trees were green, the Dnepr blue and clear. More than one hundred people came to our wedding. People wanted to see Yehuda, so when he became as famous as they predicted, they would be able to boast that they attended his wedding. '*That* is Yehuda Dubrovsky,' they whispered in awe. They even took notice of me. And now look at me. Can you believe that I was a beautiful bride? So many boys wanted to marry me, but I had no choice. My dear poppa decided that only Yehuda was good enough for me. To Poppa, having a great scholar for a son-in-law was almost the same as knowing God personally. What good is there in knowing God at all?"

Esther stopped talking for a moment. Soybel, saddened by the weariness she saw in her mother's face, tried to soothe her. "Momma, the winter will soon be over and—" Esther silenced Soybel with a penetrating look.

"Do not pity me, Soybel. I am to blame. I should have refused to marry your father. Something inside me even then warned me that marrying a scholar was an honor only for others." Without warning, a violent fit of coughing wracked Esther's body; her face turned scarlet.

"Momma, are—"

"I am all right, Soybel," Esther gasped. "I am all right."

"Why don't you take some of the money you have saved and see a doctor?"

"I have seen a doctor. He did me a favor out of respect for Yehuda and asked for no money. Only his prescription was expensive—rest, good hot food, a house with heat, and more rest."

"Then do what he said."

"To lie in bed would cost nothing. But how can I afford anything more?"

"You have some money."

"No! It is for more important things. Only a little of winter is left. I will survive. To that I have my mind made up, and nothing will change it."

"Momma, our lives will get better. I promise."

"Yes, for this year. If we survive the winter, we will certainly survive the spring and summer. But then there is next winter. And if we survive that, the winter after it. How many years can people exist like this? When can I stop worrying that next winter it might be your body I claim from the shed? And who will come for my body?" Another bout of coughing interrupted Esther.

"Shhh, Momma, shhh."

"Do you know why it is like this? Because we are Jews. And Jews give birth to sons who are not permitted to acquire educations or jobs. And the daughters of Jews marry those sons. And then they have children who are deprived of educations and jobs. And so it continues, with everyone starving like animals—begging or stealing for a piece of bread or a drop of milk."

"Not for all of us, Momma. Some have better lives."

"*We* do not have better lives, Soybel, and that is all that interests me." Esther stood erect. Her eyes became alert and fierce. "And we will never have better lives if we continue to cry and wring our hands. Nobody gives a damn about us. Nobody cares if we live or die. Not our neighbors. Not your Poppa's friends. No one. Their only concern is themselves. And we will live the same way. There is only one way for us to escape this horror without having to die first. And as long as I am alive, we will try."

The forcefulness of Esther's words aggravated the congestion in her lungs. Her small frame heaved; she doubled over, gasping for air as Soybel watched helplessly. Slowly the fit subsided, and Esther made her way to a chair. She sat down heavily, leaned back, and closed her eyes. Clasping her arms across her chest, Esther swayed from side to side. "Only you can make it possible for us to escape from this place. Only you can save us, Soybel. And I will give you everything you need to save us. If Horodetzky is willing to teach you without payment because he thinks I have agreed to let you marry his son, then so be it. Because I want Horodetzky to teach you all that he knows about history and Russian and French and mathematics. And if Pincus will teach you music for free for a similar promise, then that shall come to pass, too. Because without education and culture, you will capture nothing but the air that surrounds the *luftmenshn.* That is why I will not spare a single kopeck for anything but you. And we will need not just kopecks but rubles to get what we want. More rubles than I have. Many more. And we will get them, anyway we have to."

"And if it does not work? If after all our efforts, I fail to find a husband so rich that he will provide us with a life of luxury, then what, Momma?"

"With just your face, you could have half of the rich Jews in Kiev right now. With an education and culture, you will have anyone you want."

"But what if I fail, Momma?"

"You will not fail. You do not have my permission to fail."

"Then tell me again, Momma, how will I succeed? Please tell me."

"We will use God as He has used us." Esther's expression changed from stern resolution to anticipation. "Because soon it will be Passover, and on that day I intend for us to appear at the *Bais Midrash Hagadol,* the Great Synagogue. Where the merchants go. And the doctors." Esther grabbed Soybel's wrists, digging her nails into them. Her eyes blazed. "Because there is only one place in Kiev where a marriageable girl can meet all the wealthiest Jews, and that is in the Great Synagogue. That is where we will be. Every Sabbath. Every holiday. Every time there is a chance for us to select a prospect. And every time we appear there, I want us to be dressed as beautifully as anyone. And each time we must wear something different. And for that we need rubles and more rubles. For material so I can make dresses and gowns for you. And for me, too. We need money for gloves and hats. And I want to donate at least a respectable sum to the synagogue. Because I want no one to know our circumstances until I have achieved what I want."

"Momma, we are chancing so much on—"

"We are investing, Soybel. Like bankers. Two or three hundred rubles to try for a fortune."

"Even if we are very lucky, Momma, it would take us three, perhaps four years to save so much money."

"I want all of it—and soon!"

"How soon?"

Esther answered not with words, but with her eyes. They were blacker than ever before, and they warned Soybel that her mother would refuse to accept anything less than success. Soybel squirmed in discomfort, wanting to look away but lacking the courage. Esther slowly tapped her knuckles against the table. The uninterrupted evenness of the rhythm was ominous. Still without uttering a word, Esther stood up and with determined steps crossed the room and tore aside the curtain that hid it from the back one. Esther stopped. The icy-blue light of the winter sun cutting through a small window exposed the dreariness of the tiny room all too clearly. It was naked. Dank. The earthen floor, now frozen, would turn to a thick brown slime with the arrival of spring. The wood-slat walls were rotting. Set into one of the walls was a row of unevenly spaced pegs: hanging from the wooden protrusions was the bulk of the Dubrovskys' clothing—nearly all of the pegs were bare. Taking up most of the space in the room was a mattress resting on a wooden platform that had been occupied by Esther and her husband, and was now shared by Esther and her daughter. Covering the bed was a thin rumpled sheet, a layer of newspaper, and a red woolen blanket that was lumpy from Esther having tied hundreds of snags into knots. Partially blocking the window in the room was a cedar chest, its surface marred by gouges, its door fastened with a padlock. Esther grimaced. A surge of anger spirited her into the room and toward the cabinet. Quickly she knelt on the floor before it, thrust her hand beneath it, and withdrew a key. Esther inserted the key into the padlock and turned it. When the tumblers clicked into place, she removed the iron fastener and flung open the doors. From behind a pile of papers on the bottom of the chest, she removed a gray metal box and opened it. Her face beamed. Lovingly, she picked up a slender gold chain on which hung five tiny emeralds. There was something else in the box, but Esther hid it from view. Esther stood up and twirled the necklace. The golden chain shimmered in the sunlight. The emeralds glimmered. Esther brushed her face with the jewels.

"It is exquisite, Momma."

Esther held up the necklace against Soybel's throat.

"It will be even more exquisite on you."

Soybel took the necklace from her mother, and with one hand kept it at her throat while with the other she held a hand mirror and admired herself. "This is really for me?"

"Yes."

"How can I ever thank you?"

"Thank my poppa. He had it made for my mother. When he died he left it to me. Even your poppa never knew I had it."

"Your poppa must have loved your momma very much."

"There was nothing he would not have given her."

"Momma, how come you never sold it to—"

"No!" she cried. "This necklace will never be sold. Because to get a rich husband, a girl must look rich. And anyway, what would have been gained by selling it? Some extra food? Wood? Some clothing? And then we would have been worse off than before. Because those things would be gone. Once you eat something, you cannot eat it again. And you cannot make wood from ashes. What nonsense it would have been to buy new clothes that would have soon become rags. We became used to living the way we do, and we have survived. And we still have the necklace."

"What about a necklace for you? Shouldn't the momma of a rich-looking girl also look rich?"

An uncontrollable flush crept up Esther's neck and mottled her face. With one hand she covered the article she had left in the box. She clenched it in her fist. Esther could feel the coldness of the gold chain and the edges of the tiny ruby that was suspended from it as the gem cut into her flesh. "The only jewel a momma needs is a daughter like you," Esther said nearly inaudibly, her thoughts focused on the fact that this necklace would have to be sold. *Because if it were not . . .*

"Momma, when can I wear my necklace?"

"The very first time we go to the Midrash Gadol."

"When can we go there, Momma, when?"

Tighter yet, Esther clutched the ruby necklace. "Soon, *kinde.*" *Sooner than you imagine.*

CHAPTER 5

On March 10, 1889, the temperature in St. Petersburg dropped to twenty below zero. Church domes, blue, red, and gold in the spring, were capped by snow and topped by gleaming gilded crosses that poked skyward. Over the city's wide snow-covered boulevards skimmed sleighs and sledges, the snorting horses that pulled the vehicles kicking up swirls of flakes as they raced through the biting wind. Swathed from head to toe in fur-lined coats, people dashed from appointment to appointment, trying to cheat winter of chilblained toes and frostbitten faces. In a large room, warmed by a stone fireplace faced with blue-glazed Dutch tiles, a tall broad-shouldered youth of eighteen lay stretched out on a bed that was covered with a fluffy down-filled quilt. He ran the strong-looking fingers of one hand through his long, straight blond hair while with the other he held a letter.

"Andreana, I love you," he said, his basso voice making the Russian words sound like a song. His deep blue eyes sparkled as a vision of a girl's delicately featured face hovered above him. He laughed, pressed the letter to his lips, then dropped it onto the bed. Comfortable in the well-heated room, and warmed even more by the memory of the girl, the young man folded his arms beneath his head and drifted off to sleep. His name was Aleksandr Moisei.

It had been months since Aleksandr had seen his beloved Andreana, a willowy girl of seventeen with hair the color of honey and eyes green like mint. In fact, it was eight months since he had left Odessa for St. Petersburg to begin his first term at the university. His departure from Odessa the previous August had not been unexpected, and yet the last summer evening Aleksandr had spent with Andreana passed far too quickly; since then, not a day had gone by without Aleksandr thinking about those parting hours. He and Andreana had spent the evening in a secluded glen miles from Odessa. The grass had been thick and soft, and a steady breeze from the sea filled the air with the scent of wild roses; the moon hung low in the sky, silhouetting the trees. Aleksandr would never forget how frightened Andreana had been when she slipped out of her dress. He had been almost afraid to touch her. Still, he had taken her hand and gently pulled her to the ground. When he leaned over to kiss Andreana she rolled away, covering her breasts with her arms and drawing herself into a ball to hide herself. "No," she said. But when Aleksandr ran his fingers along her back, then slid them around to her belly, Andreana moved so she could meet his lips with hers. She clawed at his back, her mouth devouring his. After a long embrace Aleksandr pushed Andreana away and examined her body. He was pleased with its lithe fullness. He touched the smooth flesh of Andreana's legs, working his hands between them. Her skin smelled like Oriental spice. Suddenly Andreana sat up.

"Don't, Aleksandr!" She drew up her knees and clasped them with stiff arms. "I am sorry, Aleksandr. I want to . . . but I cannot." There was a tremor to her voice.

Aleksandr lay on the grass and counted the stars.

"I could never face my father again," Andreana tried to explain. "Please understand."

"I do."

"Do you really?"

"I promise I do."

Aleksandr picked up Andreana's dress. The silky material felt cool, and bore Andreana's own particular scent. Reluctantly, Aleksandr placed the gown in Andreana's waiting hands; she moved several yards away and began to dress. Only the sounds of the leaves rubbing against the breeze reached Aleksandr's ears. A few moments later Andreana returned. She looked as proper as when Aleksandr had come to call for her earlier that evening. For a long while the two of them sat side by side looking at the sky, entranced by the fullness of the low-hanging moon, trying to see it move through the night.

It was nearly midnight when Aleksandr's carriage entered Odessa. The streets were empty, giving the young lovers the courage to share a public embrace. Aleksandr held Andreana tightly in his arms, swallowing her breath as he kissed her. The young girl responded passionately and murmured something only she understood. As the carriage approached the road which led to the top of Odessa's terraced hillside, Aleksandr directed the horse to follow it. Upwards the carriage was pulled, all the while its two passengers rushing to bestow enough kisses on each other to last them for all the months they would be apart. The sound of a coach approached and, still clinging to Andreana, Aleksandr grabbed the reins, slapping the horse into the driveway which wound its way to the Vizhni villa. Knowing that her father's favorite servant would hear them well before they reached the house and be waiting outside to help his mistress to the ground, Andreana sat upright, inspected her dress to make sure nothing was awry, and carefully fixed her hair.

"What will you tell your father when he asks how you enjoyed the carnival tonight?" Aleksandr asked.

A uniformed man stood in the light of the villa's open doorway.

"I shall tell him it was wonderful."

The elderly servant hurried down the long flight of wide stone steps to the courtyard.

"Was the carnival any good at all?" asked Andreana, straining to keep herself from touching Aleksandr's face in view of the valet.

"As you said, it was wonderful," he replied, understanding the meaning of her cryptic question.

"When you come back from school in the spring, there will be a better one. I promise."

Before the carriage had rolled to a complete stop the servant, dressed in a red and gold uniform, extended his hand so it would be ready to help the girl alight.

"Good evening, Miss Andreana. I trust you had a pleasant time."

Andreana nodded her head, keeping her eyes on Aleksandr.

"And a good evening to you too, sir."

Aleksandr acknowledged the servant with a slight dip of his head.

Andreana's eyes filled with tears. Instinctively, she took hold of the servant's hand and stepped down from the carriage. "Have a good trip with your father, Aleksandr. And have a good year at school," she said, trying to sound properly formal.

"I will."

The liveried man moved discreetly away but not out of earshot.

"Write to me," said Andreana, her voice cracking.

"Every week."

No longer caring how she sounded, she beseeched, "Write to me—every day!"

"Your father is waiting for you, Miss." The servant's tone implied that Igor Vizhni would disapprove of his daughter's open display of familiarity.

"I will write twice a day," Aleksandr promised softly.

The servant started up the flight of stairs, his firm footsteps pulling at Andreana like a magnet. She followed behind him. Nearing the villa's ornate entranceway, Andreana turned and waved good-bye to Aleksandr. He waved too, but before he was able to blow her a kiss she disappeared inside, the servant quietly closing the door and sealing Andreana within. Aleksandr cried out, reaching to grab hold of the night and pull Andreana back. He wanted to run with her, to return with her to the countryside and begin the evening again. "I love you," he whispered to himself, aching because Andreana was unable to hear him. "I love you. I love you. *I LOVE YOU!*" Reluctantly, Aleksandr Moisei wheeled his carriage away from the villa, the darkness of the world around him matching his anguish.

That Aleksandr Moisei was courting the daughter of Igor Vizhni, an aristocrat by birth, seemed to bother no one. Certainly not Jacob Moisei. His son's wooing the daughter of a man whose wealth and power were well known in Odessa greatly pleased Jacob; in truth, Jacob was rather impressed with Aleksandr. Indeed, using his son as his prime example, Jacob Moisei often mentioned to his wife how different their lives had become since they converted from Judaism. Repeatedly, he would recite the names of his new friends and business associates, swelling with pride each time he recalled how he himself had changed the fortunes of the Moisei family. No longer was Jacob just a well-to-do Jew. Now he was a man of solid wealth with a degree of influence, especially at Odessa's port, where he managed the daily affairs of the Viska enterprise. The stigma of being a Jew, treated as a social pariah, had no bearing anymore on Jacob's life. He and Naomi were familiar figures at the theater, opera, ballet. Every year Jacob and his family were invited to attend the exclusive balls held at the Financial Exchange. Only once, when he realized that never would he be invited to become a member of Odessa's venerable Arkadia Yacht Club, was Jacob reminded that his baptismal certificate had not fully erased his heritage. Undaunted, he gathered together a syndicate of rich converted Jews and rich but not aristocratic Russians to organize a second yacht club. At Jacob's direction a charter was drawn, a clubhouse designed and built, and within a year Odessa was host to two yacht clubs: the aristocratic Arkadia and the newer Pamoyre; it was because of Jacob's association with the Pamoyre Yacht Club that Aleksandr was able to first meet Andreana, a fact Jacob never permitted his wife and son to forget. All in all, the life of Jacob Moisei and his family was one of great comfort, with unbounded expectations for an even richer future. Yet, of all his possessions, there was none more important to Jacob than his son. And what he cherished most was preparing Aleksandr for the finest possible future.

Naomi Moisei also considered Aleksandr most precious. She was enchanted that he had inherited her ready smile, easygoing manner, her unusual comeliness. And she was determined that her son would learn to face the world as she did: with compassion and gentleness, with a willingness to disregard the foibles of others and to cherish them for their goodness.

Naomi's resolves in respect to Aleksandr's upbringing were points of bitter contention between her and her husband. Jacob's motto was "Pragmatism at all costs." To him, Aleksandr was a raw gem to be artfully faceted for a career at the highest level of Russia's financial community, or perhaps as a jurist, and possibly, if the results of Aleksandr's careful nurturing and opportunity coincided, a position of importance in the government. Jacob believed that only a woman could afford to exist with a defensive temperament. And he chided his wife for her naiveté, for her ignorance of the myriad complications not only of the business and social worlds, but also of the political sphere, an arena where nothing but pragmatism had ever proved effective. Beneficial though it is for Naomi to acquaint her son with aesthetics, Jacob often repeated, far more essential is that Aleksandr comprehend what is most effective in dealing with those of influence and power: though the Tsar appreciates music, he does not ask the counsel of musicians on affairs of state. This disagreement between Jacob and Naomi was only one of many regarding Aleksandr's rearing and education. But these quarrels were short-lived. For, as in most things, Naomi Moisei deferred to her husband.

In fact, in all facets of life Naomi Moisei behaved according to Jacob's eccentricities. Obsessed with outward appearances, Jacob demanded "proper" behavior both at home and in public. Protocol and etiquette were never to be compromised. Propriety and only the most refined of manners were tolerated by Jacob. He shunned any display of emotion, becoming irate at those who resorted to histrionics. And when the behavior of one of his family did not meet with his approval, he retaliated with his most vile epithet: "You are behaving like a Jew." Whenever Jacob and his wife attended the theater, opera, or any social gathering, he decided what Naomi wore, selected her accessories, determined if her décolletage was excessive. And Jacob was prudish. He never disrobed before his wife; disapproved if she appeared naked before him; was discomfited by Naomi's impulsive displays of warmth. Indeed, though Naomi was a passionate woman, endowed by nature with the most feminine of charms, nothing she did could entice her husband to make love to her less perfunctorily.

Still, Naomi loved Jacob deeply. And she was truly devoted to her role as his wife. For though her marriage was not extraordinary when compared to other wives of her standing, Jacob was an unusually thoughtful husband. Often he surprised Naomi with gifts for no apparent reason. Never once did he forget to mark the day of her birth by having flowers delivered and arriving home with a stunning and expensive piece of jewelry which he would invariably present, if gruffly, with a phrase of affection, too. Always, Naomi would thank her husband with a peck on the cheek, and a reminder that his extravagance was uncalled for. Jacob would laugh, amused by his wife's bent toward frugality. For despite all the years they had lived together, and Naomi's repeating that material possessions meant nothing to her, Jacob Moisei was unable to fully accept his wife's word as true.

Naomi had not always been blasé about her husband's extravagance. Once she had been thrilled by Jacob's generosity toward her. She was nineteen years old then, possessed of vitality and beauty, unusual intelligence, and too aware of her own attributes to be easily flattered. But a dapper young man of twenty-nine, with an intense self-assured determination, caught her fancy; his name was Jacob Moisei. Their attraction was mutual, and after a brief, concentrated, and lavish courtship they were married. Immediately, Naomi was swept into Jacob's whirlwind world of parties, dinners, and exclusive social gatherings with Odessa's prominent Jews. Everywhere she went with Jacob, Naomi was treated regally, for already her husband was considered a businessman of acumen, a man to befriend. And for Naomi, every second of life with Jacob was exhilarating, overflowing with riches of all kinds, and it was quite some time before her wonderment at being Madame Moisei subsided. But that was understandable when the circumstances of her childhood were considered.

Naomi Moisei had been born Naomi Livitnov in the squalor of the ghetto in Grodno, a city in the north of the Pale. Eleven years later, after her mother succumbed to a combination of malnutrition and tuberculosis, Naomi's father and his young daughter migrated south to Odessa. If nothing else, Mendel Livitnov knew that the climate of the Black Sea city would make poverty much less gruesome. Much to his surprise, he discovered that the weather was not Odessa's only positive aspect. The easy-going cosmopolitan nature of the city made life more than tolerable. In truth, Mendel and his daughter thrived.

Being a cobbler of talent, and a man of pluck, before long Mendel Livitnov became known for his ability to fashion handsome boots and fine leather goods. Year by year his reknown and prosperity increased. His clientele grew in caliber as well as size. No longer did Mendel repair the boots of ordinary Jews; instead, he custom-crafted footwear for the men of Odessa's Jewish elite.

Released from Grodno's oppressive atmosphere, from the watchful eyes of orthodox neighbors, enjoying his unexpected financial success and desiring more gain, Mendel

Livitnov discarded his traditional beliefs. He shaved his beard and sidecurls. Donned fashionable clothing. He educated his daughter, excitedly watching her evolve from a shy withdrawn child into a mature woman of beauty and with a keenness of mind. Savoring his life-style, relishing the smattering of cameraderie he shared with his customers, and being an astute businessman, Mendel Livitnov decided to ingratiate himself even more with his clients. And so he became a member of their synagogue, the Brody—the most influential synagogue in Odessa, and the most different of all synagogues in Russia.

To the Jews of the Pale, the Brody Synagogue was infamous, despised for being more like a church than a synagogue. Its congregation, the *maskilim,* were vilified as satans. Because of the Brody and the *maskilim,* Russia's Jews considered Odessa a city filled with sinners, freethinkers, blasphemers. The *maskilim,* whose lives were so russified as to make them appear little different from non-Jews, had no sympathy for the pious orthodox *shtetl* Jews. Indeed, the *maskilim* prided themselves on how little the Brody and its religious services resembled the antiquated and restrictive traditions of their forefathers. To them the Bible was no longer considered the book of knowledge, but a collection of fables. Yiddish, the language of the ghetto, was abhorred, pointed to as a major barrier between the Jews and the rest of Russia. They ridiculed the old-fashioned dress of the Orthodox: the long black coats, high-topped hats, wild beards, and sidecurls. "If you must be a Jew, then be a Jew at home. But on the streets, be a Russian!" the *maskilim* shouted to the pious. "Even to appear to assimilate is to perish," the Orthodox retorted. "To be slaughtered is to perish even more!" came the rejoinder. Certain that theirs was the only path to salvation, the *maskilim* proceeded with the russification of their religion. The Brody was not to be a synagogue where men gathered morning and evening, day in and day out, to pray, to honor God, to perpetuate His orthodoxy. Rather, the Brody Synagogue would be a place where the moneyed Jews of Odessa assembled only on the Sabbath and holidays not to praise God, but to be entertained by Him.

The rabbi of the Brody was Joshua Eleazar, a worldly man whose primary desire was to please his congregation. He was determined to fashion the Brody into a showpiece of modernity, a house of worship where the demands of Judaism were reduced to a pleasant glossy imitation. The use of Hebrew in prayers was replaced by Russian. The old prayerbooks were discarded and new ones, Russian translations, were purchased. Rabbi Eleazar hired a choir and an orchestra to perform at Sabbath services. An organ of great size and expense was installed, and an organist, known for his virtuosity rather than for his liturgical knowledge, was engaged. Secular paintings and frescoes were commissioned. The great sums of money contributed to the Brody by its members were used to renovate the synagogue's interior, to make it resplendent, not to honor God, but to satisfy the eyes of the worshippers. No longer was the Brody a shrine, but a grand hall for socializing, exchanging gossip, and conducting business. To the rest of the Jews of the Pale, sacrilege and Odessa became synonymous. Still, the Brody's *maskilim,* protected from persecution by their version of Judaism, were certain that they had discovered the only way to prosper in Russia while remaining Jews.

Jacob Moisei certainly believed that. He had been a *maskil* long before he met Naomi, and he attributed his financial success as much to being russified as he did to his business ability. Mendel and his daughter also pursued the philosophy of *Haskalah,* the concept of integrating Judaic culture with the culture of Western Europe: in short, assimilation. But the attraction of *Haskalah* abruptly faded for Mendel, and slowly he drifted back to his Orthodoxy; his daughter, though at a great distance, followed behind him. The occasion for Mendel's turnabout, and then his daughter's, was the birth of Aleksandr Jacobovich Moisei.

From the moment of Aleksandr's arrival, Naomi Moisei believed that she had borne a perfect child. When he was a baby, she surrounded Aleksandr wiith cooing and caressing, with toys and games, and one-sided conversations overflowing with love. She spent hours reading to Aleksandr, observing him play. When he reached the age when all children struggle for their own identities, Naomi reluctantly stepped aside, adoring her son from afar. Once Aleksandr had become sure of himself, had gained the ability to verbalize his thoughts, could express his own self, Naomi was again welcomed into his world. For hours she talked to him of her own childhood, of her hopes for herself and her wants for him. With a love so strong that it bordered on pain, Naomi watched her father, Aleksandr's beloved Papu, cradle her child in his arms and rock him to sleep with memories of his yesteryears, Bible stories, with the lullabies of Judaism. After the Moiseis became Christians, Jacob forbade Naomi and Mendel to even mention to Aleksandr his Jewish origins. Only Papu had the courage to defy Jacob, telling him directly that it was the accursed Brody Synagogue which had made Jacob weak enough to convert. Defiantly, Papu embarked on a project of secretly inculcating Aleksandr with all of Jewish history, tradition, religion. But Papu died six months after his grandson and daughter were baptized. And the beliefs that prevailed were those of Jacob Moisei.

With the passing of years, Aleksandr matured into a healthy, upstanding young man, his self-assured assertiveness moderated by compassion, and Naomi adored him. Yet there was one thing about her son that disappointed Naomi: Aleksandr seemed to have forgotten his Papu and all the gentle old man had taught him. Naomi hoped that was not true. On the day that Aleksandr and his father boarded the train which would take them to St. Petersburg, to the university, it was with a sense of great pride, but even more, with a sense of suffering an irreparable loss that Naomi bade Aleksandr good-bye. For, as the train pulled out of Odessa's railroad station, leaving her standing there alone, Naomi Moisei feared that the son who had just left her would soon forget his mother as he had his grandfather.

Aleksandr's acceptance at the University of St. Petersburg was not unexpected. Beginning with his childhood, Jacob had prepared his son to achieve that goal. Aleksandr's early education, consisting of mathematics, history, Russian literature, and the Russian, French, Greek, and Latin languages, was drilled into him by tutors. Also, to ready Aleksandr for a world of wealth and rank, Jacob had him instructed in etiquette and the dances most in vogue with the nobility. Complementing the knowledge and grace he had acquired, nature had endowed Aleksandr with an unusually handsome face, classically featured, and with a smile of disarming innocence. By the time he had passed the middle of his teenage years, Aleksandr's body had developed into one of sinewy grace. His shoulders were broad and strong, his arms heavily muscled, and he stood an inch over six feet tall; Aleksandr's custom-tailored clothing further enhanced his appearance. A love of merriment, Bessarabian wine, and an apparent fearlessness made Aleksandr a leader among the young men with whom he associated, all the offspring of parents as prominent as his own. But it was the distaff side which most openly admired him, his dazzling looks and charming manners enamoring Aleksandr to every young woman in his class.

Despite the wealth of diversions available to Aleksandr, his first love was for his *Golub,* the finely crafted sailboat his father had specially built for him. Rarely a day passed without Aleksandr racing his sloop far beyond Odessa's breakwater; he risked the most stormy weather, stimulated by the challenge of rough seas and heavy winds. By his seventeenth birthday, he was a daring, skilled sailor with six years of experience. During his eighteenth year, Aleksandr was granted the opportunity to truly test his prowess. In that year the sailors of Odessa's Arkadia and Pamoyre yacht clubs finally acknowledged each other's existence; the communiqué was a challenge from the Arkadia to participate in a regatta.

The race itself was uneventful, Aleksandr finishing third in a fleet of twenty-seven boats; the first two places were captured by Arkadia Club sailors. Rather than his crossing the finish line well behind the leader being considered a loss, Aleksandr was praised by the aristocrats of the sailing community; they were surprised and impressed by Aleksandr's excellent showing. Their skills, after all, had been learned at the hands of well-seasoned skippers; Aleksandr had preferred to learn by trial and error. In celebration of the race, a party was held aboard the *Maryevo,* the most luxurious yacht in the older club's flotilla. Aleksandr was warmly greeted by many whom he had previously known only from crossing their bows on the sea. Invitations for him to crew on sailboats far more sophisticated than his *Golub* were forthcoming. Young men with titles chatted amiably with him, captivated by his affability. Girls costumed in expensive replicas of peasant outfits, and others more formally attired, all displaying expensive jewelry, vied for Aleksandr's attention, laughing at his every witty remark, but truly more interested in gaping at him than in listening to him.

With the approach of darkness, the *Maryevo*'s kerosene lanterns were lighted and an eerie orange glow covered the boat, spilling onto the water. Bottles of wine appeared, and everyone drank heartily. Couples searched for privacy. Aleksandr, having flirted with many of the young women, was interested in only one: a girl of sixteen who, when he had smiled at her, had shyly averted her eyes. Aleksandr approached her and introduced himself. Softly, she gave her name: Andreana Vizhni. Sensing a fragility about her, Aleksandr proceeded slowly. Together they sat on the *Maryevo*'s bow, talking of themselves in whispery voices. And they kissed—once, a fleeting touch of their lips. But with that kiss an ardor was born that would not be denied. After that night, unable to think of anything but her, Aleksandr pursued Andreana. And though he yearned for her, ached to sweep her into his arms, to know her completely, Aleksandr did nothing that might frighten or threaten his Andreana. Never did he abandon the utmost propriety. Gradually, almost imperceptibly, a passion awakened in Andreana; its subtle emergence entrapping Aleksandr all the more. When the night before his departure for St. Petersburg arrived, and Andreana's desire for him was unleashed, Aleksandr knew that with but a little coaxing, with reason couched in romantic terms, he could have overcome her final resistance. Instead, he refrained from doing with her what they both so desperately wanted. He refrained, because to have done otherwise would have been to desecrate the reflection of his mother that Aleksandr unwittingly perceived in Andreana.

CHAPTER 6

"Aleksandr, are you home?"

"Is that you, Solomon?"

"Yes."

"The door is open, come in!"

A dark-haired young man wrapped in an enormous fur coat entered the room. "Were you sleeping?" Solomon's voice sounded gruff; it was his natural tone. His Russian, spoken in as rapid and staccato a cadence as his Yiddish, the first language he had known, added a barbed edge to Solomon's words.

Aleksandr arose from the bed.

"I can see you weren't studying." Solomon moved closer to the fire. An ember crackled into the air; it landed on his fur wrap, singeing several of its hairs.

"Be careful, Solomon, or you will burn the entire coat."

"Then you can buy me another. Or better yet, I will stay here where it's warm until spring." Solomon stepped away from the blazing logs, removed his coat and fur-lined gloves, and tossed them onto a chair; his every move had a fierceness to it.

"You do not need an excuse to come and live with me."

Solomon looked around the room. Its opulence was overwhelming. "There is no place for me to cook my meals here," he noted ironically.

"You could dine out with me."

"Every day?"

"Why not? The food is good. And rather inexpensive."

"To you, perhaps."

"You know I would pay for it."

Solomon walked toward a bookcase. "Anyway, I could never study here. The way I scatter my books about, I would be in your way."

"I would not mind."

"Of course you wouldn't. You never study," Solomon bantered in return.

"I study. But not locked away for weeks at a time like you. And why do you bother to lock yourself away, anyway? To keep out your friends so they will not disturb you? Except for me, Solomon, you have no friends in St. Petersburg."

Amused by the drollness of Aleksandr's tone, Solomon turned and looked at him. After all these months since their first meeting, he was still impressed by Aleksandr's dash and striking good looks. *I wonder if you have any idea, Aleksandr, that with you as my friend I have no need of any others.* Solomon grinned.

"What is so humorous?"

"I was just wondering if you will still be so smug if you fail your exams."

"I will not fail them."

"You make it sound so simple."

"I read something once, Solomon, and I can remember nearly every word."

"But do you learn anything?"

"If I know the answers to the questions, what more is there?" Aleksandr walked across the room.

Solomon's intense brown eyes followed Aleksandr's every move.

"I wish it were as easy to become a doctor as it apparently is to become a lawyer."

Aleksandr opened the liquor cabinet. "Wine or vodka?"

"Vodka." Solomon peered into the cabinet and counted ten varieties of liquor. "I will miss your selection when school is over for the term."

"I have already invited you to Odessa for the summer. You could choose from a dozen times as many in my father's house."

"I will come to Odessa on one condition."

"And what is that?" Aleksandr filled two glasses with the clear colorless drink.

"You go to Mogilev for the summer."

Aleksandr did not respond. He handed Solomon one glass while he finished the vodka in his own. Aleksandr poured himself a second drink. The undertone of resentment in Solomon's voice made Aleksandr uncomfortable. More than once Solomon had depicted his life in the ghetto of Mogilev,, the hardships his family suffered, the sacrifices they had made to educate him. Aleksandr had been shocked by the privations Solomon described. And Solomon had mocked Aleksandr's horrified reactions, pointedly remarking that for all of his wordliness, Aleksandr was woefully ignorant of the world in which he lived.

"You see, Aleksandr, your invitation is not repeated so quickly, is it?" Solomon walked to the bed, picked up the letter to Andreana that Aleksandr had left there, and began to read it.

"If I wanted you to know what it says, Solomon, I would have made a copy for you."

"What is the difference if I read it or you tell me what is in it?" Solomon skimmed the letter quickly and replaced it on the edge of the bed.

"When I tell you what I have written to Andreana, I can omit what I do not want you to know."

Solomon chuckled and sprawled his stocky, muscular body across the bed. "You will be a good lawyer, Aleksandr."

"And when you need some advice, Solomon, I will only charge you half."

"And I will be your doctor, Aleksandr. And when you need treatment, I will only charge you double."

Aleksandr laughed, expecting Solomon to do the same. He did not. Instead, Solomon rolled onto his back and stared at the ceiling.

"Have you heard from Andreana yet?"

"No." Aleksandr slouched in one of the chairs in front of the fireplace. "If the snows have been half as bad in the south as they have been here, I am not surprised a letter from her has not arrived."

"I wish you would hear from her. I am tired of your love life."

"I am willing to listen to yours."

"That is because I have none. I am too busy."

"But if you wanted to, you could have. I have seen more than one girl stop and look at you a second time." Aleksandr studied the defiant face of his friend.

"How can you be sure they weren't looking at you?"

"I can tell the difference." Aleksandr understood why Solomon's perpetually arrogant expression attracted attention. He himself was intrigued by it.

"Next time, let me know and I will look back."

Aleksandr nodded his head and twirled his glass between his fingers. Reflections of the fire's flames glinted from its faceted surface.

"Do you ever stop thinking about Andreana?" Solomon asked.

"The first time I saw her, Solomon, I thought she was the most beautiful girl I had ever seen. In the sunlight her hair looked like gold. She was wearing a pink blouse and she looked like a bewitching figurehead sitting on the *Maryevo*'s bow. But more than her face, Solomon, it is Andreana's nature that I love." Aleksandr's voice had taken on a poetic quality and the expression on his face was wistful. "She is so gentle. Once we found a bird with its wing broken, and while I stood there and spoke of the pain the bird was in, Andreana carefully picked it up, then took it home to mend it. At the carnival she refused to look at the midgets and dwarfs; the sights of their deformities were too much for her to bear. And the night her father's favorite horse had to be destroyed, Andreana was inconsolable."

Aleksandr remembered how Andreana had clung to him for comfort that night, her face pressed tightly against his, her tears wetting his face, moistening his lips, the saltiness tasting like nectar to him. And he could still smell her perfume; a whisper of jasmine mingling with a trace of musk. As she wept, Andreana begged Aleksandr to hold her closer until he feared he would crush her with his arms, and still she cried to be held closer. The heat from Andreana's body blazed through her clothes, making Aleksandr light-headed, causing his blood to rush to his loins and making his manhood swell. Tighter, Andreana asked to be held. Needing no urging, Aleksandr obliged, all the while pushing his hips and thighs hard against her, and she responded, her sadness turning to desire, her ardor burning away her sorrow. She tried to consume his lips with hers. The hunger of her mouth, her tongue, was insatiable. Again and again, Aleksandr thrust himself against Andreana, and then it was over, a wetness oozing down Aleksandr's thighs making him dispirited, reminding him of how much more of Andreana he wanted. And she, still unsatisfied, could do nothing but wait for her frustration to ebb, while a heavy sweet odor that emanated from deep within her filled the air with the pungent scent of love.

"I hope that poor doctors can find the same kinds of girls rich lawyers do," Solomon said, his voice tugging Aleksandr out of his reverie. Solomon's large eyes looked dreamy and he thought for a long moment. "Did you ever think, Aleksandr, that even if I become a doctor I might be poor? But you, even if you become nothing, you will always be rich."

Aleksandr squirmed. He disliked Solomon's reminding him of his wealth, especially now. It seemed particularly mundane in comparison to his memory of Andreana. "Did you know," Solomon continued, "that there isn't a city in the Pale where the Jews do not despise the Odessa Jews?"

"Why?" asked Aleksandr, at the moment not really caring why.

"Perhaps the word should be envy," Solomon added with a touch of sarcasm.

"Envy?"

Solomon nodded his head, his condescending smile angering Aleksandr. "Because we converted?" Aleksandr asked pointedly, Solomon's sarcasm blotting out any thought of Andreana.

Solomon's expression indicated the exasperation he felt.

"Solomon, I know about that life. You have told me—"

"But you have not lived it, Aleksandr. And though I could tell you every detail of how we try to survive a single day, it would be nothing like living it for just one second."

"The day I first met you at *Tshukin Dvor* I realized more than you imagine."

"What you saw that day was someone in Paradise! But how would you know?"

Solomon jumped to his feet. He waved a hand to emphasize his words; the well-developed muscles of his arms knotted visibly beneath his shirt. "Do you know that I am risking every spare ruble my family has, to become a doctor? Every ruble my father, my uncles, and both my grandfathers have has been gambled by them for my education. And not only did they have to pay for *my* place at the university, but for the place of a non-Jew, too! It did not matter that the marks on my exams were far higher than anyone else's. I was a Jew, so I had to obey the custom of paying *two* tuitions. And now that I have been in school for two years, my family is already convinced, as is the entire ghetto at Mogilev, that I am going to be the greatest surgeon Russia has ever had. Do you have any idea what it would mean if I failed them?"

"You won't," Aleksandr replied, his assurance sounding inconsequential.

"I casually mentioned you to my parents in a letter. All I wrote was that I have a friend who comes from Odessa, and that his father is the manager of one of the largest export businesses there. Do you know how they interpreted that information? To them it is proof that all my patients will be so wealthy that I will be wealthy, too. I am sure they dream that I will be so brilliant a physician that the Tsar himself will request my medical skills!"

Solomon ripped open the burgundy drapes that covered a wall of windows. Before him stretched St. Petersburg, the snow making the buildings and thoroughfares look even more grand than they already were. "One boulevard in this city is bigger than all of Mogilev. When I told my poppa about the Winter Palace, that six thousand people live there, he did not believe me. He was certain I was exaggerating. I described the Hermitage to him. He was awe-struck by the number of chandeliers and gold statues. But when I told him about the garden on the roof, and how it blooms all year round because of its being heated by subterranean stoves, he thought I had lost my senses and was delirious with fantasies. You have no idea, Aleksandr, what this city looks like through my eyes. The palaces, the boulevards, the golden domes of the churches. I can see those things and I still do not believe it. To my father it must all sound preposterous. Yet, he still has the audacity to believe that the Tsar will be lying sick in bed and ask for the help of Doctor Solomon Levin." Turning to face Aleksandr, Solomon continued: "My poppa was so impressed with your wealth he did not even care that you are an Odessa Jew. And for his entire life he has hated the bogus Jews from the south."

"Didn't you tell him that we are Christians now?"

Solomon shook his head with resignation. "How many times must I tell you that all the holy oil in Russia can anoint you, you can attend ten thousand masses, but you will always be a Jew, Aleksandr."

Aleksandr shifted uneasily in his chair. Frequently, he and Solomon had argued about their drastically different backgrounds, and how each had been affected by his upbringing. Aleksandr charged Solomon with being bull-headed, of seeing the world so narrowly that he attacked everything with sentiment rather than reason. Infuriated by what he considered to be Aleksandr's dilettante ways regarding education and purpose in life, Solomon denounced Aleksandr for his complacency, condemning him for accepting his father's timidity, and continuing to pretend that he was a Christian. Aleksandr had stood in silence under his companion's indictment, distressed by his simultaneously feeling that he had committed no sin by adhering to Jacob's wishes and that there was more truth to Solomon's words than he was willing to accept.

"As far as I am concerned," Aleksandr finally said, "I believe in no religion. In Odessa I go to church every Sunday with my father and mother, because that is what my father wants. If he decided that we should go to synagogue, I would go there. To me they are both the same."

"You do not have the courage to be a Jew, Aleksandr."

"Damn it, Solomon, I think I proved my courage to you months ago!"

"You accepted a dare, Aleksandr, out of guilt."

Shaken by the accusation, Aleksandr looked away from his friend.

"You write a few words on a piece of paper and you are convinced that you have defied the world. I asked you seriously to do something, but what was it to you? Perhaps it was not because of your conscience that you did it. Maybe it was just a prank!"

"No!"

Solomon eyed Aleksandr with mild disdain. "Tell me something: when you converted, did the priest make the sign of the cross on your prick, too?"

CHAPTER 7

Two weeks later, Aleksandr's father arrived unannounced in St. Petersburg on the early morning train. He wasted little time hurrying from the depot to the Hotel Rozhdestvenka, where he had wired ahead for reservations. Although he was tired and irritable, Jacob bathed and shaved, then dressed in a black German cheviot suit, a white shirt with a steel-gray weave running through it, and a pearl-gray cravat. Satisfied that his appearance was impeccable, Jacob left the room, rushed through the hotel's elegant lobby and, in too much of a hurry to wait for the uniformed doorman to arrange transportation, hired his own sleigh.

"I want to go to the university!" commanded Jacob, climbing into the vehicle.

The driver nodded, barely touching his horse with the whip.

"If you can manage to take me across town before nightfall, I will pay you double," Jacob added, the derision in his voice the cutting edge of the impatience he felt within.

The driver nodded again but did nothing to urge his horse to move faster than a walk.

"Triple then, you bastard!"

With a flick of his wrist, the *ivoshtchik* whipped the

horse's flanks, sending the animal into a fast trot. The sleigh moved swiftly along the spacious boulevards, their smooth stone surfaces a perfect bed for the hard-packed snow.

As the vehicle sped through the Petersburg streets, Jacob kept his head buried inside his coat to avoid the sub-zero wind that tore across the Neva River. He paid no heed to the famous iron bridge, an engineering marvel, that was the first permanent structure to span the waterway. The Winter Palace, which had enthralled Jacob when he first saw it, did not even make him stir; none of the splendid sights of the capital intrigued him. When the sleigh finally skidded to a halt before an imposing building, Jacob quickly stepped down to the ground before it had fully stopped. Without a complaint, he paid the driver the exorbitant fare and hastened away. The *ivoshtchik* belched loudly and cackled. Ignoring the man's effrontery, Jacob hurried toward the building.

A mighty bell rang out from a distant tower. Unmindful of the sound, Jacob entered the university and briskly strode along a marble corridor, his footsteps clicking loudly against the stone floor. Deeply involved in his own thoughts, Jacob ignored the sauntering students passing by. When he reached a second corridor which intersected the first, Jacob caught the eye of a young man whose arms were laden with books.

"Excuse me, I am looking for the office of the Chancellor."

"It is to your left, sir."

"Thank you." Jacob took a deep breath, turned smartly on his heel, and proceeded down the second corridor. At the third doorway he paused. A row of gold Cyrillic letters indicated the entrance to the office of the ruling official of the Imperial University, Chancellor Viktor Yadinovich Bezobrazov. With a brisk push, Jacob opened the door and stepped inside. A diminutive man, sitting behind a large desk cluttered with papers, looked up.

"Yes?" The man seemed annoyed.

"My name is Jacob Moisei. I have an appointment with the Chancellor."

With deliberate slowness, the man ran his finger along a page in a leatherbound appointment book. "So you do."

"Would you inform him that I am here."

"I will see if he is free yet."

"Yes, would you please?"

Unmoved by Jacob's apparent urgency, the secretary carefully completed the form on which he was working. He then rose from his chair and lightly rapped on a door just to the side of his desk. After a moment's wait, he opened the door slightly and slipped inside. A minute later the man returned. There was a sneer on his face. "The Chancellor will see you now, *Mr.* Moisei."

Jacob walked past the secretary and entered the room. His eyes were drawn to the bookshelves filled with important-looking volumes. At the far end of the room, floor-to-ceiling windows let the full glare of the sun stream into the room, creating a luminous backdrop for the man sitting behind a well-polished desk. Even though he was sitting, it was obvious that the Chancellor was a man of impressive proportions. His face was hidden by a full, perfectly manicured beard, and his navy-blue uniform adorned with gold braid and military medals added an aura of invincibility to his formidable appearance.

"Mr. Moisei, I am glad to see you have arrived safely in St. Petersburg," the Chancellor said without moving, his resonant voice not unfriendly. "Sit down, won't you?" He indicated a leather armchair in front of the desk.

"A copy of the letter is in front of you, sir, and the other document is beneath it," said the secretary, assuming an air of gravity.

"Thank you."

The slight man bowed and exited from the room.

"I apologize if my letter confused you, Mr. Moisei," the Chancellor said as he read the handwritten communiqué before him.

"It also greatly disturbed me. From his last report, and his letters, I assumed that Aleksandr was doing quite well."

"He is."

"Then I am more confused than ever."

"I can appreciate that, Mr. Moisei, but in truth I should think that you would have understood what is certainly no secret in Russia."

"As I remember, your letter stated that due to recent developments, of which you were sure I was aware, it would be better if Aleksandr voluntarily withdrew from the university." Jacob quoted from an official communiqué which he had received two weeks before, and which he now carried in his inside jacket pocket.

"Yes, that is a fair summary," replied the Chancellor, setting down his copy of the letter.

"On the basis of that kind of information, or lack of it, I saw no reason for Aleksandr to withdraw. That is why I insisted you see me. He does not yet know that I am in St. Petersburg. Without facts how can I explain to him that he has been asked to leave the university?"

The Chancellor leaned back in his chair and fingered the campaign ribbons pinned to his coat. "The only reason I suggested a withdrawal was because of your son's academic record. His achievements have earned him some consideration. But if you prefer, I could have him dismissed. That would follow him everywhere, and certainly would be a reflection on his character."

"And what would that reflection be?" Jacob asked pointedly, refusing to be intimidated.

"That he lacked the manners and sense of a gentleman. Even Jews can be respected as gentlemen, Mr. Moisei," the Imperial educator responded, displaying the first sign of temper.

"I do not understand." Jacob looked stunned.

"Are you ignorant of the law?"

"What law?"

Carefully enunciating his words, the Chancellor answered

Jacob's question. "The law that states Jews cannot be members of the judiciary. They are barred from it. Is that clear enough for you?"

"But we are Christians! We converted years ago," explained Jacob weakly, perspiration beading on his forehead.

"Perhaps *you* are a Christian," the Chancellor rumbled. "But you are not attending this university." The Chancellor sat ramrod-straight and peered down at Jacob. "And by his own admission, Mr. Moisei, your son is a *Jew*."

"That is impossible!"

"Read this if you doubt my word." The Chancellor handed Jacob another document that was on the desk. "Every student who attends St. Petersburg is required to complete this questionnaire. Do you see where it asks for the religion of the student?"

With a slight nod of his head, Jacob indicated that he did. He ran a finger along the collar of his shirt, finding it suddenly too tight.

"Then please tell me, Mr. Moisei, what is written there in your son's own handwriting?"

Almost inaudibly Jacob said, "Jew."

"Yes, Jew. And since I have just schooled you in the law, you certainly must be able to see that for Aleksandr to continue studying for a career in law, to prepare for a profession he will not be permitted to practice, would be a waste of his time. And a waste of the university's time. In addition, your son is preventing a Russian youth from acquiring a jurist's education."

"Is there nothing I can do? An appeal to the Minister of Education? A substantial contribution to the university?"

"I am sorry. There is nothing that can be done. Even if your son agreed to change his field of study, our quota of Jewish students is already filled in other departments."

An expression of utter despair covered Jacob's face. "How could this have happened?" he anguished aloud.

"Perhaps you should have watched over Aleksandr more carefully."

Jacob could think of nothing to say. He slumped in his chair and stared at the document in his hands. Jew, written by Aleksandr's hand, leapt out from the page. The Chancellor stood up.

"I will ask you once more, Mr. Moisei, is it to be withdrawal or dismissal?"

Why are you doing this to me? Jacob gritted his teeth.

"Well, which will it be?"

"Aleksandr will withdraw."

"I was certain that you would do the gentlemanly thing, Mr. Moisei. In turn, if Aleksandr can secure a place in another university, I shall be more than happy to recommend him. His academic record here is excellent."

Not hearing the Chancellor's words, Jacob got to his feet, bowed politely, and quickly left the office. Without even a glance at the secretary, he stepped into the corridor and ran until he reached the street. In a whirl of confusion, Jacob hurried across the wide boulevard, his boots trying to grip the snow. A speeding sledge raced by him, its skidding runners catching Jacob's ankles and knocking him off balance. Jacob fell to the frozen ground, landing with an ugly thud. For a moment he remained motionless, tears of humiliation gathering in his eyes. Slowly he raised himself to a sitting position. Waiting until his pounding heart quieted, Jacob struggled to his feet and roughly brushed the snow from his clothing. Once he had regained his composure, he flagged down the driver of an empty sleigh: "The Hotel Rozhdestvenka!"

The sleigh hissed as it whisked across the city. The sky was overcast, threatening another storm. The cold wind from the Neva howled relentlessly. When he reached the hotel, Jacob went directly to his room, undressed, and ordered a tub of hot water and a bottle of vodka. Fifteen minutes later he was soaking in a steaming bath trying to wash away the entire morning. Fatigued from the scrubbing, he dressed in a heavy robe and lay down on the bed, his eyes fastened on the ceiling.

Hours later, when snow began to fall, Jacob was still lying in the same position; the room became dark as a fresh curtain of white flakes clung to the window. Finally, Jacob stirred; he rose from the bed and prepared himself to return outdoors. With no idea what he would say to his son, he left the hotel and headed toward Nevski Prospekt.

His uncovered head turned white from the snow. The wind lashed his face. He turned a corner onto a side street, not remembering how beautiful the now barren lime trees had been when he and Aleksandr had first arrived in St. Petersburg the summer before. He recognized the building where he had rented the room in which Aleksandr lived. Wearily, Jacob climbed the stone steps to the entranceway and stopped. He stood there trembling. Then, knowing he had no choice, he entered the building, climbing three more flights of stairs before reaching Aleksandr's door. Filled with feelings of powerlessness and failure, Jacob knocked. But when he heard Aleksandr's clear "Who is there?" Jacob stood mute, hoping the door would never open. The footsteps from inside grew louder.

"Who is there?" Aleksandr repeated, swinging open the door at the same time. "Father! What are you doing here?"

Jacob looked at his son and said nothing.

"What brings you to St. Petersburg?" Aleksandr ushered his father into the room. He laughed. "You should see yourself, you are covered with snow. Let me get you a towel."

Jacob walked to the fireplace and stood close to the flames.

"Why have you come all the way to St. Petersburg, Father?" Aleksandr handed Jacob a towel, then went to the ebony cabinet. "Whatever the reason, I am glad to see you."

Jacob studied the fire, mesmerized by the blaze.

"How long will you be here? Exams are over in a week. Perhaps we could travel to Odessa together." Aleksandr gave his father a crystal snifter filled to the brim with cognac. "Well, to what should we toast?" Aleksandr asked with a hearty laugh, raising his glass in the air.

Without uttering a word or even glancing at his son, Jacob tossed off his drink.

"Father, what is it?"

Jacob exhaled slowly, loudly, the sound rivaling the wind. He turned to his son and began to speak.

CHAPTER 8

During the train ride from the capital to Odessa, Jacob Moisei again attempted to learn why his son had lied about his faith. Jacob was surprised that Aleksandr had any recollection of ever having been a Jew. From the first day of their conversion Jacob Moisei had led his family to live an exemplary Christian life. Rarely was Judaism mentioned in the Moisei household, and when it was, Jacob raised the subject, smugly relating to Naomi how another stubborn member of the Brody Synagogue was beset by sudden and inexplicable financial difficulties. As for Aleksandr, all of his friends were either Christians by birth or faithful converts. *Could Naomi have undermined my decision?* Jacob wondered. *Could she have secretly influenced Aleksandr to disobey me?* Jacob's thoughts angered him. He ground his teeth together and nervously curled and uncurled his toes inside his shoes. It had been such a simple matter to become a Christian. All the obstacles that had once made the future ominous suddenly disappeared. And, following his baptism, not only was Jacob accepted by his Russian peers, he was admired, applauded as if he had miraculously recovered from some dread disease. Jacob turned to his son, annoyed that until now all his probing as to why Aleksandr had made such an imprudent, indeed, perilous decision had been met with obstinate silence.

"Please tell me why, Aleksandr? At least permit me to understand."

Not accustomed to hearing his father plead for anything, Aleksandr finally spoke. "It was a matter of conscience."

"Conscience?"

"I am not certain that I can really explain it."

Jacob shook his head in disbelief, his displeasure underscored by a rather unpleasant grunt.

"You see! How could you ever understand anything I might tell you."

"Why not try, Aleksandr, before you come to a conclusion?"

"It was a question of conviction," Aleksandr said. There was defiance in his face.

"You believed in what you did?"

"Yes."

"What is this belief of yours, Aleksandr? To fabricate the truth? To lie and say that you are a Jew? And by lying to threaten your future? What is more important than the future?"

Aleksandr disregarded his father's question. He turned his head toward the window and the endless purity of the unbroken white landscape.

"I am waiting for an answer, Aleksandr."

Slowly, Aleksandr began: "Did you know that when Papu—"

"Papu?"

"Don't interrupt me, father."

Aleksandr's angry look silenced Jacob. He began again: "Did you know that when Papu was a young man in Grodno, a group of peasants seized him and knocked him to the ground and then cut off his beard and sidecurls? They spit in his face. Jews are worse than pigs, they said. And when he cried because he was afraid, they beat him viciously to make him stop crying. And when he yelled from the pain of the beating, they beat him until he stopped yelling. When he finally collapsed, unconscious, they urinated on him."

"Your grandfather, who spent his entire life proclaiming devotion to his God, lived in my house and ate my food until the day he died. Even after we converted, he remained. How much of a Jew could he have really been to live under the same roof with people he considered traitors?"

"He stayed to be close to Mother."

"He stayed because he loved the comfort!"

"I wish he were still alive. I would like to talk to him again."

For two days and nights, the train rolled southward, stopping at Narva, Riga, and Minsk, pulling into stations rank with the smell of travelers crushed against one another. At each depot, passengers grappling with bulky boxes and bags crushed their way into the third-class coaches, falling this way and that as the train lurched forward, picking up speed.

Comfortable in the plush seat of the first-class roomette, Jacob stretched out his legs and unbuttoned his suit jacket. Once settled, he opened a ledger and was about to busy himself when Aleksandr began to speak.

"There is a marketplace in St. Petersburg called *Tshukin Dvor,* where almost any kind of meat can be purchased: geese, duck, rabbit, meat from oxen and calves. In the winter all the animals are frozen. Some of the small ones, like the hares, are frozen in running positions. Reindeer lie on tables, their legs collapsed as if they had just been shot." Aleksandr paused and thought of the maids of the wealthy who crowded *Tshukin Dvor,* choosing the finest sections of the animals for their mistresses' tables. *They are all so haughty the way they point to what they want. And they stand there so aloof as the butchers hack and saw through the carcasses.* Aleksandr recalled how frozen chips of pigs and oxen flew in all directions with each blow of the axes, each rip of the jagged-toothed blades. The memory of the children of the poor, scrambling after those bits of icy meat and gathering them in sacks so their families would have something to eat, made Aleksandr grimace.

"During the winter the market is tolerable. You should be there in the warm weather. Like it was when I arrived in St. Petersburg. Blood and gristle ran over the tables and onto the floor. Liquid from the eyes of oxen and sheep. Hay and manure lie in slippery rivers, making it treacherous for anyone to walk. *And still the children came, crawling along the floor, their arms and legs smeared with blood and excrement. Filling their bags with chunks of fat, discarded tripe, the heads and feet of geese . . .*

"Last summer I went to *Tshukin Dvor* with some friends from the university. We were preparing for a party and we wanted to serve the choicest meats. At first we found the sight amusing—until I saw a young man there, on his hands and knees, searching for scraps of meat with which to feed himself. He had to do that because the little money he had was not enough to pay for everything he needed, and food, too. Some of his money was used to pay his rent; he lived in a room smaller than my closet. He had to save a few kopecks to have his clothing cleaned once in a while. And a fair sum of his money had to be hoarded so he would be able to buy wood for the winter. And then, he only burned the wood when he could no longer withstand the freezing weather and feared he might contract pneumonia. He had to buy books, too, because he was a medical student." *When I saw you there, Solomon, on all fours on the floor of the marketplace, your shirt drenched with blood, your hands slimy with viscera I was horrified. I wanted to run away, to flee to my room, to my comfortable furniture, and drink some good wine, and forget about you. It would have been so easy to . . .*

"I approached him. At first he assumed I had come to eject him from the market. He got angry, and I thought he might strike me. I offered him money to buy food. He refused. I offered to take him to dinner in a restaurant. He refused that, too. He said to me, 'I do not need charity. As long as there is so much meat lying here on the floor, I can be independent. And to me, that is more important than all the charity in the world!' We became friends eventually. And until then, despite everything Papu had told me, and Mother had told me, despite everything I had ever heard, until I met Solomon Levin, I had no idea what it meant for someone to be a Jew."

Aleksandr hoped he would see compassion in his father's face, but Jacob's eyes were interested only in his hands as he anxiously tapped his briefcase.

"Do you know what the most difficult thing I have ever done in my life was, Father? What frightened me more than anything? Admitting to Solomon Levin that once I had been a Jew." Aleksandr shuddered, recalling Solomon's horrified reaction and then his uncontrollable rage, his fists so close, so threatening. His humiliating words. And yet, for a reason Aleksandr could not comprehend, he had accepted Solomon's anger, actually feeling he deserved Solomon's malevolence. Then, as abruptly as Solomon's wrath had erupted, it ceased—the tears in Aleksandr's eyes, the pain and confusion so obvious on his face, making Solomon realize that Aleksandr Moisei was not his enemy. His enemy was Jacob Moisei, and all the men like him who had buried their backgrounds, denied their history, foresaken their brethren, in order to gratify their own immediate pleasures. Determined to destroy Jacob's influence over his son, Solomon forced Aleksandr to listen repeatedly to the most sordid details of the lives of Russia's pariahs. And whether Solomon Levin spoke in quiet earnestness or ranted violently, Aleksandr never flinched, never retreated from what he heard. For it was not Solomon Levin's voice he heard, but the gentle tones of a grandfather called Papu speaking to his eleven-year-old grandson.

"It was not an easy decision for me to declare myself a Jew," Aleksandr said, his thoughts focused on his grandfather's kindly face. "Nor was it a rash decision." Aleksandr recalled his grandfather's smile and he suddenly felt warm and secure. "It is very possible that I did not appreciate the full import of the law regarding Jews and my becoming a jurist. How could I? What experience have I had where the law confronted me as an enemy? I was certainly aware of the law. Solomon saw to that." The vision of Papu vanished, replaced by Solomon Levin's determined expression. "And intellectually I understood the meaning of the law. But, I admit it was really an abstraction for me. All that was real was Solomon's poverty, the degradation I felt for him when I first saw him in the market, and the ease with which I could obtain practically anything I desired."

Again Aleksandr looked at his father and waited for him to say something. After a long pause, Jacob spoke, and though his eyes were hidden from view, the sadness within him was clearly expressed by his voice.

"Aleksandr, do you honestly think I have no idea what it is like to be a Jew? I was born and grew up in a place where life for a Jew was wretched. I saw the violence, felt the terror, that you have only heard stories about. My childhood, Aleksandr, differed greatly from yours. Did I ever tell you about Nikolai Viska's father? He was my father's employer. And if ever there was a cruel man, it was Nikolai's father. Every year, come Easter Sunday, Fyodor Viska would go to church. Afterwards he would invite the priest to his house to enjoy his selection of fine liqueurs. By mid-afternoon they were drunk, ready once again to avenge the Crucifixion. Together, Nikolai's father and the priest would rouse up a score of willing men to ride through the Jewish section of our village, crashing their horses against the flimsy doors of our houses, trampling our thresholds, purposely dragging mud and filth across the floors. Whatever they wanted they stole. Even the priest raped more than one young Jewish girl. But they left my father unharmed: he was the only person in the entire countryside who knew enough about numbers to manage the intricate calculations necessary to keep Fyodor's ledgers. And he was honest. That made him quite useful to old Viska. But you know, Aleksandr, Nikolai's father thought that my father was honest only because he was afraid. Frightened that if he cheated Fyodor of a single kopeck, he would suffer the consequences. It never occurred to Fyodor that my father was honest in his own right." Anticipating a question from his son, Jacob ceased talking. Aleksandr said nothing.

"I did not want to work for the Viskas. But my own father urged me to. He saw it as the only decent opportunity I would ever have. The only education I had was what I learned at the *heder*, and what my father taught me. Unlike you, I was not able to receive the type of schooling that would prepare me for a life far removed from that of a *shtetl* Jew. My outlook was bleak. Better to be despised as a Jew and have a little money than to be despised and have none, my father always said. I heeded his words, and I, too, went to work for Fyodor Viska. I served my apprenticeship under him. And because I was ambitious, because I knew the power which Fyodor Viska had over me, because I despised his ability to treat me as his property, to make me his slave, I deliberately made myself invaluable to him. While I acted meekly before him, at the same time I learned every facet of his business. Fyodor trusted me no more than he did my father, but he was pleased with my devotion to him. And little by little, slowly, carefully, I garnered more responsibility. Not because Fyodor gave it to me. But by making it possible for Fyodor to ignore his duties, I assumed them by default. As the years passed, I saw less of Fyodor. And when I did see him, he would clap me on the back and brag to whomever he was with, 'You see, if you had a shrewd Jew, as do I, you, too, would be free of the daily drudgery of work.' I would smile modestly at Fyodor, and thank him for his confidence. We both knew that if I failed him he would no longer clap me on the back but run a sword through me.

"I remember that time as if it were yesterday. We lived in a small nameless village thirty miles east of Kishnev. It was known as the village of the Viskas. Now, as you know, Nikolai refers to it as Dalyoki, after the summer house he has there. I thank God that Nikolai is the sort of man he is. If he had been like his father, I would have fled from his employ long ago. But Nikolai is a good man. And he hated his father as much as I did. Fyodor was only slightly more humane to his kin than he was to the others he ruled. So, when Nikolai started to work for his father, he and I already shared a bond—an antipathy for his father. And like you and Solomon, Nikolai and I eventually became friends, but, differently from you, I selected a friend who would raise me up with him, not drag me down. You see, Aleksandr, when I decided to continue to live at the whim of Fyodor Viska, when I chose to accept that suffering, I did so purely on reason. For the future. For the day after Fyodor died. For the time when, because of my friendship with Nikolai, I would prosper without fear. And I was right. Because today, all the torment I suffered is nothing but a mad memory. And I have done everything, and will continue to do everything, to further reduce any vestige of that terrible existence. Because to do otherwise would be irrational. And irrationality is the greatest crime any man can commit against himself."

When he finished talking, Jacob closed his eyes and folded his hands in his lap. He thought about how far he had come since those days more than thirty years ago. And he thought about how far Nikolai had advanced, too. Jacob smiled ruefully: if he had a choice, he would have much preferred to be Nikolai Viska.

CHAPTER 9

As the train rolled further south, leaving Kiev behind, the white landscape became spotted with brown, the early spring sun having already begun to thaw the snow. Shaggy horses tried to shake off their winter coats while peasants, bareheaded and shirtsleeved, anticipated seeding the earth and watched the rich, black soil of the steppes absorb the melting ice.

"Aleksandr, what will you say to Igor Vizhni when he inquires as to why you are no longer at the university?"

Aleksandr was startled by the question.

"Apparently, you have ignored that eventuality."

Unaware, Aleksandr rested his foot against the small suitcase beneath his feet which contained Andreana's letters.

"What kind of welcome do you think the great Vizhni will offer you? Do you think his greeting will be one of joy?" A nasty laugh escaped Jacob's lips. "What will you tell Vizhni? What will you tell Andreana?"

Aleksandr shut his eyes tightly and pressed his face against the window.

"Of course you have no answer. What possible explanation can you give to the daughter of an aristocrat for having deceived her? And do you think that Andreana's father will permit his daughter to be courted by one such as you?

Especially considering Vizhni's intimacy with the court? It is unfortunate enough that Alexander III occupies the throne. But do you know who his closest advisor is? Pobedonotsev!" Jacob looked to Aleksandr for his reaction to the name. There was none. "My son, you are dangerously uninformed about the politics of your country. Not to know Pobedonotsev, the Procurator of the Holy Synod, is never to have heard of the Devil. It is because of Pobedonotsev that you are no longer in school. He is the man who developed the solution for ridding Russia of the Jews—one-third were to be eliminated through emigration, one-third through assimilation, and one-third through starvation. Now, do you really think that Igor Vizhni will cross the power of Pobedonotsev for you?" Jacob paused, awaiting a comment from Aleksandr. When none was forthcoming, Jacob continued to speak.

"In 1882, Aleksandr, just after we took the vows of Christianity, Pobedonotsev inspired the Tsar to announce the 'May Laws.' That's when quotas were established for Jews permitted to enter the universities, and when Jews were excluded from the judiciary—and then there was the violence. Especially after it was discovered that one of Alexander II's assassins was a Jewess. Who knows what we would have suffered had we not been baptized." Again, Jacob ceased talking, expecting his son to have something to say. And again Aleksandr remained silent, his eyes focused on the muddy landscape beyond the train. An expression of irritation crossed Jacob's face and he shook his head in annoyance.

"You may not remember, Aleksandr," Jacob said, speaking more for his own ears than his son's, "you were still a boy then, but I can assure you that many, many of my old friends came to visit me again after Pobedonotsev's intentions became known. No longer was I, Jacob Moisei, an outcast. Oh no, because they finally recognized that it was I, and not they, who was right. No more did they scoff at me when I again told them that the bridge from Alexander

II to Alexander III led only in one direction: from light to dark. While I was prospering as a convert, they feared for their lives. They begged me to tell them how to become baptized. Do you know, Aleksandr, I helpèd so many of them convert that Rabbi Eleazar came to see me. He pleaded with me not to convince any more members of his Brody to become Christians. But he was always a fool. An opportunist first, but a fool, too." Jacob glanced at his son, but Aleksandr did not respond, his face taut with conflict.

"But let us return to you, Aleksandr. You are my own flesh and blood. How could *you* have acted so unwisely? Instead of your having to spend a life in misery, I handed you the opportunity to achieve everything anyone could want. Don't you know why I converted? For your sake, not mine. To protect *your* future. But because of a friend who knew how to make you feel guilty, you took it upon yourself to behave in a manner that indicated that your father is a man whose ideas are nonsense? This Solomon tells you about Mogilev, and you are ready to give him everything you have? Would *you* be willing to crawl along the floor of *Tshukin Dvor* with him? Would *you* live in filth? Did it not occur to you that as a jurist, even a Christian jurist, you might have been able to do something for all the Solomons in Russia? Do you ever think at all?"

Jacob's voice was no longer restrained. Aleksandr was taken aback.

"Father, I—"

"Do you know what your problem is, Aleksandr? Your life has been too easy, too safe. You have never had to struggle like I did. You have never had to suffer like I did. And so, despite the wealth in which you live, you are a pauper. Bankrupt of character, of thoughts of your own. And what influences you most is not you, but those around you. And that disappoints me, Aleksandr. But what is worse, I am fearful that the first time you experience something *you* consider a tragedy, you will collapse under the strain."

"Father, I am sorry that I—"

"Be sorry for yourself, Aleksandr. Not for me. Because I am not the one who wants to marry Andreana Vizhni."

Aleksandr's body was suddenly wracked by sobs. His head snapped backwards, his body jerking spasmodically, his lips twisted in anguish.

"Damn it, Aleksandr, act like a man!"

Aleksandr ground the heels of his hands into his eyes, desperately trying to control himself.

"Will you cry like that in front of Vizhni when you beg him for his daughter's hand?" Jacob looked at his son; he pitied him. "I have been through a hundred hells worse than yours, and I have never even whimpered. What is wrong with you?"

A look which frightened Jacob came over his son's face. Aleksandr raised his fists above his head, waving them uncontrollably. With all his might he pounded them against his forehead. *Leave me alone, damn you! Leave me alone!* An instant later, Aleksandr collapsed back into the seat, his body quivering, his heart racing madly, his arms numb. Slowly, exhaustion permeated Aleksandr's entire body and he slipped into a deathlike sleep. Jacob covered him with his coat, then, with nothing else to do, he opened the ledger he had put aside and used his time profitably.

Four days after departing from St. Petersburg, Jacob and Aleksandr Moisei arrived in Odessa. As soon as the porter gathered their luggage outside the depot, Jacob hired a carriage, and, while he instructed the coachman how to load their suitcases, Aleksandr wandered several yards away. The afternoon sun warmed his face, and the familiar scents of Turkish bananas and Oriental spices blended with the odors of fish and sea air were a reminder to Aleksandr that he had returned home.

"You will have the rest of your life to idle away in the sun," Jacob said brusquely to his son. "Let's go!" Jacob climbed into the coach and clucked his tongue impatiently. "Will you hurry, Aleksandr! There is still time enough for me to explain this to your mother and then devote a few hours to the office."

The mention of his mother broke Aleksandr's reverie. Quickly, he entered the carriage, settling himself next to the coach door. "*Spyshet!*" the driver shouted as he cracked his whip. The horses broke into a run, and the vehicle sped off.

The coach raced along Nicholas Boulevard, which was crowded with fiacres, lumbering barouches, and with produce-laden wagons being unloaded at the hotels. Uniformed officials passed in and out of the Veronozoff Palace. Successful-looking men strolled at leisure while clerks from the Exchange scurried to and fro. When the carriage turned onto Deribasovskaya Street the scene changed. Dozens of ladies wearing stylish, gaily colored costumes, new bonnets, and carrying parasols, their arms already filled with packages, paraded from one fashionable shop to the next. Half a mile further on they turned onto Pushkinskaya Street, driving past the Town Hall with its yellow stone facade and white columns, and past the ornate statue honoring the poet Pushkin. Rapidly, the carriage drove through Sobornaya Square and entered Preobrazhenskaya Street, the dividing line between the exclusive residential section of the lower city to the south and the slums to the north. Jamming Preobrazhenskaya Street were swarthy foreigners in flowing robes, sightseeing aristocrats, street urchins, wives of the poor bartering with vendors who were hawking hot tea, exotic melons, tiny balls of spicy meats wrapped and baked in dough, articles of clothing and housewares. Tartar women, their black hair braided into twenty tails, looking wild and savage, yet beautiful with their fine dark eyes and well-proportioned figures, strutted along the walkways. A band of gypsies, their wagons moving in single file, crowded into a side street which led to Moldavanka, the poorest of the slums, Odessa's ghetto.

For the first time, Aleksandr realized how congested and confined Odessa was, noticing that half a dozen of its broadest avenues could easily fit into St. Petersburg's Nevski

Prospekt. Even the villas on the terraces appeared insignificant when likened to the sprawling estates of the capital. Yet, St. Petersburg seemed lifeless compared to Odessa; the boulevards in the northern city were empty stone expanses; the streets of the Black Sea port city bubbled and churned with thousands of people. The driver turned the carriage south, snapped the reins, and the vehicle quickly headed away from Preobrazhenskaya Street and the crooked roads that led to Moldavanka. Again the scene changed, the tumult of the bustling multilingual, multinational thoroughfare evolving into sedate avenues graced by elm trees where gardeners trimmed lawns that ran from the walkways to sturdy stone houses a hundred feet beyond. Another corner was turned and the driver tugged on the reins, his eyes looking for number twenty-seven. He stopped in front of a large two-story stone house surrounded by a manicured lawn edged with flowers and protected by a wrought-iron fence.

"We are here!" the *ivoshtchik* announced as he climbed down to the ground and opened the carriage door.

Jacob stepped out of the vehicle and Aleksandr followed. After paying the coachman, Jacob unlocked the iron gate and hurried toward the house. He opened the door, then stood aside to let the driver, who was struggling with several suitcases, pass by.

"Leave them in the hallway," Jacob ordered.

"Yes, sir." The man grunted as he set the cases on the floor. He doffed his hat. "I will be going now, if that is all right with you, sir."

"Yes, thank you." Jacob dismissed the man with a wave of his hand.

The driver limped back to his carriage, deftly pulled himself onto the seat, and drove away.

By the time Aleksandr entered the house, his father was no longer in sight. He walked along the hallway, trying to remember if it had always been so dark and cool.

"Naomi?" Jacob's voice called out from somewhere deep within the house. There was no answer.

Aleksandr stepped into the parlor, inspecting it as if he had never seen it before. The draperies were drawn, subduing the light, but still he was able to see that the furniture was as he remembered.

"Naomi, are you home?" Jacob again inquired, his voice even more faint.

Aleksandr brushed his hand against the green velvet couch as he passed it by. For a second he paused in front of the wingchair where his grandfather used to sit and hold him on his lap, telling him stories. He thought of the time his mother had decided to have the chair recovered; Aleksandr wished she had left it the way it had been long ago. He continued toward the fireplace. The portrait his father had forced him to sit for years before still hung above the mantelpiece. Just to the right of the painting was a slender silver frame with a black velvet background on which was mounted an official letter written in perfect script; the seal of the imperial government was embossed at the bottom. Aleksandr read it:

May 16, 1888

To Aleksandr Moisei:

The Academic Committee of the University of St. Petersburg is pleased to accept your application for admission as a student for the coming year. This honor is conferred upon but a few, thereby granting you entry into the most distinctive circle in Russian academia. Both the Committee and I trust that you will conduct yourself in every facet of your life as a Russian, a gentleman, and a scholar. In the name of our beloved Tsar, Alexander III, we welcome you to the University of St. Petersburg.

Best Wishes,

V. Y. Bezobrazov

Victor Yadinovich Bezobrazov
Chancellor of the Imperial University

As Aleksandr finished reading, he heard his father enter the room. Jacob walked toward his son, stopping when he reached his side. After a brief look at Aleksandr, Jacob turned his attention to the framed letter. He lifted it off its hook and intently examined it.

"There is no need to display this anymore," Jacob said, his voice near breaking. He tucked the silver rectangle under his arm and stiffly moved away.

Aleksandr watched him, noticing that his father's hair was more gray than black, and that he walked with a slight stoop, his step leaden. *Father, I am sorry.*

"You know, I spent two days searching for the perfect frame for that letter."

Stop it, Father, please!

"I wonder why I devoted so much time to it?"

Looking disoriented, Jacob stared blankly at his son, then, clutching the framed letter to his chest, he left the room.

CHAPTER 10

The wind subsided and the little white sloop, the *Golub,* alternately heaved and rolled in the sloppy sea beyond the breakwater. The sun grew hotter. Aleksandr removed his shirt, tied it around his waist, and lay down on the wooden bottom of the boat. He was glad he had remembered to bring a blanket. *All those girls were right,* he thought, trying to cushion his body from the *Golub*'s ribs. He laughed aloud. *What an uncomfortable place to make love!* The sailboat rocked gently, the lulling motion easing Aleksandr's tensions. He wondered where Andreana could be. He had been home for nearly a month, and had gone to the Vizhni villa several times, but he could find no one there except for a gardener and a groom, and all they knew was that the family was not at home.

A gull, soaring overhead, swooped toward the *Golub,* screeching as it chased a fish darting just beneath the water's surface. "You sound like my father!" Aleksandr shouted. The seagull climbed skyward and twitched its body, its droppings staining the sea a yard away from the craft. A sudden wave made the sloop pitch. *"Asuzhdat!"* Aleksandr cursed. He scrambled to his feet to avoid the water cascading into the boat. The *Golub* yawed dangerously with Aleksandr's careless shifting of his weight. "The blanket is wet, too!" Aleksandr tossed it forward. The waters of the Black Sea became calm, glassy. The sun burned straight down, its reflection off the motionless sea a second sun that created a vise with Aleksandr caught between its fiery jaws. The *Golub* remained stationary, as if it were glued to the bottom of the sea. Sitting down, Aleksandr leaned against the mast, hoping to get some shade from the tiny shadow cast by the boom. Nothing helped. Aleksandr closed his eyes and prayed for a breeze. *I wonder which God will answer.* In the still air, the heat became intense, parching Aleksandr's body, robbing him of strength. Limp, unable to move, fatigued by the sweltering heat and nearly a month of restless sleep, Aleksandr Moisei finally drifted away from reality and into the void of a bottomless slumber.

A small wind caressed the sea; the *Golub* stirred. Like a rocking cradle, the comfortable motion of the boat dragged Aleksandr further into a dream he had been fighting for days. His mind drifted; he had no idea if he were awake or asleep, alive or dying. His face looked strained. A formless fear caused him to run within his nightmare. He stumbled and fell. A threatening mass of darkness hurtled toward him, threatening to crash into him, to annihilate him. Downward Aleksandr tumbled, forever downward, into a world devoid of shape or substance. Wildly, he struggled to slow his descent. To bring it to a halt. But no longer was Aleksandr able to resist his memory. His mind whirled through the festive ribbons of Easter week that had followed his arrival home. In unusual clarity he saw himself stroll through the endless displays of painted eggs at the fair at Alexandrovsky Park. Both priests and soldiers were kissing pretty girls while well-dressed men boasted of their fasts. Palm leaves whipped back and forth, beating the people of a processional; as they made their way toward a church to witness again the Resurrection, the worshippers chanted: "Christ is risen. Christ is risen from the dead!" The phrase echoed through Aleksandr's mind. Clouds of incense swirled around his head, its sweet fragrance perfuming the air. "*Christoss vosskress. Christoss vosskress!*" The golden embroidery of the priest's robes glittered behind his eyes. Before him rose the brilliance of thousands of flickering candles. *"Christoss vosskress."* The bruised sound of Jacob's voice made Aleksandr tremble.

"Will you never understand, Aleksandr, that it is not what you believe in that determines success, but rather what you make others think you believe in!"

Can the two never be the same, Father?

Far away, a dark cloud billowed and the wind found a new home in the north. The *Golub* shuddered until its bow settled into the freshening breeze. Aleksandr retreated further into his dream. Once again he was in his father's house watching the tears run down his mother's cheeks while he stood by feeling as if he were on trial. One by one, Aleksandr recalled each detail, remembering precisely what had happened that day he and his father had returned from St. Petersburg.

His mother had been asleep in her bedroom upstairs and it was a while before Jacob's voice disturbed her rest. Still only half awake, Naomi made her way downstairs, her voice filled with apprehension.

"Jacob, is that you?"

"Where have you been?"

"I was lonely, so I took a nap."

"I have something to tell you."

Naomi hurried to her husband, stood on tiptoe, and lightly kissed his cheek. "I am glad you are home."

"There is something we must talk about."

"Do you want something to eat?"

"Are you listening to me?"

"Are you thirsty?"

"Doesn't anyone in this house ever listen to me?!"

Naomi froze in place.

"Why are a man's words treated so lightly by his own family?"

"Jacob, what is wrong?"

"Everything!"

The wind snapped intermittently, shaking the *Golub* as

if it were a toy. Aleksandr moaned, wishing he were in Andreana's arms, but each time he reached for her, his father's face appeared just beyond her shoulder, mocking him, causing Aleksandr to hesitate. Finally, Andreana's haunting countenance vanished, her gentle laugh fading into silence, leading Aleksandr deeper into anguish.

"Aleksandr! Oh my God, it's my Aleksandr!" Naomi cried out. "Jacob, why didn't you tell me Aleksandr was with you?" Naomi laughed through joyful tears and, not waiting for her son to move, ran to him and kissed him. "Come here, let me look at you!" She took hold of his hands and pulled him to where there was more light. "I am so happy you are home! I missed you so much!" Naomi hugged Aleksandr, took a step backwards to see if he had changed, then hugged him again.

"I missed you, too, Mother."

"Are you home for the rest of the year now?"

"He is home forever," Jacob interjected.

"Forever?" Naomi was bewildered, and she looked back and forth between her husband and her son.

Wearily, Jacob sat down on the settee that rested next to the doorway. He looked tired, defeated.

"Aleksandr, what does your father mean?" Naomi extended her hands in a gesture of helplessness. "What has happened?"

"I have withdrawn from the university."

"Why?" Naomi covered her mouth with her hands.

"So he would not be dismissed," interrupted Jacob, his voice brittle.

"Please, Jacob, explain—"

"What more need be said than that a Jew cannot be a jurist, and that Aleksandr has decided to be a Jew."

Naomi spun around as if her husband had grabbed hold of her and yanked her toward him. Dumbstruck, Naomi stared at Jacob. He looked past his wife to his son; Jacob's eyes were burning with the betrayal he felt. Naomi, too, faced Aleksandr. With a tremor to her voice, Noami asked:

"Is what your father says true, Aleksandr?"

Aleksandr gazed at his mother, but remained silent.

"Since the morning the priest crossed your face with oil I have prayed for this day."

Jacob exploded. "You are lying, Naomi!"

"Jacob, you still do not understand what it meant to me to kneel before a cross. To see my son touched by a priest."

"And you do not understand that no one chooses to be a Jew."

"I do."

"Why didn't you tell me that years ago?"

"Because you wanted a Christian wife, and I loved you enough to pretend."

"And I wanted my son to have a past that would permit him a future free from fear—with every opportunity available to him. And for that he needed unblemished credentials. But now he has thrown away his future."

"Are you really a Jew, again, Aleksandr?" Naomi asked.

Aleksandr avoided his mother's steady look.

"Do you understand what it means to—"

Jacob let out a sneering laugh. "Aleksandr understands but one thing: that never will he be the husband of Andreana Vizhni."

The seas steepened into clumsy crests, tossing the *Golub* this way and that. Aleksandr clutched the sides of the boat, trying to pull himself up out of his dream. His efforts were useless.

"Do you remember, Naomi, what happened the day before we went to see the priest to arrange for our baptism? Have the years dulled your memory of Reschelevskaya Street?" Jacob asked.

"Don't, Jacob!"

"Are you afraid to remember? I am not."

"I don't want to hear about it!"

"Then just think about it!"

A violent wave raised the *Golub* high into the air, then sucked it back down with a crash. Quickly the seas grew ugly and the little sloop swirled helplessly in wild whirlpool circles.

"Will you remain a Jew, Aleksandr?" Naomi asked fearfully.

"Answer your mother, Aleksandr. Or have you changed your mind because of Andreana?"

An unsettled wind tore at the sails in a frenzy.

"Remember your grandfather, Aleksandr, and honor the past," pleaded Naomi.

The temperature fell and the air became as cold as the sea.

"Remember yourself, Aleksandr, and protect the future!" warned Jacob.

For a moment the air was windless, letting the *Golub* rest in a vacuum. Without warning, from the northwest, a gale-force wind hurtled across the sea, raising foaming waves that crashed against the boat, their crests descending on Aleksandr in a deluge.

Feeling trapped, with an anger that made him hate everything he could see, Aleksandr ran from the room and up the stairs to his bedroom, his footsteps echoing his fury. He caught a glimpse of himself in a mirror, and the sight enraged him. Facing himself fully, and with a deliberate, furious vengeance, Aleksandr smashed his fist into the silvered glass, shattering it and his reflection simultaneously.

Startled, suddenly ripped from his nightmare, Aleksandr struggled to his feet. Lines of dark scudding clouds and the churning sea dared him to escape, the wild waters trying to crush the *Golub* and rip loose its planking. The sails whipped to and fro, lashing Aleksandr's face. The boat pitched, and he lurched forward. Instinctively, Aleksandr jammed the tiller to one side until the bow accepted the deadly wind. With scrambling fingers he unfastened the main sheet and hoisted the sail to the masthead. Heading off the wind, Aleksandr eased the boat into a conservative heel. The steep waves stretched out, trying to outrace the slender hull, but nothing could catch the clean-lined sloop as it sliced though the water. Holding the course with his foot on the helm, Aleksandr reached for his shirt, careful not to disturb the tiller as he dressed.

The seas grew frenzied, the waves mountainous. And like a chip of wood on some madcap jaunt the *Golub* sleighed from crest to crest. In the far distance, the coast appeared. Slowly it loomed larger; what had seemed to be white shapeless specks became houses, minuscule dots were transformed into the boats of the Arkadia Yacht Club. Aleksandr swung the *Golub*'s bow through the wind and tacked through the staggered line of moored yachts. A hundred feet from shore, the newly scraped and varnished *Maryevo* pulled at its anchor. Playing his sails, Aleksandr circled the boat, rounding the *Golub*'s bow into the wind, stalling the sloop to a halt. For several minutes he studied the *Maryevo*, remembering how delicate Andreana had looked when first he saw her sitting in the bow, her slender fingers resting lightly on the massive anchor line; he recalled how seductive her voice was, like a muted violin rubbing its sound against the air; how lush her scent, like wild strawberries, how shy her smile, how elusive her kiss—that very first kiss, simultaneously an answer and a question. Knowing full well now what he must do—indeed, having known precisely what he intended to do from the very instant he and his father had returned to Odessa from St. Petersburg—Aleksandr yanked the *Golub*'s tiller, crossed the wind, laid the sloop on its side, and hiked down the coast to the heart of Odessa's port. With a broad wake churning at the *Golub*'s stern, Aleksandr dropped the mainsail and skimmed the craft up to the wharf at the foot of Politsiskaya Street. Quickly, he secured the *Golub* to the quay, hastened off the boat, and half-walked, half-ran up the dirty cobblestone hill.

The street rose abruptly, making the climb difficult. Everywhere there were boisterous clusters of people: sea captains loudly bargained for cargo and passengers; grain brokers argued angrily with sea hands about how best to care for the produce they shipped. Unsure of their footing, horses clumsily drew wagons up and down the hill while their drivers shouted warnings that the cumbersome wooden vehicles might break loose at any second. Garbage littered the street. Tall weather-beaten buildings sat like forbidding mountains on either side of a narrow pass. Halfway up Politsiskaya Street a stone building, its walls pitted as if it once had the pox, caught Aleksandr's attention. The windows were covered with years of grime and the entranceway was dark and musty. Aleksandr rushed inside, dashed up two flights of stairs, and hurried into a small office.

"Aleksandr!" a short, corpulent man called out.

"Hello, Maurice, is my father in?"

"Yes, of course. Go right in!" Maurice replied, his mouth stretched in an obeisant smile.

"Thank you."

Aleksandr strode past Maurice's desk to an oak-paneled door. He knocked once, his knuckles rapping against gold leaf letters which read: VISKA ENTERPRISES, *Jacob Moisei, Manager.*

"Yes?" boomed Jacob's voice.

The imperious sound of his father's voice caused Aleksandr's resolve to waver. Recalling his courage, he boldly opened the door.

"Aleksandr!" Jacob exclaimed, surprised to see his son. He stood up, put on his jacket, and extended his hand to his visitor.

"I was sailing and thought I would stop by."

"Sit down. How about some tea?" Jacob offered, silently questioning the real reason for Aleksandr's visit.

"Tea sounds perfect. I was caught out in the storm, and I am cold."

Aleksandr looked around the room, seeing on every wall the charts and graphs of which his father was so proud. Jacob's desk was crowded with stacks of documents, an atlas, and a well-thumbed book telling the day, hour, and minute of tidal ebbs and flows, phases of the moon, and prevailing winds of every major port in the world. Neatly piled on top of a filing cabinet were books dealing with agriculture, climatology, tariff laws, and exchange rates of money. In one corner there stood a large safe, its iron doors locked. On a table next to the safe was a silver samovar, several bottles of vodka and brandy, a set of four matched glasses, and a finely crafted model of a square-rigged sailing vessel mounted on a mahogany base. A set of tall, narrow windows let in light from behind Jacob's desk, and, while the room was of fair size, it seemed much smaller as Jacob strutted about.

"You must have had a good sail with all that wind," Jacob said, drawing two glasses of tea from the samovar.

"Only the last half hour or so was worth anything. Until then, I floundered," replied Aleksandr, not looking at his father as he accepted a glass of the tea.

Jacob returned to his desk and sat down. He hooked his thumbs in the pockets of his vest and watched his steaming tea cool.

"You look busy. Am I disturbing you?" Aleksandr inquired, trying to sound matter-of-fact.

"I am always busy, Aleksandr. How else do you think a man becomes successful?"

Aleksandr winced.

"And how could I not be busy? Everything you see here I must keep up to date. If not, these papers would be useless. They tell me everything there is about who is shipping what, and where, for how much, and at what exchange rate. Those charts tell me at a glance which of our ships is where, which captains keep to their schedules best. The charts were my idea. The ones behind you tell me to the last kopeck how much every one of our cargoes is worth. I know when a mouse eats a single piece of grain. And I know how to get along in this world." From his right vest pocket, Jacob pulled out a gold watch. He opened its lid and checked the time. "Ivashko will be here shortly. If you would like, I will give you a ride home."

"I tied up the *Golub* at the foot of Politsiskaya Street. I should take it back to the club."

"It's your decision. But if you prefer, I will send Maurice down to tell one of the watchmen to keep an eye on it tonight. You can return for it tomorrow."

"If it's no trouble. I see that it is starting to rain."

"At the port, Aleksandr, very few things are trouble for Jacob Moisei."

His father's boast disturbed Aleksandr, and he hid his discomfort by quickly finishing his tea and rising to refill his glass.

"I have been doing a lot of thinking since I came home," Aleksandr said quietly, his soft tone belying his anxiousness.

Jacob swiveled his chair so his back faced his son. He looked out of the window and watched the people in the street below hastening to find shelter from the rainfall.

"More than once I have wanted to talk to you, but every time I tried, we started to argue. But now, I must talk to you. In fact, there are two things specifically I want to tell you. Firstly, what I have decided to do with my life. And secondly, what I . . . what I intend to tell Andreana. I think you deserve to know those things."

Aleksandr sat down and waited, expecting his father to turn and face him. Jacob remained motionless.

"I would like an answer, Aleksandr. But talking with you has been difficult these past weeks." Jacob looked at his watch again and then down at the street to see if Ivashko had arrived.

"Until today, I refused to admit to myself that the very day we were back in Odessa, I knew exactly what I intended to do. I wanted Andreana to be the first one to know, but she is still away and I don't want to wait any longer."

Jacob's stomach began to churn and a pain radiated from his belly to his bowels. He gripped the arms of his chair.

"What I have decided is that I want to work with you. I want to learn Viska's business."

Jacob wanted to respond, but nothing seemed appropriate.

"I would like to start tomorrow."

"There is no rush, Aleksandr. Take a few more weeks before you decide. You might change your mind and want to enroll at the university here, or at the one in Kiev."

"No. I think I would have enjoyed being a lawyer. But

nothing else really interests me. In fact, no matter what the circumstances, I have no desire to return to school. And unless I learn the Viskas' business I will not have any future at all. I am certain you know that better than I do. And I must have a future. A *successful* future."

Jacob craned his neck to be better able to see out of the window. He nodded his head to someone below. "It is your life, Aleksandr. And at nineteen, you are certainly old enough to make your own decisions."

"Are you upset that I have no desire to return to school?"

"To work for the Viskas, experience is the only education necessary. It is for important things, like the judiciary, that universities are necessary."

"You make it sound as if what you do is nothing."

"From where I started life, managing Nikolai Viska's empire is equal to being the Tsar. From where you started—it is nothing."

"Are you trying to discourage me?"

"No."

"At least I will be rich working for the Viskas."

"Perhaps. Unless they make new laws against Jews."

Aleksandr wished his father would turn and look at him. "What will Nikolai say?"

"He will be quite pleased. More than once he's said that he would welcome you into the business. He thinks that you and his son, Vassili, would get along quite well."

"Does Nikolai know that I have left the university?"

Jacob nodded his head. A flash of lightning followed by booming thunder startled him.

"Does he know why?"

Imperceptibly, Jacob nodded his head again.

"Does he care?"

Jacob sat for a long moment before he replied. "Nikolai is a very liberal man," Jacob finally said. "There are few things he is unable to accept."

"I am glad." Aleksandr got to his feet. "May I start working for you tomorrow?"

"I have already told you, the decision is yours."

"Then tomorrow it is. I have had enough vacation."

"Then, I suppose, tomorrow will be fine."

"If I run down to the wharf, to make sure the *Golub* is secure, will you wait for me? It should take no more than five minutes."

"Take your time. I enjoy watching the rain."

Aleksandr set his glass down on the table and started toward the door. Jacob's head began to throb. The sound of the doorhandle turning grated against his ears. He gritted his teeth and cleared his throat. In a voice high pitched from nervousness he said, "Aleksandr?"

"Yes?"

"Haven't you forgotten something?"

The rain beat against the windows, its force threatening to shatter them.

"What?"

Again lightning flashed, its accompanying thunder shaking the building.

"You had two things to tell me, I have only heard one."

From the doorway, Aleksandr could see his father's profile. It looked strained, forced to appear composed, like the face of a man on the gallows who had sworn to die with dignity.

"What have you decided to tell Andreana? How will you solve *that* problem?"

"There is no problem with Andreana anymore."

"And why is there no problem, Aleksandr?"

Outside someone screamed and the sound of a wagon sliding out of control down the rain-slicked cobblestones cut through the air.

"How could there be, Father? I am a Christian. And there can be no reason why Igor Vizhni should object to a Christian, a wealthy Christian, marrying his daughter."

CHAPTER 11

From the very moment that Aleksandr Moisei became an employee of the Viska Enterprise and began working with his father, Jacob drove him mercilessly—and Aleksandr enjoyed it. He listened raptly as his father explained the intricacies of exporting grain and sugar, making copious notes in a leatherbound tablet and asking a torrent of questions. And in rapid detail, Jacob gladly revealed his vast knowledge of Nikolai Viska's business.

Day after day, Aleksandr shadowed his father everywhere, inquring about everything. He pored over the records and files Jacob had accumulated in the Politsiskaya Street office during the last twenty-odd years. He studied the legal details of all the contracts for which he might one day possibly be responsible. He accompanied Jacob on inspection tours of the granaries, learning how meticulous his father was about the conditions of the grain and sugar, and how cautious he was with the brokers, ship owners, and sea captains. Jacob required that his son learn the tax laws, import duty requirements, and exchange rate of money, including black market prices. And he instructed Aleksandr in the workings of international stock and commodity markets, explaining how a miscalculation in predicting future grain prices could cost Viska tens of thousands of rubles, while accurate forecasts would do precisely the opposite. As Aleksandr's knowledge of Viska's business grew, so did his responsibilities. Jacob permitted his son to draw up first drafts of contracts, inspect the dockside grain silos, arrange for produce to be shipped from Odessa to Holland and England. And in August, after three and a half months of apprenticeship, when Aleksandr asked his father if Jacob considered him a promising employee—Jacob looked at his son thoughtfully.

"I must admit, Aleksandr, that I am surprised at how valuable an asset you have become to us."

Pleased, Aleksandr smiled. Jacob scrutinized his face, feeling almost as much pride as he had the day Aleksandr had been accepted at the university. He thought about how uneasy he had been when Aleksandr first started to work at the office on Politsiskaya Street; he had felt invaded, spied upon. But with the passing weeks, Jacob finally realized that Aleksandr was following his every step, questioning his every move, only because of a genuine desire to learn Viska's business. Now, not only was Jacob accustomed to working with his son, he thoroughly liked it. Not knowing how to convey what he was thinking and feeling, Jacob Moisei glanced at his watch and brusquely reminded Aleksandr not to dally, as the contract he was working on was due by day's end.

In mid-August, Jacob informed his son that Nikolai Viska wanted to see the both of them together, and it was with great curiosity that Jacob led his son into the Exchange and then into the lift which raised them three floors to the headquarters of Viska Enterprises.

The suite of offices occupied by Nikolai Viska was tastefully, but not opulently, decorated. The walls were beige, with a few paintings of pastoral scenes used more to break up the monotony than for ornamentation. The furniture was sturdy rather than elegant, the curtains selected for their durability. Three male secretaries, who seemed to be everywhere at once, gave the place an efficient hum, and when Jacob and Aleksandr appeared they interrupted nothing, but rather blended into the activity.

"Jacob, Aleksandr, welcome!" greeted Nikolai Viska, his commanding voice filled with warmth, a broad smile on his craggy face. Nikolai bounded out of his chair as he went to vigorously shake hands with both men and usher them into his private office.

Though his frame was sparse, Nikolai's voice and great height made him an imposing figure. "Sit down anywhere. Would you like a drink? Brandy? Sherry? Vodka?"

"For me, brandy will be fine, Nikolai."

"And for you, Aleksandr?"

"Nothing, thank you."

Nikolai, who stood a full head taller than Aleksandr, looked down at the younger Moisei. "Are you trying to impress me with your sobriety? Don't bother. I do not care if you need to be drunk day and night if it helps you do the things I require." Nikolai waited for Aleksandr to change his mind, examining the young man as if he were assessing a potential acquisition.

"I will have a brandy, too."

"Excellent! The reason your father and I get along so well is that we think the same way and drink the same way. You seem to be continuing the tradition. I just hope that Vassili does the same."

Nikolai poured a fine brandy into three perfectly formed snifters. His long fingers held the glasses as casually as if they had been inexpensive goblets.

"How is Vassili?" Jacob inquired.

"His examination reports are excellent. And I am certain his social life is more than adequate. I just hope that when he returns to Odessa he won't find it dull after Paris."

"I envy his being in Paris. Someday I would like to go there," said Aleksandr.

"It is a remarkable city. As long as one does not go there the way most of our Russian aristocrats, and would-be aristocrats, do: with the belief that Paris is the Mecca of culture and refinement, of all that is worthwhile." Nikolai handed Jacob and Aleksandr each a glass of brandy.

"It is so peculiar that those at the Court prefer speaking French to Russian," Jacob said.

"Yes, how strange that the rulers of our land find their native tongue so despicable. It is as if they consider the Russian language suitable only for the peasants. French, they think, makes them somehow intellectual." Nikolai chuckled and continued. "Russia is an odd country. The government asks the peasants for their tax money in Russian, then curses them in French."

"I think they curse us all, Nikolai. Not just the peasants."

"Those of us with money are not yet cursed. At least not to our faces. Sometimes I wonder where the Tsar is leading us. His father was so liberal, but this dull-witted Alexander we now have—ah, it is foolish of me to become upset over the pupil of Pobedonotsev. Thank God I am in a position where they cannot bother me. As a matter of fact, just the opposite has occurred this week. That is why I asked you to come by today."

"From your note I assumed it was good news."

"Very good. Let me show you something on the map as I explain." Nikolai went to his desk and unfolded a large drawing of the area that began at Odessa, included the land as far west as Kishnev, north to Kiev, and ended at Krivoi on the east. Lines that wiggled, looped, and curled, following the contours of the land, and were intersected by shorter lines, ran from city to city. "This is a railroad map. As you can see, every day more miles of track are being added, until someday all of Russia, from the west to Kamchatka on the east, will be connected. In ten years, the entire country will be tied together by the railway. But what interests me are the lines from Odessa to Kiev. You see this check I have put here? It is a small village named Kodoma."

Jacob leaned over the map, noting where Nikolai had placed the mark. He motioned for Aleksandr to join them. "That is where most of your land is," Jacob said, tapping his finger on the spot for Aleksandr's benefit.

"Yes. And for years the peasants have had to drive their wagons sixty miles from Kodoma to Odessa to deliver the grain to the port, and for years it has bothered me. That trip has been the most cumbersome and inefficient part of this business. So, two years ago, I started negotiating with the State for a railroad spur to be built from the main line that runs from Odessa to Kiev—to Kodoma. That way the grain could be loaded in Kodoma. There would be more peasants available in Kodoma for the harvest. And the grain would move faster to Odessa. And something else, we would no longer have to worry about the landowners, who already live near the main rails, arriving in Odessa with their harvest before us."

Jacob stepped away from the desk and refilled his glass with brandy. "You know, Nikolai, you could even build a granary there for storage. That way, instead of loading the freight cars wagon by wagon, the grain could be brought to the storehouse, and from there loaded onto the trains in bulk."

"Exactly!" Nikolai beamed as he neatly folded the map and sat down at his desk. "The granary has already been planned for. An architect is drawing preliminary sketches at this very moment."

"Then you have convinced the State to build the spur?"

"Yes. After I finally impressed them with how much trade I personally conduct for Russia, they finally agreed. But it was more than just that. After much, shall we say, diplomacy, I was able to convince several other landowners in the vicinity of Kodoma to join me in this venture. Together we control close to sixty percent of the exporting business. That was more than the government was able to resist."

"And what did the government make you promise for all this?"

"You are right, Jacob. There were concessions. The State agreed to build the spur and schedule trains to and from Kodoma on an infrequent but regular basis *if* we landowners pay fifty percent of the construction costs, plus purchase our own railroad cars for shipping the grain."

"That is a fortune you will be paying!" Astounded, Jacob seated himself in a leather chair across from Nikolai.

"I am afraid so. When it comes to collecting money the government is very demanding. Thankfully, we can repay the debt over the next decade based on the current rate of the ruble. And you know as well as I do, world trade can only grow. And a decade from now this capital investment will seem infinitesimal compared to what our profits will be."

"Yes, and if ten years from now we were still sending our grain from Kodoma to Odessa by wagon, we would be forced out of business by our competition."

"I will lay a wager, Jacob, that by the turn of the century Kodoma will be the center of our business and Odessa nothing more than port facilities."

"You are expecting quite a change to occur in eleven years."

"I anticipate momentous events occurring once we leave this wretched century. And if we are very lucky, Russia will enter the twentieth century without Alexander III as Tsar." Indignation tinged Nikolai's voice.

"That would be a blessing," Jacob agreed.

"Yes, wouldn't it!"

There was a lull in the conversation as both men swallowed their anger along with some brandy. It was Jacob who broke the silence.

"You know, Nikolai, once the railroad spur is completed, it is conceivable that you could live at Dalyoki all year round."

Nikolai ran his fingers through his thinning gray hair. He rubbed his slightly hooked nose and sharp chin. "I get too comfortable in the country to want to do much of anything. And this will require a great deal of work, Jacob. More than we have ever done before."

"I am ready for it. And I am also ready for the part you have not yet told me about."

"Jacob, Jacob, do we really know each other that well?"

In answer, a modest smile covered Jacob's face.

"Of course we do! And I am glad. Because without you this plan would not work at all." Nikolai rose and went to the liquor cabinet. "More brandy?"

"Yes." Jacob began to get up from his chair.

"Stay there. I will bring the bottle." Nikolai refilled Jacob's glass, talking as he poured. "I am going to be perfectly frank with you, Jacob. I need everything you know to make the Kodoma plan a reality. But I need you in Odessa. Not in Kodoma." Nikolai offered Aleksandr a second drink by extending the bottle.

"Just a drop, please."

"Without you in Odessa, the entire exporting operation would crumble, Jacob. I am well aware that only because of you have I been as successful as I am. I appreciate that deeply. I hope you know that."

"I do." Jacob glanced at Nikolai, his expression thanking him for the compliment.

"So we, and I mean we, must determine how best to handle the Kodoma project. And to be honest, it is no accident that I invited Aleksandr to accompany you here today. I wanted him to hear what I have to say. Keep in mind now, Jacob, that right now he is not your son, but our employee." Nikolai looked at Aleksandr and then back at Jacob. "What would you think if Aleksandr were made responsible for the Kodoma project? Admittedly, he is as green at this business as we were at the start. But Kodoma is also the beginning. It is a good place for him to learn the business from the ground up. Even if he makes mistakes, which he understandably will, they could not happen at a better time. And eventually, when you want to relax, to enjoy what your labors have earned you, Aleksandr will have the Kodoma complex under control, and can assume some of your responsibilities."

"I am honored that you would even consider such a thing."

"Jacob, understand that I am not doing you a favor. By now you should know that I am a very practical man. And when you think about it, you will realize how selfish I truly am. I wish the smoothest transition for my business from this century to the next. I want your son, and mine, to accept responsibility for that transition. I want them to carry on what we have built. I only have two things in my life, Vassili and my business. I am not so foolish as to think that I can go ahead and die without having prepared them both for what has to be done." Nikolai paused. "How strange, Jacob. We have discussed many, many things over the years. I would imagine we must have discussed everything except our own deaths. Now, we have reached a time, I suppose, when we should at least mention them to one another." Nikolai made an attempt at smiling, but his face showed how much he disliked the thought of the inevitable. "Ah, there is nothing to talk about. I am sure we will both live to be five hundred years old. And all I meant was to emphasize the critical nature of this decision. For all of us."

"I understand that."

"Then what do you think about Aleksandr's being thrown in with the foundation of a new century?"

"I hope you believe that I will answer as your employee, and not as Aleksandr's father."

"Jacob, we have worked together for nearly three decades. Never once have I known you to lie to me, or placate me. As a matter of fact you can be a stubborn bastard when you think I am wrong."

Jacob turned to his son and carefully studied the youth's face. Aleksandr met his father's gaze, his eyes unwavering and his face filled with determination.

"Nikolai, I honestly believe that Aleksandr is capable of doing what you have outlined. If Kodoma were an already established center, I would say no. But the way it is, it's like two infants growing and gaining experience together."

"Precisely!"

"Therefore, I can recommend Aleksandr for the position."

Nikolai looked at Aleksandr. "Now that you have heard everything, this is really your decision. I don't want your answer today. Take some time to make up your mind. Discuss every detail with your father. There is not a single thing about this business he doesn't know."

"Mr. Viska, I—"

"If you are going to tell me you accept, don't. The first thing to learn is patience. Just because you kiss a frog and it becomes a prince does not mean that when you kiss the prince he will not change back into a frog."

"I was just—"

"And don't thank me. Not when what I am offering you is the opportunity to live in the middle of nowhere with a handful of ignorant peasants. Wait until you have spent eight months snowed in by blizzards, and four roasted by the sun—then see if you don't want *me* to thank *you*!" An expression of amusement touched Nikolai's face. "I cannot wait until you meet my son. I think you and Vassili will be good for one another. Don't you agree, Jacob?"

"Yes."

"By the time Vassili returns from Paris you will have a few years' experience on him. He will have to start at the beginning. I like that! There is nothing better to keep the son of a rich father humble than his having to start from the bottom."

"I am starting lower than everybody," Aleksandr said lightly. "In a hole in the ground with a building!"

Nikolai and Jacob laughed heartily. Nikolai raised his glass of brandy. "Here's to our children, Jacob. May they continue what their fathers began!"

Jacob and Aleksandr joined in the toast.

"Aleksandr, learn everything you can from your father. And even though I have an idea what your answer will be, think about it. Think a lot about it, because it will change the rest of your life." Nikolai turned to Jacob. "This has been a good day for me, Jacob. I am glad our lives worked out as they did."

Nikolai extended his hand. Jacob clasped it, the two men reaffirming their deep admiration and genuine liking for one another.

"Aleksandr, even if I am wrong, and you decide to do something else, I wish you luck. But whatever you do, do it well, for your father's sake."

"I will."

"In a little more than a decade an event of great significance will take place. The world will step into a new century. An enormous page of history will be turned, and the next one will be blank. Your father gives that to you. And I give it to Vassili. If each of you leaves just one good impression on that paper you will have done more than most everyone who has lived before you." Nikolai stared at Aleksandr, his expression solemn. Slowly he turned away and faced Jacob. A broad smile came over his face. "Jacob, let us go for a walk. I think we have earned it."

CHAPTER 12

As Nikolai Viska had suspected, Aleksandr Moisei decided to accept the challenge of the Kodoma project as soon as it had been offered to him. Out of respect for Nikolai, Aleksandr waited a week before advising Viska of his decision, and when he did, the two men sealed the bargain with a handshake. Immediately, Aleksandr immersed himself in his apprenticeship to his father, redoubling his efforts to fully understand Viska's business.

In October, when Jacob informed Aleksandr that the time had come for him to begin final preparations to leave for Kodoma, father and son spent days making lists forecasting every sort of problem that might confront Aleksandr; a steamer trunk was filled with books and notes containing solutions to the problems. Naomi packed and repacked other luggage, each time adding more warm clothing in case the coming winter was worse than even she imagined. As the day for her son's departure neared, Naomi became melancholy, spending hours making the *pashka* meat pies he loved so much. A loneliness came over her, and as much as she tried, Naomi found it impossible to hide her sadness. Aleksandr, too, was unhappy. Although he was certainly looking forward to the adventure, something was missing from his life. And though he knew what it was, there was nothing he could do about it.

It was Andreana who was causing Aleksandr's sadness—or rather, Andreana's absence from Odessa was what gave rise to Aleksandr's feeling dispirited. At least once every week since his return to Odessa Aleksandr had visited the Vizhni villa. Each time the estate was still and empty, and the caretaker could tell him nothing about where the family had gone. As time passed and Aleksandr was still unable to see Andreana, to tell her of his love for her, to ask her father's permission to marry her, a malaise began to envelop him. Constantly he dreamed of Andreana, imagining how she would smile at him, embrace him, lingeringly kiss him when again she saw him. And Aleksandr rehearsed how he would present himself as a future son-in-law to Igor Vizhni; Aleksandr had even selected the clothes he would wear on the day he asked Andreana's father for his daughter's hand in marriage. Only his fantasies prevented Aleksandr from being overwhelmed by the anguish he was beginning to suffer. But as the day he was to leave for Kodoma neared, Aleksandr Moisei was filled with a desperation that no amount of dreaming was able to ease.

Midafternoon on Sunday, a week prior to his departure, Aleksandr walked the block from his house to the stable where his father's horses were kept. He hitched his favorite, Bastray, a bay mare, to a two-wheeled chaise and within minutes was driving up the terrace road that led to the villas which overlooked the city. Below Aleksandr, Odessa gleamed white, a sea breeze alleviating some of the heat from the late summer sun. His yellow shirt billowed and his long blond hair danced with the wind. He sat hunched slightly forward, like a cat coiled for a leap; his mouth was set in a noncommittal line. Half an hour later, the sleek bay horse jauntily pulled the little carriage along the driveway of the Vizhni estate; Aleksandr sat erect, his tanned face paled, and his blue eyes glinted like diamonds. Towering trees on either side of the white pebble drive created an arched cavern of cool green. Here and there, through the leaves, the sun dappled the ground. In the distance, the villa sparkled like a jewel; before it, rows of asters and poppies swayed in rhythm with the breeze. Alongside a hedge, blazing yellow sunflowers stood like sentinels. Aleksandr slowed Bastray to a walk. A gardener, who had been absent the last time Aleksandr had visited, doffed his cap and waved hello to him. Aleksandr raised his whip in greeting and continued on. A small wagon stood outside the house, a brown pony waiting between the shafts. Aleksandr's heart leaped with excitement, and he clucked to Bastray to move faster. When he was abreast of the wagon, Aleksandr brought his chaise to a stop, jumped to the ground, and dashed up the stairs to the door of the villa. Restraining himself, Aleksandr politely tapped the brass knocker against the wooden portal. He knocked twice more before a servant he had never seen previously opened the door. The man's pants were streaked with dirt and his shirt was damp.

"Yes, sir?"

"I am Aleksandr Moisei. Is Andreana at home?"

"No, sir."

"When will she return?"

"Oh, not for a month, sir. I am just opening up the house now."

"Another month? Where has she gone?"

"To Paris first, and by now I expect the family has arrived in St. Petersburg."

"To Paris? St. Petersburg? That sounds very special."

"It was special, sir. Paris was a present for Miss Andreana from her parents. And St. Petersburg was a surprise for both ladies."

"A present?"

"Yes, sir."

"Oh?" Aleksandr looked at the man quizzically. "What was the occasion?"

The servant glimpsed behind him to make sure he was alone. "I suppose I can tell you, sir. You look like a gentleman." He quickly inspected Aleksandr from head to toe. "Miss Andreana wanted to get married. The master disapproved and offered to take her to Paris if she changed her mind, and she did."

A rush of fever flushed Aleksandr's body. "Who was he?"

"A Jew, sir."

For an instant, Aleksandr was certain the servant had not answered his question and he was on the verge of asking it again. Suddenly, a clawing sensation gripped his stomach. Rivulets of sweat chilled his body. Stumbling, Aleksandr retreated from the door.

"Sir, who shall I say called for Miss Andreana?"

Aleksandr scrambled into the chaise and fumbled for the reins and whip.

"Sir, don't you wish to leave a message?"

An uncontrollable rage exploded within Aleksandr. He raised his whip and lashed Bastray's back. Again he whipped the mare. And again. The frightened horse bolted. Wildly, the chaise careened down the hill and through the streets of Odessa. At full stride, Bastray streaked along the Arkadia road, the wheels of the nimble carriage barely holding the ground. Aleksandr cursed vilely, his words hurled back at him by the wind. His eyes stung and teared, and the world became a meaningless blur. Then, unused to such a sustained pace, Bastray's legs gave way and she fell to the ground, the chaise crashing after her. Alexsandr was thrown from the carriage, his body slamming hard against the dirt roadway. He lay there motionless and several minutes passed before he stirred. He groaned. Bastray whinnied. Aleksandr looked around: what he saw horrified him. There was Bastray trapped between the sharp points of the splintered carriage shafts. Shakily, Aleksandr got to his feet, freed the horse of the leather harness, and gently coaxed Bastray to stand. Running his hands along the horse's legs, he checked her for broken bones. There were none, but bruises crisscrossed the animal's back where Aleksandr's whip had bitten deeply. "I am sorry, Bastray. I am sorry." Aleksandr stroked the horse's muzzle. Bastray softly neighed at the kind hands and voice she knew so well. After the two of them had rested, Aleksandr led the horse a few steps, seeing if she could walk without difficulty. Gamely, Bastray followed Aleksandr's lead. Wishing there were another way, Aleksandr loosely hitched the animal to the carriage. He lashed the broken shafts around Bastray's girth, and, instead of riding in the chaise, Aleksandr walked the seven miles back to Odessa by the horse's side.

It was well past dark when they reached the stable. After unhitching Bastray from the chaise, Aleksandr carefully rubbed liniment on her back. He made warm gruel for her, stroking her neck as she ate. Aleksandr massaged Bastray's back with a currycomb and she stomped with gratification. He pitched clean straw into a stall, and boxed her in, waiting until she settled down before he left the stable. As he stepped into the night air, Aleksandr buried his face in his hands and sobbed. His fingers dug into his flesh, twisting it, trying to wrench out the agony that possessed him. And then it ended. Aleksandr wiped his face on the sleeve of his shirt, raised his face toward the heavens, and let the coolness of the evening soothe it. With no destination in mind, Aleksandr started to walk. His mind rambled. It darted here and there: to his Papu, to the priest of the Church of the Transfiguration, to his mother, his father, to Solomon Levin. His thoughts wriggled, sidestepped, backtracked, trying to avoid the one question he could not face: would he ever see Andreana again? With each slap of his soles against the stone walkways, the anguish Aleksandr felt subsided, a dull ache replacing his pain. Aware of nothing around him, Aleksandr walked blindly, taking no notice that his route was not aimless. Slowly he trod in an ever-tightening spiral at whose center was Troitzkaya Street. An impressive building loomed out of the night before him. Aleksandr came to a halt, having no idea how he had gotten there. For a long moment he stared at the massive limestone structure. He searched the depths of his memory trying to recall its interior. With deliberate steps, Aleksandr climbed the flight of broad stone steps that led to a formidable pair of high arched doors. Gathering his courage, Aleksandr grasped the handle. Cautiously, he swung open the wooden barrier and entered the edifice. Except for a single burning candle, the inside was dark. Aleksandr called out a name. It echoed back at him. From somewhere deep within the shadows, a door opened and closed. Footsteps approached, padding softly on the marble floor. Aleksandr waited, not knowing what he would say, but knowing that he wanted to talk to a man whom no one would have thought he even remembered. The footsteps grew louder, but Aleksandr heard nothing; he had become transfixed by the sight of the altar which stood at the center of the Brody Synagogue.

CHAPTER 13

When Aleksandr Moisei arrived in Kodoma he found it to be exactly as Nikolai Viska had described: a place so insignificant that it appeared to be nothing more than a temporary encampment for a handful of peasants. A cluster of twenty mud-walled, thatched-roof huts sat at the bottom of a line of low, sloping hills. Nearby stood a small domed church. A single road, really a dirt path, was the only route even remotely suitable for travel. The nearest settlement was twelve miles to the north, as isolated and undeveloped as Kodoma. Odessa, sixty miles to the south, seemed as distant as if it had been on the opposite side of the earth. Yet, it was Kodoma's very isolation that attracted Aleksandr. Here he could hide and immerse himself in the challenge set by Nikolai Viska without looking up at Odessa's terraced heights to stare at the Vizhni villa, feeling as if eyes from within were watching his every move, taunting him, the sight of the house itself reminding Aleksandr daily of how much he still yearned for Andreana. And, too, being in Kodoma permitted Aleksandr to ignore the inexplicable attraction he felt for the formidable-looking Brody Synagogue and its urbane and gentle rabbi, Joshua Eleazar.

Indeed, from the moment he arrived in Kodoma, the autumn climate of the steppes, the cool mornings, warm afternoons, and brisk evenings rejuvenated Aleksandr. And the solitude, the quietness of the vast rolling grasslands, gave him a peacefulness he had not known for years. But it was the task that faced Aleksandr which most revitalized him. Immediately, he set out to fulfill the promise he had made to Nikolai Viska. And on the second day after his appearance in Kodoma, with blueprints in hand, Aleksandr Moisei started at the door of the church and with animated strides paced off a map of the thriving town he envisioned there.

Within the next several years more changes occurred in Kodoma than had taken place there in the preceding two hundred years. A granary and railroad depot were built. A railway spur, connecting Kodoma to the main tracks six miles to the west, was completed. A hundred-yard length of the earthen roadway was widened to four times its width and paved with cobblestones. Before the church a square was laid out, and in its center a circle of grass was planted, and within that several young trees that had been taken from the nearby woods were rerooted. Year by year, as the granary operation expanded, so did the permanent population of Kodoma. Stores and shops grew up next to one another along the main thoroughfare. And by the mid-1890's, a dozen new streets had been added, some lined with small but comfortable houses belonging to the merchants, others dotted with stone cottages which housed the men who worked at the granary; the remainder were empty in anticipation of more people coming to Kodoma to make it their home. Mail, foodstuffs, and merchandise for the stores began to arrive as regularly as the trains, and soon it was necessary to give the buildings numbers and the roads names. The main street was called Mirazdanyaskaya, meaning creation, because to those who had lived in Kodoma before the advent of Aleksandr Moisei that is what this new Kodoma was: something made from nothing.

At first, the peasants had wanted to call the thoroughfare Aleksandraskaya Street to show Aleksandr how deeply they appreciated what he had done, how much they had grown to love him—for not only had he always paid them a good wage, not only was he scrupulously honest and unfalteringly fair, but from the beginning Aleksandr Moisei had worked right along with the peasants. At once he was both their foreman and their peer. Side by side with the men of Kodoma, Aleksandr had broken open the earth with a pick, dug out foundations with a shovel, raised timbers for buildings, nailed, and hammered, and painted. He had helped with spring plantings and the fall harvests. And even when most of his time became occupied with administrative duties, even when he was gone from Kodoma for weeks at a time, traveling to Kishnev, Kiev, Odessa, for business reasons, no matter how busy his life, Aleksandr never neglected the people who had toiled so hard with him to realize Nikolai Viska's plan and his own vision. Aleksandr arranged for loans to help those men who dreamed of being merchants to try their hands at business. He ordered a schoolhouse built and arranged for a teacher to live in Kodoma so the young could be educated. He purchased medical supplies for the ill, books for the curious. He counselled those who looked to him for wisdom, arbitrated disagreements for those who trusted his fairness. But what Aleksandr most enjoyed doing was sitting with the people of Kodoma, drinking with them, singing and laughing with them. For, in truth, through the years, he had become one of them. And now, the people wanted to reward Aleksandr by naming the main roadway after him. But Aleksandr refused, saying that they were as responsible for Kodoma's metamorphosis as he was. After much discussion everyone agreed on Mirazdanyaskaya Street, and no one was more pleased than Aleksandr Moisei.

By 1895 Kodoma was a thriving village, and it was with great pride that Aleksandr surveyed what he had been so instrumental in achieving. But more importantly, when he viewed Kodoma, Aleksandr felt a deep sense of belonging. Nothing reflected that more than his house. It was situated two miles outside of Kodoma and hidden from the main road by woods thick with oak and elm trees, blackthorn and lilac bushes, and was reached by a long, winding lane that led to the foot of a rambling, single-story, gable-roofed wooden house. Originally, the house had been nothing more than a hastily constructed three-room structure which Nikolai Viska had provided for Aleksandr to live in when he moved to Kodoma in 1889. Through the years, along with the rest of the village, Aleksandr had extended the house, adding rooms, improving the flooring, having a fireplace built in his bedroom, changing the decor from practical pieces to more expensive Russian ones. And while the place was not opulent, it definitely suggested that its owner was a man of substance and power.

In September of 1895, Aleksandr departed from Kodoma as he did every year at summer's end. But unlike past years, rather than travelling to Odessa to meet with his father and Nikolai Viska in order to discuss the disposition of the coming harvest, business forced Aleksandr first to journey to Kiev.

As he strode down Mirazdanyaskaya Street toward the railroad platform it was obvious that Aleksandr had changed right along with Kodoma. Unlike the nineteen-year-old youth who had arrived there six years before, a youth motivated by enthusiasm rather than thought, by intuition rather than intellect, Aleksandr was now a man. He stood tall and straight, with an almost regal bearing. The movements of his body no longer suggested the impetuousness, the blind daring of his younger days, but instead radiated a powerful litheness, a smoothly coordinated fluidity that indicated a man of authority, a man to whom other men listened, not out of fear but out of respect.

His face, too, was different. Yes, it was still startlingly handsome, but instead of bordering on youthful prettiness, there was a maturity to it, a firmness of jaw, a steadiness of eyes, an expression of prudence and a certain wisdom. Indeed, his eyes alone indicated that this new Aleksandr would never have accepted Solomon Levin's challenge to declare himself a Jew, thereby jeopardizing a prestigious career as a jurist. Never would this Aleksandr have permitted anything to interfere with his winning the hand of Andreana Vizhni. This Aleksandr was a businessman, fully understanding the theory of profit and loss, and not to win was to have lost. But this Aleksandr was only a winner. His newly developed ability to analyze all situations, to determine their pitfalls and possibilities, prevented him from erring. And while those who knew him, those who admired how successful he had become in his own right, considered Aleksandr shrewd, an unusually capable businessman, a stranger might have labeled him cautious, fearful, afraid to take a risk, lacking the courage to dare the uncharted, to gamble everything in an area where he could stamp his own mark rather than elaborating on the pattern already designed by his father.

And yet, deep within Aleksandr, invisible even to himself, the seed of what he had once been had not disappeared. For, unknowingly, Aleksandr Moisei had only put to sleep who he truly was, that germ of himself lying dormant, waiting for the moment when the opinions others held of him meant less than the beliefs he held for himself.

The weather was hot and dry, the sky bright with sunshine the day that Aleksandr boarded the train in Kodoma that would take him to Kiev. Everywhere, the rich black earth of the steppes was soft, still nourishing the golden fields of grain that were almost ready to be harvested. Here and there, already fattened cattle and sheep grew plumper on lush grasses. Along the Dnestr River, peasant women washed clothes while their husbands lolled on the banks, resting themselves for the heavy labor of reaping crops that was yet to come. With unbroken concentration, Aleksandr stared out of the train window, intently observing every detail of the scene before him, memorizing the locations of the choicest parcels of land, making mental notes to investigate who owned what and whether they would sell; on more than one trip, Aleksandr had discovered and eventually purchased a piece of farmland for Nikolai Viska, land which had proved profitable for both of them.

For hours Aleksandr sat that way, until the repetitious chugging of the engine, the clacking of the wheels against the rails, lulled him to sleep. He swayed and lurched with the train as it wound its way north and west through the countryside, constantly wriggling his body, trying to find a comfortable position. The sun streamed through the window, warming Aleksandr's face, and he dreamed, dreamed pleasantly of his father, Jacob, and his mother, Naomi. He dreamed of his mentor, Nikolai Viska. He dreamed of Solomon Levin, amused even in sleep by what he now referred to as his youthful folly, explaining away his dismissal from St. Petersburg University as an unfortunate but apparently necessary step toward his maturity. And he dreamed of Andreana Vizhni: no longer did her memory plague Aleksandr with the nightmares he had suffered after his final attempt to see her. Now his thoughts of Andreana were fond recollections remembered as if they were wonderful stories he had once read long ago. No longer was the pain of having lost Andreana, his constant companion. And the secret hope he had of recapturing her, the despair that yearning caused him, had also vanished. So, Aleksandr dreamed comfortably, easily, his sleep undisturbed, unaware that the freedom of bachelorhood about which he bragged was merely a costume he wore to hide from himself the fact that no other woman he had ever met began to compare with Andreana Vizhni. And, too, it was a convenient way to keep at bay all those women whom he feared might not be able to replenish the love he had given to Andreana Vizhni.

For two days and a night, Aleksandr Moisei was en route to Kiev. And for two days and a night he alternately slept and dreamed or sat alert, studying the documents that detailed the terms of a grain brokerage contract he would sign in Kiev. For two days and a night, Aleksandr Moisei remained in his first-class roomette enjoying the solitude, permitting himself to rest for the first time in months, reveling in the belief, excited by the belief, that he had become the master of his own fate.

CHAPTER 14

While the train that carried Aleksandr Moisei to Kiev puffed onward, the Mother City of Russia was experiencing its own excitement. Kiev's river, the Dnepr, was crowded with overladen barges hastening to move cargo before the winter ice made passage impossible. Sunshine made the city sparkle; its houses, freshly painted in May, glistened even now. People crowded the streets, their colorful clothing rivaling late blossoming flowers. And there was a joy that seemed to touch everyone. Even the Jews of Kiev felt a sense of jubilation, of promise. For soon their day of hope would arrive, their New Year—*Rosh Hashana,* a fresh dawn followed by unblemished days in which peace and prosperity might reign. Even Esther Dubrovsky and her daughter felt a surge of hope. True, a hope based on nothing more substantial than desperate faith. But, nevertheless, a hope as real as any other.

Though Esther still spent days begging for money, the warmth of summer had made people more generous and the precious hoard of money she kept stored in the hole in her floor had grown considerably. She had received a fair sum from selling her ruby necklace, enough to make a respectable donation to Kiev's synagogue; the remainder, along with Soybel's wages from the *Fabrika Relekvya,* was enough to purchase material to make dresses and buy accessories to accent the clothes so that each time Soybel and Esther appeared at the *Midrash Gadol* they were resplendent. And always a portion of the money went to purchase books and dictionaries in Russian, French, and Latin, history books, volumes on art, novels, collections of poetry, everything that Uchetyel Horodetzky suggested would fashion Soybel into a being of intelligence and culture. So, though it would have been possible for Esther Dubrovsky to improve the immediate life of her daughter and herself with the money she had saved, she chose not to do so, still preferring to forfeit present comforts for future security.

As Esther predicted, Soybel had attracted an unusual amount of attention from the very first time she set foot in the Great Synagogue. On that Passover day, six months before, Soybel's uncommon beauty, her long black hair framing her face, a natural blush heightening her perfect cheek bones, her dark eyes glistening, all set against a gown more yellow than the petals of sunflowers, turned heads from the moment she and her mother entered the synagogue until the services had concluded. From then on, Esther and Soybel attended Sabbath services as often as possible, the frequency of their visits to the synagogue determined by Soybel's wardrobe; she never wore the same costume twice. In time, mothers of eligible sons made the acquaintance of the mother of the young girl who was new to the *Midrash Gadol;* they were impressed by Esther's reserved response. And before long, a marriage broker visited the Dubrovsky house, eagerly inquiring about Soybel's availability.

Though she was thrilled at the prospect of changing her circumstances, Esther declined the first offer of matrimony for her daughter. She had no intention of making an error because of overanxiousness. Carefully, Esther listened to the credentials of each marriage candidate recommended by the broker. When one seemed worthy, a meeting was arranged between Esther, Soybel, and the suitor; these encounters always took place at the home of the broker, the purpose being not only to keep hidden the Dubrovskys' poverty, but to assure Esther that if she disapproved of the man, he would be unable to locate them.

By the autumn of 1895, Esther and Soybel had been introduced to a number of men, young and old. None of them fulfilled Esther's expectations. Many of the more youthful men were of wealthy families but without fortunes in their own rights; Esther had no desire to wait for them to receive their inheritances. Others were university students who offered little more than promises for the future. Of the older would-be beaus, some were quite affluent, but infirm; some lecherous; several were gracious, charming, witty, but lacking in fiscal resources. Rejecting all who were less than financially secure, and not wanting to impose on Soybel a husband whose only merit was wealth, Esther decided to wait. And yet, she did not want to wait too long, for during the past winter all the symptoms of Esther's pneumonia persisted, and they still did not disappear during the spring and summer. Now another winter was approaching.

With the nearing of *Rosh Hashana,* Esther's and Soybel's excitement became unbounded, for with the new year, they were certain, would come rescue from Kiev's ghetto and security in a mansion at the foot of the Lipki Heights. Soybel spent hours before the mirror, practicing her smile, her pout, teaching her eyes to convey only what she intended. Sewing into the wee hours of the morning, Esther worked feverishly to finish the dresses she and Soybel would wear. She devoted her days to searching through tens of shops for shoes and gloves to match the outfits. With the money she had been able to save Esther bought shoes imported from France, soft Italian leather gloves, and two hats, plumed, with rosettes of silk, and with taffeta bows. On *Rosh Hashana* morning, the weather sunny and warm, Esther and Soybel bathed themselves in the wooden tub. Esther washed quickly, anxious to be on her way, but Soybel luxuriated in her bath, unabashedly admiring her full breasts, flat stomach, and her smooth inner thighs. Two hours later, when they entered the Great Synagogue, Esther, and especially Soybel, looked elegant, radiant; they could have deceived anyone into believing that they were already residents of an estate at the foot of the Lipki Heights.

"Momma, straighten my collar," Soybel whispered to her mother. She glanced around at the other young girls, who were clothed in dresses tailored by Kiev's finest couturiers.

"From the amount of attention the men are paying you, it is the others who should be worrying." Esther surveyed the throngs of richly attired people around her.

Even the synagogue bespoke the opulence Esther craved. At its center stood an altar flanked by Ionic pillars with sculptured lions standing before them. The eternal light glowed brightly, and, above it, the Ark containing the Torah was carved with flowers, leaves, birds, lions, and fanciful renderings of beautiful beings. Inscribed in relief on the wall behind the Ark were the Ten Commandments. On either side of the Ark hung red silk curtains embroidered with gold and silver thread. Subdued light, filtered through stained-glass windows, shone on the pulpit, and hundreds of candles in silver chandeliers cast their reflections against the altar's golden-hued wooden frame and flooring. From the altar at the center of the synagogue to the limits of the walls, Kiev's wealthiest Jews were gathered, proudly displaying their success to each other, but, more significantly, eager to pray to God and reverently thank Him for their good fortune. Through this congestion, Esther and Soybel weaved their way, Esther graciously greeting those whose acquaintance she had already made while Soybel stood demurely by her side. At last, knowing the custom, the men and women began to part company, each moving to opposite sides of the synagogue: the ritual law of the Jews required men and women to be separated in a house of worship by a divider, a cloth curtain called a *mechitza,* which hung in loose sections from a framework that ran the length of the synagogue. This isolating of women from men in a *shul* was a reminder that women were not equal to men, not worthy of communicating directly with God, not competent enough to do so. Indeed, Talmudic wisdom said: "He who teaches his daughter the Talmud is corrupting her;

a woman of learning is a monstrosity." Only males were permitted entry into *heders* and *yeshivas.* Only males were honored with a specific religious ceremony welcoming them into manhood: their Bar Mitzvah, occurring in their thirteenth year, the time when no longer were a son's deeds and sins charged to the account of his father. But of greatest consequence was the fact that only males were allowed to recite *Kaddish,* the prayer for the dead.

Leading Soybel by the hand, Esther worked her way to the women's side of the synagogue, selecting two seats on the aisle next to the *mechitza;* Esther sat down in the second seat from the aisle, her daughter taking the place closest to the curtain. Toying with the emerald necklace which clung to her graceful neck, Soybel studied the scene around her with reserve. From the front of the synagogue a rush of silence swept backward as a distinguished man, dressed in a black robe with a cream-colored *talis* draped around his shoulders and a white *yarmulke* on his head, mounted the pulpit. The rabbi of the *Midrash Gadol* took his place behind the lectern, and, when all heads were bowed, he began the Hebrew convocation to the *Rosh Hashanah* service and then started to read a portion of Genesis from the Torah.

As the long ceremony proceeded, more than one person in the congregation grew restless. Among them was Soybel. First she scanned the women's side of the synagogue, her eyes flitting from one face to another. Then, peeking through a space between two sections of the *mechitza,* she contemplated the men. Across the aisle from her and one row forward, the profile of a young man caught her notice. Soybel watched him. As if in response, he looked up from his prayer book. His gaze began to wander. Shifting his position so he was sitting more sideways than forward, he peered through the gaps in the curtain, displaying a mild curiosity about the women across from him. The young man's eyes skimmed over their faces, moving from one woman to the next, until his look met Soybel's. Her dark eyes were locked on him. He turned his attention back to the Torah reading.

"And when they came to the place which God had told

him of, Abraham built an altar there, and laid upon it the wood, and bound Isaac his son, and laid him on the altar upon the wood. And the angel of the Lord called unto Abraham from heaven: 'Abraham, Abraham, lay not thy hand upon the lad, for now I know thou art a God-fearing man, and because thou hast not withheld thine only son, in blessing I will multiply thy seed as the stars of the heaven, and in thy seed shall all the nations of the earth be blessed.' "

Throughout the reading of the Torah, Soybel continued to look at the young man. With her right foot she surreptitiously pushed aside the curtain to see him better. There was an elegance about the young man, a fineness to his clothing, a proudness in his bearing which spoke of affluence, *puissance*. Soybel scrutinized the finely chiseled features of his clean-shaven face; never had she seen eyes as blue as his. Sensing that he was being watched, the young man glanced back at Soybel. Her gaze did not waver. Intrigued by her boldness, the young man looked at Soybel directly. She blushed. His lips parted in a smile. Without thinking, Soybel returned the greeting. Aware of what was transpiring, Esther kept her eyes buried in her prayer book. Soybel averted her gaze and let the *mechitza* fall back into place. The young man faced forward. *Just half of his face is more handsome than all the others with their whole faces,* Esther thought to herself, finding it difficult not to glimpse at the young man's profile. The service continued, the voices of the rabbi and the *chazan* a droning buzz to Soybel and Esther. Finally, hours later, the elaborate liturgy marking the Day of Judgment drew to a close. The rabbi's voice took on a joyous forcefulness.

"With the coming of Thy kingdom the hills will sing and the rivers will laugh in ecstasy that they belong to God. And through all Thy people so loud, praise of Thee shall ring that all will hail Thee as King!"

"T'keeah!" The clarion call of the *shofar*, the ram's horn, rang out, symbolizing Abraham's willingness to sacrifice his only son, Isaac, to the Lord. "T'keeeah!" the *shofar* trumpeted, reminding all of Abraham's complete faith in God. "T'keeeeah!" blared the ram's horn, summoning the worshippers to look within, to search their consciences and repent their sins. "T'keeeeeah!"

"Leshanah tovah tikkatevu—may you be inscribed in the Book of Life for a good year!"

"Leshanah tovah!"

"Leshanah tovah!"

The exultant *Rosh Hashana* greeting raced through the synagogue. The rabbi stepped down from the pulpit and walked up the aisle, stopping at intervals to shake hands and share a few words of happiness with his congregation. Swarms of people crowded into the pathways, following the rabbi. Soybel stood up, her eyes searching for the young man with whom she had been flirting. She saw him being pressed along with the crowd toward the doorway. Not waiting for her mother's approval, or for Esther to accompany her, Soybel pulled aside the *mechitza,* squeezed her way into the aisle, and pushed her way to the exit. Emerging into the sunlight, Soybel frantically looked this way and that. The young man was nowhere to be seen. In search of her mother, Soybel spun around, took a step forward, and stopped short. Before her stood the young man.

"Excuse me!" He tipped his hat, revealing a thick head of long blond hair.

Soybel's heart jumped. He was far taller than she had calculated. The young man stared down at her; for the first time in years he felt tongue-tied. Soybel's mouth became dry, her hands cold.

"I hope you did not think me rude by my watching you during the . . ." The young man's voice diminished into silence, Soybel's sparkling smile making him dumbstruck.

"To be honest, I feared that you might consider *me* irreverent for permitting my attention to wander from the service," Soybel purred.

"No such thought crossed my mind." A look of impishness tugged at the corners of the young man's mouth. "Indeed, my honor forces me to confess that I far prefer Pushkin to prayers."

Soybel looked askance at him.

"Is it Pushkin you disapprove of or, in truth, my disrespectful behavior during the service?"

Her expression became coy.

"Ah, you do not believe that I have read Pushkin."

With arched eyebrows, Soybel intimated that, in fact, she did not accept his word. The young man beamed.

" 'God's little bird knows neither care nor toil. Does not bustlingly weave a permanent nest. In the long night on a bough it slumbers; let the fair sun rise, and the little bird harken to the voice of God.' "

"Then you do know Pushkin!"

"As obviously do you."

"But certainly not as well as you," Soybel said with delight, impressed by the young man's knowledge.

"Ah, modesty forces me to admit that aside from *The Gypsies* my awareness of poetry is lacking."

"Why, then, have you memorized that poem?"

"Because it is my favorite."

"But it is so sad."

"True, but how many people do you know whose name is the same as one of the main characters in a great work of literature?"

"You are certainly not the 'Old Man,' " Soybel teased.

"Nor am I Zemfira, or do you think the role of a fiery gypsy woman suits me?"

"Then there is but one choice left, Aleko."

"Yes. Except my name is not so romantic sounding. It is Aleksandr."

"Aleksandr what?"

"Moisei. Aleksandr Moisei, originally from Odessa and now of Kodoma."

Soybel fought to maintain her composure. "Then you are only visiting Kiev."

"Yes. I am here on business. In fact, I only came to today's services out of respect for my host—you see, my business is with him."

"Then shouldn't you be with him?" The fear that Aleksandr Moisei might reply yes and leave her caused Soybel to nervously bite her lower lip.

"When I left the synagogue, he was so engrossed in conversation that for the moment I am certain he has forgotten about me."

"Will you be here for long?"

"For another week. Until after *Yom Kippur.* I had not planned to stay but my associate insisted and I could not very well refuse."

"I assume you are quite familiar with Kiev."

"Barely at all. Except for business, I never visit here. And when I do, I see little but ledgers and restaurants."

"Will your business occupy all your time this coming week?"

"My formal business is concluded. Accepting my associate's invitation to remain in Kiev is nothing more than courtesy—a way to ensure our doing business in the future."

"Then you will have time to see much of Kiev."

"It is possible." Aleksandr laughed softly, deeply, an irrepressible grin on his lips. "Would you be kind enough to show me your city?" he asked, the mellow lilt to his voice implying that he wanted Soybel to be more than an escort.

Soybel gave Aleksandr her most dazzling smile. "I would be delighted to show you Kiev—if you allow my mother to accompany us."

"Of course. I did not mean to suggest that we go alone." Aleksandr was entranced by Soybel's sensuality, and he had to force himself not to lean down and kiss her.

Knowing full well what he desired, Soybel moistened her lips with her tongue.

"You have not yet told me your name," Aleksandr said, unable to remove his eyes from Soybel's mouth.

"I am Soybel Dubrovsky, of Kiev."

"Soybel Dubrovsky of Kiev, I formally invite you and

your mother to be my guides so I may learn about your fair city."

"Aleksandr Moisei of Kodoma, we accept." *Aleksandr Moisei of Kodoma, I will accept everything you request. And like the gypsy Zemfira, I, too, sing out about my Aleko: "How young and bold he is. How he loves me."*

BOOK TWO

September 1895 to February 1907

If we do as our brothers have done,
and refuse to fight our enemies
for our lives, for what is just,
they will destroy us
until we have vanished from the earth.

THE FIRST BOOK OF THE MACCABEES

CHAPTER 15

Aleksandr Moisei married Soybel Dubrovsky three weeks to the day after meeting her. The first of those three weeks Aleksandr remained in Kiev, delaying his trip to Odessa so as to remain close to this breathtakingly beautiful young girl who was at once innocent and educated, impish and earnest, who clung to his arm as if he were a savior, and whom he had vowed to wed the moment she spoke to him at the Great Synagogue. Indeed, on the second day he had known her, as they strolled arm in arm along the grassy banks of the Dnepr River, Aleksandr had asked Soybel to be his wife. Without waiting to seek her mother's advice or permission, Soybel accepted, knowing full well that Esther would agree. In truth, Esther was prepared to offer Soybel to Aleksandr if he did not ask for her hand first. For Aleksandr quickly proved himself to be everything that Esther had dreamed of. He was handsome and wealthy, cultured, and charming. He exuded self-assurance, a power that made Esther and her daughter feel protected when they were with him, safe from all the indignities of life. He was understanding; the horrified expression on his face when he saw where Esther and Soybel lived, and then when Esther told him of their life, was obviously genuine. The distraught tone of his voice as he struggled to find something to say that might help erase Esther's and Soybel's suffering was unmistakable: the despair Esther saw in Aleksandr when she told her sorrowful tales pleased Esther, for she was certain that this unusual young man would be more than generous in attempting to soothe away the Dubrovskys' past. And Esther was right.

During that first week, Aleksandr showed Esther and her daughter things they had never seen before: a performance of the opera *Boris Goudonov* at the Municipal Theater, a French ballet in the garden setting of the *Château des Fleurs*. They lunched on pheasant at the Merchants' Club, had duckling for dinner at Semadéni. They took a steamboat ride along the Dnepr, Soybel and Aleksandr embracing, whispering words of love to one another while Esther relaxed on a lounge chair, bathing her face in the warm sunshine.

Alone, Aleksandr and Soybel climbed to the top of the Lipki Heights, and there, on a wooden knoll overlooking Kiev, they pledged their love to each other, Soybel ready to give Aleksandr anything he wanted while he, though desiring to feel Soybel's flesh against his, to lie with her, remained a gentleman. The way Soybel kissed Aleksandr, her tongue searching every part of his mouth, her teeth nibbling his lips, made Aleksandr want to run off with her, to abandon his responsibilities and live on a balmy isle in the tropics with Soybel where they would do nothing but lie naked in the sun and make love forever. When Aleksandr told Soybel of his fantasy, she snuggled against his chest and laughed, the sound of her ecstasy a song of love to Aleksandr.

The two of them spent another afternoon wandering along crowded Kreshtchatik Boulevard, browsing in fashionable stores which before Soybel had only seen from the outside. In one shop, Soybel admired a thin bracelet fashioned from gold. Aleksandr purchased it for her, leaving Soybel speechless. In another store she mentioned how elegant she found a small jade pin sculpted in the shape of a cherub. Aleksandr bought that, too, and Soybel looked at him in awe. Further on, Soybel spied a red silken shawl, saying that her mother would adore it. Without hesitation Aleksandr paid for it, laughing heartily as he caught Soybel staring wide-eyed at the amount of rubles he carried in his wallet. Thinking that Aleksandr was mocking her, Soybel became angry and turned away from him, ignoring his apologies until he put his arms around her and coaxed her out of her pique with a kiss. Immediately Soybel's gaiety returned, and, taking Aleksandr by the hand, she led him forward along Kreshtchatik Boulevard.

At the end of the first week, unable to remain in Kiev any longer, Aleksandr suggested to Esther that she and Soybel accompany him to Odessa, where they could meet his mother and father and together plan for the wedding the three of them wanted. Needing no urging to flee Kiev, Esther accepted the invitation. Two days later, with all the possessions she cared to take with her stuffed into one suitcase, Esther, her daughter, and the magnificent young man who would soon be her son-in-law boarded a train which would take them away from the misery Esther had often thought she and her daughter would never escape; a misery to which neither of them intended ever to return.

Odessa overwhelmed Esther and Soybel. The stature of the city's government buildings, the elegance of the soft-hued mansions, the constant scent of spice in the air, the way the Black Sea caressed the shoreline, made Esther and Soybel believe that this was not Russia but some exotic foreign land. The sumptuousness of the suite that Aleksandr rented for them at the exclusive Hotel St. Petersburg astounded them. And when Aleksandr advised them both to open accounts at Odessa's most chic couturiers they were dumbstruck. Jacob and Naomi Moisei captivated them, especially Naomi who, without hesitation, welcomed Esther and her daughter into the Moisei household as if they were already members of the family. But nothing excited Esther Dubrovsky or her daughter as much as did the moment on

September 30, 1895, when Soybel Dubrovsky, age fifteen, became the wife of twenty-six-year-old Aleksandr Jacobovich Moisei.

The scene of the marriage was the home of Jacob Moisei, the event filling that place with a gaiety unknown to it for years. Though only the immediate families of the bride and groom were present, it seemed as if a score of well-wishers had gathered there for the wedding. Wine flowed freely; platters of steaming meats and breads, cakes and candies were voraciously devoured, everyone eating and chattering at once. Soybel was beautiful, dressed in a gown of silky white, her black hair coiffed in curls that were held in place by a gold comb; at her throat was a necklace of tiny emeralds. Wearing a suit of maroon velvet, Aleksandr looked dashing, his strong countenance and blond hair giving him the demeanor of an invincible warrior. And at the request of Aleksandr the ceremony was performed by Rabbi Joshua Eleazar, the rabbi's delight in marrying the couple obvious; his pleasure was twofold—presiding over any marriage excited him, but officiating at the wedding of Jacob Moisei's son gave Eleazar an exquisite sense of triumph.

Unbeknownst to Soybel and her mother, Aleksandr's desire to be married by Rabbi Eleazar had created a furious argument between him and Jacob. Jacob became enraged, stating furiously that for Aleksandr to be married by a rabbi—and especially in his, Jacob Moisei's house—would be highly inappropriate. Becoming angrier than Jacob had ever seen her, Naomi defended Aleksandr, insisting that her son would be wed where he chose, and in the manner he chose.

"For years, Jacob, for far too many years, you have treated Aleksandr as if he were just *your* son. You made him your creation. You determined his life, his education. Never once were my wishes considered. Well, my husband, I, too, want Aleksandr to be wed by a rabbi. And if my son has decided to mark this auspicious occasion in his life with the blessing of the God of his forefathers, rather than your God of opportunity, than that is what shall come to pass. And if you attempt to influence or coerce Aleksandr into doing otherwise, I will curse you, Jacob. For if you cause Aleksandr to foresake his desire, you will have proven that it is not your son you love, but only yourself."

When Naomi's tirade ended, Jacob expected his wife to cry, to beg forgiveness for her audacity and accede to his wishes. She did not. So Jacob relented, fearful that if he did otherwise, never again would there be a moment of peace between him and his wife.

It was with great nervousness that Jacob Moisei watched his son being married, fearful that someone might recognize Rabbi Eleazar as he entered and left the Moisei residence and question his own Christian allegiance. Nevertheless, it was with Jacob's blessing, too, that Aleksandr Moisei solemnly exchanged the vows of matrimony with Soybel Dubrovsky. For Jacob genuinely liked Soybel, sensing beneath her romantic attachment to Aleksandr a core of practicality, a pragmatism that would compensate for his son's apparently uncontrollable bouts of impetuousness, a trait that Jacob considered a tragic flaw in Aleksandr's character.

A month after his marriage to Soybel, Aleksandr Moisei first helped his wife and then her mother down from the train to the railway platform in Kodoma. From that day, Aleksandr Moisei's life changed dramatically. The once-quiet house where he had lived in casual disarray began to evolve into a manor which truly reflected the wealth and power of its occupants. In preparation for the family he and Soybel often talked about raising, Aleksandr had a second story added to the house. To satisfy a fantasy of Soybel's, Aleksandr also had a ground-level porch constructed that bordered the front and two sides of the house. And, at Soybel's request, the house was painted yellow with white window-trim and doors. Inside, room by room, the walls were repainted and the wooden floors refinished. Slowly, one piece at a time—with Aleksandr's full agreement, indeed with his encouragement—furniture that Soybel had seen in

Odessa and that had delighted her arrived in Kodoma, Soybel's intent being eventually to replace Aleksandr's selections with ones of grace and style.

As for Esther, with nothing but tacit approval from Aleksandr, she assumed the role of managing the household. With an astute eye she hired servants: a maid, a woman to do the cooking, and a young peasant girl to wash and press clothes. At Esther's suggestion, Aleksandr engaged a caretaker and a stable boy. Free of toil for the first time in her life, and suddenly having the ability to utilize other people's labor, Esther enjoyed manipulating the staff of servants. It was with ease that she took on her role, for, after years of fantasizing about living in wealth, Esther Dubrovsky had vicariously perfected the art of being the mistress of a manor.

Oftentimes, overcome by the thought that a miracle had caused the appearance of Aleksandr Moisei in her life, the knowledge that he was responsible for the redemption of her and her daughter moved Esther to tears. Just the sight of the grand villa and its expansive, carefully cultivated grounds made Esther weep. But it was the sight of her daughter's unbounded jubilation which induced Esther to cry and laugh at once.

Yet nothing equaled the exultation Esther felt when at the end of December, 1896, Soybel Dubrovsky Moisei gave birth to a son, Grisha. From the moment her grandson screamed his way into life, Esther felt an exuberance she had not experienced since her own childhood. For hours at a time she hovered over the infant, his peaceful look as he slept, the delicacy of his skin to her touch, enthralling Esther. More than once, Aleksandr teased Esther about her devoting more time to Grisha than did Soybel. His mother-in-law's reply was always the same: "There are not enough days left in the world for me to have the time I want to spend with my grandchild." *Because his existence is absolute proof that I am awake, alive, really living amidst all this, and not caught in the cruel hoax of a dream.*

Stimulated by a vigor she had not felt in years, Esther

instructed Soybel to rest while she took charge of caring for Grisha. Esther played with him, sang to him, bathed him, dressed him. Even after Grisha was in bed for the night, Esther would stay by his cradle and watch him sleep. And Soybel was grateful that her mother was willing to be Grisha's nursemaid. Though she dearly loved her son, felt a rush of exhilaration each time she nursed him, and saw his instinctive smile of contentment, Soybel was not fond of maintaining Grisha's cleanliness, or staying awake all night long when he was colicky or showed signs of being ill. Without complaint, Esther looked after Grisha's needs, not displaying a trace of jealousy when, once Grisha was rested and freshly dressed, Soybel would take him from her and play with him until he soiled himself and required a change of clothing. A year later, with the birth of Soybel's second child, Daniella, Soybel made no pretense at even attempting to nurture her daughter. Fearful that her breasts would droop and be unappealing if she nursed her newborn, a wet nurse was hired, and then a governess from Odessa whose duties required her to care fully for the infant girl and Grisha—permitting Soybel to do nothing but enjoy her children at her leisure.

Esther Dubrovsky never saw her granddaughter, Daniella, for Esther died in February, 1897, long before the child was born. Her final illness started with a cold so slight that no one thought twice about it. Not even Esther, who was certain that at most she would be in bed for two or three days. To be safe, Aleksandr summoned his father's personal physician to Kodoma, the doctor deciding that there was nothing more to prescribe than plenty of bedrest and healthful foods. Instead of abating, Esther's condition worsened, developing into pleurisy. She lingered on for days, flushed with an acute fever, wracked by chills and painful fits of coughing. The doctor was recalled, but was unable to do a thing to help his patient, Esther's lungs having been too badly weakened from previous bouts with pneumonia to respond to any treatment. In the middle of the night, alone in the dark, delirious, her very last thoughts being of her grandson, Esther died. When she was discovered the next morning, her body stiff, a mask of tranquility covered her face. With no ceremonial preparations, without a man of God presiding over her burial, mourned at graveside by her daughter, son-in-law, and Jacob and Naomi Moisei, Esther Dubrovsky, age forty-two, was laid to rest in Kodoma's small cemetery—her final abode—further from the ghetto of Kiev than she had ever imagined she would get.

During her second summer in Kodoma, without Esther's energetic presence, having to assume the often tedious burden of raising Grisha, with the preparations for the harvest occupying nearly all of Aleksandr's time, and being near the end of her second pregnancy, her weight and fatigue restricting her mobility, Soybel Moisei became bored with her life in Kodoma. Often she found herself daydreaming about the stimulating hustle and bustle of Odessa, where she and Aleksandr had spent a month after their marriage doing nothing but indulging themselves in all the pleasures the city offered. She longed for the excitement of the opera, the ballet, the extravagance of the chic shops that lined Deribasovskaya Street, the sumptuous meals served in the restaurant of the exclusive St. Petersburg Hotel. By autumn, after having given birth to Daniella, Soybel embarked on a campaign for Aleksandr to take her on a sojourn to Odessa, especially during the winter months when Kodoma would again be snowbound and drab. Unable to resist any of Soybel's requests, Aleksandr agreed. From that time on, at the beginning of December, the house in Kodoma was closed, and the entire Moisei family and the children's governess would journey to Odessa and ensconce themselves in the luxury of Jacob Moisei's home.

For four months the household of the Odessa Moiseis was in a constant uproar. Grisha and his games seemed to be everywhere at once, Daniella's crawling about kept her always underfoot. The aromas of braised meats, roasted fowl, fruit- and nutcakes continually filled the house, Naomi doing all the cooking, her obvious delight enlivening the atmosphere with a constant gaiety. Jacob, beaming with pride, played games of peek-a-boo with his grandchildren, concocted tales of ghosts and ogres for their amusement, doing everything that occurred to him to entertain them. Almost without letup, Aleksandr and Soybel were occupied with their own interests, attending the theater, concerts, plays. They dined lavishly, frequenting the Bavaria Café for lunch, and for dinner their favorite restaurant, the St. Petersburg. They danced until dawn at the balls held at the Exchange. And several times they were guests at Vassili Viska's terrace villa, where they mingled with foreign dignitaries and Russian aristocrats. When the weather permitted, Aleksandr slipped off by himself for an afternoon sail in the *Golub*, the winter-chilled sea spray stinging his face like needles, the frosty air invigorating him. When the first thaw arrived and it was necessary to return to Kodoma, new clothing, jewelry, knicknacks capriciously purchased by Soybel, presents that Naomi had bought, plus everything that had originally been brought from Kodoma, were secured in locked trunks and loaded onto the train along with Aleksandr and his family. For six consecutive years this winter routine took place.

After a while it was not just winters in Kodoma that Soybel found tedious, but all the seasons year round. With nothing to do but idle away her days, Soybel became irritated at being confined in the unstimulating environment of rural life. Her patience grew short. The merest oversight by the servants caused her temper to flare. The noise made by her children elicited complaints. Even Aleksandr's easygoing manner and buoyant spirit added a nettle to Soybel's lackluster existence. In an attempt to entertain herself Soybel took to reading, but the novels of Balzac and Dumas, which she adored, only made her long even more for a life filled with adventure. To ward off total ennui, Soybel forced herself to take an interest in Aleksandr's work and, for a time, the complexities of learning how to keep ledgers and deciphering the jigsaw puzzle methods required to make all areas of the Viska enterprise mesh intrigued her. Eventually that, too, became dull. Again, Soybel approached Aleksandr about going to Odessa, but this time she wanted permission to go by herself, to stay with his parents for several days at a time to rejuvenate herself. Generous with his wife to a fault, Aleksandr quickly assented, and quite a few times during the years Soybel kissed her family good-bye and journeyed to Odessa alone. Aleksandr regretted each of her departures, knowing how desperately he would miss her. When she returned home, elated, eagerly displaying the gifts she had bought for everyone, including herself, and then at night when Soybel would engulf him with kisses and a passion so abandoned he thought his wife more animal than human, Aleksandr forgot everything except how much he loved Soybel. But in 1903, along with the family's winter trips to Odessa, Soybel's solo expeditions also came to a halt. The cause was the death of Naomi Moisei.

At first, only Naomi detected a difference in her body, attributing her slow but steady loss of weight to poor eating habits and winters spent in perpetual motion with her grandchildren. By the winter of 1903, when she had withered away so severely that her appearance shocked everyone who saw her, Naomi became worried and sought the advice of a doctor. His diagnosis chilled her, the prognosis was devastating. Naomi told no one what the doctor had concluded, but it was obvious to all. She grew frail and weak; the disease was rapidly devouring her body. And then she became bedridden. Naomi's blue eyes became lifeless and sunken in their sockets, her face hollow-cheeked, her skin translucent. When Naomi reached out for her husband with her once slender fingers now skeletal, Jacob would tremble with love for the woman who was slowly ebbing away from him. Gently, he would cradle Naomi against his chest. She felt weightless, and for an instant Jacob would mistakenly believe that he was holding not his wife, but her spirit. Consumed with grief, already agonizing over his wife's irrevocable fate, Jacob Moisei even consented to a request of

Naomi's that in better times he would not have even considered.

The end came quickly for Naomi, faster than anyone had anticipated or was prepared for. Jacob was so distraught, so despondent over the loss of his Naomi, that without a single reconsideration he honored his wife's vehement, pleading last wish and arranged for her burial in Odessa's Jewish cemetery in a grave next to that of her father. Aleksandr, too, was overcome by despair, the loss of his mother sapping his vitality and happiness. Two months passed before Soybel was able to coax her husband out of his despondency. A year later, almost to the day, another misfortune befell the Moiseis: Jacob died. With nothing of a terminal nature apparently ailing him, Jacob's death was attributed to heartbreak and the loneliness caused by Naomi's passing away. Again, Soybel expected Aleksandr to be incapacitated by bereavement. She was astounded not only by his refusal to attend his father's funeral, but by the anger with which Aleksandr recalled Jacob's memory. What disturbed Soybel most, even after he had explained his reasons, was that Aleksandr Moisei refused to touch even one kopeck of the large inheritance bequeathed to him by his father.

CHAPTER 16

"Aleksandr, how long do you intend to remain angry over your father's death?" Soybel asked one night while sitting at her dressing table, preparing for bed.

"It is not his death that angers me, Soybel, but his burial," Aleksandr replied as he rocked back and forth in the chair that sat next to the bedroom fireplace.

Soybel studied herself in the dressing-table mirror as she combed her waist-length hair with slow, indulgent strokes. "Your anger is expensive for us, Aleksandr."

"What would you have me do, Soybel, pretend that I forgive him so I won't feel like a hypocrite when I accept his inheritance? Anyway, forgiveness is the last thing my father would have wanted."

"I am still not convinced that what he did was so wrong."

Aleksandr looked at Soybel's reflection in the mirror. "When he actually buried my mother in the Jewish cemetery, I was astonished."

"He did that because that is what she wanted."

"But then to abandon her by having himself buried in the Christian cemetery? I cannot believe that he could have loved my mother and still have done that. And that is what I an unable to forgive."

"Aleksandr, you are making more out of this than it is

worth," Soybel said matter-of-factly as she opened a bottle of skin oil and rubbed the scented liquid on her face.

"And do you know why he chose to be buried in the Christian cemetery? So his grandson would be sure to have a history that would not have to be hidden. When he told me of his decision, he said: 'If by some chance our baptism papers are lost, if a catastrophe should strike and all records of our conversion disappear, then everything for Grisha will be forfeited. But if a priest buries me, if I am laid to rest in a Christian cemetery, then Grisha will have my remains to prove that he is not a Jew.' How could he do that, Soybel?" Aleksandr sat erect, his face lined with stress. "How could he refuse to be buried next to his own wife? Who will be my mother's husband in heaven? Who?"

"In heaven, Aleksandr? My convenient Jew suddenly believes in heaven?" Soybel lightly mocked. She smiled as she inspected her glistening skin in the mirror.

Aleksandr glared at his wife. Soybel leaned closer to the mirror and examined what she thought might be the start of wrinkles at the corners of her eyes.

"Have you forgotten, Aleksandr, when just after our marriage I discovered that you practiced no religion—and had no intention of ever doing so—how you boasted to me, to my mother, and your parents that you were a businessman. That's what you said, Aleksandr: 'I am a businessman. Because when I deal with Jews, I know how to be a Jew. And when I am with Christians, I can be a Christian, too.' "

"I remember my answer very well." There was a preoccupied tone to Aleksandr's reply.

Soybel dipped her index finger into a dish of ointment, then rubbed it on the skin below her eyes. "You know, Aleksandr, I never did fully understand why you chose a rabbi to marry us."

For a long moment Aleksandr was silent. When he finally answered his wife, his voice was unsteady. "The only other choice would have been for a priest to marry us. And that was something I could not do. Not to my mother. Not after what she did for me. No one could have comforted me, understood the way I felt, as she did."

With an inquisitive look in her eyes, Soybel tried to pry a clearer answer from her husband.

"It was something that happened long ago. There is no need to talk about it."

Shrugging her shoulders, Soybel took a towel from the rack at the side of the vanity table and wiped her face dry. Left to himself, Aleksandr's thought drifted back to the day he had announced to his parents that he wanted Rabbi Eleazar to preside over his wedding. He recalled how fearlessly, how boldly his mother had stood by his side against his father's fury, and he remembered the bond he felt with her at that moment, a closeness far more intimate than ever before. Yet, not long after that occurrence, when Soybel was pregnant with Grisha, Aleksandr did to his mother what Jacob had done.

"When Soybel gives birth to the child she is carrying, Aleksandr, then you will understand that there is far more to religion than convenience."

"Mother, please—"

"How else will you teach your child right from wrong, to have an unimpeachable morality, if you yourself do not have guidelines stronger than any made by man?"

"Mother!"

"That is not an answer, Aleksandr."

"I am sorry, Mother, but I cannot tell you what you want to hear. Because I could never convince someone to believe in something I do not believe in."

"Then why did you have Rabbi Eleazar marry you? Have you forgotten all the things we spoke of after that tragic incident with Andreana Vizhni? Have you forgotten the promise you made to me about how someday you would raise a son? Are you a hypocrite, Aleksandr?"

"I am a realist, Mother. That is why in Kodoma, living in the midst of superstitious peasants, Soybel and I are treated with respect. Because we are taken to be Christians who do not practice their religion. And—"

"You sound as if that is something to be proud of."

"And to the peasants that is far less despicable than being any sort of Jew."

"You are living a lie, Aleksandr."

"No more so than if I were a Jew who did not practice his religion."

"You are living a double lie!"

"I am living a simple truth, Mother. That those who defy history eventually succumb to history."

"Tell me, Aleksandr, who are you to dismiss religion with the snap of your fingers?"

"I am dismissing nothing, Mother. Because it is impossible to dismiss something that does not exist. Without God there can be no religion. And truly, I have no belief in God whatsoever."

Naomi was dumbfounded by Aleksandr's remarks, and wounded. Months passed before her disappointment with her son ebbed and she was able to respond to him without feeling a trace of anger. Yet there was a rift between the two of them that was never completely resolved. And the hurt that persisted between Aleksandr and his mother left him with an open wound on his conscience that had never healed.

Soybel Moisei again looked at her husband's reflection in the dressing-table mirror; that he was having a struggle within himself was plainly visible on his face. "Why do you look so downcast, Aleksandr?"

"It will pass."

"You sound as if you know that from experience, as if you have been troubled by the same thing before."

"All that is bothering me is that sometimes I think my life is passing by with nothing special to mark time."

"Are you saying that you are unhappy with your life, Aleksandr?"

"No . . ."

"I should think not. Especially when the future promises us even more than we already have."

"We have been very fortunate, Soybel."

"You are too modest, my husband. There are few men such as you, whose ambition is matched by their ability."

"Do you know, Soybel, when I hear the church bells at Easter, or Christmastime, or the Sabbath bells, they repel me. And yet, at the same time I am drawn to them. To what they symbolize; a belief by man that gives meaning to life far more lasting than anything material."

"Religion is for the poor, Aleksandr. It is they who need ephemeral treasures—because they are unable to acquire real ones." Without thinking, Soybel picked up a diamond bracelet that lay on her dressing table and stroked its gleaming facets.

"It is more than that, Soybel. A man who believes in God has something to look forward to—an eternity in Paradise or Hell. But what is the future for me except a repetition of the present, ending only when I die."

Soybel laughed. "Is my Aleksandr telling me that he is having thoughts of religion?"

"If that were the problem, I would be wrestling with the idea of setting foot in a house of worship. But I would no more enter Kodoma's church than the *shul* at the far end of the village. And yet, is it possible that a man can be satisfied devoting his life to nothing else but filling his coffers to overflowing?" Aleksandr glanced at his wife. She was busily scrutinizing the reflection of her bracelet. Soybel's apparent indifference to the depth of Aleksandr's feelings caused a surge of anger to stiffen his body.

"Damn it, Soybel, don't you care about what I am saying?"

"To be honest, Aleksandr, this subject holds no interest for me whatsoever."

"What does interest you, Soybel—besides beautiful clothes and jewels, that is?"

"Right now, Aleksandr, sleep interests me."

"Soybel, I am trying to tell you about something which is beginning to disturb me very deeply."

"Aleksandr, I detect a change in you, and I am not certain that I like it." Carefully, Soybel laid down her bracelet, making sure each diamond was in perfect line with the one next to it. "But perhaps this folly of yours will pass by morning."

"Folly, Soybel? You—"

"Aleksandr, you are not the first man known to be temporarily overcome by childishness."

Seething at his wife's easy dismissal of his thoughts, Aleksandr was unable to move or speak. Soybel stood up and approached her husband, her hair swaying with the movement of her hips. Soybel's nightgown was sheer, and her heavy breasts pushed the garment outward, stretching it so tightly that the outline of her large nipples clearly showed. Aleksandr studied his wife. She had changed considerably from the impish sixteen-year-old girl who had scampered down Mirazdanyaskaya Street eight years before, catching falling snowflakes on her tongue, squealing with delight about the enchanted village to which her impetuous Aleko had brought her. This was no longer the shy Soybel Dubrovsky whom he had married—the virginal child who, on her wedding day, was dressed in a flowing gown of white with only a necklace of tiny emeralds breaking the purity of her innocent look. No longer did Soybel consider herself to be Zemfira, the smoldering gypsy woman. Now, Soybel was sophisticated, the mistress of a resplendent estate, the wife of a man of wealth and influence. And she acted as such.

Physically, too, Soybel had changed. Her once-supple body had grown fuller, her hips rounder, her breasts heavier. Her face, still beautiful, with its small nose and long lashes fluttering over large black eyes, had become that of a mature woman; her lips always appeared ready to begin an endless kiss. But it was when she walked that the difference in Soybel was most noticeable. Unlike when she had first married Aleksandr, Soybel no longer made men's hearts race to hold her and deeply kiss her. Now when she moved, the rustling of her long silk dresses sounding like the flesh of her thighs rubbing together, her hips and buttocks undulating gently, men thought only of making love to her. Soybel was aware of that, and she enjoyed it.

"Come to bed, Aleksandr," Soybel purred. Facing her husband, Soybel let her nightgown slide down the length of her body to the floor. She placed her hands beneath her breasts, pushing them upwards, extending them outwards, offering them to Aleksandr. The scent of his wife's body made Aleksandr lightheaded. And, as always, Soybel's womanliness smothered Aleksandr's thoughts and he quickly succumbed to her seductiveness.

"Come to bed, Aleksandr," Soybel repeated, backing away from her husband.

As if in a trance, Aleksandr followed Soybel to their canopied chamber. He disrobed and lay down beside her. Soybel nuzzled his cheek. She brushed his lips with her nipples and Aleksandr took them in his mouth. Slowly, Soybel sat up, purposely tantalizing her husband by drawing away from him. Aleksandr reached up and firmly held his wife's breasts. Soybel leaned further backwards. Aleksandr tugged at his wife, trying to pull her back toward him. Soybel laughed softly, the sound low and alluring.

"Come closer," Aleksandr implored.

With a look of satisfaction on her face, Soybel bent nearer to her husband, letting him kiss her nipples. He took one of them between his teeth and gently bit it. Soybel rolled away from Aleksandr, lay on her back, and took hold of his hands, pressing them against the hair that became lost between her thighs. Aleksandr caressed the soft skin of his wife's legs until she parted them. He twirled the down into curls around his fingers until Soybel became wet. Firmly, Soybel guided her husband's hands the way she wanted.

"Touch me slower, Aleksandr."

Aleksandr lightened his touch and followed his wife's instructions.

"Even slower . . . yes . . . slower."

Soybel turned onto her side. Downward she raked Aleksandr's stomach with her fingernails. She reached lower. "You feel so strong," she murmured.

Aleksandr grunted, pushing his body against Soybel's hands. She grasped hold of him, drawing him toward her.

"So strong." Soybel breathed in and gasped.

Sitting up, she pressed Aleksandr onto his back and straddled him. With her own rhythm, and at her own speed, Soybel let her husband enter her. She raised her body so Aleksandr could penetrate her more easily. Aleksandr reached for his wife's shoulders and brought her forcefully against him. Soybel closed her eyes. Her mouth fell open. She writhed. She rotated her hips in slow sweeping circles. Suddenly, Soybel clenched her teeth and screamed. Aleksandr pushed up inside of her until he was unable to arch his back another inch. With a final violent thrust, he pierced his wife as deeply as he could. Then, Aleksandr sank back to the bed, covered his face with his hands, and tried to catch his breath. When his heartbeat had returned to normal, Aleksandr turned to kiss his wife, but she was already asleep. Exhausted, Aleksandr closed his eyes and tried to rest, but he was unable to. And for the first time since he could remember, an inexplicable feeling of uneasiness caused Aleksandr Moisei to spend an entire night in a state of restless sleeplessness.

CHAPTER 17

By Eastertime, 1904, the household of Aleksandr Moisei was a place of peace and calm. Whatever sadness and bitterness Aleksandr felt at the deaths of his parents, whatever personal dilemmas plagued him, had subsided; Aleksandr had come to the conclusion that his temporary thoughts of God and religion had been precisely what Soybel had said—folly. And everywhere Aleksandr looked he saw nothing but a life of continuing bliss.

The early spring sunshine promised a glorious summer and bountiful harvest. The Moisei house itself sparkled more brightly than ever. The spacious lawn surrounding it was thick, luxurious; rising from the very center of the lawn was a majestic elm tree, its sturdy limbs emblazoned with tiny buds of green. Beyond the house, to the east and south, saddle steeds and carriage horses lazily grazed in acres of rolling meadows lush with grass. West of the house, the barn, tool shed, and coachhouse had been freshly painted a bright yellow. Just behind those buildings, running northwest for more than a mile, was the dense stretch of woods, alive with new vegetation and foliage; only the path that led from the house to the outside world broke the solid, lofty barrier. All around, the air smelled of flowers, and the odor of rich earth rose from the ground.

On Easter Sunday, Kodoma looked like a painting. Its surrounding hills were tufted green and the trees had uncurled new leaves. The peasants' cottages were still wet with whitewash, and the rows of village shops had been painted colors as gay as the kerchiefs worn by the country women. Dressed in clothes clean and sparkling like the air, peasants and townspeople, merchants, laborers, almost everyone in Kodoma, strolled toward the town square to attend the Resurrection Mass at the village church.

North of Kodoma, a lazy twenty-minute walk from the village, the estate of Aleksandr Moisei was tranquil, the tolling church bells faint. Sitting beneath the elm tree, quietly playing a game of war with toy soldiers, were the Moisei children: Grisha, a sturdy lad of eight with straight blond hair and eyes of piercing blue, whose face so resembled Aleksandr's that there was no mistaking them for anything but father and son, and seven-year-old Daniella with hair the color of midnight framing a face that while reminiscent of Soybel's was more angular, less pretty. As the children played it was obvious that Daniella was the aggressor, her large dark eyes never once leaving the lines of soldiers with which she was attacking her brother's miniature army, her determined expression showing how important it was for her to be the victor. In contrast, Grisha's attention strayed, his gaze wandering from the game before him to the budding leaves above him, to the blooming woods beyond. Only sharp reminders from Daniella that he was supposed to be playing with her kept Grisha from completely forgetting his sister's presence.

Inside the house it was dark, the odor of roasting duck and potato dumplings drifting everywhere, the cook's dinner preparations adding a mouthwatering perfume to the fragrant spring afternoon. The hallway that ran from the front door straight back to the rear of the house looked like a tunnel, the gilt-framed paintings which hung along its length difficult to see. The first room off to the right of the hallway, the parlor, was as hushed as an empty museum. A creamy-hued Persian rug covered the floor. Stretching along one wall and half as high as the room was a fireplace; a log, as large around as a wagon wheel and three yards long, rested on polished andirons. Facing the fireplace was a deep-cushioned sofa covered with pearl-gray velvet. Before it stood a low ebony table trimmed with gold leaf; set on top of it was a silver tea set. A grouping of fragile French chairs formed a circle next to one of the tall, curtain-draped windows. Nearby, separated by a marble table on which rested an expensive copy of a Greek vase, there were two leather wingchairs. Facing a long window which overlooked the front lawn was a writing desk, an escritoire, covered with papers and charts and dominated by a tooled leather-bound ledger. Several large landscapes graced the walls, while a smaller picture of the Odessa harbor, featuring a white sailboat heeling offshore, hung in a corner above a heavily built and well-used armchair.

To the right of the hallway, thirty feet beyond the parlor entrance, was the kitchen, a bright cheerful room, its walls deeper yellow than the outside of the house, with ample working space, a four-burner coal-fueled stove, an ice box, a silver samovar sitting at the end of the work counter, and a massive square table for eating. At the very end of the hall was a staircase which led to the rooms upstairs. Just before it was another door, a hand-carved piece of wood which led to the huge master bedroom where Aleksandr and Soybel slept. In the very center of the room was their bed, where Soybel now lay curled up, her mind far away from her surroundings, a story by Maupassant having transported her to France. A sharp noise in the distance made Soybel look up from her book. A second shot, like the crack of a whip, and far louder than the first, caused her to get up and go to a window to see if she could discern anything in the distance. She saw nothing. The sounds of Grisha and Daniella clamoring into the house made Soybel hurry from her room to the parlor.

"Momma, what was that noise?" asked Grisha as he saw his mother approaching him from down the hallway.

Not replying, Soybel swept into the parlor and hastened to the windows, her children trailing behind her. Shouts, and what sounded like sporadic gunshots, echoed through the hills.

"Is it a holiday, Momma?" Daniella asked, scampering to her mother's side.

Again, Soybel peered outside. And again there was nothing she could see. Another volley of small explosive sounds broke the stillness.

"Can we go and see what it is, Momma?" Daniella pleaded excitedly, remembering the tumultuous celebration that lasted for days after the harvest was over.

Before Soybel could answer, Aleksandr burst into the house, his face pale. "Soybel!"

"Aleksandr, what is wrong?"

"Get the children, Soybel!"

"Why?"

"Just get them!"

Shoving his wife aside, Aleksandr swept Grisha and Daniella into his arms. "Hurry, Soybel! Run to the woods!"

"But Alek—"

"Listen to me, damn it!"

Fleeing the house, Aleksandr charged into the woods, Soybel struggling to match his pace. The gunfire increased and smoke from the direction of the village streamed upwards, spreading across the sky in a thin black line. Frantically, the Moiseis scrambled to hide themselves in a small area of dense underbrush.

"I'm frightened, Poppa," cried Daniella.

"Shhh. Everyone be still!" Aleksandr warned as galloping horses approached.

"What is going on? Tell me!" insisted Soybel in a panting whisper as four men, waving pistols above their heads, raced along the road just twenty yards away.

"They have come to kill the Jews," Aleksandr finally answered after the men had ridden by.

"What?"

"Fifty, perhaps a hundred men with guns and torches. They've knocked in the windows of every store. As I left the village I could see them riding their horses into the *shul*."

Crazed yells and running hoofbeats shattered their words and the men who had passed by before came racing back; close behind a band of thirty peasants on horseback chased them, screaming curses as they fired their guns.

"What is happening now?" Soybel asked, burying her head against Aleksandr's chest.

"Poppa, are they going to hurt us?" Daniella clung to her father's neck.

"No. Not anymore," he said, recognizing his foreman from the granary, Pyotor, as one of the pursuers.

"I want to go home, Poppa."

"Soon, *lyubimitsa*, soon." Aleksandr stroked his daughter's head.

New columns of black smoke funneled skyward.

"What do you think they've done?" Soybel fearfully asked, mesmerized by the ashes swirling overhead. "Do you think they have burned our house?"

"No. The smoke is too far away."

For a while no one spoke, stupefied by the increasing density of the black cloud, repulsed by its odor, jumping every time they heard a gunshot. Half an hour later all was still.

"Do you think they have gone?" Soybel asked.

Setting his children on the ground, Aleksandr said: "I will go and look."

"Perhaps you should wait, Aleksandr. Just a few minutes more, to be sure it is safe."

Aleksandr peered through the bushes. "We won't be certain then either." He crawled out from the hiding place and stood up.

"Don't be long, Aleksandr, please."

"I am going all the way into the village—so it will be a while before I return."

"I want to go with you, Poppa," Grisha said, forcing his way through the tightly woven branches.

"I want you to remain here, because while I am gone it is your responsibility to protect your mother and sister."

"I can protect them, Poppa!"

"I know." Aleksandr tousled the boy's hair.

"Poppa, Poppa, what should *I* do?" Daniella asked, poking her head through the bushes.

"*Lyubimitsa,* stay close to your mother . . . for her protection."

"Momma needs me to take care of her, doesn't she, Poppa?"

"Yes, my little teddy bear, we all need each other."

Daniella's face disappeared and Soybel made her way out of the refuge. Her hair was pulled awry, her face was scratched, and her eyes looked terrified. She clutched at Aleksandr for support.

"Be careful," she pleaded.

"I will be."

With a final word, Soybel reluctantly let go of Aleksandr, watching him as he started off toward the village.

By the time he reached the center of Kodoma, Aleksandr could see no danger. Dozens of people wandered up and down Mirazdanskaya Street inspecting the damage caused by the attackers. Bolts of materials, axes, stove parts, harnesses, loaves of bread, cakes, freshly kneaded dough, all sorts of things were scattered about. Genya the blacksmith, his spindly legs madly churning, tried to corner a wily mare that had broken her tether during the raid. Two other men, Andrei and Isaac, struggled in vain to keep a band of excited children from snatching merchandise through the broken windowpanes of their mercantile store and running off. Braunstein, the baker, watched helplessly as a group of older boys played kickball with the fresh batch of rolls that had been strewn about the square. Seeing that everyone was safe, Aleksandr hurried past the end of the stone road and along a muddy one that wound its way to the tiny section of Kodoma where a small group of Jews had established their community. Rounding a bend, he saw the smoldering remains of huts and the small mud-walled building used as a house of worship that was broken apart like the cracked shell of a nut. A circle of people stood in the roadway, all staring helplessly. The sound of pitiful sobs wracked the air.

"What happened?" Aleksandr asked a hunched-over old man who was standing on the fringe of the crowd.

"They killed Rabinowitz."

Aleksandr pushed his way through the ring of Jews. When he reached the middle he saw a white-haired woman, her face wizened and flecked with liver spots, hugging the dead man's body.

"Sholem, Sholem, why did they kill my Sholem?"

Several women approached the grieving woman and tried gently to pull her away so the men could take her husband's body.

"Don't touch him. Don't!"

Ignoring her protests, the women pried Rabinowitz's widow away from her husband and firmly led her off. For the first time, Aleksandr could see the man clearly. Jagged gashes covered his arms, his chest and face were crushed where horses must have ground in their hooves, his silky white beard was filled with mud and speckled with red clots. There was blood everywhere. Seeing the kindly Sholem lying battered in the dirt, still hearing the wry stories of the simple, softspoken man who had spent his days mending clothes, a rush of tears came to Aleksandr's eyes. He knelt by Sholem's head and tried to brush the mud from the dead man's face. But the moment he felt the splintered bones beneath the skin, Aleksandr withdrew his hand and looked away.

"Death feels terrible, doesn't it?" said an elderly man as he studied Sholem.

"He was the most gentle man in the village. Why did they choose him?"

"God chose him."

"You can accept that?"

"I accept God."

One of the men in the small crowd coughed to get the attention of the man speaking to Aleksandr. "Rabbi, should we take him away now?"

"Yes."

Four men, decrepit with age, lifted the corpse from the ground and carried it toward the only hut that had not been completely razed. They cried as they walked. Aleksandr stood up and stared after them.

"All the money cannot buy his life back, Aleksandr. It will not even buy your own life," the rabbi said quietly.

The old men slowed their pace, their arms and legs growing weary from the weight they carried. They entered the hut, and except for the rabbi and Aleksandr, the road was empty. The rabbi looked down at the ground where Sholem had died; his blood had already turned brown, nearly invisible against the earth. Without raising his eyes the rabbi said: "If God decides a man is to die, Aleksandr, he will drown in a spoonful of water."

"And if God lived here on earth, Rabbi, people would break His windows."

CHAPTER 18

At the end of July, a day after a small but particularly violent disturbance in a village just outside of Odessa, Rabbi Joshua Eleazar was startled by the angry voices of several men entering his domain, the Brody Synagogue.

"You who call yourself a rabbi, turn around!"

Frightened, Eleazar obeyed. Before him, six men armed with rifles and pistols glared at him. Standing slightly ahead of them was a short muscular man who looked as if he were ready to explode with fury.

"Come here, man of God! Come see what we have brought you!"

The rabbi did not move.

"Do not be afraid, Rabbi. It is only a dead child. But that is all right. She was a Jew, so you should not be upset."

A tearful man stepped forward and showed the rabbi the youngster he held in his arms. "Please, Rabbi Eleazar, help us."

"Do you know how she died?" asked the first man. "From a peasant's bullet in the back of her head. And do you know why? Because she was a child. That is their way of telling us not to have children!"

Rabbi Eleazar staggered backwards.

"Can you help us, Rabbi?" the man who cradled the girl repeated desperately.

"He can help us . . . if he becomes a real Jew!"

Eleazar examined the men who confronted him. They were not the fat, jovial Jews of Odessa that he knew so well. These were not the men with whom he socialized; finely dressed men in custom-tailored suits, carrying gold-headed canes, and with wives whose skins were oiled by imported lotions, whose bodies were clothed in elegant fashions. These men were dirty, their clothing soiled and patched, their hands rough from hard labor, their faces lumpy and pockmarked. They lived not in elegant houses, surrounded by every creature comfort, catered to by servants—but in poverty. The man in whose arms lay the dead girl came from a squalid *shtetl* seven miles north of Odessa. The other men lived in Moldavanka, Odessa's slum, where for decades all of Odessa's poor, traditionally religious Jews, had been relegated. Nervously, Rabbi Eleazar shifted his weight from foot to foot. He rubbed his face and ran his fingers through his graying hair.

"This is a rich synagogue, Rabbi. The men who come here and pretend to pray have money. Lots of money. So make them give us some of it!" demanded the defiant-looking man who was the leader of the group.

It was this man, Aram Zubov, who most troubled Eleazar. He was an upstart, a firebrand, who at age thirty-three was already well-known in Moldavanka and at the Brody for his fearless determination to form a partisan corps to protect Odessa's Jews against pogroms. More than once, Zubov had appeared at the Brody, berating its members, attempting to intimidate them into joining him, or at least using their wealth to support his cause.

"What will you do with the money, Aram?" Eleazar asked weakly.

"Buy guns and bullets so we can defend ourselves against Russia!"

The rabbi tried to look at Aram boldly, but the man's

black eyes were testing him and Eleazar was forced to turn away.

"Take your worst sin, Rabbi, and multiply it ten thousand times, and it will be nothing in comparison to the sin you will commit if you deny us help," continued Aram Zubov, clipping his words.

"What do you know of my sins?"

Zubov crouched as if he were readying himself to leap at Eleazar. "We do not care about your sins. We care about our lives!"

"Do you really think you can fight off the Russians with a few guns and bullets? You are Jews. Not warriors."

"The Maccabees were Jews, too! And those who are really Jews have always been Maccabees! Not the frightened ones who think being a Jew means suffering in silence, waiting to be slaughtered like animals!" a tall, thin man snapped.

"Nor are we Jews like you! We have no desire to appear to be Christians so the Tsar will permit us to live," added another man.

"Why don't you join the Zionists and run to Palestine?" Eleazar asked sharply.

Shaking his fist in the air, Aram Zubov shouted, "Because we are Russians! Russian Jews like the Christians are Russian Christians! This is our country, too. Right here. Not a piece of sand somewhere at the end of the world!"

"Palestine is our homeland. The Bible says so," Eleazar countered.

"The Bible was written for scholars and rabbis. Not for the people!" Zubov retorted.

"God never worked in factories like we do! He never tried to live on the wages they give us!" the man who held the dead girl cried out.

"Nor is He beaten by the police or shot by soldiers!"

"And He never died in a pogrom!"

"No, I just let Him die in my synagogue," the rabbi said softly.

Unsettled by Eleazar's confession, the men shuffled embarrassedly, regretful that they had raised their voices in a house of God. Aram Zubov approached the rabbi and spoke in earnest tones.

"Rabbi, each time I have come here, you have always refused us help. Can't you help us now, before any more of our children die?"

"Before I can help anybody there is something I must do. I *must*." Eleazar's last words were nearly inaudible.

"Can we help you, Rabbi?"

Eleazar stared into Aram's eyes. He said nothing.

"Will you bury the girl for us, Rabbi?" Zubov whispered.

Eleazar shook his head. "A precious child should be buried by a good man. Go to Moldavanka, where Odessa's real Jews live. Take her to any synagogue or *shul* there, and then you will find the kind of rabbi you want."

Confused and disturbed by Eleazar's remarks, Aram Zubov mumbled a good-bye and hastily led the group of men from the building. Standing there alone in the echoing silence of the empty synagogue, Rabbi Joshua Eleazar knew he could no longer put off talking to Aleksandr Moisei.

The heat was fierce on the August day that Rabbi Eleazar took the train from Odessa to Kodoma to visit Aleksandr Moisei. Even after sunset, when Aleksandr and the rabbi took their brandies and went outside, the air remained stifling. But it was far more than the weather that made Rabbi Joshua Eleazar uncomfortable.

"Now tell me the truth, Rabbi, why did you come all the way to Kodoma to see me? It is a long trip just to say hello," Aleksandr said as he led Eleazar to the garden.

"As I told you, it has been quite a while since I have seen you and I was wondering how you were." The rabbi was thankful that the darkness hid his uneasy expression.

Aleksandr settled himself in a cushioned wrought-iron lawn chair. "Rabbi, I have known you since I was a child, and without meaning to be rude, I can never remember you doing anything without having a practical reason."

"Seeing the son of a man who was my friend is a practical enough reason."

Eleazar sat down in a chair across from Aleksandr, fussing with his suit as he made himself comfortable.

"My father was no one's friend except his own."

"You should be charitable toward the dead."

"Charitable?"

"Forgive him."

"Soybel said that to me once, too."

"He was not a bad man, Aleksandr."

"You were not there when he died, Rabbi. He argued with me until he closed his eyes for the very last time."

"He was always a stubborn man."

"He was a selfish man, who cared nothing for his wife."

"Your poppa loved your mother very much, Aleksandr. More than you know."

"It is so strange—"

"Far more than you know."

"I never loved my father as much as I did the day I saw him holding my mother in his arms and weeping. And when he was going to die, I was so certain he would join her in the Jewish cemetery. How could I have been so wrong?"

Rabbi Eleazar stared across the garden into the dark woods and inhaled the scent of lush lilacs. "Many years ago, when you stole into my synagogue and called out my name, I was stunned; Jacob Moisei's son coming to ask a rabbi for help? But what affected me most was not your appearing there, or your explanation of why you had come to see me. It was not your telling me that there was no one else who would understand what you were suffering. And it was not the story of your heart being broken by a girl, or the reason for it happening, that touched me. It was the anguish in your voice that tore at my heart. I am hearing that same anguish now."

Aleksandr leaned back in his chair and drummed his fingers on his knee. "Never again will I suffer as I did then."

Eleazar shivered from a chill he could not explain.

"You know, Rabbi, when the pogrom happened here this past Easter something remarkable occurred. I did not realize how astounding it was until well after the incident was over.

When the attack began the first thing I thought of was that I must get home as fast as possible to protect my family from the men who had come to kill the Jews. But at that same instant I also thought—no, it was not a thought, it was a feeling that shook me to the very foundation of my being—I felt that they had come to kill *me*, who was also a Jew! Rabbi, I have never in my life considered myself a Jew. I wasn't a Christian. But neither was I a Jew. And yet there I was, dragging my family into the woods to hide, not for the obvious reason, the logical one: that our lives were in jeopardy because a band of marauders had attacked Kodoma and, for no reason except their need for violence, might harm us, too. I was fleeing to safety with my family because deep within me I knew we were in danger because *we* were Jews! All during the attack I was afraid. But I enjoyed the fear, because for the first time in my life I understood what it felt like to be a Jew. I finally learned what it meant to have people want to kill you for no other reason than that you are different than they are. I lived for thirty-four years before I truly understood that. Before I truly knew who I was. Before I *admitted* who I was."

"I still do not know."

"That night, Grisha asked me if the reason we were not attacked and our house not burned was because we were Christians. I had no answer for him. And Soybel said to me that she had not been afraid during the attack, but humiliated. Ashamed to have to crawl like an animal into the bushes and hide from hunters who considered her more dangerous than a wolf. She said to me, 'At least they can use the fur from a wolf for a coat. But to them we are poisonous bugs to be squashed!' She cried all night long, asking me if there were anywhere we could ever be safe."

"Did you have an answer for Soybel?"

"Not then."

"And now?"

Aleksandr grabbed the arms of his chair, his head thrust forward. "Now, Soybel no longer needs an answer. She has forgotten the terror she felt that day. With a single trip to

Odessa, following the attack, Soybel wiped clean the memory of that incident with the soft fur of a new coat and the glint of gold and diamonds. Do you know what my life with Soybel is like? When I leave the house in the morning, she is asleep. And when I return home at night, she is also asleep. For all I know, she sleeps in between times, too."

"You are still happy with her, Aleksandr, are you not?" Eleazar asked warily.

"What is happiness, Rabbi? Working from dawn until midnight with peasants who stink so badly from sweat that I cannot breathe, only to return home and sleep next to a wife who stinks so badly from perfume that I still cannot breathe? To be honest, I prefer the smell of sweat."

The contempt in Aleksandr's voice made Eleazar uneasy and he attempted to return the conversation to its original subject. "You were telling me about an answer you had uncovered, some solution—"

"What I was telling you, Rabbi, is that *I* will never forget that day when Kodoma was attacked. The thought of it is constantly with me because *I* need the answer to Soybel's question. And I think I have discovered it."

"And what is this great truth you have uncovered, Aleksandr?"

"On the day following the attack on Kodoma, I returned to the *shul* and asked the rabbi to be my tutor. To teach me about my ancestry, to unveil the Talmud to me, to school me in the language of my people, in the history of my people. And every day since then I have studied with him."

"And what about God, Aleksandr, have you come to believe in Him, too?"

"Rabbi, I could never believe in God. How could anyone, when all around us the world is overflowing with hatred and violence? Is that what God has created?"

"Aleksandr, God only created man. It is man who has created everything else."

"God is a shackle on man's mind, Rabbi, leg irons on his freedom."

"You sound like the members of my congregation who are becoming Zionists."

"And you make that sound like an accusation, Rabbi."

Aleksandr's perceptiveness made Rabbi Eleazar squirm in discomfort. "What I meant, Aleksandr, was that Jews will not be saved from their enemies just by eliminating God from Judaism."

"And since when do you believe in God, Rabbi?" Aleksandr stared at Eleazar, his gaze unwavering.

The rabbi said nothing, averting his eyes to escape Aleksandr's withering look. "What distresses you so, Rabbi—that I might give credence to Zionism?"

"Do you?"

"Until I am certain that what I believe is right, until I have worked out every detail, refuted every foreseeable argument, until I can answer the questions that no one will even ask—I will not expose my position. Because once I am certain of what I think I see, I want no one to be prepared to stand in my way."

"You make it sound as if it would take someone very brave to accept your conclusion."

"Not brave, Rabbi—frightened."

"Then I know that I, for one, will easily accept it." The rabbi glanced at Aleksandr; their eyes met and locked in the darkness.

"What could you be afraid of, Rabbi?"

Eleazar stood up and moved a few steps further into the darkness. "When I was a boy I wanted to be rich more than anything else in the world. I would have given anything to be rich. But my family was so poor that I knew my dream was hopeless. Yet I refused to give up. I refused to accept having to live my life in a ghetto as did my father. One Sabbath, at services, the rabbi of our *shul* announced that there was a partial scholarship available at the Vilna *yeshiva* for someone who wanted to be a rabbi. And he hinted that our congregation might be willing to pay the rest of the tuition if a worthy candidate could be found. I decided right then to become a rabbi. If I could not be rich, then at least I could have some status and security. I was always an excellent student, and I was not surprised when they gave me the scholarship, and the extra money. From the very first day I entered the *yeshiva* I hated it. The old rebbes babbling in Yiddish. Wasting hours arguing about the Talmud while they pulled at their beards and sidecurls. I nearly abandoned my education. But I met a group of students who called themselves *maskilim.* They had decided to devote their lives to destroying the orthodoxy. They refused to accept anything not based on reason. They ridiculed everything that had come from the past. 'No more Yiddish!' they proclaimed. 'We want everything in Russian! Even the Bible! Because Russian is the language of our country!' They demanded to be taught in Russian and would not respond to anything unless it was said in Russian. They shaved off their beards and sidecurls. The Yeshiva rebbes were horrified, and they ignored everything the *maskilim* wanted. I joined them. I became their leader. Before I left the *yeshiva,* every class was taught in Russian. Even the Bible was taught in Russian. And when I graduated from there, I was no longer a displaced Jew in a hostile land, but a Russian whose religion happened to be Judaism."

The rabbi paused to look at Aleksandr. Seeing that he was listening, Eleazar continued. "I knew that I could never be a rabbi in a *shtetl* or a ghetto. I despised everything about orthodox Judaism. Even the people who believe in it. So I decided to leave Vilna and go to the only place where I knew I would be content. I traveled five hundred miles by foot. Some days I did not eat. And I was afraid every step of the way. But I would rather have died during that journey than spend my life anywhere else except in Odessa. Even then Odessa was infamous. It was the place every good Jew loathed. And that is where *I* wanted to live."

The rabbi's body trembled with excitement. He rubbed his hands against his sides, then squeezed them together.

"The day I became the rabbi of the Brody Synagogue was

the happiest day of my life. Me! Joshua Eleazar, the son of the poorest man in Vilna, a rabbi in the richest synagogue in Odessa. For days my heart danced, and until my name was painted on the door of my new office I did not believe it. I was like a child whose father had given him a ruble to buy all the sweetcakes he wanted. And I must admit, I was very impressed with myself. How many men were rabbis in synagogues as great as the Brody? And I had such plans! Choirs. Musicians to accompany the cantor. A thousand ideas, one more splendid than the other, and whatever I wanted came to be. Everything! And do you know why? Because a man named Jacob Moisei befriended me. I was grateful to him, more than grateful. I believed I owed him my life. To tell you the things he did for me, made possible for me, would take a week. But you must know, Aleksandr, that no man could have done more for me. And no man did."

Rabbi Eleazar took a deep breath. His face became agitated.

"Then came 1881 and the assassination of Alexander II. And on Easter Sunday of that year the world collapsed once again for the Jews of Russia. Pogroms, everywhere. In Kirovo. Kiev. In more than a hundred Jewish localities. The atrocities spread to Warsaw and Podolia, and finally to Odessa. A week later your poppa became a Christian. We had an argument. I was a rabbi. Admittedly, a russified, assimilated, watered-down version of a rabbi, but nevertheless a rabbi! I could not understand why your father was running to become a Christian. The kind of Jews we were made us almost Christians anyway. He became furious when I refused to accept his reasoning, and for the next twenty-one years we did not speak. Then, two years ago, when your momma died, he came to me and asked me to bury her. Like you, I thought he had returned to being a Jew. But after the funeral he ran from the cemetery. I went to see him at his house, but he would not open the door. So, I gave up.

"Then last summer there was the pogrom in Odessa. It

was like a nightmare returning after more than twenty years. Everything looked the same again. The peasants, their clothing, the horses, the screams and curses, and the Jews begging for their lives. I did not feel humiliated like your wife. Or afraid. I was angry, Aleksandr! Furious that those men should interrupt the routine of my life. Afterwards, when those murderers had spent their hatred, when Odessa was quiet again, your poppa came to see me. He looked haggard, grim. He took me to the cemetery and showed me your momma's grave. The headstone was crushed to rubble. Half of the earth was scooped out of her resting place, the ditch that was left was filled with droppings from the horses and their riders, and the earth reeked of urine. The pogromists had been there, too. Everywhere in the cemetery there were signs of their desecration. Your father cried as he talked about your momma lying beneath all that vileness, and as he cried I thought he would want me to have her grave repaired, or to arrange for a stone building to protect her, or an iron building, anything but what he asked. When I refused to do what he wanted he became enraged. I never hated anyone until then."

The rabbi paused again, this time looking at Aleksandr. Instead of finding the man's eyes watching him he saw Aleksandr sitting with his head bowed and his hands folded in his lap. Eleazar continued, trying to be more gentle in his tone.

"All through the years, after your father and I stopped talking, I received a fair-sized sum of money every six months. It always arrived in cash and never with any explanation. I attempted to find out who was responsible for it, but no one knew anything about it. So I put it in the bank for myself. After twenty years it came to a tidy sum. The day your father took me to the cemetery, he admitted that it was he who had been responsible for it. He had his coachman—Ivashko was his name if I remember correctly—he had Ivashko leave it for me. I asked Jacob why. He looked at me in that way of his. You know that look, Aleksandr. His eyes could make you feel as if some calamity was about to befall you. He said to me: 'Eleazar, that money was to protect myself in case I ever needed you again. It was insurance for the future.' He reminded me to the ruble how much his gifts had amounted to. And he knew me well enough to know I had kept it all for myself. When I still refused to do what he asked, he laughed at me and called me a hypocrite. Then he told me that if I did what he asked he would provide for me in his will. I was dumbfounded by the sum. It was more money than I had seen in my entire life, so I agreed to do his bidding. I agreed because I saw myself getting older. Because I saw more pogroms coming and, if it were possible, I wanted to be able to buy my life. I agreed because what I always wanted most was to be like your father. Rich and free. So, I arranged for some men to dig up your poor momma's coffin and repair her grave so you would never know she was not there. I arranged to have the broken headstone replaced with one exactly like it. And I sent her body to the Christian cemetery where she was reburied by a priest. She then rested where Jacob wanted her to: next to the place he had reserved for himself. Ever since then, the grave in the Jewish cemetery has been filled with nothing but dirt. Every time you went there since then, it was like that. You talked to nothing but dirt. You cried to nothing but dirt. And I knew it. And I said nothing."

After a long moment Rabbi Eleazar gathered the courage to face the son of Jacob Moisei. Aleksandr grasped the sides of his chair and inhaled as if he were going to suck in the world. The rabbi shuddered.

"I am sorry, Aleksandr. You cannot imagine how sorry I am."

Eleazar waited for Aleksandr's huge arms to crush the wrought-iron seat.

"God, dear God, I am sorry!" Eleazar held his breath, waiting for something to happen. But nothing did. No shattering of the chair. No anguished screams. Not even a whimper. And that terrified Eleazar even more. The veins in Aleksandr's neck were distended; his mouth was a thin slash. His eyes remained unblinking. Expecting Aleksandr to explode with rage, Eleazar stood rigid, but Aleksandr remained absolutely still, not even breathing. Eleazar backed cautiously away, ready at each step to be overwhelmed by Aleksandr's wrath. But nothing happened, and the rabbi trembled, terrified by what he was unable to imagine: the monstrous violence that would be unleashed when Aleksandr Moisei finally decided to breathe.

CHAPTER 19

A man of medium height but quite broad through the shoulders hastened his steps as he walked along the dirt road that led north out of Kodoma. His black hair was cropped short making his heavy eyebrows appear as an ominous line. He moved with his head jutting forward, his stride long for someone his size. A canvas knapsack was strapped to his back, and crooked in his arm like a shotgun was a hefty walking stick. He wore a thin shirt, dark trousers, and boots. Tucked into his waistband and hidden by a woolen jacket was a revolver. Spying a break in the trees that lined the right side of the road, the stranger slowed his pace. He strained to see if there was an opening in the woods further ahead: there was nothing but a wall of timber laced together by vines and brambles. Uncertain if he had correctly remembered the directions given to him at the granary, the man paused for a moment. Then, assuring himself that this was the lane that had been described to him, he left the main road and strode briskly along the path that would lead him to the house of Aleksandr Moisei.

Spurred on by his excitement, the man took no notice of his surroundings. He locked his eyes on the path before him, anxious to catch sight of the merest speck of the man he had traveled so far to surprise. He walked faster still, and was about to break into a run when he rounded the last bend in the lane and was confronted by the estate of Aleksandr Moisei one hundred yards ahead. The man stopped short. "My God," he gasped. Against the unbroken green of the vast manicured lawn, the yellow house glowed more brilliantly than the sun. The leaves of the stately elm tree were shades of autumn gold. The meadows were amber, the hills colored straw. And the woods blazed with hues so varied that it took a moment to realize that everything was real and not a lifesize canvas painted to surpass nature.

So this is God's punishment for baptism. Now I understand everything, Aleksandr. Seeing a woman peering at him from the porch, the man forced himself to stop gaping at the house and head toward her.

"May I help you?" the woman asked when he neared the steps.

"Is this the home of Aleksandr Moisei?"

"Who is inquiring?"

"I am an old friend, and I have come a long way to see him."

"And your name?"

"I am Solomon Levin. *Doctor* Solomon Levin."

"Solomon Levin? From the university?"

"Aleksandr mentioned me?" Solomon leaned back his head and an explosion of delight erupted from his body.

"Lately he has mentioned you often."

"And who are you?"

"His wife!"

Solomon stared at Soybel. He seemed confused. Carefully he inspected her, approving of what he saw. "You are Aleksandr's wife?"

"Yes."

"You look nothing like what he described to me."

"And what did he tell you to expect?"

"You are Andreana?"

"Who?"

"Andreana Vizhni."

"My name is Soybel Dubrovsky Moisei."

Solomon laughed. "So!"

"Soybel, who is there?" Aleksandr's voice boomed, followed by his footsteps.

Both Soybel and Solomon squarely faced the door. Soybel's face was keen with anticipation, while Solomon was already relishing how astonished Aleksandr would be when he recognized him.

"Soybel?" The door swung open. "Soy . . . Solomon? I do not believe it. It's Solomon!"

In one bound Aleksandr Moisei leaped from the porch to the ground. With arms outstretched, the men greeted each other. They hugged and shouted, and pounded one another on the back.

"Aleksandr, Aleksandr, it is so good to see you!"

"Solomon, I have thought of you every day!"

"You are a liar, Aleksandr, but I do not care."

"How have you been? Where have you been, Solomon?"

"Your wife is beautiful, Aleksandr, but I am not surprised."

"I have missed you, Solomon."

The two men bear-hugged one another.

"Remember how drunk we got on New Year's in St. Petersburg?"

"You got drunk, Aleksandr. I only pretended."

"Are you married, Solomon?"

"Yes."

"Then where is your wife?"

"I am on my way to meet her for the first time."

"You are still crazy, Solomon."

Aleksandr and Solomon danced in small circles. They kissed.

"How did you find me, Solomon?"

"It was simple. There was only one place I had to go to locate a family as wealthy as the Moiseis."

"Oh?"

"To your infamous Brody. Even if you had become a pagan, Aleksandr, the Brody would always know where money tainted by Judaism resided."

"Ah, thank goodness there is still anger left in you. It makes me feel comfortable."

"But I am not angry, Aleksandr, I am grateful. A *Jewish* synagogue would have erased every trace of you, and then I would have never found you."

Ignoring Soybel, Aleksandr pulled Solomon into the house and led him into the parlor.

"Vodka?" inquired Aleksandr.

"Did you ever know me to drink anything else?"

Quickly, Aleksandr removed a bottle of vodka from a cabinet, yanked out the cork, took a hearty swig, and then passed the vodka to his friend. Solomon swilled a mouthful and gave Aleksandr another turn. Like two schoolboys suddenly free of their parents' watchful eyes, the two men guzzled the entire bottle of liquor, toasting everything they could think of. For the remainder of the afternoon, through sunset and dinner, they continued to drink. And they barely ate, the recounting of each second they had spent together in St. Petersburg far more important. Their voices grew loud, their gestures boisterous as they raced one another to repeat a story first. Rollicking laughter boomed through the house. They tippled brandy and sherry, stumbling outside, guffawing, slapping each other on the back. And if Soybel had not chased them and forcibly dragged them back to the house, Aleksandr and Solomon might very well have wobbled all the way to Odessa.

Taking charge of the situation, Soybel led Solomon to the guest room, waiting only until he had collapsed face down on the bed, then towed her husband off to their room. The moment the men lay down in their beds, they both passed out.

Late the next morning they awoke with headaches and parched throats. Solomon spent the day reclining under the elm tree, recuperating, entertaining Grisha and Daniella with tales of his adventures. Aleksandr worked at the granary from noon until nine at night. When he returned home, he hurried through dinner so that he and Solomon could have sufficient time to sit quietly on the porch and talk soberly.

"Are you glad you became a doctor, Solomon?"

"Yes."

"Good!"

"And you, Aleksandr, do you ever wish you had been able to become a lawyer?"

"Not anymore."

"Why?"

"Because most probably I would have married Andreana and I would not have Grisha for a son."

"He is a good child."

"He is a special child."

"Why?"

"Because he is my child."

"I can tell that he is going to grow up and be exactly like you."

"I am going to make him better than me."

"How?"

"I am teaching him who he is, Solomon. I am teaching my son that he is a Jew."

"And are you a Jew, too, these days, Aleksandr?"

"I have always been a Jew, Solomon. The problem was I never knew that."

"Ah, Aleksandr, if years ago you had told me that, I would have jumped up and applauded you. But today, after all the places I have been to, I am no longer so sure that it is praise your discovery deserves."

"We had a pogrom here this spring, at Easter."

"In the last year there have been pogroms in Dusiata, Sedlitz, Lodz, Konotop—"

"I know, Solomon. And at Simferopol, Murom, Vologda, and—"

"But I was there! To be accurate, I came after the pogroms were over. It was then that they needed either me or an undertaker. That is how I have spent my life. Going from *shtetl* to *shtetl,* ghetto to ghetto, sewing people's bodies back together after someone else has ripped them apart. I never did become a rich doctor."

"And the Tsar never requested your services? He never lay dying and commanded his servants to bring Doctor Solomon Levin to his bedside?"

"Even if he had called, I would not have gone. I did not have the time."

"You always said you would not attend the Tsar."

"Or any other Russian."

"You have not changed, Solomon."

"I have changed, Aleksandr. The world has changed."

"I know."

"And you?"

Aleksandr looked intently at his friend and said softly, "I am changing, too."

"It is about time."

"I was in Kishnev last year, on business. I saw Theodore Herzl walking in the streets at the head of a parade of Jews. Everyone was screaming: 'Herzl, *melech Yisrael,* Herzl, king of the Jews!' It gave me chills, Solomon, and it gave me pause."

"Aleksandr, the ideas of Herzl have given many men pause."

"Solomon, do you think the Jews will follow Herzl to Palestine?"

"*I* am."

Aleksandr gaped at his friend. "*You* are a follower of Herzl? You are a Zionist?"

"There is no other choice. The old ways do not work. They never did. Until you have seen children mutilated by the peasants, girls as precious-looking as Daniella, boys like Grisha, until you have seen the work of mobs, you have no idea how totally disastrous Russia is for Jews. I would have been a far better doctor to have let those children die, rather than keep them alive as pathetic cripples. When you see *those* things, when, with your hands, you actually touch the atrocities committed by one people against another, then you know there has to be an alternative."

"Maybe the Bolsheviks are right. Maybe it *is* time to overthrow this government and start anew."

"No! The Bolsheviks are wrong. They want us to admit not only that their way is right, but also that it was God who made all the errors."

"Do you still believe in God, Solomon?"

"I do not know." Solomon placed his hand on top of Aleksandr's. "But I am going to find out. In a week and three days I am leaving for Palestine."

Aleksandr stared wide-eyed at his friend, his jaw slack.

"I have my boat ticket. Everything I own is with me. And no matter what, I am never coming back to Russia."

"What if it is not as you imagine?"

"I imagine sand. Nothing but miles of sand, and a few places of green where others are already trying to grow fruit in barren soil."

"I have heard that the Turks do not like the Jews."

"They like the money they receive for selling us their land!"

"It is difficult to believe that there have been settlements there since 1882. How ironic that in 1881, when I was baptized, other Jews were planning to leave Russia for Palestine. While I was gaily dancing at balls, other people were struggling to survive in a desert. And now, while I am surrounded by luxury, while my wife is content to idle away her life in opulence, to do nothing more than indulge in all the pleasures money can buy—you carry all your worldly possessions on your back and are setting off on an adventure that might result in disaster."

"Or paradise."

A strange smile touched Aleksandr's lips. "How ironic life is. At the moment that my mind is in flux, my thoughts battling with themselves, Rabbi Eleazar comes to my door after more than a year with no word from him. And now, after fifteen years, you appear. It's all too convenient, too coincidental."

"It is not coincidental at all, Aleksandr. We are Jews, all of us. And, like rats on a sinking ship, we are all in different states of panic. There are men like you who are just becoming aware that the water is rising. And there are men like me who were right there when the planks gave way. But you, too, will soon realize that not to flee from Russia is to perish in Russia."

Anxiously, Aleksandr folded and unfolded his hands. "How I envy you, Solomon. How much I envy you."

"I think you always did."

"But Solomon, I am not as unaware as you might think. Yet how can I explain to you, to anyone, what is happening within me? How my mind constantly churns. How finally I have admitted to myself that I know very little of anything worthwhile. I have lived my life the same way I attended the university—on the surface, just skimming along. But now, Solomon, I want to know everything. I *must* know everything. But more important, I must put everything I learn to use." Aleksandr's words were like quiet thunder. He bound his eyes to Solomon's. "When you leave for Odessa to go to your boat, I am going with you. Because I want to take you someplace and show you what I am learning. I want you to see what Aleksandr Moisei is becoming."

"Let me warn you, Aleksandr, the more you learn the more you are going to realize that you have wasted your life."

"I am not afraid of that anymore."

Solomon smiled knowingly. "Aleksandr, the only romantic thing about fighting evil is when you dream and see yourself as the conquering hero."

Aleksandr looked away, the night hiding the flush that crept up his neck to his face. "I am not dreaming of anything."

"Aleksandr, you still do not lie very well."

There was a long pause. Aleksandr stared out into the darkness, his eyes focused somewhere far away. Solomon studied his friend's face by the flickering candlelight which trickled onto the porch from inside the house. There was a tightness to the way Aleksandr looked, a hardness, as if his flesh were made of stone and would feel cold to the touch.

Repeatedly, Aleksandr bit his lower lip, his teeth digging deeper into the flesh with each bite. Several times, clenching and unclenching his fists, he shook his head no, obviously finding it difficult to reject some secret cherished thought. Twice Solomon tried to continue their talk. But the only response he received from Aleksandr was an absentminded nod. A quarter of an hour later Solomon excused himself and retired for the night, leaving Aleksandr Moisei lost in the privacy of his mind, weighing and reweighing the worth of his existence and the consequences of a new one.

CHAPTER 20

Solomon Levin sat at the rear of the Brody Synagogue, intrigued by what was happening around him. The richly appointed hall was crowded with people whose dress and manner were incongruous with the surroundings. On one side of the room, beneath stained-glass windows, a group of indignant cleanshaven men dressed in threadbare clothing defiantly surrounded Rabbi Eleazar. Nearby, a gathering of older men, bearded and with covered heads, shouted decisively at a slender young man who stood at the pulpit, pounding his fist against the lectern. On the other side of the synagogue, beneath a mural of Moses descending from the Mount, sat dozens of women, sputtering with anger, fuming at the speaker on the platform.

"I am beginning to enjoy this," Solomon said to Aleksandr.

"You see that man there sitting on the aisle, looking as if he is ready to jump out of his skin? That is Aram Zubov, and when he gets started you will really enjoy yourself."

"Do you know what else Lenin said?" the man at the lectern yelled out, the ends of his long mustache flapping like pennants. "Lenin said that the idea of a separate Jewish people is reactionary! The proof is furnished by well-known facts of history. Everywhere in Europe the downfall of medievalism and the development of political freedom went hand in hand with the assimilation of the Jews. So it follows that the concept of a Jew is in direct conflict with the rights and equalities of the proletariat. And the proletariat must conquer!"

"Praklinat Lenin!" someone cursed, the epithet resounding through the synagogue.

"This is some education Grisha is getting," Solomon said, glimpsing at the spellbound youth sitting beside Aleksandr.

Aleksandr looked at his son, gratified by how much the boy already understood about the events unfurling about him. Aleksandr put an arm around Grisha, pleased by the sturdiness he felt in his son's shoulder. Often Aleksandr took measure of Grisha, noting that even at the age of eight his child's young body showed unmistakable signs of becoming broad-shouldered and muscular. And always he was taken by Grisha's handsomeness, ecstatic that his son had inherited his features, his blue eyes and blond hair; somehow Aleksandr knew that if Grisha had resembled Soybel, he and his son would not have been as close.

"Thank goodness his mother has no idea why he and I so often visit the Brody," Aleksandr said to Solomon, his words really meant more for himself than for his friend.

"I used to be a Jew, too!" the man standing on the platform screamed. "But I realized my mistake. That is why I agree with Trotsky's declaration that if crushing the *shtetl,* if destroying the Jews—even if it means killing them to rid Russia of their lifesucking business dealings—would accomplish our ends then it should be done. Unfortunately nobody has ever had enough courage to significantly repress the Jews."

The crowd was stupefied; never before had they heard such talk.

"You Jews live as foreigners among foreigners. With a superstitious allegiance to a Biblical idiocy called Palestine. But you have no country anymore. Nor will you ever. Nor *should* you ever! Because Judaism should perish, and with it all its symbols. It is you who insist on remaining Jews who are the cause of anti-Semitism. And it is men like me who help destroy anti-Semitism. Because it is men like me who will destroy the curse of Judaism!" The Bolshevik looked around to see if anyone would challenge his words. All were speechless. "The worst of you are the Zionists! You who dream of tilling land in Palestine. You can have a Palestine here in Russia! By being Russians! To us, the followers of Lenin, the *true* Russians—you are traitors! Worse than your brothers who are so simple as to believe that they can be Russians *and* Jews simultaneously. That is no more possible than being Russian and Christian simultaneously. Or Russian and anything else! Because there is no way that religion can be reconciled with Bolshevism. Karl Marx said that religion is the opium of the people. And I say that Jews are the root of the plant!"

Aram Zubov jumped to his feet. "Perhaps we are the root of the plant, but whether you like it or not, we will continue to flourish in this country!"

"It is men like you who ensure the continuation of anti-Semitism!"

"And it is Jews like you who would do worse things to us than the others, because you are ashamed of your heritage!"

Balling his fists, Aram Zubov marched down the center aisle toward the pulpit. The Bolshevik hurried to the end of the platform, leaped down to the floor, and hastened up the far aisle.

"Why do you move away, Bolshevik? Are you afraid of a lowly Jew?" Zubov strode back up the center aisle.

"What do you intend to do to me?" the man whined, seeing the doorway blocked by a line of stocky embittered men.

Zubov sneered. "The same thing you do to us." He continued up the aisle, stopping when he stood almost nose to nose with the trapped Bolshevik.

The slightly built Leninist prepared himself for the fist that would smash into his face. He set his mouth into an expression of contempt and waited for the blow to come. Instead of feeling a sudden, excruciating pain, he was overwhelmed by something worse as Aram Zubov spat in his face and watched his venom slide down the Bolshevik's cheek.

"I will never forget that," the man softly threatened.

"I hope not."

Enraged and humiliated, the Bolshevik shoved his way through the wall of men who barred the door and ran from the synagogue. Hoots and taunts followed him. People stood on their seats, shaking their fists and cursing.

"Do you see why we must arm ourselves and fight those kind?" Zubov bellowed. His eyes searched the room, their fierceness commanding silence. "*Now* do you understand?"

"The most stupid thing we could do is to stay in Russia," a quiet but firm voice said. "No matter what we do, we will never be allowed to be part of this country."

Zubov turned to the man who had spoken and disdainfully eyed him. Seeing who sat next to him, he snorted. "Now I understand why you talk like that. You must be a Zionist like your friend, the country gentleman." Zubov glared at Aleksandr. "So, Moisei, this time you appear with an ally. I did not think that a man like you would need help in defending his childish ideas. Is he dreaming about going to Palestine, too?" The assembly laughed.

"There is no other place where we will ever belong," Aleksandr said.

"For two months you have been coming here, and for two months that is all you have said. Don't you—"

"What more need be said?"

"Moisei, you are no different from that Bolshevik. He wants us to live in Russia with barren souls, and you want us to live in Palestine with barren land. Don't you realize that we want neither of those things?"

"For a man with your intelligence, Zubov—one would think that of all the people in Odessa *you* would understand why we must quit Russia and return to Palestine."

"And for a man with all your money, Moisei—what *I* cannot understand is why you would want to leave Russia."

"What good is my money when my existence is threatened?"

"*Your* existence is threatened? A man who is as wealthy as you is never threatened."

"Now you sound like a Bolshevik!" shouted Aleksandr.

"That is because he is a Bundist!" Solomon snarled, getting to his feet.

Zubov took a step toward Solomon. He halted when he saw that his adversary was not cowed. "And what is wrong with being a Bundist? What is wrong in believing that we, too, should be part of the mainstream of Russian life? What is so dreadful about holding to the ideal that the common Jew also deserves to live with dignity and with a sense of his own worth?"

"What is wrong with Bundists is that they are so busy being Russians first and Jews second that they do not see what lies ahead."

"Hey, Zionist, do you believe in God?" someone shouted.

"Zionists do not believe in God, they *are* God!" another voice answered derisively.

"Zionist, your mind must be dull, because any man who thinks he can do God's work is an ignoramus. And leading us to Palestine is God's work. Not that of an impostor like you," an old man cried out.

"You make me sick! All of you!" Solomon exploded. "Praying to God! Crying to Him! Begging Him to lead you back to Jerusalem. Well, you just might wait forever until God is ready to help you."

"Then we will have done something to deserve that," a calm voice responded.

Aram Zubov fumed. He stamped down the aisle, glowering at the men who had been arguing with Solomon. "I do not know who to despise more, the Zionists or you. At least they are willing to fight for their lives in Palestine. But you, you are like a bunch of women! Instead of being willing to defend yourselves, you cry out in fear and piss in your pants. You would rather curse me for the way I speak in a synagogue than do one thing to save yourselves. You cheer when I insult a Bolshevik because you know I will protect you. But when you are alone, what do you do? Hide behind your wives?"

"What would you have them do—fight all of Russia?" Solomon asked abrasively. He started down the aisle toward Aram.

"I would have them fight the world if necessary!"

"Do you really think that they, or you, stand a chance against the army, or the peasants?"

"I am not frightened. Russia is my country, too. I have a right to live here in peace and safety like every Russian does!" Zubov stood his ground, not yielding an inch to Solomon's advance.

"Then you are the only one who knows about your rights. Because the Tsar never heard of them. The peasants and the priests never heard of them. So tell me, who gave you these rights?" Solomon's eyes smoldered.

"Go ahead, run to Palestine, Zionist. Run away and make us who stay here weaker. If all of you Zionists remained in Russia, we could build an army so no one would attack us again!"

"You are a fool, Zubov! And worse, you are dangerous. Because you are going to lead everyone who believes you to their deaths!"

"That is better than leading them to a false dream!"

"Palestine is not a false dream!"

"Palestine is as useless as a piece of shit!"

With one lunge Solomon struck Aram Zubov and grabbed him around the neck. Zubov clamped one of his hands around Solomon's throat while he shoved the other one into his face. A fist, slammed into Aram's belly, was returned with a crushing blow to the side of Solomon's head. The two men wrestled to the floor. They rolled against the pews, their legs thrashing in the air. Several of Zubov's followers moved to help him; they halted when they saw Aleksandr Moisei charge down the aisle.

"Stop it!" Aleksandr roared, grabbing hold of each man by the hair and yanking their heads back. "Stop it or I will crush your skulls together!"

The pressure exerted by Aleksandr forced the combatants apart. They looked at each other with loathing. Slowly, they got to their feet. Solomon searched for something at his waist, then glanced at the floor. Seeing what he was looking for, he stooped down, and reached out his hand.

"He has a gun!" a woman screamed.

Hastily, Solomon stuck the weapon into his waistband and stood up. Aram stared at him, dumbfounded.

"Why didn't you shoot me?" he finally asked.

Solomon started up the aisle.

"Why?"

He looked at Grisha as he passed by him; the boy looked at Solomon in awe.

"Tell me!" Zubov insisted.

He opened the synagogue door.

"Why didn't you shoot me?"

Solomon paused and turned around, his eyes no longer filled with fury. He studied Aram for a moment, then in a low voice he said: "If I shot you, who else would there be to protect the lives of these fools?" Without waiting for a reply, Solomon Levin stepped outside and softly closed the synagogue door behind him.

CHAPTER 21

Following Solomon's departure for Palestine, there was a profound change in Aleksandr. Though he continued to perform his tasks and fulfill his responsibilities to Vassili Viska, Aleksandr's entire handling of the Kodoma complex was mechanical. When an unusually intricate situation arose, he had great difficulty in dealing with it, his mind no longer interested in providing solutions for the problems of grain and sugar. With the conclusion of the harvest, Aleksandr's concern with the granary ceased completely, a growing disinterest in all of Kodoma's affairs following closely behind. But of greatest import was that Aleksandr Moisei was also receding from any involvement with his family.

In November, along with the arrival of the first snowfall, Aleksandr spent a week converting one of the upstairs bedrooms into a study, building a large wooden desk and bookcases. He went to the village *shul* and borrowed dozens of books, returning home and secluding himself with them for hours at a time. When he finished the first batch he borrowed others. He traveled to Odessa, where for days on end he browsed through bookshops, haunted the municipal library, eventually reappearing at home, staggering under the weight of more books. Once back in his study Aleksandr arranged the volumes in alphabetical order and began to read. The more he read the more exasperated with his ignorance he became, and with a text in one hand and a dictionary in the other he struggled to understand the concepts of philosophy, history, religion, and politics that both Solomon Levin and Vassili Viska were able so easily to discuss. As his naturally logical mind began to move from the root idea to others' interpretations of that idea, Aleksandr resented how much his own arguments had relied on little more than emotion. He was annoyed by the way in which he had disputed the beliefs of Aram Zubov, fighting that man's passion with his own, stimulated by being thrust into a maelstrom of history by the shock of what his father had done and underscored by the men who had ravaged Kodoma. At first Aleksandr was overwhelmed, afraid that it was too late for him to learn what others had known for years. He scolded himself for not continuing his education after withdrawing from St. Petersburg University, and doubly so for his not having taken his studies seriously when he was in school. He became irritable as he immersed himself in one subject, only to be quickly distracted by another. In a single day he opened and closed Plato's *Republic,* Lermontov's *Hero of Our Times,* two novels by Dostoevsky, Herzl's *Der Judenstaat,* Gogol's *Dead Souls,* the poetry of Heine. Aleksandr's mind reeled, his thoughts racing as fast as his heart; he stomped through the house irate, frustrated by his inability to learn everything at once. Constantly he thought about the history of the Jews, dismayed by the knowledge that, since Genesis, God's pervasion of every aspect of Judaism had prevented the Jews from seeing their true destiny, had kept them from discarding their blind faith and deciding their future based on reality. Finally Aleksandr understood why Zionism, a Jewish philosophy without the domination of God, was meeting so much resistance among Russia's mass of Orthodox Jews. *They have no choice but to oppose Zionism,* Aleksandr mused. *Yet how futile their opposition is. For history is inevitable—its course, neat. It is only when one is living in history that it appears chaotic. And that is why determining what the future will be and what actions it necessitates requires nothing more than the application of logic.*

For hours at a time alone in his study Aleksandr pondered the path of man that led from the dimness of antiquity to the present. *Judeo-Christian history is like two Romes,* he concluded. *There are two centers of history from which Western man has emanated. In one center stood God, and from Him man was created. In the other stood man, and from him God was created. That the two would clash was predictable, for there can be no reconciliation between men who justify their deeds in the name of God and men who create God to justify their deeds. And therein lies the dilemma of the Western world—that deadly quarrel between God's Chosen People and the people who chose a new God.*

The theological antagonism between Jehovah and Christ greatly intrigued Aleksandr, for he knew that that ancient dispute was the root of Western man's deepest hatred. *If that were not so, then why is the world nothing more than an extension of that primal battleground—Palestine? Where the Maker of man dueled the maker of God? Where immortality warred with mortality. Can that historical jealousy ever be quelled? Must every Jew be slain before Christians can forget Christ's temporal mortality—can forgive him that mortality? And forgive him his Jewishness? Is the true curse of the Jews that they are not Christians? Or is the burden they bear that their continuing existence is a reminder to the Christians that they, too, are Jews?*

The myriad of thoughts that blossomed from Aleksandr's theories were constantly alive in his mind, each passing moment convincing him more firmly that only logic could save Russia's Jews from a grave fate. And as his studies merged one historical era into the next, past melding into present, halting at the threshold of the future—Aleksandr Moisei saw precisely what must be done. He wrote out a list. First there was God, then biblical Judaism, the Diaspora, the Orthodoxy of the dispersed, Cabalism, Hasidism, baptism, anarchism, socialism, Marxism, Bolshevism, Bundism, and—with sweet inevitability—Zionism. On one sheet of paper Aleksandr Moisei outlined the sweep of history from God to Herzl. Before him lay the chain of events which bound a five-thousand-year-old God to a godless messiah. His messiah. A flush of exhilaration took hold of Aleksandr, and all at once before him in perfect clarity was the picture of his destiny: Palestine!

And what had only been a dream, and, as Solomon had said, fancying himself as the conqueror of injustice, Aleksandr Moisei started toward that single goal. He immersed himself in the study of surveying, irrigation, the designing of buildings and roads, gaining a smattering of knowledge about things that he thought would be useful in a land where there was nothing but sand, where everything had to be built from the beginning. Aleksandr was thankful for his ability to work with tools and for his physical strength, and he displayed that thankfulness by exhausting himself in study, but even more so by inviting the most precious being he knew to learn with him, to share his passion. And while he let his dream become an obsession, Aleksandr Moisei taught his son first to have the dream.

CHAPTER 22

At first Soybel Moisei had been amused by her husband's sudden interest in Palestine. But when he absorbed Grisha into his private world, excluding Daniella and herself, Soybel became worried and then maddened. Slowly, along with the deepening winter, an ever-widening distance grew between Soybel and her husband. He living in isolation by choice, while she had no say in the matter of her solitude. But what most provoked Soybel was not her husband's absence from her, but for the first time since the inception of their marriage her inability to predict Aleksandr's behavior, to manipulate him to do her bidding.

Seeing herself caged in Kodoma by the cold snows of winter and an even colder husband, Soybel longed for the days when Jacob and Naomi were still alive and she had a place to seek refuge. Even after Aleksandr's parents had died, life for Soybel had not been too unbearable. The entire family still made excursions to Odessa, renting two suites in the Hotel London, one for herself and Aleksandr, the other for the children and their governess.

Now, Soybel was stranded, isolated, in a place void of all the indulgences she so dearly loved. By day Soybel seethed inwardly, while at night she was disturbed by nightmares, sometimes imagining herself back in Kiev, living in the ghetto, her father having returned from the dead. Soybel saw herself devoured by books snapping shut around her body, swallowed forever in musty pages whose odor made her want to retch. Other nights Soybel was pursued by devils, beings with demon bodies and the head of her husband, all of them tearing away her possessions, her clothes, bits of herself, picking at her, pinching out pieces of her flesh until nothing remained of her but a skeleton with a skull that smiled and smiled. When she awoke from those dreams, Soybel would be trembling, swearing to herself that she would force Aleksandr to change his ways. But as the weeks dragged by and Aleksandr became more remote than ever, Soybel was at a loss as to what to do. And what had started as amusement at her husband's behavior, and then became anger, evolved into the beginnings of hatred.

Other rifts, too, were coming to pass. Instead of Soybel and her daughter being drawn closer together, they drifted apart, Soybel preferring to wallow in her own misery rather than give her eight-year-old daughter the attention she desperately needed. For Daniella was becoming separated from her family, feeling like an outcast, harboring a growing jealousy of Grisha for having captured Aleksandr's attention. Often now Daniella and her nine-year-old brother argued without provocation, on two occasions coming to blows so severe that Aleksandr had to separate them. But most days, alone with nothing to do and no one to talk to, Daniella would remain in her room, staring out of the window. On rare occasions she would sit outside the closed door of her father's study, listening for any sound he might make from within. If she heard his footsteps approaching the door, she would scamper away to her room and hide. Then, she would imagine her father and brother conspiring to run off, deserting her. Tormented by that loss, Daniella would throw a silent tantrum, screaming without sound, pounding her fists against her pillow, convulsed by an unbearable agony. As for Grisha, the love he had for Aleksandr swelled into adoration, while whatever feelings he had for his mother quickly paled in comparison; for Daniella, Grisha had no thoughts at all.

As snowstorm after snowstorm isolated Kodoma from the rest of Russia, Aleksandr Moisei remained in his study for days at a time, even taking his meals there, and more often than not sleeping there, too. For Soybel, the winter dragged on, and with it her dreary life. She became sharp-tongued, lashing out at anyone who crossed her even for the slightest reason. To escape the house she now considered a prison, Soybel would trudge through the snow to the village, enjoying the stinging chill of winter. Without knowing why, she found herself drawn to the empty granary, finding solace in its solitude. With nothing else to do there but think, Soybel daydreamed, picturing herself as the manager of the granary, enjoying the feeling of power induced by her imaginings. Other times, when just the thought of the walk to the granary tired her, Soybel relieved her boredom by reading and rereading the Odessa newspapers, memorizing every display of the latest Paris fashions, devouring every article about the glittering performances at the Opera House and the spectacular productions of the ballet. She ached to walk on Deribasovskaya Street and wander in and out of the fashionable shops that lined its sidewalks. She missed staring up at the villas on the terraces, desperately wishing to be the mistress of any one of them. She spent hours arranging her jewelry, making sure each gem, each necklace, was carefully protected in a separate velvet-lined box, and when she had put them away, Soybel thought of the day when she would have twice as many jewels. She filled sheets of paper with descriptions of new furniture she wanted to buy, deftly sketching how she wanted each room of the house redecorated. But nothing soothed her loneliness, her longing for the ardor she had felt the very first time she had seen Aleksandr years before. Nothing eased her foreboding that, like her mother, she would live out her life in a cage. And it gave Soybel no comfort that the cage was gilded.

In March of that year only once did Soybel and Aleksandr

speak at length, and that time Soybel's words were spurred by desperation.

"I cannot go on living like this, Aleksandr! Can't you understand that? Do you have no feelings for me? Are you so far removed from me that you have no idea how you are tormenting me?"

"There are things tormenting me, too, Soybel," Aleksandr retorted, without looking up from the book he was reading.

"Aleksandr, I do not understand what is happening to you."

"I understand, Soybel, and that is all that matters."

"Why are you doing this to me?"

" 'In the middle of the journey of my life I came to my senses in a dark forest, for I had lost the straight path.' Dante wrote that, Soybel, and it touches me as deeply as anything I have read."

"And will Dante plant the grain and harvest the fields?"

"Is that all you care about?"

"Someone has to."

Aleksandr began flipping through the pages of his book. "I want to read you something. Then perhaps you will understand what—"

"I do not want to hear what you want to read. I am sick of your reading. We are all sick of it!"

"Grisha is—"

"You have another child besides Grisha."

"And Daniella has another parent beside me." Aleksandr looked directly at his wife. "And just as it is a mother's responsibility to teach her daughter, so it is a father's to raise his son. That is why I give all my time to Grisha. Because now is the age when he must learn the things I am just discovering. Do you have any idea, Soybel, what I might have been if I had been taught the same things when I was Grisha's age?"

"What good will his knowing Hebrew do for him? Will it get him into the university? And what is he learning at those meetings in Odessa you take him to? What are *you* learning there?"

"Why some men are less afraid to die here in Russia than to live in Palestine."

"Oh, Aleksandr, stop. The subject has become tiresome."

"No, Soybel, it is just beginning to become interesting."

"To you, perhaps. But you have no idea how bored I am with it."

"Let me read you something Cicero wrote; it is right here in this book. And I am quoting. 'Not to know what has been transacted in former times is to continue always as a child.' Do you understand that, Soybel—that if we do not know our past, we remain children?"

Soybel got to her feet; her eyes were livid and her voice strained. "Aleksandr, I know my past. And the very last thing I ever want to be again is a child."

Seeing the anguish in Soybel's face, Aleksandr changed his tone. "Maybe it is because I do not have your past, or anything like it, that I need to know so much about it."

Soybel approached her husband. "I can tell you everything about the past you need to know. It was ugly, Aleksandr—vile and ugly. And I do not wish to hear about it or know it anymore." Without warning, Soybel snatched Aleksandr's book from his hands and shook it in the air. "Just like my childhood, this book is ugly, too. All your books are ugly. And if you are not careful, Aleksandr, you will become ugly just like them!" With fury, Soybel whirled around and flung the book into the fireplace and then, as its pages charred and smoldered to ashes, a look of satisfaction covered her face.

"Soybel, Soybel, listen to me, *please*. To remain in Russia would be foolhardy. There will most certainly be more pogroms. And the possibility of a revolution is not far-fetched—the signs are everywhere. And I fear that our lives will be in jeopardy."

"If you are so worried about our lives, why don't you talk about taking us to England? Or America? Why is it always Palestine?"

"Because—"

"To me Palestine means nothing, Aleksandr. My mother did not struggle so I could go to Palestine!"

"Doesn't being a Jew mean anything to you?"

"It means as little to me as it did to your father. I would sooner become a Christian than return to being a Jew. Because being a Jew has nothing but bad memories for me. It was due to my father that I have those memories. And I will not permit my husband to give me more of them!"

Soybel began to cry, and Aleksandr went to comfort her. She pushed him away. "I do not want you to hold me, Aleksandr."

"What *do* you want me to do?" asked Aleksandr in a hoarse whisper.

With her face contorted in anguish and her cheeks wet with tears, Soybel pleaded: "Be who you once were."

"And if that is not possible?"

Your love is turning stale to me, Aleko. I am growing bored with you. Oh, how my heart begs for freedom. How I long to have the courage of Zemfira and—

"If I cannot fulfill your wish, Soybel, then what?"

"Then release me from this dismal existence."

Soybel's words stung Aleksandr, and everything he had hoped for, had so carefully planned for, tumbled down around him. He wondered if perhaps he were being unfair. It was so easy for Solomon to leave Russia; he had no wife, no children. There was nothing in his way. Aleksandr went to his study and sifted through his books, trying to find even a paragraph written by someone else who had been faced with the same quandary—he found nothing. Left to seek his own conclusions, Aleksandr was faced with questions he could not bring himself to answer. His thoughts tormented him. *If Palestine becomes my first love, as it is Solomon's, what will become of Soybel? Will she be nothing more than my mistress? Or will Palestine remain my secret beloved while Soybel continues to burden me as my wife?*

Like most people caught between a spouse and a lover, Aleksandr felt a growing resentment toward Soybel—not because she was preventing him from giving all his time to his passion, but because of the guilt she made him feel, that enraging and inexplicable feeling of sinfulness that becomes one's companion at the very instant of unfaithfulness—that momentous occasion of unannounced abandonment. And because of his indiscretion Aleksandr was unknowingly compelled to prove his allegiance to Soybel while still punishing her for the hold she had over him. So it was that Aleksandr Moisei was bound even closer to his wife.

Agonized by his dilemma, confused more than ever, torn between his feelings for his wife and a need for his dream, Aleksandr Moisei was drawn to the person whose intellect he admired most, the person he trusted most. And in a rush of desperation, he fled to Odessa to seek the advice of the only person in Russia he truly considered a friend.

CHAPTER 23

When Vassili Viska, the only child of Nikolai Viska, returned to Odessa from Paris in the summer of 1901 to attend his father's funeral, he was already a respected economist and influential advisor highly regarded both in France and Russia. Since his graduation from the Sorbonne nearly fifteen years before, Vassili had remained in France, becoming involved in the encouragement of that country's growing interest in Russia. With the passing of years, and as his prominence increased, Vassili found himself more frequently summoned to St. Petersburg, where the ministers of Tsar Nicholas II sought his analysis and counsel not only in matters involving Russia and the French government but the rest of Europe, too. This exposure to the mechanics of government, differences in economic sophistication and scientific advancement, seeing the intrigues used to acquire favorable trade agreements, technical assistance, and foreign loans, sparked in Vassili not only an interest in politics, but also an awareness of just how backward and repressive the government of his country really was.

Despite having spent his formative years surrounded by wealth and power, studying and living in Paris exposed Vassili to ideas that profoundly affected him. He fell in love with the people and atmosphere of the Moulin Rouge, the Folies Bergères, and all the bistros on the Rue Pigalle. Emile Zola's *J'Accuse* had inspired him to follow closely the Dreyfus affair, whetting his interest in the writings of men like Proudhon, Marx, the Fabians, all of whom were seeking to establish a new social order. Though his professional life involved him with the most important members of the French and Russian governments, Vassili much preferred to roam the Left Bank, especially enjoying the hours he passed in sidewalk cafés, sipping inexpensive wine, listening to passionate speeches and arguments about freedom and justice. Because of the affinity he felt for the liberal ideas of the citizens of Paris, Vassili grew tired of the men with whom he worked; he disliked their constant talk of industry, colonization, investments, and it irritated him when his attempts to discuss ideas about human dignity were dismissed as the unimportant catchphrases of the rabble—those frustrated people whose lack of success made them want to steal everything away from everybody else. But Vassili was not discouraged by the reactionary attitudes of his peers. For by the time he departed Paris and returned to Odessa, he had arrived at two significant conclusions. First, if Russia intended to be successful in international affairs, vast reforms would be needed. But more important, even though he felt uncomfortable with the philosophy of Karl Marx, Vassili Viska was determined to use his enormous resources and prominence to break the autocratic stranglehold in which Russia had been gripped for five hundred years.

Soon after his arrival in Odessa Vassili spent his energies on learning everything about the business he had inherited. In the past he had paid but scant attention to its workings, not needing to have more than a surface knowledge of what his father was doing. Now things were quite different, and Vassili was determined to involve himself in every facet of the structure of the business and reconstruct anything he thought unsuitable. He spent weeks with Jacob Moisei, meticulously checking ledgers and documents, sometimes asking to see figures and contracts dating back more than thirty years. He visited the port warehouses and cargo ships, studied inventory lists, talked to the workers, grain brokers, captains, making detailed notes about what should be added, deleted, or changed. He traveled to Kodoma several times to become better acquainted with Aleksandr Moisei, examining his employee as closely as he did his property. Vassili was impressed with the evolution from the original blueprints of the granary to what he found. He devoted hours to talking with Aleksandr, trying to discern what kind of man he was. And as the months turned into a year, then two, and three, Vassili Viska discovered that he and his employee had developed far more than a business relationship, and that his visits to Kodoma, or Aleksandr's to Odessa, meant a great deal more than just discussing the yearly harvest and profits.

"Aleksandr, you look so distressed," exclaimed Vassili as he rose from behind his desk to greet his friend.

"I am." The familiar surroundings of Vassili's office made Aleksandr uneasy, the solid beauty of Odessa's Exchange reminding Aleksandr of Russia's deep-rooted parochialism. He looked at Vassili, the Russian's broad, lazy smile and kindly gray eyes erasing some of Aleksandr's discomfort.

"What you need is a change from your routine, Aleksandr. Why don't you spend a few days in Odessa? I am certain I could find some distractions to cheer you."

"If I really thought that would help, I would accept your offer without—"

"Don't you trust my judgment? Or are you afraid the women will not be discreet?"

"It is not—"

"What every man needs is a friend who is a bachelor."

"Thank you, Vassili, but I am afraid I would not be much fun."

"The cafés by the wharf are filled with willing women. For a price they will do anything."

"Vassili, what—"

"They are Greek. Not as clever as the French, but more

passionate." Vassili laughed. "You look as if I have shocked you. Has marriage made you so straitlaced?"

"Vassili, what do you think of Zionism?"

"Is that what you want? A Jewish whore? I can arrange that, too!"

"Vassili, I am being serious."

Indicating where Aleksandr should sit, Vassili seated himself in a chair facing his guest. It took Vassili a moment to find a comfortable position for his long legs.

"Well now, Aleksandr, what is this seriousness you wish to discuss?"

"I want to know what you think of Zionism, Vassili."

"Has the disease touched you, too?"

"Is that what you think—that it is a disease?"

"I did not mean it like that."

"Then what—"

"I truly believe that Zionism is the only way that millions of people will ever find any peace or security," Vassili answered.

"What would it do for a man such as me?"

Vassili took a long look at Aleksandr, recalling how, when he had first seen him, Aleksandr was standing on the roof of the granary stripped to the waist, and that when he announced who he was, Aleksandr had swung to the ground, his arms bulging as they easily supported his weight. For an instant Vassili had wished he were physically more like his friend. "Aleksandr, for the masses of Jews, who live in squalor, the concept is vital. But for a man like you, I cannot see that it would mean a thing."

"Why?"

Vassili drew his tall, lean frame deep into his clothes and replied thoughtfully. "First, unlike others, you have nothing to run away from. Do you live in a ghetto? Are your children and wife in fear of their lives? I know, I know—you are going to remind me about the attack on Kodoma. If you analyze it, incidents like that—no matter how horrid—are politically inspired."

"How can you—"

"Aleksandr, diverting animosity from the rulers of a country, by the rulers of a country, to protect the position of power of those rulers is a political act. And our government, our Nicholas, is a master at it."

"How grateful I am that *our* government, *our* Nicholas, is teetering on the edge of collapse."

"What you should really be thankful for, Aleksandr, is that there are men like us who can do something about it, so that incidents like the one in Kodoma need never happen again."

"What would you do, Vassili, resist history?"

Vassili leaned forward, his elongated face glowing with excitement. "Until now, Aleksandr, history has moved men. But now it is time for men to move history!"

"You are a dreamer, Vassili."

"This is a new century, Aleksandr. We cannot permit the nineteenth century to tarnish the twentieth."

"I am beginning to think that this new century is not worth a damn."

"Nonsense."

"Then have you forgotten this January, Vassili, and the fall of Port Arthur to Japan? And then, three weeks later, Father Gapon's disastrous march; his failure was the worst thing that could have happened to Russia."

A look of melancholy erased Vassili's exuberance. "I have forgotten nothing, Aleksandr."

"And now, look what is happening at Mukden—"

"The best the Russian army can do is lose seventy-eight thousand men, and then retreat. Ah, this March of 1905 is a very sad March for Russia."

"The war is despicable, Vassili. It has stirred up ugly passions that will never be quelled."

"Aleksandr, even without the war Father Gapon would have led his pitiful followers to the Winter Palace." For a moment Vassili was silent, the memory of Father Gapon's peaceful march on the Winter Palace clear in every detail. He even remembered, verbatim, the petition the priest held in his hand to present to Tsar Nicholas.

> We, the wretched and abused slaves crushed by the weight of the autocracy, of despotism, of arbitrary power—we, who are deprived of all human rights, as are the rest of the Russian people, beg that your Majesty not deny us the help that the Russian people ask of you. Demolish the wall which you have erected between you and your people. Hear our pleas, heed our pleas, and you will bring happiness to Russia. If you do not, we are prepared to die right here. There are only two ways left to us: freedom, or the grave.

"It was the way of the grave that Nicholas gave them," Vassili said, more to himself than to Aleksandr. "More than a thousand marchers, men, women, and children, were killed by the Cossacks and regular troops. Innocent people, starving people begging for freedom—shot, bayoneted, beaten to death. Five thousand were wounded." Vassili looked at Aleksandr, his eyes troubled. "Do you know what the workers sing in the streets now? Do you know what has become their anthem? 'A storm, soon a storm will come crashing with the power of thunder.' "

"Vassili, *parturiunt montes, nascetur ridiculus mus.*"

"Yes, the mountains are in labor, and a ridiculous mouse will be born." A sad smile gave Vassili a dispirited appearance.

"In the face of it all, Vassili, how can you believe that things can be changed?"

"Because things have to be changed, Aleksandr! Whether we like it or not, whether the Tsar likes it or not, Russia must find a new direction. And if someone does not do something it will be Lenin who chooses the way. We cannot let that happen to our country."

"You forget, Vassili, I told you once that I am not like you. I have no concern for Russia."

"And I love this country, Aleksandr, and I fear for its survival." Vassili stood up and began to pace back and forth, his words tumbling rapidly from his mouth. "I fear that St. Petersburg will perish in a bloody inundation. And what they bury on its site will be liberty. When I am in the capital the words of Pushkin ring in my ears, words that thrill me to the center of my being. 'I love you, Peter's creation. I love your austere beauty, Neva's majestic flow, her granite banks . . . so stand, Peter's city, unshakable, like Russia.' But even more, Aleksandr, I love the earth of this country of ours. When I smell the soil of the steppes, I want to cry and shout at once. The sound of our music makes my heart soar. When I was a child and my mother was still alive, I spent all my summers at Dalyoki. You know how beautiful it is there. The rolling hillsides, the birch groves. The memories of those days are the most pleasant ones I have. When I go there now, it brings them all back. I love that place. Perhaps that is why I so desperately want to save Russia from calamity—so Dalyoki will be saved, too!" Perspiration ran down Vassili's face, and his coarse blond hair was disheveled; he collapsed into his chair.

"And for me, Vassili, there is nothing in Russia I want to save. Because I believe that for men like me this land is precisely the same as it is for every other Jew. The reason it looks different to me is because my father got on his knees and buried his dignity in the dirt. He was a coward, Vassili. Maybe to survive here it is necessary to be a coward. But that is not my way. Not anymore. If Soybel would agree, I would leave for Palestine on the very next boat. No matter how much you tried, I do not think you could ever understand what I feel inside. Things I never knew. Ideas of which I was ignorant. A million voices are telling me: 'Russia is not your home.' I want a home. And now I know where it is! And that is where I am going!"

"I did not know you had that much passion in you, Aleksandr."

"Until recently I did not know it myself."

Vassili smiled ruefully. "I did not know that either one of us had so much passion." Again Vassili stood up; he walked to the windows overlooking the square that spread before the Exchange. Even from this lofty vantage point Vassili could sense the seething of the people below, feel the foundations of Russia cracking more and more. Vassili's face became drawn, his brow wrinkled. "Aleksandr, whether you like it or not, you are a Russian. And wherever you go, you will still be a Russian."

"And wherever I go, I will also be a Jew."

"Yes. What a peculiar situation—in Russia the Jews create an imaginary Palestine. And if they should go to Palestine, they would most likely create a little Russia."

"You must believe, Vassili, that I would never want to harm your business in any way. But at the first opportunity I will leave for Palestine."

"And if Soybel still disagrees with you? Will you go without her?" Vassili turned around and looked directly at Aleksandr. The despair he saw on his friend's face saddened him. "Aleksandr, I am not trying to tell you that you are wrong. My background is not yours. Your history is not in my blood, so I cannot know if what you feel is right."

"*I* know it is right."

"Then it should not matter what anyone else thinks."

"What Soybel thinks matters very much."

"I take it that what you are saying is Soybel has decided not to go."

Aleksandr took a deep breath and nodded his head.

"Why?"

"Because we cannot take everything we have with us. Because she is afraid to lose the security we have here. You see, Vassili, I do not have *her* history running through *my* blood. So I am not afraid of being poor."

"What—"

"Even before I mentioned Palestine to Soybel, I knew she would refuse to go." A grim expression crossed Aleksandr's face, and he dejectedly shook his head from side to side. "There are many things I know about Soybel, things I have known for a long time but could not admit to myself. I love her so dearly, Vassili, and at the same time I have contempt for her. How can a man feel so opposite simultaneously—what does a man do when he has changed so drastically and his wife is no different from when she was sixteen years old?

When I look at Soybel, my heart races as madly as it did the first time I saw her. But now when we talk, her words repel me. Did I make her what she is by indulging her every desire? Was it I who transformed a naïve, awestruck child of sixteen into a woman whose need for possessions is boundless? If, when we were first married, I had been what I am today, everything would be so different now. Why are we always two steps behind our own lives? Why, Vassili?"

Aleksandr's torment clutched at Vassili's heart and he wanted to reach out and embrace him.

"What should I do, Vassili?"

"What do you want to do?"

"I must go, I have to. But . . ."

A look of foreboding covered Vassili's face. "The time has come for both of us, Aleksandr. An avalanche is roaring down on us. A storm is brewing."

"Our storms are different, Vassili."

"If only they were. But they are not, and that terrifies me. The Russian government is a divine autocracy tempered by assassination. The Russian people are a religious mass of subjugated beings tempered by the arrogant might of the Tsar. And the Jews suffer at the hands of both. There is no case in history that I know of in which a country has done violence to the Jews without also doing violence to itself. And you, my dear Aleksandr, are both a Russian and a Jew. *Wir sind alle Toten auf Urlaub.* We are all doomed men on furlough."

"You feel that way, Vassili, and you still believe that there is hope?"

"Yes."

"Then one of us is mad, Vassili. Is it you or I?"

CHAPTER 24

Following his visit with Vassili Viska, Aleksandr Moisei forced himself out of hibernation and tried to take an interest not only in his son, but in his wife and daughter and the granary. Each day he spent time with Daniella, struggling not to show how much be begrudged her the hour or so he gave to her. But Daniella was sensitive to her father's real feelings, telling Aleksandr that she knew he would like her better if she were a boy; it was Daniella's face that showed how much she was truly suffering: her dark eyes, when not viewing everything with suspicion, seemed to be on the verge of tears. She almost never smiled, and when she did there was a hesitancy to her smile, a self-protectiveness that said *I will not let myself enjoy anything fully, because if I do I know someone will immediately snatch away my happiness.* Even the way she walked showed how mistrustful Daniella was. Rather than moving with the gait of a youngster, the loping stride born of a carefree childhood, every step Daniella took was cautious, as if she were ready to flee at the slightest provocation. In response to his daughter's obvious misgivings Aleksandr made even greater attempts to be a father to Daniella, chastising himself for acting so selfishly. But Aleksandr knew that he had no real desire to alter his ways.

Attempting to fulfill the promise he had made to himself, Aleksandr tried to reestablish his relationship with his wife; more than once he asked Soybel to stroll with him in the woods or to the hills beyond, intending to seduce her the way he had years before, hoping they could be as they once were in all things. But there was far too much hostility between them for Soybel to yield; her husband's sudden attentiveness succeeded only in making her more wary. And so the constant churning within Aleksandr increased in tempo, agitating him more, further splitting his heart and mind, his son the only person with whom he shared anything of consequence.

In June, Aleksandr suggested that the entire family go to Odessa for a week of pleasure. Only the children were delighted; Soybel was suspicious of her husband's motives. But three days later she was in the carriage as Stepan directed the horses to the city by the sea.

"What can we do in Odessa, Poppa?" Daniella asked, curled on her father's lap as the coach bumped along the dirt road which led south.

"What would you like to do?"

"Can we go to the sea and play?"

Aleksandr scratched Daniella's head. "In the midst of what might become a revolution, you want to play in the sea? Aren't you afraid of anything, teddy bear?"

"What is a revolution, Poppa?" asked Grisha.

"A revolution is when people with different ideas disagree, and instead of trying to find a point on which they can both agree, they shout and yell, and sometimes they fight, each hoping to get everything he wants."

"Sometimes there is no middle ground," Soybel added.

For several minutes Grisha stared out of the coach, then, with a glimmer of understanding on his face, turned to his father. "Are you and Momma having a revolution about Palestine?"

Dusk hung low in the sky when the carriage finally reached the heart of Odessa, and to the casual observer the city did not appear different than it had a month ago, or even a year ago. Although suppertime had passed, the streets were still crowded. Couples sauntered arm in arm, some stopping to listen to gypsy fiddlers. Husbands waited patiently as their wives shopped. Trams with bells clanging cut through the streets, pursued by would-be passengers and daredevil children. Brassy music from an outdoor concert in Alexandrovsky Park ricocheted off the buildings, a counterpoint to the steamship horns from the harbor.

"From all the activity one would never know that anything was wrong anywhere in the country," Soybel said.

"Haven't you noticed the number of soldiers?" Aleksandr asked. "Never have I seen patrols like this."

Soybel peered out of the carriage window. "The soldiers make me feel safe."

"Odessa used to be safe *without* soldiers," her husband countered.

A group of fierce-looking Cossacks galloped down Nicholas Boulevard, glaring into the coach as they passed.

"How nice it would be to live here. Look at the shops. And there is the theater, concerts—just the thought of it all excites me!" Soybel opened her purse and removed a small mirror. "Where could you find a better place for children? With good schools, parks as beautiful as the countryside, and the sea where their father has a sailboat." Soybel smiled, making certain her hair was in place.

"Poppa, can we go sailing?" asked Grisha.

Aleksandr looked at Soybel, in his eyes a mixture of anger and hurt.

"Can we? Can we?" echoed Daniella.

"Of course your poppa will take you sailing, sweetheart. He is going to give us all treats. That is why we came here," Soybel laughed as she applied a subtle hint of rouge to her cheeks.

Aleksandr observed his wife carefully.

"You know, Aleksandr, there is no reason not to renovate your father's house so we can have a place to stay when we come to Odessa. And with some new furniture and draperies, and repainting the inside, it would be hardly recognizable."

"I should—"

"How silly for us to stay in a hotel as expensive as the London when we already have a house here."

"Poppa?"

"What?"

"Can we go to the *Golub*, please?!"

"If we lived in Odessa, Grisha, your poppa could take you sailing every day," Soybel purred.

Grisha faced his father, his eyes bright with hope. "Could we?"

Aleksandr looked away, regretting having come to Odessa.

"Someday, could we sail to where Uncle Solomon went?" Grisha added.

"I do not know. It is very far away."

"Don't you want to go anymore, Poppa?"

Aleksandr glanced at his wife, then at his son, and instead of answering he bowed his head and prepared for another battle with himself.

As their days in Odessa passed there was a metamorphosis in Soybel that affected them all. It was as if the commotion of the city and the summer heat were stimulants that made her lighthearted and gay. Even Aleksandr was unable to resist the way his wife bubbled awake each morning. Refusing to allow him a moment of melancholy, Soybel charmed her husband into accompanying her while she shopped on Deribasovskaya Street, asking for his opinion of every hat with feathers and ribbons, of dresses with snug bodices and revealing necklines or high collars. There was hardly a moment when she was not prattling on about how happy she was that they had come to Odessa. Without stopping to breathe, they dashed from one place to the next, from the fashion shops to the Arkadia to the promenade overlooking the sea. At Theater Square, Soybel convinced Aleksandr to buy two tickets for any performance of anything—a play, a concert, an opera—joyfully kissing him when he returned from the Opera House with passes for *Swan Lake.* They were whisked off by coach to luncheon in the restaurant on the beach at Mali Fontan, and afterward strolled the two miles to the Bolshoi Fontan and climbed the steps to the top of Odessa's old lighthouse to watch the steamers and tugboats plying the harbor. Aleksandr and Soybel stood with their heads pressed together, arms entwined around one another.

They spent an entire afternoon with Vassili at the beachside German colony of Lutsdorf, the three of them sucking on cups of crushed ice sweetened with cherry syrup. Relaxing on the veranda of the rambling Olgino Hotel, with a string quartet playing Mozart and Haydn in the background, Soybel surprised and delighted Vassili with her knowledge of French; he spoke it slowly to give Soybel time to understand him while she trilled out *"enchantée," "mais oui,"* and begged to hear gossip about *"les gens du monde."* As the sun set they returned to Odessa, Soybel walking between her husband and Vassili, her arms resting in the crooks of theirs. Soybel pulled Vassili close to her, not minding that the side of her breast pressed firmly against his elbow. They said good night in front of the Hotel London, the spreading orange dusk bathing their faces. Vassili took hold of Soybel's fingers and pressed his lips to the back of her hand. Ever so slightly Soybel squeezed Vassili's fingertips, emphasizing the implied intimacy with a fleeting but penetrating look at Vassili.

Two days later, Vassili, Soybel, and Aleksandr savored a lunch of curried fondue at an outdoor café. Afterward they ambled along Deribasovskaya Street.

"At this very moment," Vassili said, his face animated, his slender fingers expressing his enthusiasm, "right now, there are men, important men, in Moscow, St. Petersburg, in every city and town, even here in Odessa, discussing the future of Russia. Deciding how to make it clear to the Tsar that this country can no longer be ruled by his handpicked ministers, just for his benefit—but must be led by men freely elected by all its citizens by secret ballot, with a constitution that guarantees every Russian dignity, the right to an education, decent wages, and the legal right that their religious beliefs, no matter what they are, will no longer be a source for persecution."

"Whoever these men are, Vassili, they are asking for a miracle."

"No, Aleksandr, we are just asking for Russia."

Soybel gaped at Vassili. "You are one of them?"

"Yes." Vassili's face broke into a wide grin. "And by summer's end I will be in St. Petersburg as a member of the Duma."

"A member of parliament—I have never heard of anything more exciting!"

"Building a new political party, one that has real power, is the most exciting thing imaginable. Because we will have the opportunity to lift our country out of the Dark Ages and bring it into the present."

"You are more of a dreamer than I am," said Aleksandr.

Vassili laughed. "Are you denying me the right to dream?"

"I am advising you not to waste your time trying to convince Nicholas to change his policies."

"He will have to."

"He will not even listen to you, Vassili."

"But he will, Aleksandr. Our party is comprised of lawyers, doctors, landowners, bankers, industrialists. He needs us, because without us there is no Russia. But with us, the possibilities for change in Russia are better now than ever before."

"For Russians, perhaps."

"We are all Russians, Aleksandr!"

"Tell me, can laws also change people's superstitions?"

"*Tempora mutantur, et nos matamur in illis*—the times are changing, and we are changing with them."

"I am impressed by your Latin, Vassili, but it is not an answer to my question. Can laws change people's morality? Can you legislate the eradication of hatred?"

"It is a shame that laws cannot change people's stubbornness, their blindness to reality."

"The only one who is not blind, Vassili, is me!"

Furious, Vassili stopped short and wheeled toward Aleksandr. "Damn you, I think you could drive a stone to madness!" Vassili's body quivered with rage, his face out of control.

"Vassili, I am not quarreling with you," Aleksandr said, avoiding Vassili's hard stare.

"It was beginning to sound like it."

"I was quarreling with my wife."

As their walk continued the atmosphere was strained, each of them at one point or another attempting to start an innocent conversation. But that only made the awkwardness more obvious and the three of them tacitly agreed to silence. At the corner of Deribasovskaya Street and Gavanndya, just before the Deribasov Gardens, Soybel stopped to look in the window of a store that sold antique jewelry. A cameo brooch caught her attention and she asked if it would be an inconvenience if she went inside to inspect it more closely. Without hesitation, Vassili said he would be delighted to wait. Aleksandr, feeling remorse for his outburst and anxious to ease the tension, also agreed.

"Aleksandr," Vassili said, watching Soybel through the window, "if what you want so much is to go to Palestine, demand that Soybel go with you. You are a man—are you not?"

"In Russia Soybel dislikes me. There she would despise me."

"Then leave her behind." Vassili turned toward him. "If your dream is that important, that is what you should do."

"Without Soybel I would have nothing but a country."

"And without Palestine?"

Aleksandr looked at Vassili, then for an instant at his wife inside the store, and finally at the ground.

"Is there no solution?" Vassili asked gently.

"No, none."

"What will you do?"

Aleksandr gazed through the window at Soybel; she was admiring herself in a hand mirror, studying the brooch that was clasped at her throat; she smiled. The saleswoman said something to her, and Soybel laughed. Aleksandr imagined the sound. He turned away.

"It is so strange, Aleksandr. I have what you want, and you have what I want."

Aleksandr regarded Vassili quizzically.

"You have no country, and I have no family," Vassili explained.

"It is much easier for you to get what you want than it is for me."

Soybel tapped on the window to get their attention. Vassili turned toward her; she held up the brooch, pointed to it, nodded her head yes, shook it no, shrugged her shoulders—requesting him to make a choice. With an upraised thumb and a smile Vassili indicated his approval. Aleksandr ignored his wife. Soybel mouthed a thank-you to Vassili, and returned to the counter, handing the pin to the clerk. Vassili watched Soybel's every move.

"Aleksandr, you have no idea how very difficult it would be for me to get what I want."

CHAPTER 25

That evening and the next day were difficult for Aleksandr. He was torn between self-pity and reluctance to make Soybel's last days in Odessa a trial. Though Soybel did not act as if she had been upset by the way he had behaved toward Vassili, Aleksandr was certain that his wife had not forgiven him. For hours he considered ways of mending the rift between them, rejecting one idea after another as either too elaborate or overly sentimental. Finally, Aleksandr decided to write Soybel a note, requesting that she dine with him wherever she preferred; with the note Aleksandr left a single carefully selected rose.

"This has always been my favorite restaurant!" Soybel exclaimed, as a dignified maître d'hôtel escorted her and her husband through the exclusive restaurant in the Hotel St. Petersburg to a secluded corner table.

Soybel looked ravishing in a low-cut gown of purple silk, her face framed by long diamond earrings and the arch of her neck and the rise of her breasts ornamented with a diamond necklace. Aleksandr, too, looked striking in a navy-blue suit that had been especially tailored to accommodate his wide shoulders and muscular arms; by contrast, his sun-bleached hair made his tanned face appear even darker. As they passed people turned to admire them.

"Do you remember how often we used to come here when we were first married?" Soybel asked, allowing the maître d'hôtel to help her with her chair.

"Then, you were afraid to eat too much. You could not understand how anyone could afford the prices they charged."

"And tonight I am so hungry I want everything on the menu!"

Soybel scanned the room, her eyes glossing over the other guests who had come to enjoy a dinner of exquisitely prepared food. The decor was exactly as she had remembered: the chairs upholstered in maroon velvet, the golden dinnerware just heavy enough to add to the opulence, the tablecloths still the same blue that had always reminded her of Aleksandr's eyes, the paintings on the walls the work of Russia's most renowned artists. In one corner three violinists dressed like peasants played lush melodies while uniformed waiters softly padded on the deep pile carpet, carrying platters of thick beef, steaming vegetables, and *kasha* garnished with mushrooms. Courteously, the sommelier requested that Aleksandr select a wine. Aleksandr deferred to the man's knowledge and asked that he make the selection. Flattered, the wine steward hurried to his cellar and returned with what he considered one of the finest French burgundies in all of Russia. He uncorked the bottle, handed the cork to Aleksandr to sniff, set the bottle in a silver bucket next to the table and, as he departed, suggested that before they drink the wine it be allowed to breathe.

"I wish we could dine here every night," Soybel said, toying with a gold bracelet she had purchased that afternoon. "If we lived in Odessa we could. And instead of finding a performance of *Swan Lake* by chance, we could plan to go to the ballet regularly."

"It might not seem so special then; you might become bored very quickly."

"I would be willing to risk that."

"Perhaps if we came to Odessa more often—" Aleksandr began.

"It would not be the same as living here. And at least during the winter there is no reason for us to be in Kodoma. There is nothing to do there then."

"There is much to do. You know how long it takes to finish the ledgers for the previous year and prepare everything for the next. It would be impossible for me to do that in Odessa. Everything I need is in Kodoma."

"But that is no reason why the children and I cannot live here. You could work two or three days a week in Kodoma, then spend the rest of the week with us. Grisha needs to start his education in a good school so that when the time comes he will qualify for the university in St. Petersburg."

"Grisha will have all the education he needs—without a Russian university."

"It is impossible for you to teach him everything. I would like him to be as well-educated as Vassili. The amount of knowledge that man possesses is overwhelming. French, German, Latin. He is familiar with music and art. Perhaps Grisha will attend the Sorbonne, too. Perhaps someday Grisha will form a political party!"

"There is no need to worry about that now." Aleksandr picked up the bottle of wine, read the label, and began to fill his glass.

"Why don't you wait for the sommelier. He will know when the wine is ready."

"I am not interested in the wine being ready."

"Sometimes you embarrass me, Aleksandr. You are insulting the man."

"To be honest, Soybel, I would have been just as happy with a bottle of Bessarabian wine."

"There are those, Aleksandr, who would not even consider a wine unless it was perfect."

Aleksandr took a long sip of his drink. "Is this dinner going to mark the end of the one good week we have had together in months? In years?"

"No. Tonight is a celebration."

"Of what?"

"Would you pour me some wine, please?"

"I will call the sommelier to—"

"Aleksandr . . ."

Restraining himself, Aleksandr filled his wife's glass, then refilled his own.

"Once upon a time we came to Odessa almost every month, do you remember?" Soybel asked. "And do you remember how you used to love to show me all the places you knew as a boy? We would walk along the sea and talk about our dreams. About traveling to Europe. To France. Perhaps spending a winter season in Nice or Biarritz. You promised to take me to St. Petersburg. I want to see the Winter Palace, Aleksandr. I want to see what it is like to be the Tsar. To live in a palace with ten thousand rooms and twice as many jewels. I would like to dance, just once, at the Emperor's Ball. I dream of that, Aleksandr. I dream just the way my mother once dreamed. Her vision was of me marrying someone who lived at the *foot* of the Lipki Heights. She was willing to give her life for that. My dreams, Aleksandr, take me to the top of the heights. And there is no reason why that must remain merely a fantasy—not with Vassili sitting in the Duma. Do you think for a moment that despite how much he wants to do for Russia, Vassili is unaware of how much he can do for himself? And whatever he gets, we get some, too. And we can get more. I have seen your ledgers. I know what vast sums of money we earn for him. I know how vital we are to his continuing to reap such great profits. I—"

"Is that what we are celebrating—your ability to dream of a king's ransom because you have read some figures in a ledger?"

"No, Aleksandr. We are not celebrating a dream, but the fact that now Vassili Viska will make it possible for us to live as he does. It was Moisei toil that made the Viskas so wealthy. And now Viska's position will make us as wealthy.

Because Vassili will provide us with the one thing we need to achieve what we want—Russian blood!"

"And what makes you think Vassili will oblige this fantasy of yours?"

"There are many ways to induce others to do what you wish." A look of deadly earnestness came over Soybel's face. "And if necessary, we can always oblige ourselves. It would be a simple matter for us to omit ten percent, or even more, from the ledgers without it being noticed, and . . ." Soybel's expression hardened into a mask of unswervable determination.

With one swift swallow Aleksandr finished his drink and poured himself another one. "Are you listening to yourself talk, Soybel? Do you hear what you are saying?"

Soybel picked up her glass of wine, holding it without drinking. "Aleksandr, do you still love me?"

For a moment Aleksandr did not breathe, his eyes did not blink. "Do you?"

He slowly exhaled, and his shoulders sagged. "Yes, I love you."

"Then act as if you did!" Soybel said sharply. And then her voice became cooing. "Stop being so serious, Aleksandr. You never smile anymore. Did you know that the first thing I loved about you was your smile? That day in the synagogue in Kiev I wanted to touch your mouth more than anything else in the world. I thought that if I could touch it just once, I would be happy for the rest of my life. Where has that smile gone, Aleksandr? Where has my Aleko gone?"

"How can I smile when I hear the way you talk? When I hear you say all the things that I have always feared you were keeping within you. When we were first married, I never thought twice about giving you everything you asked for. No matter how expensive, how wasteful I thought it was. And through the years, after you had far more than any one person could use in a dozen lifetimes, I still permitted you to buy whatever you wanted. But now, with all of Russia's misery around you, with people barely able to feed themselves, with men and women living on the edge of death and violence, how can you think of nothing but wallowing in more money, planning callous intrigues—"

"Will it help Russia if I live in misery, too?" Soybel glared at her husband. "If your father's house remains empty, will the rest of Russia's quarters be more tolerable?"

"Soybel, just as Russia's masses do not deserve poverty, you do not deserve wealth."

"I have earned everything I desire."

"You have earned *nothing*."

"My childhood alone earned me everything I want," Soybel retorted. "And living in Kodoma, isolated from the world, with a husband who has fled from me into his books, has earned me even more. Do you think that being imprisoned in a village of peasants has made my life one of joy? Yes, for the first year or so Kodoma enchanted me. But I soon viewed it differently. I took a good look at Kodoma and I saw instead of a Jewish *shtetl* a Russian one. That is when I decided that I wanted to be more than just the mistress of Kodoma. What does it mean to be the lord of peasants, the queen of stupid, superstitious men and women? The king of the pigs is still a pig."

"And a pig at court is still a pig," Aleksandr rejoined.

"I have no intention of arguing with you, Aleksandr. If you can live your life the way you want, despite what I want, then I have a right to the same freedom. And the freedom I want begins here in Odessa."

"You will have to find your own way of being free in Odessa," Aleksandr said softly.

Soybel peered at her husband inquiringly.

"We do not have the house anymore." Aleksandr paused to make sure his wife was listening to him. "I sold my father's house."

"You sold it?"

"Right after Solomon left. Like you, there are memories I want to rid myself of."

"It is a shame you cannot sell everything you find disagreeable!" Soybel's rising voice caused the other diners to turn and stare. "These days everything is disagreeable to you—the granary, me, *everyone*—except Grisha. And all you use him for is a mirror!"

Aleksandr concentrated on arranging his silverware so each of the pieces was exactly parallel to the next.

"Don't you have anything to say?!"

Wishing he were far away, Aleksandr clenched his hand around the fork until its tines pierced his flesh.

"Say something, Aleksandr!"

Without looking at his wife Aleksandr replied: "I do not want to stay here any longer."

Minutes later Aleksandr and Soybel entered their hotel suite. Ignoring each other, they undressed and climbed into bed. Aleksandr lay on his side, facing the wall. Soybel looked toward the opposite wall. Time passed. The wine Aleksandr had drunk warmed his face and made his hands throb until they ached for something to touch. He rolled onto his back to detect if Soybel were asleep. She was not. Aleksandr turned until he faced his wife's back. His hand traced the deep curve of her hip.

"Don't touch me!"

Aleksandr leaned on one elbow and stroked her waist, letting his hand slide down to her stomach.

"Don't!" Soybel tried to push him away.

Aleksandr rolled one of Soybel's nipples between his fingers. Soybel tried not to respond to his touch, but it excited her too much for her not to react. She pushed against Aleksandr until her breasts oozed through his fingers. Aleksandr pulled Soybel down on top of him, sliding his hands along her back, across her buttocks, and between her thighs. He drew up his knees, making a space between their bodies. His fingers traveled from Soybel's breasts to her stomach and then further down. He rubbed his hands against the soft hair, feeling each strand individually, gently pulling them one by one. He buried his fingers deep inside Soybel, her sudden wetness making them both shudder. Feeling Aleksandr's fingers push against her womb, Soybel grasped his shoulders and bit the back of her hand. Aleksandr reached even deeper into his wife. Without warning Soybel yanked away her husband's hand and knelt over him, her expression as menacing as a gargoyle's. She laughed nastily. Aleksandr forced Soybel against him, struggling to find what he needed. Soybel fought him off. And she sneered: "Tell me, Aleksandr, would Andreana Vizhni have gone to Palestine with you?"

The sound of Andreana's name hit Aleksandr like a hammer blow. For an instant he was stunned, and a thousand images clashed in his mind. Soybel's continuing cruel laughter pierced Aleksandr like a knife, the pain infuriating him. Aleksandr grabbed hold of his wife's arms, trying to force her to comply with his desire. Soybel twisted and squirmed, battling to free herself. Aleksandr became enraged. He slapped Soybel across the face, then grasped her hips, thrusting upward until he was able to drive himself deep inside her. Soybel tried to wrench loose, but Aleksandr was too strong for her. His fingers bruised her back. He battered her with his fists.

"I hate you!" Soybel screamed.

At almost the same second Aleksandr released his hold on his wife, his fluid dripping out of her onto him. Soybel did not move. She stared down at Aleksandr, her face filled with loathing.

"I hope with all my heart you haven't put a baby inside me!" she hissed.

The harsh moonlight illuminated Soybel's face, exposing angular planes and shadows that Aleksandr had never seen before. Soybel curled her lips, contorting her face into a mask that frightened him. Her eyes narrowed, and a guttural rumble spewed from her throat. Aleksandr pulled away, drawing himself back against the headboard. Soybel smiled venomously. And for the first time since he had known her, Aleksandr Moisei truly despised his wife, truly wanted to cause her insufferable pain.

CHAPTER 26

For the next several days Soybel and Aleksandr avoided each other as much as possible. At night, though they slept in the same bed, they silently acknowledged an inviolable barrier. During the day there was no problem. Soybel was content to see the city by herself, leaving Daniella with the governess, while Aleksandr was glad to be able to escape with Grisha.

On Wednesday of their second week in Odessa, after breakfast in bed, Soybel decided to walk to the promenade by the sea. Two hours later, after a leisurely bath, having combed her hair for half an hour, taking another thirty minutes to apply her makeup and dressing in a sporty long-skirted suit, Soybel strolled along Nicholas Boulevard. By ten o'clock she was lingering at a table outside a café on the promenade sipping lemonade.

Swirling the sugary liquid around in her mouth, Soybel forgot all her concerns, enjoying the sight of tugboats, barges, scows, and steamers that zigzagged across the harbor. Beyond the black coal-puffs of the harbor craft, and beyond the breakwater, a small white speck flitted along the water. Soybel strained to see it, wondering if the darting glimmer was the tiny *Golub* with Aleksandr playing the sails while his son stood at the helm. Soybel closed her ears to the shrill whistles of the tugboats and the deep steamer horns, listening for her husband's deep, satisfied laugh.

"*Praklyata!* Look at what's entering the harbor!" a man in the café cried out.

Startled out of her reverie, Soybel drew back at the sight of a monstrous ironclad naval ship entering the channel that led toward the port.

Everyone on the promenade and along the waterfront paused as several long, low blasts from the great cruiser caught their attention. Hundreds of dockworkers, barefoot and dressed in rags, ran to the end of the longest quay to watch the armed vessel as it loomed closer.

"Do you think the navy has come to help the soldiers?" asked a man sitting at the table next to Soybel's.

"I do not know," she replied, trying to read the name lettered on the ship's bow.

From all over the port, shouting voices and running feet destroyed the peaceful morning.

"It's the *Potemkin*!" the dockworkers roared in unison. "It's the *Potemkin*! The sailors must have mutinied!"

Like stones suddenly hurled from an enormous catapult, thousands of men, women, and children burst forth from the bowels of the city, raced to the boulevard stairs, and scrambled down to the harbor to meet the colossus of the Russian navy. Before long the excited mob extended from the foot of the steps all the way up to the promenade and back toward the center of Odessa. Through this energized mass of people blazed the flame of revolution.

The whistle of the *Potemkin* shook the port, and, as though they were one, the people surged forward, shoving, elbowing, and jostling one another, trying to push past those who weren't moving quickly enough, all of them screaming, "Welcome, sailors of the *Potemkin!* Welcome!" Soybel, too, was pressed along with the crowd, forced from her chair on the veranda of the café toward the railing at the edge of the promenade.

"The revolution is starting! Hurrah for freedom!"

Soybel gripped the stone balustrade, terrified that the

seething mass of humanity around her would cause her to tumble over and plunge to the wharf two hundred feet below.

"Fire on the town! Let the guns of the *Potemkin* liberate Odessa! Free us from the Tsar and the capitalists, and we will make Odessa a republic!"

Everyone took up the cry. Children, too, dashed about, shouting: "Death to the Tsar! Death to Nicholas!"

Sounds of skirmishing could be heard from within the city. The massive wall of people became restive. The sun rose to noon, making the day hot and sticky; tempers grew short.

"Soldiers, sailors, and people of Odessa, unite!"

A lone Cossack caught in the crowd was pulled from his horse and beaten to the ground by a gang of youths; when they had finished with him their hands were smeared with blood. Soybel attempted to evade a group of men who roughly shoved her against the railing as they tried to find a better vantage point.

"Thank God for the sailors!" one of the men bellowed, grabbing Soybel and kissing her in celebration. She squirmed in an effort to be free of his grasp. "Do not be afraid, lady. Today there is nothing to fear. Today we are free!" The man released Soybel only to put his arm around her and lean on her for support, all the while babbling excitedly about the arrival of the cruiser. Intimidated by the man's strength and fearful of incurring his wrath, Soybel remained fixed in place.

The sun passed its zenith and the shadows changed sides. The sailors aboard the *Potemkin* wandered aimlessly around the deck and from the shore they appeared to be unsure of themselves. The crowd became anxious.

"Fire on the city, or go away like cowards!" a man bitterly shouted.

"The police are bringing up reinforcements!" another voice warned.

"Sailors of the *Potemkin*, save Odessa! Save Russia!"

Frustrated, sensing failure, people clawed and scratched

at the air as if they were trying to reach out and pluck the help they wanted from the sky.

"We will lay down our lives with you! We will fight to the last drop of our blood! Fire on the town!"

From every corner of the port people pleaded with the sailors, their waning hope turning to desperation.

"The Cossacks are here!"

"Now or never, sailors of the *Potemkin*! Now or never!"

The crew of the battle cruiser hurried to their stations and prepared their guns with ammunition. A roar jolted the harbor.

"Freedom for Russia! Death to the autocracy!"

The guns of the *Potemkin* were cranked into position, their barrels aimed at the City Hall. The crowd grew still. A flash of light and smoke belched from the muzzle of a six-inch gun. The boom of the shell launched from the cannon reverberated off the quay. A trumpeting bugle accompanied the deadly projectile as it sped overhead. Just before the missile hit there was silence, and then a deafening explosion rocked the city. A second earshattering detonation erupted, a wisp of acrid smoke following it from the barrel of the ship's large gun. Once more, a ball of light brighter than the sun thundered over Odessa. In the distance flames licked at the sky, black smoke spiraled upward.

"They've shelled the houses! They missed their mark and hit the city!"

The multitude began to fight its way back toward the Boulevard. People fell as they scrambled up the granite stairs, crushed and trampled by others behind them.

"The Cossacks are here, run!"

"Not that way, the soldiers are there!"

"The fires are spreading. Let's go!"

People swarmed everywhere, tearing through any obstacle in their path as they raced toward the heart of the city. They charged a line of mounted Cossacks and soldiers, and were met with brutal lashings from whips and clubs. Men, women, and children fought to escape the knouts and rifle butts that mercilessly battered them. Shots were fired.

Cossacks, ripped from their saddles, were stomped to death by the mob or their own horses. People were slashed and beaten, their flesh stripped off like skinned animals'. The sun began to set, and the gathering darkness heightened the fear and confusion. Soybel, her dress torn, her body bruised from being punched and kicked, was panic-stricken. Coming straight at her was a violent youth leading a pack of his friends. "Kill the aristocrat!" he snarled. Soybel closed her eyes, waiting for the attack. But the gang passed her by, assaulting a well-dressed young man behind her.

"I got him!" the brutish youth shouted triumphantly, his eyes livid as he choked the man.

"Death to the Bolsheviks!" yelled a wild-looking Cossack, whipping his horse into the thick of the crowd.

"Death to the capitalists!" a band of children shouted, backing Soybel against the wall of a building. Soybel covered her face in fear as the beast-like youngsters tore handfuls of material from her clothing, one child savagely pulling at her breasts and another at her groin. "Animals!" Soybel screamed at the top of her lungs. She hurled herself past the children, letting the ferocious mob sweep her along.

Soybel ran, unable to stop, as people from behind pushed her along faster. The incessant clatter of hoofs followed, Cossacks and soldiers riding after the mob. Here and there in dark alleyways, furtive figures waited to launch new attacks against the troops. Forced down dark streets where every noise was a threat, Soybel used all her strength to free herself from the fleeing horde. She found an empty doorway and there was able to rest.

Night settled, and the last of the demonstrators had disappeared from the streets. The city was quiet, the thoroughfares empty. Clinging to the building shadows for protection, Soybel prudently made her way back to Nicholas Boulevard, the sound of her own footsteps frightening her. Her face was streaked with dirt, the jacket of her suit so shredded that it was unrecognizable; her blouse was ripped down the front and stained with dirt and grime from the hands of her attackers, her long skirt was splattered with the blood of the injured. Soybel was exhausted. And when she found herself in the square in front of the Exchange, still nearly a mile from the London Hotel and too tired to walk another step, she began to cry. Soybel looked around; except for the lights in some of the tall windows of the Exchange, she was surrounded by darkness. A chilling wind from the sea funneled down the Boulevard and swirled around the square, cutting through to her bones. The street lamps of Nicholevskaya, the yellow patches peeking from the hotel, seemed to have receded. For an instant Soybel wondered if Aleksandr were searching the city for her. She did not care. A light in the Exchange was doused, leaving an ominous black hole. Soybel was curious whether one of the remaining illuminated offices was Vassili's. Her eyelids heavy, her limbs clumsy, her body in pain, Soybel hugged herself, wanting to sleep, wanting to be held and rocked to sleep. She closed her eyes and for a long moment thought. Then, her decision final, Soybel Moisei began to walk toward the entrance of the Exchange.

CHAPTER 27

Almost immediately following the *Potemkin* incident, Vassili Viska left Odessa for St. Petersburg, his sudden departure causing Soybel to feel as if someone had wrenched out her heart. For a month she languished in Kodoma, doing nothing but seeking solace in memories of how Vassili had flirted with her, so outrageously at times that she had feared Aleksandr would notice and take offense. She recalled the night of the *Potemkin*'s shelling of Odessa, still able to picture how hesitant Vassili had been to kiss her, how comforting his arms had felt. When he finally opened the door to his suite of offices to investigate as to who had been knocking and saw her standing there, an obvious victim of the rampaging mob, Vassili quickly ushered Soybel inside, offering her brandy and soothing words. The first glass of liquor was followed by more. And using the quantity she had consumed as an excuse, like a nun of an order of silence suddenly released from her vows, Soybel poured out all her fears, speaking urgently of her disappointment with Aleksandr. The sympathy displayed on Vassili's face spurred her on to elaborate. She cried as she confided in him, clutching his hands for strength. Soybel asked Vassili to hold her, to let her rest her head against his shoulder. Tenderly he drew her to him and she grazed his lips with her cheek. It was then that Vassili had kissed her. Soybel responded passionately, evoking from Vassili the confession that from the first time he had seen her he had been smitten by her. They talked for hours, their words the excited babblings of new lovers. And even as they talked they never stopped kissing one another, Soybel's fingers constantly moving across Vassili's face, caressing his cheeks, brushing his eyelids, stroking his neck, her fingertips sensing every change in the texture of his skin, her hands tingling with an excitement that made her body tremble, her entire being wanting to give Vassili every bit of itself, wanting Vassili to do with her as he wished. And though Vassili desired Soybel just as passionately, he was unable to comply with Soybel's urgings that they consummate their love, the specter of Aleksandr, the deep friendship he had with Aleksandr, forcing Vassili to obey his honor before his ardor.

In August, when Aleksandr mentioned that he had received a letter from Vassili, Soybel asked to read it, terrified that her husband would hear in that simple request her desperate yearning, but Aleksandr perceived nothing, handing Soybel Vassili's message with as much concern as if it had been a blank sheet of paper. Slowly Soybel read it, devouring every word. And though the letter contained nothing but news of Vassili's political life in the capital, Soybel thought she could read a secondary meaning between the lines. She could hear Vassili's commanding voice as his words burned into her eyes. She could see him standing before the Duma, demanding that the Tsar heed his words and give the Russian people the constitution they wanted, that they deserved—and she could hear Vassili demanding that Aleksandr give Soybel the freedom she wanted, that she deserved. Over and over, each time with growing excitement, Soybel read how Vassili was leading the Constitutional Democrats in drafting a constitution that would free all Russians from bondage. Vassili's eloquent statements of his belief in the rights of every Russian, of his dedication to realizing those rights, stirred Soybel's deepest passions, and her love for Vassili matched the heat of the summer's sun. At the end of the letter, where Vassili inquired after the well-being of Aleksandr's wife and children, Soybel was certain she detected a quaver as Vassili's bold script formed the letters of her name. When she finally tired of reading the letter and laid it aside, Soybel's exhilaration quickly ebbed; for in truth she had nothing to cling to but the vision of Vassili's face, his gestures, the memory of his laugh —the fantasy of making love with him.

Summer waned, autumn came and died, winter unleashed its raging storms, and then one day it was spring once again. And while Aleksandr Moisei still strode defiantly with his son through a world of his own, the life of Soybel Moisei was at a standstill. As Soybel watched her husband receding further from her, the intimacy he shared with Grisha increasing, Soybel was repelled by her husband, no longer caring if ever again he became the man she married. Only Vassili mattered, and he, too, seemed to have abandoned her.

Every month a letter came to the Moisei household from Vassili, but always addressed to Aleksandr and always circumspect—discussing nothing but the growing disregard Tsar Nicholas had for his subjects, how the humiliating terms of the treaty that ended the war with Japan were fomenting minor insurrections and massive strikes, the disaster Vassili foresaw if Nicholas did not change his autocratic methods, and how thwarted Vassili felt at being unable to halt what he perceived to be Russia's inexorable march toward revolution.

Angered by the propriety of Vassili's letters, unable to withstand his silence toward her, and no longer caring about being discreet, Soybel wrote to Vassili, pleading with him to make a commitment to her—a pledge that somehow he would rescue Soybel from her present situation. When no letter came in return, Soybel was wracked with despair. Her life became unbearable, only the thought of Vassili, the wild hope that he might suddenly appear, preventing Soybel from going mad.

Summer arrived, and with it days of constant loneliness

for Soybel, days void even of sound from her children or Aleksandr. Each morning Aleksandr and Grisha arose before dawn and tramped off to the fields to work with the peasants. From sunup until dark they toiled. Some nights they did not even bother to return home—the two of them sitting by a fire in the cool night air, listening to the peasants sing to the music of guitars and balalaikas, sharing thick pieces of cheese, chunks of black bread, and sweet red wine with the people of Russia's steppes, sleeping together on the ground, beneath a roof of stars, protected from the night's chill by a thick blanket and the warmth of each other's bodies—father and son entwined together in slumber, breathing, dreaming as one.

Daniella, too, was never at home. Her days were spent roaming the countryside with a band of peasant children, pilfering produce and livestock from neighboring farmers. At night, as she sat with her companions' parents, Daniella discovered that, though stealing was nothing but a sport to her, to these people, her friends, it was a necessity. And the bitterness she heard in those peasant huts, the hatred that poured out when they spoke of their lives, kindled the fury Daniella felt for her own life.

Often, Soybel thought of her family. She disliked her daughter. That was easy. For already, at age eight, Daniella was sullen, her face pinched in constant anger, her eyes suspicious. And the way Daniella moved—slinking, as if she were always spying—made Soybel mistrustful. Of Grisha, Soybel was jealous: nine-year-old Grisha, his body hard and brown from spending months outdoors working with his father, his sun-bleached blond hair almost white. Grisha Moisei, the spitting image of his father. Grisha Moisei, often and for no obvious reason swept off his feet by his father, lifted high into the air, then hugged close to Aleksandr's chest and kissed. But what Soybel resented most was that Grisha's love for Aleksandr was as obvious as was his disinterest in his mother. As for Aleksandr, Soybel was afraid even to look at him. His chest was brawny, his arms powerful. Yet not only was Aleksandr's size overpowering, but his eyes were so blue, so intense, his every move so precise, rippling with power, his total being so full of energy that it seemed to Soybel that her husband was invincible. Inescapable.

Finally, summer passed. The harvest was over, and with autumn well established and still no personal message from Vassili, Soybel felt a new despondency. She feared that not only had she been foresaken, but also that she was no longer attractive. More than once she made an effort to seduce Aleksandr, but each time Aleksandr fended her off. Frightened by her failure, Soybel devoted hours to arranging her hair and perfecting her makeup. Behind her ears, in the crook of her elbows, on her wrists, and between her breasts she sprinkled exotic perfumes until the house reeked of jasmine, musk, and eau de cologne. She wore her most fashionable clothes, and every day at noon made it her habit to stroll the length of Mirazdanskaya Street, stopping to talk to everyone she knew, thriving on the attention they paid to her. Soybel exulted when she noticed how many people went out of their way to look at her, assuming that when they whispered among themselves they were commenting on how beautiful she was. Late in September, as she sat at her dressing table combing her hair while Aleksandr reclined in the rocking chair, his eyes closed, his face relaxed, Soybel asked: "Aleksandr, do you think I would look better with ringlets against my neck instead of these curls pulled on top of my head?"

The squeak of the rocker moving back and forth was Aleksandr's only answer. Soybel fluffed her hair this way and that, held up a hand mirror, and turned her head from side to side. "Yes, that's better. Aleksandr, now what do you think?"

Without opening his eyes, he replied, "It is ridiculous, Soybel. As ridiculous as the way you dress. I know of no other woman who clothes herself for the opera to walk among peasants."

"I dress the way a woman of my position should dress."

Aleksandr opened one eye and peered at his wife. "Soybel, it is *my* position."

Indignant, seething, but unwilling to engage in another battle of wits with her husband, Soybel centered her attention on his reflection in the mirror. There was an unusual air of self-assuredness about Aleksandr lately, a smugness that disturbed Soybel. And whenever they argued, Aleksandr seemed to be toying with her, playing with her like an angler who has hooked a game fish that he knows will ultimately lose the struggle. Soybel studied her husband's image in the mirror. He was slowly rocking back and forth, his eyes closed, a satisfied smile on his lips. Soybel tried to imagine what secret Aleksandr was keeping to himself, what mystery that she was sure would affect her fate. Softly, as casually as possible, forcing herself to sound amiable, she asked, "Aleksandr, why do you look so happy? What wonderful thing are you thinking about?"

In his deep voice touched with the lilt of delight, Aleksandr replied: "My dear wife, all that is on my mind now is the trip to Odessa I will take tomorrow."

"You are going to Odessa?"

"Yes. It is the end of the season, and it is time to go over the ledgers with Vassili."

"Vassili is in Odessa." Soybel clutched her neck, trying to control the quivering in her throat.

"He has just returned from the capital. I received word from him this morning."

"I want to go with you."

"Why?"

"I just want to. It—"

"Are you the dutiful wife who enjoys accompanying her husband on his business trips?"

"It has—"

"What will you do there?" Aleksandr stood up, unbuttoned his shirt, removed it, then took off his trousers.

"It has been so long since I have been to Odessa. It might do me some good to get away from Kodoma."

"It would do us all good to get away from Kodoma." Aleksandr removed his underdrawers, the whiteness of his body below his waist sharply contrasting with the deep bronze of the rest of his body.

"Then why don't we all go—the children, all of us?"

Aleksandr stretched out on the bed. "I intended to take Grisha with me. If you want to go, too, that is fine with me. As for Daniella's coming along, that is your decision."

Dumbfounded by her husband's assent, overwhelmed by the thought of seeing Vassili, Soybel sat mutely and stared into space. Tears gathered in her eyes, and to hide them she covered her face with her hands. When she had regained her composure, Soybel began the slow process of readying herself for the trip. Hours dragged by before she was calm enough to lie down next to her husband. She was beset by thoughts of how to tell Aleksandr that she preferred for Daniella not to go with them. Grisha was of no concern to her—he would be constantly at his father's side—but Daniella would be an inconvenience. She was becoming unmanageable. Her unruly behavior was already too much for the aging governess to handle, and Soybel did not want to be hindered in Odessa by her daughter. Soybel slept little, using the night to select the best words to tell Aleksandr of her decision, thinking of Vassili to give her the courage to inform Aleksandr of her decision. The next morning when she calmly told Aleksandr that she thought it would be unfair to burden the governess with such a headstrong child, and that it would be best for everyone if Daniella remained at home, Aleksandr seemed neither concerned nor suspicious. That afternoon, her worst fears alleviated, looking magnificent, Soybel Moisei, along with her husband and son, boarded the train for Odessa. It was a trip she was anticipating both with eagerness and apprehension, for it was a trip on which she had decided to gamble her future.

CHAPTER 28

What started out one evening with a band of youths taunting strolling couples in Odessa's Alexandrovsky Park turned into a brawl. Girls screamed for help as their boyfriends were mauled, and when the police arrived, they began to swing their clubs indiscriminately, beating all who got in their way. Bystanders who had been enjoying the free-for-all became infuriated, some joining the ranks of the police, others the side of the rioters. It did not take long for the fighting to spread to the nearby streets, and soon the incident had erupted into a battle. The rioters swooped through the city, Cossacks on horseback and foot soldiers swelling the violence. Stores were looted, innocent people beaten and robbed. Instinctively, the marauders headed for the soft underbelly of Odessa, the slums of Moldavanka, where Odessa's large community of poor Jews lived. "To Moldavanka, to kill the *zhidis*!" was the battlecry as the mob expected to vent its rage without meeting resistance. "Let's kill the *zhidis*! Let's kill the lousy *zhidis*!" Even on Nicholas Boulevard the frenzied screams could be heard: they even penetrated the sedate office where Aleksandr and Soybel Moisei sat talking with Vassili Viska.

"What is going on?" Aleksandr asked as he hurried across the room to the window and saw hundreds of people running through the darkness. Grisha followed close at his father's heels.

"A riot, no doubt," Vassili replied. "But I am not surprised. I spent the last six months in St. Petersburg trying to convince our ministers that this would occur. They laughed at me." A surge of anger caused Vassili to kick at the floor. "We had our manifesto, a constitution, and Nicholas spat on it. *Damn* Nicholas! But how well he knows his subjects. He shows a little force, and despite what the new laws say, our most learned and influential men fall to their knees in fear and acquiesce to the Tsar's subversion of freedom. Nicholas is clever, but I fear that even he will be unable to quell the passions that are now running rampant."

"And now Odessa will suffer, too," said Aleksandr.

"With the city steaming and reeking because of the weather, I am surprised that an outbreak like this did not happen sooner."

"You mean that those people are fighting just because of the weather?"

"For two weeks now, Aleksandr, the temperature has been well over a hundred. The heat and humidity have made it difficult to breathe; the damp air prevents the fumes of garbage and waste matter from being blown away by the sea breezes. The foulness gets worse every day. And for the past two days rumors of cholera and typh—"

"Poppa, where is everyone going?" interrupted Grisha, moving closer to his father's side.

"The agitators will have a holiday now," Vassili commented. "The Bolsheviks are organizing strikes everywhere." Vassili sighed and looked at Soybel. "You have no idea how hard I tried—"

"Poppa, where is everyone going?"

"To Moldavanka . . . it looks like all of Odessa is rushing there."

"Rabbi Eleazar lives there."

Aleksandr put his arms around his son and squeezed his shoulders. He, too, had immediately thought of the rabbi.

How ironic, Aleksandr mused, that Eleazar—who only recently had resigned his position at the Brody, had given up the plush quarters provided for him, and had moved to Moldavanka to become the rabbi of a traditional synagogue—was already in danger. Aleksandr and Grisha continued to peer out of the window, far removed from the conversation that was taking place across the room.

"I am so tired," Vassili said to Soybel. "The struggle in St. Petersburg was futile. And nothing makes a man more tired than futility." Vassili stared at Soybel, his gaze unwavering.

Soybel smiled at Vassili, her eyes shouting that she agreed with him. A faint blush touched Vassili's ears.

"You know, more than once I had to force myself not to run away from St. Petersburg and return here. There is so much more for me here than in the capital."

A shiver of excitement made Soybel tremble. She wondered if her back was hiding her emotions from Aleksandr. "Tell me about St. Petersburg."

"Someday I will tell you. Now, I do not even want to think about it."

"Do you have any plans, any—"

"I am going to Dalyoki for a while to rest—then back here, I suppose."

"Will you be in Odessa long?"

"Just long enough to be sure I know what is happening with my business."

"I presume that busy men never have time for anything but business."

Vassili nodded in agreement.

"That is very sad. A man should have more than one thing to his life."

"So should a woman," Vassili whispered on a breath.

Nervously, Soybel inspected her hands, picking at a speck of dirt on one finger. Vassili forced himself to remain composed.

"I am going to Moldavanka," Aleksandr said suddenly as he turned and strode across the room toward them.

"Why?" Soybel asked, annoyed by the intrusion.

"Because they might need help there."

"And what will you do against that mob?" Soybel inquired derisively.

"I want to go, too, Poppa."

"It is better that you don't."

"Please, Poppa. I will stay right by you, I promise!"

"Grisha, a riot is not a place for a child," Soybel said angrily. "But then again, knowing your father, he most likely wants me to run through that insane mob, too."

"Of course he doesn't," said Vassili. "In fact, you should not be going either, Aleksandr."

"And Grisha should certainly not go," added Soybel.

Aleksandr, his eyes an icy blue, studied his wife. "I think Grisha should go."

"Why?"

"As part of the education you want him to get in Odessa."

Vassili glanced at Aleksandr, then looked steadily at Soybel. "I can understand why Aleksandr wants Grisha to go."

"Can we leave now, Poppa?" Grisha asked, pulling his father to the door.

"When will you return?" Soybel asked. There was a subtle change to her voice, an anticipation.

"I do not know. Maybe late tonight. Maybe before. Whenever it is over."

"Then perhaps Vassili would be kind enough to see me safely back to the hotel. That is, if you do not mind, Aleksandr," said Soybel, sounding innocent, obedient to her husband.

"If it is not an imposition, Vassili—"

"I would be more than happy to escort Soybel to the London."

"Thank you, Vassili," Soybel said softly. "I am certain that Aleksandr will be relieved knowing that I am with you."

Vassili looked at Soybel, not expecting her to be smiling at him, and his face flushed scarlet. Aleksandr noticed nothing.

"I do not want to inconvenience you, Vassili."

"Of all people, Aleksandr, you could never inconvenience me."

"Are we going now, Poppa?" Grisha impatiently asked.

"Yes." Aleksandr opened the door of Vassili's private office.

"Be careful, the two of you," Vassili said.

"We will."

"And do not concern yourself about Soybel," Vassili reassured Aleksandr as he walked him to the outer office of the suite. "She will be as well taken care of as if she were with you."

"I hope she appreciates you more," Aleksandr muttered, then added more warmly, "Thank you again for offering to accompany Soybel to the hotel."

Nodding his head in acknowledgment, Vassili opened the door to the hallway. Grisha went out first, immediately followed by his father. Vassili watched the two of them until they had rounded the corner at the end of the corridor. He waited a moment to make certain they were gone. Then, taking a deep breath, he closed the outer door of the suite, locked it, and returned to his private office, where Soybel was waiting.

Much to Aleksandr's surprise, the square outside the Exchange was empty except for two soldiers who stood at one end, their rifles held ready. Casually, so as not to arouse their suspicion, Aleksandr took Grisha's hand and sauntered across the plaza toward Pushkinskaya Street. There things were different. Cossacks galloped back and forth chasing bands of rioters who were smashing windows and looting shops. A young man, bleeding from a gash on the head, was being roughly marched away by a military patrol. Crouched in doorways, hiding in alleyways, youths waited impatiently to hurl rocks at anyone who displeased them. Keeping Grisha between himself and the safety afforded by the buildings, Aleksandr walked as quickly as he dared, hoping that neither the soldiers or the Cossacks, nor the stray groups of rioters, would take the time to annoy a father and his son. They turned left onto Troitzkaya Street and passed the Brody Synagogue, as massive and somber as a fortress.

"Does Rabbi Eleazar ever come here anymore?" Grisha asked, seeing that the heavy wooden doors were chained shut.

"No."

"I like his new synagogue better anyway."

"So do I."

From a block away curses and shouts assaulted their ears. When they reached the end of Troitzkaya and came to the cross-street, Preobrazhenskaya, Odessa's longest street, and the one that separated the rest of the city from Moldavanka, Aleksandr and Grisha could see the commotion. Dozens of policemen and a large contingent of mounted soldiers milled about. A hundred or more men and women were being herded into a police station, some of them bleeding, some shaking their fists and yelling, the rest sullenly submitting to their captors.

"Let's not walk too fast," Aleksandr said to his son.

"Will the police come after us?"

"I don't know."

Starting across the wide thoroughfare, Aleksandr was afraid to breathe, expecting at any moment that someone would command them to halt. Their footsteps suddenly seemed loud, and when Grisha asked a question, Aleksandr quickly silenced him. By the time they reached the far side of Preobrazhenskaya Street, Aleksandr's heart was racing, his breath coming in short gasps. Unnoticed, they entered Moldavanka and accelerated their pace, Aleksandr and Grisha both feeling more comfortable once they had reached the slum unharmed.

Usually from sunup until midnight the crooked cobblestone streets of Moldavanka were crowded with people. This night they were empty. Gone was the cacophony of men and women continually talking, children screeching, merchants haggling. Even the air was different. Gone were the aromas of olives, coffee beans, sardines, watermelons, and tea wafting up from the Old Marketplace; now the atmosphere was heavy with the stench of rotting food and human waste. Still, the streets were clean; the Moldavankans refused to permit their enclave to become unbearable. Every morning women swept off the walkways, scrubbed the steps of their houses; daily, weather permitting, from nearly every window sheets, blankets, and clothing were hung over the window sills to air. For despite their poverty the Jews of Moldavanka were intent on living a healthful life. And for the most part they did, Odessa's liberal environment allowing them to live generally unharmed. The tolerance of the Jews by the rest of Odessa's citizens permitted the Moldavankans an existence far more tolerable than that of their brethren in the rest of the Pale. Yet, when tragedy struck, when pogroms befell them, the people of Moldavanka suffered equally with their kinsmen. For, like all Russian Jews, the Moldavankans were also a weak and defenseless people.

"Are you afraid, Poppa?" Grisha asked, clinging to his father's hand.

Before Aleksandr could reply, hoofbeats shattered the stillness. Aleksandr pushed Grisha into a doorway, the two of them huddling there while three Cossacks galloped by into the heart of Moldavanka. When the sounds of the horsemen faded away, they continued on, into Yekaterina Street. There were loaves of bread strewn all around, shards of broken glass were everywhere. A torn sack lay in the gutter, a dozen potatoes and some fruit scattered nearby. Shreds of cloth lay twisted on the walkway. When Aleksandr and Grisha turned onto Masterskaya Street, they both stopped in mid-stride, alarmed by the sight of soldiers swarming around several corpses that were lying in the road.

"Leave them until morning!" a soldier suggested, poking one of the bodies with his rifle.

"But the dogs will eat them, and the Jews will take what is left."

"Good. Then there won't be anything to clean up!"

Aleksandr pulled Grisha away in another direction.

"What happened there, Poppa?"

"I don't know."

Grisha looked back over his shoulder. "Did the soldiers kill those men?"

"Perhaps."

"Who do you think they were?"

"Who knows? All men look the same when they are dead."

After walking a circuitous mile, Aleksandr and Grisha reached Kherson Street, a narrow roadway lined on one side by two old and crumbling apartment buildings; between them, at number nineteen, was a modest wood frame house, before it a patch of grass and a carefully tended flower bed protected by a low picket fence. On the other side of the street was a solid row of shops: a fruit store, a bakery, a place for a tailor, a cobbler, and a ramshackle shop belonging to a fixer. When they passed number nineteen and saw that it was dark inside, Aleksandr was even more anxious to reach the one-room synagogue a block away. He lengthened his stride, forcing Grisha into a half-run. The instant he set foot on Tiraspolskaya Street, Aleksandr's eyes focused on a single-story stone building. The door was closed, but light from the window tumbled out onto the street. A man of about thirty-five, squat, unsmiling, his arms folded across his chest, stood outside the doorway. Aleksandr recognized him as one of Aram Zubov's followers.

"You missed the excitement, Zionist," he said as Aleksandr and Grisha approached him. "But you are lucky, it is not over yet."

Ignoring the sentry, Aleksandr opened the synagogue door and led his son inside.

"Tomorrow, when the peasants realize it was not the soldiers who did the killing, you will not be so proud!" an elderly man was shouting, his words slashing out like a whip at the people congregated in the *shul*. "And when the peasants come back seeking vengeance, you will not be so brave!"

"Would you have preferred it, Benya, if we had let them

do what they wanted? Was it your daughter they stripped naked? Was it your child they touched with their filthy hands? No! It was mine! And I am glad they are dead!" yelled a heavyset woman, the rolls of fat at her neck shaking.

A few cheers followed the woman's words, but most of the people remained silent, their faces pinched with fear. Aleksandr pushed his way through the crowd until he and Grisha were standing against a wall near the front of the *shul*. Aleksandr looked around the room; he never had seen it so crowded before. People were backed up against the walls, every one of the wooden benches was filled; men stood in the aisles and around the pulpit, while others sat on the floor.

"Why are you worrying so much? Maybe after tonight they won't return. Don't you think they will wonder if the next time more of them might die? Maybe they learned a lesson tonight," a neatly dressed man said just loudly enough to be heard.

"Maybe, maybe. All I hear is maybes! Look at you! Fools! Every one of you. They will be back. And we will pay ten times over for what happened tonight! Since when do Jews take up arms and kill?" a white-haired man raved.

"Rabbi, tell us what you think."

"Yes, Rabbi, what should we do?"

Everyone turned toward the first row of seats and looked at Rabbi Eleazar. Those in the rear of the *shul* stood up in order to see him better. The rabbi waited until there was silence, then began to speak.

"Every law of God and man has been turned against us, in every country, and in every time. But we survived. Why? Simply because no matter where we were, or how desperate our condition, there was always a group of us who remembered the Commandments, followed them, and handed them down to the next generation."

"Amen!"

"But times have changed. The government makes laws that force us to live in the Pale and nowhere else. The rules they have imposed on us prevent us from living decent lives. Yet, we have not obliged the government and disappeared. So now more than ever Russia is trying to slaughter us. And I know of no commandment that says, Thou shalt accept death at the hands of thine enemies!"

Applause and shouts of approval interrupted the rabbi's words.

"Yet, for me to stand here and tell you what to do is impossible," he continued as the excitement ebbed. "For Benya to fight makes no sense. He is an old man who can barely walk. And I can easily understand why Luba Bobol is not sorry those men are dead. But for me to take up a gun and shoot those who would do us harm, to kill them? I could not do it. But I have no answers from God either."

"Then what should we do?"

"There must be something, Rabbi. If there are no answers for us from God, or from guns, how will we keep ourselves from vanishing from the face of the earth?"

Rabbi Eleazar's eyes jumped from one face to another, avoiding looking at anyone directly.

"If you do not have an answer, Rabbi, who does?"

"Aram Zubov has an answer!" someone loudly proposed.

"No, no. His way we saw tonight. It is no good!"

"There is another answer!"

As if all present had become mute at once, the room was instantly silent.

"And you know the answer."

The congregation strained to see the speaker.

"But you would rather argue like a bunch of old women than admit that answer. Do any of you really think the Bible will protect you from bullets? Do you believe that obeying the Commandments will save your lives? Or that violating them will mean your deaths? One way or another each of you is waiting for the Messiah. Don't you realize that each one of you *is* the Messiah? And that what you are doing is waiting for yourselves?"

Murmurs of interest rose from the crowd as the people became intrigued by Aleksandr's words. He paced up and down the aisle, his head jutting forward, his fists held close to his sides, his eyes burning, challenging them all to stand up to him.

"Why are you so obsessed with sacrificing your lives in Russia? Do you have an answer besides 'it is God's will'? Do you have an answer that makes sense?"

"Do you really want an answer, Moisei?" asked Aram Zubov, his swarthy, brooding face filled with contempt.

"If your answer is the violence everyone thinks you were responsible for tonight, that makes no sense either."

"*If* that violence *was* my violence, it makes all the sense in the world," Aram countered coldly.

"Can you fight a thousand peasants? A hundred thousand? A million? Can you stand up to all of Russia? You will have to."

"Can your money, all of your money, bring every Jew in Russia to Palestine? Can it, Mr. Rich Man? How easy it is for you to say, 'Let us run to Palestine! Let us leave Russia!' How easy for the wealthy to propose such grand plans for the poor. How dare you come here from your fancy country house and tell us we are fools. Of course we are fools—because we are not rich like you!"

"If you are so concerned about us, why don't you come to Moldavanka and live?" a woman dared Aleksandr.

"There are seven in my family. My wife and me, plus five children. When will you buy our boat tickets for Palestine?"

"If you won't buy us tickets, then buy us guns!"

"Instead of running away, join us, help us defend ourselves!"

Aram Zubov raised his arms for quiet. Immediately the room was still.

"You see, Moisei, you can sell them a dream for a moment, but no longer."

"And what they are buying from you instead is nothing!" Aleksandr spat back.

"I do not sell anything, I just contend with reality. Tonight was a reality. People came to harm us. Instead it was turned around. This time someone put bullets into them first. This time it is *their* bodies lying dead on our streets.

Whoever did that—whoever was responsible for killing those men—is a hero. Because tomorrow we will all still be here. Alive. Do you know what happened when those men were shot? In a minute the streets were empty of the mobs. They ran faster than they knew they could. They left Moldavanka alone! *That* is reality. And no one has to have that sold to them!"

"Six months from now you will still be here, doing the exact same thing," Aleksandr said with disgust.

"And a year from now, and ten years from now if necessary. We don't need your dreams, Zionist—what we need is our lives!"

"Without dreams, Zubov, there can be no future."

"Without people, Moisei, there is no present."

A strange look appeared on Aleksandr's face. He repeatedly clenched and unclenched his fists. Sweat streaked his brow, and his eyes were glazed. Zubov started to walk away, but Aleksandr clutched his arm.

"In three months I am going to Palestine. With my family. All we will need is some clothing, my books, and passage. Beyond that, nothing. Are you listening to me, Zubov? I am going to Palestine, and I need almost nothing! But you, you need many things. You need to play God! But for a man to play God there is something he must have. Money. I have money, Zubov. Lots of it! And I hate it. I hate every kopeck of it. I hate what it has done to my life. So when I leave Russia, I am going to give you half of it, Zubov. Half! Then you will be able to buy all the guns and bullets you want. You can buy cannons if you choose, or you can give the money away. Maybe you will keep it all for yourself and change your ways to those of the wealthy and strut around Moldavanka in velvet suits and perfumed underwear. I don't care. I don't give a damn about what you do with the money. That is your decision. And your problem!"

A startled rush swept through the synagogue. Aram Zubov gaped in amazement at Aleksandr.

"If you do not believe me, I will sign a paper for you right now."

"Why give away just half of your money? Why not all of it?" a man shouted.

"Yes, why just half?" others cried out.

"But I am going to give away the rest of it—to Rabbi Eleazar!"

"Oh!" the people gasped.

Eagerly, everyone pressed toward Aleksandr. They all spoke at once, bombarding him with questions and congratulations. They shook his hands, clapped him on the back, embraced him and kissed him.

"I think you must be crazy, Moisei," Aram Zubov said, still looking stunned.

"And if I am, so what?"

"Why, Aleksandr, why are you doing this?" asked the rabbi. "Are you blessing us or cursing us?"

"That is up to you and Zubov to determine."

"Does Soybel know that you are taking her to Palestine?"

"I am going to tell her tonight, Rabbi. Tonight!"

"And if she does not like the idea?"

"Then she can go to hell."

"But Aleksan—"

"I am going home, Rabbi. And no one is going to stop me. Do you understand? Do you?"

"I—"

"You and all these others can remain in Russia because you believe this is where you must repent for your sins, but I will absolve myself in Palestine. Do you know, Rabbi, that since he has left, Solomon has never written to me? I know why. He is waiting for me to visit him instead. He visited me. Now it is my turn to visit him. Do you see what I mean?"

"Yes."

"Do you think that I am crazy, Rabbi?"

"No."

"But I am!"

"Aleksandr, before you do anything rash, please think."

"Why? Because I am crazy? That is nothing to worry about. Once I leave Russia, I will no longer be crazy."

"Think, Aleksandr, please!"

"Damn it to hell, I don't want to think anymore! There is no time left for thinking! All about us stand our enemies. They are closing in on us, coming nearer, they are here!"

Rabbi Eleazar shook his head sadly. "Aleksandr, the only enemy approaching you is yourself."

CHAPTER 29

The first ribbon of dawn streamed from the sky as Aleksandr Moisei returned from Moldavanka to his suite in the Hotel London. Though Soybel was sleeping, Aleksandr charged into the bedchamber, still flushed with the excitement of the evening. He shook his wife roughly and called out her name: "Soybel, Soybel, Soybel," the repetition a song of jubilation. Soybel's eyelids fluttered open.

"What time is it?" she murmured.

"Just after five o'clock."

Soybel stretched lazily. "Then what do you want?"

"To tell you that we are going to Palestine in December."

"I know."

"How could you know?"

Soybel yawned and patted her husband's hand. "You would not have awakened me to say that we are staying in Russia."

Aleksandr was taken aback by his wife's response. He watched her wriggle until she found a comfortable position. Soybel smiled and purred, then closed her eyes and returned to the pleasant dream Aleksandr had interrupted.

The next day Aleksandr repeated the news to Soybel and then informed her that they were leaving for Kodoma immediately, so that he could begin to conclude his affairs with Vassili Viska, thereby ensuring their December departure for Palestine. Soybel said nothing, simply nodding her head in agreement and promptly packing their suitcases. Again Aleksandr was surprised—shocked—by his wife's calm acceptance of his decision. Indeed, upon their arrival in Kodoma, and every day for the next two weeks, Aleksandr continually reminded Soybel that his intentions had not changed, and still Soybel remained complacent. She actually seemed mellow, unperturbed. She spent hours curled on the sofa reading, her delicate laughter tripping through the house in response to Rabelais and Molière. She developed a deep affection for George Sand, feeling strong empathy with her tales of idyllic country life. *Les Misérables* only made her gloomy, while Maupassant's *La Parure* touched her deeply; Soybel wept disconsolately at the wretched life lived by Madame Loisel as she tried to replace diamonds made of paste with real ones. Not once did Soybel find an excuse to argue with Aleksandr, and when she willingly accepted his advances and made love with him, he was again surprised. Aleksandr's first thought was that Soybel had changed her mind and had resigned herself to going with him. When he felt her thighs squeezing his hips for the second consecutive night, Aleksandr toyed with the idea that perhaps his wife was actually looking forward to the adventure. A week later, after she had pressed her breasts against his back and run her fingers down his chest toward his stomach, he decided to pretend that he was sleeping, afraid that his wife's renewed affection was nothing more than a campaign to seduce him into changing his mind. Yet Soybel did not seem to mind her husband's rebuff, acting as happy the next day as she had every day since their return from Odessa. So when she started to complain that she was ill, Aleksandr's first reaction was that it might be a ruse, a more certain way of making him defer his plans. By mid-November it was obvious that Soybel was not play-acting, and that she was in truth unwell. Chills and nausea plagued her daily, and one morning during the last week of November, Aleksandr awoke to find her lying on the floor, hugging her pillow and vomiting.

"What is wrong!" Aleksandr exclaimed, rushing to Soybel's side and helping her back into bed.

"I need a doctor, Aleksandr, please!" Her face was ashen, and her skin was cold.

"I will send for Dr. Rahabi."

"I want a doctor from Odessa!" Soybel began to heave, bringing up nothing but air.

"Let Rahabi look at you first. Then we will decide what to do."

"I do not care. Just do *something*," she moaned, her face wet with perspiration.

Aleksandr ran from the room, shouting for his children. When he found them in the parlor he ordered Grisha to hurry in to the village to get the doctor, and told Daniella to bring her mother some hot tea. Immediately, both children raced off to do their father's bidding, while Aleksandr returned to his wife. Moments later, Daniella entered the room, carefully carrying a steaming cup of tea.

"Get it away!" Soybel moaned, the sweet scent making her gag.

Aleksandr waved Daniella out of the room and gently began to stroke his wife's forehead. "Dr. Rahabi should be here shortly," he whispered.

"Just let me sleep." Shivering under several blankets, Soybel drew her legs up to her chest.

"I will light the fire for you."

Aleksandr arranged several logs in the fireplace and ignited them. By the time the wood started to burn, Soybel's eyes were already closed. For several moments Aleksandr watched her sleep; the muscles of his face were taut, his expression blank, his mind awhirl with colliding emotions. "Damn!" he muttered to himself; he resented the peaceful look on Soybel's face. Aleksandr turned on his heel and left the room. Slipping deep into thought, he walked slowly down the hall to the parlor. Up and down the hallway he paced, simultaneously angry with Soybel for being ill, suspicious of her illness, infuriated by the feeling that Soybel would always be a burden to him—sick or healthy—and angry with himself, since he could not decide whether he should delay their departure if Soybel were seriously ill. As soon as he heard Grisha and Dr. Rahabi climbing the porch steps, Aleksandr flung open the door, took the doctor by the arm, and hastily led him down the hallway to Soybel.

The doctor asked Aleksandr to leave him alone with his patient. Aleksandr obeyed, closing the door as he left the room. For a minute he remained in the hallway, his ear pressed to the wooden partition, trying to hear what was being said inside, but the thick oak slab made eavesdropping impossible. Irritated, Aleksandr reached for the door handle, then changed his mind and headed for the parlor.

"Is Momma very sick, Poppa?" Daniella asked when her father entered the room.

"I do not know." Aleksandr stood by the fireplace and stared into the flames. "Of all the times to become ill!"

"Will she be well for our trip, Poppa?" Grisha's plaintive voice caused Aleksandr to turn and look at his son. "Yes, my little soldier. She will be well. She *must* be well."

"Momma really doesn't want to go with us, does she, Poppa?" The sadness on Grisha's face caused Aleksandr to tremble.

"I don't know, Grisha."

"But I want to go, Poppa," said Daniella, running to her father and hugging him around the waist.

"And we will go, teddy bear."

"Poppa, why doesn't Momma want to go?"

A flash of fury coursed through Aleksandr's body and he nearly blurted out all the hateful things he felt about his wife in answer to Grisha's question. Instead he forced himself to reply quietly.

"Your Momma is hesitant to go because she loves this

house so much. Because she is afraid she will never again live in a house so beautiful."

"I am not afraid of that, Poppa."

"Why?"

"Because I live in my heart. And no one could ever make a building like it."

The simple purity of Grisha's words, the glow on his face, caused tears to well up in Aleksandr's eyes. "I love you, my son." *My God, but I love you.*

"I love you too, Poppa."

Three quarters of an hour passed before the doctor returned from Soybel's room.

"I am here, Doctor!" Aleksandr called out from the parlor. "How is my wife?"

"In a few days, or a week at most, I suspect that she will be fine. At least her morning upsets will cease," the slightly built, gray-haired man said easily.

"What is wrong with her?"

Doctor Rahabi grinned. "You are going to be a father!"

"A father?"

"Yes, your wife is pregnant—her suffering is nothing more than the first sign of it, but I think that is just about over now."

"How could this have happened?" Aleksandr looked to his children for help.

The doctor laughed. "With two other children you should know exactly."

"In four weeks we are scheduled to leave on an extended trip."

"You will have to postpone it. At least for a while."

"You mean she cannot travel?" Aleksandr became jumpy, finding it impossible to remain still.

"I am afraid not. Your wife is in a delicate condition. It is not serious, but she could miscarry."

"Why a baby?" Aleksandr asked, his voice hollow and thin.

"You must ask God about that. I am just a doctor."

Aleksandr began pacing back and forth between two windows, stopping at each to glance outside, then turning on his heel and repeating the same moves. "Doctor, how soon can she travel?"

"I would not advise it until after the baby is born."

"And when will that be?"

"If your wife's calculations are correct, then I would say July—yes, July of next year you will be a new father."

"July?" Aleksandr stopped in mid-step; his mouth dropped open.

"If I could, I would make it sooner," Doctor Rahabi chuckled.

"No matter what you did, you could not make it soon enough," Aleksandr muttered bitterly. "You see, Grisha? You see what she has done?"

Doctor Rahabi gave Aleksandr a strange look. He quickly put on his coat, assured Aleksandr that he would return in a few days to check on Soybel, and then hastily departed. For the rest of the day Aleksandr rambled distractedly about the house, muttering angrily, with Grisha and Daniella trailing him everywhere. Several times he looked in on Soybel, wanting to say something to her. But each time she was asleep. That night, for the first time in weeks, Aleksandr Moisei slept in his study.

For the next few days Aleksandr avoided his wife completely, letting the servants attend to her. Hidden in the depths of his coat, Aleksandr spent most of his time tramping through the desolate winter countryside. The agitation he felt was heightened by the accumulating storm clouds which threatened a blizzard that might isolate Kodoma for months. Just the thought of that possibility angered Aleksandr, and when the snow did begin to fall, he became furious, stomping through the deepening drifts, kicking the flakes as if that would make them disappear. When Soybel's morning sickness finally ended, and she began to laugh and banter with anyone in earshot, Aleksandr became even angrier. His wife's endless prattling made him want to scream for her to stop, to be quiet for a minute so the throbbing in his head would ease. Seeking to dull his torment, Aleksandr began to drink, heavily, swigging vodka often and liberally, but instead of numbing his senses the liquor only fueled his wrath, and with each passing day Aleksandr's seething grew until every time he saw Soybel his face contorted with an explosive rage.

A second snowstorm added to the first, and more than once Aleksandr decided that he would still leave for Palestine as planned, not caring that he would be abandoning his pregnant wife. But the more determined he became to vanish from Kodoma, the more he felt compelled to remain—his malevolence binding him fast to the very things he loathed. Icicles grew from the trees, everything froze, and winter smothered the countryside. Day after day, both the sky and earth were the same endless white, confusing Aleksandr as to which was which, making him fear that the world had turned upside down. Bitter winds blew fiercely, drifting the snow into mounds higher than his head, and Aleksandr knew that soon the Black Sea would freeze and become impassable. Every sound, every thought became muffled, winter surrounding Aleksandr like a hideous cocoon. And as the New Year passed Aleksandr Moisei wondered if he would ever escape.

At the end of January new snow fell, sending Aleksandr deeper into despair. He stopped shaving, his beard quickly turning from stubble into straggly hairs. His eyes became watery and red, he was unable to sleep, and there was not a moment when he was not at least slightly drunk. His temper became short, and even Grisha felt his father's wrath, Aleksandr reproaching his son for everything he did or said.

"I hate this place!" Aleksandr roared one morning as he stumbled downstairs from his study and along the hallway. "I hate *everything* about it!" he added as he passed the closed door of Soybel's bedroom. He banged the wall with his fist. "Everything!"

Within, Soybel lay awake. She ran her hands along her

swollen stomach, wincing at her husband's shouts. *It is you I hate, Aleko, old husband, grim husband. I despise you, Aleko. I love another, and I am dying for his love.* Rubbing her fingers in a gentle circle on her belly, Soybel remembered how tenderly Vassili had touched her breasts. Her mind reeled, the same way it had the last time she had been in Odessa. Soybel recalled how her heart had jumped when she heard the snap of the lock as Vassili secured them inside his office suite. She had wanted to run to him, to fling her arms around his neck and kiss him passionately. Instead she had waited for him to come to her. Soybel closed her eyes, picturing how Vassili had looked that night, his gray eyes restless, glittering, and his mouth was softer than she had ever imagined it could be. Again Vassili told her that he had loved her from the first. *"I recollect that wondrous meeting, that instant I saw you, when like a fleeting apparition, like beauty's spirit past me you flew."* Embraced by Vassili's poetic avowal, Soybel had whispered in return that she loved him. Soybel opened her eyes and turned her head so she could see out of the window. She grimaced, thinking about how she made love to Aleksandr after that night with Vassili, pretending that her husband was Vassili. But that was part of the plan—unspoken, but part of the plan nevertheless. Soybel and Vassili had agreed that she was to bide her time, to wait until the very hour that she was to board the boat for Palestine with her husband and family—and then refuse to go with him. It seemed logical to Soybel and Vassili that with one foot on the gangplank Aleksandr would not forsake his dream, and that the worst she would suffer would be his furious recriminations. But if that did not succeed, if Aleksandr refused to set foot outside of Russia without his wife, then Vassili would confront him with the truth. For weeks Soybel had excitedly anticipated that delicious moment when she would be free of her husband, yet she dreaded the scene that would inevitably follow. She even feared that Vassili might disappoint her. To protect herself, Soybel planned to be the devoted wife to her husband while readying herself for her lover. But providence had intervened; Soybel had become pregnant. It did not matter that she did not know by whom; it was more important that her pregnancy gave her an authentic reason, a tenable excuse for not accompanying her husband on his journey. Soybel was thankful that she had made love with her husband, otherwise . . . But everything was going smoothly: her pregnancy, her scheme, her future. And there was nothing else for Soybel to do but wait, and carefully, deftly, drive her husband away from her, and then watch with satisfaction as day by day Aleksandr came closer to leaving without her.

Still lying in bed, with Vassili's image fixed in her mind, Soybel clasped her hands over her chest, repelled by the memory that Aleksandr had never treated her like a virgin. On their very first night together, he had shoved his way into her, not caring that she was frightened or that he was hurting her. But Vassili? His fingers had flitted across Soybel's neck, stroking her skin until it seemed to be aflame. He caressed her in places that Aleksandr had ignored; her husband had never known how warm and pliant his wife could be. When Vassili discovered that Soybel was not wearing any undergarments, he laughed softly, the rolling sound wondrous music to Soybel. She gasped as she felt Vassili leading her to a place where she had never been. He had made her touch him, concentrate, focus on him, then pressed her face down until her lips welcomed him. Without warning his gentleness erupted into a brutal insistence that made Soybel scream so loudly that Vassili suppressed the cry with his mouth. He forced her against the couch, crushing her until Soybel thought she would crumble; the cold leather squeaking against her bare flesh excited her even more. She kicked Vassili, clawed his back with her fingernails, shouting as she dissolved into a realm of incredible pain and pleasure. When it was over, when she was able to breathe again, and her arms and legs stopped trembling, when the pulsating rawness inside her eased and became an exquisite throbbing, Soybel began to cry.

"Are you sad because I am not Aleksandr?" Vassili asked softly.

Soybel shook her head and squeezed his hand.

"Then why are you crying?"

"Because Aleksandr is not you."

Soybel rolled onto her side, slid her legs to the floor, and sat up carefully. She looked at her feet; like everything else about her they had become swollen. Thinking that they were ugly, she hid them inside a pair of furry house slippers. Cautiously, Soybel stood up and shuffled over to the dressing table.

"Momma, Povara told me to tell you that she has just finished baking sweet rolls for breakfast."

The intrusion of Daniella's voice irritated Soybel. "Is your father eating?"

"He went for a walk with Grisha."

"Walk, walk, walk. All he does is walk," Soybel said angrily, brushing her hair with forceful strokes. *Why doesn't he just keep on walking? No one is stopping him.*

"Momma, the rolls will get cold."

"I am coming, Daniella!" Soybel put on a bathrobe and looked at herself in the mirror. *You are getting too fat,* she thought grimly. Taking a deep breath to clear her mind, Soybel opened the bedroom door and padded toward the kitchen. The house was quiet. The slapping of her floppy slippers echoed in the hallway.

"Good morning, Momma," Daniella said as her mother entered the kitchen.

"Where is Povara?"

"She's gone out to the village to shop."

Annoyed that the cook had disappeared from the house without serving her breakfast, Soybel maneuvered herself into a chair at the dining table and looked directly at her daughter. Not knowing what else to do, Daniella stared back at her.

"Well?" Soybel drummed her fingers on the table.

"Well what, Momma?"

"When it is that difficult for me just to sit down, do you expect me to get my own breakfast?"

With her eyes downcast, Daniella shook her head very slowly from side to side.

"Do you propose that I wait for Povara to return?"

Again Daniella shook her head.

"Then what do you suggest, Daniella?"

"I will get your breakfast, Momma."

Soybel sighed with exasperation. "Why is it everyone in this house thinks of themselves first and of me last?"

Daniella brought her mother a plate with two warm sweet rolls, a jar of strawberry jelly and a knife, and a cup of tea. Soybel broke off a piece of one roll, smeared it with a thick layer of the fruity preserve, took a bite, and started to chew while staring off into space.

"Momma . . . why do you dislike Poppa, Grisha, and me so much?"

Soybel stopped chewing, but only for an instant.

"Why, Momma? And why do we have to have another baby, Momma? I don't want us to have another baby. I don't want any baby!"

"This is my baby I am carrying. Not yours. Not your brother's. Not your father's. Mine!"

Slowly Daniella shrank back into one corner of the kitchen.

"*Nothing* that I have is your father's. And I will take everything I can from him, so he feels every bit of the pain and loneliness he has made me suffer." Soybel's eyes narrowed into venomous slits. "I owe your father a lifetime of pain, and I intend to give him a lifetime of pain." Soybel chewed her food deliberately, each bite an attack. "When my baby is born, Aleksandr will still want me to go to Palestine. What should I do then? Become pregnant again? Cut off my legs?" Soybel sneered. "Once I worried that your father might go and leave me here alone. Now I pray for him to go and leave me alone." Bit by bit, Soybel devoured both rolls. Sip by sip, she swallowed her tea, all the while her eyes riveted on her daughter's face, Daniella's expression of horrified sadness only feeding Soybel's anger. *Why do you look at me that way, child? What do you know of my suffering? How dare you accuse me of betraying your father? Don't you know that he is the betrayer?*

"Don't you love Poppa anymore?"

Soybel daintily wiped the residue of her meal from her lips, slid back her chair, and got to her feet. "Once, Daniella, your father was the most important thing in my life; now he is the least important thing in my life." Holding herself erect, Soybel turned her back on her daughter, and marched toward the door. As her mother's swollen belly disappeared through the doorway, Daniella was overcome by a rage she did not understand. Without realizing what she was doing, Daniella reached for a knife, ready to slice open her mother's belly and tear out the thing that was destroying her father. Daniella's eyes flooded with tears, and her face contorted with rage; she plunged the knife into the tabletop. Suddenly she felt weak, her head became light, her body heavy with grief. Weeping bitterly, Daniella slipped to the floor and crumpled in a heap. Nearly an hour passed before she moved; the sound of her father and brother entering the house caused Daniella to stir.

"Soybel!" Aleksandr's voice shook the house. "Where the hell are you?"

Daniella shuddered as her father crashed his way down the hall.

"Where is my loving wife?"

After Aleksandr had passed by the kitchen, Daniella peeked out of the doorway. She watched her father stamp down the hall, bang open the door to the bedroom, where her mother was, and disappear inside. Grisha approached Daniella.

"Poppa is very drunk, and very angry," he whispered, stopping next to his sister.

"There you are, my wonderful Soybel!" Aleksandr scoffed. "How lovely you look when you are pregnant!"

"Are they going to have a fight, Grisha?"

He nodded his head.

"Grisha, why does Momma hate Poppa?"

Instead of answering, Grisha pressed his hands over his ears, tears already streaming down his face.

"I am drunk. Can you tell?" Aleksandr grinned, his expression daring his wife to chastise him.

Soybel was sitting in the rocking chair, knitting; she contemplated her husband.

"And do you know why I am drunk? Because I have been drinking!"

Giving him a look of disgust, Soybel returned to the infant's sweater she was making.

"And do you know why I have been drinking?" The snow that clung to his boots was melting in puddles on the floor. "To put some fire back into my belly, that is why!"

Aleksandr's eyes blazed with energy. He paused, waiting for Soybel to say something. Seeing that she was absorbed in what she was doing, he snatched the wool and needles from her hands and hurled them across the room.

"Look at me when I talk to you!" he bellowed.

Soybel regarded her husband indifferently.

"What do you want from me?" Aleksandr asked, disconcerted by her lack of emotion.

"I want you to leave me alone."

"I thought you were my wife. I thought you wanted to share your life with me."

"Once I was a wife. My husband was a prominent man. A wealthy man. We had two children and a beautiful house. Then my husband disappeared. Now I am alone, and I want it to remain that way."

"*I* am your husband!"

With a caustic laugh Soybel said, "To me you are nothing. As far as I am concerned you might as well be somewhere else. I would prefer you to be somewhere else."

Shaken by her words, Aleksandr asked weakly, "Do you hate me?"

"I no longer care enough about you to hate you." Soybel

looked out of the window and watched the first snowflakes of another storm twirl through the air.

"I am going away," Aleksandr said quietly.

Soybel shrugged her shoulders.

Aleksandr approached her. "Don't you care?"

She scrutinized the snow that was coating the window like a fine gauze.

"Doesn't it matter to you? Doesn't anything matter to you?" asked Aleksandr.

"My baby matters to me."

"Is that why you wanted—a baby? To ruin everything for me?"

Soybel singled out one crystal flake, intrigued by its lacy perfection.

"I want you to come with me, Soybel."

"That is too bad."

"Then I will have to go alone."

"Yes."

Aleksandr looked down at his wife; it seemed as if he might cry. "I don't want to go without you."

"I don't care what you want, Aleksandr."

"I will make you go with me. I will force you to go with me!"

"Then you will kill my baby."

"It is my baby, too. And if I want to kill it I will!" Aleksandr punched his fist into the wall. "I wish it would die!" Aleksandr pounded his forehead with his hands. "I want it to die!"

Soybel started to stand up.

"I want you to die!" Aleksandr shouted at the unborn child inside her body. "Do you hear me? I want you to die!" He shoved his wife back into the rocker.

"Stop it, Aleksandr! Please stop! Go away and leave us alone. We don't need you anymore."

As if he had bent a young tree limb to the ground and suddenly released it, Aleksandr hit Soybel across the face with his open hand. *"I hate your baby!"*

Soybel screamed, protecting her face with her hands.

Again Aleksandr hit her, and again, and again, Soybel's head snapping from side to side. Finally, as though all the strength had been drained from his body, Aleksandr stopped. "I hate your baby," he quavered.

"You should hate it," Soybel retorted, her face scarlet from the beating. "Because it is not yours."

Recoiling from the impact of Soybel's words, Aleksandr drew back in horror; the veins in his temples looked as if they were about to rupture. "You're lying . . . you are lying."

Once more Soybel turned to the window, her thoughts drifting far away from Kodoma. Aleksandr stood motionless, his breathing sporadic. There was a long silence.

"Whose is it?" he asked, his question barely audible.

The falling snow made the glass opaque, obliterating the world outside.

"Whose is it!" Aleksandr grabbed Soybel's face, crushing it between his hands. "Whose!" His grip tightened, his powerful fingers bruising Soybel's skin.

"Vassili's!"

A rush of air exploded from Aleksandr's lungs. He released his hold on Soybel and held up his hands as if to ward off a blow. "Vassili's?" He shook his head in disbelief. *"Vassili's?"*

Soybel gazed at her husband impassively.

"Why Vassili?" He stood there, dazed. "Why him?"

Aleksandr moved backwards haltingly. Not seeing where he was going, he retreated from the room, stumbling into the walls as he lurched out of the house. The wind tore at his face; within seconds his hair and clothes became icy white and the driving snow blinded him. He began to run, his legs churning, his arms flailing wildly, tearing his way through the storm to the stable. Aleksandr cried, the tears freezing to his face, and he screamed, the primitive wail engulfing him. When he reached the stable door, Aleksandr fumbled with the latch, his numb fingers madly struggling to open it. Once inside, he saddled the horse that was in the closest stall, climbed up on its back, and without even thinking to close the stable door behind him, dug his heels into the horse's flanks and forced the animal to break through the snow-blocked lane to the road that ran south. Repeatedly, Aleksandr kicked the horse, making it plow toward and then past the deserted streets of the snowbound village. Unable to withstand the brutal pain from Aleksandr's boots, the horse stretched to full stride, running all out as the storm became a blizzard and finally a terrifying *samjot.* Violent, twisting winds ripped at Aleksandr's clothing, shredding the material into rags. His eyes and nostrils were caked with snow, his face a crystal mask. Instead of easing up and seeking shelter, he beat the horse even more violently. The terrified beast bolted, battering through frozen drifts as high as its shoulders. Jagged pieces of packed snow slashed the animal's legs and hoofs, razor-sharp icicles slit Aleksandr's face, and a path spotted red trailed behind them. The wind, even stronger now, whipped Aleksandr's body as it tried to hurl him out of the saddle and fling him to the ground. The white sky darkened. Tree limbs snapped, crashing to the ground. The horse's legs buckled, but Aleksandr yanked the reins so viciously that the animal lunged back onto its feet. He shrieked into the horse's ear, cursing it, daring it to give up. Half an hour later the horse collapsed and died. In an uncontrollable fury Aleksandr thrashed the dead animal, pummeling it with his fists, kicking it with all his might. Then, finally understanding that the horse was dead, Aleksandr continued toward Odessa on foot, pushing himself as relentlessly as he had the horse.

Night came and still Aleksandr broke his way through miles of snow which often reached his chest. By the time morning came, Aleksandr no longer seemed human but rather a mass of delirious madness that should have fallen and died hours before. Benumbed, Aleksandr was unable to feel his arms and legs. Frostbite turned his flesh gray. His toes broke off with chilblain. The sun rose, and then set once again. Aleksandr's deranged mind, fearing doom, compelled him to run. The next morning, just after dawn, Aleksandr tottered and fell. He tried to crawl: he was too weak.

Closing his eyes in exhaustion, Aleksandr promised himself that he would rise in a minute and continue. Instead he slipped into unconsciousness. For hours Aleksandr lay where he had fallen, and only when a peasant happened by and saw him there did anyone know that Aleksandr Moisei had arrived in Odessa.

Two days later, on Tuesday, February 19, 1907, in Odessa's finest infirmary, the Catherine II Hospital, under the personal care of the senior physician, Aleksandr Jacobivich Moisei, age thirty-seven, died. In accordance with a request he had made long before, he was buried in the Jewish cemetery, the Jerusalem cemetery in Odessa, next to his grandfather. As the mourners watched the shrouded corpse being lowered into the grave they listened to Rabbi Joshua Eleazar chant the final prayer for the dead; only he realized the momentousness of the occasion. Only Eleazar knew that the grave in which Aleksandr would rest was the same one in which his mother had originally been buried. The body touched the bottom of the pit, the first shovelful of earth was tossed onto the deceased, and the rabbi wailed a dirge that had never before been heard—a personal lament for the man who as he lay dying had forgiven Eleazar for everything and then entrusted him with the most beloved thing he was leaving behind. When Grisha took hold of the rabbi's hand and began to weep, Eleazar thought his own heart would shatter. Daniella stood alone at the very edge of the grave and looked down, dry-eyed, devastated, isolated. Soybel's eyes were closed, her arms clasped around the child inside her, wishing that Vassili were at her side to comfort her. But Vassili stood at a distance, Grisha's inconsolable sobs echoing his own feelings.

One by one they passed by the grave, lost in their own thoughts of Aleksandr, all but Soybel regretting some unspoken or unshown kindness, remorseful that it was too late to make amends. In single file they walked to a waiting carriage. Moments later the vehicle sped off and was lost from sight. Two peasants, silent and impassive, filled the open grave with dirt. When they were done, they trampled its surface, stamping the earth flat. Then they too were gone. The cemetery was empty, silent, peacefully white. A steady wind swirled the snow, drifting it over the acres of graves. In the distance a church bell pealed. A few stubborn leaves, brown, brittle, clinging to barren trees, fluttered. Then the wind died, and nothing moved.

BOOK THREE

February 1915—May 1916

The tree will wither long before it fall,
The hull drives on, though the mast and sail be torn.

BYRON

We are savages; we have no laws.

PUSHKIN

CHAPTER 30

Six months after the invasion of Russia by Austria and Germany, a tall young man—his face solemn, his shoulders broad, his arms muscular—stood in a doorway of a railway carriage that had just arrived at Odessa's main station. It was the end of a long journey that had begun four and one-half months before on a boat in Jaffa. With thousands of other deportees and refugees, all of whom had been uprooted by the Great War, the youth had traveled by ship from Palestine to Egypt and then to Greece, and from there by train through Bulgaria and Rumania. For nineteen weeks the sad eyes of the eighteen-year-old young man had absorbed the ravages of war—endless days and nights of seeing nothing but human agony, accompanied by the grinding noise of the iron monsters charging north; at every depot the youth had been forced to beg for food or to steal it. Then he reached Russia, and finally Odessa. As the locomotive screeched into the station, the young man raced to the door, hoping he would find one kind face on the platform, a gesture of welcome from anyone at all. But wherever he looked he only saw soldiers, their faces apprehensive, confused. There were women crying everywhere, kissing their husbands or lovers good-bye while children marched around proudly, imitating the heroes they thought their fathers would be. As soon as he jumped down from the train the young man was surrounded by nervous chatter that reverberated off the walls of the cavernous building. He pushed his way through the waiting recruits, his dark skin, sun-bleached hair, and keen blue eyes making the soldiers appear even more doomed than they already looked. An officer shouted, and a hundred men stood up, grabbing their rifles and packs. They boarded a train which would take them to battlefields where another German assault awaited them. Opening the massive doors of the station which led to the city, the young man expected a glaring winter sun reflecting off the white stone buildings of Odessa. Instead, the sky was gray with clouds; everything looked worn and old. Nicholas Boulevard was dismal, jammed with carts, carriages, and the clamor of automobiles that belched smoke and fouled the air with the noxious odors of their exhausts. The streets were topped with the blackened remains of a week-old snowfall, and even the Exchange had become shabby. The young man passed the Opera House with its gilded cornices now tarnished, and the City Hall with its walls grimy with soot from the factory smoke that polluted the atmosphere day and night. Preobrazhenskaya Street, where vendors had once peddled their colorful wares, was dreary, ugly, its buildings dun-colored, decaying. The depression which had been companion to the young man for the last four and one half months grew stronger. He scraped his shoes against the ground as if he were trying to delay rounding the next corner.

Then a sudden break in the city's oppressive corridors made the young man pick up his pace. He hurried across a street toward a low open area. A speeding truck splattered him with slush and the young man stopped, momentarily wanting to chase the man, but a more powerful urge made him change his mind. He started to run, the canvas sack hanging from his shoulders slapping against his back. Passing through a gate, he moved along a narrow path flanked by rows of stone markers. The young man saw a thick old tree, its core ringed with two hundred lines. He slowed his pace and looked at the ground. He knelt and wiped away his tears with the sleeve of his coat. Touching the earth with callused hands, the young man read the inscription on a stone slab two yards away. His body shook as a childhood sorrow returned with clarity. He kissed the ground, not knowing where the rectangle he wanted ended and the next one began. Anguished, he got to his feet and stood staring at the snow-covered plot. Minutes later, he reluctantly whispered good-bye and promised that he would return. After one last glance at the grave that lay before him, he turned, and left the cemetery without looking back.

The instant the young man's feet touched the hard, snow-packed cobblestones of Khutorskaya Street, the street that bordered the cemetery and formed the eastern boundary of Moldavanka, he began to run. His long legs covered the ground in smooth strides. Turning right on Vuisoki Place, he was assailed by the wheezing of a delivery truck roughly idling before a warehouse whose windows had been broken and whose walls had cracked even more in the four years since he had seen it last. On Yekaterina Street, he searched for the store where he had once delighted in the scents of berries, plums, apples, oranges, and the score of other succulent fruits that had always been stacked in pyramids. The store was still there, but it was empty, its shelves bare and its windows covered with cobwebs. Tiraspolskaya Street was no better: garbage filled the gutters, and horse droppings littered the pavement where he used to play kickball. Thin slashes of light escaped through warped shutters fastened over windows in an attempt to keep the cold from becoming unbearable in the rooms beyond. Two cats fought in an alleyway over the remains of a fish, and a dog slinked sullenly, unable to find anything to eat. On the next block, a mounted detail of six soldiers, protected from the freezing weather by their furlined coats, chatted amiably among themselves. They stopped when they saw the young man running in their direction, watching him as he approached a small wooden house. Seeing him knock on the door they lost interest in him, spurring their horses forward as they continued their rounds. The young man knocked again, this time more loudly.

"Who is there?" a suspicious and cranky man's voice asked from behind the door.

"It's a surprise!"

"Who are you?" the voice shot back.

"If you don't open up right now, I will never come back!"

The doorknob turned slowly, and the door opened an inch; a curious eye peeked through the crack. The door was opened farther, and a frail old man of sixty, slightly stooped, his white hair sparse beneath his skullcap, appeared in the doorway. He inspected the stranger in front of him. "Is it you?" The man's long, wispy beard began to quiver, and his mouth twisted as he tried to decide if he should laugh or cry. "Is it really you?" His body began to shake. "My Smyelchak. You are my Smyelchak!" The man clutched the youth's arm.

"Yes, it's me," the young man exclaimed, hugging the old one, tears gathering in his eyes as he heard the nickname the old man had so lovingly given him years before. "Yes, it is Smyelchak," he said, the name conjuring up a thousand memories. For a moment the youth studied the old man, surprised to see him wearing a *yarmulke* and a beard.

"I've missed you so, my Smyelchak."

"I missed you, too, Rabbi."

The old man looked up at the youth, who towered above him. "You were such a little boy when you left Russia—how did you become a man so quickly?"

"Being tall does not make me a man."

The rabbi gazed at the youth lovingly. "It must, because when you were a boy you were short!"

Smiling, the youth again embraced the old man. "Come, Rabbi, let us go inside."

"Yes, so we can sit and talk, there is so much I want to know. But first you must eat, and after such a journey you will want to bathe and rest." The rabbi led the way into the house. "Every day I prayed for you, Smyelchak. Every day I asked God to keep you from harm, and to permit me to see you once more before I died. And look, He did both! I must get some wine so we can offer thanks to God, and so we can celebrate your homecoming."

Like a spindly-legged bird scampering across the ground, the rabbit hastened from the room. He called out to his visitor, but there was no reply, for the young man had heard nothing; his attention was focused on the room he knew so well. The first time he had seen it was when the rabbi moved into the house. Then everything was so shiny. The young man remembered how his father had helped the rabbi paint the house inside and out, had built bookcases for the rabbi's countless volumes, and moved his belongings from the Brody Synagogue to Moldavanka. Now everything looked so much older. The once virginal white walls had become creamy in color, and the room seemed smaller than the young man recollected. The furniture was exactly where it had been when he left Russia—the sofa still rested against the far wall, its green upholstery now faded and rubbed bare in places; above it hung the same washed-out print, a view of Odessa from atop the terraces. Two cloth-covered chairs, brown except for the armrests, which had been worn to a straw color, remained before the window that looked out onto Kherson Street. The cabinet with the glass doors, its shelves crammed full of old photographs and letters, still stood next to the bookcases. The oval rug, a beige weaving which the rabbi had so proudly selected himself, covered the center of the floor, the stain where the young man had dropped and broken a jar of jelly years before never having been completely removed. The youth smiled as he stared at the stain. Forgetting everything else, he wandered from the parlor, along a short narrow hallway, past the room where the rabbi slept, and into the next room.

Looking around, a sense of relief overcame the young man. Everything was just as he had left it. His room—the place where he had studied, and rested, slept and dreamed, for four years after his father's death—was the same. The poorly drawn pictures he had sketched of Odessa, the harbor, the rabbi, his father, were still tacked to the walls. The desk that he and the rabbi had constructed, and the wobbly chair that he had wanted so desperately and that the rabbi had bought for him, appeared undisturbed since the last time he had used them. Even the frayed bed covering, a spread with white sailboats floating across a sea of blue wool, had not been discarded. Hanging from a wall peg was his school uniform: a white duck suit, a broad leather belt with a brass buckle, and a white cap with a bright yellow badge. The young man recalled how much he had disliked attending the tedious classes at the Peterhof Academy for Boys. He had much preferred roaming the streets and alleyways of Moldavanka, excited by the throngs of chattering people, the odors of fruits, vegetables, cooking meats, fish, horses, and the sea air all pressed together into an invisible blanket, a comforter that made him feel secure. When the warm weather of spring embraced Odessa, the young man had often not gone to school at all, sneaking off to the seashore with friends to swim naked in the invigorating, winter-cold water. He was the only one who dared to swim as far as the breakwater, to clamber effortlessly up the rocky barrier and then dive back into the sea. When he finally confessed his truancies, and what he had done instead of attending classes, the rabbi nicknamed him Smyelchak—*Daredevil.* The young man removed a book from the shelf next to the desk; it felt comfortable in his rugged, work-worn hands. And when he opened it, the binding, broken from use, fell slack, revealing a map of Europe and all the lands which bordered the Mediterranean Sea. The youth placed his pinky on Odessa and stretched his thumb toward Palestine. His span reached way beyond the mark, the distance appearing minute. A look of sadness crossed the young man's face. He closed the book softly and returned it to the shelf.

"The day will come, Smyelchak, when you will return there."

The sound startled the young man and he turned around. The rabbi was standing just outside the doorway, his expression trying to console his guest's melancholy. "Come, my Smyelchak, take off your coat, put your bag on the floor, and sit quietly, and rest." The rabbi eagerly took the canvas bag from the youth's shoulder. "It is so heavy," the rabbi grunted, letting the bag slip to the floor.

"Everything I own is in it."

"Everything you own, my child, all that you will ever need, is within you." Taking the young man by the hand, the rabbi led him into the parlor. He picked up two glasses of dark red wine and handed one to his Smyelchak, and kept the other for himself. The rabbi raised his glass. *"Baruch atah Adonai—"*

"First I come home and find you wearing a *yarmulke* and a beard. Now I hear you blessing the wine. What has happened while I was away?" the young man gently mocked.

Ignoring the question—indeed, not having even heard it—the rabbi continued the prayer said before drinking wine, chanting with his eyes closed. "Blessed art Thou, O Lord our God, for giving us this wine." Upon finishing the blessing, the rabbi opened his eyes; there was a brilliant luster to them. "And blessed is the Lord for allowing the return of someone very special to me—my Smyelchak."

The elation on the rabbi's face, the unbounded joy in his eyes, erased the aching that had accompanied the young man ever since his exile from Palestine. And through tears he was unable to control, Grisha Moisei offered his own toast to the elderly man he had come to love dearly—to Rabbi Joshua Eleazar.

By the time Grisha had bathed and seated himself at the kitchen table, Rabbi Eleazar had put a bowl of cold borscht with a steaming boiled potato in it and a slice of thick black bread at each of the places.

"Now, Smyelchak, tell me about Palestine," the rabbi said, as he sat down across from Grisha.

"First tell me what has happened to you, to—"

"It is your life I want to hear about, Smyelchak. I already know about my life."

"And I know about my life, Rabbi." Grisha's tone was mournful. Absentmindedly, he cut his potato into small chunks.

"Why did you come home?" Eleazar asked.

"Because I had no choice. Because I was arrested and deported."

"By whom?"

"By the Turks. They arrested thousands of us when the war started."

"Did they hurt you?" inquired Eleazar, his face immediately beset by worry.

Grisha shook his head, his eyes dull. "Me? No. But they killed some and tortured more than a few. They put us in wire stockades. Jammed us together and kept us like that for days without food and only a few drops of water. Then they separated us according to nationality—Russians in one pen, Rumanians in another, Bulgarians in another. It was like sorting white cows from black ones."

"Why did they arrest you? Why did they send you back?" Eleazar asked anxiously.

"The pasha was afraid that we would form our own army there and initiate an attack against him. The Turks are allied with Germany, and the pasha—Djemal Pasha, Governor of Palestine and Syria, the Commander-in-Chief of the Fourth Imperial Turkish Army—considered us the enemy. He's a bastard! There was no need to deport us, to have his soldiers swoop down on us in the middle of the night, forcing us from our beds, and marching us off to stockades in Jaffa. We were certainly not his allies, but we were just as certainly not his enemy. We considered ourselves Palestinians—Jewish Palestinians—with no allegiance to either side."

"If the Tsar had been faced with the same problem, he would have killed all of you and been done with it," Rabbi Eleazar interjected.

Grisha looked anxiously at the rabbi without focusing his eyes on him. "The day before we were to be shipped off to Alexandria a man who was in the same stockade with me raced to the fence and began to scream. 'Tirza, I am here, Tirza!' Fifty yards away a young woman with an infant in her arms stopped to see who was calling. He cried out, "I am coming for you, Tirza!' and then, using every bit of strength he had, he tried to tear through the fence. The girl saw him and attempted to push her way through the crowds of Arabs and the Pasha's soldiers who ringed the compound. They laughed at her and pinched her breasts and buttocks. When she reached the line of guards that surrounded us, one of them held a bayonet against the baby and dared her to pass. Her husband was shouting 'I will kill them!' He shook the fence like a wild man, he cursed everyone, and we cheered him on. Suddenly whistles blew and twenty, maybe more, Turkish soldiers raced into the stockade. Everyone stopped to watch. The man was still crying his wife's name, still struggling to demolish the fence, until the first rifle butt smashed against the back of his neck." Grisha could not continue; he swallowed hard, as he recalled and recounted the scene. He sniffled and wiped his eyes with his hands. "The next morning, under guard, all of us except that fellow were rowed out to a steamer that was to take us to Alexandria. From the deck we could see Turkish soldiers dragging something to the center of the compound. There were poles every few feet that held up the fencing—tall, sturdy poles so that we could not knock them down and escape. I can still hear the winch hoisting the anchor from the sea, and the screws turning as the ship moved away. I looked back so I could watch Jaffa disappear. It's a beautiful sight from aboard ship. The Arab houses are made of stone, all the doorways and windows are arched, and there is a long wall at the edge of the water. The sun was just above the horizon. Everything appeared in silhouette, including that youth. He was hanging by his neck from the top of one of the fence-posts. You could see that he was still alive, and choking. His body kept jerking. Then it stopped. A breeze came up. Slowly he twirled round and round. He was still turning when we lost sight of land."

Grisha stopped talking. There was silence. Finally with

forced lightness Eleazar said: "You could have at least written to me to let me know where you were, or sent a telegram. It was thoughtless of you to make an old man like me worry as I did."

"Rabbi, when the war started, everything in Palestine stopped."

"And when you arrived at Alexandria—you could not send word from there?"

"The British were no different than the Turks. They put us in stockades, too—for our own protection, they said. And when we reached Greece there was not time to do anything but take the first train north; no one knew if there would be any tracks left the next day. And then we entered the war zones and there were only the tracks—endless miles of track and endless streams of homeless, hopeless people."

"After the war, if you can, will you return to Palestine?"

"Yes." Grisha smiled. "You can tell that I came for a long stay. I brought one shirt and one extra pair of pants. You know, I took no more than that with me when I ran away. The only difference is, then everything was a lot smaller." Grisha laughed softly as he remembered how, bundled in a fur jacket, in the dead of a winter night, he had slipped out of the house in Kodoma. Often he had daydreamed about running away to Palestine. During the school term, when he lived with the rabbi in Odessa, he would wander along the docks, imagining himself on the deck of a freighter as it plowed through the Black Sea—its destination, Jaffa. How strange, Grisha thought to himself, that he should have chosen to flee Russia in the midst of winter, when he was in Kodoma for the midterm recess. *Why was it then that I finally found the courage to run away?* A dark moodiness crossed Grisha's face. He grimaced and shook his head. For the first time he allowed himself to know the truth of why he had decided go then.

Rabbi Eleazar placed his hands on Grisha's, interrupting his thoughts. "Do not brood, Smyelchak. It solves nothing."

"I crept out of my father's house before dawn; I did not even leave a note."

"Did you know that when your mother awoke and found you gone, she sent someone to ride after you to find you and bring you back?"

"It was a waste of time. I met a peasant driving a sled who was going to Odessa, and he gave me a ride all the way."

"And did you know that if it had not been for Vassili, your mother would have stopped you anyway? She wanted to send a telegram to the Odessa police asking them to search for you; she suspected what your intentions were. But Vassili convinced her not to. He persuaded her that it was wrong for her to force you to stay in Russia."

"Rabbi, how do you know all this?"

"Your mother also sent me a telegram, asking if you were with me or if I knew where you were. I, too, surmised where you were going, but I could not lie, not even to your mother, so I never replied to her telegram."

"How do you know so much, Rabbi?"

"Your sister told me."

"Daniella?"

"I will never understand how a fourteen-year-old boy was able to make his way by himself to Palestine."

"Daniella told you? When? Where?"

"And how he survived, by himself, in a land so hostile."

"Rabbi, I want to know about Daniella."

For several seconds there was an uncomfortable silence.

"Isn't Daniella with my mother? Didn't she go to St. Petersburg?"

"Petrograd, Grisha. Not St. Petersburg. The Tsar changed the name of the capital because he thought St. Petersburg sounded too German." Eleazar snorted. "If Nicholas worried more about the war and less about changing the names of cities, perhaps he might win the war!"

"Rabbi, *where is Daniella*?"

A long sigh escaped Eleazar's lips. "She has a life of her own now."

"Where?"

"Here, in Odessa."

"My sister is in Odessa? Why? Doing what? She's not living here with you, and she can't be alone. She is so young. Rabbi, stop fumbling with your hands and tell me about my sister!"

"She is involved with the workers' union," Eleazar said angrily.

Grisha raised his eyebrows with curiosity, waiting for the rabbi to go on.

"Your sister organizes factory workers to strike against the government."

"And she lives by herself—at the age of sixteen?"

"Today, Smyelchak, boys of sixteen are dying in the war. And girls of sixteen are already women." There was a great sadness to the rabbi's voice.

"The war!" Grisha banged his fists against the table. "With a little luck Germany will crush Russia!"

"Do not let anyone hear you say that, Smyelchak. The Jews are already being blamed for Russian defeats. Every day there are reports of another one of us being arrested as a German sympathizer. The Tsar has spies everywhere."

"I do not want to discuss the war now."

"You are right. We will have months to discuss it while they fight it."

"I want to talk about Daniella."

"Smyelchak, why must you know so soon of all that has changed?"

"What will I gain by waiting?"

Eleazar shook his head, and in a voice filled with resignation he said, "Daniella ran away from Kodoma, too. Just before your mother and Vassili left for Petrograd. She ran away with a young peasant. Twice she came to see me, to talk, to hear news of you. A few times I went to see her. But she refused to see me. I have not seen nor spoken to Daniella in a very long while. You see, Smyelchak," he finished slowly, "I have no reason to frequent places belonging to Bolsheviks."

Startled, Grisha flushed, his mouth drawn into a tight line.

"I am sorry I could not tell you something else about your sister."

Grisha picked up his bowl and quickly drank the tepid borscht.

"Smyelchak, why don't we talk of something pleasant?"

Grisha glanced at Eleazar.

"Such as what you did in Palestine."

Eleazar's mentioning Palestine again caused Grisha to picture himself fleeing Kodoma; the image merged into his last memory of his sister—a child of twelve, sullen and remote, her young face and slender body always rigid with a bitter ferocity. For the first time in months Grisha thought of his mother, and Vassili. And then Munya, his baby brother who was treated like a girl, dressed in tailored velvet suits and silk shirts. A surge of fury immobilized Grisha. A hatred he thought had dissipated long ago returned to him. Deliberately, with each word enunciated precisely, Grisha said: "Rabbi, I do not want to speak of Palestine. I do not want to speak of Daniella. I do not want to speak of anything."

"What do you want to do?"

"I just want to sit back and have you tell me why, when I left, you were a rabbi only in your *shul*. But now you even pray in your home."

"And will that make you happy, my Smyelchak?"

"I don't know. But I also don't know what else might."

CHAPTER 31

Instead of finding respite from the shock of his ejection from Palestine and the grueling journey back to Russia, Grisha Moisei found himself assaulted by painful memories, and worse, disquieting realities. The most calamitous to Grisha was the discovery that he was a prime candidate for conscription into the Russian army.

Grisha knew well the grim statistics of the war. Everywhere people spoke of the staggering losses Russia was suffering; more than a million troops already dead, wounded, or captured. And now the Russian army was being forced to retreat, slogging its way through blizzards and chest-high snowdrifts, continually giving up ground until the land of western Russia looked like a sea of gray waves rolling eastward. The thought of donning the uniform of a Russian soldier and being sent off to war agonized Grisha. He could think of nothing more wasteful than to be maimed or killed in defense of the Tsar. The only alternative he had was to become a student, to enter a *gymnasium,* where he would be legally exempt from military service. But the tuition was far more than the amount of money available to him. In fact, Grisha needed to pay two tuitions—the custom that a Jew had to pay not only his own tuition but that of a non-Jew still existed.

Rabbi Eleazar offered Grisha every ruble he had, adding that he would appeal to his congregation to make donations for the cost of his education. Unwilling to protect himself by taking money from those to whom a kopeck often meant the difference between living and dying, Grisha refused. He considered finding a job, but he knew that long before he would be able to save enough money, he would already be in uniform somewhere on the front lines. Tormented by this dilemma, Grisha came to the only conclusion possible: he would write to his mother, announcing his return to Odessa and requesting enough money to enter school and protect his life.

For days Grisha debated his decision. Several times he discussed it with Eleazar. Each time the rabbi avoided answering by asking God for guidance. Annoyed by Eleazar's refusal to give him counsel, Grisha became moody, gloomy, his painful ambivalence driving him to hide in his room and suffer in solitude. There he tried to imagine what would happen if he received a reply from his mother, if she came to visit him. And almost continuously Grisha thought of his father. Sometimes at night he would walk for hours, wandering to the sea where he would stand at its edge and shout at the convoys that he knew were slipping past him in the darkness, venting his hatred at the war. But it was far more than Russia's battles he despised. Grisha had woven together a tapestry of the lives of Soybel and Vassili Viska from the profusion of letters his mother had first sent him after his arrival in Palestine and the very few notes he had received from her in his last year there. He also recalled the bits of information Rabbi Eleazar had passed on from the newspaper articles about Vassili Viska—a great Russian patriot—and an account emerged of his mother and Vassili that left Grisha numb with rage.

In the years between 1907 and 1914 unprecedented economic growth had transformed Russia from a country with great potential as a source of industry to an important member of the European economic community. To fulfill its new role, Russia needed a way of transporting raw materials and finished goods not only within the country, but beyond. The most obvious means of transportation—the sea—was not feasible, for Russia lacked adequate harbor facilities. This meant that another transportation system needed to be developed. The only viable alternative was the railroad, an industry sorely in need of modernization. Due to the lack of technical skills and money, Russia turned to her closest ally, France, for engineers, designers, and economic aid to undertake this vast project. The only thing missing was a Russian of sufficient competence to oversee this considerable venture.

Because of the years he had spent in France, his association with French officials and financiers, and his increasing position of power in the international import-export markets, Vassili Viska was called upon by Russia to act as an advisor and emissary between St. Petersburg and Paris. By the beginning of the war Vassili had traveled between the two capitals dozens of times, rarely visiting Odessa. In 1910 he sold his villa in the Black Sea city, having decided to make his permanent residence St. Petersburg. A year later, when he married Soybel Moisei, and informed her that she would have to leave Kodoma and accompany him north, Vassili's new wife joyfully agreed. By March of that year Soybel Viska had become the mistress of the Rastrelli Palace in Russia's most important metropolis.

With great ease and uncommon grace Soybel moved from her life in Kodoma to the world of diplomats, high officials, and military men. Her beauty and charm impressed and delighted both Vassili's friends and his business acquaintances. The parties she gave were lavish, the cuisine—whether *sterlet* from the Volga, pheasant from Hungary, or *coq au vin*—was exquisitely prepared. Strolling musicians were always hired for these affairs, and often dance troupes also entertained the guests. Once she arranged for a theatrical group to perform Molière's *Le Malade Imaginaire,* though later—and much to Soybel's dismay—a performance of *Le Bourgeois Gentilhomme* had to be canceled due to an emergency meeting of the war cabinet after the Germans advanced to within twelve miles of Warsaw.

Reveling in the social whirl of the royal city, thriving on attending the ballet, opera, theater, mingling with the most powerful men in the country, gave Soybel what had been missing from her life. More than once she explained that to Grisha in her letters to him. Indeed, Soybel's longest and most effusive letter to Grisha described in minute detail the Tsar's Tricentennial Ball, to which she and Vassili had been invited.

> If only you could have seen it for yourself. Officers splendidly uniformed in blue, green, and scarlet, dancing quadrilles with the young unmarried girls, all madonna-like in white. Everywhere, there were court officials dressed in black and gold, generals with chests armored with glittering decorations. And ladies, duchesses, Grand Dames, in billowing satin dresses, with jewels on their wrists, heads, necks, ears, fingers, and waists. Servants with silver platters offered glasses of champagne and *hors-d'oeuvres* of cold sturgeon, stuffed eggs, caviar. Along with the usual music—gypsy melodies, Viennese waltzes—a new rhythm was played—the tango. It is the latest rage in the capital. For the first time in Russian history, my dear Grisha, the tango is bringing the "right couples" together with an outward appearance of innocence. You cannot imagine how amusing it is, to we who know the truth, to see the cuckold warmly applauding his wife's indiscretions, which can now be so masterfully camouflaged by this wonderful dance.

Apparently Soybel enjoyed sharing court gossip with her son, since she wrote in the same letter that—despite Nicholas's decree that French was no longer to be used at court and all state business was to be conducted in Russian—"The instant the little Emperor, he is only five feet seven inches tall, you know, but as I was saying, the moment he is out of earshot nothing *but* French is spoken."

Soybel also mentioned Grigory Rasputin, ignoring the mystic's increasing stranglehold on the royal family and revealing instead that the monk's ability to please women was well known and that his favorite ploy—aside from rape—was to explain that by sleeping with him a woman would commit a sin, and then by renouncing him and thus the sin, she would be purified. Soybel closed the letter with "A thousands kisses and my love." More than a month passed before Grisha destroyed the letter. He had read it everyday, purposely allowing it to infuriate him, using his hatred for his mother to pay homage to his father. Finally he burned the letter and hurled the ashes into the wind that swirled over the Mediterranean Sea toward Russia.

Along with the spreading rumors of war there was a dwindling of communications between the Rastrelli Palace and the barren land of Palestine. And when Austria's June 1914 ultimatum was made public and predictions that war was inevitable gripped St. Petersburg, Soybel's already sporadic messages to her son ceased completely; having obtained commitments from France and England to come to his aid if Russia were attacked, Tsar Nicholas declared that internal preparations for war should begin. Because of his expert knowledge of the railway system, Vassili Viska was immediately placed in charge of military rail transport. From June 1914 until August, Vassili and his staff worked feverishly, gathering reams of statistics about the numbers of railroad cars and engines, their present deployment, exact mileage of track and its condition, its position in relation to population centers and proximity to the most likely points along Russia's eastern border for Austrian and German invasions. When war was finally declared, Vassili became invaluable. Day and night he toiled to solve the immense logistical problems involved with transporting men and supplies from all over Russia to the war zones. The worse Russia fared in the war, the greater was the pressure on Vassili to increase the efficiency of a railway network that was woefully inadequate for such a critical enterprise.

Soybel's life also became hectic. Her calendar was a maze of impromptu gatherings for government ministers, military leaders, political architects who appeared at the Rastrelli Palace to share with Vassili their grave concern for Russia and offer advice on how best to defend the country. Along with the wives of other men of influence, including the Empress herself, Soybel devoted four afternoons a week doing volunteer work in hospital wards crowded with wounded soldiers. Soybel read to them, wrote letters for them, soothed their fears, and she wrapped scores of bandages for those who were yet to be injured. At home Soybel acted as Vassili's sounding board, his confidante, often staying up until dawn with him as he struggled with a problem. And, too, she was his wife, lover, and mother to a seven-year-old son, Munya. As the battles became more virulent and Russia's losses more severe, Soybel barely had a moment to herself, directing all her energies in support of her husband, neglecting everything else, including correspondence with her firstborn child. Indeed, after Germany's victorious initial attack on Russia, Soybel Viska gave no indication at all that she had any family other than her husband and son in Petrograd.

At the end of February 1915 Rabbi Eleazar handed Grisha an envelope addressed to number 19 Kherson Street, Moldavanka, and postmarked Petrograd. Dumbfounded, Grisha looked inquiringly at Eleazar.

"It can only be from your mother, Smyelchak."

"But—"

"I wrote to her."

"Why? I should have—"

"Would you have really written to her, Smyelchak? Or would you have been sent off to war still trying to decide whether you love your own life more than you hate your mother?"

Grisha clutched the letter tightly, the paper feeling as warm as the memory of his mother's flesh. A hush came to Grisha's mind and he recalled a vision of his mother from long ago. Grisha and Daniella had been sitting quietly in the drawing room of their parents' suite in Odessa's Hotel London. Waiting for Aleksandr to finish dressing, Soybel entered the airy chamber alone, smiling broadly, her eyes consuming everything they saw. Soybel's yellow dress made her long black hair look like the center of a sunflower. Her face shone, with just a hint of rouge highlighting her cheekbones. A shade of pink, more subtle than the petals of a rose, colored her moist and slightly parted lips. Without hesitation, Soybel swept toward her son, warmly pressing her lips to his cheek; the heat of her flesh grazed his skin and her perfume enveloped him. Now, as he stood in Eleazar's house, Grisha shut his eyes, still smelling her perfume and the fragrance of her flesh. He felt breathless, remembering how beautiful his mother was, recalling how much he had once loved her.

"Smyelchak, why don't you open the letter?"

Without thinking, Grisha carefully opened the envelope. His shock was multiplied when, along with a letter, Grisha pulled out a bank draft for a considerable sum.

"The letter, Smyelchak, what does it say?"

Grisha slowly unfolded the expensive stationery, his vision blurring at the sight of his mother's handwriting. His body suddenly chilled with sweat, his fingers shook; cautiously, hungrily, Grisha read his mother's words. When he had finished reading, Grisha handed the letter to Rabbi Eleazar without a word and walked away. With heavy steps he left the house and plodded into the gray, damp afternoon. *Momma, If you missed me so much while I was gone, if you are so overjoyed that I have returned to Russia, if you are so remorseful for not having written to me this last year—then why, Momma—damn it, Momma—why do you still write to me about yourself, and Vassili, and Munya, and not just about you and me? And why must I come to Petrograd with the money you sent me? What gives you the right to expect me to live with you and Vassili? Momma, if you so dearly want to see me, then you can come to Odessa!* The image of an application for entrance to the Nicholas Gymnasium beckoned to Grisha.

Momma, I will not use your money for fancy clothes and a ticket to Petrograd, because I am going to use your money to go to school so I can stay out of the army. I would pay ten tuitions not to have to fight for Russia. And if you and the great Vassili Viska do not like that, then you can take my place at the front lines. You save Russia! Do you hear me, Momma? The sounds of cannons boomed in Grisha's head. The words of his mother's letter screamed at him like the deadly noise of mortars.

I was so afraid when I ran away from home, Momma. When the sailors found me hiding on the boat in Constantinople and threatened to send me back to Russia, I swore that I would do anything to prevent it. Because I refused to fail at what I had promised myself I would do. And now you want me to accept Vassili's offer of an appointment to a military academy so I can become an officer in the Russian army? Will you never know your own son, Momma? Will you never understand why, when the captain of the boat wired you for money for my passage—either to Jaffa or back to Odessa—I did not sleep for three days until your answer arrived? Oh, Momma, I hated you so from the moment I slipped out of our house in Kodoma until the very moment your cable arrived. But when the captain told me you had sent the money for my passage to Palestine, I cried. I actually missed you, Momma. I actually loved you.

The crashing of waves bombarded Grisha's memory, and the glimmering image of a fourteen-year-old boy hanging over the rail of a rusting old Russian cargo ship lying at anchor three hundred yards off the shores of Jaffa caught hold of him. He saw a dozen longboats racing toward the steamer, bobbing precariously as they came alongside, waiting to accept whatever cargo or passengers that had come to Palestine. The boy scurried down the metal ladder which clung to the side of the ship, stepped into one of the boats, and settled himself next to a withered old man. One by one, the longboats pushed off from the steamer, the grimy ship the last outpost of Russia. In each of the small boats there were passengers, most of them old and none as young as fourteen. As the slender wooden craft rode the last waves up onto the beach and their bottoms grated on the sand, several men on shore grabbed the prows, an unofficial customs group pulling the boats high onto the land to prevent the sea from taking them back. Hand grasped hand, or elbow, or arm; the very old were the first to set foot on the Holy Land: all of them fell to their knees and kissed the ground. Grisha was unable to move, still not believing that he was actually in Palestine. *Poppa, Poppa, look!* He trembled as the roar of the waves filled his ears. *Poppa, this is what we dreamed about!* The awesome power of the giant sea rising like mountains, then curling into graceful hillsides as it rushed toward the land, made Grisha shiver. *Can you hear the noise, Poppa?* The incessant roar of wave after crashing wave deafened Grisha. "I am here, Poppa!" he shouted aloud at the top of his lungs. "I am here." Then, as the waves receded, there was a silence more serene, more peaceful, than any Grisha Moisei had ever known.

CHAPTER 32

Angrily, Grisha Moisei kicked his way from Moldavanka to the sea. He was repulsed by the odors of meat pies and steaming tea which rose from the metal containers strapped to the backs of insistent street vendors. The women who clutched ikons of St. Gerassim, their coats reeking of pungent incense, irritated Grisha as they brushed past him. He thought of Palestine and the brilliant sun glinting off endless stretches of sand. He pictured Jaffa, the ancient Arab city with its crowded bazaars, narrow, crooked streets, and the men whose long robes, covering them from head to foot, made the city look like a sea of bobbing whitecaps. He remembered the women, swathed in black, scurrying like schools of frightened fish, their veils showing only dark eyes that constantly flitted about, sometimes resting on an unsuspecting man's face like a cautious butterfly. Grisha grimaced, repelled by the thought of being shoved and pushed by the crowds of arguing men, darting children, donkeys, and merchants who loudly hawked anything they thought might bring a price. Open shops and stalls overflowing with foods he had never before seen still revolted him; the memory of the unceasing heavy aroma of burning lamb mixed with the sickly sweetness of dates, oranges, sweat, and garbage were things he would never forget.

His thoughts of the Holy Land led Grisha to think of Solomon Levin. More than once they had shared a meal in Palestine; in a land so small, and with so few Jews, there was nothing unusual about long-lost unseen friends meeting once again. Each time they met, Solomon would be on his way to another remote settlement in the Hula Valley; he was determined to cure the Jewish pioneers of the malaria they had contracted in Palestine's mosquito-infested northern swamp. During those few hours they spent together, Grisha and Solomon reminisced but little, their conversations overwhelmingly concerned with the present. And each time Grisha saw him, Solomon looked more grizzled than the time before, more resolute, his posture—whether he was on foot or astride his horse—always taut. All he owned he carried with him: a rifle, a pistol, one bag containing medical supplies and another with a single change of clothing and ammunition. After the outbreak of the war Grisha expected to see Solomon herded among the rest of the Jews in the compound at Jaffa. He never appeared. In Alexandria, Grisha again expected Solomon to be there. He was not. Knowing Solomon's temper and having heard him tell how he had fought off Arab attackers several times, Grisha wondered if Solomon had resisted deportation. He wondered if . . .

Unwilling to pursue his thoughts, Grisha forced the memory of Solomon Levin from his mind. Immediately the image of Rabbi Eleazar nagged at him, irritated him. Ever since his return to Odessa, the rabbi had pestered him with a profusion of questions about Palestine—about the Jews there, the aura of God there, the meaning of God there. But most bothersome to Grisha were Eleazar's relentless attempts to woo him into joining in the rabbi's mystical search for God.

Initially, Grisha was profoundly moved by Eleazar's explanation of his return to religion and his adoration of the Cabala, Jewish mysticism. The rabbi's unveiling of how his life had evolved since the death of Aleksandr touched Grisha deeply. He hung onto every word as Eleazar explained his fear at no longer having someone on whom he could rely for moral support, and, more importantly, with whom he could discuss his own destiny. Eleazar revealed that while he was teaching Grisha the history, language, and an appreciation of the religion of the Israelites, he, too, felt as if he were learning those things for the first time. An urge to delve once again into the Talmud gnawed at Eleazar, and oftentimes he took down one of its sixty-six volumes at random and scanned its pages, finding new meaning and fresh inspiration that his own youthful arrogance had kept hidden from him. The rabbi explained that other incidents further increased his desire to return to God—Grisha's flight to Palestine, the commitment of one so young to a Jewish ideal, had caused Eleazar to ponder about what things, what *one* thing, of significance he had accomplished as a Jew. The answer demoralized him. Aram Zubóv had also inspired the rabbi, for the perseverance of the militant Bundist had begun to produce results; Aram finally attracted to himself a handful of men and boys who were willing to form a partisan group, all of them solemnly swearing to risk their lives in the defense of Moldavanka. But what had swayed Eleazar most was the remorse he felt at having devised a concept of God to satisfy his profane desire for material wealth. And so, Rabbi Joshua Eleazar transcended his intellect and strode into the enigma of his own being, trying to draw everyone he met along with him to help bolster his newfound courage.

The blaring of tugboat whistles, sonorous steamship horns, and the clacking of machinery from Odessa's harbor interrupted Grisha's thoughts. Trying to awaken himself from the dullness brought on by wallowing in unpleasant memories, he breathed deeply and tightened the muscles in his arms, liking the hardness they had gained from setting miles of stone in shifting sands for roads that someday might be finished. The calluses on his hands made Grisha yearn to be far from Russia, digging more ditches to irrigate the desert. The noises of the port drove him back toward Moldavanka, the songs of the sea painfully reminding him of the impenetrable wall the war had created. Grisha felt constricted, like a prisoner caged in a cell whose walls moved ceaselessly inward. His path led him into the section where the laborers and factory workers lived; the streets were as filthy as those in Moldavanka, the houses and tenements as shabby. Grisha stopped before an old building, a squalid remnant of better days that was wedged between a church and a long row of empty stores. He opened the door and stepped inside.

A steady hum of voices filled the corridor. Grisha followed it into a large room where dozens of people were busily involved in as many different activities. The walls were covered with posters and slogans demanding the downfall of the government and the overthrow of the Tsar. Pamphlets were neatly stacked on long wooden tables, and yellow copies of Lenin's newspaper, *Iskra,* were strewn about. The people worked feverishly, some writing while others edited. Several were arguing, their loud voices accentuated by emphatic gestures. In the rear of the room stood a hand-cranked printing press. A young girl, her black hair tied up in a knot, whirled the handle as fast as she could. Her face was unusually pretty, but she seemed old and haggard, disillusioned. She wore a loose blouse and pants stuffed into knee-high boots. Grisha watched the girl for a minute, then, taking a deep breath, he approached her.

"Daniella?"

The press drowned out his words.

"Daniella?" Grisha tapped his sister's shoulder.

Daniella looked around, and when she saw who it was, she brought the machine to a halt and turned to face her brother. With arms outstretched, Grisha went to hug his sister. But Daniella made no move to embrace him; her contemptuous look caused Grisha to halt in mid-step, and he dropped his hands awkwardly to his sides.

"I was wondering when you would get around to visiting me," Daniella said, her voice husky and tinged with sarcasm.

"You knew I was in Odessa?"

"For more than a week now, am I right?" Daniella laughed, the sound a curt underscoring to her words. "Eleazar has been very busy."

"I know."

"You must still be very special to him. He has never come here before because I am a Bolshevik. You do know that I am a Bolshevik, don't you?"

"Yes. Eleazar told me you were a Bolshevik," Grisha whispered, not liking the sound of the word.

"And what else did he tell you?"

"Daniella, let's go outside and talk."

"Why? Here we share everything. We have no secrets!"

"But we have not seen each other for years. It is impossible for us to say everything standing here."

"There is not that much we have to say to each other, Grisha. Just hello, how are you, and good-bye."

Hurt by Daniella's response, shocked by her coldness, Grisha took a step back. A tough young man of about twenty came toward them.

"Anton, this is my brother, Grisha. Grisha, I would like you to meet Anton. He is my lover."

"So, you are Grisha—the brother who ran away to Palestine," said Anton, his voice nasal and caustic. He ran his fingers through his close-cropped hair. "It's a shame you wasted your time there; you could have spent it building a Palestine here."

Grisha tried to return the young man's unwavering gaze but was unable to; Anton's colorless eyes seemed unpredictable and dangerous. "It would not have been the same," Grisha said.

"Nor should it be!" Anton laughed. "I was not talking about a Zionist Palestine here. Just a place where everyone lives in dignity and decency. The world needs Zionists as little as it needs Christians or capitalists," Anton added. "And of all the people in the world, the Jews should want communism more than anyone. They should be the *first* ones to sacrifice their lives, to repay mankind for the sins they have committed with their treachery and exploitation."

"And what should those who want to remain Jews or Christians do?" Grisha asked, not knowing how to refute the arguments Anton hurled at him.

"Bolshevism has no room for religion. Throughout history, religion has made people slaves," Anton replied as if he had memorized a pamphlet.

"Then Bolshevism becomes the new religion," Grisha stated evenly, feeling uneasy under Anton's scrutiny.

"Yes." Anton smiled, liking the thought. "You might say that."

"And who will be the leader of these Bolsheviks when they gain control of Russia?"

"Control of the world. Not just Russia. Things will be changed so people everywhere can be free!" Anton's voice quivered with excitement.

"And will the Jews be treated like everyone else?" asked Grisha, his question a reflexive response.

"Are you that ignorant? There won't be any Jews, or Christians, or any religion! Do you think that Lenin has relegated himself to a life of poverty in Switzerland, preparing for the revolution, just so religion can be saved? Do you think that in the last three years we have started nearly ten thousand strikes, have fought the police and the army, for an anachronism like God? If we supported an idea as outmoded as God then we would also support the war and an idea as prehistoric as the autocracy, and we support neither!"

"And if I want to remain a Jew?"

"Then you cannot be a Bolshevik!" shouted Anton as everyone else in the room applauded. Grisha glanced around the room and a feeling of apprehension came over him.

"Don't be afraid," Anton said, shrewdly sizing up Grisha. "You will change your mind. Everyone will, when they see there is no other way. Unfortunately, for the last several years most Russians have been lulled to sleep by prosperity, by the naive belief that the peasants have ceased their violence because they are satisfied with their lot. The war is changing all that. Russia is again awakening. *We* are awakening Russia, to be ready for the arrival of Lenin. And mark my words, when the time is right, he will come. And when he comes, we will be ready."

"Does Momma know what you are doing, how you are thinking?" Grisha asked Daniella, struggling to find something to say.

"I don't know, and I don't care."

"Why should her mother know anything about her?" Anton interrupted.

"Yes, why should I tell my mother anything? When did she ever care about me?" Daniella added bitterly. "When did Poppa ever care about me?"

The unhappiness in his sister's voice visibly affected Grisha.

"Do you remember when we were children, Grisha, and Poppa took us all to the club so the two of you could go sailing—the time that Grandmamma and Grandpoppa went with us?"

Grisha nodded. He pictured his father.

"I wanted to go sailing, too. But Poppa said no, because it was too dangerous. So I remained behind, by myself. Momma went for a walk with Grandpoppa. And Grandmomma Naomi was painting a picture of the sea, and of you and Poppa sailing the *Golub*. Nobody even looked at me. So I went for a walk out onto the dock, and I fell into the water. Everyone noticed me then. Even strangers. Do you remember that, Grisha?"

Again he nodded his head, his eyes drawn to Daniella's hands as they twisted the material of her blouse.

"I did not fall off the dock, Grisha. I *jumped*!"

Daniella paused for a moment to let her words sink in. She relished the dismay in her brother's face.

"Even Poppa cared about me that day. When the two of you finally returned and they told him what had happened, he looked so frightened. I can still feel Poppa's arms around me as he held me close to keep me warm. I think that is the last good memory I have of him." Daniella clenched her hands so tightly that her knuckles turned white.

The entire room was quiet. Grisha breathed heavily, certain that everyone was looking at him.

"As long as I can remember I always wanted Poppa to like me, to play with me. But he was always too busy with you. I wanted you to like me, Grisha, to spend time with me. I used to love you. I once thought that, next to Poppa, you were the best person in the world. When you ran away, I was so happy for you. The only thing I wished was that you had taken me with you—and then you did not even write one letter to me while you were gone. Not a word. But you wrote to Momma. Why not to me? Didn't you care about me?"

"I rarely wrote to Momma, but every time I did, I always asked about you," Grisha said softly, knowing how lame his excuse was.

"But I am not Momma, Grisha. Nor am I anyone else. I am me! And I want to know when someone will care just about me. I need that."

"Poppa loved you. And Momma—"

"Momma is a whore!"

Unprepared to hear aloud what he himself secretly felt, Grisha was stunned by Daniella's accusation. His sister sneered, her expression brutally reminding him of what she had told him one Christmastime long ago, the Christmas of the year he had run away.

"Didn't Momma write to you about what she did while you were gone? Oh, until she married Vassili, of course, she ran the granary. She loved taking charge of everything, controlling the lives of the peasants, having power over them. She was so busy with her ledgers, her profits, that she never had time for me. But she was never too busy for Vassili and Munya. Didn't she tell you how often she took Munya to Odessa or Petrograd just so she could sleep with Vassili? They were not even married yet, but that never bothered Momma. Of course the first time she slept with Vassili she *was* married—to Poppa!"

Grisha's mind reeled, the echo of Daniella's words ringing in his head.

They were almost the same words she had whispered to him years before, and now he felt the same sudden stab of pain, the incredible anguish as he imagined his father's agony.

"When Momma returned from her trips," Daniella went on, "she always brought me a present—for being a good girl and not giving the servants trouble, she said. Why didn't she take me with her as she did Munya? Because Vassili adored Munya, that is why. And that is precisely what Momma wanted—because she still does not know if Munya is Vassili's child or Poppa's."

"That is not true!" Grisha stammered, unaware that he was defending his mother in an attempt to erase his father's suffering, to ease his own suffering.

"But it is, Grisha. Why do you think Poppa left the house and rode through a *samjot*? To kill Vassili, that's why."

"How do you know that was why he went?"

"Wouldn't you? If your wife told you she was carrying someone else's child?"

"He was going to Palestine then! That is why he went."

"Then why didn't he take you with him?"

Grisha stopped short; his difficulty in breathing made him incapable of speaking. His head began to ache. "I do not believe you," he managed to say.

Daniella shrugged her shoulders. "What do I care?"

For an awkward moment Grisha looked at his sister as if he expected her to tell him she had been joking, but her unwavering look and the determined set of her mouth proved that she was not going to retract her words. And he knew they were true. He had heard enough of that brutal argument between his parents to have reached the same conclusion, but until now he had forced himself to deny it. Grisha wanted to turn and leave, but he did not want the others to see how deeply he had been hurt. Anton's voice broke the silence.

"All right, we have heard enough of Daniella's sad tale. Let's get back to work. Now!"

Instantly the hum of business began again.

"You have work, too, Daniella," Anton added.

She looked at Anton, then at Grisha, and wordlessly started the press rolling.

Grisha watched his sister, noticing the sadness in her eyes. More than anything he wanted to apologize to Daniella for ignoring her, not only while he was in Palestine, but throughout her entire life. As Daniella cranked the handle of the printing press, the machine's rhythm seemed to repeat 'I am sorry, I am sorry.' Grisha ached to echo those words, but something prevented him from uttering that simple atonement. As if a great weight rested on his shoulders, Grisha sighed. "I am going, Daniella." The racket of the press made his words unintelligible. Daniella looked at her brother. He nodded his head and silently tried to express his sorrow. His sister's face remained expressionless, and with a good-bye that she saw more than heard, Grisha turned away and left the room. For a moment, Daniella stared at the doorway, hoping that Grisha would come back. *You are as lonely as I am,* she said to herself. A fresh stack of pamphlets filled the bin at the end of the press. Automatically, Daniella went to remove them, lifting the sheets so as not to smear her blouse with ink.

"Bring them here!" shouted Anton from across the room.

Daniella studied Anton. His blunt manner still attracted her, but she realized that despite all his ambitions he would never amount to much. *He is too busy proving how important he is now to be planning for the future,* she thought as she approached him.

"I'll take these with me," he said, scanning the top sheet. "And hand them out to the workers at the munitions factory when they leave to go home."

Like a puppet, Daniella nodded her head up and down, thankful that Anton had not asked her to distribute the leaflets, despising having to stand in the cold for an hour or more until the last worker had been given another Bolshevik pamphlet.

"I will see you about seven," Anton added.

Daniella wondered if he would arrive drunk or sober, alone or with a group of comrades who would keep her awake all night with their pompous talk of how they were going to overthrow the government.

"We'll spend a quiet night by ourselves." Anton gave Daniella a seductive look.

Daniella thought that she would prefer it if they had company. Anton returned to whatever he had been writing, dismissing her. With nothing else to do, Daniella went back to the press. As she crossed the room she noticed how cheerless it looked, its tan walls chipped and stained from years of neglect; a dim bulb hanging overhead was the sole source of light. A sofa stood precariously on three legs against one wall, with several of its springs poking through the bottom. A thin mattress rested on a wooden box-frame in a corner by a table littered with ashtrays overflowing with cigarette stubs, books, and half a loaf of stale bread. *Anton would be happy spending the rest of his life here. The boss of nothing!* Dejected, Daniella continued the thankless task of running the press. She whirled the handle faster and faster until the noise sounded like that of a train. *I want someone people will notice!* A fragment of her mother's face disturbed Daniella's mind. *I want someone everyone else wants!* The crank whipped her arm around at its own speed, its momentum controlling her. Daniella's thoughts froze, the motion of her arm hypnotizing her. She laughed; a peculiar vision of Anton becoming enmeshed in the printing press coursing through her mind. She imagined everyone she knew being crushed by the rollers, falling into the bin as flat as sheets of paper, and covered with words. Distracted, she let her hand slip from the crank; it smacked against her wrist, making her cry out in pain. Free of guidance the handle whirred even faster. Daniella looked at her wrist, afraid she had broken a bone. Seeing only a blotch of ugly red, she looked back at the revolving crank. It slowed down and, as if it were exhausted, creaked to a stop. She stared at it, also feeling tired. She pictured scores of people with their skins imprinted with words. *That is all anyone is—words! Everything they do is just words. Their promises are words. Their threats.* Daniella choked. *Even Poppa's love was just words.*

An uncontrollable scream of rage reverberated in Daniella's head. *I hate your words! I don't want any more words!* Without warning, a feeling of desperation engulfed Daniella. To keep herself from shouting aloud, she emptied another pile of finished pages from the bin and began to print new ones. She turned the crank deliberately, counting each revolution, with each rotation promising herself she would not cry.

CHAPTER 33

If not for the war, Grisha Moisei would never have even considered entering the Nicholas Gymnasium. He had no desire to spend his time studying Russian history, Russian literature, Latin, French, seeing no practical use for them in Palestine. Yet, knowing there was no safe alternative to avoiding conscription, Grisha was determined to become a student.

During the third week in February, after he had passed his entrance examination, Grisha petitioned to enter the Nicholas Gymnasium immediately, rather than waiting for the new term to begin the following autumn. The headmaster commented that he could recognize a sincere and devoted scholar when he saw one and also remarked how impressed he was with Grisha's enthusiasm for learning; he wasted no time in accepting the bank draft, which was large enough to cover the cost of two tuitions, and assigned Grisha to begin his first class the following Monday.

Unlike most of the other *gymnasia* in Odessa, the Nicholas school was not known for its academic excellence. It was a rowdy, noisy, multilingual institution that catered to merchants, minor government officials, and anyone else who could afford the tuition and who wanted their children to continue with their education, no matter how low the standards. But there was one thing that the Nicholas Gymnasium did have in common with every Russian school: a tiny minority of Jewish students who were despised and since the start of the war cruelly punished by their fellow students for the German and Austrian victories.

Out of the three hundred students at the Nicholas Gymnasium six were Jewish, and on the best of days their lives were made unbearable by the others. One Russian boy in particular was well-known for his hatred of the dark-haired, frightened *zhidi,* spending considerable time every schoolday indulging in what he considered a patriotic sport: Jew-baiting. His name was Alexi Gryechovnay, a tall, beefy, ruddy-skinned boy whose father was a minor official in the local government. Though Alexi tortured all the Jewish students, his favorite victim was a skinny red-haired boy named Feldman.

Alexi and Feldman were in the first class of the day together, a Russian history class, and every day, without fail, there was an incident between the two. Each morning Feldman arrived at the Nicholas Gymnasium before any of the other pupils, dashed down to the basement to hang up his coat, then clattered up the stone steps to a large classroom crowded with wooden tables, and dominated by a portrait of Tsar Nicholas II. Afraid even to look around to see if anyone else was present, Feldman would sit down at his assigned desk, open his history book, and read and re-read the pages that he had studied at home. Twenty minutes later the other students started to arrive; all of them would ignore Feldman until Alexi strutted into the room.

"Feldman, I see you are still alive—what a shame! Although I am certain the Germans would be glad to see you." Alexi would sneer as he loomed over Feldman.

Feldman always remained silent and motionless, never knowing what Alexi intended to do next. Some mornings Alexi would slap Feldman on the back, as if he were greeting a friend, only to leave a patch of wet horse manure clinging to the Jew's shirt. Other mornings it might be mud, or paint. No matter what, Feldman never complained, lacking the courage to say a word to Alexi or to the instructor who knew precisely what was occurring but was also intimidated by Alexi. More than one of the teachers had been badly beaten by the students for having reported them to the headmaster, and it was decided by the faculty that an unruly classroom was far better than risking broken bones.

The Friday before Grisha joined the Russian history class, the instructor had announced that a new student would be arriving Monday morning. Immediately speculation filled the room; Alexi derisively shouted that the new student would either be the son of a rich Jew or a pampered brat from an aristocratic family, and that he would be the first one there to greet him. On Monday morning, true to his word, Alexi arrived at school earlier than ever, even prior to Feldman. For thirty long minutes he paced back and forth at the front of the classroom. Each time he heard a sound outside, Alexi rushed to the window to see if one of the figures below might be the new student. After half an hour of the same routine Alexi became anxious and positioned himself at the window, carefully inspecting everyone who passed beneath him. The squeak of footsteps entering the room caught his attention and, throwing back his shoulders and standing as tall as possible, Alexi Gryechovnay turned around.

"Oh, it is only you, Feldman," Alexi said with disgust.

"Good morning, Alexi."

"Screw you."

Hurriedly, Feldman took his seat, opened a book, and busied himself with reading. Alexi walked toward the door, pausing an instant to knock Feldman's text to the floor.

"Did you see the new boy anywhere?" Alexi inquired.

"No," replied Feldman, trying to decide if he should retrieve his book.

Alexi moved away from the door and walked back to the window.

"Good morning," a pleasantly deep but unfamiliar voice said.

The unexpected greeting caused Alexi to halt in mid-step

and he stumbled forward as he tried to stop and turn simultaneously. Feldman, hiding his face behind a book, peeked at the youth who had entered the classroom.

"Good morning," the youth repeated.

Alexi inspected the new student, who was nearly as tall as he, and smiled. "Good morning, I am Alexi Gryechovnay."

"And I am Grisha Moisei."

Alexi approached Grisha. "*That* is Feldman." Passing Feldman's desk, Alexi again smacked the book from his hand. "They allow him in this school for our amusement!" Alexi laughed.

Grisha looked quickly from one to the other, instantly understanding their relationship. Before he could say anything the other students began to arrive, and as they entered the room, Alexi introduced Grisha to them, the Russian youth's friendliness surprising them all.

"This is *my* class, Grisha," said Alexi, surveying the other students who smiled at him obediently.

"But you are not the instructor, are you?"

"No. But it is still my class, and Feldman is my slave." Alexi suddenly grabbed a handful of the soft flesh on Feldman's arms and squeezed it tightly. "Feldman loves the Germans, so we are keeping him for them, until they are our prisoners. *Then* they can have him." Viciously, Alexi twisted Feldman's skin.

"Stop, Alexi, please. You are hurting me!" Feldman whined.

"I know, Feldman. That is why I am doing it," retorted Alexi with a grin. The other students laughed.

"Why do you pick on him like that?" Grisha asked, a surge of anger knotting his stomach.

"Don't worry about Feldman. No one cares about him."

"I am curious. What did he do to you?" Grisha inquired, measuring Alexi's size and trying to calculate his strength.

"He is a Jew!"

"So?" Grisha could feel the muscles in his forearms becoming taut.

Alexi's pink cheeks paled. He leaned toward Feldman

until he was nose to nose with him. "So—I do not like Jews. With their hooked noses and sticky fingers!" He spat in Feldman's face, laughing as the saliva slid down his cheek. "Jews are spies for the Germans. They would *love* to see Germany win the war." Like an adoring mother, Alexi pinched Feldman's cheek. He compressed his fingers tighter and tighter until Feldman began to sob. "Feldman is not a bad Jew, though. He never squeals. Of course, there is no one who would believe him, but still, he never squeals." To add a final touch to these indignities, Alexi turned his back to Feldman, bent over slightly, and farted loudly.

The entire class erupted into shouts of approval.

"And, he is a coward!" Alexi added as he stood up straight.

"*I* am not a coward," Grisha said evenly.

"So what? Who cares?"

"You should care."

"Why?"

"Because I am a Jew, too."

Alexi clapped Grisha on the shoulder. "With a face like that—you are a Jew?" The husky youth roared with pleasure.

"I am a Jew. And I am *not* a coward."

The classroom became still. Everyone stared at Grisha, even Feldman, who never looked directly at anyone. Alexi drew himself up to his full height. His ears were burning, and his lips curled into a snarl.

"How did you get that face, Jew? That is a Russian face you have. Did you get it from the Germans so you could spy on us? Did you?" Alexi advanced toward Grisha. "Does your poppa have a curly beard?"

The other students were as stiff as statues, anticipating the excitement of a fight. The instructor, who had approached the classroom just as Alexi began to rage, remained outside in the hallway. He ran his tongue back and forth across his lips, aware that he neither could—nor wanted to—do anything to stop the first challenge Alexi had ever received.

"When I am through breaking your face, *zhid,* I will finish circumcising you!" Gesturing with his hands, Alexi indicated how he would tear Grisha's testicles from his body. He came to a halt when he stood directly before Grisha. "Watch closely, Feldman, and I will show you why it does not pay to be a Jew, not even a brave Jew."

With the word *brave* Alexi shoved Grisha, trying to push him off his feet, but as he did, Grisha swung his right hand up at Alexi's face. The thick book he held in it smashed into Alexi's mouth, ripping two of his teeth out of the upper gum; like pennants, they hung by slender threads of bleeding flesh. Instinctively, Alexi took both his hands and put them around Grisha's neck while at the same time he jerked his knee upward toward Grisha's groin; it was Grisha's knee that found its mark first. Alexi screamed. The fingers he had clamped around Grisha's throat lost their strength, yet instead of falling to the floor and rolling in pain, he shoved one hand into Grisha's mouth, attempting to rip through his cheek. Grisha bit Alexi's fingers, digging his teeth into the flesh until he felt bone. Howling, Alexi yanked away his hand and waved it in the air. Dropping the book with which he had first hit Alexi, Grisha used his fists like hammers, battering his opponent's head and face. Enraged, Alexi threw his arms around Grisha, trying to crush his ribcage, but Grisha slipped beneath the encircling arms and hit Alexi's nose with the edge of his hand, splitting both of his nostrils. Alexi clawed at Grisha's eyes. Reaching into his pocket, Grisha withdrew a penknife. With one hand he opened the blade, flicking it at Alexi like the darting tongue of a snake. Alexi bellowed as the knife caught his shirt, ripping it and his skin beneath. He staggered backward, fell over a desk, and sprawled on his back onto the floor. At once Grisha was upon him, crouching over him, his knees digging into Alexi's chest, the point of the blade pressing against Alexi's throat.

"I'll kill you!" Grisha's body shook with fury. "I will kill you, you bastard!"

Everyone in the classroom drew closer—even Feldman felt

secure enough to act like the others—like vultures waiting to feed on the meat of a dead animal. Grisha's hand trembled, and he felt an uncontrollable urge to plunge the knife into Alexi's neck. Alexi turned his head slightly, then stopped when he felt Grisha jab the knife against his throat.

"Please, don't!" he begged, dreading the look in Grisha's eyes.

Grisha examined Alexi's quivering mouth, his frightened expression. He felt nothing.

"Please don't kill me!" Alexi pleaded, gulping for air, tasting the blood from his broken nose and teeth. "Don't kill me, please," he whimpered, as Grisha lightly drew the finely honed edge of the blade across Alexi's jugular vein.

Dropping his gaze from Alexi's face, Grisha saw that the slightest motion of the blade would tear an irreparable hole in the Russian youth's neck. Torn between two choices, Grisha's eyes became cloudy. He exhaled slowly, deliberately, and reluctantly removed the knife from Alexi's throat. Grisha stood up and stared down at the pathetic boy, feeling nothing but disgust.

"Next time I *will* kill you," Grisha said very softly.

"I am sorry," sniveled Alexi.

Grisha snapped his knife shut, slipped it into his pocket, picked up his book, and looked around for an empty seat in the classroom.

"I am sorry," repeated Alexi, wiping the blood from his face with the back of his hand.

Grisha turned toward him, his blue eyes dull barriers that concealed his thoughts. Alexi averted his eyes, afraid of the unrelenting expression on Grisha's face. Hesitantly, several students moved to Alexi's side, all the while keeping track of Grisha's whereabouts. When they reached the prostrate boy they helped Alexi to his feet and sat him down at his desk, directly behind Feldman. Alexi folded his arms on the desktop and rested his head on them; even when the instructor entered the room Alexi did not move.

"Good morning," the teacher said, his voice strained.

"Welcome to our class," he added, unable to look directly at Grisha, afraid of the youth whose violence had frightened him more than anything Alexi had ever done.

Grisha nodded his head. The instructor looked at the other students, seeking comfort in their expressions; but they, too, sat immobile, stupefied not just by the beating Alexi had taken, but also by the fact that it had been administered by a Jew. As much as they hated Alexi, they had wanted him to destroy the blond-haired youth who had dared to stand up to him, who had defied everything they had been taught. Grisha had made a mockery of their beliefs, of the foundations their parents had built for them. Now they were terrified. The slave had become the master, the weak had become the strong, and they had no idea as to what could be done to reverse the turn of events. They had witnessed Grisha's ferocity, and they were too cowardly to challenge it, afraid he would beat them, too. By the end of the school day, what had happened to Alexi was known throughout the *gymnasium* and everyone made certain that they knew who Grisha Moisei was. No one admired him; no one tried to befriend him. They despised him because they feared him. Even the other Jewish students avoided him, knowing that the order he had upset would return with even more ferocity once he had moved on. The Russian students of the Nicholas Gymnasium agreed among themselves to leave the Jews alone until Grisha had gone for good. They bided their time patiently, satisfied that the day would come when they could seek their revenge tenfold. In turn, the Jewish students waited in fear. And the worst part for them was that Grisha Moisei did not remain at the Nicholas Gymnasium for very long.

CHAPTER 34

"Rabbi, does Aram Zubov still hold meetings at your synagogue?" Grisha asked, two evenings after the incident at the *gymnasium*.

Eleazar looked up from the paper he was reading. "Why do you ask?"

"Does he?"

"Yes."

"When?"

"These days, every night."

"Why aren't you there?" Grisha's eyes pinned the rabbi to his seat.

The old man smiled weakly and held out his hands in a gesture of helplessness. "What can a man my age do?"

"Perhaps give him the support only a rabbi can offer."

"He wants warriors, Smyelchak, not me."

"Then maybe he will want me."

"What do you know about fighting?"

Narrowing his eyes, Grisha's face took on the same look of merciless violence that had appeared when he nearly killed Alexi.

"And why would you want to get involved with men whose craziness only brings the police? I am sure the Tsar has spies among Aram's men, and when you see what has happened to Aram, you will understand how dangerous is this thing he is doing."

Grisha set down the Russian history book he had been reading, got to his feet, and took his coat from the peg near the door.

"Where are you going?" asked Eleazar, his tone conveying his disapproval.

"Where do you think?"

"You are begging for trouble."

"That is better than being useless."

Grisha's accusing expression drove Eleazar to his feet. "I will go with you."

"What for?"

"Do I have to explain why I am going to my own synagogue?"

Grisha opened the door. "Rabbi, there is no need for you to explain anything to me." He stepped outside and closed the door behind him.

The instant Grisha entered Rabbi Eleazar's synagogue he thought he had stepped back in time. Everywhere there were men, women, children, even infants cradled in their mothers' arms, all of them with the same fearful expressions he had seen years before. Arguments he already knew from memory cut across the small assembly hall, the people releasing their anger and fright at the outrages that, because of the war, were befalling the Jews throughout the rest of the Pale, while at the same time they debated how best to prevent those very same things from visiting Moldavanka.

Shabbily dressed men and women, some with skin as yellow as the pages of an ancient text, others who looked like carcasses made of leather, their faces lined with age and worry, their eyes lackluster, gesticulating with bony hands, shouted at one another, each attempting to be heard above all the rest. Leaning against the walls, arrogantly surveying the crowd as they searched for anyone who might betray himself as a spy for the Okrahna, the secret police, were tough young men, several boldly displaying revolvers tucked into their waistbands. Grisha worked his way through the crowd to an empty seat halfway between the door and the pulpit; with hands shaking from age and disease, a rheumy-eyed old man glared at Grisha with a contempt that seemed to accuse him for his youth. A stocky, muscular man freed himself from a circle of anxious people. Adjusting his crutches, he carefully made his way to the pulpit, ignoring the scattered applause he received. He brushed away the hands that offered to help him up the steps of the platform, and when he stood at its center he waited for the noise to cease.

"Thank you," he said, with a barb to his words; the room became still. "It is nice to know that you are still willing to listen to Aram Zubov." He looked around the room and his expression softened. "For the first time in my life," he continued, in a gentle tone, "I am seeing Jews who are willing to defend themselves. If years ago there had been Jews such as you in Odessa, everywhere in the Pale, things would be different now. But there is no use in bringing back the past. Let the dead stay dead, let the cowards remain hidden, while we plan for tomorrow."

As Zubov readjusted the crutches he used for support, Grisha studied him. He had changed since Grisha had seen him last, and not just physically. Grisha was startled to see that Zubov was a cripple, his legs obviously now useless. But there was an air of authority to Aram Zubov now; a quiet self-assurance had replaced the messianic frenzy that had once been the mainstay of his personality. No longer did Aram appear to be irrationally fearless, trying to force others to join him by intimidation. Reason seemed to dominate Aram's demeanor and his tone of voice.

"Our task is becoming more difficult," said Zubov, interrupting Grisha's thoughts. "As each day passes, and Russia is wracked by another defeat, we are blamed twice as much as the day before. The soldiers lose a battle, and as they retreat they run rampant through the ghettos of the cities along the front, attacking the Jews. It must make them feel very brave when they win a battle against old men and women. And if by chance the soldiers happen to beat the Germans, they are no different. They still slaughter us, in celebration. We have been lucky here in Odessa, but only because the war is hundreds of miles away. But now we, too, are beginning to feel its effects. Not just because we cannot buy food and clothing, but because of the hatred seething in the streets. But if anyone attacks Moldavanka, they will not have an easy time of it. That I promise you!"

Shouts of approval and applause prevented Zubov from continuing. He raised one hand and silence returned.

"As we sit here there are tailors, bakers, shoemakers, watchmakers, carrying rifles and pistols, standing in the cold, hiding in shadows, perched on rooftops, protecting *all* of us. We need more men like that. Hundreds more. Thousands. Because if we want Moldavanka to remain our home, it is *we* who must make it strong. Build it as we would our own houses. For unless you have built your house with your own hands, it can never truly be yours. Your sweat must mix with the mortar, your blood with the stone. Part of your flesh must be left sealed inside the walls before your house truly belongs to you. Moldavanka is our house. Our home. And only we can make it strong."

"Tonight, I will be the first to join with you, Aram!"

"And I the second, Aram!"

"If you give me a gun, Aram, how will I learn to use it?"

"You will be taught, Kolke, as carefully as a child learning the Talmud. But more important, your desire to go on living will teach you how to use it."

"And then, Kolke, if you shoot someone, the police will come and arrest you!"

Zubov turned his attention from the straggly-bearded teenager, Kolke, to a man of fifty with a wart on his nose and broken blood vessels interrupting the whiteness of his face. "You are right, Emil, *if* they catch him."

"Remember, Emil, going to prison is better than being murdered by pogromists!" another man shouted.

"Not in Russia!"

"Aram should know that better than any of us!"

"I still prefer this," Zubov said, holding aloft one of his crutches for emphasis, "I still prefer having suffered in prison than to have remained unharmed, hiding behind my own meekness."

"But Aram, not all of us are as fearless as you. We cannot tolerate what you can."

"But you *can*, Mayer."

"How can you be so sure?"

"Because there is no other choice."

The grim tone in Aram's voice brought quiet to the room; the crowd stirred uncomfortably. Grisha looked around, aghast at the lack of robustness, the sickliness, the ragtag condition of the men and boys who were being asked to volunteer to protect Moldavanka. On their faces flickered old fears as they calculated the odds they would be facing. Slowly, without commotion, Grisha stood up and in a clear voice spoke to Zubov.

"Will you accept me in your defense group?"

Every head in the room turned toward Grisha. Zubov studied him, a look of recognition coming to his face.

"Your father was Aleksandr Moisei, wasn't he? And you are the one who ran away to Palestine. I remember that. Eleazar told us."

"Yes. And if you want me, I would like to join you."

"But why are you in Russia? Didn't you like Palestine?"

"When the war started, I was expelled," replied Grisha matter-of-factly.

Zubov nodded his head and smiled knowingly. "And now you are in the same predicament as we are. Ha! There could be no better justice for a Zionist."

"I did not come here to argue with you, just to help—if that is what you want."

"What was it like there?" a clean-shaven man of about twenty-five inquired.

"Difficult."

"Tell us about it!" someone shouted from the rear of the hall.

"Did you go to Jerusalem? Will we ever be able to rebuild our Temple there?"

Mention of Jerusalem and the great Temple there which had been destroyed thousands of years before caused several men to get to their feet and begin wailing. A tumult erupted as dozens of voices shouted questions at Grisha while others berated those who were loudly bemoaning the loss of the Temple.

"Damn it, this is no time to discuss Palestine! Or to weep over what no longer exists!" Aram's powerful voice boomed above the discord. He gripped his crutches and furious determination blazed across his face.

"If you were not so filled with vengeance, Aram, you would be more gentle with those who are drawn to you," said a short, wiry man with thinning gray hair; his large brown eyes peered directly at Zubov through wire-rimmed spectacles.

"Joseph," replied Aram, his voice lowered to nearly a whisper, "as well as you think you know me, you know me not at all. It is not vengeance that engulfs me, but love. Deep love. For you. For everyone here. For everyone in Moldavanka. For every Jew in Russia."

Aram's unexpected revelation, the raw truth of his emotions, galvanized the people in the synagogue. With their mouths agape, they stared at Aram. Only Joseph remained unimpressed.

"What you love most, Aram, is the thought that you will be able to punish Russia for the past. It is your anger which keeps you in Russia. And your hatred for what Russia has done to you far outweighs your love for anything. That is why you are unable to move an inch away from this foul soil until you have had a hand in destroying our oppressors."

"Of all the people I know, Dubrow, you are perhaps the one who has the least right to criticize my desire to crush our oppressors."

Joseph Dubrow smiled kindly at Aram. "Of all the people you know, it is I who perhaps has the *most* right to speak to you as I do."

"Do you? It was not I who was the traitor."

"Aram, the redeemed are far less suspect than those who have never fallen."

"And just because you have determined that redemption means fleeing Russia, because you believe that it is Palestine where you will find—"

"Unity, Aram. And therefore, peace of mind and soul. Aristophanes wrote that at one time men and women were not two separate beings but one. And that having angered their gods, they were sliced in half, and since then all the halves have been running madly through the world seeking their original companion selves. We were once whole—in Palestine—and then we were severed from it. And as you yourself have said, Aram, a man's house is never truly his unless his sweat and toil are intermixed with the stone and mortar. Well, we have already built our house, long ago: *Eretz Yisrael.* And just as a man can have but one firstborn child whom, rightly or wrongly, he loves the most, we have a firstborn country."

Disgusted with Joseph Dubrow's recitation, annoyed by the man's calm logic, Aram Zubov turned to the others in the synagogue. But he had lost their attention; most of them were more interested in listening to Joseph than in hearing Aram ask them to risk their lives. Realizing that any further attempt to regain control over the meeting would be futile, Aram descended from the pulpit and, followed by the small group of tough young men, hobbled out of the building in a huff. For several minutes after he left, the people flocked around Joseph Dubrow, anxious to hear more of his eloquent way of speaking about the Promised Land. But there was something of greater importance to Joseph than speaking of grandiose visions. Ignoring those who sought solace in his chimerical orations, Joseph Dubrow, a broad smile on his face, his hand extended for a warm greeting, stepped quickly toward Grisha Moisei, excitedly anticipating learning about the reality of Palestine as it existed in the present.

CHAPTER 35

Meeting Joseph Dubrow was the best thing that had happened to Grisha since his return to Russia. Until then his daily life had been tedious and often seemed hopeless. He intensely disliked his classes at the *gymnasium;* the constant threat of conscription was the only thing that kept him there. His relationship with the rabbi had become increasingly uncomfortable as day by day Eleazar slipped further into his practice of mysticism, becoming increasingly vehement in his attempts to convince Grisha that only the way of the Cabala, pursuing the real message from God by fasting, entering into ecstatic trances, would save the Jews. The more Eleazar assaulted him with mystical diatribes, the less Grisha wanted to do with the rabbi or God. As far as Daniella was concerned, Grisha had attempted to talk with her one more time. But her viciousness persuaded Grisha to accept finally the reality that she did not want to see him again. Finding nothing that gave him comfort, imprisoned in a country he despised, assaulted by memories he loathed, and faced with a future as bleak as the dreariest winter day, Grisha Moisei felt himself racing to the brink of lunacy. So, when he met Joseph Dubrow and found how easy it was to talk to him, discovered the breadth of the man's knowledge and the depth of his humanity, Grisha clung to him, thankful for the sudden release Joseph's interest gave to his outpourings.

For his part, Joseph Dubrow went out of his way to spend time with Grisha, repeatedly inviting him to visit, to roam through Moldavanka, to listen to the stories of his own life. While school was still in session, Grisha would run to Joseph's tailor shop after classes and sit with him, talking until it was so late that Grisha had little time for homework or sleep. In May, when the school year ended, Grisha arrived early each day at the tailor's shop, often just as Joseph was opening the door for business, and stayed at least until nightfall. By the time spring fully blossomed, the rest of Russia and the war seemed very far away to both of them.

Beginning on the first of June, when Aram Zubov presented Grisha with a rifle and a pistol, and assigned him to the streets he was to patrol four nights a week from sundown until dawn—Grisha was without Joseph's companionship. Each minute of those nights dragged by for Grisha, each hour seeming interminable. To compensate for time lost, Grisha spent the other three nights with Joseph in a state of intensity, both men sitting in straight-backed chairs propped against the building next to the tailor shop, conversing, arguing, discussing, sharing a bottle of inexpensive wine until long after the sun had risen, neither of them knowing or caring if it were sunup or sundown. There was no subject that was too personal for them to broach. Grisha told Joseph of his entire life, his loves, hates, and fears, finding more than just a sympathetic ear. And always, Joseph had a perceptive observation or asked a question so astute, so penetrating, that as Grisha answered it he unraveled hidden memories or came upon new insights.

Joseph, too, revealed intimacies about which he rarely, if ever, spoke to anyone. He disclosed to Grisha that during the early and mid-nineteen hundreds he had been a Bolshevik, another Jew who also believed that Jews were responsible for anti-Semitism. Joseph had dedicated those years to ridding Russia of Judaism, because it was Karl Marx whom he worshipped as God. With self-derision, Joseph admitted that he had been involved in acts of destruction; once he had helped to blow up a police station and a small military barracks, believing then that he was a hero. He added sadly that while he was donating his time and most of the little money he earned to the great cause of Bolshevism, he had forced his wife and daughter to live in penury. But that was not the worst iniquity he had committed as a Bolshevik. Nor was it when he had to make speeches and write pamphlets denouncing his own people, the Jews. Locating historical facts to prove that Judaism was a despicable way of life, and when there were none, falsifying facts, or if necessary creating facts, to prove the perfidy of the Jews, was still not the most vile thing Joseph Dubrow had done. That came when he was ordered to use force against the Jews, commanded by the paramilitary organ of the Odessa Soviet to use a club to beat his neighbors. His greatest sin, Joseph confessed, was that he had not refused immediately. "I still avoid questioning myself about that," he said to Grisha. "There is a possibility that I did not give my answer as soon as they asked me because I actually considered carrying out their orders. This way I can pretend that I was too afraid of them to say no to their faces then and there." But eventually Joseph did refuse and the Bolsheviks beat him for his decision, reviling him as a traitor, a filthy swine who would rather protect the *zhidi* than dedicate his life to Bolshevism. His usually placid face wrinkled with anger, his evenly modulated tenor voice as thin and piercing as a tautly pulled strand of fine wire, Joseph said: "Thank God I escaped them. Thank God I saw that their way was just another form of oppression. That is why now I am their worst enemy. And as long as I am alive I will remain their worst enemy!"

His face wet with perspiration and his hands trembling, Joseph continued: "In 1913, Grisha, while you were in Palestine, a mob of drunken Bolsheviks went on a rampage in Moldavanka. They did exactly what Russians have always done to Jews. They robbed, looted, and raped. And they killed a woman. Despite their words of peace and dignity, they, too, proved themselves to be animals. I ran into the street with a stick and began fighting them by myself, screaming for others to help me. And when it looked like I might be killed, Nessa ran out to help me. She had a bread knife in her hand, and she fought by my side like a madwoman. But by the time other Jews had found enough courage to help, it was too late. Oh yes, they drove the Bolsheviks away. But for Nessa it was too late. They killed my wife with her own knife."

Tears flowed freely down Joseph's face, and with fingers deformed by years of being a tailor he clutched Grisha's hand. "The Bolsheviks never tried anything like that again in Moldavanka," Joseph said, his voice cracking with torment. "They have never returned. But for me, for my daughter Sara, it is the same as if they had never left."

It was because of the Bolshevik attack on Moldavanka that Joseph had become involved with Aram Zubov. For on that day, when informed of what was happening, Zubov had raced to the scene, brandishing a revolver and leading a handful of his partisans. And more than the bullets that Aram and his followers fired at the Bolsheviks, the fury of their attack, the frenzy with which Aram Zubov and a dozen men launched themselves into battle, drove the Reds away. The very next day Joseph Dubrow became a member of Aram's self-defense brigade; he had finally understood what Aram's attraction was. It was not that he was a leader of inspiring stature or a great orator, for in fact he was neither of these things. Rather, Aram Zubov's magnetism was explained by his audacious defiance of Russia, his commitment to risking his own life to save the Jews.

"Every summer since that time I have patrolled the same street three nights a week," Joseph told Grisha. "Nothing has ever happened, and God forbid it should. I would not know what to do. But now with reports from the north that Petlura is gathering an army of followers, I must stay with Aram. You do know of Petlura, don't you, Grisha?"

"I have heard his name."

A look of dismay crossed Joseph's face. "I fear you will

hear much of his name someday. Semyon Petlura might be the single greatest force of evil Russia's Jews will ever meet. Did you know that he is being hailed as a Ukrainian hero? And why not? He has sworn to rid the steppes of Jews and Bolsheviks. He has been quoted as saying that he will scourge the land of the diseased who worship Lenin and the pestilence which glorifies Jehovah. And he has proven himself as good as his word, Grisha. There are accounts that he has already launched his promised journey of death—methodical crisscrossing of the Pale from east to west, back and forth, moving south from Kiev, stopping everywhere to kill the enemies of the Ukraine. So far his progress has been slow—there are many Jews to kill in the north."

"Then everything Aram has said is true."

"Yes. And there is more. For along with Petlura, there is a select circle of men known as the Black Hundreds whose aims are the same as Petlura's. But while Petlura gains his support from the peasants, the Black Hundreds are encouraged by the government, by the Tsar himself. They are led by the most reactionary aristocrats and military officers in Russia, and the government supplies them with funds to pay the local police throughout the Pale to instigate pogroms. In these times that is an easy thing to do. I do not dare to wonder what will happen to us if Petlura and the Hundreds ever join forces."

"Aram has always been right, hasn't he? From the very beginning."

"I am afraid so. And even though I disagree with him about many things and even though to me Russia is not my home, I will stay with Aram and do whatever I can to protect Moldavanka until the day comes that I can leave for Palestine."

"Perhaps Aram will leave then, too."

Joseph shook his head. "He will never leave. Not until he can punish Russia for his feet and for his son." Joseph took a deep breath. "If what happened to Aram's son happened to my Sara, I, too, might be like Aram. I *would* be like Aram. Just to imagine someone doing harm to my child . . ." Joseph stopped in mid-sentence, not wanting even to consider such a tragedy.

"It was last spring that they arrested Aram, wasn't it?" asked Grisha.

"Yes."

"How did the Okrahna know what he was doing?"

"The secret police have spies everywhere. Even Jewish spies. And anyway, Aram was never close-mouthed about his attempts to form a defense league. So it was no great surprise to anyone that he was arrested for being an agitator, a rabble-rouser. The shock came when they arrested his son too. Did you know his son, Grisha?"

"No."

"A momma's boy. A sickly child who always stayed at home—and just sixteen years old when the police carried him from his mother's house to jail. Then they turned their attention to Aram. For three days they tortured him; for three days they beat him so he would confess that he was a dangerous man, a traitor to the Tsar. He refused. So they hung him upside down and burned his feet. They held matches against the soles until his skin burned, until the flesh was charred black. Eventually, Aram confessed that years before he had killed several peasants. You know, I remember that incident as if it were yesterday. Sara was a child then. But even she remembers that night."

"So do I," Grisha added softly, vividly remembering how he and his father had rushed to Rabbi Eleazar's synagogue during a night of violence and had seen soldiers on horseback riding in tight circles around a handful of men who lay dead in the street.

"When they heard Aram's confession, the police stopped torturing him. At first, Aram said, he thought they were going to put him on trial and then execute him. He would have preferred it if they had. Instead they took his son and sent him to the army. To fight at the front. That was the worst thing they could have done to Aram. He knew that his child would not survive an hour in the war, and so did the authorities. Two months later word came that his Yaakov had been killed. Now, for Aram, it is as if he is in a prison where they execute him every day."

"And he still wants to remain in Russia?"

"His life is totally committed to revenge, to destroying Russia."

"But everyone has something to punish Russia for!" Grisha shouted, jumping out of his chair.

"Not everyone. Not I. If I did, I would want to remain here, too. But I want to leave, because I no longer have anything to prove to Russia. No longer have I a grudge against Russia. I do not care about Russia. You cannot plant new ideas in old soil, because every time you turn the earth you uncover the graves of your own family. So you must go someplace else, someplace new, and start over again."

"And what place could be better than Palestine?" Grisha asked with a tremor in his voice.

Joseph looked at Grisha; there was a radiance to his eyes. "Yes. There we will start at the very beginning. We will recreate the earth, turning sand to soil, desert to gardens. Each day I think about the only real difference between those who choose to remain here in Russia and those who do not. The difference lies in how they view the future. To those who only want to use the future for retribution, the future does not exist. But for those who want to use it to create life, the future awaits them with open arms."

Aside from Joseph, there was another reason that Grisha spent every possible moment in the tailor shop: Sara, Joseph's sixteen-year-old daughter. From the first Grisha had been taken with Sara. Her long brown hair, which she wore in a single thick braid, made her face look innocent, but her large black eyes hinted that she knew far more than anyone suspected. Her voice was husky and mysterious. Though she was a head shorter than Grisha, her sultry, self-assured walk made her seem taller. But it was Sara's smile which had truly captivated Grisha. It promised everything while at the same time promising nothing, and Sara tantalized Grisha with it. More often than not while Joseph rambled on Grisha would be oblivious, listening only for the sound of the girl's footsteps approaching from the living quarters at the rear of the shop. Yet, when she did appear, Grisha became tongue-tied; Sara's sparkling eyes were too mocking and wise, her sharp wit and keen mind made Grisha fear that whatever he said to her would seem foolish.

Weeks passed, and the fondness shared by Joseph and Grisha evolved into a deep affection that obviously touched Sara. When the hour became late, and her father and Grisha were still talking, Sara no longer angrily reminded them of the time, or that it was she, not they, who had to be up with the sun to get ready for work, and that their meandering conversations kept her awake. Now, a mellowness removed the edge from Sara's attitude; her silky laughter caressed Grisha's ears, the love she displayed for Joseph, the gentle way she spoke to him, nuzzled his face and stroked his gnarled hands, made Grisha long for her to treat him in the same tender manner. Still he was unable to reveal his feelings for her; his uncertainty about how she would respond shackled him. If not for Joseph, months might have passed before Grisha found the daring to expose his desire for Sara.

"Do you see these pants?" Joseph asked Grisha and Sara on a musky June afternoon. "If Zlotnick rips them once more, he will have to go naked. There is more thread in them than material." Shaking his head, Joseph held the pants up to the light and inspected his work. "Can you imagine? Having this hole repaired will make him feel like he is wearing something new!"

"You would think that in these times his wife would fix them herself," said Grisha.

"If she did, we could not afford to feed you as often as we do," Sara retorted, staring directly at Grisha.

His face turned pink and he looked away.

"Be careful, my *ditya,* or Grisha will start eating at Zlotnick's."

Sara's eyes met her father's; they shared a secret.

"Instead of standing here, why don't you deliver these

pants to Zlotnick," Joseph said suddenly to his daughter. "It will save his wife a trip."

"If you want me to, Poppa."

"Grisha, why don't you go with her? It is such a beautiful day, and I have some other work to do." Joseph stood up and stretched, then went over to a shelf and pulled down several shirts. "It will take me hours to fix these."

Grisha glanced at Sara, seeking a sign of encouragement; she was engrossed in carefully folding Zlotnick's pants.

"The two of you, go, so I can get some work done!"

Sara smiled at her father and left the shop, not looking back to see if Grisha were following her.

"Go with her, Grisha, or do something else. I have no more time to talk now."

Grisha started out of the door.

"But come back to eat!"

As Grisha hurried after Sara, Joseph looked at the shirts he held in his hands and laughed. "I am not crazy enough yet to mend rags." He replaced the tattered garments on the shelf and, feeling happier than he had in weeks, pushed aside the curtain at the rear of the shop, wandered into his bedroom, and lay down to take his first afternoon nap in as long as he could recall. Closing his eyes, his breathing becoming slow, deep, all Joseph hoped was that he had given Grisha another reason other than conversation to return for supper. If he had known that Sara was now Grisha's main reason for visiting so often, Joseph Dubrow would not have been insulted.

CHAPTER 36

Though Joseph Dubrow was unaware that Grisha had fallen in love with his daughter, Sara was as certain of that as she was of her own feelings for Grisha. And if she had any misgivings at all about how either of them felt, they were dispelled that night, after she and Grisha returned from delivering Zlotnick's pants. Indeed, that evening Joseph Dubrow also discovered how much his daughter and Grisha were attracted to one another, and he was pleased.

Yet even after that night, despite the closeness they had shared, the mutuality of feelings they had admitted, there was still an awkwardness between them: an uncomfortableness for Grisha caused by Sara's worldliness, an independence coated with a veneer of sarcasm, a touch of cynicism, while Sara found Grisha's idealism hard to believe, certain that, behind his utopian thoughts and apparent fearlessness, somewhere below his outward artlessness there lurked a blemish in Grisha, a flaw that was destined to hurt Sara, or worse, cause harm to her father.

Nevertheless, the pull between Sara and Grisha was far stronger than either of their misgivings. And, too, from observing the youngsters, Joseph Dubrow correctly assessed the trouble between them, and unbeknownst to either of them deftly involved himself with them, his only purpose to mitigate their worries, to smooth the path they hesitantly walked together.

It was obvious to Joseph why his Sara made Grisha feel uncomfortable. Here was a young man who, between the ages of fourteen and eighteen, had spent his life quite differently from ordinary youths. While others his age had the time to deal with their developing manhood, had friends of the same age who were experiencing the same problems, permitting them to share their concerns and curiosities, Grisha had grown to manhood in a social vacuum. While in Odessa boys of fourteen, fifteen, and sixteen gathered in Alexander Park or along the Arkadia to ogle the girls, clumsily clustering around any female their age who showed the slightest interest, experimenting with the patter of courtship, learning the rules and techniques of romantic parrying, Grisha Moisei toiled to build roads in shifting sands that led from villages that had been built on hope to villages that were being built on hope. While young men in Odessa pursued the prettiest girls they could find, escorted them to the sea, to outdoor concerts in the pleasure gardens along Deribasovskaya Street, here and there stealing a kiss or a caress, a few able to convince some young maiden to lie with them in thick woods well hidden from prying eyes, Grisha Moisei helped patrol the perimeter of a town that was beginning to take shape at the edge of the Mediterranean Sea, protecting a handful of buildings called the Hill of Spring, *Tel Aviv*, from marauding Arabs. While the maturing youths in Odessa were able to select the young girls whom they wished to woo and bed, Grisha Moisei found it necessary to seek an outlet for the stirring in his loins with husky women pioneers, Zionists from Eastern Europe who after years of physical labor had rough dry skin, hands hardened with calluses, and muscular limbs more appropriate for beasts of burden than for lovers. Unlike the playful couplings of his peers in Odessa, the lovemaking of Grisha Moisei was as basic and unromantic as the mating of animals. So it was no wonder that Sara Dubrow's glib coyness, her sophistication, disturbed Grisha Moisei.

And Sara was sophisticated. For not only was she exotic-looking, making her fascinating to a wide variety of admirers and would-be suitors, she was educated, too; schooled from childhood in poetry, art, music, history; taken by her mother and father to operas and ballets, to concerts and plays; urged by her parents to express herself by writing and painting. Politically, too, Sara was mature. Her father's involvement with Bolshevism, the years he had spent reading and discussing Marx and Engels, arguing the philosophies of Hegel, Kant, Rousseau, investigating ways of thought both Occidental and Oriental and then trying to devise his own system for bettering the lot not only of the world's Jews, but of all mankind, had exposed Sara to ideas that made her wise far beyond her years. But perhaps of greatest influence—Sara Dubrow was reared in an atmosphere of freedom, in an environment in which the curiosities of the body were considered no more sinful than the curiosities of the mind, where satisfying the desires of the senses was deemed as natural and right as satisfying the needs of the intellect. And if one were to err, it would be from blindly following social convention, and not from experimenting with the pleasures of life.

Yet, like Grisha, despite her unusual upbringing, Sara Dubrow dreamed of a life filled with romantic love, a life predicated on the belief that the basis for happiness, for a fulfilled life, was spending that life with one person with whom she could share her fantasies, trust her feelings, hone her intellect, practice her ideals: a person with whom she could create one child or many.

Careful not to appear meddlesome, Joseph Dubrow often suggested that Grisha and Sara accompany him to places he thought they might find interesting. Several times they visited the Museum of Antiquities, where Joseph happily enthralled his daughter and Grisha with his vast knowledge of the collection of Greek artifacts on display there. Twice they wandered through the archeological and natural-history exhibits at the Russian University, the three of them excitedly discussing the effect of Darwinism on religion. Sara was convinced that if anyone was descended from the apes it was Grisha, and she laughed aloud as Grisha tried to prove her correct by loping down a corridor like a chimpanzee while scratching his chest and mimicking the chattering noises of a monkey. At other times Joseph took Grisha and Sara on walks along the Arkadia where they were cooled by sea breezes and talked of nothing more serious than how many grains of sand there were on all the beaches in all the world.

But most often Joseph Dubrow invited Grisha and Sara to come with him to Alexander Park to have a picnic supper of roast chicken and wine while they enjoyed the outdoor concerts at sunset. Alexander Park was where, years before, Joseph had often taken his Nessa, first to court her, and later on to perpetuate the romance in their marriage that neither one of them was willing to let die. Shaded by broad-leafed trees from the long rays of the low sun, perfumed by the scent of roses and lilacs and the gentle odor of the evening's dew-touched grass, surrounded by the familiar lush melodies of Tchaikovsky, Joseph, Sara, and Grisha allowed themselves to be swept away by the beauty of their surroundings, each of them convinced at those moments that all the world felt as peaceful and harmonious as they did. Swaying slowly to the sentimental strains of Tchaikovsky's *Romeo and Juliet,* charmed by his delightful *Nutcracker Suite,* Joseph, Sara, and Grisha would talk quietly of their hurts, their happinesses, revealing some of their most personal thoughts, each of them feeling secure enough to entrust the others with their most vulnerable beliefs. And if by chance there occurred a misunderstanding between Grisha and Sara, a confusion between what was said and what was meant, at the first sound of a barbed comment from Sara or a self-righteous declaration from Grisha, Joseph would deftly take charge of the situation, his diplomacy invisible to Grisha and Sara, his skill so refined at helping them circumvent the traps they unknowingly set for one another that soon Grisha and Sara avoided these pitfalls themselves. It was not long before Joseph, having had his fill of food and drink, felt relaxed enough to doze off, blanketed by the heroic music of Tchaikovsky and warmed by the knowledge that as the sun sank below the horizon, its golden strings tugging the night over Odessa, Sara would slide closer to Grisha, rest her head on his shoulder and snuggle close to him as he encircled her waist with his arm. It was not long before Sara and Grisha were going to Alexander Park by themselves, leaving Joseph home alone where happily he went about his work knowing that his fine young daughter was in love and loved by the finest young man he had ever met.

By mid-summer it was obvious that both Grisha and Sara had changed considerably. Now, rather than being shy, Grisha was quite open about his love for Sara, having no hesitation about telling her how much he cared for her, dreamed of growing old with her. And Sara, instead of being mocking, almost insolent, had become softer, gentler, more trusting of Grisha and therefore able to permit herself the luxury of wanting him to protect her. But there was more, too. For whether they just sat and shared a quiet hour together, or talked, or laughed, or held hands, or kissed, or made love, there was an unusual depth to their relationship —a commitment, a bond that had been forged so strongly that it seemed to be unbreakable. And yes, there was passion. But not a passion that suddenly blazed from nothing only to consume itself and then struggle to become reignited. It was a passion that glowed steadily like a perpetual ember; a passion that grew slowly in intensity to a flaming climax and then ebbed to a constant heat that nothing could douse. And if either Grisha or Sara had any doubts that their love was to live for more than a fleeting moment, by the end of August 1915 every uncertainty had been quelled.

There was nothing unusual about a heat wave beginning in September and stifling Odessa for several weeks at a time, the temperature soaring to a hundred degrees or more. During the day, in spite of the war, the beaches along the

Arkadia were crowded with bathers, swimming and frolicking until long after sunset. Thousands of people took advantage of the warm weather by visiting the Kuyalnitzki Liman, a lagoon five miles north of Odessa that extended for twenty miles, where they soothed themselves in mudbaths and in saline springs that were nearly as hot as the air. Others traveled two hours by train to the south, to the Liman of Xenievka, a lagoon seven miles long, separated from the Black Sea by a narrow strip of land. Beyond it stretched miles of coastline, sparsely populated even in the warmest weather because of the distance from Odessa. Whenever it was possible, Grisha and Sara went there, sometimes walking for an hour or more beyond the depot at Xenievka until they found an isolated beach where they could remove their clothing and wander naked on the sand or swim in the sea. Of all the time they spent together these were the occasions when Grisha Moisei and Sara Dubrow felt closest to each other and farthest from Russia.

"When I was a child," Sara said as she and Grisha strolled hand in hand at the water's edge of a small inlet, "Poppa would take us to the Arkadia. He would buy Momma and me seltzer mixed with strawberry syrup, and for himself just seltzer. We would walk along the water, Momma and Poppa holding hands while I played. They never went swimming, never even took their shoes off. The just walked and held hands. Once in a while they would stop and sit on the sand, close their eyes, and face the sun. Momma would put her arms around Poppa's neck and kiss him. He would smile. He would beam! He still doesn't know it, but I always watched them when they were like that. I can't think of anything that ever made me happier than seeing them that way." Sara put her arm around Grisha's waist. "Except for you." She rested her head against Grisha's arm, his muscles making her feel safe.

His eyes filled with tenderness, Grisha looked down at Sara and said softly: "I love you." A dry, hot breeze, really nothing more than wispy puffs of air, ruffled Sara's long brown hair. Her black eyes, fringed by gently curling lashes, gazed into his, telling him that she would give her life for him. Grisha nuzzled Sara's face, gently kissing her. As they walked in the wet sand their feet made sucking sounds.

"I wish we could spend all our days by the sea," Sara murmured.

Grisha stared out across the water. On the horizon there were dark clouds. He squinted, seeing a long convoy of naval ships moving from east to west, plying the sea placidly, clouds of black smoke drifting upward from their stacks.

"What are you thinking about?" asked Sara.

"If there will always be a war."

Sara took Grisha's hand and pressed it against her heart. "We have no war," she said in a voice softer than a whisper.

"Do you really want to marry me?"

"I have to marry you."

"Why?"

Sara rubbed her smooth, flat stomach. "What if you have made me pregnant?"

"Are you pregnant?"

"I don't know. I could be. I should be, considering how much we make love."

Sara studied Grisha, her Grisha, not the only man she had known intimately, but the only one, aside from her father, whom she had ever loved. Sara scrutinized Grisha and wished she were pregnant. She ran a finger along Grisha's bicep. *You are so powerful, my Grisha. And so wise. I can make love to your intellect, and converse with your body. I am the flesh of my mother and the wisdom of my father. And just as my father was to my mother, you are to me, the poetry of Lord Byron.* Sara smiled, recalling her mother's deep, rich laugh. *"While the rest of Russia worships Pushkin, your father reads me Byron."* Sara remembered how even after her mother had died, Joseph often repeated the two lines that best described his feelings for his beloved Nessa. *"I loved her from my boyhood; she to me was a fairy city of the heart."* First Joseph would quote the lines in the original and then translate them into Russian, his voice quavering with awe at Byron's genius and the love he himself felt for his wife. The poem was *Childe Harold,* and it was as much Sara's favorite as it was Joseph's.

Sara nestled against Grisha. "Make love to me while you talk to me, Grisha. Make love to me and make me pregnant."

"What would your father say if I made you pregnant?"

"He would instruct us to forsake everything for our child's life."

Grisha kissed the top of Sara's head. "How come Joseph doesn't mind that we make love, even in his own house?"

"What is the worst of woes that wait on age? What stamps the wrinkle deeper on the brow? To view each loved one blotted from life's page, And be alone on earth as I am now." The melancholy voice of Joseph Dubrow tugged at Sara's heart. *Poppa, Poppa, if I could only ease your anguish when you sit and weep over Momma.* But nothing Sara did could alleviate her father's loss, and though the sorrowful lines from *Childe Harold* only added to his grief, Joseph Dubrow recited them often.

"Sara, why does your father permit us to make love in his own house?"

"Because he knows how terribly simple it is to be suddenly left with nothing but memories. And that the more things two people share, the more memories there are."

"I love Joseph."

A shiver of happiness rippled across Sara's skin. "Poppa loves you, too." *And I loved you from my girlhood, Grisha, for you are the substance of all my dreams.* "Oh, my Grisha, my fairy-tale prince, you have no idea how much I love you," Sara whispered, holding him close.

A low moaning horn from far out at sea caused Grisha to turn from Sara and look again for the convoy, but it was gone, only the fading sound of its deep-toned whistle proof that it had ever existed. Grisha thought of Aram Zubov, wondering if, like the vanished armada, the Moldavanka defense group was so far from the enemy that it was really protecting nothing—*or is it just that the enemy has not yet appeared?* Grisha stopped walking; his face was grim. He squatted on the ground, and drew Sara's name in the sand. "How many uniforms did you make this week?"

"I cut out a hundred pairs of sleeves and—"

"How can you tolerate working in that factory?"

"What is wrong with spending eleven hours a day sitting in a room with two hundred other girls making clothes for the army? What else do I have to do with my time?"

The anger in Sara's voice caused Grisha to scoop up a handful of sand and fling it into the sea. "If I were you, I would quit. I would make everyone quit!" he added with fury. "So this winter the soldiers would be naked and freeze to death. *That* would end the war."

Sara knelt down next to him, touched her tongue to his shoulder, then lay her head against it. "Maybe this winter there will no longer be a war."

"The winter is almost here, Sara, and all around us there is nothing but war."

"You sound like an old man."

"I am doing what old men do. I wait. Every day, all I do is wait." Grisha pinched a few grains of sand between his fingers and rubbed them together, listening to the gritty sound they made. "I still remember how rich the earth in Kodoma was. A man could run through the fields there and blindly scatter seeds anywhere and then forget about them. And at the end of the season there would be a perfect harvest. In Palestine it took ten seeds, each tended as carefully as a baby, to get one plant. That is what I am waiting for. To go back there and take sand like I am holding now and make it as fertile as Russia. But I am so scared, Sara, that waiting is all I will ever do. Do you know what happens inside me every day when the sun sets? I want to scream, to tear everything to shreds because one more day has been wasted. Because the sun has had one more chance to make a barren land more barren. What am I doing with my life? Wasting it at the *gymnasium* so it will not be stolen from me? Painting the walls in a room so we will have a clean place to wait together? How long can I talk to your father about what we *will* do instead of doing it?" Grisha got to his feet, his eyes filled with despair. He stretched out his arms to Sara. She stood up and embraced Grisha while he clung to her. "Do you know why I like patrolling for Zubov? Because it is the only thing that makes me feel like I am doing something. Sometimes it gets so cold near dawn that I cannot stop shaking. But I would not give up five minutes of that cold for an hour of warmth."

"When we are married, I will make you so warm that you will never be cold again." Sara held Grisha tightly, forcing her breasts against him, wanting their heat to reach the very depths of his body.

"Some nights, Sara, I wish something would happen, so I could—"

"So you could be a hero?"

Grisha shook his head. "That is not what I want."

"What do you want?"

They began to walk again, their feet kicking up splashes of water.

"In Palestine we trained two mornings a week to learn how to be soldiers. The Arabs would watch us and snicker; they could not believe that the cowardly Jews they had known for centuries had any courage at all. But we did not care that they mocked us; we were too busy learning how to defend ourselves. We were ordered to run until we could not breathe, panting from the heat and thirst, men and women, and children like me. We would want to rest, but instead we would be ordered to flop on our bellies and do a hundred pushups. And then we would have to stand at attention for an hour, until we thought the sun would burn out our brains. We were shown how to use rifles and pistols. Hour after hour we practiced how to load them, unload them, dismantle, clean, and assemble them until we could do it with our eyes closed. We learned how to shoot standing up, sitting down, lying on our bellies in the sand.

Some mornings we would run for perhaps two hours with our rifles held above our heads, or we would do situps with them clasped behind our necks. And we marched until we had blisters on our feet and our throats were so dry it felt as though we were being strangled. Then we were taught hand-to-hand combat, told that it is the most difficult kind of fighting there is. Our instructor said: 'Shooting a man is nothing. That is impersonal. At a hundred yards it is easy to kill a man and believe you are doing it for an ideal. But when two men are locked together in a struggle for survival, and they can smell the other's breath, feel the sweat and heat from the other's body, it takes more than belief and courage to be victorious. You have to know how to respond automatically to everything an attacker might try. Because in personal combat he is doing exactly what you are: fighting like an animal for his life!' " Grisha paused for a moment, his face agitated. He grabbed Sara by the shoulders. "We were taught how to press a finger against a man's throat and strangle him. We were told that an ear peels off the side of a head as easily as the skin off a banana. We learned how to insert a finger into a man's eye and wiggle it, removing an opponent's eyeball as effortlessly as you would a seashell imbedded in wet sand. Or crack the bone in a man's nose with your fist, and with the palm of your hand shove it up into his brain and kill him instantly. Then they gave us penknives, because there were not enough guns for all of us. And because there was not a moment when we might not be attacked, we learned how to use *them* best!"

"Grisha, please!" Sara begged, pushing him away from her. "Lately all you talk about is guns, about fighting. You speak of everything in terms of violence. Is there nothing else to your life?"

A strained expression came over Grisha's face. "I learned to be a surveyor in Palestine. To farm. To build roads. Can I do any of those things here? But I learned to fight, too—and I *can* do that here!"

"But you said—"

"Sara, for Moldavanka, I *will* give a drop of my blood!"

"If I believed in God, I would pray that we leave Russia before that happens."

Grisha opened his arms and Sara came to him. "If there were a God, Sara, there would be no Russia."

For a long while Grisha Moisei and Sara Dubrow stood in silence at the water's edge, the swirl of the waves caressing their legs.

"Sara," Grisha finally said, his words riding on the sound of the sea, "tell me you love me."

In response, Sara kissed Grisha, her lips clinging to his face.

"Tell me in words, Sara."

Sara laughed gently. "Someday I will show you the poems I have written about you."

"Tell me, Sara."

"I'm a very poor poet, Grisha."

"Sara."

"If I told you that your golden hair is a miniature sun to me, the blueness of your eyes the source of my Don, your arms the Urals of my country, your smile its rich earth, would you laugh at me? I would. I *do*!"

Grisha drew Sara to him and kissed her. She pressed her body against his, her lips and thighs straining to meld with him.

"Do you have any idea how much I love you?" Grisha asked, his lips attempting to devour hers.

"I know exactly how much you love me." A tiny smile graced Sara's lips. "I knew from the first time you looked at me you loved me. Every time you visited Poppa and found it impossible to even peek at me, I knew you loved me." Sara's eyes sparkled devilishly. "Do you remember what you did that night after we took Zlotnick's pants to him? Do you have any idea what you looked like, and sounded like?" Sara stepped back, her eyes mocking Grisha, a broad grin playing with him. "Do you remember how much wine you guzzled and how you began showing off by—"

"I didn't know what else to do!"

"Getting drunk was a *wonderful* idea. You have no idea how impressed I was by your stumbling around and by your speeches."

A smile shattered Grisha's serious look. "I thought I sounded as intelligent as your father."

"You did, because you were using his words for your speeches. Except when you kept raving on about how you intended to return to Palestine and conquer the country single-handedly!"

"Did I say that?"

"Over and over until I thought you would smash up our kitchen to prove how much you meant it!"

Grisha's face flushed with embarrassment.

"And not only did you make Poppa and me suffer through *that,* but you went outside and lay down in the street like a drunkard and we had to carry you back inside!"

"I felt awful."

"Good!"

"I thought the air would make me feel better."

"It certainly must have for you to lie down in the street."

"My head felt like someone had dropped a boulder on it. I got sick to my stomach—"

"You deserved it."

"Then everything started spinning around, and my legs collapsed from under me."

"I told Poppa we should leave you there."

"I do not believe you."

"Ask him!"

"Then why when you brought me inside, did you hold my head in your lap and sponge my face?"

A sound of pleasure, like vibrant golden chimes, tumbled from Sara's throat. "Because even though I thought you were a braggart and I did not like you very much then, I thought I might change my mind."

"And did you?"

"No!"

"But you kissed me!"

"It was a mistake."

"And you told me you liked me!"

"It was a mistake."

"You told me I was handsome."

"It was a mistake."

"When we made love—"

"That was a terrible mistake!"

"You said you liked it."

"I lied."

"You said you loved me."

"I lied."

"You said you wanted to make love again."

"I lied again."

"And again, and again, and again!"

"And I lied, and I lied, and I lied!" Sara began to run, her legs churning the beach into fans of spraying sand. Her hair streamed behind her and she stretched out her arms, her face raised skyward. Swooping along the arc of the cove, Sara shouted with joy, her cries of ecstasy rushing at Grisha from every direction and embracing him. In a long sweep she completed the circle by racing into the blue-green sea; she dived deep beneath its surface. Grisha waited for her to reappear, and when he saw her emerge in a geyser of water, twenty-five yards from shore, he laughed until his body rocked back and forth. He unfolded his arms and charged into the sea, rushing to catch her. They swam until they were so far from shore that the sandspit looked as tiny as a crumpled piece of paper.

"I think we have gone far enough," Sara gasped as she started to tread water.

"Should we go back?" Grisha swam over to her, wrapping his arms and legs around her, Sara's wet, squirming body exciting him. Easily slipping free of his grasp, Sara turned over on her back. "Let's float a while."

Silently, with nothing to break the stillness of the afternoon, Grisha and Sara rested on the water, bobbing up and down, drifting, their faces scorched by the sun hanging low in the sky. The sea lapped at their bodies, its purling song lulling them toward sleep.

"I am going back now," Sara said.

Not waiting for a response from Grisha, Sara rolled onto her stomach and dove back into the sea, her strong arms bringing her close to shore while she was still underwater. Grisha chased after her, but Sara reached the beach first, ran past the swirling edge of the sea, shook thousands of glistening droplets from her hair, fell to the ground, and sprawled on her back. Grisha swam until his chest and legs scraped the sloping sand. He got to his feet and raced over to where Sara was lying and stood above her, dripping water from his hair onto her face. Then he lay down beside her. With eyes closed, their faces turned toward the sun, Grisha and Sara groped for each other's hands. Within minutes both of them fell asleep.

Whether it was the unusual chill in the air or a sound they both heard in their slumber or something else, neither of them knew, but they awoke together, their lips pressed close, their bodies entwined. Sara gripped the sand with her back and buttocks and Grisha kissed her nipples, taking one between his lips and lightly holding it with his teeth.

"Do you like them?"

Grisha nuzzled his face against Sara; the smell of her skin made him quiver.

"I like it when you touch them."

Gently, he suckled at her breast.

"I like it when you touch everything."

Grisha laid his head on Sara's stomach, tasting the salt that had dried there; he closed his eyes and listened to her breathe. Sara raised her hips, the motion a request to be touched. Grisha swirled the hairs that curled below Sara's belly, then placed his hands so they covered them all. A scent that only Sara had, at once both pungent and fragrant, surrounded him. So tenderly that at first Sara thought the breeze was caressing her, Grisha kissed her thighs. He placed his hands beneath Sara's legs and guided them apart. Again he kissed her. And then, with a delicate tongue, he tasted the juices that flowed from deep within the garden of his woman.

On October 19, 1915, at the age of eighteen, Grisha Aleksandrovich Moisei married seventeen-year-old Sara Ruth Dubrow. The ceremony was small, with only Joseph Dubrow in attendance. Rabbi Joshua Eleazar officiated, tears coming to his eyes when Grisha recited the vow of matrimony.

"By this ring you are consecrated unto me in accordance with the laws of Moses and Israel."

After sealing their vows with a kiss, Grisha and Sara Moisei pledged to spend their lives in Palestine, going there as soon as they were able to leave Russia. The meal that followed was one of joy: the wine was plentiful, the food—compared to their usual fare—was lavish, and for a little while they all forgot about everything except their own immediate world.

When the merriment finally subsided, Grisha and Sara left the rabbi's house and walked hand in hand from Kherson Street to Mikahilovsky Place a mile away. There, in one room, with the walls painted white and decorated with inexpensively framed reproductions, amidst a table for eating, a secondhand sofa and armchair, clothing, mementoes, books and three boxes from Joseph containing sheets, pillowcases, dishes, utensils, two pots, a frying pan, and twenty-five rubles tucked inside a sugarbowl, in a bed given to them by Eleazar, Grisha and Sara Moisei spent the first night of their lives as husband and wife. Clutched in each other's arms, their breathing and bodies entwined, resting, they waited for morning when they would be born again and begin their life together.

CHAPTER 37

The Rastrelli Palace, named after its designer, was built in 1765 on the Great Prospekt in what was then St. Petersburg. It was only one of many palaces situated in the neighborhood of the Fontanka Canal, and while it was neither the handsomest nor the most impressive building in that quarter, it was a residence of which none of its inhabitants had ever been ashamed. Built in the center of a large garden whose perimeter was protected by lofty trees and an iron grille, the palace had always seemed more like a summer house than a year-round home. Its corniced white stone walls gleamed brilliantly above green summer lawns and long rows of fragrant blossoms. In the winter the palace seemed like a crystal doll's house set in a field of snow.

By 1916 the exterior of the palace had become worn, but its interior remained as exquisite as on the day it had been completed and furnished. Mosaic furniture of Florentine workmanship graced every room. Tapestries and paintings covered the walls. Settees and divans in the French and Italian styles were arranged more for visual appreciation than for convenience. Cabinets in *pietra dura* and a table of malachite stood proudly in the drawing room. Gold ikons inlaid with jewels hung in the hallways. A central staircase of Carrara marble swept up from the main floor to long corridors that led to bedroom suites, sitting rooms, and a solarium overlooking a garden. But it was the stateroom that was most breathtaking. Over its entranceway hung a painting on blue silk entitled *Genii Paying Homage to Venus.* Stepping over the threshold, one could not fail to be captivated by the sight of eight decorative pillars of black marble encircled with gilded foliage. On either side of the room there was a fireplace; the marble mantelpieces inlaid with lapis lazuli. Every inch of the walls was covered with paintings of the Venetian school, and the ceiling was a mosaic mural of scenes from the Bible. In the center of the room was a canopied bedchamber made of ebony, decorated with pastoral landscapes created in pearl. A brocade spread was neatly folded back so that it hung over the edge of the bed without touching the floor.

Sitting in the center of the bed was Soybel Viska, wearing a flowing white-silk nightgown, her hair knotted at the back of her head and held in place by a gold comb. Facing her was Munya, a slightly built child of eight with features and coloring identical to his mother's. Soybel was manicuring her son's fingernails and at the same time conversing with her husband, who was slumped in an oversized armchair, the floor around him littered with charts, maps, and documents.

"I have never seen you look quite so tired," Soybel said.

"I have never been so tired." Vassili took a long sip from his glass of vodka. "Even this tastes like water these days. Do you know what the figures have been readjusted to? Almost four million! That is how many men we have lost since the start of the war. And those figures are four months old. The new ones are still being totaled."

"Give Momma your pinky, *petit,*" Soybel said to Munya, making sure the nail on the finger next to it was perfectly rounded.

"Ici, maman," replied Munya, with an aristocratic clip to his French.

"*Merci.*" Glancing at Vassili, Soybel said, "If you continue as you have been, you will be one of those numbers, too."

"I sometimes wonder if Petrograd will still be standing next year." Vassili picked up a thick sheaf of documents. "You should read these. If not for the marshes around Pinsk, Germany would extend all the way to the Urals by now." Vassili kicked aside several large documents, revealing a map of Europe. "I truly thought that in 1916 we would be able to help the French as was planned—to force Germany to keep as many troops as possible occupied fighting us so as to ease the situation on the Western front. But the Germans are not afraid of us. They have already shifted half a million troops from here to France, and still we are retreating. How far can we retreat?" Vassili stared at the map for a moment, leaned back in his chair, closed his eyes, and placed his hands over his face.

Soybel held a finger to her lips, signaling Munya to be quiet; she continued to buff his nails.

"It is not even humiliating anymore," Vassili finally said, dropping his hands in his lap. "It is terrifying. And why shouldn't our soldiers run away? They are exhausted. The winter is killing them as fast as the enemy. They are nearly out of ammunition. And even if they weren't, we do not have enough guns for them."

"There!" Soybel said, examining Munya's fingers. "Go show your Poppa your hands."

Munya climbed off the bed and ran over to Vassili, who carefully inspected the boy's nails. "I see your mother put clear polish on them."

"Just like she does for you, Poppa."

Vassili laughed and tousled Munya's hair. "I hope that when you are my age, you have a wife who does everything for you as your mother does for me."

"Munya, come sit by Momma so Poppa can rest." Soybel patted the spot beside her on the bed.

Vassili kissed Munya on the forehead, his eyes following the boy as he scurried back to his mother.

"I was at the war ministry today," Vassili said, resting his head against the back of his chair. "I saw statistics on how many soldiers have deserted or surrendered. The figure is approaching one million. Who can blame them? I would also prefer being a German prisoner or risking our own jails to freezing and starving to death, or dying from the effects of chlorine gas. Here it is twenty centuries since Christ died and look at how much we have learned: to murder men with chemicals! Aah! You should hear what some men are doing. Maiming themselves, amputating their own fingers so they cannot pull a trigger or load a cannon. Anything not to have to fight. But Nicholas is not worried, because he has new recruits to call on. Do you know how they are being trained, Soybel? With broomsticks and axe handles because there are no weapons for them to use. We are sending boys into battle who have never loaded a rifle, much less fired one. And they are being asked to face the best-disciplined soldiers in the world! At the present rate it is estimated that by the end of this year we will have mobilized twelve, perhaps fifteen million men. And it is also estimated that unless there is a drastic turn of events, eight to nine million of them will be killed or captured. How long can it go on? Until there is not one Russian left alive?"

Soybel hugged Munya, resting her head on his. "You are making me afraid, Vassili."

"I am afraid, too, Soybel. Because I am almost convinced that the country is going to collapse. There isn't a city or town where there are not strikes and riots. The Bolsheviks are doing a splendid job of using the war for their own purposes."

"Can't anything be done about them? How many of them can there be?"

"By now, millions. If the war had not gone so badly for us they would not have had such perfect circumstances. But along with the army the rest of the country is starving, too. And hunger has always made better fuel for revolution than ideals." Vassili opened a folder and leafed through some papers and notes he had made. "If only Nicholas would relinquish his command of the army to someone more qualified it is possible, remotely possible, that the war could be turned around. That might put a halt to the Bolsheviks. And if Nicholas took his wife in hand—he *has* to take her in hand! Rasputin manipulates Alexandra as if she were a toy doll, and then she goes and does the same to Nicholas. You know, if Rasputin is permitted to remain at court I am not sure that saving the monarchy might not be worse than the catastrophe we already seem to be heading for. I just do not know . . . I just do not know."

The strain and exhaustion Soybel saw on Vassili's face worried her. For the first time since she could recall, he had deep dark circles beneath his eyes. He was eating poorly. His hair was gray at the temples, and lines of worry had permanently creased his forehead. It was a rare occasion when Vassili came to bed before two or three in the morning; he spent hours after he returned home from the Office of the General Staff pouring over plans, logistical charts, and an endless array of other material as he struggled to find an efficient way to feed, clothe, and supply the army. It infuriated and frustrated Vassili that despite all his efforts the railroads were in worse shape than ever, and the railway system transported more dead and dying soldiers from the front than replacements, weapons, and ammunition to the front.

"You need a rest, Vassili." Soybel got up from the bed and went over to him. She massaged his temples, and he pulled her to his lap. "It seems senseless for you to go on this way," Soybel continued softly. "You have accomplished miracles, obtaining help from the French for the railroads, and now, all the work you do for the war, it is more than one man should even attempt." Soybel ran her lips across her husband's face and Munya stirred on the bed. Soybel glanced at him, motioning for him to join them. Munya climbed down to the floor and ran to his mother, wedging himself between her and Vassili.

"You are right, Soybel, a rest might be perfect," Vassili

said as he stroked Munya's hair. "What else can I do? What can anyone do?"

Soybel rubbed Vassili's hands, working each finger individually.

"You arrive at a point where you have what looks like a decent constitution—even the Tsar is willing to accept it, until the Empress tells him that it is too liberal, that the new laws will weaken the autocracy. And Nicholas listened to her. Alexandra was actually able to persuade Nicholas to reject the constitution. In truth, though, it was Rasputin's idea to reject the constitution. Everyone in the government knows that. And everyone is asking what kind of man Nicholas is to let his wife remain that monk's captive. Everyone is also asking what will be left of Russia if that monk is not stopped—rubble?"

"Perhaps if Rasputin were to disappear, things would change." Soybel touched Vassili's hands to her face and then to Munya's. She kissed them, and so did the boy.

"The only way things will change is if Nicholas heeds us and retrieves his wife from that monster."

"I have heard the wives of other men who know what you do, who feel as you do, speak of rumors that some are thinking of removing Rasputin altogether."

"Yes, that is true," Vassili grunted.

"And?"

"And what?"

"It *would* make matters different." Soybel watched for Vassili's reaction.

He peered at his wife, surprised at how directly she was looking at him. "I could not be a party to that."

"How much does one man weigh when he is balanced against an entire country?"

"There are some things a man cannot do," replied Vassili, cupping Munya's face with one hand.

"Some men can do anything, Vassili," Soybel purred, her fingernails scratching his chest.

"There are times when I think that we should flee to the

country—to Dalyoki—and lock ourselves away there until the war is over and only then step outside."

"I would like that. We would like that." Soybel lightly ran a finger under Munya's chin, making him smile.

"Perhaps we will. If things do not improve, there is no reason for us to remain in Petrograd."

"When can we go?"

"I do not know. I refuse to give up just yet. I cannot!"

"By Eastertime? There still might be snow on the ground at Dalyoki, and I love it like that!" Soybel sat up straight, her eyes consuming Vassili's.

"Dalyoki will be just as beautiful after Easter."

"Please, Vassili, let's be there for Easter."

"If we can." Vassili gazed at Munya; his love for the child was obvious. "If there is any way, any sensible way, to shift Russia onto a safer course, I do not want to miss it because I rushed off too fast. I owe that much to you, to myself, but most of all to Munya. I think I would rather see him . . . I do not want him to have to live in the kind of chaos and terror I foresee in the years ahead." Vassili kissed one of his fingers and then touched them to Munya's lips. "If the worst comes, if Bolshevism should triumph or anarchy prevail, we can always leave Russia and live in Switzerland or France. And if Germany conquers the world, we can stay right here and live in Germany."

"Let's go south, Vassili, as soon as possible."

"I will promise that if it is feasible we will be at Dalyoki for Easter. If we are not, it means that we will have something better. A new hope for Russia."

For the next six weeks Vassili Viska drove himself unsparingly, trying to do everything conceivable to move Russia one inch from its disastrous heading. He badgered every government minister with proposals, suggestions. Because of his name and his services to Russia they listened to him politely, but once he had left their offices they shook their heads in dismay, wondering if Vassili Viska truly understood how an autocracy functioned. Vassili petitioned the

Tsar for an audience but was refused. He even sought permission to speak to the Empress; that request was also denied. From then on, with nowhere left to turn, with Russia beginning to feed on its own flesh, the spirits of Vassili started to sink.

"Soybel, I think today was the worst day of my life!" Vassili exclaimed, as the two of them, bundled in fur-lined coats, walked through the snow-covered gardens of their estate. "By now, everyone of importance must be discussing it. There must be a thousand different conspiracies hatching at this very moment, every one plotting to rid Russia of its most vile enemy."

"Rasputin?"

"My mind is whirling with talk of a deed so foul—to plan such a monstrous thing, just to *think* of it frightens me. And when I hear my own answer to the request that I be party to it, I have no idea if I am a hero or a coward. And yet, it grieves me to see Russia perishing at the hands of that monk. He is using every deceit to mold our country into the realm *he* desires: a Russia where his scandals and debaucheries will be permitted while everyone else will be forced to do nothing but supply him with flesh and money to satisfy his needs. A less calculating man who behaved the same way would be judged insane and dealt with accordingly. But Rasputin, despite whatever else he might be, is brilliant. And so far he has held his enemies at bay. But not for long . . . not for long."

Soybel clutched Vassili's arm and looked straight at him, her eyes flaming with excitement.

"It pains me to see Petrograd twisted inside out, to see this grand city of Peter reduced to a place of raw nerves. You know, Soybel, it does not matter if the Germans destroy us, because even if they do not, the Empress and her crazed monk will."

Soybel stopped walking and stared at her husband. "Then you have made up your mind?"

Without breaking his stride, Vassili said, "Yes." Soybel ran after him, tugging at his coat sleeve when she caught up with him. "You have agreed to join with them? To, to eliminate Raspu—"

"You wanted us to spend Easter at Dalyoki, and we shall do so," Vassili interrupted curtly.

Soybel shivered as a sharp wind raced across the Neva, piercing through her heavy ankle-length coat. "Are you telling me you told them no? That you refused to act to save our country?"

"What good would it do?" Vassili gestured helplessly. "As far as I am concerned, this monarchy is not worth trying to save." He strode on.

"But only a week ago—"

"That was a lifetime ago. Let others—"

"But Vassili, what will be left if Rasputin is allowed to go on?"

Tears came to Vassili's eyes. "The same thing if he is killed." Two glistening drops rolled down his cheeks. "There will be nothing, Soybel, nothing." Vassili stopped walking; his arms hung limply at his sides.

"Then what alternative is left for you? How will you save Russia? How will you prevent Rasputin from becoming our emperor? How will anyone prevent that?"

"The first thing we must do is escape from Petrograd. We will find refuge in the south. The war is not there, at least not yet. And Rasputin's hands have not reached that far either."

"Will we be able to get there with so many of the railways destroyed? Are there any trains left at all?"

"If you do not mind sharing a compartment with vermin and refugees, we will make it."

"To be with you, I would share it with anything."

"I am glad, because I have already begun to make preparations." Vassili shuddered. "Suddenly I feel compelled to run from Petrograd. This is not the capital of my country. This place is foreign to me." As if in pain Vassili cried out, "If I do not find Russia at Dalyoki, Soybel, I think I will go mad!"

Soybel looked up at Vassili, her heart aching for him. "For the first time, I hope the Germans do win. To rid Russia of everything that is hurting you, and to prevent the Bolsheviks from assuming control. I would certainly prefer living under the Germans than under the Bolsheviks."

"No! At least the Bolsheviks are Russians."

"Vassili!"

"Until I am nothing but bones, less than bones, I am still a Russian, Soybel. And perhaps even after that."

"What is happening to you, Vassili?" Soybel hugged him tightly.

"I am just tired. Very tired. All I want to do is go to Dalyoki so I can think. Too much has happened. Too many terrible things for the mind to comprehend." Vassili paused for a moment. "Right now I do not care if I never see Petrograd again."

"What about the house?"

"We will close it up as best we can and leave it. If Russia falls, it will too.'"

"We could leave Annushka to watch it for us."

"As long as you do not mind having to care for Munya yourself."

"And you will be his tutor, instead of a stranger. He will love that!" Taking Vassili by the hand, Soybel began to walk, pulling him along with her. "If there is snow on the ground at Dalyoki, can we go for sleigh rides? And spend our evenings by the fire and talk, like we used to?"

"We will do everything as we used to."

Soybel stepped in front of her husband, grabbed him by the coatsleeves and spoke rapidly. "Do you remember how we used to drive through the countryside in your automobile? How Munya and I would wave at the peasants? You were so occupied with trying to stay on the road, you never noticed how startled everyone was when we passed. Who wouldn't be, with all the snorting and hissing it does?"

"I wonder if Volodya has kept it in condition."

"Can we polish it, Vassili? And take it out for a ride as soon as the snow melts? Now I hope there is no snow at Dalyoki!"

"Munya would get so excited when we raced past a farm house and I squeezed the horn and made the horses whinny and run in fright."

"Would you teach me how to drive it?"

Vassili looked down at his wife and smiled, enjoying the image of Soybel in a large bonnet held fast by a ribbon under her chin, trying to wrestle the big red Mercedes-Simplex over the rutted dirt roads.

"Would you?"

"Yes."

Soybel threw her arms around Vassili's neck and stood on her tiptoes to kiss him. "You know, I always wished you had brought it to Petrograd. But now I am glad you did not. Because now we will be able to drive to Odessa, too. We can go for rides along the Boulevard. Or along the Arkadia. It will be the most fun we have had in years!"

Vassili watched the delighted expressions that touched Soybel's mouth and eyes. It had been months since he had seen her so happy. He felt a great need to seclude himself with his wife and ignore everything except the delicious sweetness of her face, wanting to hear nothing but her laughter when she awoke in the morning and rolled over to hug him, resting her head against his chest as she had long ago. Vassili thought of the summer days just before and immediately after they were married, when the two of them had spent countless lazy mornings and drowsy afternoons dallying in bed, making love, then relaxing with Munya lying between them as they played with one another's fingers on the pillows behind their heads. Vassili placed his hands on Soybel's shoulders. Surrounded by the white fur of her coat, her face glowed. "I will tender my resignation this week; I will plead exhaustion. And that is the truth. At least partially. Then we will leave for Dalyoki."

"I am so happy, Vassili. So happy."

"Everything will be like it once was," he said softly.

"Do you promise?"

Vassili brushed a loose strand of hair back up under Soybel's hood. "I promise."

Soybel buried her face against her husband's chest. Vassili put his arm around her, holding her snugly. He rested his chin on top of her head and stared into the distance, unmindful of the bitter-cold wind that reddened his face and stung his eyes; his expression was unsure.

CHAPTER 38

The railway trip from Petrograd to Kishnev was long and uncomfortable. And as Vassili had predicted, the train was crowded with refugees and soldiers, all of whom looked as if there was nothing left for them but despair. They told terrifying tales about the war, recounting brutalities, tortures, and carnage so monstrous that after a while their words held no impact. They spoke of epidemics and starvation; their own oozing sores, battle wounds dressed in soiled bandages, their emaciated bodies, attested to their lack of nourishment and medical attention. They reeked of filth, and lice infested their bodies and clothing. By the time the train reached Kishnev, Soybel, Vassili, and Munya looked and smelled as badly as the others, and when they saw Volodya, who had been instructed by wire to meet them and take them the remaining thirty miles to Dalyoki, the three of them rushed up to him, greeting the caretaker of Dalyoki as though he were a savior.

It took Vassili and Soybel a week to recover from the bruises and indignities of their journey. During that time they did little else but bathe in scented water, read, sometimes talk, but mostly they rested by the fireplace and made love. It was Vassili who led the way, Soybel waiting until her husband fastened his eyes on her and slowly let them rove over her body. Wherever they were, whatever they were doing, they stopped and retreated to their bedroom. Undressing one another, they caressed, their hands exciting them to move to the bed. There Soybel made Vassili lie face down while she kneaded his back until the knots of tension eased. Handspan by handspan, she worked her way down to the base of his spine, across his buttocks, and down the backs of his thighs. When she had finished with his legs and feet, Soybel would rub Vassili's toes one by one, then slide her hands along the insides of his legs. Rolling over, Vassili positioned himself so that Soybel's face was directly above his thighs. Sitting up halfway, he watched Soybel touch him, gently stroke him. Then when he was ready, Vassili would nod his head and Soybel would lower her face, her lips encompassing him, drawing him into her mouth, swallowing him until he had released all his anxieties. Afterward they would lie side by side, holding hands, not saying a word. And then, when Vassili felt rested, they would begin to make love.

Once they had adjusted themselves to their new life, all thoughts of the war and of politics disappeared; the very few times that Soybel and Vassili did talk of those things, it all seemed to belong to a period far in the past. Most of the time they fantasized about what they would do when the war was over, planning an itinerary for a trip to Europe, deciding to purchase a villa on the French Riviera. They discussed how they would redecorate Dalyoki, agreeing that every room needed repainting and refurnishing. The only news of the outside world came from Volodya when he returned from his shopping trips to Kishnev, and the more they learned of how violently the country was reeling from one blow to the next, the more Soybel and Vassili Viska enclosed themselves in a world where there was room for nothing but themselves and Munya.

Toward the end of their second week at Dalyoki, a new powdering of snow fell, covering the ground and trees with a thin layer of frost that made everything look like sugar. Each afternoon for an hour or so Soybel, Vassili, and Munya walked along the sloping hillsides or through the nearby woods, the beauty of the landscape and the stimulating climate helping to revitalize them. Every so often a waft of spring air floated over the countryside, and Vassili decided that it was time to uncover the red Mercedes. He and Volodya pushed the vehicle out of the carriage house and opened the hood. Vassili was pleased at the way the caretaker had kept the automobile clean and covered with a tarpaulin. Despite the fact that the Mercedes had been indoors, it took the two men an entire afternoon of adjusting the engine before it would start and keep running. Vassili thanked Volodya for his help and instructed him to let the motor idle for half an hour, then he entered the house to wash and change his clothes. When Soybel saw Vassili, she teased him about his appearance. His hands and face were smudged with grease, his hair was disheveled, and the place where he had cut his finger on the throttle spring was stained with a small clot of blood. His clothes were rumpled, and a tear ran the length of his shirtsleeve where he had caught it on the raised engine cover. Vassili laughed, playing along when Soybel asked him if he was indeed the same man who once dressed so elegantly in another city where he had been considered an important member of the government. Vassili replied that he was not, and that the person she was speaking of was his brother, and that he, Vassili Viska, was a poor mechanic whose life consisted of nothing more than working with the temperamental engines of automobiles.

Then, early in May, with the ground still frozen, a dozen peasants on horseback rode into Dalyoki. Politely, they asked to see the master of the house and were surprised and delighted when Vassili stepped outside to talk with them without making them wait. After a courteous greeting and a few pleasantries about the weather, their spokesman asked Vassili if he would be willing to discuss the possibility of giving them some of his land so they could become independent farmers. The question caught Vassili by surprise, and he gave no answer. An instant later he was smiling; the seriousness and extreme politeness of the peasants amused him. Studying the group of men before him, Vassili found it difficult to believe they would approach him in such a manner. He had heard of similar requests made by peasants, but those stories always included details about how force had been used. Already several hundred estates had been burned to the ground and the landowners murdered. It took Vassili aback to be approached so civilly, and when he finally regained his composure he agreed to talk with them if they would return in a week or so when he had come to a decision, adding that he would send Volodya to fetch them so that they would not waste their time by arriving before he had completed his deliberations. For several moments the peasants talked among themselves, and then told Vassili that his proposal was satisfactory. Doffing their hats, they turned their horses around, and left Dalyoki peacefully.

When Vassili returned to the house and informed Soybel of what had occurred, she, too, found it entertaining, until she asked her husband what he intended to do.

"Give them some land, what else? If the Tsar will not permit us to have a constitution, then we must find other means to achieve the same thing."

"But Vassili, it is our land. Why should we give it away for nothing?" Soybel asked, continuing to slice the cold meat that had been left over from the night before.

"You did not mind when giving up land was part of the legislation we wanted Nicholas to support." Vassili took a piece of the meat and chewed it slowly.

"If something is a law, and everyone is required to do it, I do not mind. But to be the only one to give away something as valuable as land is another matter."

"All they want is a few acres," Vassili said, following Soybel to the dining table.

"That is all they want for now. What will you do when they want everything?"

"Why should they want everything? They acted like reasonable men. And I am a reasonable man." Vassili replied loudly enough so that Soybel could hear him while she called Munya to lunch.

"Today they were reasonable. Tomorrow, who knows?" Soybel said, returning with her son. "Sit here, Munya. Your poppa will give you some meat."

"What do you think I should do?" Vassili held the serving platter toward Munya.

"Leave some for others, Munya."

"We have more land than we have a right to. And you know as well as I do what needs to be done if Russia is to survive."

"We are not discussing Russia's survival, Vassili, but the illegal demands of the peasants."

"But we *are* discussing Russia's survival. Dalyoki is not an island, and unless we anticipate the future we, too, will become victims of our history." Vassili held out the tray of meat for Soybel.

"Our history also tells us, Vassili, that Russia has survived similar periods."

"That is not true."

"Maman, du pain, s'il tu plaît."

"There is mint jelly, too, Munya. Would you like some?"

"Oui, maman."

"Soybel, never before have we been faced with events such as these, and that is the danger of history. Because past circumstances are never identical with present ones. That is why we err when we attempt to use history to foretell the future."

"Maman, plus de confiture!"

"Furthermore, when we look to the past for answers, there are only facts to refer to," Vassili continued as he passed the plate of mint jelly to Munya. "But it is a combination of man's reason and passion that shapes events—and perhaps far more passion is involved than intellect. But history is only facts, and that is why only fools commit themselves to dealing with the present based solely on the past."

"Perhaps. But a man who stakes everything on the future

is also a fool, because he is a gambler, risking the known against the unknown. And for us to jeopardize what is rightfully ours because *you* have calculated the events of tomorrow is senseless, perilous. What if you are wrong? How will we retrieve what we have lost? And tell me this, Vassili, how much of what is ours will you give away? When will you say no to their demands? How will we be reimbursed for your generosity? Who will pay us—"

"Soybel, I am not interested in the worth of our property. All that concerns me is the worth of people!"

The sharpness of Vassili's tone made Soybel pause. She smiled coyly at her husband. "Please do not be angry with me. I am just upset because I know how hard you have struggled for Russia, and it hurts me to see how much you have suffered without achieving what you wanted to."

"I am not angry with you, Soybel."

"And all I have really been trying to say is that we should think about this situation and not rush into a decision."

"And I agree. That is exactly why I did not give them my answer right then."

"Still, Vassili, a week, even two weeks, is not enough time to make such an important decision."

"How long should we think about it?"

"Forever," Soybel replied lightly, a playful smile brightening her face.

Vassili laughed. "The peasants might become restless waiting that long."

"If they do, I will be happy to teach them patience."

Almost continually, Soybel and Vassili discussed the peasants' request, and by the end of the week Soybel announced that she agreed with her husband's initial decision. But she did make one request: that Vassili should wait a few more days before sending Volodya to arrange for a meeting, in the event that they themselves had overlooked something. Vassili consented.

In the middle of the following week Soybel gave Volodya a sealed envelope containing a note written in her elegant handwriting and instructed him to take it to the village ten miles away. Immediately, Volodya scrambled onto his horse's back and whipped the animal into a run, unmercifully forcing it to fly across the frozen steppes. For too long, Volodya had accepted the taunts and angry words of the members of his village who chided him for continuing to work for a landowner. Nevertheless, Volodya had steadfastly refused to say anything against Vassili Viska, never doubting that the man was honorable. Now, he had proof of it, and Volodya could not wait to boast about how right he had been. He felt his jacket pocket, making sure he still had the letter. Imagining the expressions on the faces of his kinsmen, Volodya was overcome by exhilaration. And he urged his horse to run even more swiftly.

The morning sun climbed higher, burning away the chill in the air. In the distance Volodya could see the tiny specks he knew were straw-thatched mud huts, and his stomach growled for some vodka and a large bowl of steaming groats. He shouted a greeting when he was still a mile away, repeating it until it became a constant clanging, like celebration bells. Men and boys ran to see why this usually reserved man was raising such a clamor; heavyset women, aproned and with babushkas covering their heads, followed close behind.

"I have it!" Volodya shouted, pulling the envelope from his jacket and waving it wildly above his head. "I have Viska's answer!" He yanked his horse to a halt.

Volodya dismounted and handed the letter to the first man who reached his side. The peasant ripped open the envelope, withdrew the paper from inside it, then studied it carefully. When he was finished he handed the letter—which had the light fragrance of a woman's perfume on it—to another man, who also passed it on when he had finished, the process continuing until each of them had felt the expensive writing paper and had run their coarse fingers along the lines of the handsome writing. Then it was handed to a white-haired old man who slowly began to read the words, reciting to the others what their uneducated eyes had been unable to decipher.

It was nearly sunset when the countryside trembled under the immense weight of fifty running horses. The snapping sound of whips cut through the late-afternoon light as the leather thongs commanded the animals to run as fast as possible. The riders, bundled up in fur jackets, had rifles slung over their shoulders; frosted breath belched from their mouths. They charged across the barren grassland toward a house that was still out of their sight; they swung north for a mile, then turned east again. The outline of their destination became distinct, its size making them move faster. Nearing the mansion, the horsemen unslung their rifles, holding them across their thighs until they were twenty-five yards from the house. Then they raised them, firing bullet after bullet into the grandly designed wooden structure. They cursed and yelled, bellowing with rage as their metal shells tore into the walls. Their leader leaped from his horse and kicked open a door. He entered the house, followed by the others, and in a frenzy they ran from room to room, smashing everything in sight. They destroyed paintings and books, sent chandeliers crashing to the floors, and started a bonfire with the velvet-covered furniture. They smashed expensive statuary and trampled delicate chinaware into dust. A wooden hobbyhorse the size of a pony lost its head to the repeated blows of an axe; beds and draperies were slashed with knives, then set ablaze. Burning torches were tossed into every room. Then they stepped outside, standing silently, listening for a sound from someone other than themselves. In the distance they heard the whine of an automobile. Quickly, they gathered their horses, remounted them and dashed eastward along the dirt road; they had no difficulty following their quarry. The distance between the peasants and the machine they were chasing closed rapidly. The automobile disappeared around a bend in the road, its shiny red body mocking the peasants. Their fury increased and they slammed their heels against the sides of their mounts. Moments later the pursuers entered the curve, bending low over their horses' necks, racing along the arc. When they reached the next straight stretch, the peasants raised their whips, ready to beat their animals into an even faster pace. But what they saw stayed their hands. Directly ahead of them, crumpled against a tree and lying on its side, was the red automobile; pinned beneath it was the master of Dalyoki. Reining in his horse, the leader dismounted and walked toward the man he had once served. He grabbed his head by the hair and, seeing that he was still alive, motioned to the others to lift up the car. When they did, Volodya slid the body of Vassili Viska out from under the Mercedes and dropped him back to the ground. Confused, frightened, Vassili's eyes flickered from one hate-filled face to the next. He tried to move, but he could not. His back was broken; Vassili could only move his eyes. Someone knelt by his side. Shifting his focus, Vassili saw the man who for twenty-five years had worked at Dalyoki.

Volodya stared at Vassili, not a glimmer of recognition on his face. Wordlessly, the peasant removed an envelope from his jacket, and from it extracted a letter. He held it for Vassili to see. Vassili's eyes grew wide with horror as he read the lines he had never seen and did not even know had been written. He tried to talk; only blood gurgled from his mouth. He screamed silently as he read the words again and again. Volodya removed the letter from Vassili's sight and pressed it against the landowner's chest. The paper crackled as Volodya smoothed it flat. To Vassili, the sounds were as loud as explosions, each one reminding him of the lies Soybel had written. Fury raged within Vassili, struggling to erupt from his throat. He wanted to yell to Volodya and the others, he wanted to shriek to them that the letter was false, that he *had* decided to give them the land they wanted, but it was impossible for him to speak. Volodya ceremoniously removed a knife from his belt. He looked around to make sure the others were watching him. Every one of the bearded, leathery men nodded in approval. They tightened the circle they had formed around Vassili and peered down at him, their faces weary, their eyes showing the betrayal they felt. Vassili looked from one face to another, begging for mercy; the group of men remained impassive. Volodya waited until Vassili's eyes met his. Suddenly, with one violent thrust, Volodya stabbed his knife through the letter and deep into Vassili's heart. A moment later the red Mercedes-Simplex was engulfed in flames. For a minute the peasants watched it burn, then, satisfied with their revenge, they mounted their horses and rode back to their village.

Darkness covered the earth before Soybel and Munya crawled out of the woods and stealthily approached the still-smoldering automobile. Soybel's face was scratched and bleeding, and the boy limped, both of them having been bruised when Vassili pushed them out of the vehicle. It had been a desperate plan, but Vassili could think of nothing else; so he had ordered his wife and son to run into the woods and hide while he led the peasants away from them. Unfortunately, he had negotiated a turn in the road badly, and now, revealed by the moonlight, the result was clearly visible. Soybel stumbled as she rushed to her husband's side. Her eyes were glazed, and she collapsed next to his body, screaming so frightfully that Munya was terrified to come near her. Maniacally, Soybel shook her head back and forth, beating herself with her fists. Munya stood motionless, horrified. Seeing the letter she had written, and where Volodya's knife had pierced it, the words blurred by dried blood, Soybel tore the paper from her husband's chest and squeezed it into a ball. Then she opened her hand and watched as it skittered away on the wind.

"Help me!" she demanded of her son, grabbing one of Vassili's arms.

Munya looked at her blankly.

"Do what I said!"

With difficulty, mother and son dragged the body of Vassili Viska into the forest, stopping beneath a tree where the ground was free from any trace of snow. Soybel searched for a stick, and when she found one she fell to her knees and scraped at the earth. It took her until dawn to dig a shallow grave. When she was done, she rolled her husband's body into the pit, covering him with dirt. Soybel placed rocks and branches over the mound to protect Vassili's corpse from hungry wolves and wild dogs. For hours she stood beside the grave, and not until the mid-morning sun drove away the chill that numbed her mind and body did Soybel move.

Noticing his mother stir, Munya took hold of her hand and looked up at her, his expression asking her to explain what had happened. Anguish distorted his face; tracks made by his tears ran from his eyes to his chin. Munya put his mother's hands to his lips, his body wracked with grief. Soybel pressed his head against her hip.

"Let us go home," she said, her words dry, cracked.

After one last glance at her husband's final dwelling place, Soybel Viska gripped her son's hand and very slowly began to walk, the two of them clutching one another more tightly with each step.

CHAPTER 39

With the first step he took from the road onto the lane, the uneasiness he had suffered for the last two days seemed to increase many times over. All around him, events far beyond his control were pressing toward him, trapping him in the center of a vise that was relentlessly tightening about him. Four hundred miles to the north, Semyon Petlura and his army of Haidamacks had just attacked Kiev. Now they were leisurely riding south, stopping often to punish their enemies, their objective—Odessa. From the west the German and Austrian armies were steadily advancing eastward. To the east the Turks were threatening, while the escape route to the south, across the Black Sea and through the Dardenelles into the Mediterranean, was effectively blockaded by warring battleships. And now there was this. Unexpected. Foreboding. At once repulsive and compelling. Like omens, trees that had fallen during winter storms lay across the lane, while in other places, the underbrush, vines, and prickly plants, all entangled, obstructed the path.

Carefully, he worked his way past the ends of jagged branches and snarls of thorns, each step heightening his agitation. When he rounded the last bend in the trail and saw the manor house in the distance—the house where he was born and had spent his childhood—he stopped in mid-step, shocked. The walls had lost all their paint, the vivid yellow he remembered now showed only in small flakes. There was hardly a board that did not require some repair, many hanging loose, some warped, broken, or missing entirely. The porch railing was shattered in one place, as if something large and bulky had charged its way through it. Every pane of glass had been smashed. The lawn that had always been so neatly clipped and green during the warm months was waist-high and dead, like hay. Where the barn and carriage house had once stood there was nothing but piles of wood chips; the timbers of the buildings had been demolished by an axe. The inside of the house was even worse. Rain that had leaked through the broken windows and the roof, then had frozen during the winter storms, had melted and lay in stagnant pools. The furniture in the parlor was scattered everywhere, upended, slashed with a knife. In front of the fireplace and strewn over the Persian rug were chunks of bread as hard as stone, partially eaten fruit as petrified as the pits at the center, and empty wine bottles. A trail of silverware, much of it bent and twisted, encrusted with food, led to the kitchen and from one end of the hall to the other. Every room was in disarray, touched by at least some destruction, but nothing was in as vile a condition as the master suite. Painted on every wall in brazen strokes were epithets, curses, and threats. The dressing-table mirror lay scattered in ten thousand slivers; the table itself was scarred with frightening words deeply carved into its top. The canopied bed had been defiled, the once-white sheet was yellow, putrid, and in its very center were animal droppings. The French doors leading to the veranda were open, decomposed leaves and twigs making a trail to the outside.

Sitting on the swing in what had once been a beautiful flower garden was a woman in a filmy blue dress and a bonnet, holding a parasol of the same shade. She swung back and forth, the chains which supported the seat squeaking. Her face was heavily powdered and rouged, her lipstick caked from several layers having been applied one on top of the other. Around her neck was a necklace, a gold chain on which were strung tiny emeralds. Her eyes were shining and alive, too alive. Next to her, curled like a cat against her side, was a child, dark-haired, slender, clothed like a boy but beautiful enough to be a girl. Neither of them spoke or even stirred, their eyes transfixed into space, swinging, swinging, back and forth, gently swinging.

"Hello, Momma," Grisha barely managed to whisper.

In the distance a bird screeched as it swooped after its prey; it was the only sound there was.

"I received your telegram, Momma."

The mouse was dead, the bird, nervously twitching its head from side to side, ate in silence.

"Are you all right, Momma? Did they hurt you?"

Overhead a hawk circled, waiting for the bird on the ground to finish eating and fatten itself up with its meal.

"I . . . I am sorry about Vassili, Momma."

"The peasants killed him. Bolshevik peasants. Did you know that he wanted to give them some of his land? All Vassili wanted them to do was wait until it was made a law. I wrote it down in a letter, just like Vassili told me to. He made me write the letter. I did not want to. I did not want him to be killed. Why did they kill Vassili?" Soybel rested her head against the side of the swing and slowly twirled her parasol.

Having eaten its fill, the bird stepped away from the remains of the mouse, fluttered its wings, and lifted itself into the air, flying straight toward the sun. Noiselessly, effortlessly, the hawk overtook the smaller bird and in mid-flight snatched it in its talons. A moment later the sky was empty.

Soybel began to hum softly, the tune a monotonous two notes that she repeated, up and down; up-down, up-down, up-down. She stopped abruptly. "After the war is over, Munya and I are going to France." Soybel gazed at her son and scratched him behind the ears. "We may never leave once we get there." The youngster snuggled closer to her. "We will only speak Russian there, so no one will be able to understand our secrets."

"Momma, I never wrote to you about this. I should have. I, I wanted to, but I didn't. I am married, Momma."

"When everything is straightened out, I will inherit all of Vassili's money and his land. I intend to sell the land. Then the peasants can steal it from someone else."

"My wife's name is Sara, Momma, and—"

"Grisha, rub my head. It has been so long since anyone rubbed my head."

"Yes, Momma." Carefully, Grisha removed his mother's bonnet, letting her black hair fall free.

"I loved Vassili. Everyone knows how much I loved Vassili." Soybel leaned her head back, rolling it against Grisha's fingers. The afternoon sun beat against her face. "It is so warm here. For three years it was winter in Petrograd. I was always so cold there. Even at Dalyoki it was winter." Soybel hugged herself and swayed from side to side. "I am cold, Grisha, get me a blanket."

"Everything in the house is ruined, Momma." Like a lover, Grisha stroked his mother's silky hair.

"The house is ugly now. I *hate* it." A strand of Soybel's hair became caught in one corner of her mouth, sticking to her lipstick. Grisha went to brush it away—his mother grasped him by the wrists. "Did you see what they did to my bed?" Soybel dug her nails into Grisha's flesh. "It was not enough that they made love in it, but to do those other things!"

Prying his mother's fingers loose, Grisha took a step away. "Who would do such a thing?"

"I do not know, Momma."

"You are lying, Grisha. Everybody knows who did it. It was Daniella!" Soybel laughed, the sound short. "She did it to hurt me. Just like you got married to hurt me."

"No, Momma, I—"

"I despise Daniella!" Soybel glared at Grisha. "And I despise your wife . . . I despise everyone's wife." Very slowly Soybel's anger receded. "Are you happy with your wife, Grisha?"

"Yes. Like you and Poppa once—"

"I do not want to hear about that." Soybel turned to Munya and smiled at him. "Is your wife very pretty, Grisha?"

"Yes."

"Did you know that I was the most beautiful woman among all of Vassili's friends? Some said I was the most beautiful woman in Petrograd. No man who knew me did not want to make love to me." With an easy push, Soybel started the swing moving, a wistful look settling on her face. It was a minute before she said anything.

"Grisha, I will not go back into the house until it is cleaned."

"There is so much—"

"*All* of it."

"Where does one start?"

"I want you to fix everything the way it used to be."

"It is too much for one person to do, Momma."

"I want every wall, inside and out, repaired and repainted. I want all the furniture thrown out and replaced. I want every book burned, and the ashes buried. Every piece of clothing that is in there, every scrap, everything—I want everything destroyed!"

"No."

"I will not move from this spot until everything has been scrubbed a hundred times, *do you understand me?*"

"But, Momma—"

"*Do you understand?*"

"Yes, Momma, I understand very well."

"Then do it!"

Soybel kicked out her feet and the swing moved faster. Her eyes had a brittle glitter to them. A breeze rustled the leaves, stirring the soft curls that framed her face. The long hem of her dress flapped, brushing the ground, the sound muffled by the long grass. And all Soybel saw was a vision. A manicured lawn, vast and green; two small buildings—a barn and a carriage house—newly constructed, freshly painted yellow with white trim; a majestic elm, thick-limbed, broad; woods, a wall of oaks and maples, ripe with pear and apricot trees, garlanded by lilacs; a garden, its border edged with stone, and flowers, hundreds of flowers in a riot of reds, violets, blue gentians. At its center there was a new swing of white wicker; an enclosed chamber designed for two. And then there was the house—every board perfect, the windows reglazed, the porch railing repaired and painted white like the door and the sashes, and everything else yellow, vivid yellow to rival the sun! Soybel sat rigid, her eyes ablaze.

"Momma."

"Is that you, Vassili?"

"I am leaving, Momma."

"Vassili?"

"Momma, I am going."

"*Vassili?*"

"Good-bye, Momma."

BOOK FOUR

September 1917—March 1920

He will put on uprightness for armor,
wear justice for a helmet,
sharpen his anger for a sword,
And with him the world will go to war
against the madmen.

THE APOCRYPHA

CHAPTER 40

By mid-September 1917 the weather in Odessa had already turned cold, and after half an hour of patrolling the empty streets of Moldavanka, the night air made Grisha Moisei's teeth chatter. He was tired, especially now that Aram Zubov had increased each man's patrol from four nights a week to seven.

"Damn the Bolsheviks," Grisha muttered. "And damn the Germans, too." He yawned and forced himself to concentrate. He knew that since March the ghetto had been without incident. But he also knew the lull was temporary. There were certain to be more riots, as there had been all through March after Tsar Nicholas' abdication from the throne. Especially now with the entire country on the verge of chaos. *And why shouldn't anarchy rule? With the people beginning to starve. Germany coming ever closer to conquering Russia. The Bolsheviks using every means to foment strikes and insurrections in order to topple the provisional government. So Nicholas abdicated—so what? Perhaps he can escape Russia's hatred for him, but Moldavanka will still suffer because of the Romanovs' three-hundred-year precedent of using Jews as scapegoats.* Throughout March and well into April there had been an inordinate number of assaults on Moldavanka. Then they abated. Aram Zubov attributed the cessation of attacks to the increased vigilance of his self-defense group. Others claimed that life was beginning to return to normal, as it would in all of Russia. Grisha agreed with Aram Zubov.

Grisha became numb, and he breathed on his fingers to warm them. He was alert, his hands ready to snatch the carbine off his shoulder and challenge or, if necessary, kill. The clatter of distant hoofbeats caught his ear, but when they faded away he relaxed. Nervously, Grisha adjusted the ammunition belt strapped around his waist. A child's crying made him jump, and he put one hand into his jacket pocket, feeling the cold metal of the hand grenade at its bottom. His fingers recoiled. Gingerly he touched the small bomb again, checking to make sure he had not dislodged the firing pin. Finding it still in place, Grisha sighed with relief. A stone rattled behind him. Grisha grabbed hold of his rifle, released the safety catch, and turned, ready to fire. All he heard was his own breathing and a moaning boat whistle. He peered into the darkness, searching for the source of the sound. He saw nothing. Cautiously, Grisha inched forward, his body in a crouch.

"I will count to three. And if you do not answer, I will shoot!"

There was no response.

"One."

Only a slight breeze from the north replied.

"Two."

Grisha waited.

"Three!"

He cocked his rifle.

"Stop, *malchik*!" a voice ordered.

Grisha froze, aiming his weapon in the direction from which the voice had come. "Step out where I can see you!" demanded Grisha.

A slight man dressed in high boots, a fur-collared jacket, and a woolen cap stepped out of a doorway. "Don't shoot."

Grisha held his finger against the trigger. "Who are you?"

The man snickered and slapped his forehead. "My life depends on you? On a child?"

"Who *are* you?" repeated Grisha.

"You still have your mother's milk on your lips."

"What do you want?" Grisha asked, the rifle beginning to feel heavy in his hands.

The man laughed deeply, his eyes flashed, and his thick black beard wiggled with amusement. "You think you are protecting me? Ha! I am protecting you!"

"Hold your hands above your head!"

"If Mishka could see you, he would laugh even more than me!" The man ignored Grisha's order.

"Your hands, *raise* them!" Grisha aimed the rifle between the man's eyes.

"Of course. But do not be afraid of me." The man chuckled as he obeyed. "Come with me to our headquarters. It is nearby." Then with his hands held above his head the man began to saunter away.

"Stop!"

"Come, child, let's go."

"Stop, or I will shoot!"

"You would shoot a Jew in the back? What kind of crazy world is this?"

Not knowing whether or not to fire at the man, Grisha followed him. They walked for two blocks; Grisha with his rifle pointed at the man's back, the man with his hands raised high in the air. When they came to a street called Petrovskaya, the man turned right.

"In here, momma's boy," said the man as they approached a one-story building that covered half the length of the narrow thoroughfare. "Mishka wants to see you." He opened the door, above which hung a hand-painted sign that read Malinas Zala.

A rush of boisterous laughter bounded into the street. The man motioned for Grisha to accompany him. Grisha hesitated. Again the man gestured. Warily, Grisha approached the building, still pointing his rifle before him.

Reaching the doorway, Grisha halted and peered inside. Through a thick swirl of blue cigarette smoke he discerned a large room, perhaps eighty feet long and half as wide, with a bar at one end and at the other a large fireplace. The sawdust-covered floor was crowded with circular tables around which motley groups of men sat and drank; everyone was talking at once. Grisha started to count them, stopping when he reached sixty and estimating that there might be a hundred and fifty or more. The man who Grisha had captured stepped inside and walked to the center of the room, his hands still held above his head.

"Hey! I brought another momma's boy!" he shouted.

"Where is he?"

"Trying to decide if he should shoot me or not!"

"If I were him, I would shoot you!" someone shouted.

The roomful of men laughed and whistled, pounding the tables with their fists.

"Does he know that he belongs to Mishka now?" a wiry man asked.

"He knows nothing except his mother's milk!"

Hesitantly Grisha entered the café; his eyes, along with his rifle, swept the room. Everyone became silent. Grisha looked from one man to another, feeling naked as they stared at him: each one was more fearsome than the next. Some wore short beards, others full ones, a few were clean-shaven. Their clothes were coarse, their faces weathered, their hands thick and raw from labor. Everyone sat except Grisha, his prisoner, and a giant of a man who had been leaning against the bar. With deliberate steps the man walked from the bar across the sawdust-covered floor toward Grisha. He wore black pants, with the trouser-tops stuffed into high leather boots. Around his waist was cinched a wide leather belt decorated with rows of bullets, and from both hips hung leather holsters, each one cradling a blue-black revolver. Over his dark shirt he wore a lamb's-wool vest. A wide scar slanted from the bridge of his nose to his ear, and his mustache hung well below his chin. His straight black hair fell below his massive shoulders. His eyes were the gray of a cold winter's dawn.

"Sit down!" he roared at Grisha. "And point that rifle at the floor!"

Grisha took a step back and obeyed. His prisoner finally dropped his arms to his sides.

"What was he guarding?" the large man asked.

"The almshouse and the cemetery."

"Borisov! Go there and take this child's place!"

Without a word a man rose from one of the tables and left the café.

"Don't worry, child, Borisov is a good guard," the burly man said, some of the gruffness gone from his voice. "Do you smoke?" he added, offering Grisha a cigarette.

"No," Grisha replied, still awed by the size of the man he faced.

"A drink then?"

Grisha nodded, hoping that liquor would calm his pounding heart.

"A *malinas shalost* for our guest!" the man shouted to a tall, well-proportioned woman who stood behind the bar.

Quickly she took down a bottle of raspberry juice and poured a glassful. The room was suddenly filled with cheers, and Grisha squirmed with discomfort.

"Do you know who I am?" the man asked, diverting Grisha's attention from the woman who was approaching him. The man lit a cigarette, dropped the match on the floor, grinding out its flame with his boot heel.

Grisha gaped at the man and said nothing.

"Is your momma's tit still in your mouth, or don't you have a tongue?" The force of the man's voice made Grisha flinch.

"I know who you are," Grisha replied weakly. The woman set down the fruit d_ink in front of him.

"Ah, so you've spit out your mother's nipple. Good. Now drink!"

Grisha lifted the glass. Every eye was on him. He raised

the vessel to his lips, and to hide his uneasiness gulped the juice down at once. A flash of heat with the intensity of a flame surged through Grisha's body. His face flushed red, and he gasped for breath. The man laughed uproariously.

"Do you want another *shalost*?" the buxom woman inquired; her low voice was as smooth as velvet. "Or just vodka this time and no juice?"

"Give him another!" someone shouted.

The assembly of men noisily approved the suggestion. The woman grinned and returned to the bar to refill Grisha's glass.

"Now! Who am I?" the herculean man asked, his voice drowning out the crowd.

"Mishka Yaponchik," Grisha answered, feeling dizzy as the vodka entered his bloodstream.

"No, I am not Mishka Yaponchik."

Grisha stared at the man in disbelief. He would have sworn that he was talking to the one whose name was known throughout Moldavanka. He was certain that the man was Mishka Yaponchik. "Who are you then?"

The man drew himself up to his full height. He shoved out his imposing chest as far as it would go and rested his hands on his revolvers. "I am *Mishka Yaponchik*!" he bellowed, his voice sounding powerful enough to knock down walls. "I am a thief! A real live Jewish criminal! I rob. I steal. I even kill when I have to. But I never cheat or rape. I never rape because I do not have to. And I never cheat because I am honorable." Mishka Yaponchik glared at Grisha, daring the youth to dispute his words.

The woman who had brought Grisha's first glass of the spiked raspberry juice returned with a second.

"Do you know how many men are in my gang?" Mishka asked, studying the woman's voluptuous body.

"People in Moldavanka say thousands," Grisha replied, the vodka allowing him some of his courage back.

"Do you hear that, Mala? The little fart says thousands! And he is right. Forty thousand, child! Forty thousand Jewish thieves, *my* thieves, *an army*, roam Odessa!"

Mishka grabbed Mala, crushing the woman in his enormous arms. She laughed, and everyone else joined her. Grisha looked away and sipped his drink. A roar of voices dared him to gulp this one down, too. They taunted him, angering him, and Grisha swigged the raspberry-colored vodka as if he were drinking only the juice. A round of thunderous applause and shouts of congratulations surrounded him. Mishka shouted with delight and swatted Mala on the rump as he swaggered toward the center of the smoke-filled room.

"We even do honest work, child," Mishka began, his words overpowering the din. "You see that ugly man there who looks like a village of peasants shit on his face? Everyone thinks he sells coal, and he does. During the day he gets so damned black he looks like his own shadow. But at night he becomes the best safecracker we have. And look at that one—Karmanchik. Look at his nose. It's so long it looks like it belongs between his legs. He sells candy, but he is a pickpocket, too. Right now, Skakum is somewhere in the city going through the house of a rich merchant, stealing anything he can. Tomorrow morning he will go to work in the leather factory, and no one will suspect that his life is devoted to Mishka Yaponchik. And Urka, my own special Urka. Aside from me he is the best thief there is. Do you know what he does for a living? He works as a clerk for the government. All of us have cover-ups, but we are an army, a Jewish army. And now, with the revolution, we are more important than ever. And we need more men, like you, and the others from Zubov's brigade, because we will have to fight both sides: the revolutionists *and* the monarchists. And only Mishka has the men and weapons to make that possible. Not the cripple, Zubov. All he has is words. That is all he has ever had. But Mishka has power!" Mishka slammed his fist against a table to underscore his words.

Dumbfounded, Grisha stared at Mishka Yaponchik, wondering if any other man in the world was as awesome.

"When I was your age, child, I had already been fighting for the Jews for years. Do you know that I was with the first strikers in Vilna? I helped build up the Bund there, with my fists and clubs. Then I became an enemy of the state, and the police chased me from city to city. But they never caught me, and now they are afraid to. They know that if they hurt Mishka Yaponchik, his men will destroy their city!"

No longer afraid, Grisha scrutinized Mishka Yaponchik, remembering how Joseph Dubrow had once mentioned the man, recounting the day in 1913 when a wild-eyed, violent Russian Jew had ridden through the streets of Moldavanka shouting curses and daring the frightened Jews who ran to hide to face him.

"What is this?" Mishka had shouted that day, riding along the streets astride a black horse. "What is this, a little fucking village somewhere in the forest? What are you, pieces of shit? Is that why you let them kill you like nobodies? Like dogs with fleas? Is everyone a stinking woman here? Isn't anyone a man? Well, let the Russians try anything in Odessa now that Mishka Yaponchik is here! They will see if Jews are cowards! I will show them if we are weak. And you! All you little girls down there, wearing pants and beards, do not run away anymore. I despise cowards! So join with me! Fight with me! Let us show the Russians the strength we really have!"

For the rest of the night, until dawn, Grisha listened to Mishka rave on about his thieves and how they stole from the rich Russians and Jews, giving the money to the poor. Mishka bragged about how he and his men robbed banks, assassinated police officials and soldiers. He strutted from one end of the café to the other, describing in detail his most daring exploits, and though Grisha believed only part of what Mishka said, it was still enough to make him admire the man's courage and daring. By morning the café was empty except for Mishka, Mala, and Grisha. Mishka's voice became lower and his words came more slowly, the large quantity of vodka he had consumed affecting him.

"Without Mala nothing would matter," Mishka said,

resting his head on the shoulder of the woman who sat next to him.

"And if not for Mishka, there would be no Mala," the woman added, snuggling her breasts against Mishka's large hands.

The tension Mishka felt was evident. He filled his glass with more vodka and sucked the liquid through tight lips. He looked directly at Grisha. "Have you ever heard of Semyon Petlura?"

"Yes."

"Semyon Petlura is the scum of the Ukraine." Mishka sat upright, his voice getting louder. "He is a murderer of children, an animal who hangs Jews until they are dead and then castrates them. He takes their balls and carries them in his saddlebags, so that when he attacks the next Jewish ghetto he can display them like war booty! There is not a Jewish family in the Ukraine who will escape Petlura unless *Mishka* stops him!"

Mala began to weep quietly.

"Her poppa was killed by Petlura. She was lucky. They only made her watch." Mishka gently touched Mala's cheek with his massive hands. "That was a long time ago, before anyone ever heard of Petlura. Now the entire Ukraine knows who he is, and soon they will know who Mishka Yaponchik is!"

Mala pulled away from Mishka, glanced at Grisha, then stood up and hurried away.

"Don't be ashamed to cry in front of anyone, Mala. Especially not a Jew. Because either he will understand what things are really like or he should learn." Mishka folded his hands on the table and stared out of the café window; the early light exposed the grim ugliness of the ghetto street. "Do you have a girlfriend, child?"

"I have a wife."

"Then perhaps you can understand how far a man will go to avenge someone else's pain. For me, I do not care. But for Mala, for others like her, and like her poppa, I would do anything to crush Semyon Petlura." Mishka placed his hands on Grisha's; his eyes were subdued, his voice soft, but strength lurked within him, a force that was ready to erupt like a volcano. "Patrolling the streets of Moldavanka will not accomplish anything. It will not even help to protect Moldavanka. The enemy is far greater than what we feel here in Odessa. It is bigger than all the Russians who are alive today. Because the enemy was here before your birth and mine, before our fathers and their fathers. Maybe it goes back to the very beginning. I do not know. I am not smart enough to understand history. But I am too smart not to have learned from my own life that wherever we are, we have enemies. And wherever we are, we must fight them. There is no other way for us."

"Even when I was in Palestine we had to fight."

"So! You were one of those who ran there, too. Once I thought about going. Now I just think about having a place to live tomorrow. Do you ever think of going back?"

"Yes."

Mala reappeared carrying a tray with three glasses of tea on it. Mishka watched her approach.

"Do you have children?" Mishka asked.

"No."

"I would like a child. Can you imagine how beautiful Mala would look pregnant? She could suckle a titan with her breasts!"

"I do," Mala retorted, setting the tray on the table.

Grisha's smile vanished when Mishka gave him a disapproving look.

"Don't be afraid of him. I am not," Mala said, kissing Mishka on the lips.

"And how is it that you, a woman no less, are not afraid of Mishka?" Mishka tried to pull Mala onto his lap, but she pushed him away.

Mala laughed softly. "Who could fear a man once they have seen him sleeping naked, rolled up in a ball like an infant?"

Mishka slapped Mala's behind. "When this *malchik* and I go to Palestine, I am leaving you here!"

"So now you are going to Palestine. What will you do there, be a farmer?"

"Why not?"

"Shouting at the ground will not make plants grow."

"Then I will steal to stay alive—from the Arabs."

"The Arabs are the best thieves in the world," Grisha said.

"Impossible!" Mishka hit the table with an open hand. "*I* am the best thief there is!"

"We need more than thieves now, Mishka," Mala replied soberly.

Mishka looked at her, surprised by her words. It was rare that Mala was so serious, preferring to indulge in the lusty humor they both enjoyed so much.

"What do we need?" he asked evenly.

Mala looked at Mishka and said: "The army you have always talked about."

"I have an army."

"An army of thieves. But not an army of soldiers."

"When it becomes necessary, they will be soldiers." Mishka's eyes, red from liquor and fatigue, were as deeply colored as the blood-hued curtains that were touched by the morning sunlight.

"I hope you are right."

"I *am* right. My thieves will steal our lives away from the enemy. If I have my way, Petlura and his Haidamacks will no longer run wild, raping and murdering. And if we have to fight the Monarchists, we will—and the Black Hundreds. And if necessary, the Bolsheviks, too! You do not know me, *malchik*, but I fear no man. Mala says I am crazy. Maybe she is right. But it does not matter. Because one crazy Jew who lives is worth a hundred sane ones who are dead. Do not be a fool, child, and waste your time with the Zubovs of the world. I know them. I have been watching them for the forty years of my life. They speak beautiful words, but they lack the ability to make men follow them—because they have only the courage of one man. I have the courage of twenty, and each of my men has the courage of a dozen! When you find out how brave you are, *malchik,* let me know, and then I will decide if I want you."

Abruptly, Mishka got to his feet and stamped out of the café.

"Does Mishka frighten you?" Mala asked as Grisha watched the man through the window. "He frightens almost everyone, except those who have courage. In all of Russia there is no one else like him, and I do not say that because I love him, though God knows I would do anything for him because of that. But he is more than just brave. He is a good man. He would willingly give his life to save us from another moment of terror. His father was a rabbi. Can you imagine that? He killed a policeman when they came to take his only son into the army. They arrested Mishka's father, and did not even bother to give him a trial. They beat him to death the same day they arrested him. Mishka was sixteen then, and he has been running and hiding ever since. How could the Tsar even begin to understand what it meant for a father to have his son taken away to serve in the army? A Jewish son in the Russian army. Mishka is proud of what his father did. Ever since then he has sworn that he would make Russia pay for what they did. And now he can. He really does have his own army. If the police truly believed it, they would arrest him. But to them, that is too absurd to be true. They think the rumors about Mishka are nothing but fairy tales. Thank God the only things they can understand are what their small minds permit them to. And thank God for the revolution. The confusion gives Mishka protection. Maybe he *will* find Petlura and destroy him."

Grisha saw the same courageous defiance in Mala's eyes as he had in Mishka's. "Are there really forty thousand thieves?" Grisha asked.

Mala laughed heartily. "Yes! In this city of three hundred thousand people, nearly half are Jews. So it is not surprising that so many of them are thieves, especially since most of them live like dogs. What is surprising is that all of them are not thieves."

"And Mishka is their leader?" Grisha pictured the swaggering giant at the head of a huge army.

"Not officially. But they all know who he is, and will do almost anything he asks. If they do not, they know what he will do," Mala said, explaining her last sentence by running her index finger across her throat. Grisha looked dismayed.

"Does that upset you? Mishka has killed at least two dozen men."

Grisha's mouth hung open.

"Would you respect a man who allowed others to trample on him?" Mala asked, her voice becoming firm. "Who will follow a weak man? No one! And now there is no time for weaklings!" She added sharply, standing up and starting to clear the mugs, empty bottles, and dirty ashtrays from the table.

Mala worked swiftly and efficiently, her body exuding an energy Grisha had never before seen in a woman. He understood why Mishka loved her. Grisha got to his feet, knocking his chair to the floor.

"Are you going?" asked Mala, stopping her work to look at Grisha.

"My wife will be worried. It is way past the time I usually return from my patrol."

"Mishka likes you, you know," Mala said casually. "If he did not, he would have sent you home long ago."

Grisha shifted his weight from one foot to the other, not knowing what the woman wanted him to say. He set the chair back up on its feet, stalling for time.

"He would like you to join his army."

"But I am not a thief. I would not know how to be a thief."

"Mishka has enough thieves. Now he wants soldiers." Mala inspected Grisha and added huskily, "You look strong enough to be one."

Grisha avoided looking directly at Mala and asked: "What would I have to do?"

"Whatever Mishka wants you to." Mala walked toward Grisha, halting when she was but inches from him. "Did you know that once there was a raspberry patch that covered this part of Odessa. That was long ago. Then buildings were put up, and the raspberry patch was destroyed, except for a tiny piece of it behind this café. It lay untended for years. Like the people who came here before Mishka arrived, the ground was barren, without life. Now the men who come here to drink have joy in their bellies, and out back the raspberries grow again. Every spring Mishka tends the plants so the fruit will be big and juicy. He crawls on his hands and knees in the raspberry patch, struggling with the stubborn soil, just to grow a few berries. Because of Mishka, the Malinas Zala is more than a café now. It is becoming the heart of Moldavanka. And Mishka tends the people who come here as lovingly as he does his raspberry plants. Both need Mishka to keep them alive. But the task is becoming more than Mishka can handle alone. That is why I hope that you will decide to become one of us. And then someday when another stranger enters the café, you will be the one to order him a *malinas shalost*. And I will bring him a glass of raspberry juice mixed with vodka. And together, the three of us will enjoy someone else discovering the secret of the raspberry trick."

Mala turned away from Grisha and returned to her work. The morning sun streamed through the windows, making the wooden tables appear rich and dark and the sawdust on the floor glitter like specks of gold. Grisha wanted to say something to Mala but she kept her back to him, as if she were telling him to leave and think before he made his decision. Grisha began to feel his weariness, and he remembered that Sara would be worried about him. He walked to the door and looked back to say good-bye to Mala. She was at the far end of the long room, facing the wall, cleaning a table with brisk, strong strokes. Grisha felt foolish trying to catch her attention, and he opened the door of the café and stepped outside into the crisp autumn morning. His mouth felt dry and stale, his clothes were rumpled. He started toward his apartment, only realizing when he was more than halfway there that he had left his rifle at the Zala; he had never forgotten it before, no matter what; Grisha wondered why he was not upset. The thought of his weapon reminded him that his jacket pocket still bulged with the hand grenade he carried, and that the cartridge belt at his waist was clearly visible. Trying to act inconspicuous, he closed his jacket, holding his arms against his body to conceal the grenade and the ammunition. With every step Grisha feared he would be caught by the police. And by the time he reached Mikhailovsky Place, he was sweating. Grisha hurried into his building, rushed up the stairs, calling out Sara's name as he entered their apartment. The room was empty. Sara had already left for work.

Grisha removed his jacket and shirt. His head ached from the vodka. He searched for something to eat, but there was nothing except some lukewarm tea and a roll that Sara had heated for his breakfast; the roll was cold and hard. Grisha filled a glass with tea and quickly drank it, refilling the glass twice more before his thirst was quenched. He washed his face with the water Sara had left in the basin for him, then put on a fresh shirt. Removing the cartridge belt from his waist, and the hand grenade from his jacket, Grisha returned to the streets of the ghetto, having no idea where he was going. He thought of visiting Joseph, but he was in no mood to listen to his father-in-law's recriminations about his quitting the *gymnasium*. Joseph had been furious when Grisha informed him that he was not going to enroll for the fall term. *He was angry because he was afraid for me,* Grisha told himself. *Why should he be afraid if I am not? The war is as good as over. Why should I waste my time at school?* "Instead I waste it waiting for Sara to come home from work," he grumbled. A gang of men wearing red armbands on their coat sleeves sauntered toward him, defying anyone to tell them they had no right to be Bolsheviks. Only Grisha looked at them, everyone else on the street too occupied with their own troubles to care about a few tough-looking Reds. *I wonder if they carry weapons like I do? How many secret armies can there be in Odessa now? Like Zubov's and Mishka's. But Zubov has no army. Mishka has an army!* The events of the night and early morning flooded over Grisha and he relived every second of them. He could still feel the heat of Mishka's body, hear the passion of his voice: Grisha was still struck by Mishka's size and strength. The sun stood overhead before Grisha realized that he had wandered in a circle which had led him back to his apartment. He went inside, knowing what he yearned to do, though not why. While he searched for reasons for his wanting to join with Mishka Yaponchik Grisha sat by the open window and chewed on the stale roll. The day became warm. He stripped to the waist and lay down on the bed, rolling over to the stone wall against which the bed rested. Grisha pressed his sweating chest and face against the cool limestone. Finding some relief from the heat, he fell asleep, dreaming of the things he had seen and heard at the Malinas Zala.

Hours later, with the evening sky streaked red, Grisha awoke, his body hot and clammy. Taking the basin filled with water, he leaned over the tub and poured the tepid liquid over his head, hoping it would remove the throbbing pain at the back of his neck. He sat down in a chair by the window, staring outside, waiting for Sara to come home. There, in the dying light of day, Grisha finally understood why he would do whatever was necessary to become a member of Mishka Yaponchik's legions. And while he was aware that Mishka was the only other man besides Aleksandr he would have liked for a father, it escaped Grisha's notice that Mala intrigued him even more. For hidden deep within him was the knowledge that it was she whom Grisha Moisei had always wanted for his mother.

CHAPTER 41

Joseph Dubrow's eyes swept the room. Everything looked so familiar, so comforting, as if it were his own home. The strong sunlight made the orange curtains and bedspread glow. The white walls were spotless, the tinted seascapes hanging from them seemed three-dimensional. Light reflected off the polished surface of the dining table, and the cushions on the sofa and armchair were fluffed high. The air was scented with the fragrance of the oranges and lemons that were on the windowsill. Joseph regarded his daughter and son-in-law; despite everything he had said, they continued to pack their clothes in a large trunk. Joseph's face tightened with fury. "Don't you understand that Mishka Yaponchik is a thief!" he sputtered.

"Joseph, I have—"

"These days everyone runs in packs like wild animals—revolutionists, Tsarists, and especially gangsters! Is that what you are, Grisha, another weakling who needs the courage of other people's convictions?"

"Joseph, every day and night for a month now I have been with Mishka—"

"I know."

"And I have never seen him steal a thing. And even if

he had, what good does it do to be honest these days?" Grisha looked at his father-in-law with annoyance.

"That is not the point, Grisha."

"What is the point?"

"The point is that I do not understand why you are leaving this place to live in the back of a café. Has this man taken over your life? In just four weeks you are able to decide that this Mishka Yaponchik is—"

"Joseph, after just one minute I decided about you."

Joseph turned away, refusing to let his son-in-law disarm him.

"Why would you leave a place as beautiful as this to live behind a café?"

"Because there is no rent to pay there. Because Sara will be able to quit her job and help Mala while I—"

"First you leave school telling me that you are going to work in a factory, and instead you are going to live with a thief? Tell me, Grisha, what kind of thief will you be?"

"Poppa, please!"

"You agree with him, Sara? You want to live with a thief, too?"

"Joseph, have you ever met Mishka Yaponchik?" Grisha asked pointedly.

"I know about him. *Everyone* knows about him."

"And what is it that they know?"

"That he is worse than a thief."

"Why? Because he has killed some people? So has Zubov."

"But not for the same reasons. Aram does not kill so he can steal!" Joseph retorted.

"Tell me, Joseph, is Aram building an army to hunt Petlura? No! All Aram is doing is sending a bunch of old men and boys parading up and down every night to protect Moldavanka from the wind!"

"Have you told Aram you are quitting the brigade?"

"Yes."

"And what did he say?"

"If he could have walked, I think he would have attacked

me," answered Grisha. "I have never seen him so angry."

"Can you blame him? A man who has devoted his life to gathering together a group of men to protect Moldavanka? A man who sacrificed his own son and his own health for that one purpose. Can't you understand how he feels?"

"Joseph, Aram Zubov could spend the next twenty years standing on the streets of Moldavanka with a thousand men keeping Jews free of harm. But his efforts would be meaningless. What good will it do when the heart of the enemy is riding across the Ukraine far from Zubov's guns?"

"And Mishka will chase Petlura? Is that what you are telling me?"

The muscles of Grisha's body tensed as if he were preparing to strike out at something. "Yes, Joseph. Forever, if necessary."

"And now, with the Tsar gone and Kerensky about to fall, this savior of Moldavanka is preparing to fight the Bolsheviks and the Monarchists too? And the Germans?" Joseph shook his head in disbelief, finding it difficult to comprehend that his son-in-law had fallen victim to the well-known bravado of Mishka Yaponchik.

"I believe he will, Poppa." Sara's gentle voice startled her father.

"You also believe in this Mishka?"

"Yes." Sara walked to her father and touched his cheek. "If you could witness the people's faces when they come into the café and see Mishka, or when he walks in the street, you would understand what he is really like."

"They do not mind that he is a thief?" Joseph kissed his daughter's hands.

"Mishka is only a thief to those he has stolen from. To the rest he is a saint."

A look of irony covered Joseph's face.

"Some people think the world will be saved by a saint. Others, by a sinner. Now there is a man who is both. I wonder what he will save?"

"It might even be you he saves," said Grisha kindly.

"It is you and Sara I am worried about."

"Joseph, I am not afraid for us."

"You are brave, Grisha, but you are still young. If you and that thief actually do chase Petlura, you will discover as you ride across the steppes that you will be hunting more than that despicable man. You will be attempting to change the history of the world. I hope you are not disappointed when you finally realize how fruitless a task that is." Joseph studied Grisha for a moment. "And I hope that when it is over you will not have forgotten about Palestine."

"I will never forget that," answered Grisha, too quickly.

"Then you are still planning on returning there?" Joseph persisted, disturbed by the tone of Grisha's response.

"Yes. When it is possible."

"Is that what it has come to—when it is possible?"

"Joseph, we will be on the very first boat that leaves for Palestine. I promise!"

Nearly a minute passed while Joseph looked at Grisha. Finally he said softly, "Even if we take the second boat, I will be happy."

Grisha rushed up to Joseph and hugged him, then suddenly released him and turned away; he had never done that before. Tears came to Joseph's eyes. He walked slowly over to Grisha and squeezed the young man's shoulder. With a gnarled hand, with fingers bumped and lumpy from his years of tailoring, Joseph stroked the smooth skin of his son-in-law's face. He smiled at Grisha, his mouth quivering. Then without a word Joseph went over to his daughter and kissed her, his lips touching her eyes, her nose, her cheeks; Joseph held Sara's hands for a moment, clasping them to his heart. Barely able to whisper a good-bye, he left the apartment. As he made his way through the crowded streets of Moldavanka, a warmth filled Joseph's body as he imagined the three of them in the Holy Land. *Perhaps four,* Joseph said to himself, seeing a grandchild tugging at his hand. Joseph sighed, his shoulders relaxed, and the ache at the side of his head eased. And when he reached his tailor shop and began to mend the clothing that long ago should have been used for rags, Joseph Dubrow contemplated nothing except a journey that someday would lead him to Palestine.

Four days later, on October 24, 1917, promises and dreams no longer mattered. The Provisional Government of Russia was overthrown by the Bolsheviks. Within hours of the uprising Petrograd was in the hands of the revolutionaries. The Winter Palace was stormed and taken, and the telegraph stations, railway depots, and all the main bridges leading to and from the capital were under the control of the Reds. Without delay Vladimir Ilyich Lenin assumed full control of the country, abolishing private ownership of land and proclaiming that all of Russia belonged to the peasants. Banks were nationalized, accounts frozen, safety deposit boxes broken into—the contents confiscated by the Red Guard—and the right of inheritance was abolished. Roused by the news of the Bolshevik success, armed rebellions erupted throughout the country, dozens of cities and towns capitulating to the Bolsheviks. Everywhere armies were raised. On one side were the Reds, Bolsheviks, flaunting their red armbands and the tenets of Lenin. Opposing them were the Whites, Monarchists still loyal to the Tsar and determined to destroy everyone who swore allegiance to the new government. A gruesome, brutal struggle commenced, both the Reds and the Whites prepared to decimate Russia to gain control of the country.

Odessa, too, girded for battle. At mid-morning, on November 3, with skirmishes between the Reds and Whites breaking out throughout the port city, Monarchist soldiers and sympathizers attacked what they were certain was a stronghold of Bolshevism. Hundreds of loyalists converged on the Brody Synagogue, smashed its interior, and set it ablaze. The rabbi of the Brody, terrified that his building would be destroyed, ran to the fire department for help. But when he arrived the firemen refused to do anything, explaining that the Whites had threatened their lives if one of them so much as spat at the flames. Frantic, the rabbi raced back to the Brody, determined to do whatever he could, only to be confronted by a crowd that had come to watch the synagogue burn. People cheered and shouted as flames leaped from the windows in great roars. They applauded when the soldiers formed a double column and marched back and forth before the burning building, daring anyone to try to extinguish the fire. Fearing for the precious books and scrolls inside, the rabbi attempted to push his way into the synagogue. A soldier knocked him to the ground with his rifle butt. The elderly man struggled to his feet and, as fast as he was able, hurried to Moldavanka seeking the one named Mishka Yaponchik.

When he reached Petrovskaya Street, the rabbi found his way blocked by hundreds of people shoving one another toward the Malinas Zala. In front of the café, sitting on the bare backs of their horses were Mishka, Urka, Karmanchik, and Grisha. Behind them, stretching for three blocks, were five hundred men, also on horseback, and armed with rifles, revolvers, and grenades. Like their leader, each man sat ramrod straight, head held high, eyes and mouth grimly defiant.

"Let's go!" Mishka commanded, digging his heels into the flanks of his horse.

The instant the black stallion bolted, the others jabbed their heels into the sides of their mounts, and the curious-looking army charged through the streets of the ghetto.

Riding at a gallop, Mishka Yaponchik led the way to the firehouse, and when he arrived there began shouting out orders, detaching a hundred of his men as fire fighters while the remainder forced the real firemen to barricade themselves inside the station. It took but moments for the fire wagons to be readied, and as soon as they were Mishka bellowed out more orders: five hundred Moldavankans, riding at breakneck speed, headed for the Brody Synagogue. Swooping around a corner into Yekaterina Street, the extent of the disaster was clearly visible. Smoke billowed skyward, the crackling flames and the crashing of structural timbers deafening. Screaming at the top of his lungs, Mishka Yaponchik hurtled toward the jubilant spectators, firing his revolvers into the air. The crowd panicked; in front of them the burning wreckage of the synagogue was falling into the street while behind them a wild army led by a crazed-looking giant bore down upon them. Not knowing which direction was safer, the people ran pell-mell. The Monarchist soldiers drew their sabers and unholstered their pistols, preparing to fight the horsemen. But before they could act, the Bolsheviks in the crowd wrested away their weapons and started a melee.

While the Reds and Whites battled with their fists, Mishka and his men attacked the fire. Feverishly, they pumped, pailed, hurled water from the fire wagons and hoses onto and into the blazing building. As one group of Mishka's men tired another stepped forward, until gradually the flames diminished. As the fire died down to nothing so did the fighting and clamor. Unmindful of the smoldering embers and weakened supports of the synagogue, Mishka stepped inside, disappearing from sight. Everyone fixed their eyes on the empty doorway. No one moved; no one spoke. Ten minutes later Mishka emerged into the daylight, his expression forbidding. He strode over to his horse and with one hand on its black mane and the other on its soft back, pulled himself astride and trotted off. Five hundred men followed suit. Within minutes, except for a small crowd of bewildered Monarchists and Bolsheviks, the street was empty. Those who remained at the scene looked around, stunned by the great mass of confused hoses, pails, fire wagons, axes, pikes, and the badly damaged but still-standing synagogue. They scratched their heads, asking one another if they had all seen the same thing. And while they tried to put the pieces together, Mishka Yaponchik was sitting at his table in the center of the Zala surrounded by scores of celebrating men. Across from Mishka sat Urka and Karmanchik; next to him was a youth of nineteen with straight blond hair that hung well below his shirt collar, with hollow cheeks, high cheekbones, and intense blue eyes. His frame was solid, the slope of his shoulders and size of his neck indicating that he was uncommonly strong. He was costumed almost exactly like Mishka: over a dark blue shirt he wore a lamb's-wool vest; his black pants were tucked into knee-high boots, a wide leather belt studded with bullets was strapped around his waist, from his hip hung a leather holster with a revolver. The young man leaned forward, not wanting to miss a single word. He watched the broad smiling face of Mishka and he smiled too, drawn to the man, wanting to embrace him.

Word by word, Mishka addressed more of his talk to Grisha. The night wore on; the others became drunk. Grisha and Mishka Yaponchik spoke to no one but each other, and nobody suspected the depth of their relationship, not even they themselves. Only Mala saw it, understood it, but she never said a word, knowing that if she did, the man and the boy might taste the fruit before it was ripe, and that might destroy everything.

CHAPTER 42

For days after the fire Odessa buzzed with stories about a Jewish army led by a man of immense proportions that had appeared out of nowhere to save the Brody Synagogue. In Moldavanka the excitement was tenfold, the people of the ghetto wildly enamored of the man whose bravery gave them a feeling of security and pride. Even Joseph Dubrow agreed that what Mishka Yaponchik had done was not the work of a common criminal whose only purpose was to benefit himself. After being forced by Grisha to come to the Malinas Zala to meet him, and after spending a long and boisterous evening there, Joseph grudgingly admitted that he found himself liking the man. Indeed, from then on Joseph Dubrow spent a considerable amount of time at the café, intrigued by Mishka Yaponchik, admiring him, drawn to him. And, too, Joseph enjoyed the exuberant confidence that affected everyone who entered the Zala. But most important, Joseph Dubrow found a special happiness in the joy he saw reflected in his daughter and son-in-law.

Riding with Mishka's army through Odessa, helping to put out the fire at the Brody, mingling with the exultant crowds that jammed the Malinas Zala from morning until night for days afterward, and being treated by the ghetto populace as one of its heroes had transformed Grisha Moisei. Once again he felt an enthusiasm that made him babble for hours to Mishka, Mala, Sara, and Joseph about Palestine. No longer did he complain about his stifling existence in the land of his birth, but instead spoke of his homeland, predicting its future with assurance, planning to be part of its future. He laughed as easily as when he had first met Sara; the smile that had first attracted her was once again ready to light up his face at the slightest provocation. And Grisha was overflowing with energy. He polished all the tables and chairs in the Zala, and the long wooden bar. In the room where he and Sara lived he painted the walls sky blue, refinished the dressing table and the chest of drawers, fixed the broken leg on the bed, reslatted the back of a chair, helped Sara hang their old orange curtains. He devoted hours to reading poetry and novels, often reciting aloud to Sara a particularly meaningful or beautiful passage, his voice rising with passion as he learned to love what she did—the literature of clarion calls, of righteousness, of romantic adventure. He spent even more time excitedly explaining to Sara how he saw himself as a noble conqueror, a soldier-poet whose pen was the gun, whose verse was war. Grisha boasted to his wife that he was a redeemer, not a Maccabee of the mind as was his father, but already a seasoned warrior. He claimed to be a better poet than even Lord Byron, because he, Grisha Moisei, was a Russian poet, not born in Albion's ice which first had to be melted away before even an ember could be sustained, but born in flame, nurtured by fire! "The pen is not mightier than the sword," proclaimed Grisha, "it only inspires new swords, for it is not reasonable men who need to be swayed by humane ideas, but unreasonable men. And unreasonable men succumb only to the threat of force, and more often only to force itself." Stirring his fervor even more, keeping ablaze his dream of returning to Palestine and reclaiming that land for his dispossessed people, were Byron's *Hebrew Melodies.* A couplet from those poems became his battle cry:

How long by tyrants shall thy land be trod!
How long thy temple worshipless, O God!

Seeing her husband return to the way he had once been, Sara found herself even more easily excited by him, and she looked forward to the mornings when he refused to allow her out of bed until they had made love, until Grisha's hands fondled her soft breasts, his knees parting her legs, until his belly, hips, thighs met Sara's with equal urgency. Still warm with sleep they would press their bodies together, moving together, their tongues darting everywhere, stroking each other's bodies, swallowing one another's breaths, inhaling each other's existences, their hands clasping each other's faces, hair, backs, buttocks, both of them feeling exquisitely alive and safe, the only world that existed for them being their own world, a place where the reality of life in Russia was erased by their total absorption in one another.

When there were only a few customers in the Zala, Grisha and Sara took long walks through Odessa, pretending that there was no war, but rather peace and calm, making believe that Moldavanka's open-air market was really in Jerusalem and that the merchants were haggling with their customers in Hebrew, not Russian. Some nights they would sneak away from the café and stroll down to the sea, arms entwined, stopping often to kiss as passionately as when they first became lovers. Standing at the water's edge with the sea lapping at their bare feet, the moon guiding their steps, Grisha and Sara would whisper words of unabashed love to one another. Grisha, swept away by the fragrance of the sea air and Sara's skin, murmured the poetry he had created to express how deeply he felt about Sara, his Sara, his wife, Sara.

The obvious closeness between Grisha and Sara, the feelings they had for one another and for Mishka and Mala, overwhelmed the thief of Moldavanka and his woman. Instinctively, they were drawn to the youngsters, loving them, finding fulfillment in them, and for the first time the Malinas Zala truly became the home of which Mishka Yaponchik and Mala had dreamed. And for a while Moldavanka felt secure because of the presence of Mishka Yaponchik, while the people of the Zala felt safe because of each other.

Although the defeat the Monarchists suffered at the Brody Synagogue helped the Bolsheviks to take power in Odessa, the stronghold the Reds thought they had in the city was, in reality, shaky. While the people of Odessa seemed to prefer the liberating policies of Lenin to the strictness of Tsarism, there were challenges to the Reds that appeared to be insurmountable. Along with the snows of December came renewed attacks by the Monarchists and a critical shortage of food, coal, and wood for the winter. And then, in February of the following year, the Germans invaded the Ukraine, occupying the steppes from Kiev to Odessa. As a final indignity, the Germans installed *Hetman* Paul Skoropodski, a former Russian general of Ukrainian descent, as their puppet ruler.

"Well, how do you like living in the German Pale?" Mishka Yaponchik asked Joseph Dubrow as the tailor entered the Zala.

"It is no different than the Russian Pale."

"You are wrong, Joseph," said Mala as she wiped off the bar. "The Bolsheviks at least noticed Mishka. The Germans have never heard of him."

"What do you mean, the Bolsheviks noticed me?" Mishka put his hands on his hips and thrust out his chin at Mala. "They respected me! They said I helped them get control of the city because of what we did at the Brody—"

"The Bolsheviks needed you, Mishka, that is all."

"Without me they would have had more trouble than they could have handled. And if they know that, why don't you?"

"It does not matter anymore," Mala replied. "The Bolsheviks are gone. And thanks to Lenin and Trotsky, the whole Ukraine is part of Germany now."

"Sara!" Joseph Dubrow exclaimed, seeing his daughter

enter the café from the back. Going to kiss her, he asked, "And where is your husband?"

"Getting dressed."

"Not anymore," Grisha grumbled, scratching his head as he trudged into the café.

"Ten o'clock and you are just waking up?" Joseph commented.

Grisha went behind the bar and drew himself a glass of tea from the samovar. "If I could, I would sleep until the Germans leave, or until I knew that their stay was permanent." Nodding a noncommital good-morning to Mala, Grisha scuffed his way over to the table where Joseph, Sara, and Mishka were sitting. "Damn, I hate the Germans!"

"After getting out of bed at ten o'clock, you must have enough strength to smile just a little," Joseph gently teased.

"If I go out in the streets today, and I don't see the Junkers anywhere in Odessa, then maybe I will smile," Grisha replied bitterly. His expression became one of anger as he thought of how Sara or Mala had to waste three to four hours each day standing in line just to buy a loaf of worm-infested bread or a piece of smoked salmon so small and expensive that it made as much sense to eat the money.

"Do you think anyone has a good life under the Germans?" Joseph inquired. "Do you think I enjoy coming here every day to do nothing but sit and talk about the same things?" He sighed. "At least being here is better than waiting in my shop for customers who never come to have their clothes fixed anymore."

"Who can afford anything these days?" added Mala.

Mishka looked around the empty café. "Before the Germans came, the place used to be half-filled by now. What a world, when a man cannot even afford to drink!" Mishka rubbed his stomach and leaned back in his chair. "It is difficult to believe that in February we could have had peace. Instead we have Skoropodski."

"Skoropodski," muttered Grisha. "The great Tsarist general, a Judas. He and the Germans deserve each other."

"The Junkers selected the right man when they put him

in charge of the Ukraine." Mishka shook his head in disgust. "Skoropodski sits in Kiev like a king, ordering German troops to kill his own countrymen. Someone should murder that bastard."

"Now Skoropodski is encouraging the landowners to return. To again—"

"More Russian bastards!" Mishka boomed, interrupting Joseph. "*They* are the ones who are urging the Germans to kill the peasants. And because he wants even more power, Skoropodski generously approves the landowners' requests. How many deaths will satisfy them? When will they feel they have been repaid for their land? How many dead men equal the price of an acre of land?"

"The slaughter will stop soon, Mishka."

"Oh? What makes you so sure?"

Joseph removed his spectacles and cleaned the lenses with a handkerchief. He stared myopically at Mishka. "It will stop because it is April."

"Is that it? Skoropodski wrote on his calendar, in April we let the Ukrainians live?"

"Now is the time for planting, and Skoropodski needs the peasants to work the land. Don't you think he wants to impress his German masters with an abundant harvest? So of course the Ukrainians will be spared—at least until the harvest has been gathered."

"The peasants won't do it. They will never work for the Junkers, and especially not for the landowners!"

"Yes they will, Mishka," Grisha said softly. "The landowners know very well how to get the peasants to work."

Mishka slouched in his chair. "You know, now I miss the Bolsheviks. Mala, bring me a beer, and one for Joseph, too." Mishka paused for a moment to make sure Mala was doing what he had asked. "Remember how good things were when the Bolsheviks first took control of Odessa? The city was alive again! People actually smiled in the streets. It was like the old days, before the war. Now there is nothing."

Mala brought two mugs of beer to the table.

"Mishka, the kind of control the Bolsheviks had over

Odessa was the kind of control a baby has over its parents. When it stops screaming, you realize how weak it really is." Joseph peered at Mishka, pleased with his analogy.

Mishka took a long, noisy sip of beer, then smacked his lips with satisfaction. "But we *felt* free! Even you were glad when the Monarchists ran away."

"When an oppressor is driven off, Mishka, the relief you feel can blind you to the fact that the liberator is also an oppressor."

"Are you saying that Mishka was blind?" Mishka questioned.

"Everyone was. Because all we did was lose one autocracy with the Tsar and gain another one with Lenin."

Mishka kicked an empty chair away from the table and used it for a footstool. "Things have been so different since we saved the Brody."

"Did you really think that one act would change the world? Even Mishka Yaponchik is not that powerful," said Joseph, a tiny smile on his lips.

Mishka studied Joseph for a moment, then said, "Joseph, sometimes I wish you still did not like me."

"Sometimes I don't."

Mishka laughed. "Why do you make me like you? That is what really bothers me!"

"Eleazar thinks you should have let the Brody burn to the ground," Sara said. "He said that of all the synagogues in Russia, that one deserved most to be destroyed."

"Mala, did you hear that? I risk my life to save a synagogue and a rabbi, no less, says I should have let it burn. Ah, the whole world is filled with lunatics!" In a gentler tone, Mishka added fondly, "But what else should I have expected from a crazy mystic?"

As if on cue everyone looked across the café to a table by the fireplace. There, once or twice a week, Rabbi Eleazar would sit for hours, sipping a single glass of wine while reading esoteric texts on mysticism, carefully copying down fragments of prayers he found especially beautiful, ideas that were enlightening, even composing verses of his own.

Sometimes Eleazar would do nothing but sit and stare at the men who frequented the Zala, stroking his white beard which now hung below the middle of his chest and was nearly as wide as his bony body, a beatific smile on his face, a faraway look to his eyes. There was a saintliness to Eleazar, a holiness to his demeanor and manner that caused everyone around him to speak in hushed tones, to treat him with reverence.

"Did you know that Eleazar may be the most fortunate man in Russia?" Mishka said, breaking the peaceful quiet of the Zala. "He has no idea that his life is controlled by a Beelzebub. To him Skoropodski does not even exist."

"Then he is a fool," said Grisha.

Everyone looked at Grisha. Though recently he had begun to display an increasing hostility toward everything around him, never before had he spoken ill of Eleazar. Grisha laced his fingers together and pulled them so tightly that his knuckles cracked.

"Perhaps we are the fools," said Mishka gently, "because it is we who are living in misery. It is we who at any moment can have everything taken away from us. But who can take God away from anyone? Even death does not remove the existence of God from someone who believes in Him."

"You are right, Mishka. We are the fools. The only one who is not a fool is my mother." Grisha recalled the letter his mother had sent him months before, shortly before Nicholas had abdicated the throne. It was a long letter in which Soybel described in detail how she had returned the estate in Kodoma to its original condition. Grisha could still see the words of his mother's message, each sentence stabbing him like a knife.

> If only you could see your father's house, and your father's town. Everything in Kodoma is wearing a mantle of white. The village looks like a fairy-tale land, bejeweled in sparkling icicles. The golden dome on the church in the square is encased in a thin hat of ice that shimmers in the sunlight. And the house, my son, sur-

rounded now by silent snowbound woods and sugar-loaf hills, is once again vivid yellow, with a porch, window trim, and the door painted white.

Grisha forced himself to forget his mother's description of how "her peasants" had planted and harvested a crop so large that she was "almost embarrassed at the profit she had made in times so troubled." Grisha's fury at his mother was evident.

"Grisha, come have a beer and forget about it," Mala called from the bar.

"Damn, is this Armageddon we are fighting already conceded to the enemy? Is there really no justice?" asked Grisha, his voice strained.

"For men like Eleazar there is most definitely justice because there is Paradise. But for men like you, like Jacob, for men like me, there can never be justice. At best we can seek satisfaction in legal retribution. And in times such as these there is nothing for us except revenge."

"Then, Mishka, I embrace vengeance."

Mishka stood up and put a hand on Grisha's shoulder. "Come my friend, come *malcheshka,* let us have a drink while we talk," Mishka said gently.

Grisha's anger sank into gloom. "What is there to talk about, Mishka?"

"Then we'll just drink. At least you and I can give the Zala some business."

Grisha got to his feet and with Mishka's hand still on his shoulder went with him to the bar. Sara and Joseph stared after them, both their faces somber.

"Someday, *malcheshka,* we will go away from here. Just you and I. And Mala and Sara, and Joseph."

Grisha tried to smile but his attempt only underscored his misery. Mishka and Mala touched eyes, the woman nodding that she understood what he wanted; she filled two mugs with beer.

"The world is so upside down now, *malchik,* that even I am confused." Mishka made himself comfortable on a stool and swirled the beer in his mug. "German soldiers controlling our lives. Stealing our food. Raping our women. Me liking the Ukrainians because they are fighting back. Do you know what Urka told me? That if the peasants catch a Junker who has raped one of their women, they split open his head with an axe. Or sometimes they invite the Junker to share some food and serve him cabbage soup with needles hidden in it. That must be a terrible way to die. Even I would not kill a man that way." Mishka took a long draft of his beer.

"Mishka, how long must we do nothing but wait? How long must I remain in this cage?" Grisha leaned heavily against the bar, his beer untouched. He thought of all the people around him. Joseph, who had lost a wife, and Sara, a mother, to the Bolsheviks. Mishka, whose father was murdered by the police. And Mala, exquisite Mala, wondrous Mala against whose bosom Grisha wanted to rest. Faithful Mala, at once staunch and gentle, who watched in horror as Semyon Petlura killed her father, then looked on as his corpse, along with dozens of others, had its throat and the side of its head slit. And finally, after the carts that followed Petlura's army everywhere had been loaded with all the valuable possessions of the Jews of Mala's village, saw the Haidamacks take the dead and hurl their bodies into a swamp to prevent them from receiving a Jewish burial. Now, Petlura was coming ever closer to Odessa. Every day stories of his grisly deeds were whispered in Moldavanka. Grisha looked up at Mala. She was engrossed in Mishka who was rubbing her fingers one at a time. Mishka stopped when he came to the one where wedding bands were placed. He stroked the skin where a ring might have been.

"More than anything in the world, I want to kill Petlura," Grisha said quietly, dangerously.

Mishka's gaze drifted to the youth's face.

"If only Petlura could be killed twice," Grisha continued, still not removing his eyes from Mala. "The first time to avenge those he slaughtered, the second time as a gift to those his death spared." Mala contemplated Grisha, her face pale, her brown eyes downcast and moist with unshed tears.

"Sara, stop talking to your father and take care of your husband," Mishka demanded. "He is beginning to sound crazy like me."

Joseph whispered something to his daughter and then glanced at the bar, his attention fixed on Grisha. Breathing deeply, and forcing himself to sound cheerful, he said: "If Grisha is becoming crazy, it is your fault, Mishka. I predicted you would ruin him."

Only Sara laughed at her father's retort, but her response was strained and unnatural. She got up from the table and went over to the bar.

"From the beginning I warned Grisha to be wary of you," Joseph continued, his words purposely barbed.

"Do we look that miserable?" Mishka asked Sara, seeing her reaction to him, Mala, and Grisha.

Joseph chuckled. "When Grisha told me he was going to live with Mishka Yaponchik, the great thief, I said to him: 'Mishka Yaponchik is a windbag who struts up and down Petrovskaya Street acting like a German zeppelin that is landing. All he does is let out hot air!' "

Toying with Mala's hand, Mishka squirmed uncomfortably.

"And when I heard about the fire being extinguished at the Brody, the first thing I asked was if you blew it out by yourself. Did you, Mishka?"

"What I did, tailor, everyone knows. But what I *can* do, *you* should know." Mishka turned on his stool and glared at Joseph. "You, I could snuff out like this!" he said, snapping his fingers.

"You see, Mishka, I can get you every time."

Getting off the seat, Mishka strode over to the table. "What do you mean you can get me every time?"

"You see, I just did it again! That is twice in a single minute!"

"You did nothing, tailor!"

"Yes he did, Mishka!"

"*Malcheshka,* shut up!"

Grisha slammed his beer mug on the bar and headed for the table.

"Tell him, Grisha, does he rise to the bait every time or does he not?"

"*Malcheshka,* you better tell him what *I* want to hear."

"Your father is an incredible man," Mala whispered to Sara as the two of them watched the three men arguing.

Mishka and Grisha both grinned at something Joseph was saying. Mishka put his foot on a chair and leaned on his knee; without realizing it, Grisha did the same thing.

"I wish Grisha always looked as happy as he does now," Sara said. She bit the insides of her cheeks. "But most of the time he looks so sad. And if he is not sad, he is angry." Sara rubbed a spot on the bar. "Even when he sleeps he is in torment. I know that he is plagued by nightmares." Sara drew a circle on the bar with a tiny puddle of beer, adding two wet spots for eyes, one for a nose, and a frowning line for a mouth. "There is no more joy in Grisha's life. I feel as if we need something new between us, something for us to—"

"Maybe what you need is a child."

Sara looked surprised. Mala looked across the room at the men, who were still bantering. She let her eyes rest on Grisha for a moment then shifted them to Mishka.

"I know what I am talking about," Mala continued. Mishka laughed, sending shivers along Mala's spine. "I know very well what I am talking about," Mala repeated, speaking more to herself than to Sara. "If he saw you with a big belly, he would laugh day and night. He would be insane with happiness!"

"I should have been pregnant long ago, but—"

"Do you know what a man feels like when he sees his woman carrying his child? Or when it is born and he holds the son that you have given to him?"

"Mala?"

"I can see his face—"

"Why haven't you given Mishka a child?"

Sara's question stopped Mala as surely as if someone had clamped a hand over her mouth. She stood up straight and began to set up rows of clean glasses on the bar.

"Why, Mala?"

Tears welled up in Mala's eyes and she worked more rapidly. "I have tried. Every night for fifteen years I have prayed that I was pregnant. Now I am thirty-eight years old, and I am afraid it will never happen. I do not know why, but that seems to come easily only when you do not want it to."

"Then pretend you do not want it to."

A sad smile touched Mala's face. "I have even tried that, but something inside me knows how big a lie it is, so it does not work." Mala gazed fondly at Mishka, amused by the way his mustache whipped the air as he angrily shook his head at something Joseph had said. "If I thought it would help, I would try a dozen times a day to get pregnant." Mala swallowed to keep herself from crying. Mishka crashed his hand against the table, startling both Joseph and Grisha. A soft laugh came from Mala and a tear rolled down her cheek. "I can do it that much—it is Mishka who cannot." Instead of sounding like the joke she had intended, Mala's words were touched with sorrow. She lowered her eyes and in a voice meant only for herself added: "But all it takes is once."

Slowly, deliberately, Mala continued to place the mugs and glasses in rows on the bar. She wondered if Sara would be luckier than she had been. She hoped so. The conversation at the table ebbed. Grisha called to Sara, and she hurried over to him. Mishka said something to them and headed for the bar. Mala watched him, inspecting every detail of his face. She counted the lines and scars. She could feel how his mustache brushed against her skin. She thought how she had done everything for Mishka—except give him a child. When he reached Mala, Mishka kissed her. Taking his hand, Mala led him down the length of the bar. He asked where they were going. Wordlessly Mala ushered him through the doorway that led to their living quarters. Mishka laughed and touched the back of Mala's neck.

When they were inside their bedroom, Mala turned and faced Mishka, running her fingers along the scar that ran from his ear to his eye; she continued along the bridge of his nose and across his lips. Mishka hugged Mala gently. She kissed him, not minding that his mustache tickled her. Mishka picked Mala up and placed her on the bed. He unbuttoned her blouse and pushed it over her shoulders. Mishka looked at Mala, his eyes honoring her body. He bent toward her, and Mala promised that not only would she someday give Mishka Yaponchik a child, but that it would be a son.

CHAPTER 43

When the Germans arrived in Kodoma in April of 1918 and discovered the agricultural complex, they immediately realized its worth; the railroad spur which ultimately led to Germany made the village even more valuable. Adding to their satisfaction was the fact that the town was relatively small and isolated, making it an easy place to patrol. But most impressive was the land surrounding Kodoma. It was already being planted by the peasants, not in haphazard personal plots, but obviously according to someone's direction. The Germans were ecstatic, for they knew that at the end of the season it would be a simple matter to load the trains with the harvest and transport it home. Within twenty minutes of their entry into Kodoma the Germans learned who was in charge of the granary and the endless acres that were being cultivated and where to find her. To their delight the woman who claimed ownership of all they coveted proved to be more than cooperative. Without hesitation she led the Germans on an inspection tour of the granary buildings, showing them the quality of the farming equipment, the capacity of the railway facilities, opening up her ledgers to them, all the while displaying her knowledge about managing such a vast and complicated enterprise. Seeing that their needs would best be served by someone already familiar with the land, the Germans offered the woman terms to which she quickly agreed. In return for producing an abundant harvest and shipping it to Germany, Soybel Viska was promised a substantial sum of money, an amount that would increase each year if the harvest increased too. Also, the Germans guaranteed that the land would be defended against bandits or insurgents and, for her own protection, they would put a lieutenant and a dozen soldiers at her disposal. A day later a formal document was signed by both parties, the German commander making it clear that the peasants and townspeople were in effect German prisoners, and were to be treated as such. Then, after gallantly kissing Soybel's hand and with a crisp salute, the German commander departed.

Flushed with her sudden return to power and potential wealth, Soybel wrote a long and excited letter to her son Grisha, explaining her turn of success and asking him to return home to help her manage the peasants. Writing in her most graceful hand—and with an abundance of endearments and much praise—Soybel used every turn of phrase she thought might lure her son to her. She professed to have a deep longing to meet Sara and welcome her as her own daughter. And she recounted to Grisha the beauty of Kodoma, the place of his birth, the home of his father, where every acre of fertile land paid homage to Aleksandr; as an added inducement Soybel enclosed a thousand rubles and the offer of more money if Grisha did her bidding.

A week later his answer arrived. As she slit open the bulging envelope, Soybel congratulated herself on the success of her coldly calculated ploy. But her pleasure was short-lived. Rather than the grateful thank-you note and an indication of when Grisha and Sara would be departing for Kodoma that Soybel was expecting, out fell the thousand rubles shredded into countless tiny fragments. Enraged, Soybel cursed her son, and then, consumed with vengeance, she swore to do anything and everything she could to prove her gratitude to the Germans.

Knowing that only the crop yield mattered to the Germans, Soybel was determined that the year's harvest would be the largest ever. She drove the peasants mercilessly, instituting floggings and the withholding of pay for the slightest infractions. Two and sometimes three times a week she would visit the fields, flanked by her German contingent, or as she referred to it, her honor guard. Sitting in her chaise, holding a parasol to protect herself from the sun, imperious, Soybel would survey the workers and the budding crops. The day was rare when she did not find at least one peasant who met with her displeasure and suffered her rancor. Each night Soybel filled her ledgers with the most minute details, noting how many acres had been plowed, the number of planted rows in each acre, the total number of sprouts which had appeared in each row, and the average size of the plants. She devised scores of charts depicting temperature variations, the numbers of days that were cloudy and sunny, the moisture level of the soil. Once a week she sent a report to German Military Headquarters in Kiev, anxious for those in charge of the occupation to see how diligent her efforts were, how loyal her behavior. And though the information she dispatched was never acknowledged, Soybel was certain that the Germans were waiting for the results of the autumn reaping and gleaning before issuing any compliment.

Eleven weeks after the Germans arrived in Kodoma the peasants disappeared. They left most of their possessions behind, taking only a few pieces of clothing and whatever objects of sentiment they could stuff into their pockets or carry with them. When she was informed of this, Soybel flew into a rage, ranting and storming through the town, directing the German soldiers to search everywhere, to rip the houses and huts apart, to interrogate everyone who had remained in Kodoma in order to uncover any clue as to where the peasants had gone. When they found nothing, Soybel ordered the soldiers to hunt down the peasants, not caring what was done to capture them. The soldiers departed immediately, each day increasing the distance between themselves and the town. By the end of the third day they were a hundred miles from Kodoma and still there was no trace of their quarry. Frantically, Soybel tried to decide what to write in her weekly report. She paced the parlor floor, her face twisted by wrath. Her temper flared. She smashed the mantelpiece clock, not wanting to hear her triumph tick away. On the fifth day after the disappearance of the peasants the pounding of galloping hoofs raced toward the house from down the lane. Running up to his mother, Munya declared that the soldiers were returning. Together Soybel and her son rushed outside to the porch to meet the Germans, to thank them for what they had done.

Soybel stood at the porch rail, anxiously waiting for the lieutenant to emerge from the narrow dirt path. There was a smile on Soybel's face and her hand was poised to wave a warm welcome to the officer and his troops. Rounding the final bend in the lane, the first horseman came into view. Rather than the German field-gray she had expected to see, his uniform was blue, cinched by a yellow sash, and he wore a billed cap with a cockade. Even though he was on horseback, it was obvious that he was short, but his bearing was that of a military man and he appeared formidable. His face was strong, very strong, with a Roman nose, lips that were sullen, and cruel-looking eyes. He was clean-shaven, and the hair that was visible beneath his cap was dark and close-cropped. A revolver hung from either hip, ammunition belts crisscrossed his chest, and he carried a rifle loosely crooked under one arm. Behind him followed two hundred men similarly armed, and uniformed in trousers tucked into high leather boots and blue cotton shirts worn under leather vests. Bringing up the rear were fifty horsedrawn carts. The first man yanked his horse to a sudden stop five feet from the porch while the others fanned out across the manicured lawn, the horses trampling it, the carts digging ruts into the soft grass.

"I have come to honor you with presents!" the horseman at the foot of the porch announced to Soybel. His voice was thin and deadly sharp, like the point of a needle.

"Who are you? Where are my soldiers?"

The man turned in his saddle and motioned with his head. Several men jumped down from the carts and unloaded the first thirteen wagons. One by one, each man lifted a headless German body from the carts, carried the mutilated corpses to the house, and dropped them in front of the steps.

"*Maman*!" Munya cried out, grabbing hold of his mother's skirt, unable to take his eyes from the barbaric sight.

Soybel stood frozen in place, her face ashen.

"Do you like my presents?" The leader glanced at the decapitated bodies, then directed a smile at Soybel. "Petlura brings good presents, yes?"

Clutching the porch railing for support, Soybel stammered: "What do you want here?"

"Everything!" Petlura glared at Soybel and Munya, his burning eyes looking through Soybel's high-necked pink dress. Slowly his gaze wandered from his captives to the house. "Are you just landowners? Or *Jews*, too?" Petlura turned suddenly to look at Munya, and Soybel clutched at her son, pulling him close to her. She quivered and her mouth became sticky with saliva, making it impossible for her to swallow.

"Answer me. I want to know if you are Jews!"

Soybel shook her head and held Munya more tightly.

"I want to see!" demanded Petlura.

Two riders dismounted and swaggered up to the porch, the leather of their swinging holsters squeaking. They climbed the porch steps, their boots banging against the risers, their faces blank, their eyes, as motionless as those of a fish, fixed on Munya. Soybel grabbed her son's hand and ran for the door. A bullet splintered the wood just above her head.

"If you do not stop, the next one will not miss," threatened Petlura.

The two men wrenched Munya from Soybel's grasp. She scratched at them. Roughly they shoved her away, causing her to fall. Then they tore Munya's pants from his body and stood him naked before Petlura. One of the men held Munya's penis for inspection.

"So, he has a foreskin!" Petlura looked at Soybel, a smile twisting his lips. "Bring her with you," he ordered the two Haidamacks on the porch. "And if she wants, the boy can come, too." Petlura wheeled his horse around. "Now, empty the house!" he shouted to the drivers of the carts. "Then burn it!" Firing his rifle above his head, Petlura kicked his horse into a gallop. Seconds later he was leading his two hundred Haidamacks down the lane and back toward the center of Kodoma.

Seizing hold of Soybel and Munya, the men on the porch dragged them over to one of the carts and shoved them into the back. One man climbed behind the horse while the other placed himself with the prisoners. With a crack of the driver's whip, the horse broke into a trot, and the cart rumbled away from the house and into the clouds of dust kicked up by Semyon Petlura's army.

By the time the wagon had traveled the two miles to Kodoma's square, thirty people who had not fled the town with the peasants—all of them Jews—had been herded in front of the church and cowered before the Haidamack rifles.

"Burn the place! All of it!" Petlura ordered, riding into the square at a canter.

Men brandishing torches methodically went from house to house, building to building, setting each one afire. Several headed for the main granary building next to the depot. Petlura, seeing the group of terrified people, reined in his horse and with savage eyes vilified them.

"No Germans! No Bolsheviks! No Jews! Only Petlura!"

The captives, most of them old except for two young couples and five children—one an infant—wailed and moaned. They looked to Soybel, imploring her to help them. Soybel neither saw nor heard them, her face pressed against Munya's, kissing him, crushing him to her breast, her heart beating madly, deaf to everything but Munya's pitiful sobbing.

"Don't kill us. Please do not kill us!" begged the Jews.

Petlura sat on his horse, his eyes focused on the burning village as if he were studying a sparkling jewel. He smiled as the Jews began to pray.

"My beloved brother—"

"Poppa—"

"Momma, in this solemn hour I remember the days when we lived together."

A wind kicked up, fanning the hot air into turbulent circles.

"I remember the loving friendship we shared."

The roar and heat of the fire were like the inside of a blast furnace. The Jews huddled together, touching one another's faces, hands clasping hands. Their clothing hung from their bodies like loose, uncomfortable skin, the growing intensity of the conflagration singeing everyone's hair. A building collapsed, the thundering crash of timbers and bricks ear-shattering. An infant shrieked with hunger and its mother, kneeling on the ground, exposed her breast so the baby could suckle. A father wept in agony, clutching his five-year-old son to his chest. A palsied old woman smothered her husband's face with kisses. A white-haired man with pale blue eyes and skin like parchment clasped his *yarmulke* to his head and fell to his knees, his beard bobbing up and down to the trudging rhythm of the mourner's prayer which he chanted.

"V'yisgadal, v'yiskadosh . . ."

A shot rang out. The man tumbled forward and lay still.

"You see what happens to traitors to the Ukraine?" Petlura shouted, his revolver still pointed at the corpse.

A woman threw herself on top of the dead man and screamed.

"I know you are Jews just by the smell!" Petlura fired his revolver again, killing the woman. He yanked his horse around in a tight circle, signaling to the other horsemen, then motioning to the two men in the cart with Soybel and Munya. Spurring his horse, Petlura dashed from the square toward the hills. A line of Haidamacks, their rifles at the ready, advanced toward the Jews. The driver of the cart raised his whip and with a vicious slash beat the animal into a run, spiriting Soybel and Munya away from the center of Kodoma.

In groups of twos and threes or a dozen or more Petlura's men gathered around him on the hillside. Then came the two-wheeled wagons, each overflowing with stolen possessions. The crackling sound of the fire could barely be heard from the hilltop, but the spreading smoke told Petlura what he wanted to know. A fusillade of shots rang out, and human screams floated upward to the crest of the hill. An entire wall of the granary building collapsed. It crumbled slowly, gracefully, like flowing lava. Shotgun shells that had been stored in the cellar of Isaac's and Andrei's mercantile store exploded. Another volley of shots followed—rifle shots—and Petlura exclaimed, "Now this place is free of Jews, too!"

Below, only the golden dome of the church resisted the flames. Petlura rested one leg crosswise over his saddle, inspecting the destruction at the bottom of the rise. "What do you think now, landowner?" His eyes lighted on Soybel's face. "How will you explain this to your German masters?"

Soybel began to shake violently.

Petlura stared down at her. A leer curled his lips as he dismounted. Half a dozen men pulled Soybel from the cart. She attempted to kick herself free. She squirmed and sank her teeth into one of the men's hands. Someone punched Soybel in the belly—she doubled up, her body going limp. The Haidamacks dragged Soybel along the ground by the hair. The men laughed. And they argued about who would have her first, after Petlura. Soybel's clothes were ripped from her body. She was rolled over and over. Fists pummeled her everywhere. Handfuls of hair were torn from her scalp and elsewhere. Her flesh was scratched and gouged until she was covered with blood. With their fingers, whip handles, and gun barrels Petlura and his men left no part of Soybel unviolated. Compelled to lie on her belly, her legs doubled under her and forced up to her shoulders, her face shoved into the dirt, Soybel was mounted like an animal. Fingernails raked her back and buttocks until her skin was gashed raw. Saliva, stained with tobacco and phlegm, was spat on her everywhere. And all the while, riveted to the scene, unable to take his eyes from his mother's tormented body, Munya stood in silence.

By sunset, having had their fill of Soybel and then having eaten and rested, Petlura and his Haidamacks readied themselves to depart from Kodoma. The riding horses were saddled, the cart horses hitched, and without a command from Petlura the marauders headed due west, riding in double file. Ignoring Soybel and the boy who stood rigid above her lifeless form, Petlura took one last look at the charred remains of Kodoma. Satisfied, he mounted his horse and gently shook the reins: the animal began to walk. Petlura snapped the reins harder, and the animal trotted. With all his might Petlura lashed the horse and it uncoiled into a full run. Petlura gripped the saddle with his knees, keeping his balance by grasping the horse's mane with one hand while with the other he triumphantly waved his rifle. He let out a cry of exultation that could be heard above all the pounding hoofs of his horsemen's mounts. Petlura laughed, throwing his head back in unbounded joy. But as he rode toward the fading light of day, and the distance from Kodoma rapidly increased, the memory of the town disappeared from Petlura's mind, replaced by thoughts of all the other towns, villages, and hamlets he had yet to visit. His expression became grim. His eyes narrowed. Semyon Petlura bent low over his horse's neck and pushed it to run even faster.

CHAPTER 44

By mid-July it became apparent to even the least observant of people that Sara Moisei was pregnant. And as Mala had predicted, there was a noticeable change in Grisha: his constant irritability was displaced by an attentive devotedness to his wife, a gentleness that surprised everyone. Each morning Grisha sat on the floor by the bed he and Sara shared, dabbing her face with a damp cloth as she leaned over the edge, heaving up little more than air. To ease the discomfort caused by Sara's swelling belly and the constant aching in her back induced by the additional weight and pressure against her spine, Grisha was almost always at her side, supporting her as she walked, placing pillows behind her when she sat, massaging the small of her back, rubbing her stomach, pressing his ear to her abdomen to try and hear their child growing inside her, continually telling her how beautiful she looked. On the days when the heat made Sara cranky and short-tempered, Grisha would fill the tin-lined bathtub in their room with cool water and carefully bathe her with lightly perfumed soap. And so his adoration grew.

Mala, who had noticed the change in Sara long before anyone else, immediately guessed the truth. She watched over the girl as though she were her own daughter, refusing to permit Sara to work in the café, admonishing anyone whose boisterousness might disturb her when she was resting. As for Mishka, the moment he was informed of Sara's pregnancy, he kissed her, patted her stomach, then proceeded to tease Grisha mercilessly about his becoming a father. Grisha took it good-naturedly, knowing that Mishka's comments were inspired by the same happiness that he felt himself. Joseph was overwhelmed with excitement, prancing around the café, already behaving like a grandfather. He sat for hours in the Zala, sipping beer, his face beaming, his thoughts focused on all the things about which he, Grisha, and Sara had talked so often. When Eleazar heard the news, he began to babble that the child would be the most special ever born. He shouted huzzahs and hallelujahs, and he quoted from the *Wisdom of Solomon*:

"So born from mortal man, also a descendant of Adam who was created from the earth, so will this child be shaped in the womb of Imma, the Mother. And this child, too, will don righteousness for his corselet. Justice for his helmet. Holiness will be his shield.

"Purity will hone his sword. And by his side, the world will wage war against the madmen. And his reward will be with the Lord."

When finally the initial reaction to Sara's pregnancy wore off, an aura of love and protection surrounded her, a quiet joy permeating the Zala and all the people in it. The growing life within Sara seemed to revitalize everyone, and if a stranger from the outside world had first looked at Odessa, and then inside the café, he would have been startled. For amid the growing hardships of the German occupation, he would have seen a small group of people waiting for the birth of more than just another child. He would have witnessed those people attending a pregnant woman from whose body they expected paradise to emerge.

The hot days of July moved into August, the humidity rising, becoming unbearable, and the only refuge was the café, so the Zala was never empty. But even if the weather had been pleasant, there was little for anyone to do except spend their days there, passing the hours reminiscing, planning for the future, making endless lists of names for Sara's baby, or just sitting and waiting for something decisive to happen to Russia so they would know in which direction to move. "Indeed," they asked one another, apologetic for their powerlessness, "what else can we do but wait?"

On the third Tuesday in August Rabbi Joshua Eleazar rushed into the Malinas Zala shouting at the top of his lungs for Grisha, his body shaking as he repeatedly called out the name.

"Eleazar, what is wrong?" Mala asked, hurrying into the café from the living quarters in the back.

"Where is Grisha? I need Grisha!"

"He is not here—what has happened?"

"At my house. As if they have been in the war—Soybel and her young son! And all she does is cry out the name Petlura."

Not waiting a second longer, Mala ran to Kherson Street. The sight that greeted her as she flung open the door and burst into Eleazar's house stopped her short. Crumpled on the floor like a sack of rags was a woman. The shredded remains of the dress she wore were barely recognizable, its pink fabric smeared with mud and blood, and things more foul. *This cannot be Grisha's mother,* thought Mala. This woman was ugly, her hair tangled with knots and dirt. Her face was blackened from soot and blue from being beaten. Her arms were scored with abrasions, gashed, crusted with dried blood. The skin on her fingers was torn, enflamed, her nails broken and jagged.

A figure standing across the room caught Mala's attention. At first, because of the piece of tattered burlap tied around its waist and hanging loose like a skirt, Mala thought it was a girl. On closer inspection she saw it was a boy, his face caked with dirt, the skin on one cheek ripped open, his shirt torn, and his arms and hands covered with clotted blood.

"What happened?" asked Mala softly, trying not to frighten the child.

"Is Momma dead?" the boy asked, his words barely slipping past his cracked lips.

"No," Mala said, bending over Soybel to make sure she was not lying. Feeling Soybel's breath against her face, Mala picked her up and placed her on the sofa. "You will be all right," Mala said, brushing the dirt away from Soybel's eyes and nose. "Everything is all right now. You are safe."

A tiny sound stole through Soybel's closed lips. Her eyes darted from Mala's face to the ceiling and back again. The sound became louder, growing into a laugh, an incessant laugh that increased in volume. Soybel's expression became wild, and with an unearthly shriek she lunged at Mala, clawing and scratching at her. Forcefully, trying not to hurt Soybel, Mala grabbed hold of her wrists, bending them until Soybel was forced to lie back down on the sofa.

"We searched the entire village for food," she began hysterically, "but the only thing to eat were the corpses. We crawled through the remains of the houses to find a place to sleep. They burned everything. Even the—"

"Shhh, it is over now."

"Help me."

Before Mala could reply, Soybel closed her eyes and slipped into an exhausted sleep, the pain she had suffered etched deeply on her face. Deciding that she was in no immediate danger, Mala prepared to care for Munya.

After boiling a pot of water and gathering several of Eleazar's sheets and towels, Mala cautiously approached Munya. Quietly she talked to him, holding out her hands to show the child that she meant only to help him. Munya ignored her, his eyes still glued to his mother. Trying not to startle the boy, Mala slowly unbuttoned his shirt, starting at the bottom and working up to its high collar. She slipped the garment off his shoulders.

"My God!" Mala exclaimed. Fastened around Munya's neck was a gold chain with several small emeralds attached to it. Mala wondered if Soybel always dressed her son in a necklace. *No wonder Petlura did not steal your momma's jewels, little one. Who would think of looking for a neck-*

lace on a boy? But why did Petlura let you live? Mala dipped a towel in the hot water and washed Munya's chest and back. His body felt stiff, his little muscles brittle. Wetting the towel again, she wrung it out and washed Munya's face. Next, she unwrapped the burlap from around his waist, completely uncovering the boy. Without looking at him, Mala tenderly cleaned his legs and thighs. A tremor of fear made Munya shake. Mala ceased washing him, intending to wait until he calmed down. She looked up from Munya's feet toward his face. When her eyes had nearly reached his hips, they froze; Mala understood why the child had survived. Seeing that Munya had become quiet again, Mala continued to bathe him. When she was finished, she dried him with a second towel, and wrapped him in a sheet. Pulling a chair over from next to the window, Mala positioned it near the sofa. She led Munya to the seat and placed him in it. First making certain there was nothing else she could do for him, or that he wanted, Mala turned her attention back to Soybel.

Before she was able to attend to Soybel, it was necessary for Mala to remove the woman's clothes. When she saw the massive bruises and welts that covered her body from her breasts to her knees, the black-and-blue marks that had begun to turn green on her thighs, the missing tufts of hair, and the sores between her legs, Mala knew why Soybel had also not been killed. It was well-known that when Petlura and his men finished raping a woman, she rarely survived. As she inspected Soybel's body Mala felt sick to her stomach. She took a deep breath and began a chore she did not want to do. After wiping the dirt and blood from Soybel's body, Mala untangled her hair, undoing the knots strand by strand. She searched Soybel's scalp for lice; there were none. Next, she moved down to the hair between Soybel's legs, and there she did find a residue from Petlura and his Haidamacks—minute red insects that resembled the spindly-legged creatures found by the seashore. Mala tried to pick them out with her fingers, but there were too many, and the nearly microscopic brown eggs of the vermin clung too tightly to Soybel's hair to be easily removed. Leaving Soybel for a moment, Mala went to the rabbi's room, returning with a dust-covered straight razor. She washed it. Then, spreading Soybel's legs apart, Mala took one of the towels and placed it beneath Soybel, and, trying not to nick or irritate the skin any more than it was, she shaved the hair, letting the short, infested curls drop onto the cloth. When the area was shaven clean, Mala checked it again. Certain that she had rid Soybel of any trace of the parasites, Mala folded the towel into a wad, wrapped it in a rag, and placed it by the door so she would remember to take it outside and burn it in the street.

Limb by limb, torso, breasts, back, and shoulders, Mala bathed Soybel. She washed her hair, combing it until it shone black. She dried it until the dark tresses squeaked with cleanliness, brushing them until they lay across Soybel's shoulders, hiding her breasts and stomach. Mala covered Soybel with a sheet, watching for a moment to see if she would stir. But Soybel never moved, her fatigue verging toward unconsciousness. Not knowing what else she could do, Mala turned to Munya, slowly explaining to him that she was leaving and would return shortly with a doctor. The boy nodded dumbly, his eyes never wavering from his mother, his head continuing to bob up and down long after Mala had gone.

Well over a month passed before Soybel was able to walk without pain. During that time she remaïned at Eleazar's house, her recuperation supervised by Mala. As she regained her strength, Soybel recounted in bits and pieces the lurid details of Petlura's visit to Kodoma. Soybel was dismayed when no one reacted to her stories with horrified shudders. She would stop her recitation, waiting for someone to cry out in anguish, sympathy. When she heard nothing but silence, and saw nothing but wide-eyed stares, Soybel would complain that she was tired and ask those who were present to leave so she could lie down and rest. When the house was empty except for Munya, Soybel would sit by the window and study the passersby, wondering why everyone seemed to be so unaffected by her tragedy. When she finally asked Grisha about it and he told Soybel that her story was so gruesome that it was difficult for anyone to react with anything but shocked disbelief, Soybel felt little relief. Yet she persisted in retelling the story, especially to Grisha, who indulged his mother only out of pity. Grisha felt little warmth or affection for Soybel. In truth, it took great urging from Mala for him to continue to visit his mother. For her part, Soybel interpreted the time Grisha spent with her as the return of her son to her, never thinking that his feelings were anything less than love. *Perhaps he even feels remorse,* Soybel told herself, *because he knows that if he had come to Kodoma as I asked, he might have been able to save me from Petlura.*

Day by day Soybel filled in all the pieces until Grisha, Sara, Mishka, Mala, and Joseph knew every detail of her ordeal. Soybel described how, when the two men in the cart were busy watching the Jews being herded together, she had slipped her necklace around Munya's neck. She told how on the day following the attack she had crawled down the hillside and into Kodoma, and what she found there. In the square before the church, the bodies of the old Kodomites and the five children and their parents were charred, burnt black in the fire, their arms and legs entangled; the bodies of all the men and the infant boy were naked, castrated. Omitting only the most vile items, Soybel gave a moment-by-moment account of her own violation. She reported every step that she and Munya had taken to Odessa. And when she reached the end of her story, concluding at the point when Mala had entered Eleazar's house, Soybel never again mentioned it. Instead she basked in the gentle attention she received from Munya, and delighted in the candies that Sara made for her and the meals Mala cooked for her.

When Joseph stopped by on his own, just to say a few kind words and ask if she needed anything, Soybel enjoyed his quiet pleasantness. She told Joseph how much she had been looking forward to meeting him, and that now, more than ever, she wanted her family to be together again, and that included both him and Sara. In response to her warmth Joseph took Soybel's measurements with his practiced eye, on his own found the best material in Odessa, and two weeks later presented Soybel with a dress as fine as any in the city. Soybel reveled not only in Joseph's gift, but in all the attention that was being lavished on her, finding it as soothing as the healing ointments the doctor gave her. She began to smile again, her voice recapturing its birdlike, trilling quality. The greatest discomfort she suffered was the itching as the hair grew back between her legs, and when Mala would visit, Soybel would pretend to be angry and scold Mala for giving her a coiffure which she had not requested. Then she would laugh, saying that at least Mala had the sense to do such an amateurish job where no one would see it. Only once did Soybel inquire why Rabbi Eleazar was no longer living in his own house and why all his books and personal possessions had been removed. When Grisha stated that the rabbi believed that Soybel's presence had defiled his home and that he preferred to reside in the room in his synagogue that had previously been his study, Soybel shrugged her shoulders, smiled sweetly, and said that it was a shame he had come to such a rash decision and that she hoped he would change his mind. Never once did Soybel offer to leave the premises and live somewhere else. The thought never even occurred to her.

By October Soybel was well enough to take short walks each day to regain her strength. Often she and Munya ventured beyond Moldavanka, idling away the crisp autumn afternoons on Deribasovskaya Street, Soybel commenting about how fashionable the shops there had once been. Some days she arranged for a coach to drive her and her young son up the terrace road to the top of the cliff that overlooked the lower city, pointing out the still-occupied but deteriorating villas where once she had sumptuously dined and danced. She spoke of the day when the Germans would be driven from Odessa, the Bolsheviks soundly defeated, and the villas restored to their original beauty. She selected the estate she desired, chirping excitedly about how utterly exquisite it would be, once her flair for selecting decor was given a free hand. Soybel made a mental note to inquire as to who owned the imposing stone mansion at the summit of Odessa's terraces, certain that someday in the near future—when the Germans were gone, the Reds no longer a force, and the monarchy restored—she would be permitted to inherit Vassili's fortune, enabling her to offer a price for it that could not be refused.

Stimulated by her fantasies, invigorated by the return of her health and the bracing fall weather, Soybel often strode spiritedly through Moldavanka, her carriage stately, her head held high, her eyes proud, sweeping regally into the Malinas Zala. Aware only of her own sentiments and totally fascinated by her own exhilaration, Soybel had no idea that from her very first visit to the café she was at best tolerated. If Mishka were there, he would quickly disappear from sight, followed closely by Grisha, who, despite Sara's imploring looks, found it impossible to remain for very long in the presence of his mother, her condescending chatter causing unbearable knots in Grisha's stomach.

"So this is the Raspberry Café!" Soybel warbled on her initial visit to the Zala. "It is surprisingly cheerful," she said, looking around the room. With a nod of her head she acknowledged Mala. "Red curtains can make the gloomiest place seem gay." Soybel smiled at Sara who was sitting by herself at a table and eating. "My, but you are becoming fat!" She inspected Sara's enormous stomach and clucked her tongue. "*I* was always careful with myself when I was pregnant. How many months along are you?"

"Seven."

"My grandson is going to be a giant!" Soybel gave Sara a peck on the cheek. "I want it to be a boy. My two boys are my best children. Where is Grisha?"

"He is not here," replied Mala, her tone daring Soybel to press her inquiry.

"And Mishka?"

"He also is not here."

"And I wanted to see him," Soybel said sweetly. "It has been so very long since he has come to visit me. Will he return soon?"

"I have no—"

"It does not matter. Sara and I have many things to talk about." Her face aglow, Soybel sat down next to Sara. "With a baby coming, I am certain that you could use the experience of a woman who has had three."

Sara tried to smile. She shifted her weight several times, unable to find a comfortable position.

"Grisha was the most difficult of all my children. Though Munya was not easy either. But when Grisha was born, the doctor said I was the bravest woman he had ever met. I was in labor for forty hours. Forty hours! So *you* could have a husband!" Soybel's bell-like laugh echoed in the empty café.

"Sara, would you like to lie down, you look—"

"Oh, is Sara tired, Mala?" Patting Sara's hand, Soybel laughed. "I am so sorry, dear, I should know how tired one can get at this stage."

"To be honest, Mrs. Moisei—"

"Please call me Soybel. There is no need for formalities." Soybel smiled sweetly. "But if it makes you uncomfortable—though it never did me, I called my mother-in-law Naomi from the first day I met her. She asked me to. And I thought it was such a pretty name I was unable to resist. That was my first husband's mother. I never met Vassili's mother. She died long before I ever met him. But as I was saying, if you prefer not to call me Soybel, then call me Mrs. Viska; it is entirely up to you."

Sara looked to Mala for help.

"I think that it is time for Sara to rest," Mala said coldly.

Soybel looked from Sara to Mala and then back to Sara again. She ignored their unfriendly expressions. "I suppose that I am being selfish by making you sit up and talk to me," Soybel said to Sara. "When there is tomorrow and the next day, and next week—when there is a lifetime for us to talk."

"You are quite right," Mala said flatly, slowly advancing toward the table, the deliberateness of her step, the menace in her expression reminiscent of Mishka. Mala paused next to Sara, protectively resting a hand on her shoulder.

"You know, my dear, it is rather sad that Grisha did not bring you to Kodoma before that terrible incident. We had such a lovely house there. I wish I had a picture to show you. As soon as all the uncertainties caused by the occupation and the chaos caused by the Bolsheviks come to an end—and both adversities will be dealt with severely by the Monarchists, though I must admit that there would be great sympathy for the Germans—indeed support for them—if they advanced against Lenin and his bandits. Nevertheless, as soon as the situation permits me to again have access to my inheritance, I am going to buy a house here in Odessa, overlooking the sea. Then we can all live together."

"Unless Sara takes care of herself, unless she rests, she will not have the strength to enjoy your money," Mala interjected. "And I am certain that you would not want to deprive her of that."

"Forgive me, please. And you must remind me when I forget my manners and stay too long." Soybel got to her feet. "You are like a good husband, Mala," she said lightly. "You are protective." Soybel laughed. "Good husbands always are."

Ignoring Soybel's comment, Mala walked toward the door. Soybel followed her.

"I will see you tomorrow, Sara. And I will bring Munya. Soon you will know why I consider him the dearest thing that ever lived."

Before Soybel could stop and say something else, Mala opened the door and with measured sarcasm said: "We will look forward to seeing your dearest son." With a grand sweep of her arm, Mala indicated that Soybel was to continue walking straight out of the café and into the street. "And most of all we look forward to seeing you again."

As if Mala's gesture was still propelling her along, Soybel left the Zala, stopping momentarily when she was outside to smile and wave good-bye. Before she had concluded her farewell, Mala closed the door.

CHAPTER 45

On the morning of Monday, January 13, 1919, a chill wind swept through Odessa, hardening the frost that had formed overnight into ice. The sun, though without warmth, shone with unusual brilliance in the cloudless sky, exposing the city in brittle clarity, and everywhere, bundled in heavy coats and caps, their heads bent low to protect them from the cold, people walked hurriedly, anxious to avoid being exposed to the biting winter air.

In Moldavanka, in an atmosphere remote from the rest of Odessa, in a large room that looked like a prehistoric cave, its walls dark, its fireplace sizzling like a Bronze Age spit, a rite prescribed by the Book of Genesis was about to begin. Lying on the center table, protected from the wood by a spotless white sheet, was Isaac Grigorievich Moisei, the eight-day-old son of Grisha and Sara Moisei. The infant was naked, his body bright red from his kicking and crying. Surrounding him were his parents—his mother, who was nineteen years old and his father, just twenty-three, little more than children themselves. Next to them, unable to stand still, was the baby's maternal grandfather, Joseph Dubrow, whose slender fifty-year-old body, for the moment, felt as agile as a youth's. On Joseph's right—fashionably clothed in a lavender dress that had been made especially for her, her expression disdainful, the arch of her neck and tilt of her head indicating that she felt superior to the others—was the child's paternal grandmother, Soybel Viska. On her right, holding her hand, was her eleven-year-old son, Munya, the infant Isaac's only uncle. Across the table from Soybel Viska stood Mala Katyov, a robust woman of forty who had devoted her life to the man beside her, Mishka Yaponchik, age forty-three, a thief and worse, yet revered by countless numbers of people who found solace in his daring. Hovering over the infant was Rabbi Joshua Eleazar, sixty-five years old, his life now almost entirely spent in a world populated by spirits, angels, disembodied voices, and glimpses of blinding light which he was certain was the Countenance of the Lord. At his side was the *mohel,* another old man who was holding several sharp instruments that would be used to slice away the foreskin, draw a drop of blood, and thereby formally introduce a new son to the God of Abraham, another Isaac, and Jacob.

"Can you imagine anyone but a child having the nerve to enter Russia? And especially now?" Mishka Yaponchik said with a soft chuckle as everyone waited for Rabbi Eleazar to begin the ceremony.

"Wherever a Jewish child is born, no matter what city, what country, in truth he is always born in *Eretz Yisrael.* For wherever a Jewish child is born, he resides in the realm of the Lord our God. In the covenant of *Adonai,*" the *mohel* commented.

"That is true, but if it were possible, I would be far happier if my grandson's body, along with his spirit, were in Palestine."

"Ha! Listen to Dubrow. The child has barely left his mother's belly and already he has him on a boat!"

"The moment he was conceived, he was ready to leave Russia," Sara said, her eyes caressing her son.

Mishka looked at Sara, warmed by the way her face expressed her love for Isaac. "You are as stubborn as *malcheshka.* And he is more stubborn than anyone, except me!"

"You never met his father," Soybel noted, her words clipped.

Mishka took a step toward her, halting when Mala kicked him in the leg. Rabbi Eleazar cleared his throat, and everyone turned to watch the man who was about to perform the circumcision ritual.

"Please be careful," said Sara.

"He had better be, or instead of a son you'll have a daughter," Mishka joked.

"Do you realize that this same moment has occurred for every one of our sons for five thousand years!" Joseph Dubrow said.

"Listen to how loudly he is crying," Eleazar exclaimed. "He is trying to make sure that God is watching!"

"He is announcing that he is about to become a Jew!" the *mohel* added.

"Yes, and from this day on both he and the world will know that the children of Abraham still exist!" Mishka said emphatically.

"And from this day on he will have to suffer the burdens of your selfishness!" Soybel Viska retorted.

Everyone stared at her.

"Instead of the old man cutting the sign of the Jew on him, he would do better to plunge the knife into the baby's heart—because anything is better than the persecution he will suffer," Soybel continued, her voice icy cold.

Shock stunned the others into silence. Joseph Dubrow moved a step away from Soybel. Instinctively Sara moved to protect Isaac with her body. The veins in Mishka's neck pulsated violently; he clutched the edge of the table with all his strength.

"If that is the way you feel, then why did you have that sign put on me. And on Munya?" Grisha questioned, his voice even and extremely soft.

Soybel squeezed her young son's shoulder. "Munya was not circumcised."

Grisha glanced at his brother, then back to his mother.

The expression on his face was a mixture of surprise and bewilderment.

"You did not know? Your gallant Mishka did not tell you?" Soybel brushed a lock of hair from Munya's eyes. She looked pleased with herself.

Grisha slid his eyes from his mother's face to his son's. "And why should Mishka have known?"

"Because I knew," said Mala hesitantly.

Tenderly, Grisha touched Isaac's hand, marveling at his son's tiny yet perfectly formed fingers and nails.

"Malcheshka, we said nothing only because we wanted to spare you—"

"Mishka, I care nothing about my mother's other son."

"Tell me, Grisha," Soybel interrupted, "what is this thing that compels you to circumcise your son?"

"Do you hate being a Jew that much?"

"What I hate, Grisha, is the thought that if circumstances had been different, the wrong decision would have been made, and Munya would have been circumcised, and so condemned to death. I am grateful that I was free to come to my own conclusion."

Grisha studied his son's face and wondered how he would feel if Isaac should die tomorrow, on his ninth day of life, just because he had been circumcised

"Which is better, Grisha, a lie, or being responsible for your own son's murder?" Soybel asked, feeling the hostility of the people around her. Pulling Munya closer to her, she said, "I gave birth to this child. It was I who gave him life. And when it came to the choice between endangering his life and protecting it, I decided to protect it. When Petlura's men stripped him naked, made him stand exposed for the world to see, *my* decision saved his life. What will you say when your precious Isaac is exposed, and because of you they take his life?"

Grisha looked at the faces of the others, wishing that one of them would say something to help him. He looked at Sara, her expression showing she was fighting the same doubt. Joseph's face was filled with consternation. Rabbi Eleazar was paralyzed, shaken that anyone would corrupt this simplest proof of faith. The hatred Mishka had been harboring against Soybel was on the verge of erupting. His eyes darted back and forth between her face and Isaac's, his huge hands clenched into fists. For the first time since he had known her, Grisha saw anger on Mala's face; she seemed ready to pounce on Soybel. Yet, despite the animosity they all felt toward Soybel, they were intrigued by what she had said, especially the men. They, too, had been circumcised when they were eight days old. From that moment on they had had no choice but to learn to survive as Jews. Now they were witnessing a man who could decide his son's future. His choice could mean that by a stroke of the knife his son would join a history filled with tragedy, be faced with death the instant the ceremonial blade completed its work. Except for Eleazar, the men shuddered as they wondered if somewhere deep in their souls they wished that their fathers had made the same decision Soybel had made for Munya, and they truly comprehended the overwhelming decision with which Grisha was wrestling. They looked at his mother, understanding why they hated her. With a few words she had not just scorned their lives, and their fathers' lives, but worse, she had unmasked the selfishness of a belief which meant to pay homage to the past even as it ignored the realities of the world in which they all had to live. Even Mishka became confused, no longer certain that it was better for his father to have been killed because he was a Jew than to have been permitted to live as a Gentile. He thought of the horrors he had witnessed in his lifetime, the bodies crippled and maimed, the minds driven insane. He looked at Mala; he remembered her description of her father's mutilated corpse, and for the first time in his life Mishka Yaponchik was unsure of everything.

The silence continued, everyone waiting for an answer that lay not in themselves, not in the woman who had challenged a way of life that had endured for millenia, not even in the youth whose fatherhood and manhood had been placed on trial. Truly, the answer they awaited would be found in each breath the innocent Isaac would need to walk the earth instead of being buried beneath it. The decision should have been his. But that was impossible. Grisha looked at his mother, then at his brother. Munya's face was emotionless, his big round eyes empty, staring back at Grisha. Isaac squirmed and gurgled. Grisha brushed the petal-like skin of the baby's cheek. He drew a line with his index finger across the infant's palm. Isaac grasped Grisha's hand, his little fingers making his father ache with love for him. Grisha began to speak softly, his tone firm.

"The last thing in the world I would ever want would be for Isaac to die. I would never want to be responsible for his death. But I am responsible for his life. Not just for helping to bring him into this world, but for every second that he is in it. And that is a greater responsibility. And there is something else, perhaps even more important than me or my son. For if I should refuse to make the choice that he will be a Jew, then what I am doing, what I am saying, in essence, is that every Jew before me has done something horrendous. I am accusing them, as you have done, of sentencing their own sons to death. I would be accusing my own father of the same thing, and I would have to despise him for it because I would be calling him—and everyone back to the beginning—a murderer. But I think there is something worse than that. Because if I refuse to have Isaac circumcised, I am admitting that every enemy we have ever had was right in wanting to destroy us."

Slowly, with each word, Grisha's voice became louder, his posture straightening, his muscles tightening.

"But worst of all, if I deny my son his heritage, if I surrender to the terror of our enemies, it will mean I believe that the future will be no better than the present, that I am incapable of making it any better. And that makes me a failure."

As Grisha continued he gestured with his hand, his forefinger stabbing the air, emphasizing each thought, his face vividly displaying the passion he felt.

"And if I consider myself a failure, act as if I am a failure, that means I live without hope. By not circumcising Isaac, I am surrendering because I am afraid. And if that is the way I feel, circumcising my son is not what will condemn him to death. My having allowed him to be born is the thing that condemned him!"

Hunching down his body, looking as if he were preparing to leap forward in attack, Grisha dropped the level of his voice, again letting it rise with each word, his tone making each sentence sound like a warning.

"My selfishness was in conceiving Isaac. And by permitting that to happen, it is my duty to do whatever I can to protect his life and make it safer than mine. By having Isaac circumcised, I am doing two things. I am telling him that the future will be better, because I am telling him that there will be a world where Jews will be allowed to live like human beings. But more important, I am swearing an oath to Isaac. An oath that says my life is no longer just for me, but for both of us. I am swearing to Isaac that I will do everything I can to give him something better than I have. I am swearing on his life that, if necessary, I will sacrifice mine. I am giving to Isaac the most precious thing I have. Because to give my son what he deserves, I am willing to offer him my death!"

For several seconds there was silence, then Soybel stepped away from the table on which Isaac was lying; Munya moved along with her. "I was wrong, Grisha, you are not a fool like your father. You are more of a fool than he was!"

"No, I am not nearly the fool he was. Because there is *nothing* you could do that would cause me to jeopardize my life for you as he did. And unlike my father, I have the courage to drive you from my house, from my life!"

Soybel put her hand to her face as though she had been struck. Grisha glowered at her, the force of his expression driving his mother further backward. He took two steps toward her. She moved ten away.

"You are putting a curse on your son," Soybel hissed.

"Not like the one you put on yours."

"And because of that he will dishonor you."

"Like me, he will honor his father. And unlike me, he will honor his mother, too."

Soybel hugged Munya to her and backed toward the door, opening it. "You will suffer for what you are doing. All of you!"

"We do not want you here in our house, so go!" Grisha moved toward his mother.

"But especially that child, he will suffer most! And while you weep for him, while you live out your days in despair I will prosper, and I will do nothing to comfort you."

"Go!"

Soybel stepped outside and stood in the street. "Whatever tragedy befalls your son, you will deserve it. Because you have doomed your son, and there is nothing more despicable than that!"

"Go!" Grisha closed the distance between Soybel and himself.

Pulling Munya along with her, Soybel hurried to the middle of the road, pointing at Grisha for everyone to see, and shouted: "There is a father who will murder his own child!"

"Go!"

Grisha's fury reverberated off the buildings of Petrovskaya Street. Passersby stopped to stare, gaping at the sneering woman who stood in the road, shaking her fists at a tall young man whose face was contorted with fury.

"I curse you, Grisha! Just like I cursed your father!"

"Go to hell, Momma!" Enraged beyond control, Grisha dashed into the street after his mother. Soybel turned to run. She stumbled, then regained her balance, ready to flee. But Grisha was upon her. Soybel backed against a building, her body shielding Munya, her fingers blindly clawing the

stone to find a way to escape. Grisha grabbed her wrist, twisting it until his mother was forced to her knees. He clamped his fingers into a fist and drew back his arm, prepared to strike.

"Go ahead, Grisha. Your father did the same thing!"

Just as his muscles uncoiled to release a lethal blow, something hard slammed against the side of Grisha's head, hitting him with such force that his feet flew out from under him and he crashed to the ground. Standing with his hands on his hips, towering above both Grisha and Soybel, was Mishka Yaponchik. Consumed with hatred, he glared at Soybel. She cowered, shrinking against the wall of the building, silently begging Mishka not to hurt her. With a single swift motion, Mishka leaned past her and swooped Grisha into his arms, holding the unconscious youth as if he were as light as a child. Mishka looked menacingly at Soybel, and for an instant he considered shouting at her to vent his anger. Instead he turned his back to her, cradled Grisha against his chest, crossed the street to the café, and not caring who was looking, in truth, hoping that everyone was looking, Mishka Yaponchik bent his head over Grisha Moisei's face and kissed him.

CHAPTER 46

Early in 1919 Semyon Petlura, who by now reportedly commanded the allegiance of 100,000 Ukrainian fighting men, led a division of soldiers in an assault against the main German force in Kiev. In the ensuing battle Hetman Skoropodski was killed and the Germans forced into a hasty retreat westward. Without delay, the Red Army marched on Kiev, engaging in battle with Petlura and his troops and handily defeating them. Within days of their victory the Bolsheviks had absolute control of the Mother City of Little Russia, their intention being to firmly entrench themselves from Kiev all the way to Odessa. Immediately the entire Ukraine became a battleground.

Everywhere Petlura and his Haidamacks, armies of peasants, and bands of Monarchist marauders fought the Reds. Tens of thousands of Jews were slaughtered. Countless numbers of homeless people roamed through the farmlands and pillaged the countryside. The steppes were littered with the bodies of those who had perished from bullets or from starvation. Corpses spiked to trees adorned the forests, while streams and lakes hid the remains of those who had been drowned with rocks tied to their necks. Rats as large as cats invaded villages and cities, spreading pestilence. Smallpox and typhus became widespread, and peasants with festering sores, driven mad by the fear of a horrible death, were prepared to kill anyone for a bite of bread. Girls of twelve and thirteen slept with any stranger for a morsel of food, or just to be able to spend the night next to someone to keep warm. Abandoned children wandered aimlessly, killing as often and as ferociously as their elders when they became cold or hungry. Wolves and wild dogs devoured the flesh of the dead. And the first signs of famine were seen in Samara, Bashkiria, and Kirghizia.

In Odessa the sounds of carbines and light machine guns continually shattered the air, the Bolsheviks and Monarchists battling for control of the city. But it was no contest. In ever increasing numbers the Reds descended on Odessa from the north, their Maxima guns spewing bullets in every direction. The Whites were overwhelmed. And even as the opposition was fleeing, Lenin's soldiers imposed a new martial law on the easygoing people of the Black Sea city.

Unlike the earlier Red occupation of Odessa, the returning troops of Lenin no longer relied on the citizenry of any town to welcome them. For the last year the Bolsheviks had fought too many battles to believe that persuasion by reason and idealistic philosophizing was still possible. Now, military strength was their way. From the heights of the fashionable terraces, along the great boulevards, wedged into every narrow street that touched the harbor, amid all the dirty cobbled roads of the poor sections, and mingling among the decaying tenements and houses of Moldavanka, tough, humorless Bolshevik soldiers demanded obedience. The strict policies of Lenin were instituted without delay, and instead of feeling liberated, the people of Odessa considered themselves prisoners of yet another invader.

"You should see the Opera House!" Urka shouted excitedly as he ran into the Malinas Zala, his nasal voice piercing through the thick clouds of boisterous laughter. "It's the new Bolshevik headquarters. They've torn everything out of it. The red velvet drapes. The gold trimmings. Even the scenery! And they're burning all of it in the street! And do you know what they're bringing in? Huge pictures of Lenin!

They are hanging them all over the Opera House walls. Why? Can Lenin sing, too?"

"Ah, a musical tyrant, and a castrato no doubt," Karmanchik sneered, picking at a wart on his nose.

"When he appears for his debut, you distract him with a bouquet of flowers, Urka, while I pick his pockets," said Skakun with a laugh.

"All you will find there is empty promises and old threats dressed up in a new coat." Joseph Dubrow's somber tone stilled the gaiety.

"Already the Bolsheviks are destroying the churches, turning them into hospitals and recreation centers for their soldiers. Soon there will be no more churches in Odessa. And then they will come to Moldavanka for our synagogues," added Urka, his comment further subduing the patrons in the Zala.

"They will *never* take away our synagogues!" Mishka Yaponchik loudly promised.

"What will we do? And how will we do what we will do?" Karmanchik asked, wiping his very long nose on his sleeve.

"It is simple. We will not permit the Bolsheviks to enter Moldavanka!" someone shouted.

"But they are already here. There is not a street they do not patrol."

Mishka banged his hand against a table. "When the time is right, there will be no more patrols in our streets!"

"And who is to know when the time is right?" asked Urka.

"Mishka Yaponchik will know when the time is right!" Mishka replied.

For the next ten days life continued as usual in Moldavanka until shortly after dawn on one day in the third week in May—when three hundred Bolshevik soldiers on horseback entered the ghetto. They were heavily armed, and strapped to each saddle was an axe and a pike. Leading the column was a pimply-faced lieutenant who was barely twenty years old. His posture was straight, and the expression on his face displayed the contempt he felt toward everything around him. The soldiers kept their horses to a nervous walk, the clicking of the hoofs against the street a fearsome alarm for early risers. None of the horsemen spoke, their attention concentrating on anything that might signal resistance. Occasionally the face of a man would peer around a corner, or from inside a doorway, then suddenly disappear. The lieutenant, an officer named Veronozeh, smiled when he saw the scurrying figures, pleased that the citizens of Moldavanka feared the Red troops. He withdrew a notebook from his pocket, looked inside it, comparing what he had read with the street name painted on the corner of a building. Replacing the booklet in his leather jacket, Lieutenant Veronozeh scanned the street in front of him. He saw what he was looking for and spurred his horse into a trot, reigning it to a halt when he came abreast of a small, shabby, stone building. Raising one hand to signal his troops to stop, the lieutenant surveyed the building. It was minuscule compared to the churches he had visited, and he found it difficult to believe that the Jews would have such an insignificant house of worship. Once more he withdrew the pad from his jacket, checking the address written in it against the sign on the building. They were identical: 31 Vinogradskaya Street. He studied a hand-drawn map at the back of his notebook, tracing a finger from Pushkinskaya Street along pencil lines indicating Preobrazhenskaya, Yekaterina, Tiraspolskaya, Kherson, and Komitetskaya Streets, through Mikhailovsky Place, and stopping at Vinogradskaya. Shrugging his shoulders, Veronozeh put the notebook away and carefully scrutinized the surrounding area. Except for his soldiers, the streets were deserted. The lieutenant sat motionless in his saddle, listening for any sound; the faint hum of men's voices emanated from 31 Vinogradskaya. The lieutenant grimaced. Climbing down from his horse, he ordered his men to remain where they were and approached the building. As he opened the door the sudden increase in the volume of praying made Veronozeh pause. He was surprised by the number of Jews, white shawls draped over their shoulders, their heads bowed, swaying in rhythm to a slow chant, who had come so early to pray. With firm steps the lieutenant strode down the aisle toward the pulpit, his boots clicking against the floor. No one in the congregation turned to look at him, not one word of the prayer was missed. Halting at the foot of the raised platform, where a bearded man dressed in a black caftan was leading the services, the lieutenant smartly saluted.

"Good morning, rabbi, or should I say *comrade*." Lieutenant Veronozeh's raspy-voiced curtness stabbed through the gentle fabric of the morning prayers. "I am Lieutenant Ilya Veronozeh of the people's Bolshevik Army!"

The chanting faded into silence. Every eye was on the young officer.

"I am sorry to interrupt the last religious service you will be holding here, but the revolution frowns on superstition. I hope you understand that, Comrade Rabbi."

The man on the dais stepped to the very edge of the pulpit. "Good morning, Lieutenant."

"You are Rabbi—"

"Levin?" the man on the pulpit said as the officer reached for his notebook.

"Yes, Levin, that is it."

He shook his head.

"But I was informed that the rabbi of this synagogue was named Levin."

"Yesterday there was a rabbi named Levin here, and tomorrow there will be a rabbi named Levin here. But today a rabbi named Yaponchik is here. Rabbi Mishka Yaponchik!"

"Are you the head rabbi of Moldavanka?" the lieutenant asked, confused by not being able to recall a Rabbi Yaponchik.

"I am more than that. Like your commissar who rules the rest of Odessa, I rule Moldavanka," Mishka answered, quickly removing the prayer shawl from his shoulders and then the caftan. Lieutenant Veronozeh's eyes bulged when he saw two revolvers strapped to the belt of the man he had thought was a rabbi. Without thinking, the lieutenant placed his hand on his own pistol, immediately realizing the futility of his gesture when the others in the room removed their prayer shawls, revealing that they, too, carried weapons.

"You see, Lieutenant, just as your Commissar has an army, I have an army. And as your Commissar worships Lenin, we worship God. And as your Commissar wants to take away our synagogues, we want to protect them!"

Veronozeh looked toward the door.

"Are you expecting someone?"

The lieutenant sneered at Mishka. "I am calculating how fast this building will crumble when my soldiers start tearing it apart!"

"Is that what you want to do here?"

"It is what we want to do *everywhere*. Nowhere in Russia will we allow any building to be used for worship, because no longer in Russia is there any need for God. So, obviously there is no need for a place in which to worship God."

"I do not care about the rest of Russia. I do not even care about the rest of Odessa! You can have *all* the churches. That is for the Christians to decide. But you cannot have the synagogues. They do not belong to you. And as long as Rabbi Levin wants his synagogue, and Rabbi Solomon his, and all the other rabbis want their synagogues—Mishka Yaponchik will make certain that no one takes them away! No pimple-faced Bolshevik will take what is ours. No commissar. No general. Lenin himself could come here and we would tell him to go to hell, too!"

The lieutenant's face was smug. "I have three hundred soldiers outside who say that you are wrong."

Mishka smiled broadly, and as if he were explaining something to a child he replied: "All you have outside are three hundred men who are too terrified to move." Mishka jumped down from the pulpit, and standing at least a head taller than the soldier, he peered down at him. "Would you care to see?"

Boldly, Mishka strode past Veronozeh, hurried up the aisle, and threw open the doors of the *shul*.

"Good morning, Bolshevik soldiers! Did you come to pray with us?"

The lieutenant retraced his steps through the synagogue and stepped into the street. His assured manner abruptly changed when he saw his men sitting on their horses with their hands held above their heads. Mishka pointed upward. The lieutenant's eyes followed the direction of Mishka's finger. He was startled. On every rooftop along the block dozens of men armed with automatic rifles trained their weapons on the soldiers below. In the street directly in front of the soldiers and led by a man with a machine gun was another contingent of men with rifles aimed at the hearts of the Bolshevik horsemen.

"Now, my important lieutenant, do you want these children of yours to ride out of Moldavanka sitting up, or tied to their saddles, dead?"

The officer fumed, restraining his anger so as not to jeopardize his troops. Without a word he mounted his horse, and with a deadly look directed at Mishka kicked the animal and cantered off.

"You can go, too!" Mishka bellowed at the lieutenant's soldiers.

Needing no further encouragement, the Bolshevik troops wheeled their horses around and galloped after their lieutenant.

"If you want to see me again, or your Commissar would like to shake my hand, come to the Malinas Zala!" Shouting at the top of his lungs, Mishka added: "That is where Mishka Yaponchik lives! That is where the king of the Jews lives!" Then, unable to control himself any longer, Mishka fell to the ground and rolled around in a fit of uncontrollable laughter.

For one day Moldavanka was in a state of excitement, the people of the ghetto feeling like heroes because a thief, Mishka Yaponchik, had defied the Bolsheviks. The Raspberry Café was crowded until dawn, hundreds of people straining to be near the heroic gangster who swilled vodka and merrily recounted every detail of his exploit again and again. Everyone laughed and drank, honored to be in the presence of the self-proclaimed king of the Jews as he noisily held court.

"Did you see the lieutenant's face when he saw my pistols?" asked Mishka with glee.

"I thought he would piss in his pants!"

"You should have seen the soldiers in the street, Mishka, especially when Grisha held up his machine gun for them to see!"

"One move by any of them, I warned, and I threatened to kill them all!" said Grisha.

"A child could have frightened those cowards away," Karmanchik snorted.

"A child? An infant!" sneered Urka.

"Little Isaac could have done it!" someone else shouted.

"If they ever return, we will attach my machine gun to Isaac's crib—can you imagine their faces when they see that?" exclaimed Grisha.

"Grisha, Isaac has no need of your machine gun. With one look he could scare away a thousand Bolsheviks!"

"Grisha, have another son, and let him free *all* of Odessa from the Reds!"

"Have a dozen sons, Grisha, and free Russia!"

The celebrating continued until daybreak, and as the rising sun touched the ghetto, trucks could be heard rumbling through the streets surrounding the Zala. From both ends of Petrovskaya Street hundreds of Bolshevik soldiers ran for doorways, alleyways, up to the rooftops, crouching for protection. At either end of the street a truck blocked the way, a machine gun mounted on each of them, a Red soldier ready to shoot at anything suspicious. When their positions were secured and the street was under control, one man walked toward the café; in his hands he held a rifle, cocked, his finger held against the trigger. He kicked open the door of the Zala and surveyed the room, his weapon riveted on the two men who sat at the center table.

"King of the Jews, the Commissar of Odessa would like to see you."

Neither Mishka nor Grisha moved.

"Today *we* sit on the rooftops. Today *we* own the streets. Today *we* are the kings of the Jews!" Lieutenant Veronozeh snarled. "Now, outside. The two of you!" he ordered, remembering the blond-haired youth who had been in charge of the Jewish combatants in the street, holding his soldiers at bay with a machine gun.

Mishka spat on the floor. He stood up, telling Grisha to do the same.

"Put your guns on the table!"

Both of them followed the order.

"What will you do to them?" Sara asked the lieutenant, clutching at Grisha's arm.

Mala said nothing. She stood immobile, the blood drained from her face.

"Outside!" Veronozeh commanded. "And I want each of you in a different truck!"

Mishka narrowed his eyes to slits and looked at the lieutenant. Again he spat.

"Now!"

Slowly, insolently, Mishka and Grisha, accompanied by Sara and Mala, swaggered to the doorway.

"Just the two men!" the lieutenant said. "We do not want the women. Not yet."

In the distance the splattering of machine-gun bullets tearing into stone made Mishka and Grisha jump.

"I guess we have found some of your friends, too," the officer commented. "Now, if you do not want more trouble than you can imagine, get into the street and go to the trucks!"

Grabbing Grisha by the arm, Mishka pulled him out of the café; the lieutenant followed, ordering them to separate, sending Mishka off to the right and Grisha to the left. The Bolshevik looked back at Mala and Sara.

"If there is the slightest disturbance because of this, there will not be a ghetto here tomorrow. There will not be anything here!"

Turning his attention to the prisoners, Lieutenant Veronozeh watched Mishka and Grisha climb into separate vehicles. They were manacled, and each of them was placed under the watchful eyes of a guard. Satisfied with his precautions, the Red officer signaled for the soldiers on the rooftops and along the street to vacate their positions and return to the troop trucks. The vehicles started simultaneously, their engines exploding like artillery fire. Lieutenant Veronozeh climbed into the cab of the truck in which Mishka was being held and, as quickly as he had arrived, led the Bolshevik convoy out of Moldavanka.

Before the day's end rumors circulated through the ghetto that Mishka and Grisha had already been executed. Other stories said that hundreds of Jews had been arrested and were also to be shot. Instead of attempting to quell the growing number of tales, the Bolsheviks increased their patrols in Moldavanka. On the second day of Mishka's and Grisha's disappearance the destruction of the synagogues commenced. Bibles, Torahs, prayer books, prayer shawls, skullcaps, were heaped in piles in the streets. Soldiers wielding axes and pikes smashed the pews, pulpits, the Holy Arks, adding them to the mountains of debris. Lighted matches were tossed onto the pyres, and within minutes all that was left of the religious effects of Moldavanka's synagogues were ashes that blew away with the wind. The following morning carpenters started to rebuild the insides of the synagogues, erecting walls and rooms, converting the buildings into hospitals, recreation facilities, barracks for the Reds. Rabbi Eleazar's synagogue met with the same fate as the others. Grief-stricken, alternately cursing and wailing, Eleazar shouted that the legions of Rome had no right to desecrate the Temple. He called upon God to send down the plagues of Egypt and destroy the accursed heathen. Possessionless, irrational, dispossessed, Eleazar dumbly followed Mala to the café, not comprehending that she was inviting him to live there. Days later, having drifted back into reality, the rabbi visited his *shul,* wandering the planks of new wood flooring, confused by the framework for walls where his congregation had once sat. He became terrified in the confines of the cubicle where his pulpit had been, the banging of hammers and the singing of the workers blasphemous to him. Feeling as though there were nothing left for him anywhere, Eleazar retreated from the building, deaf to the taunts and laughter of the Bolsheviks. With great effort the rabbi returned to the café, passing blindly through the crowd of disconsolate drinkers. He entered the room at the rear of the café that was now his home and closed the door behind him. Without removing his clothes, Eleazar lay down on his bed and shut his eyes. At dusk, when Mala looked in on him, she was certain he was dead.

Two weeks after Mishka and Grisha were arrested, a new rumor traveled through Moldavanka. "They are at the trainyard. They are being held prisoners in a cattle car!" By word of mouth the message was quickly passed along. By nightfall Urka had confirmed the story.

"There are perhaps fifty others with them. Some are our men, and the rest those who were unfortunate enough to be in the streets too early that morning," he told Mala and Sara in confidential tones.

"What are the Bolsheviks doing to them?" Mala asked.

"The guards thought I was drunk. I made certain I smelled that way. So when I approached the train and cursed Mishka and the others for being Jews, they left me alone."

"Are they all right?" asked Sara, holding Mala's hand for comfort.

"A little crowded, but safe."

"Did you talk to Mishka?" Mala inquired urgently.

Urka gave her a look indicating that he was disappointed that she should have thought otherwise.

Mala clutched his arms. "What did he say?"

"To alert the Bolsheviks to the fact that Mishka Yaponchik is too powerful for them to keep captive."

"Is he mad? He is their prisoner, and he still thinks they are going to be afraid of him?"

"His body may be their prisoner, but not the memory of him. We made a plan."

"What? Tell us!" Sara urged.

Urka shook his head. "You will see."

"Urka, tell me!" Mala insisted angrily, grabbing a hank of his long hair.

Urka pushed her fingers away. "When Mishka is gone, *Urka* is Mishka!"

"And when Mishka returns, Urka will be in trouble!"

"You see!" Urka squealed with delight. "Already you believe that he is coming back!" Without waiting for a reaction from Mala or Sara, Urka leaped up from his chair and hurried out of the café.

The first inkling that something was astir in Moldavanka occurred the very next night. Just before dawn, in various sections of the ghetto, several Bolshevik patrols were ambushed and taken prisoner by small bands of masked and armed men. Hidden in the deepest shadows of alleyways, the Reds were lined up against walls, rifles pressed to their foreheads, their deaths imminent. But in every case one man among their captors invoked the name of Mishka Yaponchik, saying that Mishka did not want the Bolsheviks to die. Immediately, the threatening weapons were lowered, and instead of being executed, the Bolsheviks were ordered to undress, and their pistols and rifles were confiscated.

"Remember to tell your officers that it was Mishka Yaponchik who saved your lives," the Reds were admonished. "And tell them that they should save Mishka's life. If not, then you Bolsheviks will have an army of two hundred thousand Jews to fight, not so that we can take over Odessa, but just so we can keep our Moldavanka. But if you want Odessa, never forget that you need us to let you have it."

The Bolsheviks hurried away from the ghetto, convinced that if not for this Mishka Yaponchik they would have been killed. When they returned to their commanders and explained what had happened, emphasizing the mysterious way that their lives had been spared, the commanders went to see the Commissar. The Commissar immediately recognized the incidents for what they were—a plot to undermine his authority. He fumed, declaring that he was not about to be intimidated by a handful of Jews, or by a prisoner who pretended to wield such great power. But Urka was not finished. Day after day, at night or in broad daylight, Bolshevik patrols were spirited from the streets of Moldavanka into dingy shops and stores, into the cellars of buildings, into the darkest recesses of the Old Marketplace. Each time the Reds came perilously close to execution, only to be reprieved after one of their abductors mentioned the name Mishka Yaponchik. Again, the soldiers were stripped of their clothing, disarmed, and forced to walk naked through Moldavanka, shamed by jeers and catcalls. But not one person raised a hand to harm them. Upon hearing of the continuing abuses and learning that the Red soldiers were refusing to enter the ghetto, the Commissar of Odessa was enraged. He ordered his officers to establish absolute occupation of Moldavanka, to shoot and arrest as many Jews as necessary, to show the *zhidi* who ruled them and who did not. The officers declined.

"If this man has so much control over the Jews, perhaps we can use him," a major argued reasonably.

"How can we possibly have any use for a Jew?" the Commissar asked, finding the idea ludicrous.

"By making him think we are his allies. By making him think we need him. So through him we will be able to control all the Jews."

"Why should we care if a degenerate Jew likes us or not?" the Commissar asked, a reptilian hiss to his question. "Our soldiers can control the Jews."

"Two hundred thousand of them? And if Denikin should advance as far as Odessa, do you want him to have two hundred thousand sympathizers?" a colonel asked.

"Armed sympathizers!" the major added for emphasis.

The Commissar looked at the officers and nodded his head. "All right. For now, release this Mishka Yaponchik, but the time will come when we no longer need him. And then we will not even bother to arrest him!"

The major and the colonel wholeheartedly agreed, and at the beginning of the fourth week of their incarceration

Mishka, Grisha, and the fifty other men who had been detained in the cattle cars at the rail depot were released. And as they returned to Moldavanka and then to the Zala, where they received a welcome fit for heroes, the name Mishka Yaponchik was placed near the top of the enemy list of Odessa's Bolshevik regime.

CHAPTER 47

The house was shabby. The white paint that had once gleamed in the sunlight was gray and cracked. The wooden fence which had enclosed a small flower garden was broken, most of the slats split or missing, and where asters and poppies used to grow nothing remained but earth covered with refuse and the droppings of stray dogs. The large window overlooking the street was nearly opaque with a thin layer of grime, and it was easy to see where someone had made an attempt to rub it clean, then stopped. Yet the house was in no worse condition than the others on the street. Even the stone apartment building on the corner was in need of repair. Its limestone walls were pitted, large chunks having been gouged out by winters of ice, and bigger chunks by bullets that could have been fired by any number of men during its fifty years of existence. Many of the windows were broken while others had been stuffed with newspaper and rags. Across the street from the building what had been a thriving fruit market was now empty, its windows boarded up, the door padlocked. Nearby, four Bolshevik soldiers leaned against a pushcart joking among themselves, disinterested in everything around them. The whining of an engine made them turn and look, and when they saw a truck with a red star emblazoned on its door, and driven by an army major, they stood at attention and saluted. The truck squealed around the corner and into Kherson Street. The soldier sitting next to the driver pointed to number nineteen. A grinding downshift and a heavy application of the brakes brought the truck to a sliding stop. The officer said something to his aide. Receiving an affirmative reply, he climbed down to the ground, walking briskly to the door, banged his gloved fist against the flimsy wooden partition and shouted.

"Open up, before the door is broken down!"

Nothing happened. The tall, broad-shouldered officer kicked the door. He lowered his shoulder, readying himself to break it down.

"I'm opening it. I'm opening it," a weary female voice said.

"Hurry up!"

The door was unlatched. The officer flung it open, almost knocking the woman who faced him off her feet. She quickly studied the soldier. His uniform—a black leather jacket with a red armband attached to one sleeve, jodhpurs stuffed into a pair of well-polished boots—and the rifle slung over his shoulder frightened her. She scanned his face, trying to decide how to act before him. The Bolshevik revealed nothing, looking at her vacantly.

"What do you want?" The woman's fingers clasped the open bathrobe she was wearing to hide her nightgowned body from sight.

The officer ignored the question and pushed his way past her into the house. She turned to see what he was going to do. The soldier circled the small front room, running his fingers over the worn furniture.

"So this is where you used to live," he said gruffly, the arrogance of his tone adding to his authority.

"Yes," came the reply from the other soldier, similarly dressed and also with a weapon hanging by a strap from the shoulder.

The woman swiveled her head to see the second intruder. "Daniella!"

The female soldier stared at the woman, her dark eyes coldly surveying Soybel Viska as if she were inspecting an enemy for a weapon.

"Daniella, what are you doing here?" Soybel took a step forward, letting her robe fall open as she extended her hands to her daughter.

"What are *you* doing here?" the girl asked, shocked at seeing her mother.

"You have grown. You are a woman," Soybel said, taking another step toward Daniella. "I am so glad you have come."

"Is anyone else here?" the major asked, looking into the kitchen, then moving toward the narrow hallway which led to the three small bedrooms. Holding his rifle in front of him, he carefully stepped from doorway to doorway.

"Daniella, I need you. You must help me!"

The tall girl looked at her mother quizzically. She glanced at Soybel's hands, which were still outstretched. "*You* need me?" Daniella asked, her tone bitter.

Soybel nodded vigorously.

"Momma needs her Daniella?"

Soybel started to cry. "Yes!" She ran to hug her daughter.

Daniella pushed her away.

"What are you doing?" Soybel asked, stunned by the reaction.

Daniella turned her back on her mother and walked across the room. Soybel started to follow when the officer returned with Munya.

"Look what I found!"

"Munya!" Soybel exclaimed, rushing to protect her son from the soldier.

With lazy insolence Daniella survey her brother. "Do you still treat him like a girl?" she asked bitingly. "Where is your father, little brother?"

"Dead. Killed," replied Soybel.

"Not by the Germans, I hope." Daniella's eyes met her mother's. A soft chuckle escaped from her throat as she correctly interpreted the answer she saw in Soybel's expression.

"Good," she said softly. "I am glad it wasn't the Germans who killed him."

"He was not the kind of man you think."

"I do not care." Daniella underscored her words with a disdainful smile. "Where is Grisha?"

"Grisha is with his wife and son."

"My brother has a child? What is his name?"

"Isaac."

"Matushenko, did you hear that?" Daniella said to the officer. "*Another* Isaac. We will have to change him, too!"

"How about this one?" Matushenko inquired, indicating Munya.

"All I know about him is that he is a bastard."

"Still, he will make a fine Bolshevik someday."

Soybel put her arm around Munya, as if Matushenko's words were something she could deflect with her body.

"Tell me, mother," Daniella asked, "why does the widow of the capitalist Viska live in such pitiable surroundings? Have you donated your wealth to our cause?"

"I do not have my money, Daniella. No one will give it to me."

Matushenko laughed. "And your land, do you have that?"

Soybel moved closer to Daniella, her words came rapidly, each one touched with the hope that her daughter could do something to help her. "After Vassili died, the war made it impossible to claim his inheritance. Then the Bolsheviks came, and they told me there were no more inheritances. When the Germans arrived I went to Kiev, to the administrative headquarters there. But they dismissed me, saying they had no interest in Russian inheritances. Now, with the Bolsheviks in control again, I have no idea what to do. But with you here, you could tell me who to see, who to talk to. Perhaps you could even—"

"If I could, I would burn every ruble of yours before I gave you a single one," Daniella said, the strain showing on her face.

"But we need that money. It is so hard for us to live these days."

"There are millions of Russians who have *nothing* because of what the Germans did, because of monarchists like you and your Vassili! Be grateful that you have food and a place to live."

"But it is *my* money!"

"Nothing is yours anymore," shouted Daniella. "It is everyone's!"

Soybel reeled back. "You will not help me?"

Matushenko loomed over her. "Help you? We would rather—"

"Matushenko!" warned Daniella.

Soybel moved away from the officer and toward her daughter. "Tell him he has no right to speak to me like that, Daniella."

"Oh, but he does. I just do not want him to take the pleasure away from me."

Daniella glanced at Matushenko. He nodded his head and walked to the door.

"I'll wait outside. I don't like it in here."

"I will be out in a minute."

"There is no hurry." With that, Matushenko left the house.

"Thank you, Daniella. He frightened me."

Daniella watched the Bolshevik officer through the window. He lounged against the front fender of the truck and lit a cigarette.

"Is he your husband?"

"No. Just my lover."

"He is very handsome."

"Yes. Much handsomer than any of the others I have been with. And much more important."

"You have done well for yourself." Soybel released her grip on Munya. She buttoned her robe and straightened her hair.

"Your way works well, Momma."

Soybel looked at Daniella, wanting to ask her what she meant, but she hesitated and her daughter changed the subject.

"Do you have a job?"

"What?" Soybel asked, surprised by the question.

"Do you work?" Daniella's voice was firm.

"No."

"That is not the way it is going to be anymore. From now on those who can work and don't, will not eat."

"Is that why you came here? To tell me that?"

"I had no idea you were here."

"Then why did you come?"

"To see Eleazar. To inform him that his house is to be requisitioned."

"You are taking the house away?"

"Yes. For our soldiers. There is little room for them to live in Odessa, and they deserve a house like this."

"Where will I live? I need a place to live, too."

"You can stay here. Someone will be needed to keep the quarters clean and cook the soldiers' meals."

"I will not do it. I am not a servant."

"You will learn."

"I refuse to—"

"Matushenko will arrange it. Today! From here we will go directly to the Commissar, and Matushenko will inform him that there is a house in Moldavanka that would make a billet. And when he tells him that there is a woman who is willing to look after things, the Commissar will be ecstatic!" Daniella faced Soybel, smiling too sweetly at her.

"I refuse to do it!"

"You refuse? Who are you to refuse anything? You should be thankful that we are permitting you to stay here!"

"If, if I do this will you help me get my inheritance?"

"There are no more inheritances!"

"But you are a Bolshevik. You could find my money and—"

"Even if I could, I would not do it."

"I would give you part of it."

Daniella's expression hardened. "I was in Petrograd when the old government was overthrown. I was one of those who stormed the Winter Palace."

"I will give you half—even more!"

"Matushenko was one of the first to be shot in Petrograd."

"Don't you hear what I am offering you?"

"Since then he and I have been in Moscow, Kiev—"

"At least help me get out of Russia, help your brother—"

"I cannot remember all the places we have been to. Everywhere there was a battle."

"Please, Daniella!"

"Matushenko still has a bullet lodged in his leg. Shrapnel in his back. Friends of ours, comrades, have died in our arms. We could not bury them because we did not have time. We could not stop to dig a single grave because we were constantly being pursued. We have walked hundreds of miles through rain, freezing temperatures, blizzards, sometimes without food and water. Do you think we went through all that just so you could get your money? Do you really think I would give you your money? Fuck your money!"

"Is that what I taught you? To—"

Grabbing her own crotch, Daniella looked directly into her mother's eyes and said viciously: "What you taught me is that this little place here between our legs can get us anything we want. Isn't that right? My father would have agreed, wouldn't he? And Vassili, too? Matushenko does. Everyone does!"

"You cannot talk to me like that!"

Daniella pushed her mother across the room, forcing her to the glass-doored cabinet, shoving Soybel's face against it so she could see her own reflection.

"Look at yourself!" Daniella demanded.

"You have a reflection, too!"

"Yes, I have a reflection, and I hate it! Because when I look at myself, I see you!"

Soybel broke loose from her daughter's grasp. "Whatever you are, you did to yourself."

"Is that what you said about Poppa when he died? That it was his fault you fucked Vassili? Did Poppa strip you naked and spread your legs and push Vassili on top of you?"

"What happened between your father and me, between Vassili and me, is none of your business!"

"Is what happened between you and me my business?"

Soybel slinked backwards toward the hallway, keeping Munya hidden behind her.

"Was that my fault?" Daniella asked, pursuing her mother. "Was it my fault that you were too busy with Vassili and *his* son to remember that you had other children? Well, my dear mother, what happens to you *will* be my fault. I am a Bolshevik, and I intend to destroy everything that is left of your way of life. The only wealth you will have will be the wealth you remember. The only palace you will live in will be the palace you remember. Unless you work here for the soldiers, you will not live here. And unless you work somewhere, you will not live at all. And I do not give a damn!" Daniella looked at her mother with hatred.

"I have no need of a thing from you!" Soybel snarled.

"Then you are very lucky, Momma. Because that is exactly what you will get from me, nothing!"

Not wanting to spend another second with her mother, Daniella left the house, slamming the door so violently it shook the building. Soybel watched through the window as her daughter climbed into the truck, next to Matushenko. The vehicle sped off. Soybel remained at the window, staring outside, letting her anger subside. Fear overcame her, and panic. Soybel's legs started to shake and she sat down in a chair, her mind atumble with jumbled thoughts. Frantically she tried to decide what she would do when the soldiers arrived to take away her home. She had no answers. For the rest of the day, Soybel did not stir from the chair. She took no note of the disappearing sun and the arrival of nightfall. From somewhere in the city, a churchbell tolled midnight. Still sitting in the chair, Soybel fell asleep. When she awoke the next morning, her neck and back aching, Soybel resumed her vigil, every second expecting to see Bolshevik soldiers marching toward the house, terrified at having no idea as to what she would do when they knocked on the door.

CHAPTER 48

In July, with the southern weather unbearably hot, a train sped toward Odessa from Kiev. It stopped at every village and hamlet along the way, and while still a hundred miles from the seaport city, the long line of railroad cars was already overflowing with half-starved, half-alive refugees who hoped to find sanctuary along the Black Sea from the increasing dangers of the revolution. When the train was seventy-five miles north of Odessa, speeding along tracks which divided an endless wheatfield in two, the engineer was startled by heavy timbers blocking the rails ahead. Shoving the brake handle all the way forward, he brought the train to a screeching halt. Immediately, the tall wheat plants on either side of the tracks rustled and parted as several hundred horsemen emerged from hiding. Needing no orders from their leader, the men broke ranks and galloped along the length of the train. Stationing themselves from one end to the other, they awaited their commander. As if he were conducting a parade-ground review, his blue uniform rumpled, sweat-stained, his yellow sash soiled, his head bare, his hair long and greasy-looking, with a week of stubble growing on his face, armed with pistols, a rifle, and a sword strapped to his side, Semyon Petlura slowly rode alongside the train, his nervous bloodshot eyes glancing into each car through the windows. When he reached the end, Petlura turned his horse and cantered back, stopping at the first car behind the engine. He slid out of his saddle, unsheathed his sword, and climbed the steps into the train.

The railroad car was crowded with gaunt, half-clothed people. Those who were lucky enough to have found places to sit on the wooden benches clutched ragged bundles containing their meager possessions. Some held children too weak from hunger to stand or sit by themselves. The aisle dividing the rows of seats was jammed with those who had no choice but to stand. And the stench of urine and fecal matter permeated the long compartment. The intruder ambled through the car, aimlessly moving his sword like a schoolmaster contemplating where to place his pointer; the people in the aisle squeezed themselves between the seats, receiving no complaints as they fell on the seated. Backed against the wall at the far end of the car was a swarthy young man of about thirty with a short beard and large, brown, fearful eyes. He watched with horror, following the sword which steadily came nearer to him. When its point pricked his chest he wanted to slip along the wall and fall to the floor, but his muscles were unable to function.

"I want to hear a word from you that has an 'R' in it," Petlura softly demanded.

The man opened his mouth to ask why; the only sound he uttered was a rasping noise as his vocal cords constricted. The tip of the sword dug into the man's flesh and a searing pain tore through his body.

"I want to hear you say something with an 'R' in it!"

"Why?" the man managed to mumble, his eyes riveted on the blade.

The sword jabbed him again, and a trickle of blood seeped through his shirt.

"Because Jews are not able to pronounce words with 'R's' like Russians do!" Saliva sprayed from Petlura's mouth, collecting on the victim's cheek. "One word, or I will kill you anyway!"

"Radooga."

"Another!"

"Razborchivay."

"Another!"

Carefully pronouncing his "R," the man said, *"Rastyr-yatsya."*

The word sounded strange, the "R's" having a Yiddish lilt to them rather than the rolling Russian pronunciation.

"Rademay," the man continued on his own. *"Razmaznya."*

Petlura shook his head.

"Razmolvka! Razmolvka!"

Wildly shouting: "This is a mistake, a misunderstanding!" the man sank to his knees, tacitly begging for his life to be spared. *"Razmolvka,"* he whimpered, watching the sword that was aimed at his right eye, staring at the point relentlessly moving toward his pupil. *"Razmolvka."* The blade pierced the man's cornea. He screamed. The weapon was thrust deeply into his skull. The Jew shrieked, and shrieked, his nerve endings blazing with heat, his limbs flailing every which way. He vomited bile. His sphincter muscles collapsed. And he lived long enough to feel the sword being twisted, wrenched loose, freed. Before the blade was withdrawn the man was dead, his head hanging limply against his chest, his mouth agape, his face covered with blood. Petlura wiped the red stains from the saber onto his trousers. He sheathed his weapon and strode back down the aisle to the doorway of the car. Tersely, he ordered everyone to disembark, grabbed hold of the handrail, and swung himself down to the ground.

Without resistance Petlura was obeyed. From one end of the train to the other, the passengers were forced into a line along the edge of the wheatfield. One by one they were made to take the same test the dead man had failed. One hundred and seven of the five hundred refugees were unable to pass it. Fifty-three of them were men, fourteen young boys ranging in age from four to sixteen, and the rest women. There were three infants. One was a girl. Quickly, efficiently, Petlura's horsemen separated the males from the females, herding the men and boys into a cluster. Methodically, displaying no emotion, the Haidamacks shot the bearers of the seed of Abraham, slit open their temples, and then castrated them, the two male babies included. When the task had been completed, Petlura gave the order for his men to mount their horses and follow him. Within moments the attackers had disappeared among the tall wheat plants, the sound of their leaving rapidly fading, replaced by the weeping of mourners and the soft rustling of stalks of grain as a gentle summer breeze caressed the steppes.

Nearly an hour passed before the bodies of the dead were loaded into one of the railroad cars and the tracks had been cleared of the wooden obstruction. Then, with an enormous amount of steam building in the boiler, the train lunged forward, rapidly picking up speed. The engineer opened the throttle all the way, hurtling the train past villages and towns, having no intention of stopping for the hundreds of other refugees who had waited a week for the train to arrive and spirit them south. He yanked the whistle cord, warning everything ahead with its incessant howl to stay clear of the tracks. Faster raced the train, the corpses glued in position by their own drying blood.

Within half an hour of the train's arrival in Odessa, the news of the slaughter sped through the city, the name Petlura whispered by Jew and non-Jew alike. For months the people of Odessa had been hearing sporadic rumors of the vicious war the Ukrainian was waging against the Jews and Bolsheviks in the north. To most, the threat he created meant little, the miles between Kiev and the southern city giving them a sense of security. But now the news of his return to the south sparked fear. Even the Bolsheviks were afraid, remembering how often Petlura and his Haidamacks had ambushed Red military units, treating them no better than the Jews. And with General Denikin's slow but uninterrupted advance toward Odessa from the east, Petlura's appearance in the south made the situation acute.

When word of the massacre reached Mishka Yaponchik the unbridled fury that contorted his face and body petrified even those who knew him well.

"I will give my life to kill the worst fucking man the worst fucking country in the world ever produced! I will find him and crush his balls into nothing! I will tear out his heart with my bare hands, and I will butcher him inch by inch so he will die for weeks!"

Mishka smashed chairs and hurled bottles of vodka, turning the café into a shambles. His rage carried him into the street. People ran to hide, Mishka's insane fury making him a threat to everyone. A pathetic group of women entered Petrovskaya Street, trudging toward the Zala, searching for someone named Mishka Yaponchik. Seeing the fuming giant, their ears ringing with his hatred, they were certain they had found him. When they approached Mishka and told him their story, his manner became even more violent than before.

"What do you mean the Bolsheviks refuse to let you bury your dead in the Jewish cemetery? Who dares to stop you?"

"The officer at the gate and his soldiers."

"WE WILL SEE IF HE STOPS MISHKA YAPONCHIK!"

With cold precision, Mishka prepared for the burial of the Jews in the cemetery at the edge of Moldavanka, the Jerusalem Cemetery. He sent Grisha to find Urka, Karmanchik, Skakun, and as many other men as possible. Very gently he asked Rabbi Eleazar if he would say *Kaddish* for the dead.

"Please, Eleazar, I want *you* to say the prayer for them."

"Whoever knows the measure of our Creator is certain to share in the world to come."

"Rabbi, hear me, please hear me."

"The height of the Lord is thirty million parasangs. And each parasang of the Creator is three miles, and each mile has ten thousand yards, and each yard is three of His spans, and a span fills the whole world."

"Eleazar, this is Mishka. A tragedy has occurred and you are needed."

"In this world there are nothing but tragedies."

"Will you say *Kaddish* for those who have perished—"

"Every morning and every night I say *Kaddish,* for my father, for my mother. And for every other Jew who is dead. And for all the Jews who are alive, too."

Mishka studied Eleazar's emaciated face, not knowing how the rabbi survived when he did nothing but spend his days locked in his room, praying to God, chanting without letup in unintelligible tongues. "Will you come to the cemetery with me, Rabbi?"

Very slowly, Eleazar nodded his head, and in a voice quieter than the sound of his breathing said, "The cemetery is the only place where I can still be a rabbi, so how could I refuse?"

The next afternoon, supported by Mishka and Grisha, Rabbi Joshua Eleazar made his way to the door of the café. His legs seemed incapable of holding him upright without help. His body shook from age, and from the deep emotions he felt. Mishka lifted Eleazar into a wagon and placed him on a thick blanket. After making certain that the rabbi was comfortable, Mishka nodded to Grisha and the two of them strode to the head of the long cortege. Behind them, stretching the length of several streets, were more than two hundred armed horsemen. To their rear were twenty-three carts carrying the dead. Next to the carts stood the wives, daughters, the mothers of the dead. Trailing behind them were hundreds and hundreds of Moldavankans who had gathered to pay their last respects to strangers with whom they had a kinship as close as any family tie. At the head of the procession sat Urka astride a brown mare, holding the reins of Mishka's black stallion and Grisha's roan charger. Both men mounted their steeds, Grisha backing his horse behind Mishka's, his customary place.

"I want you up here!" Mishka said.

Grisha did not move.

"Urka on one side. You on the other. That is the way I want it!"

Grisha followed Mishka's orders. Immediately, Mishka kicked his horse, and one by one, like the legs of a millipede, the rest of the procession followed.

Thousands of people lined the ghetto streets to watch the cortege pass. Bolshevik soldiers stood aside, letting the mourners proceed without incident. The long line snaked its way to the cemetery that cradled the bodies of Odessa's dead Jews. At the gates of the cemetery, a Bolshevik officer, backed by three dozen soldiers with their rifles ready to fire, ordered the funeral march to halt.

"What do you want?" the officer demanded.

"We have come to bury the dead!" Mishka answered, reigning in his horse less than a yard from the Bolshevik.

"No more people are to be buried in this cemetery."

"Who told you that?"

"The Commissar."

"Tell the Commissar to go fuck himself!"

"I have my orders. If you enter the cemetery, I must shoot!"

"What is your name?"

"Furmanov. Sergeant Yadin Furmanov!"

A thought crossed Mishka's mind and he raised his eyebrows in curiosity. "Furmanov, *ferstaste Yiddish*?"

The momentary glitter in the man's eye revealed that he understood more than just the Russian he spoke.

"We have come to bury Jews, Furmanov!" Mishka said, continuing to speak in Yiddish. "And I will put a bullet in your brain if you try and stop us."

"Why are you bothering with dead Jews? Bolsheviks do not care about them even when they are alive!" the sergeant retorted.

"Then they will not mind when you are dead, too, will they, *Furmanov*?"

The soldier licked his lips, looked at his soldiers, then at the scores of men who waited behind Mishka. "You will pay for this," he said, stepping back, afraid to instigate a confrontation he would certainly lose.

Mishka signaled for Urka and Grisha to lead the procession into the cemetery, and as the carts and horses passed through the gates the Bolshevik seethed. Ignoring Furmanov, Mishka waited until the mourners were safely inside the cemetery, then he entered. Hours later, when Eleazar's prayers of mourning and his personal lament had been concluded, the shrouded corpses lowered into the ground, and every man had tossed one shovelful of dirt into each of the graves, the living started the sorrowful return to the ghetto. Watching the grieving Jews was Sergeant Furmanov, ridiculing the weeping men and women who shuffled past him. Mishka avoided looking at the Bolshevik, following the marchers until the last one had entered the outskirts of Moldavanka. Certain they would be safe in their own enclave, Mishka pulled his horse to a halt and called to Urka. The two men spoke, and when they had finished, Mishka proceeded to the heart of the ghetto while Urka rode in another direction. That night, as the tragedy was being discussed at the Zala, and plans were proposed as to how to avenge the dead, Urka was conspicuously absent. He appeared well toward dawn. Tapping Mishka on the shoulder, Urka nodded his head imperceptibly. Mishka's eyes flitted across Urka's face, and then he returned to listening to something Karmanchik was saying. The next morning the body of Sergeant Yadin Furmanov was discovered dead in an alleyway, a single bullet through the heart. And though the Bolsheviks were certain that Mishka Yaponchik had either arranged for the murder, or had done it himself, they had to let him remain free, having no evidence on which to base a warrant for his arrest.

CHAPTER 49

Grisha and Sara Moisei had been lying awake in their bed since dawn. The warm August morning, coupled with a sea breeze, filled their room with the delicate scent of raspberries. This year, as every year, Mishka Yaponchik had tended the garden behind the Malinas Zala, nurturing the berries until they were ripe, and each morning Grisha and Sara awoke to the voluptuous perfume they relished during the summer and hungered for each winter.

"I am glad we did not disturb Isaac," Sara whispered, taking her husband's hand and holding it against her thighs.

"Do you think he would know what we were doing?"

Sara laughed, the throaty sound making Grisha wish he were ready to make love to her again.

"He probably knows more than his poppa does."

"Is his momma complaining?" Grisha propped himself up on one elbow and peeked into the infant's crib to make sure he was still sleeping.

Sara inspected her husband's naked body. She touched his lips, then his nose and eyes, etching his face in her fingers. "Mommas never complain," she said, hugging him tightly.

"I suppose I should go and see if Eleazar needs anything," said Grisha, as Isaac stirred. "Every morning I expect to walk into his room and find that he has died during the night."

"He looks so old. So frail. And it is so painful for him to walk."

"Everyone gets old."

"Even my poppa looks old these days. The whole city looks old." Sara closed her eyes and lay deeper into her pillow. "Do you think the revolution will ever be over?"

"I do not know. It seems as if Denikin has been advancing toward Odessa for as long as I can remember." Grisha sat up so he could see Isaac rub his eyes with his tiny hands and yawn himself awake.

"Do you want Denikin to win, or the Bolsheviks?" Sara studied Grisha's profile, recalling how childlike his handsomeness had been when she first met him. Now his face looked aged, its vibrancy diminished, every muscle always taut.

Isaac began to cry.

"Bring him to me, Grisha, so I can feed him." Sara tucked both of their pillows behind her and sat up, leaning against the wall.

"If only we could do something," Grisha said, getting up to bring the infant to Sara. "If we could catch Petlura. If we could stop him before he reaches Odessa; if, if, if, that is all anything is these days, if!"

Sara took Isaac from Grisha, nestling the infant against her breast, helping him put her nipple in his mouth. Grisha stroked the baby's cheek and Sara's breast simultaneously.

"If the Bolsheviks would permit it, Mishka would lead an army against Petlura. He has already offered, but they refused." Grisha kissed the tip of Sara's nose.

"Why doesn't he go without their blessing?"

"Because we need their help. We need better weapons, and more men who can really fight than we can get ourselves."

Sara looked at her husband sadly. "You would go with him, wouldn't you?"

"Of course."

She pulled Grisha's head against her other breast, pushing it against his cheek, her dark nipple becoming hard. "You know, until just now, I never really thought about that."

"Does it frighten you?"

"Yes."

"Would you prefer it if I had said no?"

Sara paused to listen to Isaac's contented sucking sounds. "Grisha, if not for Mishka, would you still want to go?"

Before Grisha could answer, the bedroom door was banged open and in charged Mishka, his face livid, dragging a terrified-looking youth behind him. "You see this scum, *malcheshka,* he claims to be one of Denikin's soldiers. Sent to Odessa to spy, because Denikin expects to be here by the end of the month." Holding the young man by the back of his neck, Mishka shoved him into the room for Grisha's inspection. "When did you ever see a soldier dressed like this?"

Unconcerned about his nakedness, Grisha sat up and scrutinized the young man. He, too, was curious about the youth's dark trousers, white shirt, and black jacket.

"If I had worn my uniform, the Bolsheviks would have shot me before I got here," the soldier explained, the pressure exerted by Mishka on his neck making it difficult for him to speak.

"And do you know what else he said?" Mishka bellowed. "That he knows of a plot involving Moldavanka and the Black Hundreds!" Mishka spun the young man around, grabbed him by the throat, and held him less than an inch from his face. "If this plan of the Hundreds is so secret, why would they tell you?" Before the youth could reply, Mishka threw him out of the room and into the hallway. *"Malcheshka,* I want you in the café, now, so we can interrogate this *supposed* soldier without interruption."

Immediately, Grisha jumped out of bed, pulled on a pair of pants, boots, put on a shirt, and chased after Mishka. Together, with the young Monarchist forced to sit squeezed between them, Mishka and Grisha drew out everything he knew. While Mishka threatened the soldier for information,

Grisha sweet-talked him, pretending to protect him from Mishka's wrath, plying him with drinks. In less than an hour, Mishka and Grisha knew everything the soldier was privy to.

First, because the Black Hundreds had only a handful of men in the south, they had recruited the young White and dozens like him from Kiev southward, intending to turn them into recruiters who would then enlist others to further add to the ranks of the Hundreds, and so on. The reason for this plan to quickly multiply membership in the Black Hundreds was simple. In less than a month, General Denikin had predicted he would enter Odessa. And because of the rate at which he and his monarchist army were slaughtering Bolsheviks and advancing westward, his claim was taken seriously. The Hundreds determined that when Denikin launched his attack on Odessa they would have the perfect environment for carrying out their war against the Jews. To further insure their success, the Hundreds had used General Denikin's hatred for Jews and Bolsheviks to convince him to ally himself with Semyon Petlura, who let it be known that he could supply the Monarchists with more than 100,000 men, armored cars, and seven airplanes for their assault on Odessa. Boldly, the plan to squeeze Odessa between vast armies, thereby splitting the Bolshevik forces into two fronts, was progressing. And now, the leaders of the Black Hundreds had arrived in Odessa, more fearful of their plan going awry than of being uncovered by the Bolsheviks.

"Tell me, Monarchist, do you also know where these brave Russian patriots are hiding?" Mishka asked, his voice low, threatening.

"Yes. Do you know the small church called St. Mark's?" The Russian twirled an empty glass of vodka on the table. His eyes were bloodshot.

"If it is the one on the road that goes past the almshouse, about five miles beyond that—"

"That is the church."

"Then I know it very well. There is a story that each of

the four corners of the foundation rests on the crushed head of a male Jewish baby. It is the right place for their meeting."

"There is to be a special meeting there five days from now. On Saturday. At midnight."

"The Sabbath is a fitting day to plan the death of Jews," Mishka noted.

"How many leaders are there?" asked Grisha.

"Five. Two soldiers. One is a captain, the other a lieutenant. The captain commanded one of Kornilov's divisions during the war. The other three are aristocrats, Tsarists who have lost everything." The Russian's eyelids drooped, the great amount of vodka he had been convinced to drink having its effect.

"Will Petlura be there?" Mishka inquired, his voice soft and steady.

The Russian looked at Mishka, unable to keep his eyes focused on him. "I do not know."

"How come you know everything—except that?!" The unexpected loudness of Mishka's voice startled even Grisha.

"Because I am a soldier. And I only know what I hear in the army. Not what happens among a gang of Ukrainian peasants!" the Monarchist yelled back.

In a conciliatory tone Grisha asked, "How come you know so much about what happens in the army? Do generals talk to ordinary soldiers these days?" Grisha picked up the military identification papers the soldier had given him and held them before the soldier's face.

"There are very few secrets in the army. Especially when it comes to how the officers feel about the Jews."

"If all that you have said is true, and you are found out, they will kill you. So why are you risking your life?" Grisha's tone was friendly.

"For money! That is how he first approached me!" shouted Mishka. "But when you asked some poor ghetto Jew who you should talk to, so you could inform him of more monarchist treachery, you had no idea you would be sent to see Mishka Yaponchik. Do you think I am an ass?"

Mishka grabbed the young Russian by the lapels of his jacket, lifted him out of his chair, and hurled him to the floor.

"I no longer want your money," the soldier said, picking himself up off the floor. He sat down in his chair, filled his glass with vodka, drained it, refilled it, and drank that one, too. "In every town, as soon as we had control, the officers would enter the ghetto and murder Jews." The young man paused, rolling his tongue around his mouth as he tried to keep from slurring his words. "At first, I did not care. They were just Jews. But the last time I became sick. For two days afterwards, I was sick. They made me shoot a child." The soldier rested his head on the table. A single sob escaped his lips. "The meeting on Saturday is very important to the Black Hundreds. They are expecting word from General Denikin to see if he will offer direct help. I can assure you of this; I was the one who delivered their request to the general." Slowly, the Russian pushed himself upright. He reached for the bottle of vodka and knocked it over. Crestfallen, he watched the liquid run out of the bottle, off the table, and into a puddle on the floor. The Monarchist looked at Mishka. "Now, I am a deserter from the army."

Mishka scrutinized the young man's eyes, and when they remained unwavering he dropped his own gaze, reached into his shirt pocket, pulling out a stubby pencil whose point had been sharpened with a knife. He drew a fan of dark black lines on the table. Wrinkling his brow like a displeased artist, Mishka carefully darkened each line, then, with the side of the writing tip, he lightly shaded the spaces between the lines. Engrossed with perfecting his design, Mishka ignored the soldier and Grisha, unaware that they were watching him. When he was satisfied with his effort, Mishka looked up at the Russian, then down again at the table. He took the pencil, and in wide, boldly stroked letters wrote several words: "Black Hundreds. Meeting: Saturday, August 10, St. Mark's rectory. One captain. One lieutenant. Three aristocrats. Purpose: new recruits. Purpose: to kill Jews." Mishka picked up the military documents and scanned them. He began to write again. "Information given by: Dmitri Luchka, Corporal. Age 22." Mishka raised his eyes, resting them on the soldier's face. The Russian squirmed. "I want you to sign your name under what I have just written," Mishka said sternly.

The soldier looked at him blankly. "Why?"

"Just sign it."

The Monarchist leaned over the table, took the pencil Mishka handed him, and in perfect penmanship signed his name below the facts Mishka had listed. He returned the pencil and sat back in his chair. Mishka read and reread each square-lettered word written on the table. His brow furrowed and unfurrowed. He twisted the pencil in his mustache. He wet the index and middle fingers of his right hand with his tongue and erased the shaded design he had drawn so carefully.

"Twenty-two-year-old Dmitri Luchka, thank you for your information. You are now free to go."

The young man looked at Mishka curiously. "Why did you make me sign my name there?" he asked hesitantly, standing up and moving toward the door.

"All informers must sign affidavits," replied Mishka matter-of-factly.

"But anyone could rub it out. Like you did your pattern."

"Dmitri Luchka, this table is my table. And as long as I am alive, your affidavit will be here."

"But why did you want it?" the Russian asked, certain he was trying Mishka's patience.

Mishka permitted a smile to graze his lips. "So everyone will know that what we do is legal."

"And what will you do?" Fumbling with the latch, the soldier opened the door.

"By the weekend, all of Odessa will know. And so will you."

The Russian wanted to ask another question, but he remained still, feeling Mishka's danger from across the room.

"Don't you want to know why I am not going to kill you for having murdered a Jew?"

Dmitri Luchka shivered, realizing that Mishka had considered it.

"I will tell you. Even Mishka Yaponchik has a heart. Even he knows when a man has repented. Now go! BEFORE I CHANGE MY MIND!"

The monarchist soldier turned and ran from the café, praying that his vodka-wobbly legs would not give out from under him. The sound of his running footsteps could be heard for more than half a minute. When they disappeared, Mishka looked at Grisha.

"Do you want to really know why I did not kill him? Because when we are through with the Hundreds, who else will be able to confirm that it was Mishka Yaponchik who punished them?"

Mishka wet his fingers and deliberately rubbed out the words he had written and that Dmitri Luchka's signature had corroborated.

"There is your affidavit, Dmitri Luchka!" Mishka exclaimed, every trace of the writing gone. "Mishka wants everyone to know who dealt out justice to the Hundreds. But Mishka does not want them to have proof!"

Mishka began to laugh, the intensity of the sound increasing until it filled every inch of the café. Standing up, Mishka stretched out his arms then struck himself in the chest with his fists. The more he laughed, the harder Mishka hit himself. Five minutes later the café was quiet except for the words of a sober conversation. And for the rest of the day and well into the night Mishka Yaponchik devised a plan to try and save Moldavanka from the Black Hundreds.

CHAPTER 50

It was nearly Saturday midnight when a monarchist colonel and two lieutenants, all dressed in full uniform with large capes drawn around them to hide their apparel from observation, rode into the courtyard of the Church of St. Mark's. The main building of the church was dark, but lights stole out of the rectory behind it. Without interrupting their horses' easy gaits, the horsemen rode directly to the side of the church, ignoring its ancient cemetery, and aiming for the entryway that led to the room where priests counselled weary saints and sinners.

"Halt, or I will shoot!"

The three soldiers reined in their horses.

"What do you want here?" A rifle pointed straight at the heart of the monarchist colonel.

"I have a letter here from General Denikin," said the colonel, a trace of arrogance to his voice.

"What letter?"

"It is in my pocket," the officer replied, his tone implying that the questioner was ignorant.

"Dismount!"

The colonel climbed down from his horse. Before his feet touched the ground a bayonet was pressed against his chest. "I am impressed by your precautions," he remarked.

"Show me the letter."

Reaching beneath his cape, the soldier withdrew it and showed it to the sentry.

"I want to look at it." Holding his rifle with one hand, the guard reached out for the envelope.

"My orders are to deliver it directly," said the colonel.

"And now your orders are to give it to me."

From within the shadows of the cemetery, the click of a bullet being snapped into the chamber of a rifle indicated the presence of a second sentry. The monarchist officer handed the envelope to the man before him. The guard tried to inspect it in the patch of light that came from the rectory window. Muttering, he moved closer to the window. In the momentary stillness, a gush of low voices tumbled outside through the thin pane of glass in an unintelligible blur.

"The seal looks genuine enough," the man said, more to himself than anyone else. "And the paper feels good. Wait here!"

Leaving the three monarchist soldiers under the watchful eye of the still unseen second sentinel, the first slipped into the building. Several minutes passed before the rectory door was opened again. From within emerged a tall sandy-haired man. Briskly he strode up to the officer.

"Welcome to Odessa, Colonel Kovalenk. I am Captain Yurino."

The colonel threw back his cape and briskly saluted. "I hope we have not kept you waiting."

Captain Yurino smiled. He liked the military posture and precise salute of this formidable-looking officer. "You are exactly on time, Colonel. And let me add that you are quite brave to wear your uniform in the middle of enemy territory."

"The enemy is in the middle of *our* territory, Captain."

The look on Captain Yurino's face showed how much he agreed with Colonel Kovalenk's reply. "Shall we go inside?" the captain said. "Your aides can remain here with my guards—their professionalism would add immeasurably to our security."

"My soldiers will come with me," said the colonel, as he strode toward the rectory door.

"As you wish, Colonel."

Quickly, Colonel Kovalenk and the two monarchist soldiers followed the captain into the church annex. When Colonel Kovalenk entered the main room of the rectory, there was immediate excitement among the men already gathered there. Without delay Captain Yurino introduced the colonel to them.

"Gentlemen, this is Colonel Kovalenk, personal emissary of General Denikin, commander of the loyalist monarchist armies in the South."

One by one, Captain Yurino then introduced the leaders of the Black Hundreds to the colonel. There was Volodomyr Butovo, a rotund gentleman who, prior to the revolution, had been one of Russia's largest landowners. Leonid Bunin, a tall, elegant man of fifty, who had spent his years doing little more than living off the vast fortune left to him by his father. Gregori Sudzha was an ex-minister of finance in Tsar Nicholas's government, and Lieutenant Ilya Allilueva was Captain Yurino's personal assistant and confidant.

"A toast, gentlemen?" Captain Yurino said, filling six glasses with vodka and handing one to Colonel Kovalenk, one each to his four compatriots, and keeping one for himself.

After a flurry of flattering statements about General Denikin, the association between the Hundreds and the general, and an oath of allegiance to the restoration of the monarchy, the six men gulped their drinks in unison.

"This is excellent vodka, Captain," Colonel Kovalenk said graciously.

"We are pleased you like it, Colonel. When you leave, I will give you several bottles for General Denikin."

"He will be most appreciative." The colonel set his glass down on the small table at the far end of the room which had been set up as a bar. He cleared his throat and his manner became formal. "Shall we get down to business?" The colonel looked at the others, his eyes announcing that any more socializing would be a waste of time. "When I have finished here tonight, I intend to rejoin my troops. It will take us some time to work our way through the Bolshevik-held territory to reach our forces. And if you want troops to help you, they will need time to return."

"Yes, of course," Volodomyr Butovo replied, his tone assuaging. He pulled his vest down over his ample girth. "Gentlemen, let us take our places. We have wasted enough of Colonel Kovalenk's time." Butovo gestured for the colonel to sit at the head of the table.

As the five men of the Hundreds and Colonel Kovalenk settled themselves at a large table in the center of the room, the colonel's aides stationed themselves behind their officer, facing the doorway, ready to protect him in any dispute. The soldiers stood at attention, their hands clasped behind their backs, carbines slung over their shoulders, eyes and ears alert to every sound and movement.

"Now," began Colonel Kovalenk, "as you know from the letter I delivered to you, General Denikin has offered you five hundred soldiers to be used at your discretion—if I approve of your plan." The colonel leaned back in his chair and eyed the man who sat at the opposite end of the table. "Now, would someone tell me about that plan."

Everyone looked to Captain Yurino. He bowed his head just a bit, modestly acknowledging their recognition of his leadership. Then, the captain faced Colonel Kovalenk and began to speak. For forty-five minutes the captain explained the plan in detail. He spread a military map of Odessa on the table, his fingers working their way from grid to grid, pointing out the routes that would be used to surround and crush Moldavanka. He told how the troops General Denikin would supply would be used to infiltrate the ghetto just before the general launched his attack on Odessa. Then, while the Bolsheviks were involved in fighting the forces of the White Army, the Black Hundreds would be able to easily annihilate the most perfidious enemies of Russia.

"We are assuming, Colonel, that General Denikin will reach Odessa as he predicted—sometime during the third week in September. And by then, in all likelihood, Petlura will have heard about his arrival and will be in position to attack the city from the north," Captain Yurino said.

"That is why it would be best, Colonel, if the troops your General Denikin is sending could arrive here no later than the second week in September," Lieutenant Allilueva added.

"Will they be able to slip through the Bolshevik lines?" asked Volodomyr Butovo, his watery blue eyes appearing worried.

"Of course, if they dress like Bolsheviks," the colonel replied.

The men of the Black Hundreds laughed heartily.

"Now, tell me about Petlura. Do you have any idea what his route will be? To coordinate our efforts, that information is vital." Colonel Kovalenk looked directly at Captain Yurino.

"Unfortunately, Colonel, we know nothing of Petlura's intentions. He seems to be everywhere at once, or at least everywhere where there are Jews. All we know is that he has been moving southward for the past several weeks and, hopefully, he will want to take advantage of General Denikin's attack on Odessa. We can certainly use the distraction his men could create," answered Captain Yurino.

"I must say, even though we are in total disagreement with his desires for an independent Ukraine, Petlura's efforts against the Bolsheviks and the Jews have been outstanding," Leonid Bunin said in his usual offhanded manner; he sat slouched in his chair, one arm hooked over the back.

"Especially his efforts against the *Jews*," the plump Butovo added.

Lieutenant Allilueva sat up as straight as he could, his shoulders held back as if he were at attention. "If the Jews had one tenth of Petlura's courage, they and the Bolsheviks would already rule Russia. Thank God they do not!"

"The Jews only have courage when it comes to money," Butovo wheezed.

"If not for the war, we would have been rid of them by now!" Leonid Bunin snarled, sitting erect for the first time all evening.

"If not for the Jews we would have won the war!" Gregori Sudzha shouted, his deep voice reminiscent of a cannonade, his pinched face reddening with anger. "Why in God's name they just don't do everyone a favor and leave Russia, I do not know."

Butovo sneered. "They do not leave, Gregori, because they do not know when they are not wanted. Perhaps we have been lax in showing the Jews exactly how much they are not wanted."

Lieutenant Allilueva leaned forward, his index finger jabbing the table. "The Jew I would like to kill personally is Trotsky. He is the one who ruined Russia singlehandedly!"

Gregori Sudzha rose half out of his chair. "Of all the *zhids* he is the worst. Of all the filthy Jews, Trotsky is the most treacherous!" Bits of saliva sprayed from the ex-finance minister's mouth.

"Yes, Trotsky is a lousy Jew. And I, too, would like to kill him, personally," Colonel Kovalenk said, rising to his feet.

Everyone looked at the colonel. The fury they saw stretching the muscles in his neck excited them. His breadth and height emboldened them. And as he continued to speak, they fed their loathing on his.

"Do you want to know why I hate Trotsky so much? Because he pretends that he is not a Jew. And like you, he, too, wants to see the Jews destroyed. Because he agrees with you that Jews are vermin. Speculators. Thieves. And he is right! But *we* are like that because you would never let us be anything else. You are bastards. All of you! Stinking, fucking, murdering, slimy bastards! You have caused more tragedies than hell itself will be able to hold!" The colonel drew the revolvers that hung at his sides and waved them threateningly. "And if nothing else, at least none of *you* will ever kill one more Jew!" He looked from one man to the next. "Now let us see how brave you are! Let us see you try and kill *this* Odessa Jew!"

The five men at the table were aghast. Their jaws dropped, their eyes darted wildly about. They looked to the door, but the ominous sound of the colonel's aides releasing the safeties on their carbines made them freeze in their places.

"Is this a joke? This must be a joke!" Volodomyr Butovo cried out, losing control over his bladder; his legs and trousers became warm and wet.

"Yes, this is a joke. On you!"

"Who are you? The letter from General Denikin, how did you get it?" asked Butovo, his stomach, bloated with gas, relieving itself and filling the room with a foul stench.

"The letter was a forgery. This uniform is a forgery. My lieutenants are forgeries. Everything is a forgery except me, *Mishka Yaponchik*!"

Lieutenant Allilueva clamped his fingers on the edge of the table for support. "What are you going to do?"

"What else would a filthy *zhid* do? He is going to kill us!" Leonid Bunin spat nastily.

"*You* call Jews filthy? You call me filthy? How can you call anyone filthy after you told me what you and these others intend to do in Odessa. I am filthy, while it is you who were planning to shoot, stab, tear apart every Jewish man and boy in Moldavanka? Kill every male child! Even slicing the testicles from the bodies of infants! I am filthy, and you intended to bash in the heads of old women with your clubs? You call me filthy while you sit here and dream of raping Jewish girls? I am not filthy! Don't you ever say that any Jew is filthy!"

Mishka's voice was so violently loud that the windows of

the rectory shook. His words smashed the ears of the Black Hundreds with the force of a thousand *samjots.* The veins at the sides of his head and in his neck were distended and ugly blue. His lips were contorted, his face a grotesque mask.

"KILL THEM!"

An enormous explosion filled the room.

"KILL THEM!"

Again and again, Grisha and Urka, who had posed as Mishka's lieutenant's, fired their weapons.

"KILLLL THEMMMMM!"

Blood poured onto the floor as dozens of bullets ripped into the bodies of the men of the Black Hundreds. Their limbs convulsed, their torsos twisted, their heads snapped backwards, cracking their necks and spines. Gray slime ran from their skulls and over their bulging eyeballs, their faces dissolving into indistinguishable masses of pulpy flesh. Their muscles twitched in death spasms and slowly each one of the Black Hundreds toppled to the floor. Mishka stood in the silence and stared down at the dead men. He began to walk, stepping in their blood, in the shreds of their flesh, on their dismembered limbs, in the remains of their minds. As he passed each one of them, Mishka fired a single shot into their already lifeless bodies; Butovo received the last bullet. Mishka walked out of the rectory and into the courtyard. There amidst several dozen of his men lay the guard, his body sprawled on the ground, face down. Mishka placed his boot under the man's belly and rolled him over. There was a bullet hole between the man's eyes.

"He is dead, too," said Skakun. "And Karmanchik killed the sentry in the cemetery."

Mishka exhaled slowly, loudly. "And the real messenger from Denikin?"

Skakun said nothing, his piercing look conveying everything he had to say. "Urka, you take the men home. I want to walk with Grisha for awhile." Mishka sounded old and tired.

Without delay Urka obeyed Mishka's order and within minutes was leading a long line of Mishka's men back toward Odessa. While alone, leading their horses by the reins, and without a backward glance, Mishka Yaponchik and Grisha Moisei plodded away from the Church of St. Mark's.

CHAPTER 51

The murder of the six men was discovered the next morning by the priest of St. Mark's. He ran and stumbled all the way into Odessa, screaming insanely until he reached the Bolshevik headquarters in the old Opera House. When he finally managed to tell his story coherently, a detail of Bolshevik soldiers, along with the Commissar, went to investigate. It did not take them long to put the pieces of the mystery together. Still lying on the table was the military map Captain Yurino had shown Mishka. A leather pouch, containing a detailed breakdown of both Denikin's and Petlura's pincer attack on Odessa, and the plan for the pogrom, lay on the floor next to the captain's body. The forged letter Mishka had presented to him was in the jacket of his uniform. The Commissar frowned as he read the documents. When he was through with them he handed the papers to Major Lukoyanov, the commander of the Bolshevik military forces in Odessa. Stepping away from the soldiers who were burying the dead men, the Commissar and the major discussed the matter, both of them arriving at the same conclusion: that what they had found must be the work of that Jew, Mishka Yaponchik.

Fearful that the power of Mishka Yaponchik might undermine his own if knowledge of the mass execution became publicly known, the Commissar was determined to keep the discovery as quiet as possible. He ordered the troops who had been at the church not to reveal anything to anyone, and he threatened the priest with the loss of his church and imprisonment if he so much as said a word about the occurrence. The Commissar's precautions were to no avail. The priest found it impossible not to talk, telling everyone he met of the desecration of St. Mark's. The soldiers got drunk, retelling the story a dozen times, each time making it worse than the time before. And by the end of the following day, hardly a person in Odessa had not heard some version of the incident. Here and there, Mishka Yaponchik's name was mentioned in connection with the massacre, and though there was no evidence of his involvement, speculation evolved into rampant rumors, the facts so exaggerated that Mishka was credited not only with saving Moldavanka, but for delivering all of Odessa from a secret monarchist invasion.

By noon of the next day, Moldavanka was crowded with Jew and non-Jew, with factory workers, laborers, people from every level of Odessa society, including hundreds of Bolshevik soldiers and even some officers. The streets surrounding the Malinas Zala were so jammed with people that no one could move. The multitude began to chant Mishka's name. Inside the café, men and women besieged Mishka, begging him to say whether or not he had been responsible for the executions. Flushed with excitement, Mishka admitted that he had masterminded the plot. Bedlam broke loose. Cheers that gave Mishka chills steadily crescendoed. The sound was contagious, the people outside of the Zala screaming for Mishka to show himself. Proudly, Mishka strutted into the street. Everyone grabbed at him, wanting to touch him, to have a piece of his clothing for a souvenir, and if not for Mishka's bulk and strength he would have been stripped naked. Mishka shoved his way along Petrovskaya Street. The crowds parted, making a narrow passageway so the hero of Odessa could pass by. Mishka marched back and forth along Petrovskaya Street, then turned onto a side street and paraded through the rest of Moldavanka. Everywhere he went, people tagged along straining to see him, shouting and whistling, cheering him. A Bolshevik officer dashed up to Mishka and shook his hand, thanking him for what he had done. Mishka laughed. He stopped walking, turning in a circle to survey the throngs of Odessans. He raised his hand. The street became quiet, only the humming of breathing and a few appreciative murmurs breaking the stillness. Mishka began to speak, his voice strong and clear, his words decisive.

"Today, Mishka Yaponchik is a hero. To *all* of Odessa! And no one cares, not even the Bolsheviks, that he is a Jew. But what happened at St. Mark's was done only for the Jews. And if Odessa gained anything from that, it was an accident. But I do not mind that. Even though I am a Moldavankan, Odessa is my city, too. And if helping the Jews helps all of Odessa, so what! But there is more that has to be done. There is a more dangerous plague approaching this city. Petlura! And until Petlura is dead not even the Bolsheviks are safe. Again Mishka is willing to help the Bolsheviks. I will hunt Petlura. Let the Commissar know that. Tell him that Mishka Yaponchik wants weapons to hunt Petlura. Tell him Mishka Yaponchik wants some of his soldiers to ride with mine. Tell the Commissar that Mishka Yaponchik will fight Petlura for Moldavanka, and so for Odessa, too!"

Wild shots obliterated Mishka's words and it was several minutes before he could speak again.

"Bolsheviks, tell your Commissar that if he gives me what I need to fight Petlura, he can keep our synagogues. But if he refuses to help me, not only will Mishka take the synagogues back, but after that I will help the Christians get their churches back!"

Again the thousands of people who were squeezed into the ghetto screamed their approval. "Bolsheviks help Mishka! Bolsheviks help Mishka!" The crowd started to move, becoming a joyous parade that was led by a Red

Army officer. Intoxicated with happiness, the marchers, at the top of their lungs, sang the "Internationale," the hymn of the revolution. They pressed along Yekaterina Street, across Preobrazhenskaya to Pushkinskaya, across Deribasovskaya to Lanzheronovskaya, finally arriving at Tyatre Square and the old Opera House, the Bolshevik headquarters. "Bolsheviks, help Mishka! Bolsheviks, help Mishka!" the throngs chanted. They surrounded the building, their voices engulfing it. The officer who had led them to the Red headquarters ran inside, demanding to speak with the Commissar; even within the building the rhythmic slogan, "Bolsheviks, help Mishka," could be heard. A quarter of an hour later the officer stepped back outside. He raised his fists in a signal of triumph. The excited multitude became impassioned, frenzied. The people mobbed the officer, lifting him to their shoulders and marching him in circles around the Opera House. High above them, peering down out of his office window, the Commissar of Odessa watched the celebration below. An expression of great pleasure covered his face.

The following day Mishka Yaponchik was invited to accompany a captain in the Bolshevik army to a meeting with the Commissar and the chief military officers of the city. Mishka was ecstatic. He carefully instructed Mala how to trim his long hair. He hovered over Joseph as the tailor ironed a pair of dark pants and a bright blue shirt for him. Grisha volunteered to shine his knee-high leather boots.

"Maybe the Bolsheviks will make me the Commissar of Moldavanka!" Mishka laughed as he dressed and inspected himself in a mirror.

"Maybe the Bolsheviks will make you the buffoon of Moldavanka if you are not careful!" Mala countered, her words meant to be more serious than they sounded.

"Do you think they would be idiots and do anything to harm me? Especially now?"

Mala knew that Mishka was right. It would be suicide for the Bolsheviks to do anything to him. Overnight, Mishka had received the full support of the city, and for the Reds to do anything but honor his request for help to fight Petlura would make no sense.

"Did you hear how clever I was?" Mishka said, combing his hair several times before he was satisfied. "I told them they could keep our synagogues." Studying his face, Mishka twirled his mustache. "That was a lie. Because after I kill Petlura, I will take back our synagogues from the Reds. And if they want, I will do the same for the Christians and their churches!"

"What are you intending to do, start your own revolution in Russia?" Mala asked.

"No. Just in Odessa!"

"I think you are crazy. No, I know you are crazy. But I hope you do it!" said Joseph Dubrow.

Five minutes later Mishka strutted into the crowded café and informed the Bolshevik escort, who had patiently waited for him, that he was ready to meet the Commissar. The Red captain stepped outside, signaled his driver to start the engine of the army truck. Mishka kissed Mala, waved to the others in the Zala, and strode into the street. When the officer held the door open so Mishka could enter the vehicle, the crowd that had gathered outside the café applauded. The Bolshevik closed the door, then climbed into the rear of the truck. Immediately the vehicle began to roll. Cautiously, the driver weaved the truck through the line of people who shouted wishes of luck, and as the lorry disappeared around the corner, roaring off with a sudden burst of speed, as many well-wishers as possible forced their way into the café.

By the time the sun had set, Mishka had still not returned from the Bolshevik headquarters. The crowd in the Zala had thinned considerably, and those who remained were quiet. A feeling of apprehension pervaded the café, everyone wondering if Mishka had been duped. Sitting at the center table where Mishka always held court were Joseph, Mala, Grisha, Sara, Urka, and Eleazar. Some were drinking beer, Urka and Grisha vodka, and the rabbi sipped a glass of wine. Their faces showed tension as they awaited Mishka's return. Urka was angry that he had let Mishka go without him. He considered going to the Opera House to look for him, but he knew that if things were going well he would be useless. If they were not, he would still be useless. Eleazar stared into space, his thoughts meandering far from the present, his intellect as decrepit as his body. A verbatim conversation he had once had with someone, sixty years before repeated itself in his mind; the rabbi was confused, uncertain as to whether it was his father or God who had spoken with him. Someone coughed, causing Eleazar to look around the table. He tried to remember why he and the others were sitting there. Sara watched her father. He had grown much older than she had realized, and now that there was nothing to do but look at him, it became quite apparent. Sara touched Joseph's hands, and he covered her fingers with his. She assumed it was because it comforted him. Joseph thought the gentle touch was that of his wife. Grisha put his arm around Sara, and her thoughts changed. She pictured how her husband played with Isaac, swinging the infant high above his head and making him laugh gleefully. She remembered how she had cried at the horror she saw on Grisha's face when he described what had happened at St. Mark's, how ill he had been that night when he and Mishka returned to the Zala. When Grisha declared that he would do it again, and why, Sara understood. She more than understood. Indeed, if similar circumstances arose, she wanted Grisha to repeat what he had done. A dispute seethed within Sara, a personal war. If Mishka received the help he sought, Grisha would go with him to hunt Petlura. And part of Sara lusted for that, demanded that Semyon Petlura be killed. A portion of the being that Sara was longed to see her husband standing on the soil of Russia, "upon this place of skulls," with one foot resting on the ground, the other on Petlura's corpse, announcing that he whose life was dedicated to scourging the Jews was, by a Jew himself, scourged. And yet there was another element in Sara, arguing, fighting with the first, refusing to yield her husband to anyone, to any cause but her own. Mind fought heart. The woman wrestled with the mother. The person struck the lover. Passion returned a blow to reason. One freedom challenged another. Who would win, the people or the individual? The Jews or the Jewess? Who had a greater right to win? Should either supersede the other? And the battle raged on.

The distant sound of a truck startled everyone in the café. Every breath was held and not one body moved. Mala's heart raced, blood rushing to her face. Grisha squeezed Sara's hand until she pulled it away in pain. The sound of the motor subsided for an instant, and just when everyone felt a new letdown it suddenly reappeared. No one stirred, not even when the unmistakable sputtering of an engine roughly idling in neutral clattered outside. The metallic squeak of a truck door opening and then being slammed closed increased the tenseness. A single set of footsteps approached. They stopped. Then with a loud bang the door was thrown open.

"The first bastard who moves is dead!"

"Mishka!" Mala screamed.

"Who else did you expect?!"

Mala ran to Mishka. He swept her off her feet and lifted her high into the air.

"You're not hurt?" Mala asked as Mishka set her down on her feet.

"Hurt? I am wonderful!"

Scores of questions bombarded Mishka, and before he answered he filled a glass with vodka, drank it, then hurled the glass against a wall. The rumbling of the truck pulling away made Mishka turn, and he shouted as loudly as he could: "Give my regards to the Commissar!" Then Mishka Yaponchik sat down and laughed deeply for a long time.

"You know, I did not even need these," Mishka finally said, unstrapping his revolvers and placing them on the table. "And I got this paper without even asking for it."

Mishka unfolded an official-looking document and ran his fingers along the creases.

"What is it?" Mala asked, trying to read over his shoulder.

"When I arrived at the Bolshevik headquarters every soldier saluted me when I went inside. Even the officers. The captain I was with took me right to the Commissar's office and we went in immediately. We did not wait for ten seconds. As soon as he knew I was there, the Commissar wanted to see me. He offered me a cigarette and I accepted it. Then some vodka, and I took that, too. He told me how grateful he was for what I had done at the church. He said that since he was a young Bolshevik the Black Hundreds had been special enemies of his. He showed me a communiqué that Lenin sent to all his commissars and officers regarding how the Jews should be protected from Petlura and the other pogromists. I never knew that Lenin felt that way. I asked him why the Bolsheviks took away our synagogues and the churches. He said that too many priests were monarchist sympathizers, and that taking away the churches helped to weaken the Whites. And that for now, the synagogues had to be treated the same way, so everyone would be the same. There are to be no more special people in Russia. Just the proletariat. Then he asked me what I wanted. I told him: men and weapons to hunt Petlura. And do you know what? He agreed! The Bolshevik Commissar agreed to give Mishka Yaponchik what he asked for! Three hundred soldiers with automatic rifles and machine guns! Ammunition! Good weapons for my men, too! And better horses for us! In addition, and here it is in writing, no homes in Moldavanka will be used to house Bolshevik soldiers without the agreement of the people who live there. Jews will be treated exactly like all Odessans. The Bolsheviks will defend Moldavanka against any enemy as strongly as every other part of the city. When the revolution is over, we will have jobs like everyone else. Our children will be allowed to attend school *without* quotas. Can you imagine that? And there is more, much more, but the most exciting thing of all is who will lead the troops, the Red troops. Me! Mishka Yaponchik! I am going to lead an army of their men and mine, and everything we hoped for we will have!"

Mishka beamed proudly. Mala threw her arms around his neck and covered his face with kisses. Grisha clapped his hands and shouted hurrahs. Everyone else in the café, with one exception, cheered.

"Joseph, what is wrong? You do not look happy," Mishka said, noticing how pensive Sara's father seemed.

The tailor peered intently at the large man. "Tell me Mishka, how do you know the Bolsheviks will keep their word?"

"Everything is on this piece of paper. The Commissar himself signed it!" Mishka held the document for all to see, pointing out the official signature.

Joseph was unimpressed. "What makes you think he will not change his mind and take it away from you and tear it up? Or just ignore it?"

"Do you think they would give me an army to lead if they intended to lie to me? Would that make sense?"

Joseph ran his hands through his sparse, graying hair. He pursed his lips, his eyes were lackluster. "Mishka, besides Petlura's head, what else did you promise the Bolsheviks?" Joseph's voice was low; he sounded disappointed. "What did they ask of *you*?"

Mishka's mustache quivered as he tossed his head in anger. He banged a chair against the floor and dug a beefy hand into his pants pocket. "They asked for something so simple a child could do it!" He withdrew his hand, holding something in his clenched fist. "I was glad to agree to what they asked. To give them what they wanted. Because what they gave me is ten thousand times more valuable!"

"Show me what they asked of you, Mishka. Show me!" Joseph yelled, standing up so quickly he knocked over his drink.

"This!" Mishka opened his hand and hurled a red star and a red armband on the table.

Joseph Dubrow was stunned. "You agreed to be a Bolshevik?" His voice was filled with abhorrence.

"It is nothing more than something to pin on my hat and jacket. And that is all!"

"A Jew wearing the symbols of Bolsheviks?"

"Yes! Because by doing so it says thank you for their help. That is why *I* will wear them. Urka will wear them. Skakun and Karmanchik will wear them. That is why Grisha will wear them! Anyone who wants to ride with me will wear them! Because without the Bolsheviks there is no way we could fight Petlura! Sneak thieves and forgers are not soldiers! Burglars are not soldiers! Maybe there are two hundren men in Moldavanka who really know how to fight. That is not enough to hunt Petlura. But you add to that more than three hundred Bolshevik soldiers, men who have been in perhaps a hundred battles, we become an army! And if *you* want to wait for Petlura to visit Moldavanka, then wait! But I will not wait. And to me, those who can fight, and refuse because of symbols, are traitors!"

Joseph looked around the room, searching for someone who would support his position. No one came to his aid. He rested his eyes on Grisha. "And you will wear them, too?"

Grisha took a long breath, his eyes fixed on the star and armband, their redness glowing against the dark wooden table.

"Do you see where they landed, *malcheshka?*" said Mishka. "Over the very spot where Dmitri Luchka signed his affidavit. Do you understand what I am saying? His confession is gone, and so are the Black Hundreds. And now, because of the Bolsheviks, Petlura will be gone, too. And that is enough reason for me to wear these." Mishka picked up the armband and slipped it over his shirtsleeve. "Tomorrow we all wear them!" He glared at Urka, Skakun, and Karmanchak. "Here, Grisha, take this star. It is for the soldier's hat you will be wearing."

Grisha looked at Joseph. The hurt he saw touched him

deeply. Yet, the price Mishka was asking him to pay for something he so desperately wanted to do seemed so small. Slowly, he reached for the star.

"Don't you understand what you are doing?" Joseph said. "If the people of Moldavanka see Mishka and you and the others wearing those things, they will trust the Bolsheviks. Because they trust *you*. I know the Bolsheviks, Grisha. They are thieves and liars like the Tsar was. They are worse!" All too vividly, Joseph remembered the sight of his wife's dead body lying in the street of the ghetto with a knife stuck in her throat.

"What is the matter, *malcheshka*, does his fear frighten you, too?" Mishka asked quietly.

Grisha thought he could feel heat coming from the fiery red symbol.

"Would I lie to you, my *malchik*? Of all people would *I* ask you to do something I thought would hurt you?" In a sudden rush of words he never thought he would ever hear himself say, Mishka blurted out, "I love you, *malcheshka*."

Tears came to Grisha's eyes. The café became still, the only sound the rustle of the cloth star as Grisha pinned it to his shirt. Mishka shouted a cheer, others joining with him. The clinking of glasses touched together in toasts rang out like music. The noise swiftly increased and Rabbi Eleazar opened his eyes wide, bewildered. Suddenly he clutched the glass of wine before him, certain it was he that everyone was toasting. *They must be*, he thought to himself. *This is August. And my birthday is in August. They are celebrating my tenth birthday!* Shakily Eleazar raised his glass to his lips and swallowed his drink, adding his cheer to the rest. His words, congratulating himself on his own birthday, were lost among the other voices. Mishka slapped Grisha on the back. The youth turned to his wife to see her reaction, but she was too busy attending to her father to notice. Joseph looked defeated, his posture was stooped, as if in the last few moments he had aged twenty years. When Grisha stepped into his line of vision, Joseph stared at him, a bruised expression on his face.

"Come, Poppa, let me take you home," said Sara gently.

As if it did not matter where he went, Joseph meekly followed his daughter out of the Zala. Grisha chased after them.

"Wait, please!"

Sara paused, making her father do the same.

"Joseph, what I am doing is only so we can find Petlura. Please believe me!"

"Even for that, I do not know if wearing the star of Bolshevism, of infamy, is worth it," the tailor said softly.

"*Anything* is worth it."

Joseph shook his head, recalling the words his wife used to repeat to him when he had defended Bolshevism to her:

But those scarfs of blood-red shall be redder, before
The saber is sheathed and the battle is o'er.

A sorrowful smile touched Joseph's lips. *To use the poems I taught you against me, Nessa, ah, but that was unfair. But you were so right, my darling wife, just as I misread Marx, so I misread Byron. For Childe Harold was no hero, but a man consumed by personal strife, who wandered through life burdened by guilt for the sins of his past. My beloved Grisha, who could ever explain to you that you, too, are enflamed with passion, yet lack compassion? For you, whom I love as dearly as my own flesh, in truth shun humanity.*

"Are you incapable of understanding, Joseph, what Mishka has accomplished? What we will further accomplish?"

" 'And must they fall, the young, the proud, the brave, to smell one bloated chief's unwholesome reign?' "

"Have you grown so old that, like Eleazar, you are unaware of reality? Would you really permit anything to stand in the way of destroying Petlura? How can anyone, and especially a Jew, speak against something that aids in Petlura's annihilation? And as I will reject nothing that furthers that cause, I would also crush anything that hinders that cause!"

" 'Can tyrants but by tyrants conquer'd be?' Grisha, I have

never interfered about where you followed Mishka, or why. But to follow him into this? I cannot accept that. Today he sweet-talks you, but what happens tomorrow when the Bolsheviks make harsher demands on him and he has to fulfill them or be arrested? Will he tell you then that he loves you? Or will he order you to do what is required for him to save his own life? I already know the answer, Grisha. Do you have to discover it when it is too late?"

"Mishka would not do that. I know he wouldn't!"

"Maybe he would not want to, but he might have to."

"If he does, Joseph, I will be his worst enemy. But until then . . ."

Joseph studied Grisha's face. "That kind of strength I know you have."

"Then what frightens you so, the possibility that I will fall victim to Bolshevism?"

"No."

"Then tell me what?"

"Partly, that you do not see that far more than you are using the Bolsheviks, they are using you."

"Does it—"

"But that is not my primary fear. Because what worries me most, my Grisha, is if, when the time comes, you will have the courage to relinquish your past, to flee Russia. I worry that when there is a lull to this interminable slaughter, when for an instant Russia's perversity rests, you will not want to leave."

Grisha reached out to touch his father-in-law's hand: "I detest this Russia, and since I cannot destroy it, though I want to, I will run from it at the first opportunity. Believe me, Joseph, I am telling you the truth."

"You are telling me today's truth."

"And when will I tell you the truth you want to hear?"

Joseph clasped Grisha's fingers. "On the day all of us are on a boat that has left this country far behind and, like me, you offer only your back to Russia while your face looks ahead to the future."

"I promise that will happen. I swear it!"

"Never make a promise before you keep it, Grisha. That way you will never disappoint anyone."

Grisha hugged Joseph to him. "I promise never to promise again." He kissed Joseph's cheek. Then, taking his father-in-law by the hand, and Sara, too, Grisha Moisei led the way through Moldavanka, their forms lost in the ghetto darkness, their minds lost to themselves, each of them tortured, each of them desperately seeking his own peace.

CHAPTER 52

A strong wind broke apart the storm clouds, patching the leaden sky with blue. Swirling through a shattered windowpane, a steady breeze billowed a pair of frayed pink curtains. And the cold rays of a filtered sun exposed the dreariness of the room where Rabbi Joshua Eleazar had once slept. A bureau, leaning to one side, was marred by hundreds of scratches, its varnish entirely gone. A stuffed chair sagged on lifeless springs. A dressing table, covered by a white sheet stained with spots of old makeup, was littered with open tubes of lip coloring, a vial of rouge, a comb, and a tin of caked face powder. The bed where Soybel and Munya Viska lay sleeping creaked, its mattress bellying to the floor. Soybel shivered, the rain that had fallen continuously for the last three days making everything damp and clammy. Soybel rolled onto her side, hugging Munya when she felt the warmth from his body. A thousand disturbing thoughts prevented Soybel from sleeping soundly, and even through her closed eyelids she knew it was daylight. The knowledge that if she did not arise now she would be late for work irritated Soybel. She despised her job at the *Fabrika Amunetsya*; ten hours a day, six days a week, filling mortar casings with gunpowder. Aside from the tedium and the paltry amount of rubles she earned, what Soybel disliked most about her work was that she could never completely bathe away the odor of sulfur and saltpeter; sometimes Soybel worried that she herself would explode if she came too near a flame. And the way the Bolshevik foreman shouted at her infuriated Soybel: "Faster, work faster. Our comrades are dying at the front because of the lack of ammunition. Work faster, or you will be held responsible for their deaths!" Soybel was thankful that so many Red soldiers had been sent off to fight the armies of Generals Denikin and Wrangel to the east and south. Otherwise, she reasoned, the Bolsheviks would have requisitioned the house long ago, as Daniella had threatened. *But they never came, did they? I wasted my time by the window for days, waiting for them to come. But they didn't. And they never will.* Sluggishly, Soybel rolled onto her back and opened her eyes. *The rain has stopped!* Soybel sat up and shook her son. "Munya, the sun is shining!"

"What did you say, *maman*?"

"I cannot go to work today, Munya, the sky is too blue."

"If it gets warm, *maman*, can we go for a walk?"

"Yes! And I hope there is a wind, a strong wind to blow away this stench of war that still clings to my body."

"Can we go to the Promenade by the sea, *maman*?"

"Where else would one walk on such a fine day?" Soybel leaned over and kissed her son. "I have a secret to tell you," she whispered in his ear. "I have a ruble. So we will buy some lemonade at the promenade. And maybe we will have enough for two cookies, too. Would you like that?" asked Soybel, her excitement increasing.

"Let's go soon, *maman*."

Soybel yawned and stretched, then climbed out of bed, pulled her nightgown over her head, and stood naked in a warm shaft of sunlight. "As soon as I am dressed, I will get you ready and we will leave."

Munya watched his mother, his eyes absorbing every detail of her movements.

Soybel sat down at the dessing table, picked up the comb and removed long strands of hair from between its teeth.

She glanced at herself in the mirror, not liking how she looked without makeup. Folds of skin lined her brow, her cheeks were hollow, and her hair was dry and split. She saw the reflection of her breasts. Putting her hands beneath them, Soybel pushed her breasts upwards to the position they had once held by themselves. She let them go; they hung loosely, unattractve, like two small empty sacks against her bony chest. Soybel combed her hair, having difficulty with the brittle tangles. She cursed, then used the comb more forcefully. She asked Munya to bring her the dress Joseph Dubrow had given her when she first arrived in Odessa. The last time she had worn it was the day she and Grisha had fought at the Zala; that was the last time she had seen Grisha. Standing up to step into the lavender gown, Soybel noticed how flabby her thighs were and that her legs seemed to be marked by more veins than she had seen a week ago. When she wriggled herself into the gown, she asked Munya to fasten the hooks at the back. Then Soybel sat down at the dressing table and continued to comb her hair. It took her twenty minutes before each strand lay neatly against the next; the black tresses, not as shiny as they once were, still flowed below her shoulders and to her waist. Opening the tin of powder, Soybel daubed her face with the flesh-colored talc. Next she applied rouge to her cheeks, using it liberally to try and hide the hollows. She painted her lips with red, adding a trifle higher arch to the upper one, thinking it made her look more sensual. Satisfied with her appearance, Soybel turned to Munya, telling him what he should wear. She watched as he put on a pair of navy-blue trousers, a yellow shirt, and well-polished black boots. She thought he looked beautiful. Soybel straightened Munya's collar and fixed his hair the way she liked it. *"Tu es le plus bel jeune homme dans toute la Russie!"* A sparkle touched Soybel's eyes. Impulsively, she kissed Munya. A laugh that had a trace of the trilling way Soybel used to make her happiness sound caused Munya to smile. *"Je t'aime, mon petit. Je t'aime, je t'aime, je t'aime."* Filled with anticipation, Soybel took hold of Munya's hand and pulled him outside.

"Smell the air, Munya. The day is exquisite! It was certainly meant for walking by the sea. And we will have such a wonderful time!"

Jauntily, Soybel led Munya along Kherson Street, oblivious to the people who snickered at the two of them. They all pointed to Soybel, commenting about her, mocking the way her face was always overpowdered, too rouged and lipsticked, and about how she never allowed her delicately boned and featured son away from her side, refusing to let him play with other children on the street. Soybel rhythmically swayed her hips, enjoying the motion. All she received for her effort was an obscene request from a group of young men lounging against a building. Quickening her pace, Soybel hurried Munya across Preobrazhenskaya Street and out of Moldavanka, heading for the Great Boulevard. All along their route, strapped to every building, were pictures of Lenin; despising the portraits, Soybel avoided looking at them. The streets were crowded with jobless men with nothing to do, prattling women queueing up to wait for the markets to open, and soldiers, dozens and dozens of armed Bolshevik soldiers. Soybel ignored the Bolsheviks, not wanting to even brush against them lest they infect her with the Red disease she hated. An image of the clubhouse on the Arkadia where Vassili used to take her flashed through Soybel's mind. She was about to suggest to Munya that they go there when Soybel remembered that the clubhouse had decayed and rotted, and the once exquisite grounds were choked with weeds and littered with garbage. In Sobornaya Square, Soybel and Munya were confronted by a crowd of indignant people and an obstinate Bolshevik patrol arguing about something on the steps that led to the entryway of the Church of the Transfiguration. Soybel went to turn back and take another route, but her way was blocked by a group of Red soldiers trying to prevent anyone else from entering the square. The dispute grew bitter, several women attempting to climb the church steps and the Reds threatening the group with arrest if they did. Defiantly, the women proceeded upwards to the church doors. The Bolsheviks chased at their heels. Frightened, Soybel grabbed Munya's shoulders and pushed him in front of her as she hastened to the far side of the square. Angry curses and an answering chorus of fierce shouts pummeled Soybel's ears as she rushed toward the Deribasov Gardens, hoping that the way was not blocked by soldiers. It was not. A loud cheer suddenly erupted. Not looking back to see which side was announcing victory, Soybel began to run, dragging Munya behind her, instinctively heading toward the promenade that overlooked the sea. Dashing madly, Soybel had trouble breathing, her face felt sticky and she worried that her makeup would be ruined by her exertion. People yelled at her as she barely missed knocking into them. Her ankles felt as if they would twist and break, but Soybel did not care, all she could think about was the promenade she could see in the distance, the beautiful promenade where she used to buy sweet lemonade and watch the sea. She recalled how once she had thrilled to the sight of the *Golub* cutting across the dark water, the sailboat looking so sleek, so clean and white against the sky, looking so free! When she reached the once elegant veranda, Soybel stopped, shocked by what she saw. The little outdoor café where she had once sat for hours, day after day, lazing in the sunshine, was now crowded with Red soldiers, and plump girls in gaudy dresses. Everyone was joking and flirting, drinking vodka or beer, kissing one another boldly on the lips. Here and there girls pretended to protest as young men standing before them fondled their breasts while others, pressing closely behind, touched their buttocks. Soybel was horrified. *You do not belong here! You are ugly! All of you!* But the pleasure she saw on their faces showed how little they would have cared for her thoughts. A pretty girl, with long blond hair and very blue eyes, looked coyly at a handsome Bolshevik officer who approached her. *I was pretty, too. I was beautiful,* Soybel wanted to tell them. *Everywhere I went, men would stare at me.* The girl shyly avoided the officer's daring eyes. He said something Soybel could not hear. The girl smiled, nodded her head, and the two of them strolled away hand in hand. Near the end of the stone walkway, a woman sat facing the sun. Her hair was unkempt and her clothing disheveled. Every so often a drunken soldier would taunt her, but the woman did not seem to mind. Soybel hated the woman. She hated all the old women in the city. But what Soybel detested most was being pushed against them, squeezed among them, when she stood in line to buy food. She hated their coarse words and gossiping tongues. The thought of their rough clothes touching her, their foul breaths becoming the air she breathed, made Soybel's skin crawl. That was not where she belonged. Where were all the fashionably dressed women who chatted about Paris and the Empress? Where were the robust men with perfectly trimmed mustaches and beards who sipped brandies and cognacs that glinted like their wives' jewels and spoke of shaping Russia's destiny? *I wish those old women would die,* Soybel thought, jostled by the young girls and their companions. *I wish all of them would die!* she added, knowing that tomorrow, or the next day, she would again be forced to stand in line with them to buy food. Soybel could feel the old women surrounding her, pressing against her, causing her to fall. And they would not care. They would step on her. Trample her into the ground as they fought to take her place. Soybel envisioned their large-knuckled hands and the scarlet veins on their noses. She cringed at the thought of their horny-skinned fingers pawing at her back, and she knew what made them repugnant. It was not they she abhorred. It was herself. It was not *their* faces she loathed, but her own. Because she was one of them. *Even they do not stop to look at me. Why should they? I look just like they do!* Soybel moved to escape from the victorious soldiers and the girls who looked at them with adoring eyes. *Don't you know they do not love you? They just need you for a moment. Then they will disappear. They always do.* Consumed by her ruminations, Soybel wandered aimlessly along Nicholas Boulevard, unaware that the streets had become uncommonly empty of people. Soybel grabbed hold of her son's hand, squeezing it so tightly that he pulled it away. She clutched at his arm. Munya twisted free, his mother's grasp hurting him. He ran ahead, looking back every once in awhile to see which way his mother would turn, which street she would follow. Once again Soybel's steps led her past the Deribasov Gardens. An overwhelming clamor made her look up. From every direction mobs of people were hurrying toward Tyatre Square. Curious as to why everyone was running in the direction of the Opera House, Soybel followed them. Munya wormed his way through the crowds, his mother incurring furious looks and words as she shoved her way after him. "Munya, come back," Soybel shouted to her son. He ignored his mother, his slender body having no trouble slipping past everyone until he reached a line of Bolshevik soldiers who formed a human wall fifty yards away from the Red headquarters.

"Munya!" Soybel called frantically as two people pushed their way in front of her, blocking her path and view. Soybel forced her way forward, her lipstick smearing the back of a man's shirt. "Munya!" she cried out, catching sight of the boy squatting so he could see between the legs of the soldiers. When she reached Munya's side, Soybel started to bend down to make sure he was all right; what she saw beyond the barricade of soldiers made her pause. Before her was the Opera House, gleaming in the rainwashed sunshine. Red banners, draped from its roof, fluttered in the freshening breeze. Hanging above the arched entranceway, at least thirty feet in length and fifteen in breadth, was a poster of Lenin, his face sparklingly clear, each detail crisp. Just in front of the building, standing in the back of a truck, was the Commissar of Odessa, flanked by two high-ranking military officers. The three Bolsheviks stood at attention, the army men displaying a salute. Before them, astride a black horse, was Mishka Yaponchik, a red star pinned to his army cap and a Bolshevik armband pulled over his jacket sleeve. On one side of him was Urka, on the other, Grisha, they, too, wearing the Red insignias, each of them with a pair of revolvers at his waist, a carbine slung over his shoulder, and ammunition belts crossed over his chest. Behind them, on champing horses, were two hundred and seven Moldavankan men who had volunteered to join Mishka's army, their motley clothes made uniform by the red spots of Bolshevism which gaily decorated their shirts and hats. Facing Mishka, sitting erectly on the back of a dappled mare, dressed in a proper uniform, was Lieutenant Ilya Veronozeh, who had personally requested that he be permitted to ride under Yaponchik's command. Behind the lieutenant's lead was a Bolshevik calvary unit consisting of three hundred and fifty soldiers, a string of seventy-five pack animals carrying ammunition, a dozen Maxima machine guns, heavy winter clothing, and rations. The Commissar made a short speech thanking Mishka and the brave Moldavankans for the danger they were willing to face. Lieutenant Veronozeh rode up to Mishka and with a smart salute showed that he would willingly obey the Moldavankan's orders. The crowd, numbering at least fifty thousand and spilling beyond Tyatre Square, cheered. Mishka raised his arms, waving in gratitude. The crowd waved back. Mishka rubbed his legs against his horse and the animal trotted toward an honor guard of soldiers before whom stood a tall, dark-featured woman whose handsome face glowed with pride. Mishka came to a halt directly in front of her, leaned down from his saddle, and with one arm lifted her off the ground. He kissed her. She clung to his neck. He kissed Mala again, then gently put her down. With thunderous shouts of adoration, the people displayed their approval. Mishka sat up straight and blew Mala a kiss. He turned his steed and surveyed the five hundred and fifty-seven men who were under his command. Mishka barked an order to Lieutenant Veronozeh and a similar one to Urka. Instantly, the Bolshevik officer directed his men to form a single column behind him and to Mishka's right; Urka told the Moldavankans to do the same on the left. Only Grisha was permitted to ride alongside the commander. Mishka tipped his hat to the Commissar, shouted to Urka and Veronozeh, nodded to Grisha, and grazed the flank of his horse with the end of the reins: Mishka kept the animal at a walk until his troops were moving, too. The crowd kept pace with the soldiers. Their shouts and the clattering of hooves enveloped the city, the tumult heard everywhere.

Mishka eased the pressure on his horse's bit, urging the animal into a canter. The soldiers behind him followed suit, the long calvary line sweeping through the city. Excited, the crowd picked up its step, matching strides with the departing army. Soybel, too, rushed along with the throngs, running with them, stimulated by them, trying to keep abreast of the two men in the lead. She riveted her eyes on Grisha, memorizing every feature of the dazzling warrior. His erect bearing, the proud tilt of his head, and his blond hair flowing behind him gave her chills. Glints of light sparkling off the rows of bullets strapped across his chest made Soybel think that Grisha was surrounded by gleaming stars. Her ears were stuffed with the frenzied screams of love and adulation from the mass of people around her. "We love you! We love you!" erupted in unison.

The troops rode at a gallop. The people ran faster. "WE LOVE YOU!" Soybel was pushed along, hurtling forward, arms outstretched, her legs moving without her control. Repeated volleys of rifle shots exploded, the cannonade wishing Mishka and the others triumph. The noise of the detonating bullets, the acrid odor of gunpowder, the powerful rhythm of pounding hooves, the impassioned energy of the crowd itself further inflamed the multitude. And in chorus fifty thousand people voiced their hope, rupturing the air, the roar deafening: "WE LOVE YOU!" Soybel screamed with them: "I love you. Grisha, I love you!" Again and again, she hurled those words at the only soldier she saw. She shrieked them. "GRISHA! GRISHA! I LOVE YOU, GRISHA!"

The column of mounted soldiers and pack animals disappeared, replaced by a swirl of dust—when it settled there was nothing but an empty road. The crowd dispersed; only a lone woman, trailed by a young boy, continued to follow the invisible soldiers northward. A mile further, exhausted, her legs weak, gasping for breath, Soybel halted. Tears streamed from her eyes, her extended arms aching to hold someone close, her heart breaking. Sobbing, she hugged herself, caressing her cheek with her shoulder. Her body heaved with despair. Soybel shut her eyes, and as she wept she kissed the air, her lips brushing against the wind, pretending that the breeze was the face of her son.

CHAPTER 53

On August 23, 1919, exactly one week after Mishka Yaponchik and his army departed from Odessa to fight Semyon Petlura, the military forces of General A. I. Denikin attacked the city. While the main body of Whites fought their way along Nicholas Boulevard, Deribasovskaya Street, Tyatre Square, and other key points of Odessa, mercilessly slaughtering the Bolsheviks, hundreds of other monarchist soldiers stormed Moldavanka.

Not fearing any resistance, the White soldiers moved brazenly through the ghetto, shooting everything in sight, killing dogs and cats when there were no people about. Frightened beyond anything they had ever known, trampling one another as they rushed to find shelter, the Moldavankans crammed their way into buildings and stores, anywhere to escape the deadly fusillades. From Mikhailovsky Place on the north, Yekaterina on the south, and east along Masterskaya Street came the Monarchists, attempting to encircle the ghetto. As they moved deeper into Moldavanka, with nothing standing in their way, their confidence increased, and the Whites entered each new street with less caution.

On Tirapolskaya Street the Monarchists suddenly became aware that Moldavanka was still alive. As the first group of White soldiers stepped around the corner and moved down the block, a machine gun, placed in the doorway of what had once been Joshua Eleazar's synagogue, cut them in half. From overhead, from windows and rooftops, riflemen further decimated the invader's ranks. And what had been a one-sided massacre became a battle.

Throughout the ghetto, scared but determined men, inspired for years by Mishka Yaponchik, took their weapons and fought for their lives. Wheezing and coughing, they dashed from building to building and street to street. Each time a Monarchist fell, a Moldavankan would grab the dead soldier's gun and turn it on those who still lived. Joseph Dubrow, weak-eyed, ignorant in warfare, terrified, crouched in the doorway of the Malinas Zala, firing a pistol at those who dared to come near the café. Standing next to him, dauntless, fearsome, using a rifle with murderous vengeance, was Mala, both of them barricading the entry to the building with their lives. Inside the café, playing games of peek-a-boo with her son, Sara Moisei, alert to any threatening sound, kept an eye on the revolver at her side, prepared to use it against anyone who even intimated harm.

Half a mile away Aram Zubov, hobbling on crutches, stationed himself on Troitzkaya Street within sight of the Brody Synagogue. His carbine, aimed with lethal accuracy, caused almost every soldier at whom he fired to fall. When he had no more ammunition, Zubov crawled along the walkways until he found a loaded gun in the stiff hands of one of his victims. Ignoring the difficulty of moving about on his crippled feet, Aram dragged himself from one place to another, wishing he could be everywhere at once.

The sound of gunshots slowly abated, the Whites forced to retreat. Uniformed soldiers backed out of one street into the next, trying to make their way back to the main part of the city—sniper fire reduced their number. From a building corner at Preobrazhenskaya Street Aram Zubov peeked out of Moldavanka and watched the enemy flee. He looked pleased.

The actual number of people who perished in the attack on Odessa was far fewer than had been feared. Stoically, the dead were collected and buried while the living struggled to exist under the harsh monarchist rule, a domination of unrelenting cruelty.

The Whites, suspecting everyone of being Bolshevik saboteurs, instituted a policy of stopping and searching people on the street, breaking down doors and ransacking apartments, houses, or businesses, and interrogating everyone present. Mass arrests became routine. Inhuman tortures applied to prisoners became common. And scores of Odessans were summarily executed. In addition to the monarchist threat, rats fled the dock, bringing typhus and cholera along with their hunger. Talk that the city would soon be infested with straw-lined carts carrying the corpses of those killed by the plague created panic. But nothing incited as much fear as the prospect of starvation. Reports that a real famine had struck Kazan, Ufa, Astrakhan, and Tsaritsyn trickled into Odessa. There were stories of butchers, in the parts of Russia hit worst by hunger, who sold the flesh of humans ground into other meat. By late autumn it was impossible to find vegetables and potatoes that were not rotten, or bread that was not infested by bugs. Whatever meat was available was alive with maggots, and by December the situation in Odessa, for almost everyone, was desperate.

Just before Christmas, after the season's second snowfall, Soybel Viska, her face ghostly white, trudged along Stiglitza Street from the *Fabrika Amunetsya,* where now she filled mortar casings with gunpowder for the Monarchists. Soybel drew her collar up around her neck and plodded through the snow. On Masterskaya Street she came to a restaurant crowded with White officers. Stopping, Soybel pressed her nose to the window and watched the soldiers eat. Some of the men swilled chunks of black bread in bowls of steaming cabbage soup. Others poured themselves glasses of oven-boiled milk from pitchers decorated with painted flowers. In one corner a corpulent major laughed at something his female companion said as he tore off bits of duck meat from the slender bone he held. Without thinking, Soybel walked around to the rear of the restaurant, attracted by the odors of food from the kitchen. A pile of refuse where waiters had scraped away uneaten food caught her attention. Spying a drumstick, Soybel grabbed it and stuffed the piece of roast goose into her pocket. A pastry with but a single bite having been taken from it also went into her pocket. Soybel searched for more food, but she found nothing else in the heap of garbage that she could bring herself to take. Shuffling away from the restaurant, not looking at anything but her rag-wrapped legs, chilled by the snow coming through the holes in the bottoms of her shoes, Soybel did not see the bulky form of a man approach her until he was on top of her. The man stopped directly in front of Soybel, blocking her way. Startled, she gasped and stepped back. The night kept the stranger's features hidden from view, but his presence was ominous. He said something to Soybel, his rapid words stabbing her, his foul breath making her avert her face; Soybel's eyes were filled with disbelief. The man repeated what he had said and pointed to a nearby building. Soybel's eyes traveled the length of his arm to the tip of his index finger: it appeared to be touching a window filled with light. Soybel gave the man her hand. He held it tightly while with his other hand he grasped Soybel's arm, holding her fast like a jailer keeping possession of a fleet-footed prisoner. Without a word between them, they proceeded down Masterskaya Street, the pressure the man exerted on Soybel's arm a constant reminder that he was in control. The man led Soybel to a ramshackle old building, down a flight of warped, creaking stairs, and into a small room. The walls were unpainted, damp with moisture, the plaster peeling away. The wooden floors had long ago lost their polish, the dark stain now scuffed light. A single window, uncovered, looked up onto Masterskaya Street, giving a spectator a clear but oblique perspective of the world outside. The only furniture in the room was a table, one chair, and a straw-mattressed bed. The wavering light of a burning candle looked like an old man praying. Shadows undulated on the walls, giving the place a peculiar life of its own. A one-burner stove glowed brightly, its heat making Soybel realize how cold she really was. She began to shake. Wordlessly, the man placed the chair next to the stove and indicated for Soybel to sit in it. As she did so, he drew a glass of hot tea from the samovar and pressed it into Soybel's hands. She rolled the steaming glass of tea against her cheek. The man brought her a tin of sugar and a spoon. Greedily Soybel took the little red and gold container and poured half its contents into the glass. Slowly she stirred the white granules, and when they dissolved she sipped the drink, letting each sweet drop rest on her tongue before swallowing. Gratefully Soybel looked up at the man. His pocked face beamed with pleasure. His lips were drawn back into a grin, exposing a mouth minus many teeth; the ones that were there were crooked, stained brown. The heat from the stove made the man's nose run, and a single strand of mucus hung from one nostril and dripped to the floor. He removed his coat and threw it on the bed, then walked behind Soybel, slipped his hands under her wrap and grasped hold of her breasts, pinching them. Soybel winced with pain. But instead of saying anything she continued to drink her tea. The man wormed his hands inside the top of Soybel's dress. Roughly he manipulated her, splaying her dangling flesh every which way. The calluses on his fingers were coarse, made dangerous with sharp nodules of horny skin that nicked Soybel's breasts. The hook of a hangnail caught the tip of Soybel's nipple and cut it. Ignoring the sudden burning sensation in her breast, Soybel indicated with her glass that she wanted more tea. The man shook his head no and laughed. Soybel repeated the gesture. The man mocked her and reminded Soybel of their bargain. Resignedly Soybel got to her feet. And with no trace of emotion showing on her face she began to undress.

CHAPTER 54

At the end of January 1920, the Bolshevik army launched a massive attack on Odessa. With a force superior in numbers and weaponry, the Reds appeared invincible, swiftly routing the monarchist army and eradicating all traces of White rule. When the battle was over, the victorious Reds celebrated for days.

Despite their relief at having been freed of monarchist tyranny, the people of Odessa remained apart from the rejoicing. To them, with little to eat, barely any fuel for heat, the triumphal parade of Lenin's troops offered no solace. Though the Bolsheviks often and earnestly announced that for Odessa the revolution was finally over, no one believed them; with the arrival of each new occupation force the same proclamation had been offered. Even the pictures of Lenin, which were again hung everywhere, seemed to belie the hope the Reds attempted to inject into the populace: the portraits were worn, ripped, and faded. Indeed, the spirit of the city was reflected by its dreary buildings, its outlook as gloomy as the grimy windows, the clouds that threatened new storms a fitting hat to the somber face of Odessa.

As the Bolsheviks had promised, there was now an equality among the citizens of Odessa. No longer was there any difference between the people of Moldavanka and those of the rest of the city. They were identical. The jobless, freezing, hungry inhabitants of what had once been the most vibrant city in the Ukraine were all alike, each filled with desperation. Only the Malinas Zala thrived on the return of the Reds. There, Mala and Sara, sparked with expectation, scrubbed the café until it glistened, polishing every table and chair until it shone brilliantly. Ever since the first Bolshevik soldiers had streamed into Odessa, the two women prepared for Mishka and Grisha to burst into the Zala, rushing to swing their women high into the air, hugging them, kissing them, hurrying to undress them and make love with them. But they never appeared, and by the end of the second week of the new occupation the two women were no longer cheerful, their tempers becoming short as they hid their worry behind anger. To Mala and Sara it seemed as if all of Russia was arriving in Odessa except the men about whom they cared. Each morning they would awaken with renewed hope, but with the coming of evening the women would once more succumb to gloom. More days passed, more snow fell, and more soldiers came, too. But there was still neither word nor sign from anyone about Mishka and Grisha. Then, at the end of the second week in February, there was news.

Midnight had long passed, and except for Mala who was sweeping the floor, the Malinas Zala was empty. The door opened and Mala looked up, discovering a tall, raggedly dressed man with rheumy, jaundiced eyes, the features of his face obscured by a thick beard matted with snot. A large bundle strapped to the intruder's back made him appear deformed. Slowly, deliberately, the man surveyed the room. Annoyed at having to serve a customer so late, and just as she was beginning to clean up, Mala made a noisy fuss about leaning her broom against a table and walking to the bar. The stranger studied Mala, all the while sniffling and wiping his runny nose on his coat sleeve. He coughed violently. The hacking sound of the fit made Mala look at the man again.

"Grisha?" Stunned by his appearance, Mala stood immobile.

The man nodded his head and dropped the bundle that was on his back to the floor.

"Grisha?" Mala repeated, her voice filled with tenderness, and love, and gratitude. Suddenly, crying and smiling simultaneously, Mala ran to Grisha and hugged him tightly, repeatedly kissing his face. "Oh, Grisha, Grisha. *Sara! Joseph! Grisha is home! Grisha is home!* Oh, how I have hoped for this day, prayed for it, begged for it. How I love you. How I missed you."

"I missed you, too," Grisha whispered, his voice rumbling with congestion. Gently he held Mala close, the familiar scent of her soap-scrubbed skin comforting him.

"But why are you alone?" Mala took a step backwards. "Where are the others?" She grabbed hold of Grisha's arms. "Where is—"

"I am the first one back."

"When will Mishka be here?" Mala began to shake uncontrollably. "When?"

"Soon."

"Is he, is he—"

"Nothing can hurt Mishka."

"But why are you not with him?"

"Urka is with him."

"Are they—"

"If Mishka and Urka were in trouble, would I be here?"

Before Mala could reply, Sara's voice softly called out her husband's name. "Grisha." The sound was like a love song. "Grisha." Slowly, Sara crossed the room, with each step singing out—"Grisha . . . Grisha . . . Grisha." Sara carefully looked at her husband, the distress she suffered at seeing his threadbare clothing, his battered appearance, the gauntness—the sorrow she felt at seeing how much the past months had marred Grisha's features was obvious in Sara's expression. Sara wondered what tragedies Grisha had endured and she shuddered. "Grisha." Sara locked her eyes on her husband's face, trying to retrieve every minute that she had been unable to see it. "Grisha." As the distance between them closed, Sara's step grew firmer, her stance more erect. Her face glowed. "*Grisha.*" Tears flowed freely from Grisha's eyes. He smiled. He grinned. He laughed. "Sara!" his voice boomed out. "*Sara!*"

Grisha engulfed his wife in his arms, crushing her to him, trying to feel the heat from her flesh through the thick wool of his coat. "Sara," Grisha murmured, the name lost in the depth of the first kiss they had shared in six months. *Sara!* Grisha wanted to shout out as he held his wife tighter and tighter, his mouth attempting to devour her lips, her nose, her eyes . . . "Sara," Grisha whispered.

"Now that you have proven you remember how to greet a woman, let's see if you also remember how to say hello to an old man."

The wry tone of Joseph Dubrow's voice caused Grisha to grin.

"Grisha, either kiss me or laugh, but don't try to do both," Sara said with mock annoyance.

"Hello, Joseph," Grisha said, moving quickly to his father-in-law and hugging him.

"Welcome home, my son."

The two men kissed.

"Where is Mishka?" Joseph inquired.

"Where is Isaac?" asked Grisha.

"Sleeping," Sara replied.

With strides that approached a run Grisha hastened across the Zala to the bedroom, where his son rested. There, in the dark, hovering above Isaac's crib, Grisha Moisei stood silently, listening intently to the infant's snuggled breathing. Grisha began to tremble. He reached out a hand and gently stroked Isaac's face. The child's soft warm breath caressed his skin. Grisha leaned down and kissed Isaac. *Sleep now, my son, and tomorrow I will introduce you to your father.* Grisha began to cry, not hearing Sara enter the room, ony realizing that she was there when he felt her breasts against his back, her arms encircling his chest, her breath warming his neck, her face nestling against his cheek.

"Sara, you have no idea how much I missed my son," Grisha said softly.

"He missed you, too."

"And you?"

Sara moved until she was face to face with Grisha. She hugged him tightly, talking as she kissed him. "For as long as I have known you, my husband, I have missed you."

"Even when we were together?"

"Especially when we were together."

"Why?"

"Because I was afraid of the times when you would go away."

"I will never leave you again."

Sara cried, her tears of joy and relief bathing Grisha's face, slowly washing away the grime that covered his memories of the recent past. The ardor of her embrace drove away the cold that had gripped Grisha's body ever since he had left Odessa.

"You have no idea how much I longed for you, my Sara. Every day, every night, all I wanted was you." In an uncontrollable rush Grisha kissed Sara, the urgency of his ardor making Grisha want to swallow Sara, to simultaneously engulf her and be engulfed by her, to lose himself so completely with Sara that their bodies became one, to be so totally united with Sara that, rather than each of them being a separate self, they melded together, becoming a single being, neither of them knowing where one ended and the other began.

Releasing a passion that she had kept in check for months, Sara responded to her husband's yearnings, her movements urging him to hasten to fill the void in which his absence had caused her to live. "Make love to me, Grisha, make love to me right now."

In the midst of a kiss, and while forcing himself to push Sara away, Grisha said: "Now is not the right time, my wife."

Startled by her husband's response, Sara stammered: "Have you stopped loving me?"

Staring directly into Sara's eyes, Grisha softly replied: "I love you more than ever."

"Then you should want to make love to me more than ever."

"I do, I do."

"Then—"

Tenderly, Grisha brushed Sara's face with his lips. "But to do so now would tarnish that love; it would make me dishonor that love."

"Grisha, I do not understand."

"Before I can make love to you, before I do anything, I must be sure that Mishka has arrived home."

"Mala won't be jealous, just like I wouldn't be if Mishka had returned first and they—"

"Sara, before I can rightfully take claim to the present, all the pieces of the past must be put together so that everyone involved can see and understand."

"Why?"

Gently, Grisha hugged Sara to him. "Because until the past is gathered up and put away there can be no present."

"Mala, bring my bundle to the table," Grisha said as he took a bottle of vodka from behind the bar and sat down between Sara and Joseph. "Why is the Zala so empty tonight? There should be a hundred men here to celebrate our homecoming, like in the old days."

"When Mishka arrives, there will be ten times a hundred men here to celebrate," Mala said, placing Grisha's bundle next to his chair, then sitting down across the table from him.

"They should be here already," Grisha said. "They should have felt that we were coming home, just like I felt the warmth of the Zala every step of the way back."

"After more than fifteen years of war and revolution, of starvation, after nearly half a generation of violence, I doubt if there is anyone in Odessa who can feel anything anymore," said Joseph Dubrow.

"Then they should come here to get drunk and forget," Grisha retorted.

"I do not think they know that they still have that much freedom left."

Grisha picked up the bottle of vodka and waved it in the air. "Freedom. That is exactly what we have with the Bolsheviks—freedom" Grisha toasted his statement with a long swig of vodka.

"Grisha, how soon will Mishka be here?" Mala's subdued voice seemed like a shout.

"Mala, right now Mishka and Urka are swooping toward the Zala. And by the time I have finished telling you about what we did, they will be right here before you."

"Then talk quickly, Grisha," Mala urged.

Grisha took another swallow of vodka from the bottle and immediately began to tell of the courageous battles he, and Mishka, and Urka, and Karmanchik, and Skakun, and all the others had fought.

Grisha started at the beginning, telling Mala, Sara, and Joseph how in four days Mishka had led his troops nearly three hundred miles from Odessa as they chased rumors of Petlura's whereabouts. The first place they had raced to was Grebla, but by the time they arrived there, Petlura had gone. The remains of his work, though, were unmistakable.

Fifteen Jewish families had been butchered, hacked to death with axes by the pogromist and his Haidamacks. Mishka then pushed to reach Obrush in time to kill the murderer there, but again they were too late to stop Petlura. The Jews of Obrush had been machine-gunned to death, concertinas played by the peasants accompanying the savagery; every Jewish corpse was mutilated, ears and fingers torn away by the pogromists when they robbed the dead of wedding bands and earrings.

"We almost caught Petlura in Kiev," Grisha said, his eyes leaping with fury. "We had a battle with him there. We found him and his men on Bolshaya Vasilovskaya Street. There was the corpse of a young man stretched out and a woman hugging it, screaming words Petlura was ordering her to say while one of his men held a knife to her throat. I can still hear her. 'This is good for me, because I am a damned Jew!' That is what Petlura made the woman shout. We killed the man who held the knife to her throat. But not before he killed her. And then we chased Petlura and his men all through the city. We killed two more pogromists—but Petlura escaped."

Grisha paused to take another drink.

"In Ladzhin, Petlura left two girls alive out of the entire Jewish population. They had been raped at least a hundred times each. Their noses had been bitten off, their flesh scraped raw, their hair shorn from their heads. You know, when we took those girls to a hospital in Kiev, the doctors refused to do anything because they thought Petlura would come back to retaliate. But they had never seen Mishka before. By himself he began to smash the place apart. He broke tables and beds. Kicked out windows. Put holes in the wall with chairs. He threatened to tear down the entire building unless someone agreed to help the girls. When the hospital staff saw that Mishka meant what he said, they all agreed."

Grisha stopped talking, looking from Joseph to Sara to Mala.

"In Tripole, Petlura's birthplace, he killed forty-seven Jews, even the sick and the children. They were left lying mortally wounded in the street. Not one villager came to help them, to ease their suffering. When those Jews finally died, the pigs came and rooted among the corpses, eating them. Unable to stand the atrocity of the situation, a kindly Gentile came and chased the pigs away. He took a shovel and dug a grave for the Jews who had been his neighbors and buried them. He made a Star of David from wood to mark the spot. When Petlura found out about it he made a special trip back to Tripole and murdered that man. That is what we were trying to catch! A man so wicked that his own mother must have cursed him! We found him again, just as he left another little town. We had a big battle that day. I think more horses died than men because we rode so hard. We covered seventy, maybe eighty miles, chasing Petlura. We cornered him in a forest. Mishka ordered the Bolsheviks and our soldiers to form a line and ride through the forest to flush them out. We killed dozens of Haidamacks. And we had him cornered. *We had Petlura cornered!* Then he charged. Like a maniac! He and his men rode straight at our lines and broke through! And do you know why they broke through? The Bolsheviks gave way! I never saw Mishka so enraged. I think if he had not chased after Petlura, Mishka would have shot the Bolsheviks instead. When we were finally outdistanced by the Haidamacks, we returned to the town where we had originally come upon them. There was not one Jew left alive. An old peasant woman told us that first Petlura made the Jews eat their own shit, then dig their own graves and climb in so his men could bury them alive. You know, if I could have saved just one of those Jews, if I could have filled just one of their mouths with a honey roll so they could taste something sweet just once more, I would have been willing to give my life for that."

Grisha ceased talking, his breath coming fast.

"That night we camped in the open. There was snow on the ground, and it was cold. It was the coldest night I can remember. We built little fires and huddled close together. We wore our saddle blankets over our coats. All over tiny fires burned, three or four soldiers squatting around each one. We were drained, exhausted from fighting. Eighty of our men died that day. Petlura lost more. I was at a fire with Mishka and Urka. The three of us were always together. Mishka was happy. 'Well, we got the big fight we wanted,' Mishka said. 'But if only I knew exactly who we killed.' I understood what Mishka meant. To have come so far, for so many to have died, and then not to get Petlura? That would have been more than any of us could have taken. So, for the next two days Mishka had us search for Petlura's body. But we hardly saw any bodies at all. We knew we had killed well over a hundred Haidamacks. Including our own dead, we should have found more than two hundred bodies.

But the snow was deep, and when a man fell from his horse he sank below the surface. It even snowed while we were looking, and that covered everything for sure. We made a promise to return in the spring after the snows melted, to see if we could find Petlura—except we all knew that there would be nothing left but skeletons. And anyway, all we wanted to do was return home and remain there. That is all we talked about that night." Grisha looked directly at Mala. "Mishka said that if you were with us, just your presence would melt all the snows on the steppes and warm the air until it rivaled the summer's heat. Urka spoke of his wife and children. And I of Sara and Isaac, and Joseph. We stayed up all night singing songs our fathers had taught us. And a few they hadn't. The next morning we started for Odessa. We had to cover four hundred miles. Four hundred miles with enough battles going on to fill all the history books in the world. We headed south, and for three days we just rode. We saw no one. The steppes were pure white. There was just the snow and our long lines of soldiers. Then we saw a village, the whole thing maybe one quarter the size of Moldavanka. It was a place to rest, to sleep, perhaps inside a barn, to be warm. Mishka ordered us to ride fast, so we could get there sooner. Everyone raced to be first. When we got there we wished we had all been last. Instead of finding food and shelter, we found gunfire. They waited until we were inside the town, and these were real soldiers—Monarchists! And they almost trapped us. We fought our way from one street to another, doorway to doorway. I never saw so much blood or heard so much screaming. Mishka and Urka were just ahead of me. Skakun and Karmanchik were off to one side. The Monarchists fought hard, but we fought harder. One of our machine guns opened fire and the Monarchists fell so fast it surprised even us. Then the battle was over. And even though we won, we were pretty badly cut down. Immediately, Lieutenant Veronozeh ordered his Bolsheviks to ride off, to press on toward Odessa. He could not even wait to help bury the dead. But you know who did help? The peasants. The ground was so hard it might as well have been stone, but the peasants dug anyway. And one by one they gently lifted our dead and placed them in graves. If they could have, they probably would have put them in shrouds or coffins, but there weren't any. So they just put them in the ground and covered them up with earth. I made them put Skakun's body next to Karmanchick's. That was the least I could do for them—they were good friends. And I did something else. I made them bury Mishka and Urka together."

Grisha's narration stopped, his grief making it impossible for him to go on. Mala, Sara, and Joseph sat in shock, and it was a moment before Grisha's last words penetrated their minds.

"Mishka is dead?" Mala whispered, as if she were afraid just to say the words. Her face filled with despair and disbelief, she looked at Grisha, her eyes pleading with him to say that he had lied. She grasped Grisha's hands and squeezed them, hoping the force of her grip would extract a retraction from him. When Grisha said nothing, Mala let her hands slip away from Grisha's and back onto the table. She dug her nails into the wood, splinters working their way under them, making them bleed. "My Mishka is dead?"

Grisha reached for the bundle on the floor and lifted it onto the table. He untied the rope that bound it. When the last knot was undone, the blanket that had protected its contents slipped open, exposing a fur-lined coat with a red armband sewn to one sleeve, a fur-lined cap with a red star pinned to the crown, and two revolvers.

"I brought the coat home for proof," Grisha said somberly.

Mala reached for the coat, her fingers touching a cluster of six small holes encrusted with dried blood.

"Not to prove that Mishka died—but why." Grisha's tone was foreboding.

Mala looked at the rips in the coat which might have been caused by a thousand other things but were not. She stared at the coat, transfixed by the tears in the material. She did not move a muscle. She barely breathed. Gently, Grisha slipped the coat away from her and spread it across the table, opening it fully, with the back facing upward.

"On the day we left to hunt Petlura Mishka was laughing like a child. His delight thundered above the sound of our horses. 'I, Mishka Yaponchik, have gotten what no other Russian Jew has ever gotten—a Russian government to actually help Jews!' As we galloped north you could feel his excitement. It galvanized us all. And not once, no matter how weary we were, how horrifying the sights, how grisly the battles, did Mishka's determination waver. The troops, Jews and Bolsheviks, were drawn to him, ready to obey his every command. And they fought valiantly—every man. Until the loyalty of the Reds to Mishka was undermined by one of their own." Grisha pointed to the bullet holes in Mishka's coat. His fingers punched at them as he spoke. "You see these? Mishka was shot in the back. Not in the front by Monarchists—but from behind! And do you know by whom? By Lieutenant Veronozeh. Who would ever think that in the midst of a battle anyone would watch where bullets come from—except those being aimed at them by the enemy. Everyone is too busy trying to save their own lives to keep a lookout for others. So why should a Bolshevik lieutenant worry that someone might be a witness to his committing murder? Who would see a Bolshevik lieutenant shoot a Jew in the back? No one, right? So he did it. And Mishka almost had enough strength to turn and kill the bastard. But he died a second too soon. And the lieutenant was wrong. There was a witness. Me. I was crouched in a doorway half a block away. Pinned there by enemy fire. And as I was looking for a way to escape I saw Veronozeh creeping up behind Mishka. I thought he was going to join Mishka—to fight side-by-side with him. It was only after he fired the first shot into Mishka that I realized his true intention. Then it was too late. I wanted to get a shot off—I wanted to kill Veronozeh, to murder him, to watch the same agony on his face as I had seen on Mishka's. But the enemy gunfire was so savage I could not move from my cover. And when the battle was over and I was free to move the lieutenant was already surrounded by his men. And to have accused him then, to have shot him, would have resulted in my death—and if I died, there would be no one who would know the truth. No one to tell the truth. To shout the truth!"

Mala clutched Mishka's coat, her fingers slipping into the jagged holes, in the back of it. Imagining what Mishka must have felt as the first bullet struck him from behind, the thought of the shock, the pain that Mishka must have felt as the first bullet pierced him, the staggering realization he must have come to when he turned and saw from where those deadly pellets came, made Mala shiver and a sickening nausea made her gag.

"Before the lieutenant ordered his troops to return to Odessa, he walked among our dead—acting as if he were concerned. I watched him carefully, and I knew better. All he wanted was to make certain that Mishka was dead. And when he stood over Mishka's body, there was satisfaction on his face—not the pleasure of personal vengeance, but the contentment of a man who has competently carried out his orders. The Bolsheviks must have planned Mishka's murder from the beginning."

"Why, Grisha, why? Did they hate Mishka that much?" Mala cried out in despair.

"I think the Reds were that agraid of him, afraid that they could never control him. Afraid that someday he might start his own revolution in Odessa and overthrow them. They knew how popular Mishka was—not only here in Moldavanka, but all over the city. I have an idea that their agreeing to give Mishka troops and weapons was also part of the plan. And what a wonderful plan it was. The Bolsheviks gave Mishka what they knew he wanted most—men and weapons to fight Petlura. And in thanks he gave them what he thought they wanted: the most influential Jew, the most beloved Jew in Moldavanka, and by then the most worshipped man in Odessa, openly displaying his acceptance of Bolshevism. And now the Reds have what they really wanted. Not just Mishka dead, but a hero, too! A real Jewish Bolshevik hero! And not any hero, but the greatest hero the Commissar could have ever hoped to find. Because now he can hold up the memory of Mishka Yaponchik and say: 'You see, the man who ruled Moldavanka, the king of Moldavanka, the *king of the Jews,* died for Odessa and Russia! As a Bolshevik patriot!"

"Why did they do it like that? Why didn't they just arrest him? Exile him, threaten to kill him. Anything but—"

"It was not just removing Mishka from Odessa that the Reds wanted, nor just his death. They could not come out and arrest him, and certainly not attempt to execute him. Because how he died was equally important to his dying! Have you forgotten what happened when they *did* arrest Mishka? No, Mishka Yaponchik had to die as a Bolshevik!"

Mala rubbed the fur lining of Mishka's coat against her cheek, pretending he was touching her.

"Mala, I am going to tell everyone how Mishka really died. I will not let the Bolsheviks get away with what they did. Even if they kill me for it, I will tell the truth. I will tell the world what really happened—I must!"

Grisha looked at Mala, waiting for her to agree with him. Mala did not move, her eyes did not stray from the table. Her mind reeled with memories of Mishka strutting through Moldavanka, his presence and bearing making the people feel safe. She saw the faces of joyful men as they poked their wives so they, too, would wave at Mishka Yaponchik, the thief of Moldavanka. The king of Moldavanka! *All he ever stole was an extra moment for everyone else to be happy.* A smile created by precious remembrance touched Mala's lips.

"Grisha, do you remember the very first night you came here and learned about Mishka's *malinas shalost*?"

"Who needs raspberry tricks anymore?" Grisha muttered.

"Do you remember what Mishka used to say? Give a stranger a *malinas shalost* and he drinks the fruit juice he sees with the innocence of a child. But all of a sudden, when he feels the vodka that was concealed by the juice, he has to struggle to be a man."

"The Bolsheviks had their *malinas shalost,* too. Except inside their fruit juice they concealed death," Grisha angrily interrupted.

"It was a good trick," Mala continued. "It still is. And that is why I do not want you to tell anyone the truth. Promise me that, Grisha. Promise me you will let everyone live with what they already believe—that Mishka Yaponchik, a Jew, even outwitted the Bolsheviks. Because if you tell them the truth, you will rob them of something that might give them a second of pleasure, or pride, or most important, hope. And if that happened, Mishka's death will have been wasted. Promise me, Grisha—let this be Mishka's last raspberry trick."

Grisha looked at Mala and he was drawn to her eyes, held fast by how they glistened. He saw Mala's face grow strong, her expression peaceful. Mala turned the coat so the bullet holes could not be seen, folding it neatly, then laying Mishka's hat and revolvers on top of it. Grisha touched Mala's hand to get her attention. He looked directly at her.

"I will never tell anyone, Mala. I swear it. And for as long as the memory of Mishka Yaponchik lives, there will be a *malinas shalost.*"

CHAPTER 55

A week and a half later, with new snow falling, Grisha Moisei strode through the streets of Moldavanka. There was a marked change in his appearance. His beard was gone and his clean-shaven cheeks were bright red from the cold. Beneath his wool cap his hair was neatly trimmed. His eyes looked rested, clear, once again filled with the fearless determination that the somber, exhausting past months had dulled. His bearing was erect, and there was a vitality to him, a healthfulness that ten continuous days of rest, warm food, and excessive love from Sara, Isaac, Mala, and Jacob had restored to him. Grisha moved quickly, his long bulky coat whipping behind him, looking as if it were hurrying to catch up with him. With each stride his boots kicked up clouds of snow specks. And with each breath, air escaped his lungs in steamy bursts. Alive with curiosity, Grisha looked everywhere, eagerly absorbing the sights of Moldavanka. All about him children fashioned snowballs out of the damp flakes, hurling them at one another while men went from store to store searching for work. Women roamed the streets, hunting for bits of wood or anything else to burn in their stoves to keep their families from freezing. A few people greeted each other with a glance or a slight nod of the head, but most kept to themselves, not allowing their eyes to meet anyone else's, not wanting to see their own futility reflected in the face of another. Every so often horse-drawn carts, the sound of their wheels hushed by the snow, rolled through the ghetto, the drivers hunched on their seats, wrapped in blankets, while in ones and twos Bolshevik soldiers, shivering, lonely, stood guard on the street corners, eyeing everyone suspiciously. Grisha turned onto Kherson Street, its buildings and stores ugly sores on a bleak landscape. Number nineteen had its broken windows and the gaping hole in its door covered with cardboard. Newspapers were jammed into the cracks in the wood-slat walls. From the outside the house looked deserted, and what could be seen through the few uncovered windowpanes was dark and lifeless. Nearing the walkway that led to the front door, Grisha slowed his pace; he knew what awaited him; Mala and Sara had forewarned him. A flood of past memories combined with present feelings of pity and not caring made Grisha uncomfortable. For an instant Grisha regretted having come to number nineteen Kherson Street, wishing he had heeded Sara's advice to send word of his return to Moldavanka rather than giving it in person. Grisha wanted to halt and turn around, to return to the safety, the warmth of the Malinas Zala. But something compelled him to proceed forward. He slowed his steps even more. When he reached the door he stopped, and for a long moment stood motionless. Finally he knocked. A woman opened the flimsy barrier. Her hair was uncombed, her complexion wan. Deep lines etched her wizened face, and there was a toughness, a permanent hostility to her expression. Her once perfect teeth were covered with tartar: one tooth was missing, another chipped, while a third was broken off into threatening spikes. When she saw who stood outside, the woman shrank back in disbelief. Suddenly, she drew her lips into an angry line. She looked savage.

"Hello, mother," Grisha said softly.

Soybel scratched her face and then her hair.

"May I come in?"

Soybel stepped backward, letting Grisha enter. He stole

a look at the floor. It was covered with newspapers to make the room a little warmer. The bubbling of water could be heard from the kitchen, and the odor of boiling noodles permeated the air. Soybel was thankful that Grisha had not arrived a few moments later. Otherwise he would have seen her struggle with the heavy iron pot in which she hauled *lapasha* through the streets of Odessa. No longer was Soybel an employee of the *Fabrika Amunetsya*. There was no one employed there anymore. For there was nothing left with which to manufacture bullets and mortars. So, Soybel was now forced to roam Odessa, pleading with people to buy a cup of *lapasha* for a kopeck.

For several seconds Soybel and Grisha stared at one another. Soybel's expression was contemptuous, an angry wall which she dared Grisha to breach. His mother's look conjured up recollections in Grisha which repulsed him. But other remembrances and Soybel's desperate appearance made Grisha want to hug her. "How have you been, mother?"

"How could I be? If I do not buy wood for the stove every week, we have enough money to buy food. Yet, most of the food is so rotten, it is better not to eat." Soybel's tone became menacing. "It is not an easy choice between starving to death or freezing to death."

"It is a difficult time for everyone."

"I do not care about everyone."

"If you need some food, some firewood, we could spare a bit. It is not as it used to be at the Zala but—"

"Just like I told your wife that I want nothing from her, I want nothing from you, either."

"But—"

"Nothing!"

Grisha shrugged his shoulders, indicating that the offer still held, and the choice to accept was Soybel's.

"But tell me, why, after all this time, have you come here—to mock me?" Soybel looked intently at Grisha, her expression hateful.

"To tell you that I am alive. That Mishka is dead—"

"I am glad Mishka is dead."

Soybel's words made Grisha want to slap her.

"And as far as I am concerned, you are dead for me, too," Soybel added with fury.

The *lapasha* boiled more vigorously, the steaming water that foamed over the sides of the pot hissing as it splattered against the hot stove. Soybel was unable to stand still. She fidgeted with her hands and nervously shifted her weight from foot to foot. Her eyes were tormented. His mother's obvious despair caused Grisha to feel a touch of sorrow for her and it showed on his face.

"Don't look at me like that!" Soybel shouted.

"Mother, let me help you, let me—"

"Why?"

"Because—"

"You don't care about me!"

"Mother, please," Grisha implored, moving to take hold of Soybel's hands, thinking that might calm her anger, ease her anguish.

Soybel avoided her son's touch. "You hate me. All of you hate me."

"No one hates you, mother. We have no time to hate."

"Well, I have time to hate." Soybel glared at Grisha. "And I do not want you in my house now or ever again."

Feeling his compassion quickly fading and a swell of anger replacing it, Grisha retreated to the door. "If you ever want help, Mother—"

"Get out."

"You are welcome—"

"Go!"

Not caring to say another word, Grisha hastened from the house and, without a single glance backwards, briskly retraced his steps along Kherson Street.

To assure herself that Grisha was really going, Soybel went to the doorway and watched his diminishing figure. "You have always hated me, Grisha. And you have made your wife hate me. And you will make your son hate me." Grisha turned the corner and disappeared from sight. As if someone had flipped a switch, Soybel's expression changed from one of venom to despondency. "Why do you hate me so, Grisha," she whimpered. "Why have you gone away from me again?" Soybel extended her hands in helplessness. "Why," she asked. "Why, why?" she asked again. "Why, why, why?" Over and over, Soybel repeated the question, each time her voice growing louder, shrilly demanding, sounding insane.

CHAPTER 56

Soybel Dubrovsky Moisei Viska lay awake in bed, watching the early March moon make its concentric circle around the earth. Despite all her efforts to the contrary, she was unable to think of anything except that she was two months shy of her fortieth birthday. *Can you see me from up there, Momma? Or when you look down at me, is it yourself you see?* A grim image hovered before Soybel's eyes—a woman's face, withered, deeply wrinkled, brow furrowed, her skin rough, her lips cracked, with lifeless eyes, and once luxuriant black hair that was now streaked with gray, coarse and unkempt. *We look the same at forty, Momma. And we live the same, too. Can you see my child and me lying here in bed together, dressed, covered up to our necks with blankets and newspapers, and we still cannot get warm.* Soybel watched herself exhale, the breath from her lungs a cloud that was visible in the sub-freezing air. *Have you witnessed, Momma, how I pay you homage? Every day now, I pick through the garbage, searching for something to eat. And I am teaching my son to do the same.* The painful sound of a dry, hacking cough startled Soybel. She rolled to her side and touched Munya's cheek. It was hot, burning with fever. *Don't be sick, Munya. Please don't be sick.* Munya stared at his mother, pleading for help. His features were no longer delicate, but angular, wasted, and he was aflame with disease. *Don't die, my Munya, don't die.* Soybel turned away from her son. *Once you were so healthy, my Munya. So beautiful. You looked like I did—everyone said so. Now you look as if I, myself, were perishing as a child.* Soybel stroked her own face. It was grotesque, even to the touch. The skin was as thin, sunken as deeply against her skull, as that of a mummified corpse. A fierce scowl was always upon her lips.

Soybel shut her eyes, trying to blind herself to everything. She thought of a photograph someone had taken of her standing on the foredeck of Tsar Nicholas' yacht. Soybel looked exquisite in the picture, her skin glowing in the soft light of sunset, her expression vibrant, electrifying. Suddenly, Soybel became confused, unsure if it were she who had been in the photograph, someone else, or if there had been any photograph at all.

Another coughing attack caused Munya's almost fleshless body to double up. Wracked with convulsions, he clawed at his mother. Saliva oozed from his mouth and with it blood. *Momma, Momma, my son is dying! There is blood on his lips and I know it is from his lungs.* Munya's face became ashen. *Help me, Momma.* His listless eyes were terrified. *Please, Momma, tell me what to do.* Munya's teeth chattered and Soybel covered him with herself, attempting to warm him with whatever heat she had. *But, Momma, I have no money for a doctor.* Soybel snorted with contempt. *How can I heat the house, Momma, when all that is left to burn in the stove is the house?* Soybel sneered. *And as for food, Momma, even the rats will not eat the garbage that is left in the streets. So what would you have me do—burn the house, start eating the rats?*

Munya choked on his phlegm, his body twisted and jerked spasmodically.

"No, Momma, do not ask me to do that," Soybel pleaded aloud.

The anguished sound of his mother's voice aroused

Munya. He stared wide-eyed at her, crying out in fear. Mucus and tears collected around his nose and mouth.

"There must be another way, Momma," Soybel begged.

Munya choked. His arms thrashed about, his spindly legs wrenching in pain.

There must be another way, Soybel silently implored. She touched her neck, fingering the tiny emeralds that hung there from a slender golden chain. *No, Momma, no. Don't make me sell my necklace. Because when the money from it is gone, what will I sell then?*

Terrified by the thought of having to part with her necklace, Soybel became irrational, her expression demonic. She was plagued by the images of a thousand familiar faces, each of them leering at her, laughing at her, taunting her. Their voices ridiculed her.

"Cup your hands and walk through the streets on your knees and beg for anything with which to save your child," said the grinning illusion of Aleksandr Moisei.

Gleefully the specter of Yehuda Dubrovsky said: *"Your Petrograd is no more, Soybel. Your Dalyoki is no more. Nor your Kodoma, or Odessa. Even the foot of the Lipki heights is no more. All that is left for you is Moldavanka."*

No, I will not live out my days in another slum, another ghetto, Soybel silently shouted. She flailed about, her fingers clawing the air, trying to tear out the eyeballs of the apparitions who hovered above her. *I did not escape one Kiev to return to another!*

The apparition of Vassili Viska peered down at Soybel, his face oozing contempt. *"Despite everywhere you have been, Soybel, you really never left Kiev. The stink of that ghetto, the stench of it, is still imbedded in every pore of your body."*

Stop, please stop! Soybel's eyes beseeched.

"If it were not," Vassili continued with amusement, *"how would you remember so well how to make* lapasha, *how to stuff newspapers into the cracks in the walls, and how to wrap your legs in rags? Do you think that true aristocrats know such things?"*

"Stop, damn you, stop!" Soybel shrieked aloud.

The shadowy figures began to laugh hysterically. They clutched at one another, supported each other to prevent themselves from falling down in fits of mirth.

"Stop!"

As if on cue the phantoms Soybel saw became quiet and watched her in hushed expectancy. Soybel glared at the specters before her, infuriated by their smug expressions, those looks of condescension she had seen on the faces of priests as they awaited someone's confession.

"Maman, j'ai peur," Munya plaintively cried.

Without removing her gaze from her visitors, Soybel clasped Munya tightly to her and said: "Do not be afraid, my precious."

"J'ai peur que je vais mourir, Maman."

"Momma will not let her Munya die."

"Maman, Maman," Munya mumbled deliriously. *"Maman!"* Munya's head flopped to one side. His breathing became labored. His eyelids drooped, closed. There were no more sounds from his lungs.

"Munya?" Soybel shook her son, then pressed her ear to his chest. *"Munya!"*

And as quickly as they had appeared, the unearthly callers to number nineteen Kherson Street disappeared.

False dawn lightened the slate-colored sky. The snow had ceased falling and the street outside looked fresh and clean. A cold strong wind rustled the newspapers stuffed into the ill-fitting wall slats, and the only windowpane not broken and covered with cardboard rattled incessantly. Soybel Moisei got out of bed and carefully wrapped Munya in the bedcovers. She bent over him to reassure herself that he was still breathing. The sound was almost too faint to hear, but Soybel could feel a trickle of heat from Munya's nose graze her face. Standing up, Soybel hurried from the room, returning a moment later wearing her shabby winter wrap. Gently, Soybel picked up Munya, making certain that he was completely swaddled. The child hung limply in her arms.

Quickly, Soybel departed from the house and hurried toward the street.

Lashed by icy blasts of air, Soybel labored through the deep powdery snow. The wind howled. Swirls of frozen flakes nicked Soybel's face, and she tucked Munya's head inside the folds of her coat. On one side of the street drifts of snow were piled high against the buildings, while the walkways on the other side had been blown clean, exposing a slick sheet of ice. A sudden gust of wind pushed at Soybel's back and she was forced to run to keep from falling. Snow sprays leaped from her shoes. Her lungs burned inside her chest. The skin on her face felt as if it were ready to crack, and her fingers turned blue. When she turned from Kherson Street onto Tiraspolskaya, the wind abated, the buildings holding it at bay. Munya moaned. Coughed violently. And moaned again. Overhead a scudding cloud broke open and permitted the sun to poke through. Moldavanka glistened as though it were wearing a coat of ermine. And a steamer whistle broke the white silence, announcing the first rays of morning. Turning another corner, Soybel again met the wind. It ripped through her body. Her thighs froze, chafing as they rubbed against the hard material of her dress. The hem of her coat beat against her legs, stinging them, splotching them red. Her arms became stiff, and Soybel no longer worried about Munya slipping from her grasp. Her forehead ached, the winter cold piercing her skull. A patch of ice crackled beneath Soybel's feet, making her scramble to maintain her balance. At the next corner Soybel began to run, racing toward a building that covered nearly half the length of the block. When she reached the structure, Soybel pounded on its locked door; again and again she beat her fists against the formidable barricade.

"Who is there?" shouted a voice from inside.

In response, Soybel pounded more loudly.

"I said, who is there?"

The snap of the latch being unfastened ticked along the entire street. The door was opened an inch. When the person within saw who it was, the door was pulled back as widely as it would go. Stepping inside, Soybel staggered and Munya fell from her grip. Simultaneously, Grisha Moisei grabbed hold of the boy and prevented Soybel from collapsing.

"Sara! Mala!" Grisha roared. First making certain that Soybel was able to stand unaided, Grisha set Munya in a chair.

"He's sick, very sick," Soybel blurted out.

"Grisha, what is—"

"Make some tea, Sara!"

"I'll go for a doctor," Mala said, hurrying into the café immediately behind Sara.

"I'll go," Joseph Dubrow volunteered as he followed on Mala's heels.

"First get some dry blankets for the child," Mala ordered.

"Munya will live with you. He has to!" said Soybel. "I cannot go on like this. No more. Never again!" Soybel's wild eyes jumped crazily from one person to another.

"You are welcome to stay here," Mala invited. She felt Munya's forehead and winced.

"You have everything now, everything," Soybel continued, her words popping into the air with bits of moisture. Without thinking about it, Soybel touched her throat: beneath her collar she could feel the tiny bumps of the emerald necklace. "You have everything except me!" Soybel's eyes blazed, the large black pupils widening until they appeared as if they would consume not only the people in the room, but the room, too. "No one gets that!" A frightening laugh that chilled the others to the bone escaped from Soybel's throat and tore through the café. *"No one! No one! No one!"* Without warning, Soybel collapsed to the floor and sobbed: "No one, no one, no one." And then she was still, sitting mutely, hugging herself and rocking back and forth, back and forth —Soybel's fierce expression dissolving into slack-jawed desolation, her eyes peering into a world far from reality, her thoughts focused on a young girl she thought she had once known, a sultry gypsy girl named Zemfira who had captured the heart of a gallant hero with hair like the sun, eyes like the sky, and a smile of infinite joy. "Aleko," Soybel whispered to herself and smiled. "Aleko," she said even more softly. *Aleko.*

The silence in the Zala was agonizing—awesome. No one moved, everyone watching Soybel. Waiting. Having no idea what to expect, or what might be expected of them. They listened. There was nothing to hear: even the fierce wind had become quiet. And the Zala was shrouded in a vacuum of silence. Then the soft gurgling of brewing tea rippled through the stillness. Joseph reentered the café, his footsteps carefully subdued, the blankets he carried barely rustling. Munya stirred, his eyes fluttered open. From the furthest reaches of the room, hidden away from the light of the flames in the fireplace, from within shadows blacker than night, floated hushed words, and gently, Rabbi Joshua Eleazar's benedictions for the sunrise lilted across the café. Glasses clinked as Sara set them on a tray along with spoons and a bowl of sugar. The doorlatch clicked, Mala sealing the entranceway to keep out the cold. From the living quarters behind the Zala, Isaac Moisei's awakening song, a potent cry, let it be known loudly and clearly that it was time for him to be fed. And then, without hesitation, his step firm and decisive, Grisha Moisei went to his mother, bent down and gathered her up in his arms, and carried her across the Zala and into the room he shared with his wife and child. There, he gently placed Soybel in his bed and covered her up to her neck. For an instant Soybel looked up at Grisha and smiled. Then, as her eyes slowly closed and she slipped into the safety of sleep, Grisha Moisei leaned over his mother and tenderly kissed her.

EPILOGUE

May 14, 1948

"We will turn our plowshares into swords."

GRISHA MOISEI

A green lizard, no bigger than the index finger of a man's hand, scampered among the white rocks atop the hillside, its tongue darting here and there in search of insects. Suddenly the reptile stopped, every muscle frozen; before it was a formidable brown obstacle. Cautiously, the lizard twitched its head.

"Go ahead, little one, I won't step on you," a man's deep voice said with a laugh. The man stood immobile, waiting for the lizard to gather its courage and scurry off past his booted foot. "Go ahead, you'll be safe." As if his words had reassured it, the tiny creature raced off, its tail leaving a fine line in the dusty earth. The man chuckled. "Be sure to find good cover, my little friend, or the war might get you, too." A glint far below him and to the southeast caught the man's attention and he studied it, squinting his eyes in the hard light of the noonday sun. The Sea of Galilee looked inviting, and the man wished he could be swimming there now. Sweat poured profusely down his sun-browned face, and he wiped it away on the sleeve of his uniform. He unscrewed the top off a canteen, raised the container above his head, and poured the contents over himself. The cool water soaked his close-cropped silver-gray hair, the refreshing rivulets that ran down his cheeks glistening like diamond rivers. The man yawned and stretched; he was tired. It had been more than thirty hours since he had last slept. Yet, despite his fifty-two years, he was still alert, his work-hardened muscles limber, his senses acute. Opening up a leather case that hung from a shoulder strap, he removed a pair of field glasses. He held them up to his eyes and scanned the distant landscape in every direction. To the northeast he could see hundreds of tiny shapes moving to and fro. And though they were too far off to bring into detail, the man knew exactly what was there: the Syrian army, several thousand troops, well-armed and eager to invade the portion of Palestine allotted to the Jews six months before by the United Nations partition. To the north, beyond his vision, he knew that the army of Lebanon awaited orders to attack. To the east and southeast, fighting men of Iraq, TransJordan and Saudi Arabia were poised, while to the west, the Egyptian army readied itself.

"You know," he said softly to all the opposing armies, "if even one of you were missing I would feel slighted. But this way you have admitted that we are a formidable opponent." The man grimaced and thought: *if there is to be a full-scale war, then let's be done with it with everyone at once.* He searched his memory for an epithet, but the Hebrew he now spoke had none to offer—so, he cursed in Arabic.

"Shalom!" a voice boomed out.

"Shalom," the man replied, recognizing the voice as that of his son. He turned to watch the young man as he briskly climbed up the hill to the lookout post at the crest. *How unlike me he looks,* the older man mused. Indeed, no one would have taken the two men for father and son. The younger man was several inches shorter than his father, but he was broader and far more muscular, unusually muscular. Rather than being fair-haired as his father had been, the son had dark hair, and he had inherited his mother's black eyes, not his father's blue ones. He was quite handsome. Not striking-looking in the classical way as was his father, but appealing in a heavy-lidded, sensual way. His youthful face belied his thirty years of age. Only his smile suggested that the two men might be related, both of them having the same easygoing, quick-to-appear grin that charmed all those on whom it was bestowed.

"Has anything changed?" the young man inquired as he scrambled up the last few yards of the hill. He unslung his rifle from his shoulder and leaned it against a tree next to his father's Sten gun.

"Everything is the same—our enemies are all around us."

"When has it ever been different?"

"Now, my son, you understand our past, our present, and have gazed into our future." The man glanced at his son's weapon and then at the army uniform he wore; he could not recall when he had last seen his son dressed differently. "Is there any news yet?"

"The radio is still silent. But Momma and Tziporah will let us know the moment there is anything." The young man peered into the distance, wondering from which direction the enemy would strike first. "Will they attack right after Ben-Gurion makes his declaration?"

"Isaac, the enemy has never stopped attacking."

Grisha Moisei studied his only child; he displayed the pride he felt openly. This healthy young man was even more than he had hoped for. Grisha tried to remember back when Isaac was an infant and they were still in Russia. It was difficult; that was twenty-eight years ago. And so much had happened since Grisha and his family had arrived in Palestine in 1920—so much.

There were the years spent transforming the malaria-infested Hula Valley into rich, fertile farmland. Years of building barns and bunkers, farms and fortresses. Years of living out in the open or in tents, and more years building homes above ground and shelters below. There were years when the crops withered under the merciless summer sun, the winter's drought making irrigation impossible. And other years when Arab marauders set entire fields of grain afire. There was the constant need for vigilance, to be armed always, ready to fend off Arab attacks. And there was the constant presence of the cruel British administration. But always, Grisha Moisei persevered, spurred on by a love for this land, a fervor that coursed through his body in blazing heat. And he was further urged on by the dedication of others to the same ideal—a wife, a son, a brother, a father-in-law, and a robust woman, his beloved Mala, all of whom were determined to make real what had only been a cherished hope. But there was still more for Grisha Moisei to do.

There were the years that Grisha devoted to helping organize the Haganah, the Jewish defense army of Palestine. And more years serving as a commander in the Palmach, the Haganah's commando unit. From north to south and east to west, Grisha had led his small corps of highly trained soldiers to battle the enemy, to protect the brave pioneers who had come to Palestine to give reality to their dreams and life to the desert. Yet, the challenge that Grisha most enjoyed was the raising of his son.

From early on Isaac had been an unusual child, but then again, he had had an unusual childhood. As an infant, Isaac had been nursed on revolution, had teethed on warfare, had been nourished on the idea that for *Eretz Yisrael* to exist, *Eretz Yisrael* had first to be built. And unlike other youngsters, Isaac Moisei had not marked his passing years, his birthdays, with gaily wrapped presents. Rather each year was noted by more necessary things.

At age three, Isaac had learned to withstand the violence of tempestuous spring seas as he, his father and mother, his grandpoppa Joseph, grandmother Soybel, cousin Munya, *Tante* Mala, and Rabbi Joshua Eleazar huddled for two weeks on the open, wind-swept deck of the *Russlan* as the steamer made its way through the angry waters of the Black Sea, the Dardanelles, the Aegean Sea, and finally the Mediterranean; the *Russlan,* the first Russian vessel to leave Odessa for Palestine after the end of the revolution.

By age five, Isaac spoke Hebrew fluently, and a fair amount

of Arabic, his recollection of Russian slowly dimming. By his sixth birthday, Isaac worked in the fields of the kibbutz, helping his family and other members of the cooperative farm to till the land. In his seventh year, Isaac was taught to use a rifle and a pistol, to dig battle trenches, to fill bags with sand and place them, for extra protection, along the edges of the deep ditches which surrounded the outer perimeter of the kibbutz. By age eight, Isaac had already helped to fight off several Arab attacks. And in his ninth year, he actually killed one of the enemy with a well-aimed bullet. For the next several years Isaac perfected his skills as a farmer and defender of the kibbutz. At age fifteen, he was accepted in the Haganah, trained as a soldier, and sent off to hold the enemy at bay, or fight if necessary, while new immigrants to Palestine established their settlements. A year later Isaac volunteered for the Palmach, quickly learning the art of guerrilla warfare. He was assigned to the commando unit captained by his father.

From 1936 until the outbreak of World War II, Isaac Moisei, along with several dozen other troops, followed Captain Grisha Moisei from one end of Galilee to the other, defending their brethren from the increasing number and deadliness of Arab attacks. In 1939, when many young Palestinian Jews were volunteering to join the British armed forces and fight the Axis in the Mediterranean theater, Isaac elected to remain with his father and protect their homeland. For a while there was relative calm in Palestine, the war with Germany diverting both the Arabs' and Jews' energies. Grisha and Isaac wondered if they had erred by not fighting Hitler. But in 1944, both father and son were glad they had remained behind. Instigated by the Nazis, renewed outbreaks of Arab terror, murder, and arson raged throughout Palestine. Captain Grisha Moisei was promoted to colonel, his son became a lieutenant. In daring daylight raids on Arab strongholds, in furtive nighttime missions that took them deep into enemy territory, Grisha Moisei led his commandoes with a fierceness, a boldness that made each of his troops feel invincible. Following the United Nation's partitioning of ancient Palestine in 1947, the advent of war—not just a war with the Arabs within Palestine, but a full-fledged invasion by all the Arab states surrounding Palestine—appeared imminent. On March 9, 1948, the Haganah declared a formal mobilization and began to accept every able-bodied man from seventeen to forty-five. Regional and local commanders were assigned territories, made responsible for training new troops and sharpening the skills of existing troops. Colonel Grisha Moisei was given command of the northeastern sector of Upper Galilee, a hilly region that overlooked his kibbutz and half a dozen others, but, more important, gave the Haganah control over the road that led directly south from Lebanon to Jerusalem, the focal point of Arab military intentions.

Day after day Grisha waited impatiently, anxious to have the struggle begin. His troops were also growing impatient. They had never been more ready for battle, nor more inspired, for this would truly be the war that would establish *Eretz Yisrael,* or the permanent shattering of their dreams. All around the air was electric with anticipation. Sentries were posted on every hilltop, soldiers camouflaged among rocks and bushes, snipers wedged into the crooks of trees. And at the most forward position stood Grisha Moisei and his son Isaac.

Again Grisha inspected the surrounding countryside. His eyes skimmed along distant ridges, then down into the valley below where he saw two figures hurrying toward the base of the hill. In the lead was his beloved Sara, who, even now, in her fourth decade in life, was as beautiful to Grisha as she had been on the day he met her thirty years before. Grisha marvelled at how spryly Sara climbed up the hillside, seemingly unburdened by the heavy rifle slung over her shoulder. The shorts that Sara wore revealed her strong, dark-brown legs, thighs made muscular by years of physical labor; thighs that still welcomed her husband, held him fast while her strong slender arms encircled his back and her lips caressed his face. Half a yard behind Sara climbed Tziporah, Grisha's daughter-in-law, a woman of twenty-three whom Grisha loved as dearly as if she had been his daughter. Tziporah reminded Grisha of Sara. Indeed, the two women closely resembled one another, even to their personalities.

Grisha looked beyond the women, examining the buildings of the kibbutz he had helped to build from nothing, at the fruitful earth he had helped to retrieve from mosquitoes and snakes, and at the small cemetery he had helped to carve out of the floor of the Hula Valley. The cemetery, resting place for too many comrades who had died defending their right to a five-thousand-year-old contract; resting place for too many Jews who had spent their lives wanting nothing but to die and be buried in Palestine; resting place for Soybel Dubrovsky, who died shortly after arriving in Palestine, never realizing that she had left Russia; resting place for Rabbi Joshua Eleazar, who, upon setting foot in the Holy Land, immediately made his way to Safed, an ancient mountaintop city where for centuries the most esteemed devotees of mysticism had retreated; where Cabalism was enshrined in ornate houses of worship. For nine years Rabbi Eleazar resided in Safed. He returned to the kibbutz only when he was certain he was dying, desiring to be buried in the ground closest to Grisha Moisei. The kibbutz cemetery was also the resting place of Joseph Dubrow, who for fifteen years toiled alongside his family, finding each new bud, each sprouting plant cause for celebration; resting place for Mala Katyov, who, until her death in 1943 at age sixty-three, was the matriarch of the kibbutz, its emotional foundation, its communal teacher of children, nurse for the wounded and ill, comforter of the fearful and bereaved, and bearer of love for all, though there was no one whom she loved as dearly as Grisha Moisei. For a moment Grisha mourned the loss of his Mala. And then he thought of his brother. He wondered if Munya were safe. It had been months since Grisha had seen him, Munya's secret activities with the Irgun, a paramilitary terrorist organization, having kept him distant from his family for many years. Breathing deeply, Grisha forced himself to ignore the memories and worries that were vying for his attention.

"Isaac, your mother and Tziporah are coming," Grisha said to his son.

Needing no further word, Isaac scrambled down the hill-side to help them up to the top. Grisha watched the three of them intently, a swell of satisfaction making him puff out his chest and smile.

"Did you hear anything yet?" Grisha shouted as his son took hold of the women's hands and helped them maneuver the last few steep yards to the crest. "Sara, did Ben-Gurion make his declaration?"

Flushed from the exertion of the climb, Sara Moisei gasped for breath.

"Sara, you can breathe later, but now tell us if Ben-Gurion made his declaration," Grisha insisted, needing to know if this was the day that Palestine was to become Israel.

"Tziporah, what is happening?" Isaac asked his wife.

"Ben-Gurion made his speech," Tziporah said softly.

"And?"

"And he declared that we are now an independent state," Sara said, her voice trembling. "He said that we are a country," Sara continued, her face radiant. "He said that as of today we are citizens of the State of Israel," she added, her eyes filled with joyful tears. "He said that today we are Jews with a homeland—did you hear that, my Grisha, we are Jews with a homeland!"

Shaking with excitement, Grisha Moisei hugged his wife to him, pressed her so tightly against him that he could feel the heat of her body penetrate his uniform and touch his skin. Then, extending his arms, Grisha invited his son and daughter-in-law into his protective embrace. Together the four of them stood hugging one another, crying and laughing with one another. Together, they stood atop a hill in a land at the end of a journey which had begun five thousand years before in the very same place. And together they waited to begin a new journey that was barely minutes old.